THE EYES OF THE COMET
AN AMERICAN SLAVE ODYSSEY

THE EYES OF THE COMET
AN AMERICAN SLAVE ODYSSEY

A CONTROVERSIAL HISTORICAL NOVEL

BY DENNIS LEE HAGUE

Rawhide Book Publishing
Lake Geneva, Wisconsin

The Eyes of the Comet
An American Slave Odyssey
Published by:
Rawhide Book Publishing
P.O. Box 5
Lake Geneva, Wisconsin 53147
Email: dennishague@genevaonline.com

Dennis Hague, Publisher
Yvonne Rose, QualityPress.info, Book Packager
Creative Ankh Designs, Interior and Cover Design
Cover Concept by Bruce Sabatka

For more information, please contact Rawhide Book Publishing via email: dennis hague@genevaonline.com. For book signings, speaking engagements, interviews or other media related questions. In addition Rawhide Books are available at special discounts for bulk purchases, sales promotions, fund raising or educational purposes.

Copyright © 2015 by Dennis Lee Hague
Paperback ISBN #: 978-0-9965371-0-0
Hardcover ISBN #: 978-0-9965371-1-7
Library of Congress Control Number: 2015945048

DEDICATION

This book is dedicated to the proud brothers, sisters and children who had to endure for so long the suffering generated by the bondage system and with the further hope that one day we may all realize the dream that in "God's eyes we are all one".

ACKNOWLEDGEMENTS

I would like to acknowledge my wife Kathy; my parents, Frank and Doris Hague; my son, Shane; and my brothers, Frank and Michael. In addition, my long-time friends, Robert Burnette, Jerry Dubin and Tiffany Burton.

INTRODUCTION

Every once in a while something great comes along that sends the reader on an epic journey. Carefully crafted and intensely researched, *The Eyes of the Comet: An American Slave Odyssey* represents a historical novel whose time has finally arrived.

Launched into the ante-bellum period of American history from 1835 to 1843, the "soul" for the novel reveals to the reader, mankind's search of spiritual and social equality.

The intrigue begins at the Marshall plantation in Virginia where in 1835 Halley's Comet is first witnessed by our protagonist, Reggie Marshall. Unfortunately, he is enslaved, but he is unique in that he is very bright, handsome, while being able to pass for white, which nevertheless, poses numerous problems for him throughout his enslavement.

While gazing at the comet, completely spellbound, it is revealed to Reggie, a vision of America's approaching Civil War. A compelling adventure follows where Reggie is forced to endure being sold to "twisted" slave masters resulting in sufferings that are physical, emotional, and inhumane while forewarning others of the impending crisis facing the North and the South.

Driven by his survival instincts, eventually Reggie escapes to the North where he becomes a successful salesman for a large manufacturing corporation. The plot further thickens as he is reunited with his wife Anastasia, who in so many ways is his "carbon copy", and with her by his side, he eventually ventures on a quest to free his enslaved friends in Georgia.

The finale provides us with a "shining light", which is emotionally riveting as his dearest friend, Joseph, a fellow slave, takes on a role that could be described as larger than life while in the backdrop of the Great Comet, which makes an appearance in 1843.

Written in the vernacular of the old South, the reader is allowed the opportunity to escape into an era of American history that is both intriguing and insightful. Providing a fresh and objective analysis of the period, the book offers new and exciting perspectives, while drawing upon timeless themes that are relevant today.

Brilliantly written, the novel represents a "must read" that will mesmerize the reader from start to finish.

CHAPTER ONE

In November of 1835, Halley's Comet reached its nearest position to our planet. Dubbed by many as "the year the star shot", it was viewed around the world. Superstitously, many perceived it as the start of apocalyptic times. However, there were other inspired visionaries who considered it as a sign of great change to come.

Dinner guests and house servants had gathered outside of the Oak Manor plantation near Richmond, Virginia to witness the spectacle of Halley's Comet. It was a clear and cool star-filled evening that gave a breathtaking view of the comet as it passed the earth at its closest approach.

The assemblage stood along the James River in a large arbor surrounded by formal gardens which had sacrificed their beauty for the approaching winter. Since the river traffic was the main mode of transportation and commerce, the front yard of the Oak Manor plantation home faced the river like the other frontage plantations in the area.

The captivating atmosphere was heightened by the gentleness of the flowing, trickling water and occasional glimpses of what appeared to be flickering lights from the nighttime river activities. The panorama was further accentuated by pine tar stacks illuminating the grounds. Outside of normal conversation, there was an odd absence of night sounds that would normally punctuate the early evening. Large oaks with fallen leaves and pines surrounded the property. Altogether, there was something mystical about the night.

Adding the final touch was the sheer magnificence of the large, white-framed, Grecian styled home with columned opulence. The overall feeling of the house in its setting evoked an image of old Greece in all of her splendor.

The host, Colonel Andrew Marshall recognized the chilly air, and saw that it was time to invite the guests into the parlor. The servants meanwhile had returned to their tasks of serving while nervously glancing at the comet as they believed it to be a sign of the end of the world.

Colonel Marshall was a handsome, dignified man in his fifties. He wore an immaculate, soft gray dress coat with silver buttons that were so polished that they glistened as they caught the light. His hair was black with only a slight touch of silver at his temples. His light gray eyes were complimented by a square chin and an aristocratic nose.

He cleared his throat and then announced to his guests, "Dat' was quite a show. If yu' want to retire to dah' house, drinks an' desserts are bein' served in dah' parlor. We kin' discuss dah' comet 'long wit' other tidbits inside. Now, if yu' would be so kind, please foller' my lovely wife Evelyn an' me up to dah' house."

Evelyn was exquisitely beautiful and complimented him perfectly. In her mid forties, she obviously was a possession he enjoyed showing off to his guests. Her face was pale, a delicate rose tinting her cheeks. Her hair streaked with silver was arranged in a coronet atop her head. She looked like an angel with her heart-shaped face and striking green eyes. Her gown was a beautiful light green satin, setting her off like a sparkling jewel.

The parlor was a study in Federal and American Empire style furniture. A beautiful harp stood alongside some exquisitely styled walnut furniture with the centerpiece of the room being a rich, red Persian rug. An older harpsichord in the corner appeared almost as an anachronism to the room.

Colonel Marshall continued in a commanding tone, "As yur' hosts, my wife Evelyn an' I welcome our guests to Oak Manor. An' on dis' special occasion honorin' Halley's Comet, it gives me great pleasure to introduce our guests from Boston—Miss Sarah Clark, Miss Emma Eton 'long wit' Emma's aunt, Miss Opal Eton. My daughters fortunately befriended our visitors while 'tendin' Payne's Finishin' School in Boston an' now on vacation, dey' have gifted us by bein' our guests."

With a warm smile on her face Evelyn added, "We'd like to introduce yu' to our neighborin' guests, Robert an' Dora Carter. Dey' are from one of dah' most prominent families in Virginny an' have graced our plantation wit' thar' company. It is indeed a pleasure to welcome 'dem. Neighborhood courtesies always 'bound wit' callers commonly stayin' fo' at least two weeks. Announced or unannounced, it does not matter, as dis' is dah' accepted practice down hyeh'." The intent of mentioning the prominence of the Carters was perhaps by design to impress the guests. Further, to specify, they were neighbors would imply the South was more hospitable with each other than the North. Additionally, the Williamsburg area of Virginia, where Oak Manor plantation was located, socially represented in the biased hearts of the people in this community, some of the finest families in the entire country. This conviction was established well before the Revolutionary War and further supported by the fact that most of the very early Presidents came from the region. While showing respect for their three visitors, the Williamsburg social set would never accept Northerners as their equal.

Colonel Marshall was curious. "Are things similar in Boston as well? Do Bostonians open thar' homes to hospitality as we do?"

Sarah, who appeared to be the most outspoken one of the trio, responded, "Of course we maintain our Bostonian hospitality, but, owing to the fact that we lack the staff you have in the South, it creates problems if caught off guard by friends and relatives visiting without advance notice." The implication was obvious. In the North there would be no staff of slaves available to provide the work necessary to accommodate people who visit unannounced.

Evelyn recognized the implication of Sarah's answer but chose to gloss over it. "Of course havin' a large staff would make matters easier as it facilitates our nature an' our pleasure in bein' able to entertain an' serve y'all." It is amazing how Evelyn, being quick witted, was able to use the word facilitate to gloss over a controversial subject.

Colonel Marshall, aware of where the conversation was headed, quickly changed the subject. "Y'all may have missed our own special bread served earlier fo' supper. Be sur' to partake of some now. It's a tradition in des' parts to take pride in yur' own recipes, an' we think our cook, Aunt Fanny, bakes terrific bread."

Evelyn took this opportunity to make a comment that was dear to her heart. "In fact our bread is dah' very best in des' parts an' even better din' dah' recipe in Mrs. Randolph's cookery book." Mrs. Carter sat quietly, choosing not to say anything about the bread baked at her plantation.

"Well, maybe Aunt Fanny's almost rivals dah' bread at dah' Carter plantation," exclaimed Colonel Marshall smoothing over an obvious faux pas as everyone chuckled. "I would also like to mention my own special Madeira, which I'm also 'bery proud of—please partake in some with me now."

As the guests were made comfortable, the colonel made another announcement. "I invite y'all to enjoy dah' pleasure of dah' drinks an' desserts dat' are bein' placed at dah' buffet table, an' be sur' to 'member to have some of Aunt Fanny's bread."

Donald, the oldest son of Colonel Marshall was good looking but he lacked the same aristocratic bearing and fine features of his father. He had his father's square chin and gray eyes, although not as striking, and he wore his sandy colored hair rather long. He was a sarcastic, spoiled, and annoying young man; forever ridiculing his brother Albert for things he did or didn't do. "It's really somethin' to be able to witness such a spectacle as Halley's Comet on such a clear evenin'."

"I understand dat' it only returns every seventy-five years, which means dat' we are goin' to have to wait 'til 1910 to see it 'gain," added Robert Carter in a humorous manner. Robert's intelligence along with his good looks, medium length black wavy hair and sparkling blue eyes gave him an aristocratic appeal. It was obvious that he was Colonel Marshall's counterpart in many aspects.

"Which means we'll all be dead an' buried," Donald exclaimed with a smirk on his face. Everyone nervously appeared to appreciate Donald's attempt at humor. He then added, "What really 'mazes me is dat' only two years ago from dis' month we were visited by a huge meteor shower dat' was really somethin' to witness."

"Dah' night of dah' fallin' stars," Robert further commented, "I wonder what is goin' on? Is God givin' us some sort of message? Many think dis' is dah' signal of dah' Apocalypse. I know dat' dah' servants on my plantation believe dis'."

Donald interjected, "We fo'got 'bout somethin' else. Jus' a few years ago, didn't we have a terrible earthquake not too far from hyeh'? I know I'm addin' fuel to dah' fire, but it does give more weight to what largely our servants are sayin'."

"Donald, yur' right! I don't know when an' whar' dat' took place an' normally, my memory is razor sharp," Robert added.

Everyone in the parlor was trying to remember the date of the earthquake when Reggie, the personal servant to Donald's younger brother Albert, spoke up. "Master Robert, I know when dat' happened." There was a stunned silence in the room. Reggie had entered into the conversation because he was the only one who knew the answer. This behavior was normally unacceptable from a servant in the South, but in Reggie's mind he was only sharing information that he felt was pertinent and should be appreciated. He was well aware of the negative implications of a servant joining the conversation but hoped his brief participation would be accepted since nobody knew the answer to the question.

Reggie represented an anomaly as a house servant. Reggie was strikingly handsome with dark wavy hair and brown penetrating eyes. He was of medium build and height with a slightly tanned appearance. He possessed a special carriage about him that commanded attention; his overall looks could allow him to pass for being southern European. His presence was imposing and accentuated with an intellect that couldn't help but shine. It was obvious that women would be attracted to him while men could only envy him, and yet he was, ironically—a slave.

Robert quizzically asked in a pompous manner, "If yu' know, tell us!"

"It occurred in December of 1811 an' continued on an' off 'til 1813. Dah' epicenter was located near New Madrid, Missoura'," Reggie answered with confidence.

"Did we ask fo' dah' location? Anyhow, epicenter is a fancy word fo' a servant to know. How did yu' learn dis'?" Donald's words were dripping with sarcasm as he tried to get a reaction from the guests. He knew that Reggie had been allowed to learn to read and write and simply hoped to only belittle him.

"Master Albert was instructed on dis' matter by his tutor, an' I was present," replied Reggie very respectfully.

Donald, displaying both irritation and resentment, exhorted, "If Master Albert was instructed by his tutor, din' why didn't Master Albert answer dah' question? Albert, aren't yu' as smart as yur' servant?"

Albert, a frail looking young man in his early 20's, appeared very gaunt and tired. He looked a lot like his mother, only more pallid with gray eyes and curly sandy colored hair with a pale complexion indicating how seldom he was able to get out in the sun. Albert was obviously embarrassed at his brother's confrontation, and he replied in a defensive but timid manner, "Donald, I'm so tired I'm simply unable to think."

"Oh, I see," Donald retorted. Let's be honest—dah' servant knows more din' dah' master." The guests stirred uncomfortably as Donald berated his younger brother. In the past Donald had freely made comments intended to hurt him—this display was not new.

Abigail, the youngest daughter of the Marshalls, was in her late teens and was an attractive, raven-haired young lady with green eyes. She was a copy of her mother without the maturity needed to have acquired her mother's elegance. She recognized that Donald was about to launch yet another insulting attack on Albert, and she entered the conversation to soften the tone. "Like Mr. Carter, I

18

keep hearin' some of dah' servants talkin' like Halley's Comet is 'nother message dat' dah' world is comin' to an end."

"Abigail, I wouldn't listen to any of dat' conjurin' talk from dah' servants. It seems like everythin' dat' comes up is a sign of dah' end times," Donald countered.

Albert meekly contributed, "Abigail, sometimes I wonder if God works in mysterious ways." Then he asked, "Reggie, what does it say in Isaiah 'bout dat'?" It would almost appear that Albert was showcasing his personal servant, Reggie by posing the question as he did.

"Master Albert, in Isaiah 13:6 dah' Bible says, 'Hear ye', fo' dah' day of dah' Lawd' is at hand. It should come as destruction from dah' Almighty'." Again, everyone was amazed at Reggie's acumen. This was especially true of the guests from Boston who had been taught that slaves were not permitted to learn to read and write.

Donald was furious. "'Nough of dis' talk! We really don't need spiritual messages quoted to us from a common house servant. How do we know if his quote is even accurate?"

"Donald, if yu' think he didn't' answer dah' question correctly," Albert countered, defending Reggie, "go 'head an' check dah' Bible." Clearly, Albert was intent on standing up for Reggie against his brother.

"I'm not goin' to take time from our guests to check dis' servant's knowledge of dah' Bible," Donald replied, knowing that Reggie would most likely be right and therefore avoiding being proven wrong.

"I have read dah' Bible, an' I do recollect dah' book of Isaiah does make some references similar to what Reggie quoted, but I honestly couldn't recall Isaiah as well as Reggie," Albert added.

"Let's drop dah' subject," Donald dryly submitted.

Emma, an eighteen-year-old Bostonian, who was fairly attractive with long, light brown hair and a quiet demeanor, broke into the discussion. "I must admit that I'm impressed with everything I have seen and heard, and I know my Aunt Opal is equally impressed."

"I agree with Emma, but may I be candid? I must admit that I have not seen all the suffering and cruel forms of punishment associated with slavery that I read about before I arrived here," Sarah remarked. Suddenly, stillness entered the room, and you could almost hear a pin drop. Sarah realized she had said something to offend and knew she had made a major faux pas.

Colonel Marshall, patiently observed and listened before speaking up. "Pardon me, ladies, I hope yu'll forgive me fo' bein' a little fo'ward. In fact da' 'ministration of corporal punishment in dah' South toward a servant happens to be much rarer din' dah' punishment 'ministered to criminals up North. Incidentally, dah' word slave is not used in dah' South. Dat's one of dose' inflammatory words used by rabid 'bolitionists to stir up trouble in our beloved South. We are God-fearin' people. Dah' Bible does not mention treatment of slaves but only servants. Hyeh' in dah' South we honor dah' Bible. I know in dah' North many don't read dah' Bible, so dey' wouldn't be expected to know dat'. " Of course this statement was insulting to the guests from the North but was intended only as an assumption designed to make his case.

Sarah, a very attractive young lady in her early 20's with blue eyes and long flowing chestnut hair was very intelligent and well-mannered. Out of respect she chose not to dispute Mr. Marshall, however in her mind she still questioned his analogy. Comparing a house servant to a criminal in jail made absolutely no sense.

"Now yu' got me all riled up." As Robert turned to face Reggie, "Let's ask yur' house servant, who knows the Bible an' everythin' else, to tell us what dah' good book says 'bout slaves." Robert smirked at his condescending comment while emphasizing the word slaves.

Reggie, proud of his knowledge, quickly answered, "Ephesians 6:5 states, 'servants, be obedient to dem' dat' are yur' master accordin' to dah' flesh wit' fear an' tremblin' in dah' singleness of yur' heart as unto Christ'."

"Dat's right, an' notice dat' he said servants an' not slaves—dat's 'cause dah' Bible doesn't use dat' word." Robert continued with conviction, "Yu' know, we are God fearin' people in dah' South, quarterin' only servants an' field hands, not slaves. An' 'bove all, we don't want Northerners who don't know dah' Bible to talk 'bout dah' South an' our 'perculiar' institution when dey' do not know what dey' are talkin' 'bout." Robert's emphatic comments made it very clear that this particular misunderstanding was a very sensitive subject in the South.

"With all due respect, Colonel, I'm truly sorry if my words offended anyone," Sarah backtracked. "I meant no harm. It's intriguing information we should all know, and I don't think many Northerners are even aware of this. However, I feel that we do know the Bible as well, although some in the North may not have noticed that the Bible does not explicitly use the word slave." Sarah felt a definite defensive presence amongst the Southerners by the tone of the conversation.

Robert Carter had correctly addressed one of the main justifications for the bondage system. Until the King James Version of the Bible was revised in 1881, Ephesians 6:5, like other parts of the Bible, avoided the word slaves, using instead servants. This was critically important since it justified how the South was able to successfully argue they only followed the Bible, adhering to the word servants. The word slaves could then be passed off as a Northern term used by the abolitionists designed to stir up trouble.

"I jus' want yu' ladies to know dat' we have a two-sided coin 'tween dah' North an' dah' South, an' y'all are learnin' 'bout dah' other side. 'Member to take back with yu' what yu' learned down hyeh' to help educate Northerners wit' regards to dah' Southern point of view," Robert stated politely but forcefully.

The very insightful Colonel Marshall made a poignant comment. "Yu' know, I've never given much thought to what I'm 'bout to say, but havin' dis' conversation wit' our friends from dah' North has put me to think 'bout somethin' dat' I never considered 'fore. It has always been clear to me how far apart dah' North an' dah' South are from one 'nother in their thinkin' on a lot of issues. Would it be possible dat' our division could be so great dat' we could even eventually take up arms ovah' it? I know dat' sounds somewhat outrageous, but I can't git' it out of my head."

Robert added, "Colonel, yu've asked an excellent question, but who's goin' to respond? Everybody in the North has convinced 'demselves dat' dey' are right an' we are wrong. Of course we're not willin' to listen to 'dem no more din' dey' are willin' to listen to us. Dose' meddlin' 'bolitionists only four years ago incited dah' Nat Turner 'surrection right near hyeh' in South Hampton. Innocent men, women, an' even children were unmercifully slaughtered by dat' mad dog an' his bloodthirsty followers. We're still tryin' to recover from dat'. It only made a bad situation far worse 'tween dah' North an' dah' South. How kin' we listen to 'dem when dey' support such a horrible act 'gainst us?"

"Robert is right," replied Colonel Marshall, his eyes glistening with passion and anger. "As I said earlier, dey' send des' trouble-makin' 'bolitionists down hyeh' to cause havoc wit'out even knowin' 'bout our feelins' or how we treat our servants." After carefully considering his words, the colonel continued, "Wouldn't yu' wonder jus' how many conflicts have occurred simply 'cuz' people cannot communicate wit' each other? Better yet, is it possible fo' society to understand dat' nothin' is totally black or white? As much as I hate to admit it, I believe each side will have to make concessions 'fore we kin' ever come to a meetin' of dah' minds."

Robert added with strength, "Dat's true, Colonel, but still dat' doesn't belie dah' fact dat' dah' North is more culpable din' dah' South fo' our strained relations. Think 'bout it—dey' are tellin' us how wrong we are while sendin' dose' dreadful 'bolitionists down hyeh' to stir things up. Who are we sendin' up thar' to agitate 'dem? We all know dey' are havin' thar' own problems. Thar' festers a mighty big rub an' 'sides, are dey' really in love wit' thar' own 'bolitionists? As I jus' stated, we have 'bery little evidence of Southerners goin' North wit' any intent of changin' things up thar', instead, goin' to dah' North only fo' social or business reasons. I do think it's obvious to yu' ladies why we have a right to be upset regardin' dis' matter."

22

The colonel saw his opportunity to shift the conversation to a more positive note. "Let's try to be optimistic in dah' face of dah' fact dat' we have been able to openly discuss dis' subject hyeh' today."

Sarah demurred, "You folks have raised many points we had not considered before. Thank you for enlightening us."

Abigail had been listening quietly and finally said, "While at school in Boston, I talked to a so-called free Negro. Yu' know what he tole' me? He said dat' in many ways he was better off livin' in dah' South. He said dat' up North he had restrictions on votin', couldn't sit on a jury or sue in court. He was forced to live segregated from dah' whites—dis' included havin' to ride in a separate railroad car. Worse yet, he couldn't find a job, so he had to live on dah' streets beggin' fo' food to survive 'cuz' nobody would hire him. Do our Negroes have to endure such sufferin' as dat'? Of course not, all their needs are provided."

Donald, who had also been restless but silent, added, "Our servants at least know whar' dey' stand—not like dah' hypocritical North! Dey' always have a roof ovah' thar' heads; three square meals a day an' clothin', an' medical care are all taken care of. Why, I have even seen poor white Southern trash come 'round hyeh' beggin' fo' food from our field hands knowin' dey' are better off din' 'dem." Then in a heated tone, he continued. "It's time fo' dose' despicable 'bolitionists to git' out of hyeh' an worry 'bout thar' own Negro people who need more help din' ours! An' 'member dis', as dey' continue to hamper relations 'tween dah' North an' South, things will only git' worse." It was made perfectly clear to the Northern guests that the Southerners viewed the abolitionists as a big part of the problem between the North and the South.

Emma, who now had become somewhat more sympathetic to the Southern point of view, politely commented, "Abigail, I want to return to what you just said. As a Bostonian, I have noticed the same thing. In fact I have heard the free Negroes referred to as 'temporary residents' or 'inhabitants'. The word citizen is carefully avoided."

Robert couldn't restrain himself when he heard Emma's remarks. "Do yu' know why dey' call 'dem 'temporary residents' or 'inhabitants'?"

"No, I don't believe I do," she replied. "I really never gave it much thought."

"Well, I have! 'Cuz' up North, yur' own American Colonization Society an' President Jackson want to ship 'dem all back to Afriky' to become citizens thar'! Under dah' political guise of promotin' democracy in Afriky', which dey' call 'dah' dark continent', dey' kin' dispatch dah' Negroes in an attempt to keep dah' North white." Robert continued in a condescending manner, "Dey' sur' don't want 'dem to git' too comfortable hyeh'. Dey' jus' wanta' wash thar' hands of 'dem completely an' git' everythin' back to lily white. Add to dat', a lot of Northerners aren't happy wit' dah' influx of Afrikys' goin' to dah' South from Afriky, but as long as dey' stay in dah' South, dey' kin' tolerate it. Incidentally in dah' North, dah' 'back to Afriky movement' is politically supported as a humanistic agenda, which I personally find rather interestin'. Now if my history serves me right, the ACS was founded in 1816 by Robert Finley as a humanitarian cause. Are yu' sur' dat' dey' jus' don't want to git' rid of 'dem? Anyhow, talkin' 'bout des' matters, I honestly 'lieve dat' Southerners are actually more tolerant toward Negroes din' Northerners. Wit' dah' North, it's all a facade." Of course Robert failed to mention that the South was economically dependent on the labor of the blacks for their cotton production, which requires what is called the "gang system" of labor. Meanwhile, the North had no real need for the labor of black people since they did not have any cotton production, nor were they suffering from any real labor shortage since Europeans continued to enter the United States filling any labor shortfall. A good portion of the new immigrants were Irish.

Everybody chortled at what Robert had just said. The conversation appeared to have swung over to putting more blame on the North for the problems between the North and the South with the South objectively able to support their beliefs with credible evidence.

"I 'gree wit' what I heard earlier. I have never said dis 'fore, but I have wondered why dah' Southerners don't send people up North to stir things up jus' like dah' Northerners do to us. 'Sauce fo' dah' goose is sauce fo' dah' gander'," Abigail added with a smirk on her face.

Robert agreed. "Well put, Abigail, an' let me jus' add one more 'portant matter. Have y'all heard of our 'peculiar institution' in dah' South? Well, in Federalist Papers—I'm sure it's article number fifty-four, our own beloved Virginian, James Madison, touches on it. It simply refers to our guardian institution dat' does not recognize full citizenship fo' our house servants an' field hands. But is dat' any different din' a Negro who becomes a full citizen in dah' North bein' referred to as a temporary resident or inhabitant while carefully avoidin' callin' him a citizen an' din' wantin' to dispatch him back to Afriky. Now dat's' what really burns Southerners up. It's jus' 'nother example of dah' hypocritical North not takin' care of thar' own problems. In fact, dah' North is much worse to thar' Negroes din' us 'cuz' dey' do everythin' under dah' guise of equality an' citizenship. Maybe dey' better learn to rein in thar' own prejudices." Robert successfully presented a strong argument that addressed the failure of Northerners to want to accept blacks as free citizens equal to white people.

Arguably, while Robert did make an adequate defense for the South, he failed to elaborate on the implications of the "peculiar institution"—slavery and why it was looked upon unfavorably in the North and throughout most of the world. The problem for the South arose when confronted with the words of the Declaration of Independence—"All men are created equal". How can you justify in the United States that all men are created equal while a bondage system exists in the South? Again, the mystery of this question was resolved by the Southerners. They recognized in their own twisted reasoning that slaves could not be citizens, and therefore, the Declaration of Independence and the Constitution could not apply to them. Since they could not be citizens legally, then they fell under the special category of being members of the "guardian institution" with the same rights as livestock or any other animal. It is truly disgusting to understand what the "bondage system" really entails. Therefore, the term "peculiar institution", a euphemism was adopted to avoid having to directly address this egregious issue.

The situation in the North was different, insofar as slavery was not legal, and therefore, the "guardian institution" did not exist. However, the Northerners as said earlier did commonly use the terms "temporary residents" or "inhabitants", which meant they were very reluctant to legally render "true" rights upon their fellow black citizens.

After Robert presented his criticism, Donald added, "Dah' South does not have to defend its actions to dah' North or anybody else!"

"Well put, son," said Colonel Marshall.

Sarah asked, "You folks make a good case, but what about the violence that we hear of in the South?"

"Violence!" echoed Robert. "Our violence comes from outside agitators like we discussed earlier wit' dah' Nat Turner 'surrection. Incendiary 'bolitionists, dat's what dey' are. In a recent book, a Mr. Estes pointed out dat' dah' 'mount of violence is ten times greater up North 'mongst dah' so called free Negroes din' 'mong our own Negroes. Dis' is jus' 'nother example of why dah' North should worry 'bout thar' own problems." Perhaps Robert was given to a bit of a hyperpoble in his description to make his point.

In a compromising manner Emma mused, "When I get back to Boston, I'm going to start asking some questions."

"When y'all git' back North, help to educate 'dem to worry 'bout 'demselves an' not us," Robert suggested. "'People who live in glass houses should not throw stones'."

Sarah politely decided to change the subject. "Colonel Marshall, where did you get your title?" Perhaps Sarah thought she was putting Colonel Marshall on the spot.

"Sarah, dat' is a question dat' I'm very proud to answer." Then Colonel Marshall, holding his head up and his chest out, bellowed, "I'm a rock-ribbed Virginian, an' as one of her loyal sons, I command dah' local state militia to help protect her. I know dat' up North dey' do not take des' matters seriously. Quite simply, hyeh' in dah' South military life, huntin', fishin', an' even duelin' to resolve differences are a way of life." The implication was clear—men in dah' South are more manly than men in the North.

Sarah couldn't resist asking another question—one a Northerner might pose. "Doesn't the presence of an active militia mean having armed camps throughout the South?"

"Sarah, we consider yu' a friend, so let me answer yur' question wit'out takin' yur' words as an insult. Do yu' see any armed soldiers marchin' 'round in ole' Virginny'?"

Sarah awkwardly replied, "Honestly, I meant no harm since I have not witnessed an active military presence. In fact, it's not any different than Boston."

Colonel Marshall was not quite finished. "Let me explain dat' we do have to be vigilant 'gainst 'bolitionists. In addition our federal government does not maintain a standin' army. What would happen if we were invaded by 'nother country? Dah' South is better prepared fo' trouble din' dah' North wit' our state militias prepared to fight coupled with our conditioning due to our outdoor livin'."

Politically, Colonel Marshall's answer to the question—justifying an active militia presence throughout the South successfully evaded what many would believe to be the real reason. Slave insurrections had occurred both in the United States and throughout the world, a situation that helped to create paranoia throughout the South. The presence of an active militia represented a response to any potential slave uprising. In addition, militia members provided a practical value since they were required to periodically serve as patrollers, overseeing enforcement of a variety of rules the slaves had to abide by. This included apprehension of runaway slaves or just a slave who wondered off the plantation, and of course there were additional matters that had to be dealt with.

Evonne, the oldest daughter of the Marshall's, had remained silent throughout the discussion. Not nearly as attractive as Abigail,

Evonne looked almost dowdy by comparison. Her brown hair was fine while her skin remained pale next to it. It was apparent that her younger sister overshadowed her. She felt compelled to speak. "Father, somethin' was said earlier 'bout duelin'. I jus' want to make dah' point dat' a lot of dah' women in dah' South find dat' practice to be barbaric." After the comment Evonne sensed that she had said something that was better left unsaid.

Donald quickly seized the moment. "In addressin' our father like dat', I sometimes think dat' yu' have dah' manners of a Yankee!" Not everyone laughed at Donald's comment including Colonel Marshall and Evonne.

The colonel's face was flushed with emotion. "Donald, yu' meant Northerner, not Yankee! Des' are our friends who happen to be Northerners an' our welcomed guests, an' referrin' to yur' own sister, Evonne, as a Yankee—yu' know, dat' we consider Yankees to be dah' most vile, crude an' spineless people on dah' face of dah' earth! All des' 'bolitionists, a good chunk of dah' overseers an' slave traders are dirty Yankees from dah' North comin' South fo' pure greed an' represent dah' most despised class of people anywhar'—not my daughter."

It's interesting that the colonel made this clear distinction between a Yankee and a Northerner. Most Northerners would not be aware that the use of these two words, in the South was not interchangeable. This further emphasized the wide communication gap that existed between the two regions.

Evelyn commented, "Andrew, darlin', yu' are right. I must apologize to our guests. I'm sur' Donald meant to say Northerner an' not Yankee."

Andrew quickly added, "'Dah' matter is 'water over dah' dam'. Dey' know yu' meant no harm—jus' a slip of dah' tongue." Andrew recognized that it was a good time to make a toast. "Yu' know, I think as yur' host it's time to raise our glasses to our beloved Virginny', mother to our Presidents—'member, we are first Virginians, second Southerners, an' third Americans, an' we warmly welcome our guests hyeh' to Virginny' an' want to share our passion an' love fo' our beloved state."

The South was a strong defender of states' rights, and Colonel Marshall's bellicose toast—putting Virginia first, certainly personified that passion. Unfortunately, the South's strong political conviction toward states' rights could only further strengthen the division between the North and the South, since the North supported a stronger federal government with less states rights.

Everybody clicked glasses and sipped their wine. At this point Colonel Marshall offered his guests the opportunity to retire. "With dat' toast I might add dat' if any of yu' want to retire fo' dah' evenin', please do so. It's been a long day."

Sarah quickly responded, "Colonel Marshall may I be excused? I am rather tired."

"Miss Sarah, yur' room has been prepared. We sincerely hope yu' enjoyed our soiree, an' we bid yu' adieu." It's notable that he emphasized the word soiree to possibly demonstrate that he could be bilingual, perhaps to further impress his guests.

"Colonel Marshall, I've had a delightful evening between watching the comet and being a small part of such a stimulating and educational conversation. I bid my hosts and everyone a good evening," Sarah said in well-mannered fashion.

***

Sarah left the parlor and went up the stairs and through the hallway where she accidentally came upon Reggie. Startled, she exclaimed, "Oh my, how fortunate to run into you. I really wanted to meet you, but nobody bothered to introduce us."

"Miss Clark, I'm a house servant, an' dat' would not be 'ceptable at a social gatherin' of dis' level. At an informal gatherin' introductions might be more acceptable. Protocol always rules in dah' South."

"Reggie, I've been intrigued by your appearance. You don't look like a typical house servant at all. As a matter of fact, you even bear a slight resemblance to Donald and Albert."

Reggie suddenly became red-faced and nervous, "Miss

Clark, dis' conversation could git' me in deep trouble. Dis' is one topic dat' must be 'voided."

"Reggie, I understand and sincerely apologize for making you uncomfortable." Sarah had touched on a subject that the South was extremely sensitive to acknowledge—miscegenation, the mixing of the races. Sarah realized this was not to be expanded upon and shifted the conversation. "Well, what did you think of the comet?"

"Miss Clark, I was in total awe of dah' spectacle. In fact tonight standin' out thar' watchin' dah' comet put me into an unreal, dream-like trance. While others interpreted dah' comet as a sign of dah' end times, I saw it as a positive omen of better things to come."

"Reggie, please call me Sarah, now tell me what you meant by that."

"To me, I felt dat' dah' comet represented God's eyes watchin' ovah' us to see if we could better understand dat' in his eyes we are all one throughout dah' world an' not jus' separate races, unequal to each other."

"Reggie that is truly amazing. While most interpret the comet in a negative manner, you can see it in a positive light. This is certainly a reflection of a very vivid mind."

"Miss Sarah, please don't mention dis' discussion to anyone," Reggie pleaded. "It could make things difficult fo' me." His training as a slave was so complete that he could not call her Sarah, even when requested.

"Oh no, Reggie, you can trust that I will never say a word." Sarah gave a quizzical look, "Reggie, just what do you do for the Marshalls besides assisting Albert?"

"Miss Sarah, I'm dah' personal servant to Albert an' have dah' full responsibility of takin' care of his needs. We have been together our entire lives."

"How did you learn to read and write? I thought, as a servant, you were forbidden to have an education."

"Miss Clark, I'm an 'ception," Reggie told her. "In fact, Virginia statutes forbid me from learnin' my letters an' numbers.

The Marshalls permitted me to be educated alongside Master Albert 'cuz' he's had a bit of a struggle wit' his schoolin'.'"

In the 1830's throughout the United States, public education was not provided. In Virginia, education was largely administered through tutors who came to the plantations. Unfortunately, the majority of the people could not afford a tutor, so formal schooling was not available.

"Does this help extend to other areas?" Sarah queried.

"I've instructed Albert in swimmin', boatin'·an' even horseback ridin' as best I could."

Sarah was obviously impressed with his resume. "Reggie, you are an inspiration. You are a house servant, and a well educated house servant at that—how unique that you know so much."

Pleased at what Sarah said, Reggie added, "Who knows, maybe it might serve me well in dah' future."

"Yes Reggie, it just might help you in a big way someday."

"Miss Sarah, I jus' want yu' to know how much I 'preciate yur' interest." Reggie said.

"Reggie, there's one other thing." As Sarah whispered," My father happens to be a man of influence. If you ever find yourself up North, look me up in Boston. I live at 418 Beacon Street. Now be sure to memorize that address for future reference—it could be extremely important for you in the future. With your intelligence and good looks father could possibly help you build a new life," Sarah promised with a smile on her face and a wink in her eye.

Reggie responded in a in a lowered voice, "Miss Sarah, what yu' have jus' tole' me has helped to give me dah' incentive dat' I will need to make my way up North someday soon. I love an' respect Albert, an' deep inside, I'm torn 'part knowin' dat' my best friend is so deeply ill. I sense dah' end is 'bery near fo' him," Reggie sadly went on. "Yu' saw dat' he could barely make it to dah' party. I pray every night for him to recover, but I jus' don't see any improvements. In many ways, he is my only reason fo' 'ceptin' my life in bondage. If he would die, I think my life would change drastically an' most likely not fo' dah' better, which would force me to flee."

Not wanting to further explore Reggie's sensitive comments, Sarah asked, "Reggie, what does the doctor say?"

"Not much—he jus' keeps givin' him laudanum," Reggie replied dolefully. "'Round hyeh' dey' don't do much curin' but keep yu' goin' wit' pain killers. I've read laudanum is a highly addictive tincture of opium dat' is 'ministered throughout dah' United States fo' a variety of ailments as a pain killer."

"Between you and me," Sarah offered, "if he were in Boston, he would get better treatment. I think they would come up with more then just laudanum."

"Miss Sarah, I'm not at liberty to explore dis' subject." Reggie cast his eyes downward.

Sarah changed the subject when she saw that Reggie was becoming sad and a little tense. "On a positive note, I do look forward to seeing you in Boston someday—you never know what the future might hold. By the way, something else is troubling me. It appears that Donald dislikes you almost to the point of being obsessed with jealousy."

Just as Reggie was about to respond, Donald emerged in the hallway and witnessed the conversation. It was obvious that he was going to take aggressive action as he advanced toward Reggie with a crazed look. He shoved Reggie away from Sarah and exploded. "Reggie, I saw yu' havin' a conversation wit' our guest as if yu' were one of us. Such liberty represents a serious breach of conduct! Yu' have to know yur' place!" He smashed Reggie in the face with his fist and then began punching him in the stomach. Reggie fell to the floor while the pummeling continued with Donald kicking him repeatedly in the ribs.

Sarah screamed as she backed away, her face drained of color as she witnessed the brutal way that Donald was attacking Reggie, "Stop, stop, Donald! I beg you to immediately stop this barbaric treatment! I am absolutely appalled at what I'm seeing!"

"Okay, Sarah, I'll quit." Donald's beating ended as quickly as it began—Donald realized his temper had gotten the best of him. Southerners were carefully trained not to display any facet of the dark side of slavery to outsiders, and he knew he had violated the code of conduct.

"I was only asking Reggie about the health of Albert! I had no idea this would put him in peril." Sarah was breathing heavily, angered and in shock as she went on. "We were given the impression that everybody is happy in old Virginia, and then I'm a witness to this horrible reality!"

"Sarah, I'm truly sorry, an' I beg yur' fo'giveness, but hyeh' in dah' South dah' power of dah' master must be absolute over dah' servant," Donald explained. "I have been taught dat' dah' punishment must be immediate an' harsh. I trust dat' yu' will understand dat' we still have a wonderful relationship 'tween dah' master an' dah' servant as long as dah' servant 'knows his place.'" The expression, "as long as he knows his place" is significant since it clearly defines the absolute separation between the white people and the slaves.

"I would have preferred that your actions were alcohol related and not the ridiculous justification that you have just given me!" Sarah was enraged. What he had said and done illustrated to Sarah how cruel and inhumane the bondage system really could be.

Donald didn't like having to defend himself. "It does not have to be dah' wine! He must learn—now he will be better off atter' bein' reprimanded. Does improper behavior in dah' North go unchecked?"

Sarah's utter disgust with Donald continued. "We would never administer to a servant a physical beating such as this. For one thing, it wouldn't be legal"

Reggie, who had risen with difficulty from the floor, was now standing, slumped against the wall.

"Reggie, be off wit' yu'," Donald demanded.

"Yes, Master Donald," Reggie meekly replied as he slowly limped away.

Sarah watched Reggie leave and was visibly shaken seeing the pain that he was in. "I feel guilty," she confessed to Donald. "I never should have approached Reggie to ask him about Albert."

Donald recognized that Sarah was still very upset. "It was

his fault fo' not declinin' to talk to yu'. But I do have a request of yu'. I have an ider' to take yur' mind off dis' whole affair. May I have dah' pleasure of yur' company fo' a horseback ride tomorrow so dat' I kin' show yu' dah' plantation?"

"Regretfully, I must decline—I don't think I'll feel up to it." With that she turned abruptly, her skirts rustling and angrily walked away without a backward glance.

"We kin' discuss dis' matter 'morrow atter' yu' have had a full night's rest an' are in a better frame of mind. Goodnight, Sarah," Donald called after her in a confident tone, dripping with arrogance, and sarcasm. The wine had only accentuated what he truly was, and Sarah had seen enough.

CHAPTER TWO

Early the next morning Albert was lying in his bed, very ill and uncomfortable having spent a sleepless night. He looked toward Reggie, who was sitting on a blanket on the floor watching him. "Reggie, please talk to me," Albert whispered.

"Master Albert, what is it?" Reggie's voice was filled with concern as he quickly drew himself to his master's side.

It was obvious to Albert that Reggie had been in a fight and had gotten beaten up. "Reggie, it looks like yu' were in a terrible scuffle. Who did dis' to yu'?"

"Master Donald saw fit to comb me over fo' talkin' to Miss Sarah in dah' hallway atter' dah' party," Reggie responded.

"Why, what did yu' do to deserve dis'?" Albert wondered out loud.

"Master Donald explained to me dat' I acted dah' role of a white man by talkin' informally to a guest."

"He really does resent yu', Reggie." Albert's voice was filled with contempt. "It's obvious to me dat' he was jus' lookin' fo' an excuse to hurt yu'. Nobody knew dah' answers at dah' party 'cept yu', an' I think dat' he resents yu' since yu' are so smart. He really should be happy dat' yu' were thar'. "

"Master Albert, I do 'preciate yur' interest, but we both know how dah' system works." In the South, the slave stereotypically was accepted for his physical prowess and not his mental capacity. Reggie represented an aberration—an intelligent slave who would then be viewed unfortunately as a potential threat to the maintenance of the bondage system. In fact, educated slaves would often be hesitant to acknowledge their educational level to whites for fear of reprisals that have led to death.

"A system dat' would do dis' is horribly wrong—it's jus' plain cruel. Reggie, yu' have suffered a beatin' an' din' yu' have to come to dah' bedroom to sleep on dah' floor 'cuz' a servant must always sleep lower din' his master. It's inhumane not bein' able to put yu' in a bed whar' yu' kin' rest comfortably." Albert's response spoke volumes to Reggie about how fortunate it was to have such a kind master; who, like himself was caught in such a wretched social environment, which he also abhorred.

"Master Albert, don't worry 'bout me," Reggie replied. "My only fear is yur' health."

"Reggie, yu' must stop frettin' 'bout me. It's too late. Last night I saw dah' grim ferryman arrivin' to take me." As Albert said these prophetic words, tears emerged from his eyes.

"Master Albert, yu' cannot talk 'bout death. Yu' must think of dah' future an' realize how much yu' have to look forward to. I beg yu' to hold on an' git' ovah' dis' hump. Pray wit' me to God fo' yur' restoration."

"Reggie, I'm really tired. I could barely make it to dah' party. It was such a struggle, an' I was completely powerless even to defend myself from Donald's insults."

"Master Albert, yu' acquitted yur'self in fine fashion under dah' circumstances."

"Reggie, I think it's time fo' me to reveal somethin' dat' I have held back from yu' a long time. What I'm goin' to tell yu' is a deep, dark secret dat' yu' cannot repeat to anyone. Do yu' know dat' my father is yur' father?" Albert paused to see Reggie's reaction. "Reggie, we are half brothers!"

"Yes, Master Albert, I have known fo' a long time dat' Colonel Marshall is my father makin' yu' my half brother. I also know dat' dah' entire bondage system of dah' South rests on an absolute law dat' determines dat' since my mother is a slave, I have to be a slave as well. We both know Colonel Marshall could never acknowledge dah' truth to anybody."

"Reggie, do yu' know who yur' mother is?"

"Yes, Master Albert, I know my mother. Have yu' ever wondered whar' I used to go on Sunday when dah' colonel issued me a pass?"

"Whar'?" Albert became emotional as the two shared their information.

"My mother, who has since passed 'way, lived on a plantation down dah' pike. Colonel Marshall use to let me visit her, maybe out of guilt. I never could figure dat' out. I knew dat' it had to remain a secret or he said he would punish me severely if I ever tole' anyone."

"Reggie, I always realized dis'. I didn't quite know dah' whole story, but I knew not to ask questions. 'Nough of dat', I know dat' I'm rapidly fadin', an' I want yu' to know dat' yu' are dah' brother dat' I love an' respect as well as my best friend. I also know dat' God granted yu' dah' good looks an' intelligence, which I've always been a little envious of. I've even had to depend on yu' fo' most everythin'. So now I have somethin' fo' yu' that I know yu' are gonna' be needin' in dah' future. In dah' bottom drawer of my dresser is a fair amount of cash dat' I have set 'side. I want yu' to have it, an' please do not argue wit' me. Take it an' use it fo' when yu' decide to seek a new life in dah' North. Don't say a word—it means a lot to me to give yu' somethin' to fall back on fo' all yu' have done fo' me! Trust me, Reggie dat' one day yu' will flee from slavery an' dah' funds I have provided will be a major help. At dat' time yu' will learn why Southerners forbid slaves from havin' money—it greases dah' wheels' to make it easier to git' to freedom!"

"Master Albert, I can't take yur' money." Reggie could barely believe Albert would do such a thing for him, and his mind raced with fear that the funds would be missed by someone in the family. However, he was grateful and overwhelmed with Albert's display of gratitude and brotherly love.

"Yu' must, Reggie—'lieve me when I say dat' yu' will need it on dah' road to freedom. Please take it, as yu' have more din' earned it, an' don't worry 'bout anybody lookin' fo' it as dah' money has long been fo'gotten 'bout," Albert pleaded.

Albert was emphatic and Reggie knew he had to accept the money. "I do understand yu' want me have dis' money, an' I 'cept it wit' gratitude. Words of thanks fall short in expressin' how I feel 'bout dis' gift. Master Albert, last night I tole' Miss Sarah dat' yu' have always been my best friend, an' I'm holdin' out fo' yur' speedy recovery. Now yu' need yur' rest. Is thar' anythin' I kin' do fo' yu'?

"I'm glad yu' will 'cept dah' cash. Now I jus' need to sleep, but I'm 'fraid I won't wake up. Reggie, does dah' night of death have a mornin'?" Again, tears emerged from Albert's eyes.

"Of course Master Albert, an' someday both of us will be in heaven pickin' up whar' we left off hyeh' on earth." Reggie was taken aback by what Albert had said.

"I do believe we will be together whar' thar' is no more pain, meanness, or death—only love an 'ceptance in dah' presence of our God almighty. An' I kin' almost see heaven now as I feel dat' I'm rapidly fadin'."

Reggie became alarmed at Albert's words. "Rest peacefully, Master Albert. Jus' 'member dis' is not yur' time to go to heaven," as Reggie slowly closed the bedroom door.

He then went to alert Albert's mother sensing that Albert's condition appeared to be deteriorating. He soon found Evelyn in the parlor reading the Bible, "Missus Evelyn, yu' need to see Albert. He looks extremely tired, an' he's not at all himself."

Evelyn gasped and rushed out of the parlor and up to Albert's room. Entering the bedroom, she quietly knelt down beside him. "Albert, my dear Albert, how are yu' feelin'?"

"Mother, I'm rapidly fadin', an' I don't think dah' doctor kin' help me anymore. What I need is prayer."

"Now, Albert, let your mother decide dat'," she pleaded. "Fortunately, dah' doctor lives close by, an' I'm goin' to dispatch Reggie to git' him right now! Yu' know dat' he's our tried an' true rider."

"Mother, I jus' hope dah' doctor. . ." His voice faded and

his words became inaudible as he wept.

"Don't yu' worry, Albert, he will be able to help yu'. Let me leave yu' fo' a short time while I go git' Reggie an' send him on his way to bring dah' doctor." Evelyn rushed downstairs to the kitchen where she found Reggie. "Reggie, I want yu' to bring Doc Jamison hyeh'. Don't waste any time, an' ride like dah' wind— take our fastest steed, Hermes. Now yu' best be goin'."

"Yes, Missus Evelyn, I'm on my way." Reggie went to the stables and quickly saddled up Hermes. Pushing open the stable door, he rode off at top speed. He could be heard riding out bellowing, "Come on Hermes let's ride 'boots an' saddle'. Now git' movin' like da' debil' is tryin' to catch us. Yah'!"

By midday, everyone in the Marshall home had learned of Albert's deteriorating condition. Sarah and Emma joined Abigail and Evonne in the dining room for lunch. "Abigail, you look so sad. Is Albert going to be all right?" Emma inquired.

"My brother Albert had what appears to be 'nother setback. Dis' has happened 'fore, but dis' time it appears more serious, but we are still confident dat' he will pull through," Abigail revealed.

Emma responded, "Is there anything we can do?"

Abigail burst into tears. "I'm so scared, Emma. I love my brother so much. He has always recovered 'fore an' dis' should be no 'ception. Let's all pray fo' 'nother miraculous rally."

"Abigail, Evonne, we promise you both that we will pray with all our hearts for Albert." Emma responded.

"Mother has dispatched Reggie, our top rider, to git' dah' doctor. Fortunately, he lives a short distance down dah' pike," Evonne stated.

As the four young ladies nervously picked at their lunch, Donald entered the parlor. He gently approached and said, "Sarah, I do apologize fo' dah' misunderstandin' last night. Perhaps I was a little ovah' zealous, but yu' have to understand we do have our Southern traditions. Abigail kin' explain it an' do a better job." Donald brought up the previous evening, perhaps out of a certain amount of guilt knowing that Sarah was highly offended, and he wanted to rectify the situation as quickly as possible.

Abigail volunteered. "Well, Donald was a little hard on him, but yes, he only did what would be expected. Donald was respondin' to dah' fact dat' our servants have to 'know thar' place'. Wouldn't yu' accept dat' up North servants are expected to 'know thar' place' as well? I'm sur' dat' Reggie will only be better in dah' end. Distinct lines of social positions are strictly adhered to in dah' South 'tween whites an' servants. Dah' confrontation 'tween Donald an' Reggie represented a normal reaction to a perceived threat from a servant dat' must be suppressed—dah' line 'tween a white man an' a servant cannot be breached under any circumstances."

"I've been taught to always let a sleeping dog lie, but my conscience still dictates that what happened to Reggie was not right," Sarah replied.

"Sarah, in time yu' will understand," Donald said.

Both Sarah and Emma, demonstrating the good manners of guests, chose not to say anything more about the issue.

Gently, Abigail changed the subject. "Let's jus' pray fo' Albert's speedy recovery. Dat's what's important."

Donald concurred and suggested they see if Albert was up to having company. The five set out for Albert's bedroom with Abigail and Evonne reaching the bedroom door first and Donald and the others right behind them. They then knocked softly.

Albert responded weakly, "Who is it?"

Abigail cracked the door open and whispered, "Albert, kin' yu' see yur' two sisters, brother an' our guests from Boston?"

Evelyn, who had never left Albert's side, answered for him. "Come in quietly."

Albert spoke just above a whisper with great difficulty as they entered his room. "It's so hard for me to lie in dis' bed when I would like to be havin' fun wit' all of yu'."

Albert's sister, Evonne, tried to comfort him. "Albert, yu'll be jus' fine. Dah' doctor will be hyeh' any time, an' he'll fix yu' up jus' like 'fore."

"Sis, I hope yu' are right, but dis' time it's really bad. I tole' Reggie dat' dah' end is near—I have dat' sinkin' feelin'." Albert responded.

Evelyn interjected, "Albert, my dear Albert, don't talk morbidly like dat'. Yu' have always battled back, an' dis' time will be no 'ception," Evelyn pleaded with her son.

"Mother, please believe me dat' I'm tryin' hard to not depart dis' earth fo' some unknown adventure dat' is one big mystery dat' I'm in no hurry to be a part of." Albert's words were interrupted by a knock at the door. It was Doc Jamison.

"Doctor, please come in. Albert is lookin' fo'ward to seein' yu'." Evelyn breathed a sigh of relief as she spoke.

The doctor entered the room along with Colonel Marshall and announced, "I'm gonna' ask all of yu' to leave fo' now while I tend to Albert."

Quickly, everyone left the bedroom and returned to the parlor to wait for the doctor's report on Albert's condition. There was still food on the table, and the servants continued to provide food and drink to everybody. The women nervously chatted while the men anxiously paced the floor.

An hour later the doctor entered the parlor with the update. Parsing his words carefully, he stated, "Albert is declinin' all medication. He has always 'cepted laudanum in dah' past, but he's refusin' it." Albert probably knew his only hope was in a cure and not laudanum that would only numb the pain.

Evelyn's hands were trembling, while she cried as she spoke with Doc Jamison. "I'll talk to him an' try to change his mind. Doctor, I'm pleadin' wit' yu'—please stay wit' us 'til he's out of danger."

"Of course I'll stay," the doctor replied. "Oh, he requested to see his Mammy Bertha."

"We'll git' her right away." Evelyn immediately dispatched one of the servants to run and fetch Mammy Bertha.

Mammy Bertha had been Albert's black nursemaid while he was a child growing up. She was the stereotypical black mammy. Her dark features were set off by silver-gray hair that she wore in a bun. Her ample frame was clothed in a multicolored dress dominated with red and designs similar to the clothing worn in her village in Africa. Topping off this strong figure was a bright red headscarf that accentuated her appealing features. She was a matronly woman who appeared to be in her early sixties, and, like others in her position, had been rewarded with her own small cottage in which to live in retirement. She had been hoping to be called on to care for Albert ever since he was ill, and when the servants came to get her, she eagerly responded and rushed to Albert's room.

Evelyn called out, "If it's yu', Mammy Bertha, come right in as Master Albert wants yu' to be wit' him."

She entered the bedroom and pulled up a chair, sitting next to Albert along with the doctor, Colonel Marshall and Evelyn.

"Marse' Albert, yur' Mammy Bertha is hyeh' to see yah'." She leaned over softly so he could hear her.

"Oh, Mammy Bertha, I'm so glad to see yu'." Albert looked up at her with a child-like glance and a weak smile.

"Marse' Albert, yu'll be jus' fine. Jus' like in dah' past, yu'll come 'round an' be back to yur' ole' self," Mammy Bertha said with assurance.

"Not dis' time, Mammy Bertha. I fear dis' is dah' end of my time hyeh' on earth." Albert whispered to her with finality.

"Marse' Albert, don't talk like dat'. Let me go 'bout dah' business of makin' yu' well. Yur' Mammy Bertha will take good care of yu' an' fix yu' up right fine!" Mammy Bertha conveyed her message with strength and conviction.

"Mammy Bertha, I'm scared, real scared. My legs are even turnin' blue. Dat's never happened to me. What does dat' mean?"

"Marse' Albert, dat's a matter for dah' doctor. I'm sur' he'll know what to do fo' dat'." She knew this could be a sign that the body was beginning to shut down, but of course she had no intentions of conveying anything negative to Albert.

"Mammy Bertha, please give me one of yur' big hugs an' kisses. Dat' would comfort me an' warm me up more din' anythin' else."

"Oh, yes, Marse Albert, I'll warm yu' up wit' a big hug an' a kiss jus' like when yu' were 'knee-high to a grasshopper'." She held him warmly for a few moments, kissed him on his cheeks, then laid him back and placed a cool, damp cloth over his forehead. "Marse' Albert, would yu' like yur' Mammy Bertha to sing yur' favorite song, *Go Tell It on dah' Mountain?*"

"Would yu' please, Mammy Bertha? Dats' so kind of yu'— it would ease my pain."

"Of course, Marse Albert." Mammy Bertha sang in a soft melodic voice that had a very positive, comforting affect and briefly took his mind off of his rapid decline and what appeared to be his inevitable death.

Go tell it on dah' mountain,
Over dah' hills an' everywhere,
Go tell it on dah' mountain,
Dat' Jesus Christ is Lawd'.
When I was a seeker,
I sought both night an' day.
I asked dah' Lawd' to help me
An' He showed me dah' way.
Go tell it on dah' mountain,
Over dah' hill an' everywhere,
Go tell it on dah' mountain,
Dat' Jesus Christ is Lawd'.
He made me a watchman,
Upon a city wall.
An' if I'm a Christian,
I'm dah' least of all.
Go tell it on dah' mountain,
Over dah' hill an' everywhere,
Go tell it on dah' mountain,
Dat' Jesus Christ is Lawd'.

When Mammy Bertha finished, Colonel Marshall spoke. "Albert, I know yu' are goin' to recover. It's important dat' yu' keep fightin' an' not give up. Dah' doctor is stayin' to render whatever care yu' may need, an' he'll remain wit' yu' 'til yu' feel

43

better. Yu' know dat' Doc Jamison has always done dah' job fo' any ailments yu' have faced."

"Father, I do hold out fo' a miracle, an' Mammy Berthas' presence instills dat' hope, but I still fear dat' dis' time it is different," Albert whispered as he seemed ever weaker. "Somethin' else—regardless of what happens to me, please make sur' dat' dah' 'cawn' shuckin' party goes on as planned. I wouldn't want dah' party cancelled on my account."

"Of course we are goin' to have dah' 'cawn' shuckin' party', an' yu'll be a part of it," Evelyn assured. "Albert, yur' father an' I are leavin' now so dah' doctor kin' care fo' yu'. If yu' need anythin', Reggie will be right outside yur' door to assist Doc Jamison."

The annual "corn shucking party" was one of the major events every year. Common in the North as well, it represented a celebration for harvesting the fall corn. Each year a different plantation in the area hosted the event, and it was Oak Manor's turn to host the festivity. This meant the neighbors along with their servants and field hands all be in attendance. It was a huge gala with whites celebrating in and around the "big house", while the slaves celebrated in the barn and quarters. With separate facilities, food was plentiful for the whites and the blacks. Music and dancing could always be observed, especially among the slaves. The gala would last throughout the night and into the morning hours as it was always intended to be a long, spectacular occasion.

The doctor left to join the others in the parlor after he had tended to the needs of Albert. Reggie then reentered the bedroom to continue his vigilance over Albert. Albert sensed it was Reggie and he awoke. He looked over and saw Reggie by his bedside. "Reggie, I'm so glad to see yu'. I heard yu' were dah' one who brought dah' doctor to me. Thank yu', Reggie, fo' bein' so loyal an' carin'."

"Albert, yu' know how much yu' mean to me. I know yu'd do dah' same fo' me jus' as sur' as dah' sun will rise." Reggie said, trying to muster up a smile.

"Reggie, I would throw my life in peril to save yu'. Yu' an'

Mammy Bertha are dah' two people closest to me in dah' world. I know yu' rode long an' hard fo' me. I'd like fo' yu' to git' some much needed sleep." It was notable that even on his deathbed Albert was worrying about Reggie and did not mention his parents, brother, or sisters.

"Master Albert, don't fret 'bout me. I'm more worried 'bout yu'." Reggie wanted Albert to know that he would be there through thick and thin, which was something that they both had always known.

"Good night, Reggie," Albert stated in a halting fashion, almost as if this could be his final night of sleep. There was a haunting finality in the way he said it, and it weighed heavy on Reggie's heart as he tried to dismiss his foreboding feelings and go to sleep.

CHAPTER THREE

Toward daybreak before the others awakened, Sarah and Emma became engaged in a rather serious conversation in the parlor. "Sarah, maybe I should not say this, but I was surprised by what I saw last night."

"What was it, Emma?"

"Albert was gravely ill, perhaps on his deathbed, and he appeared to be more calmed by the presence of Mammy Bertha than by his own mother. Isn't that a little unusual?"

"Perhaps it would be considered strange in the North, but this is the South," Sarah explained.

"Sarah, that's not all," Emma went on, "Albert even had that old colored woman hug and kiss him. To be hugged and kissed by an old colored woman—I think I would rather be kissed by a dog."

"Emma, don't be silly. I'm sure that Mammy Bertha nursed Albert and helped to raise him," Sarah said. "If you study Southern customs, you will find that the upper class women find it degrading to nurse their children. That is the job of the black mammy."

"I never knew that."

"Furthermore, Emma, it's possible that Evelyn may have distanced herself from Albert by relying too much on Mammy Bertha."

"Sarah, perhaps I spoke in haste," Emma concluded. "Still, you know in the North few people would let an old colored woman hug and kiss them."

"Emma, it is ironic that Northerners' feel so strongly about discrimination in the South. Perhaps in some ways it's worse up North or maybe just different. I will always remember my uncle telling me the difference between the North and South regarding their attitude toward Negroes." Sarah continued, "In the North we don't care how rich or powerful they may become—so long as they stay at a distance from us. In the South they don't care how close they get to them—as long as they stay poor and of course in servitude."

Emma thought for a moment. "That's really insightful, and quite frankly, the best that I have ever heard it put. In fact, I have to admit that I fell right into a trap when I made my thoughtless comment. Perhaps, I expressed a narrow view taken from a Northern perspective without realizing the South could see it differently. Could that be a part of what the heated discussion at the party was about when Colonel Marshall and Mr. Carter were explaining the Southern position on things."

"You're right," Sarah answered. "Yes, Colonel Marshall did state that you have to examine both sides of an issue to reach an objective understanding. I think he meant it to be applied to many situations; and moreover, he broadly believed that our leaders need to do a little more of that."

While they were talking, Abigail quietly entered the parlor with her personal servant. Sarah and Emma quickly changed the subject. "Abigail, we are so devastated by what your family is going through," Sarah offered. "Our hearts go out to you. Is there anything we can do?"

"Albert has always recovered. Dis' will be no 'ception," Abigail stated in a positive tone.

"We feel confident you are right," Emma agreed.

Abigail then turned to her personal servant, Anastasia, who was with her almost all the time. "Anastasia, yu' kin' leave now."

"Thank yu', Missus." She gave a small curtsey and left to continue with her duties.

Emma looked perplexed. "Abigail, I couldn't help but

notice just how beautiful your personal servant is. I was also a little perplexed at her light skin. May I ask about her background?" asked Emma.

Abigail's face became flushed as she responded, "Hyeh' in dah' South thar' are certain things we don't discuss. Dis' is a topic we find to be in 'bery poor taste." Emma was commenting on the stunning looks of Anastasia. While only a house servant, she seemed out of place. Long, smooth black hair in a bun, beautiful, piercing black eyes and a flawless olive complexion—she stood out from everyone else on the plantation. Interestingly, it was known by some that Anastasia and Reggie had developed a close relationship.

Emma could see that her inquiry was an error and apologized, "I'm sorry for prying into matters that are considered to be in poor taste. I meant no offense."

"Emma, I fo'give yu'," Abigail said. "But let's not speak of dis' matter 'gain. I'm sur' it's time dat' we take breakfast, an' din' we kin' go an' check on Albert." Emma had unwittingly opened up the topic of miscegenation, an area carefully avoided in the South. The South was faced with the inability to confront a deep-seated problem that would increasingly become even more difficult. How do you classify people of mixed blood in a system that deals supposedly in only absolutes? Perhaps you ignore the problem and "kick the can down the road" and let the next generation worry about it.

Evelyn awakened early and rushed to Albert, finding him considerably weaker. The doctor was already in the room tending to Albert. In spite of of his state of health, Albert was cognizant of everything and wanted to talk to Reggie alone. He asked the doctor and Evelyn to leave for a short time and motioned for Reggie to come closer.

"I want yu' to know somethin', Reggie. If I die, be wary of Donald. I fear he will do more harm to yu' din' what is imaginable."

"Master Albert, why do yu' think dat' Donald would hurt me more din' he did dah' other evenin'?" Reggie had known matters between him and Donald had worsened, but he needed to hear Albert's opinion.

"He has told me 'fore dat' he doesn't like yu', an' if he has his way, yu' would be transferred to dah' quarters to work as a common field hand."

"Master Albert, I've known fo' a long time dat' he doesn't like me, but to put me in dah' quarters? Surely, Colonel Marshall would recognize my loyalty to yu' an' yur' family."

"Reggie, I have discussed dis' subject wit' father, an' I could tell dat' my words were fallin' on deaf ears. I'm not sure dat' loyalty 'tween a master an' servant kin' ever exist. Dah' servant's loyalty is required. However, no loyalty kin' be required of dah' master to dah' slave. Everythin' must be absolute fo' dah' system to work an' father is well aware of dis'. He knows he kin' never acknowledge dat' yu' are his half son. Father once tole' me dat' he understands dah' warm relationship 'tween dah' two of us, but trust me, Reggie in dah' end, dah' system must always rule, dat' makes yu' a slave an' not his half son. As yu' like to say Reggie, 'dah' bondage system requires absolutes—nothin' in dah' middle.'"

"Master Albert, thank yu' fo' carin' 'nough to try to protect me by warnin' me 'bout Donald."

"I'm on my death bed, an' I have to put my cards on dah' table. Reggie, wit' yur' light skin an' intelligence yu' could pass fo' white an' simply head north to freedom. Do it, Reggie! Yu' are my brother an' best friend. Now mark my words—I'm dyin' so I have to tell yu' dis'. Circumstances fo' yu' will be a lot worse 'round hyeh' when I'm gone. Wit' dah' money yu' have yu' have a good chance to make it to freedom an' begin a new life. I'm only thinkin' of yu', Reggie," Albert pleaded. "I want yu' to have a new life, a new beginnin'; an' up North, yu' kin' have dat' along wit' yur' freedom. Reggie, yu' deserve all of dis'!

"Master Albert, I love Anastasia, an' I couldn't leave wit'out' her." Reggie was moved to tears by Albert's sensitivity toward his well being while on his deathbed.

"Please call me Albert an' not master when we're 'lone—we're brothers. As fo' Anastasia, she is light skinned as well. Dah' two of yu' could flee together, although it's gonna' make it more difficult if yu' travel as a pair."

"Albert, yu' have a rich imagination. But what's important now is dat' yu' are goin' to recover. Didn't Aristotle say dat' 'hope is a wakin' dream'? I jus' know dat' yu' will maintain hope while yu' git' better." As they spoke, the doctor knocked on the door to resume tending to Albert.

When Doc Jamison entered, Reggie excused himself and took the dishes downstairs to the kitchen where Anastasia had begun her morning chores. She looked up and gasped. Taking a deep breath, she stood in front of him, and raising her hands, she gently touched his face. "Dear God—Reggie, what happened to yu'?"

"Donald saw fit to punish me fo' talkin' to one of our guests in dah' hallway atter' dah' party," Reggie explained.

"Reggie, my love," she softly said, "I love yu' so much, an' to see yu' punished by dat' evil Donald enrages me. What did yu' do dat' was wrong other din' oblige dah' house guests when dey' needed an answer to a question dat' nobody else knew dah' answer to? Dis' whole evil system dat' we have to live under jus' sickens me."

"Anastasia, don't worry 'bout me—I'll be fine. 'Sides, dah' doctor looked me ovah' an' said I jus' had a few bumps an' bruises. Pray fo' Albert—dat' is who we need to worry 'bout!"

"Reggie, if Albert would die, din' dat' wicked Donald would do yu' even more harm. I 'lieve he would turn yu' into a field hand wit'out any hesitation."

Reggie tried to sooth her. "Anastasia, Colonel Marshall has dah' final word, an' I am confident dat' he would never put me out into dah' field—'sides, wit' my skin color I wouldn't be welcome in dah' quarters. Yu' know as well I do dat' dah' true African slaves regard people wit' our color suspiciously. Dey' 'cept me as a house servant, but as a field hand? I would think dey' would look at me distrustfully, thinkin' I'm an informant. Colonel Marshall knows all dis' as well as we do. He surely wouldn't 'throw me to dah' wolves.'"

"Don't be too sur' of dat'." Anastasia answered, fear entering

51

her voice as she spoke. "We kin' never let our guard down. Wit' Albert gone, no tellin' what Donald would do. 'Member, he is his son an' dat' carries a lot of weight. Maybe Colonel Marshall wouldn't 'throw yu' to dah' wolves', but I'm not so sur' 'bout Donald. He's so jealous. He knows dat' he is half dah' man yu' are! He would jus' love to bring yu' down."

Reggie did not want to alarm Anastasia by informing her that Albert had said the same thing. "Anastasia, let's put dis' matter 'side fo' now. I haven't had a chance to hold an' kiss yu' fo' so long, an' we are all 'lone. Come hyeh' an' let me embrace yu'."

They held one another close while Reggie gave her a quick kiss. "Oh, Anastasia, I love yu' so much."

"My dearest, I love yu' wit' all my heart," Anastasia responded. The strength of their love made all things seem bearable.

"I have to git' back to Albert. 'Member, Anastasia, yu' are always in my heart."

"I understand, Reggie, but please try to return to me soon," she pleaded.

Reggie departed and immediately went to see Albert. Entering the bedroom, it was obvious to Reggie that Albert's condition had deteriorated even further. He was alone and awake. Reggie asked him, "Is thar' anythin' I kin' do to make yu' more comfortable, Albert?"

"Yes, please bring me some water," he weakly requested.

Reggie assisted Albert with the water and told him, "I'm gonna' run an' git' dah' doctor. I'll be right back."

Albert quietly reacted. "Go 'head, but it's not gonna' matter—I'm slippin' fast."

Reggie immediately ran downstairs and found the doctor in the parlor talking to Colonel Marshall and Evelyn. Hesitant to interrupt but needing to get their attention, Reggie went up to the colonel. "Master, it 'pears dat' Albert's condition is worsenin'."

Evelyn was in a near panic state as she, the colonel, the doctor, and Reggie rushed back to Albert. The four entered the bedroom as Albert was lapsing into a semi-coma. Evelyn turned to the doctor, sobbing, and asked, "What kin' we do?"

After quickly examining Albert he turned to her slowly, his eyes and face reflecting his sadness and quietly stated. "Evelyn,

I think dat' at dis' stage we have to prepare to put Albert in God's hands."

Evelyn frantically begged the doctor after hearing the crushing news, "Isn't thar' somethin' yu' kin' do dat' yu' haven't tried yet?" She frantically stated, very quietly so Albert would not hear, "He can't die. He simply can't."

"Evelyn at dis' point I kin' only make Albert as comfortable as possible," the doctor informed her.

"Dah' thought of losin' our son in dah' prime of his life is extremely difficult," Colonel Marshall said quietly.

"Andrew, let's jus' keep prayin' fo' a miracle an' not give up hope," Evelyn cried out to her husband.

Through the next few hours, the family and Reggie never left Albert's side. It was evident he was slipping into a deeper coma. Finally, the doctor announced that the end was very near, and everyone should now pray for a peaceful passing.

Toward midnight with everyone present, Albert took his last breath and Colonel Marshall announced, "Albert is now wit' dah' Lawd'." He then said a short prayer over his son's body.

Evelyn was sobbing hysterically, her body stretched across Albert's. Overtaken with grief, she repeatedly begged Albert to wake up. "Albert, Albert, Albert, yu' can't do dis' to us. We all love yu' so much. Yur' mother can't live wit'out' yu'."

Colonel Marshall tried to help her. "Evelyn, don't fear fo' Albert—he's in Gods' hands. If anybody who ever walked dah' face of dis' earth deserved heaven, it would be Albert—he was almost like a sinless baby. He never caused harm to anybody, an' I'm sure dat' he is right up in heaven lookin' down watchin' us an' lettin' us know dat' now he is happy an' at peace."

"Andrew, thank yu' for tryin' to comfort me, but dah' loss of Albert will always be an' unbearable pain in my heart," she replied. As was the custom, the mirrors in the room were covered with dark cloth and windows opened so his soul would go directly to heaven.

***

In the morning, arrangements were being made for the funeral. Everyone had gathered in the parlor. Meanwhile, Colonel Marshall had assured Evelyn that all the important details were being taken care. "During dah' night I asked Jacob, our carpenter, to craft a special pine coffin an' as I speak, he is linin' dah' coffin wit' a dark blue fabric."

"It all sounds so morbid, Andrew," Evelyn wept. "Puttin' my Albert— my baby, in a coffin—I jus' can't face it."

"Evelyn, we have no choice." The colonel stated, "Circumstances require dat' dah' funeral must be swift, an' we have to move quickly. Jacob will be bringin' dah' coffin in, an' we must properly prepare Albert for viewin' in dah' parlor." A speedy funeral was paramount, since embalming to preserve the body was not an option.

"Andrew, I'm sorry, all of dis' is on yu'—I can't be helpful in any way. I must admit, it will be all I kin' do, jus' to git' my black mournin' dress an' jewelry on."

"Dis' is my responsibility," Andrew informed her. "I dispatched Luke to town to git' black buntin' at dah' general store, an' Devon was sent to git' Reverend Daniels fo' dah' service arrangements. Also, Monroe is on Hermes, an' he is out notifyin' everybody 'bout Alberts' death an' dah' impendin' service."

This caused Evelyn's voice to rise hysterically. "Dah' reverend lives quite a distance from hyeh', an' I'm worried he may not 'rive in time."

"Don't fret, Evelyn." Andrew tried to calm his wife by placing a hand on her shoulder. "If he doesn't 'rive in time, I kin' 'grab dah' bull by dah' horns' an' conduct dah' service myself."

In this time of deep sorrow, the house servants continued to be busy preparing for the funeral. Luke had returned, and the all-important black bunting was being draped conspicuously throughout the house. The minister had not yet arrived, which meant that Colonel Marshall would probably have to preside over the services. Meanwhile, Jacob had placed the coffin in the parlor after Mammy Bertha had done an excellent job of lovingly preparing his body.

Albert looked so calm and peaceful laying there that it appeared that he might awaken at any moment.

In the general quarters Mr. Eggers, Colonel Marshall's

overseer, had already instructed the field hands to take the day off to attend the funeral services. Further, they were instructed to clean up and wear their Sunday best. Notably, they knew this was an important social matter, and it represented an insult to them, thinking they would not know any better.

As two o'clock drew near and Father Daniels had not yet arrived, Colonel Marshall decided to begin the service. Many of the neighbors were present, including the Carters and of course, the colonels brother, Lawrence and his family. The field hands gathered in the rear and sang spiritual songs in honor of Albert. It was a very somber occasion, but the feeling was more of a celebration for Albert's life while here on earth, because it was felt by all that he would be receiving his just reward in heaven.

Colonel Marshall called everybody to the parlor while the overflow crowd assembled in the hallway. He then announced, "Services will be exact to dah' standards of dah' Episcopal Church. I have my *Book of Common Prayer* 'long wit' my trusty Bible, so let's now git on wit' dah' services knowin' dat' Albert is in good hands an' we will now put our son to rest wit' dignity."

The words evoked an emotional outcry from Evelyn, who started sobbing again over Albert's coffin. "Albert, my dear Albert, please listen to yur' mother an' come back to me."

Colonel Marshall broke in. "Evelyn, our dear son is in heaven, not hyeh'. He no longer has to suffer. He is pain free an' livin' in a better place."

"Andrew, our son is in heaven, an' I want to join him. I want to be in heaven wit' my beloved son," replied Evelyn as she wept. She was visibly shaking and speaking incoherently.

The colonel continued, "Evelyn, someday we will all be joined in heaven wit' Albert, but it's not our time jus'yet." He then opened the *Book of Common Prayer.* "I'm now goin' to read a short passage to celebrate our son's departure to be wit' our Father in heaven."

Oh God, who's beloved Son did take little children into his arms an' bless dem': Give us grace, we beseech thee, to entrust to

dis', our youngest son, Albert, to thy heavenly kingdom; through
dah' same thy Son Jesus Christ our Lawd' who liveth an' reignth
wit' dem' dah' Holy Spirit, one God, now an' fo' ever. Amen.

Everyone repeated the "Amen" as the colonel reached for his Bible to find the readings for the burial service. He said, "I'm now goin' to read from dah' Old Testament, dah' Book of Isaiah":

He will swallow up death fo' all time,
An' dah' Lawd' God will wipe tears 'way from all faces,
An' He will remove dah' reproach of His people from all dah'
earth; Fo' dah' Lawd' has spoken .

Departing from the Book of Isaiah, the colonel then added some words of his own. "Fo' all of us gathered hyeh', dis' scriptural readin' tells us dat' Albert 'chieved a victory bein' wit' dah' Lawd', an' not to despair, he is in heaven wit' Jesus." After a moment's pause he continued, "Finally, from dah' New Testament, dah' Book of John, 5:24."

Truly, truly, I say to yu' he who hears My word, an' believes Him
who sent Me, has eternal life, an' does not come into judgment, but
has passed out of death into life.
Amen.

"All of us know, an' most importantly, dah' Lawd', dat' Albert lived as good of a Christian life as anyone could live. He believed in his Lawd' an' practiced what dah' Bible says. In addition, he gave nothin' but kindness to everybody. Dat's why none of us should have any fear fo' dah' passin' of Albert. He is indeed in heaven wit' our Heavenly Father. Amen." The Amen was echoed by those gathered, and then the coffin lid was closed. It was now time for the journey to Marshall Hill, the family grave site.

Pallbearers lifted the coffin and carried it to a wagon decorated with black bunting for the cortege to the cemetery.

Sadly, even though Reggie was the half brother and best friend of Albert, he could not be a pallbearer because of his status as a house servant. Active participation in the services by Reggie would be forbidden since the chattle system wouldn't allow a slave to be directly connected to a death service involving a white person. Reggie was a slave, and that would have to take precedence over everything else even though he was the closest to Albert. Everything must remain absolute.

All of the servants and field hands moved close to the wagon as they sang in unison, *Swing Low, Sweet Chariot:*

Swing Low, Sweet Chariot,
Swing Low, Sweet Chariot,
Swing Low, Sweet Chariot-
Don' yu' leave me 'hind,
O, don' yu' leave me 'hind.
Good old chariot, swing low,
Good old chariot, swing low,
Good old chariot, swing low-
Don' yu' leave me 'hind,
O, don' yu' leave me behind.
Good old chariot, take us all home,
Good old chariot, take us all home,
Good old chariot, take us all home-
Don' yu' leave me 'hind,
O, don' yu' leave me 'hind.

The coffin was set in place on the wagon, and Colonel Marshall addressed Uncle Eustis, an old, trusted servant. "Uncle Eustis, it's time to take dah' reins an' move dah' cortege." Everybody fell in behind the wagon. Following protocol, the white folks led while the servants and field hands followed last. Through the entire ritual, the servants and field hands continued to sing while the white people remained silent and prayed to themselves.

Arriving at the burial site, Marshall Hill, the pallbearers picked up the coffin and placed it on the bier, and Colonel Marshall then opened up the coffin for one final viewing. Everyone, both white and black, began to weep and moan out loud. The immediate family, especially Evelyn was sobbing uncontrollably at this point. Mammy Bertha who had to remain close to the rear was also grieving loudly as everyone viewed Albert for the last time.

Colonel Marshall allowed ample time for the people to pay their respects. Finally, he announced, "Let's lower dah' lid an' consecrate dis' grave site now. All bow yur' heads."

O, God, whose blessed Son was laid in a sepulcher in dah' garden:
Bless, we pray, dis' grave,
an' grant dat' Albert's body may dwell wit' Christ in paradise,
an' may come to Yur' Heavenly Kingdom;
Through Yur' Son, Jesus Christ, our Lawd'.
Amen.

Colonel Marshall motioned to Donald to come up. "Lead us in dah' *Lord's Prayer*, son."

Donald moved to the forefront, bowed his head and in a clear voice recited the *Lord's Prayer* while everyone joined in:

Our Father, who art in heaven,
hallowed be thy Name,
thy kingdom come, dey' will be done,
on earth as it is in heaven.
Give us dis' day our daily bread.
An' fo' give us our trespasses,
as we forgive dos' who trespass 'gainst us.
An' lead us not into temptation, but deliver us from evil.
Fo' thine is dah' kingdom, an' dah' power, an' dah' glory,
fo' ever an' ever.
Amen.

The coffin was lowered into the ground as people were outwardly grieving. Mrs. Marshall as expected was crying uncontrollably and the colonel went to her aid. Finally, family and guests slowly made their way back to the house where food and beverages were being served. Interestingly, only a token force of house servants tended to the guests, most remained with the field hands at the grave site while Mammy Bertha led everybody in a spiritual song, *"Jesus Goin' To Make Up My Dying Bed."*

(CHORUS)
Yu' needn't min' my dyin', needn't min' my dyin',
Yu' needn't min' my dyin', Jesus goin' to make up my dyin' bed.
(LEADER)
In my dyin' room I know, somebody's goin' to cry,
All I ask yu' to do fo' me, jus' close my dyin' eyes.
(CHORUS)
I'll be sleeping in Jesus, I'll be sleepin' in Jesus,
I'll be sleepin' in Jesus, Jesus goin' to make up my dyin' bed.
(LEADER)
In my dyin' room I know, somebody's goin' to mourn,
All I ask yu' to do fo' me, jus' give dat' bell a tone.
(CHORUS)
I'll be restin' easy, I'll be restin' easy,
I'll be restin' easy, Jesus goin' to make up my dyin' bed.
(LEADER)
When I git to heav'n, I want yu' to be thar' too,
When I cry out 'holy', I want yu' to say so too.

The spiritual singing continued as everyone milled about as the grave was filled in with dirt. Then the slaves carried out the African tradition of leaving an object on the grave site. Mammy Bertha set a piece of pottery on the ground, and Reggie left a treasured token while others placed fragments of pottery, bones or little metal objects. These articles all represented something personal from each of them. They wanted to send along an object that meant something to them for Albert to have. In their eyes he was an exceptional person who clearly understood and respected them as individuals—white or black, it did not matter to Albert.

Eventually, everyone returned to the plantation except

Reggie, Abigail, and Mammy Bertha, who now stood beside the grave. Tears ran down Mammy Bertha's face as she said to Reggie, "I know how difficult dis' will be on yu'—he was yur' brother an' best friend."

"Yes, he was, Mammy Bertha," Reggie somberly responded. "In my heart what always stands out 'bout Albert was dah' fact dat' he could understand us better din' any other white person I have ever known. In fact in many ways he was one of us. I truly love him, an' he will always be wit' me."

"Reggie, I felt dah' same," Mammy Bertha concurred. "He was like my own son an' not jus' a little white boy dat' suckled off me who I gave no love to."

At that moment, Abigail came forward, almost appearing mesmerized and recited this unknown poem:

Sleep Dear Albert, sleep softly.
Hyeh' whar' dah' zephyrs sigh,
whar' I may come.
To shed a tear,
from sorrowin' eye.

And then as she turned to leave, she left one single lily at the head of his freshly given grave.

Slowly, they walked back toward the house filled with mourning over Albert. In their hearts they felt that life without Albert would never be the same.

As Mammy Bertha, Abigail, and Reggie arrived at the house, they could hear everyone sharing their memories of Albert. The guests remained for quite some time, and those who were staying overnight eventually drifted off to their bedrooms, exhausted from the emotions of the long day.

Reggie, who still maintained his quarters in Albert's room, knew this was the opportune time to secure the funds Albert gave him. Out of respect for Albert, he had purposely avoided taking the funds until he had passed away. Now his status as personal servant would soon change, and it behooved him to act before it might be too late. He chose a quiet, wooded location where he and Albert had played as children and toward evening he buried the money in a jar at the base of a weeping willow tree.

CHAPTER FOUR

In the morning Colonel Marshall and Donald met to discuss the death of Albert. It was a difficult conversation, but necessary. "Donald, I feel a little guilt 'bout havin' dah' 'cawn shuckin' party so soon atter' yur' brothers' death," the colonel sadly stated.

"Father, Albert wanted dah' 'cawn shuckin' party to go on. It would be 'nother way of honorin' Albert's memory," Donald offered consolingly.

"Perhaps yu' are right," the colonel agreed. "I sorta' thought 'long dose' lines too, but I wanted yur' 'pinion."

Donald's demeanor abruptly became very serious, "Father, yu' might have a bigger concern or problem din' dat'."

"What is it?"

"Have yu' given much thought to what yu' are goin' to do 'bout Reggie?"

"Of course not, Donald, yur' brother jus' died. I'm aware dat' since Reggie was Albert's personal servant, he will need to be reassigned."

"Father, I have given it a lot of thought. Haven't yu' noticed dat' Reggie seems to have fo'gotten his place 'round hyeh'? Didn't yu' spot him struttin' 'round at dah' party comportin' himself like a dignified white man? Later, I saw him personalizin' wit' one of our guests. Dat's when I put my foot down an' put some bumps an' bruises on his face."

"I did notice his condition, an' I was upset to hyeh' dat' yu' 'ministered dah' punishment in front of one of our guests. Donald, we don't ever want to promote dose' types of actions in front of guests from the North—our image is important. Yu' know dat' I shoulda' reminded yu' more often 'bout yur' responsibilites! But, jus' what are yu' gittin' at?"

With a smirk on his face Donald replied, "Since he has to be reassigned anyway, why not put dat' rascal in his place an' reduce him to a field hand? Let him think 'bout whar' his place is out in dah' quarters. He really needs to be 'seasoned', an' I can't think of a better spot fo' him."

"Donald, yu' know dat' Reggie's a 'display niggah'", an' when he gits' out into dah' quarters he may not mix well. Dah' darkies don't 'cotton to a yaller' colored niggah". Dey' would give him a rough time. Do yu' really want me to bring dat' on Reggie?"

"Father, thar' is some more mischief goin' on wit' Reggie dat' yu' may not know of."

"What? I have always felt dat' Reggie could do no wrong?"

"Yu' apparently haven't spotted him romancin' Anastasia while shirkin' his duties. Everyone knows dey' are carryin' on together 'cept yu'. Doesn't dah' master decide who his servant kin' court? Dat' should not be Reggie's decision."

"Donald, let me git' dis' straight. Reggie's 'carryin' a torch' fo' Anastasia—dah' pretty, light skinned, young servant dat' I have sorta' watched ovah'." The tone in Colonel Marshall's voice suggested something devious was now going on in his mind.

"Dat's right, father," Donald confidently answered.

"'Donald, dat's a horse of a different color'!" It appeared that Reggie was tampering with the colonel's private property, a young woman who had been reserved for him and him alone!

Donald displayed an insidious smile while saying, "Father, I kinda' thought yu' would see it my way once yu' knew dah' whole story." He knew that his father's concern would be raised when he learned that Reggie had designs on Anastasia.

"I jus' wish I had known dis' sooner. I would have nipped it in dah' bud, but Donald, yu' might jus' be onto somethin'. Reggie

64

does need to be 'taken down a peg or two' based on what I'm learnin'. Dis' is serious business. 'Dat' niggah' is tryin' to pull dah' wool over my eyes'. Yu' are right, we gotta' git' dat' rascal out of hyeh' an' into dah' quarters whar' we kin' keep an eye on him, an' he kin' be taught a lesson." The colonel, showing no remorse, demonstrated his sudden contempt toward Reggie, manifesting in his decision to reassign Reggie to the slave quarters. He made this determination even though he knew Reggie was his biological son, and this arrangement could very well bring egregious harm onto him.

"Father, how soon do yu' want him dispatched to dah' quarters?" There was joy in Donald's question as he knew Reggie was soon going to suffer in his new environment.

"'Immediately! Go see Mr. Eggers 'bout his 'signment. Atter' hyehin' all dis' it jus' warms my heart to git' dat' yaller' niggah' out of hyeh'. While yu' are at it, have Mr. Eggers put some stripes on his nice clean back jus' fo' 'further seasonin''." The colonel had surprised himself ordering Reggie to be whipped. He knew that his allegiance as a slave master toward his servant was very fragile and easily broken without much thought, and when push came to shove—the whip had to emerge. Little forethought went into his past relationship with Reggie as a slave master, he had to take decisive action. It always had to be absolute.

Donald smirked as he answered his father, "I'll dispatch him to Mr. Eggers dis' mornin'." It was apparent that Donald was excited to be a part of Reggie's downfall.

After breakfast Donald found Reggie in the kitchen. "Reggie, may I have a word wit' yu'?" Donald said it in such a sarcastic manner that Reggie knew the conversation would not be a pleasure.

"Master Donald, what is it?" Reggie replied in a rather hesitating tone.

"Well, Reggie," Donald sneered, "Now dat' my brother has died, it means dat' yu' have to be reassigned. My father has decided dat' yu' would make an excellent field hand. Yu' kin' have some food in dah' kitchen as yur' farewell party an' din' report to

Mr. Eggers atter' yu' have gathered yur' meager possessions. Now doesn't dat' jus' 'tickle yur' fancy'—a whole new chapter in yur' life?" Sarcasm flourished as Donald spoke.

This was the worst news Reggie could possibly have received, but he knew he had to appear satisfied. "Master Donald, I'm so happy to be able to move to dah' quarters."

"Oh, I bet yu' are yu' miserable piece of humanity," Donald retorted, wildly amused. "I'm glad to git' rid of yu' an' I know dat' all dah' niggahs' in dah' quarters will be in seventh heaven to see yu' show up. Yu' know, a 'yaller niggah" like yu'—why dey'll jus' love yu', won't dey' Reggie?" It was obvious that Donald delighted in knowing that Reggie could suffer immeasurable harm in the quarters.

"Master Donald, I'm sur' it'll be jus' fine," Reggie answered, demonstrating no dread. Reggie's pride commanded that he would not allow Donald to see him fearful. Furthermore, Reggie realized that all of his years of dedication to Albert meant absolutely nothing.

"Yur' damn right, an' yu'll even love it." Reggie's unfearing attitude galled Donald. "Now go eat, an' din' git' yur' cheap little grip an' report to Mr. Eggers." Donald really wanted to see fear emerge on Reggie's face, but it didn't happen.

"Yes, Master Donald," Reggie confidently responded.

Reggie quickly went to find Mammy Bertha and tell her the bad news. "I have been transferred to dah' quarters fo' permanent assignment as a field hand," he told her.

Mammy Bertha's face dropped, but she quickly gathered her thoughts. "Reggie, I'm goin' to talk to Benson, dah' driver. I know him 'bery well. He needs to know dat' yu' are not bein' sent as an extra set of eyes an' ears fo' dah' master. Yu' well know dat' yu' look like a white man, but dey' will still take yu' in as one of thar' own as long as I talk to Benson an' everybody knows what's goin' on wit' yu' an' why yu' are bein' transfered to dah' quarters." Benson, the driver was a black man, and second in charge in the quarters, answering only to the white overseer, Mr. Eggers. This arrangement represented the typical hierarchical system. Rarely was it any different.

"Mammy Bertha, I knew yu' would help me." Reggie was thoroughly relieved and grateful for her assistance.

"Reggie," Mammy Bertha instructed, "yu' go 'head an' eat an' we'll see each other 'gain real soon."

"Mammy Bertha one last thin'." Reggie made a soulful plea, "I may not git' to see Anastasia on dah' way out, so be sur' to tell her what happened an' let her know dat' I will contact her as soon as I kin'."

"I'll let her know as soon as I see her Reggie, an' don't yu' worry 'bout dat'," she responded.

Reggie's hopes of seeing Anastasia soon faded, even though he took his time gathering up his meager possessions. After failing to see her, he departed and went directly to Mr. Egger's cottage. Fortunately, the money Albert had given him was safely buried. As he approached Mr. Eggers' cottage door with trepidation, he knocked on the door and said, "Mr. Eggers, Mr. Eggers, are yu' thar'? It's Reggie."

"Come right on in. I've been 'pectin' yu'," Mr. Eggers said in a sinister tone, eagerly calling out, which brought to Reggie's mind the old saying, "'said dah' spider to dah' fly—step right in an' visit wit' me'," which put a chill down his spine.

Reggie tried to shake it off and entered the cottage finding Mr. Eggers sitting at his kitchen table playing checkers with Donald. Forgetting the checker game, they quickly looked up, both staring at Reggie with menacing grins and not saying a word. Reggie knew circumstances did not bode well for him, especially with the presence of his nemesis Donald. His greatest fear was about to be confirmed.

The cottage was located near the slave quarters. It was a small, white framed house rather typical of that time. Clearly, a marked contrast from any of the slave dwellings, it was nevertheless austere and plain with three rooms. The kitchen served as the central feature of the house.

Mr. Eggers, the overseer, was a rather ordinary looking man. He was a short, obese, and middle-aged man. In addition he was unkempt with a scraggly beard and long salt and pepper hair. He wore a lengthy, white cotton shirt with dirty beige trousers. On his head was a round, wide-brimmed hat, often called a 'Panama hat' and at his waist he wore a sash where he tucked in his derringer. Placed next to him conspicuously at the kitchen table was his trusty bullwhip which represented the standard issue for the typical overseer in the South.

"Well, well, Donald, looks like we have a sweet clabber-colored niggah' standin' in front of us," he mocked.

"Reggie, yu' yaller' niggah' rascal. Do yu' know why yu're' hyeh'?" Donald asked.

Reggie looked stunned as he replied, "Master Donald, yu' ordered me to come an' see Mr. Eggers."

"Dat's right," Donald glared at him as he started to slowly strut around the room, his eyes on Reggie. "But let me explain somethin' to Mr. Eggers. Yu' know dat' Reggie's quite dah' the social gadfly, a real conversationalist—sort of a know-it-all. He's way too big fo' his britches, he definitely needs to be reined in. Why, Mr. Eggers, he even takes liberties to personalize wit' white folks in a flirtatious manner as if he was a white man—now doesn't dat' jus' 'beat dah' Dutch'? An' by dah' way, Mr. Eggers, I already put him in his place fo' dat'. Gittin' back to dis' knucklehead, Reggie, don't yu' take special liberties dat' other niggahs' would never consider?"

"I never meant to act 'bove my station, Master Donald." Formality was required, but Reggie knew that he was in serious trouble.

"Oh, yu' never meant to act 'bove yur' station—how dignified. Do yu' know dat' 'fore Mr. Eggers 'rived hyeh' he had developed a reputation as a 'niggah' breaker'?" Donald exclaimed, "Now we all know dat' under my father's urgin' he has softened somewhat; however, we do have 'ceptions dat' have to be dealt wit' severely from time to time. Yu' happen to represent one of dose' 'ceptions, Reggie! Now, Mr. Eggers, what should we do wit' dis' swine?"

Mr. Eggers in a sneering manner, replied, "Sorta' sounds to

me like dis' yaller' niggah' is full of rascality, Donald. Sorta strikes me dat' he's a wanta' be white man and dat' is dah' worst kind. He definitely needs to be taken down a peg or two. I think we should give him 'thirty-an'-nine lashes'." Of course Mr. Eggers had been instructed earlier by Donald that Reggie was to be beaten.

"Sounds good to me—let's get it done!" Donald was very excited about the prospect of what was about to happen to Reggie. He could hardly contain himself at the thought of seeing Reggie suffer.

Mr. Eggers speedily answered, "I'll fetch my rope, an' we kin' tie him to dah' tree out yonder."

Reggie was numb with fear realizing he was soon going to be flogged. What was happening to Reggie was something he should have known could happen to him. He was now being reminded of how fragile the relationship between the master and the slave really was, and how easily it can be broken.

Reggie recalled Albert as a youngster playing with a select group of black boys and girls who were the children of field hands. This recreation continued through the years with Albert developing a close friendship with them. When these same boys and girls reached around eleven years of age, they were forced suddenly to separate themselves from Albert and made into full time field hands. It was cruel because they had been close friends with Albert, and now were compelled to sever all ties, never associating with Albert again. Reggie found this particularly disturbing but understood it was part of the cruel bondage system, which always required a clear separation between the races, even amongst the children, regardless of the feelings they might have for each other.

Once outside, Mr. Eggers led them to a tree. Mr. Eggers looked at his whip as he talked to Reggie. Donald didn't wait and ripped Reggie's shirt off. "Reggie, git' jaybird naked. It's time for yu' to have dah' privilege of 'kissin' dah' rod' of yur' master." A rope was thrown over a strong branch, and Reggie's hands were tied to one end of it, and then he was hoisted upward until his feet were nearly off the ground.

Mr. Eggers continued in a taunting tone. "'Fore we proceed,

I'm told yu' are one of dose' learned niggahs'—one of dose' 'two-headed niggahs'', yu' know, an educated niggah' who knows his letters an' numbers. How 'bout dah' Bible? Do yu' know whar' dah' 'genteel floggin'', 'thirty-an'-nine lashes' comes from? I'll tell yu' what I'm gonna' do fo' yu'. If yu' know dah' answer, I'll spare yu' dah' beatin'. I kinda' know I'm makin' a safe bet. Thars' no way in hell yu'll know dah' answer to dat' one, even though I'm tole' yu' are a know-it-all."

Donald quickly chimed in, "Mr. Eggers, be careful—he probably knows. Go 'head, Reggie."

Reggie answered, "Mr. Eggers, sir, it refers to dah' 'thirty-an'-nine lashes' dat' dah' apostle Paul received from dah' Romans."

Donald asked, "Is dat' correct, Mr. Eggers?"

In an almost speechless reply Mr. Eggers said, "Dat' would be correct, Donald. I jus' can't 'lieve dat' niggah' would know dat'," as he replied in dismay.

Donald countered, "I warned yu', Mr. Eggers—dah' niggah' knows everythin'." Then he turned to Reggie and said, "I'm so sick an' tired of yu' an' yur' smart mouth. Maybe Mr. Eggers let yu' off dah' hook, but I didn't 'gree to dat' ridiculous offer. Dat' means dah' beatin' goes on Mr. Eggers, an' I'm goin' to relish dah' honor of givin' dis' scoundrel his 'thirty-an'-nine lashes'. Dis' will be a real privilege. Do yu' mind if I grant myself dah' honors?"

"He's all yurs' Donald, 'sides I'm dah' one who made dah' silly wager," Mr. Eggers said laughingly.

Mr. Eggers handed his whip over to Donald knowing he would take great satisfaction in the administration of the punishment to Reggie. "Dis' is fo' yu'—a miserable wretch! I've waited a long time to have dah' privilege to put some welts on yur' back. Oh, how I'm gonna' love dis'!" Brandishing the whip, Donald practiced cracking it in the air while menacingly glaring at Reggie.

Reggie braced for the flogging, anticipating the pain. After taunting Reggie a little longer by cracking the whip in the air in an amateurish way, finally Donald began the administration of the punishment. Donald counted out loudly to thirty-nine, no more or no less, as he administered the whipping. Each time the whip made contact with Reggie, tearing at his flesh, Donald intensified the beating, letting out all the hatred and jealousy that he harbored toward Reggie.

Even though Donald was schooled to always be humane with the slaves, the contradiction was soon evident when he went completely out of control, becoming a brutal slave master who could only demonstrate sheer rage. This change in character raised the question about who the real Donald might be. Perhaps having the power to administer a flogging on an individual made it difficult to understand the meaning of compassion and kindness. It was evident that Donald's demeanor changed dramatically once he had the whip in his hand. His actions earlier when he punished Reggie in front of Sarah were very harsh but not nearly as hate filled as this occasion when he could administer the punishment unleashed with a bullwhip.

Through this horrible experience, Reggie vividly recalled an account he read, given by an Englishman who interviewed a young slave owner in the South. The young slaveowner told the story of when he went to England to be properly schooled. He left behind the bondage system, which he so often questioned for making him feel very uncomfortable since he perceived his father as a cruel slave owner. He related to having a happy childhood growing up and developing a close relationship with one of the slaves, a man named Edgar, who lived with the other slaves in the quarters. Unfortunately when the slave reached around ten years old, his father separated the two, and they were no longer permitted to see each other again.

The story darkens from this point on. When the young slave owner returned from England to eventually help take over the duties of running the plantation with his father, he was given the responsibility to administer any punishment over the slaves. One day, Edgar, his former close friend who he had grown up with, was involved in a little mischief. Unhesitatingly, the young man grabbed his bullwhip and delivered a severe punishment on his old friend. After the beating, he related to slumping over on his horse lamenting that he had become what his father was—just another cruel plantation owner. Whatever happened to his compassion and kindness that he so coveted when he was younger? Perhaps uncontrolled power to hurt people does indeed corrupt the heart.

Finally, Reggie who was slumped over in agony with all these thoughts still racing through his head, could only hope that the punishment was over.

Mr. Eggers looked at Reggie in a very satisfied manner. "Looks to me like dah' rascal learned a lesson."

Donald was pleased by Reggie's obvious pain and asked, "Yu' scamp, now do yu' have all dah' answers?"

"No, Master Donald," Reggie groaned, "I don't have all dah' answers." Reggie wanted to tell Donald what he really thought, but he knew he was defenseless and would be better served to remain quiet and obedient.

Donald lashed out at him verbally once again. "Yu' rogue, yu' don't have all dah' answers, an' don't yu' ever forgit' it! Yu' are nothin' more din' a dirty rotten niggah' an' dat's all yu'll ever be!"

Mr. Eggers, who was looking Reggie over, turned to Donald with a smile on his face. "Looks to me, Donald, like his back is raw. I'll go git' some 'Negro plaster' to help soothe dah' pain." In short order he returned with the mix.

"What is dat'?" Donald queried.

Mr. Eggers smirked, "Donald, have yu' fo'gotten dat' I was once a 'niggah' breaker'? Dis' hyeh' is a concoction of salt, pepper, mustard, an' vinegar. I've heard it often called 'Negro plaster'. It's applied to dah' back to sorta' ease dah' pain atter' a good beatin'," he said laughingly.

Donald was thrilled at the thought of causing Reggie even more suffering. "Mr. Eggers, I always tole' father dat' yu' knew what yu' were doin'. I wanta' have dah' honor of givin' our varmint dah' application to sorta' help soothe dah' pain. Do yu' think dah' learned niggah' will wonder what dah' principles of chemistry could be dat' would cause dah' 'ditional pain?"

Mr. Eggers chortled and replied, "Dat's a good one,

Donald—chemistry, I love it!"

While Reggie was stretched out on the ground in utter agony, Mr. Eggers with a glint in his eyes said, "Oh Reggie, dis' is jus' what dah' Doc Jamison ordered fo' yur' discomfort. Dah' honor is yurs', Donald."

Donald with great satisfaction applied the concoction over Reggie's savaged back while he screamed out and finally lost consciousness. When he slowly opened his eyes a short time later, Mr. Eggers announced, "I have some more good news fo' yu'. Yu've' already been tole' 'bout yur' reassignment to do field work, but dah' good news is dat' it will be permanent. Aren't yu' jus' tickled pink havin' dah' opportunity to work wit' all dah' darkies day in and day out in dah' field."

"Yes, I am, Mr. Eggers," gasped Reggie.

"Good, now do yu' know Carl?" Eggers bellowed. "Dat's who I have 'signed yu' to be wit'. When yu' kin' pick yur'self up, take yur' scanty possessions an git' over to Carl's."

"Yah', Mr. Eggers," Reggie responded with as much strength as he could muster.

Donald was still not finished. "Oh, one other thin' yu' miserable wretch,, enjoy yur' new assignment. I'm sur' yu' are jus' goin' to love yur' new quarters. As I said earlier I know dah' darkies will welcome yu 'wit' open arms, dat' news should be music to yur' ears!"

"Shall we leave dis' miserable creature while he thinks 'bout how lucky he was to have 'tasted dah' rod of his master'?" Mr. Eggers salivated.

"Yah', an' I'll be seein' yu', Mr. Eggers," Donald gloated. "I have to git' back to our guests. Oh yes, it was a real pleasure, yu' allowin' me dah' opportunity of givin' Reggie dah' privilege of experiencin' my superior strength, 'gainst his miserable an' feeble body." Donald was anxious to leave and inform his father that Reggie's punishment had been administered. He had even convinced himself through his twisted and insecure mind that all the suffering administered on Reggie by him demonstrated that he was stronger and the better man of the two.

"Donald, I'll be sur' to keep yu' posted on our yaller' niggahs' progress, now Godspeed." Mr. Eggers soon left as well, leaving Reggie agonizing in the dirt to fend for himself.

Suffering great pain and exhaustion while lying on the ground, Reggie lapsed in and out of consciousness not being able to fully comprehend what was happening to him. Under these abject conditions, an apparition came to him that was nothing like anything he had ever experienced in his life. It was not just a dream, it felt very real. Suddenly, he could vividly see a tall, bearded man wearing a top hat, which he removed as he stood up to a podium. In the vision, Reggie could see it was a bright, late autumn day. The setting appeared to be a rural cemetery with a large throng of people present. It was apparent the assembly was there to honor military personnel who had died at the site. The man, who was speaking, emanated greatness. Clad in black, he looked very important. Then suddenly, Reggie saw Halley's Comet emerge hovering over the man as if to provide additional cover and to add strength and shine grace upon him as he delivered his monumental speech.

The words consecrated the site of a tremendous battle waged between the North and the South, now a graveyard for those who had died in that battle. While slavery was not directly mentioned, implications of it were made within the speech. In the vision Reggie could feel that slavery was coming to an end in the United States. This battle represented the apex of the conflict that would soon bring freedom to the slaves. The date was November 19, 1863, and it was the *Gettysburg Address* that he witnessed in his vision with President Abraham Lincoln delivering the address.

Four score and seven years ago our fathers brought forth on this continent, a new nation, conceived in Liberty, and dedicated to the proposition that all men are created equal.

Now we are engaged in a great civil war, testing whether that nation, or any nation so conceived and so dedicated, can long endure. We are met on a great battle field of that war. We have come to dedicate a portion of that field, as a final resting place for those who here gave their lives that that nation might live. It is altogether fitting and proper that we should do this.

But, in a larger sense, we can not dedicate—we can not consecrate—we can not hallow—this ground. The brave men, living and dead, who struggled here, have consecrated it, far above our poor power to add or detract. The world will little note, nor long remember what we say here, but it can never forget what they did here. It is for us the living, rather, to be dedicated here to the unfinished work, which they who fought here have thus far so nobly, advanced. It is rather for us to be here dedicated to the great task remaining before us—that from these honored dead we take increased devotion to that cause for which they gave the last full measure of devotion—that we here highly resolve that these dead shall not have died in vain—that this nation, under God, shall have a new birth of freedom—and that government of the people, by the people, for the people, shall not perish from the earth.

Seeing the *Gettysburg Address* given in the future, provided Reggie with an inciteful glimpse of the horrendous Civil War, a war waged between the North and South at the expense of thousands and thousands of American lives. His immediate thoughts shifted to recognizing his responsibility to inform the people that prompt actions must be taken to heal the differences between the North and the South in order to avoid a horrific conflict in the near future. Reggie knew that he had an extremely difficult assignment ahead—he had to help reverse an unfortuate course of history that was about to take place.

If the war was conducted, it would end with the South vanquished by the North and being forced to accept a treaty on the North's terms, leaving the South in almost total devastation and economic ruin, by a war largely fought on their soil. In addition, the slave owners would receive no compensation from the federal government for the loss of their slaves. Significantly, for all those who had predicted a gradual end to slavery, they would be proven horribly wrong.

Knowing that a bloody civil war was on the horizon unless immediate preventative measures were taken compelled Reggie to believe that he must be a messenger for God. Again, he knew it would be an awesome assignmnent, but one he must follow for the benefit of mankind.

He slowly picked himself up and staggered to Carl's quarters where he would have to pick up the pieces knowing that a heavy assignment awaited him. Turning the course of history around would not be easy.

***

Colonel Marshall was left shocked at knowing that a relationship had developed between Reggie and Anastasia. Knowing intervention was necessary for his personal interests, he found a good opportunity to speak with Anastasia. Following her into Abigail's bedroom, he confronted her, "Good mornin', Anastasia. Isn't it a fine day?"

"Yah', master," she timidly replied, eyes staring at the ground while continuing to do her work of straightening things up.

"Yu' know, Anastasia," the colonel went on, "I kin' 'member when yu' were jus' a cute little playthin' 'round hyeh'. My, oh my, how yu' have grown up. In fact yu' have grown up to become a beautiful Afrikan' Venus."

Anastasia felt uneasy with his comments that made the hairs stand up on the back of her neck. She knew this was going to be a very unpleasent experience, but managed to cautiously say, "Thank yu', Master."

"Something else, Anastasia—I've always protected yu' by not sellin' yu' to one of dose' wicked speculators who would take yu' down South to New Orlens' fo' thar' own benefit. Someone wit' yur' beauty, dey' would put in one of dose' sportin' houses to be at any man's 'beck-an'-callin''. Now, jus' how are yu' goin' to thank me fo' bein' such a kind master?" Brothels in New Orleans were a flourishing business. Beautiful light skinned slave women brought tremendous prices at auction. From there, they would be placed into prostitution.

One of Anastasia's worst fears was now unfolding in front of her. She had always known she was attractive and had expected that Colonel Marshall would possibly demand her for his own sexual pleasure someday. She fought for her composure. "Oh, master, I'm so happy yu' never sold me to one of dose' dreadful speculators. I do thank yu', but I'm at a loss as to what yu' are askin' of me now." She knew what he wanted and realized it was better to act naïve.

"I have 'nother question, Anastasia," the colonel posed with a puzzled look. "Is it true dat' yu' have feelins' fo' Reggie?"

"It is true dat' we are 'bery good friends, but dat' is all." Anastasia lied in an attempt to protect Reggie from the colonel's wrath.

Colonel Marshall, fighting to hide his anger, said, "I'd have a real problem if dah' two of yu' have strong feelins' fo' each other. I never 'ranged anythin' 'tween yu' an' Reggie. I'm dah' master as yu' well know, an' everythin' must go through me. 'Sides, I think yu' should know dat', Reggie was flirtin' wit' one of our guests from Boston. Wouldn't yu' think dat' his actions would call into question his loyalty to yu'?"

Anastasia reacted defensively. "Master, we are jus' good friends an' nothin' more."

The colonel ranted on, "'Nough of dis' rubbish. Yu' know I could never give my consent fo' yu' to marry dat' scoundrel. Now, let's talk 'bout how yu' could repay me fo' how kind I have been to yu'."

The colonel reached out and put his arm around Anastasia, and she quickly responded. "Master, I'm scared."

The colonel assured her that there was no need to be afraid. "Anastasia, I'm dah' kind master who has always protected yu' from evil, an' I will continue to protect yu'."

"Thank yu', Master." While thanking him, she could only think that she could not stand the thought of him ravaging her body which just sickened her.

"Anastasia, do yu' know dat' my brother is yur' father? Yu'

have seen him when he visited. I think yu' knew he was yur' father, an yu' wisely kept it a secret—didn't yu'?"

"Yah' Master, I have known dat' my skin color comes from yur' brother."

Colonel Marshall's tone softened as he spoke. "An' of course dat' is a credit to yu'. Honestly, yu' are truly a beautiful woman who I'm 'tracted to, an' who I prefer seein' as a lovely, dark complexioned Venus, not a Negro."

Tearfully, Anastasia replied, "Thank yu', Master."

"If yu' were smart yu' would grow to like me an' forgit' dat' scoundrel Reggie," the colonel suggested. "Yu' need not say anythin'. I have decided to give yu' new responsibilities an' 'sign yu' to yur' 'bery own quarters near dah' row." It's interesting that Colonel Marshall would believe that she could automatically turn her affections away from Reggie, simply because he was the master and ordered it.

Anastasia knew exactly what this meant. Slave girls of her caliber knew that it was not uncommon for the master to set them up in separate quarters where they could be used to fulfill the master's sexual gratification. "Master, I have always enjoyed bein' dah' personal servant to Missus Abigail all des' years an' would love to continue in dat' capacity."

"'Nough of dis'!" the colonel bellowed at her. "Yu' are a grown lady, an' yu' need yur' own quarters."

Anastasia pleaded, "Master, I fear dat' Abigail will be very upset wit' dis' 'rangement."

"Anastasia," he demanded. "Don't talk back to me like dis'. I'm her father, an' I make dah' decisions 'round hyeh'."

"I understand, Master."

To make matters much worse for Anastasia, the colonel added, "One other matter yu' need to know—Reggie was jus' punished fo' not knowin' his place an' has been 'signed to dah' quarters whar' he will be one of our field hands."

This news caused Anastasia to cry out loud. "Oh no, not my poor Reggie," she exclaimed, and as soon as she heard herself cry out those words—she clasped her hands over her mouth.

The colonel upon hearing her words immediately knew that she had given herself away. Her strong feelings that she harbored toward Reggie emerged. "Shush, as it's his own fault, an' he had to be punished, an' dah' punishment had to be absolute. Maybe yu' better take stock in dis' an' start to mind yur' own 'p's and q's' 'round hyeh'. 'Sides, yu' are actin' like yu' have some fondness fo' dat' miserable blackguard."

"Master, please," she begged.

"I told yu' shush!" Colonel Marshall was done with her complaining. "One last matter—atter' yu' git' moved into yur' new cottage, I will be by to see how yu' are doin'. Don't say 'nother word, 'pecially 'bout dat' rascal, Reggie, an' do not see him 'gain!" The tone of his voice displayed anger and jealously. "Liza, my most trusted an' loyal servant, will be helpin' yu' git' settled into yur' new quarters. In addition, she will be stayin' wit' yu' temporarily jus' to make sur' thar' are no shenanigans," with that he turned on one heel and abruptly exited the room.

It was as if he had sucked all the oxygen from the room, leaving Anastasia feeling light headed and weak. She had to sit down to collect her thoughts at what had just taken place. Anastasia realized that her time had come, and with that, brought a deep foreboding realization of what her future might be under the present circumstances. Additionally, with a heavy heart, she worried about her beloved Reggie, and longed to be with him. She prayed that God would look over him as well as her and protect both of them from harm.

CHAPTER FIVE

While Anastasia was having serious problems dealing with the colonel's advances Reggie was dealing with his own set of problems. He arrived at Carl's residence as ordered and knocked on the door, which Carl opened and witnessed Reggie who nervously stated, "Carl, it's me, Reggie from dah' 'big house'." Carl was in his twenties, short and thin in stature with defining features of a native African. Non-aggressive and kind, Carl would prove to be the ideal person for Reggie to live with while facing this difficult transition in his life.

Carl, surprised, said, "Reggie, what are yu' doin' hyeh'?" He could see that Reggie was not steady on his feet and was in obvious pain. "Oh my Lawd', looks like yu' were jus' chewed up by a black bear an' spat out fo' dah' wolves. I'm goin' to guess, yu' jus' got beaten."

"I was jus' whaled on by Mr. Eggers an' Master Donald. Carl, dey' really went atter' me. Dey' have 'signed me to dah' quarters, an' Mr. Eggers tole' me dat' I would be livin' wit' yu'."

Carl looked dumfounded as Reggie told him the news. He tried to make Reggie feel welcome. "We'll jus' have to make do. We don't have a choice, but it's not a problem. Me an' my wife, Letty don't have any pickanannies—jus' dah' two of us. Dat's why dey' put yu' heyh'. 'Sides, it will be easier fo' yu' to git' 'long wit' us din' some of dah' folks, especially dose' who came more recently from Afriky'. Dey' don't take to niggahs' at all dat' look white."

"Carl, dah' way I feel now, yur' kindness is a God send, and Lawd' knows, I really need a little lift in my life.

"Did Mr. Eggers put dah' 'plaster to yur' back'? Once in 'while he kin' git' full of 'Old Scratch', himself."

"I got 'thirty-nine lashes', which was bad 'nough, an' din' dey' applied dah' plaster on me.'"

Carl called to his wife. "Letty, this is Reggie, dey' jus' 'signed him to live wit' us. He jus' got beaten an' plastered, an' he needs yur' help tendin' to his wounds. Oh yah' Reggie dis' is my wife, Letty." In her early twenties like Carl, she was short and slim with unassuming features.

Fortunately for Reggie, their kindness and caring were exceptional as he was in such dire straits and needed their full attention and understanding.

Letty calmly took action. "Reggie, when I first saw yu' at dah' door I done thought yu' were a spy. But when I hyeh' yu' done got whooped an' plastered to boot, I feel right 'bout changin' my mind."

Reggie quickly exclaimed, "Letty, believe me I'm not an informant. Dey' even tole' me 'fore I came hyeh' dat' yu' would look at me suspiciously. Fo' what it's worth, Mammy Bertha done talked to Benson to let him know dat' I'm no informant. Knowing that Reggie had the support of Mammy Bertha would go along way in helping Letty and the others to believe that Reggie could be trusted.

Letty said, "Come on ovah' heyh' Reggie an' lay down—so I kin' git' down to business. I'll wash off yur' back, lard yu' up an' wrap yur' back in cloth. Yu'll be jus' fine—believe me I've done dis' 'fore. Now lay down hyeh' an' let me take good care of yu', an' don't make me say it again." As Reggie was lying down, Letty attended to his back. "I see how severely yu' were punished, which tells me dat' yu' fell out of dah' good graces of marse'. Yu' need to know, Reggie dat' down hyeh' in dah' quarters we have to stick together. Dat' is how survive. Tyrants surround us while we fight fo' our survival. Obviously, yu' already know dat'." The word tyrant was commonly used by the slaves throughout the South to describe a slave master or his overseer.

"Letty, dat' is dah' truth." Reggie was relieved and reassured by the care, kindness and understanding of Carl and Letty. He went on to say, "I'll always 'member what dah' two of yu' did fo' me. I have to say dat' I kin' take a lot of pain, but when dey' plastered me, dat' was dah' worse pain I ever felt. 'Nough of dat 'as I have somethin' else to share wit' both of yu'. I jus' can't wait—I have to spread dah' word."

Carl curiously asked, "What is it Reggie?"

Reggie poured out his feelings. "It's still fresh on my mind. Right after dah' beatin' I had a vision dat' was a lot more din' jus' a day dream. It came like a thunderbolt out of dah' sky."

"What was dah' vision?" Letty asked in a perplexed manner.

"Carl an' Letty—freedom is not far off," Reggie told them. "In my vision I could see dat' a terrible war will be fought ovah' slavery. It will be 'tween dah' North an' dah' South, which dah' North will win, bringin' freedom to all of dah' slaves."

Carl, who was puzzled at what Reggie was saying, stated, "Yu're jus' cloggin' my head. I hope yu're right, but yu' know dat' nothin' ever changes 'round hyeh'. Dah' colored man in dah' South is like a one-armed man in a fist fight, which represents some bad odds."

Reggie elaborated. "Carl, dis' was a 'bery powerful vision. I could see Halley's Comet churnin' overhead as dis' tall man 'livered his speech. It was so real dat' it was frightenin'. 'Lieve me, I'm passionate 'bout what I saw an' what it signified."

"Reggie, it was only a dream. Dat's all," Carl stated with assurance.

"Carl, pretty much in dah' history of man no war has ever been fought ovah' slavery. Dis' will be dah' first except fo' maybe Haiti. Dah' white people are lulled into thinkin' dat' slavery will end gradually in a peaceful manner. It will not, an' dey' will suffer immeasurably amongst 'demselves."

"Reggie, me an' Letty have no learnin'. We don't know what yu' are talkin' 'bout, but I do know, Reggie that sounds like a half-baked ider' or an impossible dream. I think yu' may have been hit in dah' head a few times too many! Yu' need yur' rest, as dey' won't let yu' lay up in dah' sickhouse ovah' a beatin', an' Mr. Eggers will be blowin' dat' shell horn all too early at daybreak." Carl's response to Reggie's dream represented the prevailing attitude of the blacks in the South. While hoping for freedom, they could see little or no chance of any positive changes in the future.

***

At the "big house" Andrew and Evelyn had retired to bed. Restless, Evelyn began speaking as she adjusted her pillow. "Andrew, somethin' has come up dat' really disturbs me."

"What is it, Evelyn?"

Obviously upset, she continued. "I was told by Abigail dat' yu' had Anastasia 'signed to new duties, which include puttin' her in yur' cute little cottage near dah' quarters whar' yu' have always kept yur' cute little playthings in dah' past." Evelyn was casting dispersions in a belittling manner intended to arouse Andrew.

Always prepared with an answer, the colonel replied, "Dat' is correct. It's good fo' her character to take on new tasks. Is thar' somethin' wrong wit' dat'?"

"Yes! All yu' have to do is look 'round hyeh' an' see all dah' light skinned servants. People talk 'bout Colonel Marshall an' his Congo harem. Andrew, it is appallin'—an' embarrassment to all of us." The presence of light skinned servants was not at all uncommon in the South. This always led people to gossiping about miscegenation and the prattle was not just restricted to the South. How can a system that requires such absolutes survive with the infusion of people who are of mixed blood—where do you place them socially? Southern women were further perplexed in dealing with this double standard since the Southern gentlemen's persona called for such strict self-righteousness—except regarding this subject. It was apparent that miscegenation was a "necessary evil" accepted by the white Southern males for their enjoyment. It simply represented a very dark and incidious situation that would not go away.

Andrew angrily countered, "I believe dat' dis' conversation is at an end."

"Andrew I'm yur' wife. Why do yu' have to soil our reputation wit' an unmentionable sin an' shame on yur' family?"

"Evelyn! Yu' know dat' God made dah' Negroes different—animals really. Yu' yur'self call 'em creatures or fine pets. Why, God even made 'dem to be sort of playthins' fo' dah' master. I've even thought dat' God made 'dem jus' fo' sex. Dah' women have sex wit' anyone. An' dah' men, dey' go from one plantation to 'nother providin' stud service like hawses'. Aren't yu' an' all yur' lady friends always complainin' 'bout dah' loose morals in dah' quarters?" The argument used by Andrew was commonly expressed by the Southern white male—slaves were not quite human so the rules of adultery need not apply. God intended that adultery be applied only to having sex with white women. Understandably, the women of the South in no uncertain terms took issue with this conclusion.

Furthermore, many of the younger black women were ordered to have sex with male slave breeders who were assigned to impregnate them. Virginia was the number one slave breeding state in the South, and the motivation was obvious. Slaves were bred for economic reasons since only a very small part of Virginia was involved in cotton production; hence, slaves were treated similar to cattle to be bred and sold for profit. It represented an economic profit making venture for Virginia while helping to provide for the necessary labor to maintain the ever growing gang system in the cotton fields further down south.

Evelyn was very upset listening to her husband, and she countered, "Dat's' true, an' it's yur' actions dat' cause it." Southern men purposely sought light skinned blacks for their pleasure while maintaining they were only slaves. Understandably, many Southern women openly discussed their disgust with slavery and wished it had never been introduced to the South. In fact, it was not uncommon to hear a Southern male state that Southern women were abolitionists in their hearts. Clearly, miscegenation ranked perhaps as the one aspect of the chattle system that the Southern women abhorred the most.

The comment irritated the colonel and he retorted, "'Nough of dis' talk!"

"No, Andrew, I'm not finished! I jus' knew yu' would eventually covet Anastasia. Oh, I knew it was comin'! I know yu' like a book, yu've been sorta' savin' her up, as she is yur' light skinned beauty to covet as a prize an' to have at yur' disposal. Why, yu' will even make all yur' friends jealous! Yu'll be dah' talk 'round dah' tavern wit' yur' prize Venus, dah' number one beauty in dah' county. Andrew, why don't yu' make me less upset an' pick out a true darkie in dah' quarters to be wit' instead of somebody who looks like a beautiful, exotic, white lady?"

"Evelyn, my dear, yu're bein' rather silly talkin' like dis'." He had no intention of passing up on Anastastia.

"Am I—how kin' I ever forgit' Reggie's mother? Andrew, she was beautiful, an' she could pass fo' white jus' like Anastasia. Let's face it Andrew, yu' always have to try 'to have yur' cake an' eat it too'!"

"Don't bring her up to me ever 'gain," the colonel thundered.

Evelyn was obviously not ready to let the subject go: "Andrew, I love yu', but it's difficult not to be resentful. I will give yu' dis'. I know dat' yu' are not dah' only one dat' does dis'. Yu' an' yur' male friends talk wit' each other 'bout light skinned female servants almost like dey' are a prize, but let me play dah' devil's advocate. In dah' South we have a terrible double standard. Andrew, how would yu' feel 'bout a white woman who was caught havin' sex wit' a black Mandingo buck?"

"Are yu' outta' yur' mind? Yu' are takin' dis' matter too far! If a white woman ever got caught wit' a black buck, he'd be strung up, an' she could only wish fo' dah' same punishment!" Notably, of all the African tribes, the Mandingos were the most sought after because of their strength and size, and with this comment Andrew became enraged as Evelyn continued.

"I jus' wish dat' Negroes had never been brought hyeh'. Talk 'bout 'a castle in dah' sky'—yu' git' dah' best of two worlds. Yu' an' yur' friends like to extend dah' olive branch to all of us women by tellin' us dat' all dah' Negroes will someday be dispatched back to Afriky', knowin' dis' is what we want to hyeh'. Yet, we see ever increasin' numbers of Negroes 'riving daily from Afriky' 'long wit' mixed home grown servants like Reggie an' Anastasia. Somethin' else too—do dey' git' sent off to Afriky' as well, or do dey' jus' stick 'round as a lastin' trophy of our chattel system? Well Andrew, what is yur' answer to dat' question!"

"Evelyn, I've never seen yu' like dis' 'fore—when did yu' git' dis' 'bee in yur' bonnet'?"

"I knew yu' wouldn't have an answer to dat' one since thar' is no easy answer. Andrew, I'm upset knowin' dat' yu' are goin' to be wit' dat' half-breed Anastasia in her 'bery own special cottage, an' wit' dah' finest of clothes—no Negro cloth fo' her! An' to add insult to injury, dah' same cottage whar' dah' mischief went on 'tween yu' an' Reggie's mother."

"Evelyn, quit talkin' nonsense! She's nothin' more din' a little playthin'—nothin' more, nothin' less. I could never have designs on a house servant. I am dah' master, yu' are dah' mistress an' she's jus' a worker. Put it like dis'—yu' are sorta' like dah' queen bee, an' she is jus' one of many workin' bees—don't git' yur'self all worked up ovah' dis' foolishness!"

"Oh Andrew, I have thought 'bout it, an' I know it's jus' not right. Do yu' really think it's dah' Christian thin' to be doin'?"

"Now, Evelyn, what do yu' have to do 'round hyeh'? I'll answer dat'— nuttin', everythin' is done fo' yu'! How would yu' like to develop calluses on yur' beautiful little hands? Better yet, how would yu' like to prepare fo' friends comin' to visit fo' three weeks? Yu' heard our guests reply when asked 'bout friends jus' showin' up uninvited to stay fo' a time in dah' North. Dey' wouldn't be happy 'cuz' dey' wouldn't have special servants 'round to instantly do all dah' work. Let's face it, yu' wouldn't be happy either doin' all dat' work fo' unannounced guests. I know dat', an' yu' know it as well, so stop talkin' nonsense! Yu' know when dah' North talks up dah' American Colonization Society, dey' don't have any financial interests in dah' Negroes. Well, we have a lot of money tied up in 'dem. So stop frettin'! Slavery will always remain in dah' South—we're not sendin' 'dem back to Afriky', so forgit' dat'! 'Sides, financially we couldn't 'ford to ever give 'dem up anyhow. Evelyn, git yur' head back on yur' shoulders an' quit talkin' nonsense!"

Evelyn was obviously not satisfied with Andrew and his words. "Why should I bother to talk to yu'? Yu're not goin' to feel what I feel an' will never truly understand dah' thinkin' of a white woman in dah' South an' her compassion for mankind includin' our servants an' field hands. Perhaps it's dah' unnaturalness of dis' system dat' disturbs me an' a lot of other Southern women. Havin' to twist dah' Bible an' everthin' else to justify a cruel an' evil system is wrong. Yu' have not convinced me dat' puttin' people in bondage does not have problems. Andrew, I listen to yu' all dah' time but yu' cannot tell dah' future. Personally, I think dah' bondage system will only git' worse leadin' to more serious problems one day."

"Evelyn yu' should be mournin' dah' loss of our son an' not worryin' 'bout such silly matters—now good night!" With that, the two turned away from one another and drifted into a restless sleep, it was apparent that the issue would be left unresolved as it had always been. He had no intention of listening any further, and Evelyn was equally determined not to let Andrew simply dismiss her wishes to not allow him to maintain Anastasia as a concubine.

***

In the quarters Mr. Eggers blew the conch shell at 4:30 A.M. for everyone to rise for the workday. Reggie, who was in terrible pain, slowly sat up and said to Carl, "First time I ever had to rise to somebody blowin' a shell."

"Git' use to it," Carl replied hastily. "Sometimes Benson, dah' driver, conducts a mornin' sweep of dah' quarters, an' yu' better be up an' at it."

"Carl, do yu' think Mr. Eggers would let me lay up in dah' sick house? I kin' hardly move, an' dah' pain has gotten worse overnight," Reggie moaned as his open wounds appeared to be crusted and oozed with a foul odor and puss.

"If yu' would try to lay up 'cause of a whoopin', Mr. Eggers would make trouble fo' yu'." He would 'cuse yu' of shammin'," he responded.

"What's shammin'?" Reggie asked, confused.

"Fakin' an illness to git' out of work," Carl explained.

The reality of living in the slave quarters was sinking in with Reggie. "Carl, it's like a 'Hobson's choice'—yu' have a choice, but yu' really don't have a choice."

"Reggie, don't be talkin' wit' big words down hyeh' in dah' quarters," Carl told him. "We keep things simple. I'll talk to our driver, Benson. He's one of us, an' I'm sur' he'll make yu' a 'half-strainer'."

"A 'half-strainer', now what's dat'?" Reggie looked puzzled again stating, "Yu' keep comin' up wit' des' funny words."

"It means yu'll only have to work when Mr. Eggers is 'round," Carl answered. "An' make sur' dat' yu' talk to Benson 'bout yur' food 'lowance."

"I'll do dat'. Thanks, Carl, an' by dah' way, it looks like I might have to learn a whole new language down hyeh'. An' yur' help is much appreciated."

Carl laughed and added, "Yu' must be hungry—yu' need some victuals? Letty is fixin' her hoe cake, an' it's really good." Carl knew Reggie would need a lot of energy to make it through his first day in the field, and Letty's cooking would provide him with some necessary strength.

As the three enjoyed Letty's hoe cake, Reggie asked about the necklace Carl was wearing.

"Dat's my asafetatida'," Carl told him. "Keeps out measles, whoopin' cough an' mumps."

"Really?" Reggie displayed a slight smile.

"Reggie, yu' orte' git' wit' a conjurer. Yu'll learn a lot."

"I suppose dat' hawsshoe' ovah' yur' door has somethin' to do wit' conjurin'?" Reggie wondered aloud.

"Dat's right, Reggie. Dat' helps to ward off dah' evil spirits of my enemies. Dey' could be dead set on trickin' me an' dig a hole at night near my front door an' put dead snakes, spiders, tadpoles, an' lizards in a bag an' bury 'em. Dat'll bring evil to my house, but my hawsshoe' stops dah' curse from happenin'."

"Yu' really believe all dat' mumbo-jumbo?" Reggie asked.

"Reggie, I know it's true, an' yu' should too."

Letty interrupted the conversation. "Now let me clean up yur' wounds an' change yur' cloth 'fore yu' go to dah' field."

The same ritual played out every day for the workers. They filed out of the quarters, went directly to the field while the women took their children to Aunt Bess, who acted as the babysitter. The women would later join the men for field work. Benson, the driver, oversaw the entire operation.

On this day Benson led everyone to the field where he ordered the singing of *The Drinking Gourd*. He stated, "All hands to work, to work, to work, to work we go. I wanta' hyeh' all yu' niggahs' sing, an' jus' keep singin'. Mr. Eggers is 'way. Go 'head an' sing to yur' heart's content. Dat's one freedom song I like. Dexter, yu're dah' lead row niggah', begin dah' singin', I wanta' hyeh' y'all loud an' clear. Also, we have a new man wit' us, Reggie. He's done been beaten an' plastered so don't be too hard on him, an' excuse his skin color—he's still one of us." There was usually more than one lead row leader on a typical plantation, and they were under the driver in authority.

The Drinking Gourd was a spiritually inspired freedom song that was popular amongst the slaves throughout the South. A metaphor, the drinking gourd represented the Big Dipper constellation, which included the North Star. In addition, the song makes reference to crossing the Ohio River to freedom. It was this star they followed northward as their guide to freedom.

Dexter began the singing and all joined in.

Foller' dah' drinkin' gourd,
Foller' dah' drinkin' gourd,
Fo' dah' old man is a-waitin' fo' to carry yu' to freedom,
If yu' foller' dah' drinkin' gourd.

Dah' riverbank will make a very good road,
Dah' dead trees show yu' dah' way.
Left foot, peg foot, travelin' on.
Foller' dah' drinkin' gourd.
Dah' river ends 'tween two hills.
Foller' dah' drinkin' gourd.
Thar's 'nother river on dah' other side,
Foller' dah' drinkin' gourd.
Whar' dah' great big river meets dah' little river,
Foller' dah' drinkin' gourd.
Dah' old man is a-waitin' fo' to carry yu' to freedom,
If yu' foller' dah' drinkin' gourd.

While everyone cheerfully sang, Benson pulled Reggie aside to explain how he was aware of what happened. "Reggie, Carl done tole' me 'bout yur' whoopin'. Well as long as Mr. Eggers is 'way, yu' kin' go lay up, if he shows up, yu' jump in an' git' to work."

"Benson, I'm in such agony, I kin' hardly move, thank yu' so much—I'm in yur' debt."

"Reggie, I'm on yur' side," Benson confided. "I'm a slave jus' like yu', dah' only difference is dat' my job puts me in dah' middle, sorta' like a sergeant. I carry a whip, but I only use it when dat' old overseer is 'round. Yu' gotta' have a driver. Better dat' it's me. Thar' are plenty of drivers who forgit' dey' are also a slave, an' dey' kin' be meaner din' dah' overseer. I know dat's hard to 'lieve, somebody who would turn on thar' own people, but it's true." Interestingly, throughout the South the slaves harbored more hatred for a harsh driver than a harsh overseer since the driver was one of their own who they felt had turned on them.

"Benson," Reggie said, "history has always had people given positions of responsibility who turn on thar' own people when given authority—it's 'dah' nature of dah' beast'. I think it's thar' own insecurity requirin' 'dem to exercise unnecessary power to make 'demselves feel better."

CHAPTER SIX

Reggie quickly adjusted to living in the quarters, while Anastasia was forced to move to the cottage Colonel Marshall had chosen for her. For Anastasia, this represented a horrible change as she was now forced to stay with Liza in the cottage knowing that she was there to be available at the "beck and call" of Colonel Marshall to fulfill his carnal needs and for no other reason.

The interior of the cottage was rather sparsely furnished, but it was clean and adequate for the two young women. Knowing she had no choice, Anastasia unpacked and organized her few belongings, while Liza wanted to make her feel better, "Chile', do yu' know how lucky yu' are? Take a look at all dah' new clothes dat' Marse' has provided fo' yu'?"

"I really don't care to look," Anastasia firmly stated.

"Well, Anastasia, Marse' really cares fo' yu'. Look at all dah' nice clothes he got yu', an' dey' are not niggah' cloth." She said as she pointed to the new wardrobe hanging in the corner of the room. "All yu' have to do is be nice to him." It would not be unusual for the master to provide a new wardrobe under these circumstances, and it would usually not include Negro cloth. The underlying motive was to make her physically as "white" as possible while recognizing that she is still a slave. Perhaps, Colonel Marshall was making an attempt to "have his cake and eat it too".

"What do yu' mean by dat', Liza?"

"Don't be foolish. Jus' give into his wishes, an' yu' kin have 'bout anythin' yu' want 'round hyeh'. 'Sides, yu' have to admit dat' he is a fine specimen of a white man."

"Liza, please, I find dis' whole thin' disgustin'!"

"Nobody ever questions Colonel Marshall. Whatever he wants, he gits'. Yu' are a slave, chile'. Yu' have to give into his desires. 'Member, he could even kill yu' an' feel none dah' worse, an' 'bove all, don't mention Reggie to him. He tole' me 'bout Reggie. I'm suppose to make sur' he doesn't come 'round. I'm jus' tellin' yu' dis' fo' yur' own good an' Reggie too! Yu' have no choice." Liza represented the stereotypical plantation informant who served the master for her own selfish interests.

"Liza, I do thank yu' fo' dah' warnin', but I want yu' to know dat' I will resist dah' master's advances no matter what."

"He already tole' me he would be stoppin' by to see yu' today. Jus' give into what he wants. God is understandin' an' knows yu' have no choice. Yu'll be fo'given," Liza suggested.

"Liza, I told yu', I will not give into him!"

"Oh Lawdy', Anastasia, yu' are goin' to bring on a lot of trouble fo' yur'self."

As they spoke, Colonel Marshall, not waiting very long knocked at the door and rudely entered the cottage without waiting for someone to open it. Liza greeted him with a warm smile, "Marse', we were 'pectin' yu'."

"Thank yu', Liza, now don't yu' have somethin' to do outside?"

"Oh yah', Marse'!" Liza quickly scurried out the back door and into the yard where she had a chair set up far enough away from the cottage so she wouldn't interfere, yet near enough to be available should the master need her for anything.

Colonel Marshall with beads of sweat rollin' down his face sat down in a chair while Anastasia sat on Liza's cot. She was cautiously staying away from the larger bed provided for her use. "Good mornin', Anastasia, how do yu' like yur' new quarters?" The colonel began with a lustful smile on his face.

"Master, dey're really nice, but I think so much of Miss Abigail an' would like to be back in dah' big house helpin' her 'gain." Anastasia made the request while exhibiting a fearful look.

"Anastasia, don't be silly," he assured her. "Yu' are a grown woman wit' yur' own quarters now wit' a nice feather mattress an' other nice features. Yu' are dah' only servant other din' Mammy Bertha wit' facilities dat' measure up to des' standards. I think I kinda' wanted to spoil yu' a little since I do care fo' yur' well bein'."

"Dis' is all so strange to me, Master."

"Anastasia, yu' look so beautiful. Do yu' like dah' new clothes I bought fo' yu'? Dey' are clothes dat' would be worn by fine European ladies—not jus' ole' niggah' cloth'! I hope yu' 'preciate what I have done fo' yu'. Yu' do have dah' look of a fine European specimen—not a niggah', an' I think yu' should be treated better din' dah' other niggahs' 'round hyeh'. Shall we say, yu' have a touch of class 'bout yu'." It was obvious that Colonel Marshall expected Anastasia to be appreciative for what he had done for her and would expect something in return.

"Thank yu' fo' yur' kindness, Master."

"A beautiful woman deserves all dah' accouterments dat' kin' separate her from dah' others. Anastasia, please understand dat' I want to be more din' jus' yur' master. I want to be yur' lovin' friend as well."

"Jus' my friend?" Anastasia quickly asked with an apprehensive look knowing she omitted the word 'loving'.

"Well, yur' friend, an' maybe a little more." The colonel stood up and went over to sit next to Anastasia on the cot. At this point the colonel's demeanor changed dramatically, and friendship wasn't what she saw in his eyes—they suddenly became the eyes of a predator.

"Anastasia, how are yu' goin' to show yur' 'preciation to me?"

"Master, I'm so grateful." She was in absolute terror but knew she had to exhibit kindness.

"Well, answer me, how are yu' goin' to show yur' gratitude?"

"Master, I'll find a way. I haven't had 'nough time to think 'bout it." Anastasia knew this simple statement would not stop his advances. She well knew what would be expected of her.

"Well, I have Anastasia!" He put his arms around her and pulled her to him. She was trembling as he lifted her face to his and kissed her passionately on her lips. She wanted to pull away, but she was terrified at what would be his reaction. His kiss deepened as his passion rose. He then pulled back and stated, "Anastasia, I find yu' to be so 'citin'. Please understand my need fo' yu'. Right now my desire fo' yu' is so intense. I gotta' have all of yu'."

Out of fear she cried out, "Uncle, please stop!"

The colonel retracted with a startled look and asked, "What did yu' jus' say?"

"Master, yu' are my uncle!"

The colonel was so enraged at being called her uncle, he slapped her face. "Now look what yu' made me do. I cannot take such insolence. Anastasia, yu' are my servant, do yu' understand? As yur' master, I cannot permit yu' to call me uncle!"

"My father is yur' brother, doesn't dat' make yu' my uncle, Master?" Anastasia knew that he could not recognize her as his niece even though it was biologically true. It was a ploy she used to confuse and frustrate him and hopefully, put him off. In matters like this, the absolute separation between a white man and a slave cannot be breached, especially under these circumstances.

"Anastasia, why are yu' talkin' like dis'? Colonel Marshall's rebuttal would suggest it was almost as if Anastasia hit "a soft spot" in her comment. "Yu' are never to mention dis' to me 'gain! Do yu' understand?" The colonel grabbed her by her shoulders and threw her back on the cot. She had reminded him of the one thing that was considered taboo to ever discuss.

"Master, I'm frightened," she sobbed.

The colonel exhibited absolutely no sympathy, he was furious! "I'm leavin' now, but when I return, I expect yu' to show me jus' how grateful yu' are, an' I better not find out dat' yu' had any contact wit' dat' rascal Reggie either."

The colonel stormed out of the cottage to speak with Liza.

"Liza, watch ovah' her, an' I must remind yu' dat' she is not to have any contact wit' Reggie. If he comes 'round, run him off an' din' contact me 'mediately!"

"I'll sur' watch ovah' her Marse', an' I'll let yu' know if anythin' seems suspicious." She agreed, knowing that Anastasia had to have resisted his advances judging by his demeanor.

The colonel departed in a huff as Liza ran into the cottage to see if everything was all right. She was somewhat shocked to find Anastasia sitting quietly. "Chile', are yu' all right?"

"Of course I am, Liza," she replied with assurance. But she knew that while her actions staved him off for now, the next time he would not stop until he got what he wanted, and that could be soon. Assessing the gravity of the situation, she knew it was time to quickly make a major decision. She needed Reggie to help her decide what to do. Wisely, she waited until evening when Liza fell soundly asleep and then slipped out of the cottage and into the night to find him.

Liza was a deep sleeper, which made it easy to quietly exit the cottage. Fortunately, she knew enough about the basic layout of the quarters to put her in the right direction to find Reggie. She spotted a couple of field hands walking near the quarters and approached them. "Pardon me—I'm lookin' for a man named Reggie. He was jus' 'signed to dah' quarters. Could yu' help me locate him?"

"Sur', we know him. He's dah' 'yeller niggah" dat' dey' are talkin' 'bout dat' jus' got a beatin' from Mr. Eggers. He's stayin' wit' Carl—we'll take yu' thar',," one of them offered.

Arriving at Carl's, Anastasia thanked them and then knocked softly but repeatedly. Soon Carl called out, "Who's dat'?"

Hearing that Reggie had been beaten made matters much worse as she feared they had really hurt him. Frightfully, she answered, "I'm Anastasia, an' I'm hyeh' to see Reggie."

As soon as Carl opened the door, Anastasia saw Reggie and ran to him. "Oh Reggie, something dreadful has happened. Colonel Marshall has 'ranged separate quarters fo' me, an' he wants me to give into his desires. I love yu' so much Reggie. I can't stand him, an' I'd rather die din' give into his wishes." As Reggie held her in his arms, he stroked her hair, and she finally felt safe, while she was able to calm down, "Reggie, darlin', dey' jus' tole' me yu' were beaten by Mr. Eggers."

"I've been beaten by Mr. Eggers an' Donald. Dey' put dah' whip to me an' din' follered' it wit' a concoction on my back dat' Donald put on me dat' burned real bad."

Carl spoke up. "Reggie jus' went through a 'Negro plaster', which is as painful as it gits'. I've never felt it, but all of us knows 'bout it. It's a treatment dat' Mr. Eggers uses once in a while when he let's dah' debil' git' dah' best of him."

Reggie assured Anastasia, "Don't worry, I'm all right—I'll heal. It's yu' I'm worried 'bout."

"Reggie, my love, are yu' sur'? I'm so worried dat' des' wicked people are goin' to cuz' yu' further harm."

"Anastasia, don't fret 'bout me. I'm concerned 'bout yu' now dat' Colonel Marshall has sexual designs on yu'."

"Reggie, I'm so 'fraid of dah' master. When he tried to force himself on me, I called him uncle in desperation. He exploded an' slapped me an' din' he stood up an' said he would return, an' said dat' I'd better have a better attitude next time an' show him jus' how grateful I am fo' dah' fancy clothes an' livin' quarters he provided fo' me."

"Anastasia, dis' is real bad," Reggie told her. "I guarantee he'll be back an' soon. Next time nothin' will stop him. Dat' was clever callin' him uncle. It caught him off guard an' saved yu' from a further attack. Anastasia, yu' know as well as I do dat' slave owners struggle wit' bein' related to thar' slaves an' yu' jus' hit dah' nail on dah' head."

Anastasia, looking helpless, dropped her arms to her side as she looked at the floor while shaking her head. "Reggie, what are we goin' to do?"

"Let's step outside so we don't disturb Carl an' Letty anymore." Once outside, Reggie told her his plan. "I have a bold ider'. On dah' night of dah' cawn' shuckin' party, we're goin' to flee. Dat's dis' Saturday, an' I don't think dah' colonel will bother yu' fo' 'while since he'll be tied up plannin' fo' dah' party as fo' Liza, we all know dat' she loves her whiskey. We'll 'range to git' her drunk at dah' party an' din' we'll be able to slip 'way knowin' she'll be occupied."

"Reggie, I love yu', but how kin' I flee wit' yu'? We're not married, an' I'd have to sleep wit' yu', an' things could happen."

"Anastasia, I understand, an' I have dah' solution." Reggie's mind was racing full speed. "Anastasia, difficult situations sometimes require quick decisions. I know yu' have not properly had dah' time to think 'bout gittin' married since I have never brought dah' subject up. However, our situation has dramatically changed. My love, we have to act now 'fore it's too late. Anastasia, I'm askin' yu' wit' God as my witness if yu' will marry me tonight? I do love yu' so much, an' I feel yur' love fo' me is as strong."

"Reggie, I'm stunned. I always pictured yu' playin' dah' role of the coquet 'fore proposin' to me." She took his hands in hers, and they drew close. "Reggie I love yu' so much, an' I 'cept. I'm jus' so fearful, an' yet, I'm so happy. Hold me tightly as yu' will soon be my husband to have an' to hold an' cherish fo' all time. I understand dis' has to be hastily 'ranged, but I know dat' our love fo' each other is rock solid an' sometimes difficult matters require adjustments.

"Anastasia, I'm so happy to know dat' I will be yur' love fo' life, an' yu' know dat' even though we may have to go through thick an' thin, we will always remain together. We could stay out hyeh' all night, but maybe we better git' back inside an' git' down to gittin' married."

Reggie and Anastasia entered Carl's home with broad smiles on their faces. "Letty, git' out dah' broomstick!" Reggie exclaimed.

Letty looked at Reggie and said, "What are yu' talkin' 'bout, Reggie? Dis' is not dah' time fo' house cleanin'. Dat' comes on Saturday."

Reggie exclaimed, "Not house cleanin'—tonight we are goin' to have a good ole' fashioned broomstick marriage."

Broomstick marriages were a traditional marriage ceremony for the slaves. This practice called for the prospective married couple to jump over a broomstick and into marriage as part of the ceremony. As a caveat, if one of them tripped over the broomstick while jumping, then the other spouse would become the leader in the marriage.

When Carl heard what was going on he interrupted, "'Broomstick marriage'! Reggie did yu' git marse's' permission?"

"No, Carl, we don't need his consent. Even wit' his permission, in dah' eyes of dah' laws of Virginny', our marriage will not be considered legal since a slave cannot enter into any legal contract includin' marriage," Reggie pointed out. "Wit' dat' in mind, what's dah' difference?"

"Reggie, I don't know. It doesn't seem right not havin' dah' permission of marse'. I guess I'm ole' fashioned an' jus'don't know what I'm talkin' 'bout."

"Carl, look at it dis' way, we are gittin' married in dah' eyes of God. Isn't dat' more important din' dah' master's eyes or Virginny's laws anyway? We'll be jumpin' ovah' dah' broomstick—doesn't dat' make sense?"

Letty commented, "Reggie, yu' have a good way of sayin' things."

"Thank yu', Letty. I think it's time to git' dah' ball rollin'. Letty, go git' yur' broomstick, an' yu' an' Carl kin' hold it up. We are fixin' to jump right into marriage."

Quietly Anastasia said, "Reggie, I'm so nervous."

"No need to be, Anastasia. 'Member, it's in dah' eyes of God," Reggie told her. "One other thin', Anastasia, if one of us trips jumpin' over dah' broomstick, we'll foller' dah' tradition of dah' broomstick marriage, an' dah' one who didn't trip will be dah' boss in dah' marriage."

Carl with a smile on his face said, "Reggie, jus' don't trip."

Reggie caught his humor and replied, "Carl, yu' kin' be 'bery funny. Now, Anastasia look right at dah' broomstick an' git' ready to jump into marriage in dah' eyes of God. One, two, three—jump!"

At the moment that Reggie said jump they both jumped, but Carl raised his end up to cause Reggie to trip and fall. Carl and Letty both started laughing. Carl looked at Anastasia and said, "It looks like yu' are gonna' be dah' boss."

As Reggie picked himself up, he stated with a broad smile on his face, "Carl, I shoulda' known yu' would put one ovah' on me. Well, Anastasia looks like yu' will be dah' boss even though I know it was rigged."

"Oh no, Reggie, yu' will be dah' boss!" Anastasia assured.

"My love, yu' better git' back to dah' cottage, we'll soon have plenty of time to be together. We kin' discuss later who will be dah' boss." Reggie urged with a wink and a warm embrace. "Let's jus' hope dat' Liza doesn't wake up. If she sees dat' yu've been gone, jus' tell her yu' had to slip out to take a walk an' think things ovah' an' didn't want to disturb her. Meanwhile, I'll keep in contact. 'Member, Anastasia, dat' I love yu', an' I'm so proud to be yur' husband." Reggie then kissed her knowing he would have to reserve his passion for later.

"Reggie, I'm so proud to be yur' wife," Anastasia replied, tears of joy filling her eyes. "I better head back now, an' I want yu' to thank Carl an' Letty fo' me fo' thar' kindness an' help."

As both were standing outside, Reggie confidently repeated, "'Member our plans, Anastasia. As soon as Liza gits' drunk at dah' cawn' shuckin' party, it will be dah' time fo' us to go into action an' flee on dah' "road to freedom". Anastasia, I love yu', an' I know dah' Lawd is on our side, an' everythin' will work out, so don' yu' fret now."

"Good night, my love. I'll see yu' at dah' cawn' shuckin' party dis' Saturday." She gave Reggie a wink, and Reggie gathered her into his arms, once again kissing her passionately goodnight, never wanting to let her go.

CHAPTER SEVEN

Saturday arrived without a full moon, robbing the annual corn shucking party of its full resplendence. Tradition required that the corn shucking party be held on a full moon, but the lateness of fall combined with the lunar calendar made this date a very special time. Invitations had gone out to five neighboring plantations, which guaranteed a large number of attendees since the owners included the slaves from their plantations as well. The more notable included the Carters and the Monroes, all very prominent families, along with Colonel Marshall's brother, Lawrence and his family.

The main focus of the corn shucking party was the husking of the corn. The corn had been provided earlier by field hands who brought the ears in from the fields. For several evenings after working hours they worked to gather up the ears of corn. Prior to the party, the ears were stacked in a large heap around the main corncrib providing a huge mound of corn, which would be shucked by the field hands until the mound had disappeared. This would serve as one of the main features of the party.

Cooking for the gala began early Saturday morning with two kitchens in full service. The kitchen at the plantation house provided a full course meal for the family and their guests, while the house servants and field hands served themselves at the "niggah' kitchen" in the rear. Extra large kettles, boiling pots, turn spits and stew pots were utilized as this kitchen would have to provide for a lot more people. Burning logs supplied ashes and coals to bake the sweet potatoes and corn bread. A number of lean young porkers, geese and turkeys would be served. In addition, some of the slaves had brought dressed raccoons from a successful hunt to make coon stew, which was always a crowd favorite. In addition to raccoons, another special treat according to many blacks was opossum, which always found its way to an event such as this. More than one slave would swear that opossum was their favorite meat.

Toward evening everyone began arriving. Mother Nature was kind enough to provide a comfortable, clear, crisp autumn evening. The lack of lighting due to the absence of a full moon was solved by placing pine tar stacks liberally around the grounds, which added a certain level of mysticism to the night. The plantation owners, their friends and relatives came in carriages and buggies. The house servants and field hands without a doubt provided the most color and flavor to the event. They could be seen in separate throngs marching and singing spiritual songs, almost in unison along the way. They came from all directions, using cart paths and deer trails as they converged upon the gathering. Reminiscent of their African heritage, the women were dressed in brightly colored dresses and bandannas, which provided style beyond description. The men tended to dress in the more subdued colors of Negro cloth, topped with wide brimmed round hats. As a group by far, they infused the most color, joy and vitality to the party as they sported their "Sunday best", and it all rightfully fit.

They mingled and sat around the huge stack of corn husks that would soon be unhusked and tossed into the large corn crib. Singing and playfully having fun while under the light of the pine tar stacks and in the barn was a true Southern vignette mixed with a bit of African tradition. It was truly a delight to see.

The Marshalls were excited about introducing their Northern guests to the sights, sounds, and colors of this uniquely Southern experience. Sarah, Emma and Aunt Opal were totally absorbed in the spectacle as Donald, Evonne and Abigail led them to the area where the slaves had largely congregated. Donald commented,

"Dis' is one event of dah' year dat' I really look fo'ward to. I jus' wish dat' Albert could be hyeh' wit' us."

Evonne put her hand on his arm. "Donald, Albert is up in heaven, pain free, watchin' dis' party right now. I'm sur' he'll want everyone to have a good time. Yu' don't have to worry 'bout him.'

Sarah sensed it would be appropriate to change the subject. "Donald, can you tell Emma and me a little about this evening? Coming from Boston, I can assure you that we have never seen anything quite like this."

Donald exclaimed, "Of course, Sarah. Dah' cawn' shuckin' party is a yearly event to honor dah' harvestin' of dah' cawn'. It's held on or near dah' a full moon. Typically, dis' party will last well into dah' mornin' hours."

Abigail added, "It's a one of a kind event. See dah' mountain of husked cawn' stacked near dah' cawn' crib? All dat' cawn' will be shucked by dah' Negroes, an' when dey' finish, dah' night festivities will be filled wit' a feast of eatin' an' dancin', which will last into dah' mornin' hours. Dis' will be really somethin' fo' all of yu' to take back to Boston! An' be sur' to tell yur' relatives an' friends dat' dis' is jus' 'nother example of dah' closeness 'tween dah' white folks an' Negroes in our beloved South. Sarah, do dey' have events shared 'tween dah' Negroes an' whites up North similar to dis'?" Sarah questioned to herself why it was necessary for Abigail to make such a defensive statement.

Without hesitation Sarah answered, "Quite honestly, we don't, but the numbers of Negroes up North are far less." Sarah wanted to further remind Abigail that the racial divide at the party was quite clear and not equal. She knew courtesy required she not dare say anything that could be construed as putting Abigail further on the defensive.

Abigail recognized it would be wise to just discuss the party. "Everythin' dat' dey' prepare, includin' dah' coon stew, I have tried, an' it's all 'bery tasty. However, I have never been able to bring myself to eatin' 'possum."

"I've heard some Negroes say it is dah' best thing out

hyeh'—I jus' don't 'lieve I'm ready to try dah' varmints. Let us jus' say dat' 'possum is niggah food an' jus' leave it at dat'," Donald stated.

"Oh yes, y'all kin' see dat' dis' happens to be our year to stage dah' celebration. It always rotates from one plantation to dah' next," Evonne added.

Aunt Opal approached and thanked them for the invitation to be a part of the corn shucking party but indicated they would have to begin preparing for their trip home. She felt obliged to give them the bad news at this time. She wanted them to fully enjoy the party while also treating it as their sendoff.

"Aunt Opal, do we really have to leave so soon?" asked Emma.

"Emma, you know that I promised your parents and Sarahs' that we would only stay for a reasonable time," Aunt Opal answered.

Abigail spoke up, "We understand y'all have to return home, but we are so glad dat' yu' were able to be a part of dis' colorful event—it's always one of the big highlights of dah' year."

While everyone was enjoying the spectacle, Mammy Bertha came up and asked Donald a question. "Oh Lawdy', Marse' Donald, it's gittin' said dat' y'all made Uncle Frank dah' Cawn' General. He' out an' 'bout tellin' everybody he sees. Why, he's even runnin' 'round cuttin' dah' pigeon wing. He' jus'so happy. Is it true?"

"Dat's true, Mammy Bertha."

"Well, Marse' Donald, y'all couldn't have picked out a better niggah'," she exclaimed. "Marse', I've got to keep movin'—I got a lot to do."

"So long an' have a good evenin'," Donald replied.

Emma queried, "What's she talking about?"

"Dah' Cawn' General will sit at dah' top of dah' unhusked cawn' as dah' husked cawn' is stacked up into one big pile. He'll be wearin' a hat wit' an ear of cawn' stuck right in dah' front so yu' can't miss him. An' as dah' cawn' is thrown into dah' crib, he'll lead everybody in singin'. Din' when all dah' cawn' has been unhusked, dah' Cawn' General will call fo' dah' harvest feast to begin. Dat' will be follered' by a barn dance dat' should last 'til mornin'," Donald further explained, "It's interestin' dat' bein' selected as dah' Cawn' General is such a major honor wit' dah' Negroes."

Sarah with a puzzled look on her face asked, "What on earth is 'cutting the pigeon wing'?"

"Sarah, dat's a good question. It's a type of Negro dance. Dey' move thar' arms an' hands in a swayin' motion an' dance while thar' head remains fixed. It must come from Afriky'. I must admit dat' it is enjoyable to watch," Abigail responded.

When everyone returned to the main house, Emma and Sarah became engaged in conversation about their vacation. After discussing some trivial matters Sarah became quite serious. "Emma, I've been wondering if this Southern experience we are witnessing is being merely staged for our benefit. Are we seeing the whole story or just what they want us to see?"

"I haven't given it as much thought as you," Emma responded. "I do know that if I ever ask the house servants any questions, they quickly become very quiet and some even appear fearful. It does make me wonder."

"Think about this, Emma. Have we ever been invited to take a tour of the slave quarters? Have we ever had the opportunity to talk to Mr. Eggers, the overseer?"

"Sarah, you are right."

"Emma, if we could see the complete picture, I believe we would see a dark, disturbing side. It's like a two sided coin. You saw what happened to Reggie, it was right in front of me! I witnessed him being beaten! Now Reggie's been dispatched to the slave quarters right after Albert's death and made a field hand. Tell me if that's not cruel." Interestingly, other Northerners who vacationed in the South during the ante-bellum years typically reported that they felt things were being staged for the purpose of presenting a good impression. Speculation centers on the South being forced to uphold an "unnatural system", which to an outsider might appear somewhat obvious. This in turn could then create a defensive posture for the South to maintain.

"One other thing is bothering me, Sarah. What happened to Anastasia?"

"One of the house servants told me in strict confidence that Anastasia was taken from Abigail and provided with separate quarters. We all have heard of the rumors that went on with President Jefferson—people talked about the mulattos on his beloved Monticello plantation running wild. Could this be Oak Manor's own version of Monticello? Is something going on with Anastasia right in front of our own eyes? Emma, she can pass for white, and she's beautiful. You're not naïve! You have to know that plantation owners throughout the South have a reputation for lusting after women like Anastasia."

"Sarah, I think your imagination might be getting the best of you. If you are wondering about Anastasia, why don't you ask Abigail?"

"You can't be serious, Emma. Don't even think of asking her anything about this matter! Remember when she told us there are certain things not to be discussed? Trust me, this is one of them. Searching in that direction would almost represent an unmentionable faux pas that would not be dismissed lightly."

"You're right, Sarah, let's just forget about this subject for now. We can talk more after we leave."

Meanwhile, near the barn as evening descended, everyone gathered around the mound of corn as Uncle Frank led the singing of a song with an unknown title.

Solo – *Religion's like a bloomin' rose,*
Chorus – *We'll shuck dis' cawn' befo' we go!*
Solo – *As none but dem dat' feels it knows,*
Chorus – *We'll shuck dis' cawn' befo' we go!*
Solo-- *I'll praise dah' Lawd' til I git' threw'*
Chorus—*We'll shuck dis' cawn' befo' we go!*
Solo—*I was a sinner jus' like yu',*
Chorus—*We'll shuck dis' cawn' befo' we go!*
Solo—*But sing His praises! Bless dah' lamb!*

Chorus—*We'll shuck dis' cawn' befo' we go!*
Solo—*Fo' I am saved, indeed I am!*
Chorus—*We'll shuck dis' cawn' befo' we go!*
Solo—*Now stan' up squar' in yur' own shoes,*
Chorus—*We'll shuck dis' cawn' befo' we go!*
Solo—*An put no faith in solem' views,*
Chorus—*We'll shuck dis' cawn' befo' we go!*

After an ample amount of time Aunt Harriet, Sarah, and Emma departed with Donald, Sarah, and Evonne to the main house where the festivities were in "full swing".

Reggie, Carl, and Letty meanwhile were participating in the corn shucking festivities around the barn. Reggie's intensions were obvious—maintaining a lookout for Anastasia. "Carl, I'm 'fraid dat' dah' Colonel Marshall will forbid Anastasia to come to dah' party," Reggie anguished.

"Don't fret Reggie, Anastasia an' Liza will be hyeh' soon. Even if dah' colonel did say somethin' to Liza, knowin' her, she'd probably sneak Anastasia down hyeh' anyhow since we all know dat' she likes to drink an' have fun," Carl reassured him.

"Carl, I'm still scared. I'm not even sur' if dah' colonel hadn't gone back to see Anastasia 'gain," feared Reggie.

"Reggie, yu' would have heard somethin' 'bout dat'. Jus' 'member dat' Liza is sweet on Ralph, an' he's been tipped off to git' Liza good an' drunk. She loves her whiskey, so it won't be a problem fo' him to git' her thinkin' of other things 'side Anastasia."

"I know, Carl, but I'm still nervous."

"Don't worry, everythin' will be jus' fine, Reggie.

As Carl and Reggie talked, the Corn General made an announcement. "Folks dah' cawn' has been shucked, an' now it's time to dig into dah' harvest feast, an' dat' will be follered' by a good ole' shake down in dah' barn."

Everyone eagerly descended on the food that had been prepared. Anastasia and Liza finally appeared, and Reggie let out a big sigh of relief. Anastasia was extra friendly to Liza as part of the plan. Meanwhile, Ralph approached the two carrying a jug of whiskey and said, "How are dah' two of yu' doin'?"

Liza purred, "Ralph we're doin' mighty fine, but I could be doin' a lot better if yu' would let me take a pull off dat' whiskey yu've got thar'."

"Liza," Ralph warmly replied. "How could I ever turn a friend like yu' down?"

"Ralph my lips are so dry. I jus' need somethin' to wet my whistle. It's been a long time."

"Of course I'll share some of my whiskey with yu'," Ralph handed the jug over to Liza and she tilted it upward and took two or three large gulps. "Oh Ralph, dis' whiskey sur' tastes good— real good. Do yu' have yur' dancin' shoes on? When dah' party gits' to dah' barn, I wanta' see yu' cut dah' pigeon wing."

"Yu' bet, Liza." Ralph smiled and took Liza by the arm, leading her out back for some private imbibing. She completely forgot about Anastasia, which played right into their plans.

For the slaves, the harvest feast was finally over with everybody commenting on how full they were. The festival then moved to the barn where the dancing began in earnest. Two fiddles, a ukulele, and bones provided the music. Music represented a major part of the slave's life, expressing a legacy from their African heritage. Since they often had to sneak around to make music, it forced them to be innovative in the process. Fiddles and ukuleles were not unique, but the bones were as they were fashioned into homemade percussion instruments. The combination worked well and made an interesting sound.

The music was loud and clear. The one song that was repeated throughout the night and early morning was *Joshua Fought dah' Battle of Jericho.*

Joshua fit dah' battle of Jericho, Jericho,
Jericho;
Joshua fit dah' battle of Jericho,
An' dah' walls came tumblin' down.
Yu' may talk 'bout yur' king of Gideon,
Yu' may talk 'bout yur' man of Saul;

Thar's none like good ole' Joshua
At dah' battle of Jericho.
Up to dah' walls of Jericho
He marched wit' spear in hand;
"Go blow dah' ram horns," Joshua said,
"Cuz dah' battle is in my hands."
Then dah' lamb, sheep horns began to blow;
Trumpets began to sound;
Joshua commanded dah' children to shout,
An' dah' walls came tumblin' down.
Dat' mornin' Joshua fit dah' battle of
Jericho, Jericho, Jericho;
Joshua fit dah' battle of Jericho,
An' dah' walls came tumblin' down.

The party was just that—a real party. Meanwhile Liza and Ralph continued to drink from the jug and dance the jig until it became apparent to Ralph that Liza was about to pass out. When she finally did, Ralph made his way to Reggie and Anastasia to inform them of Liza's drunken state. "It's time fo' dah' two of yu' to make yur' getaway. Liza's as 'drunk as a skunk' an' she's done passed out."

Reggie and Carl had briefly discussed a strategy for fleeing into the night, and it was now time to put their ideas into action. "Now when yu' cut North, jus' foller' dah' North Star like a line on a kite. Yu' can't go wrong," Carl stated with assurance.

"I promise yu' I will foller' dah' North Star." Reggie was already aware of the importance of the North Star, but he felt it was polite to let Carl think he was giving him some sound advice.

"Thank yu' Ralph, we're on our way." Reggie thanked him again profusely, and then firmly held his wife and whispered, "Anastasia, it's time. We kin' git' an early start, an' 'member, dah' die is cast—thar' will be no turnin' back."

"Reggie, my love, I'm ready to foller' yu' whar'ever yu' go."

"I brought some food an' dry goods in my gunny sack,

includin' pepper. We will scatter dah' pepper to throw off dah' scent makin it difficult fo' dah' dogs. Somethin' else, Anastasia, 'fore he died, Albert gave me a fair amount of money, which he instructed me to use on dah' road to freedom. I have dah' money, but I'm not goin' to use it until we git' well down dah' road."

"Whar' are we goin'?" Anastasia asked.

"Albert an' I played in dis' ole' 'bandoned plantation north of hyeh', we kin' lay low thar' til' Colonel Marshall 'bandons dah' search. Near thar' I might even look up an old scamp 'bout a debt he owes me."

"Reggie I'm terrified dat' we could git' caught. I jus' hope dat' yu' thought dis' through, an' also, yu' didn't tell me 'bout dis' old scamp, who I never heard 'bout until now."

"I'll tell yu' later 'bout dis' man, if yu' kin' call him dat'. Lets talk 'bout somethin' more important. Anastasia, dis' ole' plantation is set deep in dah' woods. It's small an'only a few even know it's back thar'. Dis' was one of dah' favorite roosts fo' me an' Albert. Also, yu' don't have to worry 'bout us gittin' lost. I know dah' way like I know dah' back of my hand."

Anastasia felt anxious and excited as Reggie promised they would soon be on their way. Even though she was somewhat fearful of what might happen, she knew she loved Reggie and trusted him with all of her heart and soul. She was ready to go.

The "road to freedom" was upon them, and they both knew that no matter what the outcome would be—their lives would soon be forever changed.

CHAPTER EIGHT

The two slipped away from the festivities, and fled toward the old, abandoned plantation. Fortunately, they could travel the route without having to fear about being pursued since it would take until morning for the Colonel to learn they had fled. Reggie learned from others that pepper would be effective in throwing off the dogs, and he also made sure they waded in water as much as possible. Between the two ploys, he hoped they would be able to throw the dogs off-track. Reggie and Anastasia moved at a swift but comfortable pace, knowing that their interests were best served by remaining calm and level-headed.

Time was of the essence since the colonel would take immediate action once Liza reported to him that Reggie and Anastasia were missing. Instinctively, fleeing slaves will attempt to put as much distance between themselves and their pursuers; however, Reggie determined that their best strategy would involve hiding out in a secure location, hoping the colonel would assume they were running to gain distance on him and he would counter by covering a wide area and not concentrate on the immediate area. Meanwhile, their destination would serve their purpose as they would be successfully concealed by the time the search for them began. They were also aware that Colonel Marshall would show no mercy if he tracked them down—a miscalculation could prove to be fatal. The stakes were high but the alternative—remaining on the plantation could be even worse.

It took Reggie and Anastasia about three hours to reach the abandoned plantation. Normally, it wouldn't have taken that long, but they had carefully covered their trail as they moved through the woods and countryside, backtracking a few times, once again to confuse the dogs. Approaching the property, Reggie cautiously neared the abandoned plantation to ensure it was safe while Anastasia hid in the woods. There was no trace of human inhabitants, but it appeared that small animals had claimed the house as their own. Nature had encroached on the exterior covering it with overgrowth and climbing vines. Unfortunately, a quick search revealed that nothing had been left by the last residents that could be used for their comfort. This was not a problem since they were only going to stay temporarily. Their plans were to "let the dust settle" for a few days and then leave when the intensity of the search to find them had eased.

Once Reggie ascertained that the home was empty and there was no danger, he returned for Anastasia, and together they walked toward the house. Upon entering, Reggie tried to lessen the disappointment. "Anastasia dis' is jus' a stoppin' off place. We won't be stayin' hyeh' long, but it will offer us shelter from the weather. I'm so sorry, but dis' is dah' only place I could think of whar' it might be safe fo' us to hide an' rest, while providin' us wit' a roof ovah' our heads. I must admit dat' I didn't 'member it bein' quite dis' bad, but dat' was a while ago."

"Reggie, it will be all right, but I feel a little bit uneasy stoppin' hyeh'." Fear rose in Anastasia's voice as she spoke. "I'm jus' scared dat' Colonel Marshall will catch up wit' us. Are yu' sur' it wouldn't be better to jus' keep movin' on so we kin' put more distance 'tween ourselves an' dah' trackers?"

"We'll only be hyeh' fo' a short time, an' din' we kin' move on," Reggie assured her. "My emotions tell me to keep runnin', but my common sense tells me otherwise. Dose' dogs are a lot faster din' us, an' dat's whar' dah' mischief lies. If we run, dey'll catch us. 'Gain, we have to outsmart 'dem. If we jus' 'hole up' hyeh', dah' pursuit will eventually lessen—din' we'll leave. Right now I'm goin' outside 'hind dah' house an' stash our money in dah' ground in case somethin' unexpected occurs while we are hyeh'. We'll retrieve it when it's safe to head north."

"God, I hope yu're right 'bout all dis', Reggie." Anastasia's voice trembled as she spoke. "If yu're' wrong, it could cost us our lives, but I'd still rather take a chance under des' difficult circumstances as yur' wife, din' to stay in dat' cottage—dat' would be a fate worse din' death."

"Try to relax, Anastasia," Reggie replied with strength in his voice masking his own rising fears. "We should be jus' fine hyeh'. Atter' we're settled in I'm goin' to see Mr. Blanton. Fo' now please come wit' me so yu' know whar' I hid dah' money."

As Reggie was digging a shallow hole with a sturdy piece of wood, Anastasia asked, "Who is Mr. Blanton?"

"He's white trash, pure white trash," Reggie answered. "I mentioned dah' scamp earlier. He makes a livin' retailin' whiskey to dah' slaves. Dah' slaves steal whatever dey' kin' git' an' bring it to Mr. Blanton an' in exchange he keeps 'dem in whiskey. He has a general store dat' he works out of, but he doesn't really sell dat' much legally. Dah' mischief of it is if he ever got caught 'ceptin' merchandise from dah' slaves, he would be off to jail fo' a year, lose his business an' git' a $1,000 fine. Virginia has 'bery strict laws governin' dis' practice. People like him live on dah' 'bery edge, it's a 'bery dangerous business." Throughout the South, it was not uncommon to find white people like Mr. Blanton bartering with slaves even though they knew the penalty for getting caught would be very costly. The authorities were always seeking them out since they represented a serious breakdown in the bondage system. They afforded the opportunity for the slaves to acquire some money and provisions. Having money and provisions makes the "road to freedom" much easier.

"Has anybody from our plantation ever been thar'?"

"Of course, Anastasia, dey' come from all parts to git' thar' whiskey."

"Why would yu' ever trust somebody like him?"

"Fo' two reasons—first, he knows dat' I know all 'bout what he's been up to an' second, he owes me a big favor—Albert an' I possibly saved his life a few years ago."

"What happened?"

"Albert an' I were approachin' Mr. Blantons' store on horseback when we observed some 'spicious things goin' on outside. Three horses were tied up wit' a stranger appearin' to stand lookout over dah' area. As we advanced, he looked at us menacingly an' din' ran into dah' store. Immediately, he an' two other men came runnin' out, got on thar' horses an' rode off. Fortunately fo' us, dey' left us alone."

"Did Mr. Blanton git' harmed?"

"No! Follerin' dah' confrontation, we tied our horses up an' ran into dah' store to check on Mr. Blanton. Outside of takin' some provisions, dey' did not harm him. He explained dey' were threatenin' him, an' dah' threats were gittin' worse, an' din' we appeared like an act of God an' chased 'dem off by merely ridin' up."

"Reggie, why didn't yu' ever tell me 'bout dis' 'fore?"

"Anastasia, dah' long an' short of it is dat' I was ashamed of myself fo' savin' him. He shoulda' died or at least been badly beaten fo' all of his past transgressions. He feeds on dah' misery of others, pure an' simple, his life was not worth savin'. We jus' rode up not realizin' dat' our presence could have saved his life. Dah' thin' is, he promised dat' if he could ever do anythin' fo' either one us, he would as pay back."

"Do yu' really feel safe trustin' him wit' our lives?"

"I don't see dat' we have any choice. He kin' give us all dah' provisions we need, an' when dah' dust settles down', he kin' 'range transportation fo' us. We're light skinned 'nough dat' we should be able to git' by wit'out bein' questioned atter' we git' out of dah' area. Our money will help in gittin' us dah' proper clothin' to pass fo' white. God willin', it really shouldn't be dat' difficult."

After Reggie reassured Anastasia they were safe, he started a small fire in the fireplace, making sure not to use any green wood that would give them away by the smoke. Then he took out a blanket he'd had in his pack and spread it out on the floor in front of the fire. It was very warm and cozy after their long trek. In addition, he pulled out a collection of fruit, cheese, smoked meat, and bread that Mammy Bertha had given him just before they left. In the autumn air, it created a warm ambience with the flickering fire as the background. Reggie settled on one end of the blanket, and Anastasia sat opposite him. They sat there glancing at the food he'd set between them. She hadn't eaten much at the corn shucking party as her nerves wore her out from contemplating what lay ahead. They ate in silence at first, Anastasia merely nibbling on the food. She also found herself nervously thinking about being alone with Reggie and she slowly raised her eyes, cautiously glancing his way only to find him looking at her. He moved beside her and reached out with his hand, catching her behind the neck. He drew her forward to gently kiss her lips. He had dreamed of making love with Anastasia and now it was soon to be a reality. He pulled her up against him, and Anastasia rested her head against his chest. There was a contented sigh knowing all was right with his world as long as he and Anastasia were together. They would be heading for freedom shortly, and the two of them could dare to dream whatever they chose, not governed by the dictates of Colonel Marshall or anyone else. Their own determination and their own dreams would guide them. Anastasia responded to Reggie, her arms slipping up around his neck, her lips drifting open in invitation, as her body melted into his. He gathered her close in his arms. They were finally, truly together as man and wife and were prepared for a night of lovemaking as they became lost in each other's charms.

***

Several days went by, and despite their happiness with being with each other, it was proving to be very difficult living in an empty, abandoned home. Supplies were running low, and conditions were getting worse. It was apparent the next phase of their journey had to be put in motion. "Anastasia, I think it's time fo' me to sneak over to Mr. Blanton's store an' pay him a call dis' evenin'. Dah' moon isn't out, enablin' me to move wit'out bein' seen."

"Oh Reggie, I'm so 'fraid fo' yu'."

"Anastasia, I'll be careful. I know dah' area 'bery well, better din' our pursuers."

"Reggie, I'm not worried 'bout yu' knowin' dah' area, I'm more concerned 'bout Mr. Blanton, especially if he's such a no-count. I have a fear dat' he's not to be trusted even though he owes yu' his life. Don't yu' think he wouldn't be 'bove turnin' us in fo' a reward?"

"Anastasia, thar' is always a risk in every adventure, but we have little choice. He kin' provide us wit' dah' means to git' to freedom quickly. Let's give dah' devil his due—'member, 'necessity is dah' mother of invention'," he said with a smile on his face.

"My love, I trust yur' judgment, but I'm still 'fraid." Reggie was having a difficult time convincing Anastasia that Mr. Blanton would be helpful and trustworthy.

That evening as they were standing on the porch, Reggie held Anastasia, knowing the time had arrived for his departure as a tear rolled gently down her cheek. He tried to reassure her. "Anastasia, I love yu' so much, an' I promise yu' dat' I will return by mornin'." They held each other for a long time, than he kissed her tears away and departed for Mr. Blanton's store.

Even in the black of night Reggie knew the way to Mr. Blanton's as he had been there with Albert many times before. Throughout the night he did not hear any dogs, nor encounter any difficulties. Winding along a by-path that he had traversed on more than one occasion, he knew exactly where he was. Fortunately, it was a route that only a few ever traveled, making it safer for him to move without fear of apprehension.

Upon arriving he knew to knock at the rear door leading to Mr. Blanton's apartment. Blanton was in bed when he heard Reggie's knock and his dog began barking frantically as it was very rare to have a customer at this time of night. Mr. Blanton was fearful and picked up his shotgun. "Who is it, dat' would be at my door at dis' hour?" he called out.

"It's Reggie, an' I come in good faith."

"I'm goin' to open dis' door." Mr. Blanton hollered. "If thar' is any shenanigans, I have a loaded shotgun pointed at yu'." He opened the door, his shotgun aimed at the visitor and was amazed to see Reggie standing there. "Reggie, what are yu' doin' hyeh'? Never mind, come on in—don't jus' stand thar'."

He put down the shotgun as Reggie entered. "Mr. Blanton, I need yur' help like I have never needed help 'fore." Reggie spoke hurriedly, knowing that Anastasia was waiting for him at the abandoned plantation. "'Member when Albert an' I helped yu' git' rid of dose' three intruders who were bent on causin' yu' harm, an' yu' said dat' yu' owed us a huge favor?"

"Of course I do, Reggie," Mr. Blanton answered. "I was possibly at 'deaths' door' when yu 'rived an' chased dose' robbers off. I tole' yu' I would do anythin' fo' yu'—jus' ask."

"Mr. Blanton, Anastasia an' I are 'holed up' 'round hyeh', an' we are dangerously low on provisions," Reggie told him. "I thought yu' might be able to help us out wit' some necessities. Also, could yu' include a small amount of clothin' dat' is not Negro cloth fo' dah' two of us." Reggie knew that the combination of regular clothing along with their skin color would make their escape immeasureably easier. He also realized that if necessary, he could provide the funds to pay for the clothing.

"Provisions—includin' dah' clothin', I kin' help yu' wit'," Mr. Blanton obliged. "It's really risky business. If I git' caught jus' givin' yu' anythin', I'd be ruined. On top of dat', dah' two of yu' are fugitives. Dat' would make matters much worse if I got caught helpin' yu' out. Yu' should know dat' yu' an' yur' friend are wanted by dah' law. Today dey' came into my store an' posted a wanted a sign fo' dah' both of yu'! Dat's why I was shocked to see yu.' Dey've been combin' dah' countryside, an' I hear dat' dah' colonel has hired Buzz Weaver, dah' famous niggah' hunter. He's got dah' best niggah' dogs' 'round. I hate to say it, but dey' say he always gits' who he's atter'. I jus' hope dey' are wrong."

"I'm not surprised dat' he hired Weaver. I knew dat' Colonel Marshall would want us bad. Jus' how much is dah' reward?"

"Dah' wanted poster dey' left in my store has a $500 reward fo' both of yu'." Mr. Blanton eyed Reggie curiously to see his reaction to this news.

Reggie's eyebrows went up, and he stepped back as he exclaimed, "Dat's a lot of money Mr. Blanton, but I can't worry 'bout dat'. If yu' could jus' give me dah' provisions, yu' kin' consider yur' debt to me paid in full." Under the circumstances, Reggie decided to forgo telling Blanton about his money especially since he gave him the clothing. Instead, he would just take the supplies and leave.

"Wait hyeh', Reggie, while I git' 'dem fo' yu'." Mr. Blanton acted like he was becoming on edge fearing that someone would show up and find him assisting a runaway slave. "But if yu' git' nabbed, yu' can't mention my name," he forewarned.

"I brought a gunny sack' Mr. Blanton. Jus' fill it fo' me, an' don't worry, we won't say a word, even if we git' caught. 'Sides, thar' would be no reason fo' me to have to say anythin'. Yu' need not worry Mr. Blanton," Reggie promised.

Mr. Blanton went into his store and returned with the gunnysack full of provisions. He handed it to Reggie, looking at him squarely into the eyes as he held up a wanted poster. "Dis' is dah' poster I was tellin' yu' 'bout—now git' out of hyeh', an' good luck." Reggie quickly looked at the poster, amazed that the colonel had been so quick in distributing it. He commented to Blanton that he would be on his way while declining the poster as a souvenir. Reggie explained that if he was caught with the poster, it might bring deep trouble to Mr. Blanton. He didn't want him to have any problems after helping him and Anastasia.

"I want to thank yu' fo' dah' supplies, but I also know dat' yu' kin' 'wish a man good luck as yu' throw him into dah' sea', which means yu' kin' skip wishin' me good luck since my trust fo' yu' is lukewarm. Jus' so yu' know, it wouldn't be wise to double-cross me, knowin' what I know," Reggie warned him, while knowing that he was sending a veiled threat against a white man, which overstepped the boundaries between a white man and a slave.

"Oh no, Reggie!" Mr. Blanton reassured. "Yu' kin' trust me—jus' 'member, if yu' git' caught, don't ever mention dat' I helped yu'."

Reggie picked up the gunnysack and left quickly. He wanted to get back to Anastasia by daybreak. It was a relatively short distance, but it would take longer carrying the heavy gunny sack. He labored tirelessly, carrying it over his back while worrying over Anastasia's welfare in his absence. When he arrived back at their hideaway, Anastasia ran out to him and threw her arms around his neck. "Reggie, I was so worried dat' somethin' happened to yu'.' Did everythin' work out as yu' planned?"

"Take a look." Reggie showed her what Blanton had given them. "We kin' leave any time now. Dah' colonel hired Buzz Weaver, dah' famous niggah hunter, but I don't think he kin' pick up our trail atter' all dis' time. Let's git' goin'."

"Reggie, lets rest fo' awhile. Yu've been out all night. Git' some sleep first, an' din' we kin' leave refreshened," Anastasia pleaded.

"All right, Anastasia, but jus' fo' a little while. Din' we're goin' to have to move out. 'Member, freedom is our goal, not layin' up 'round hyeh'."

Settling into their makeshift bed, the two fell asleep almost immediately. They slept soundly and much longer than they had expected, not realizing that several men were approaching the abandoned plantation—Colonel Marshall, Donald, Mr. Eggers, and Mr. Blanton. They moved quickly and stealthly, hoping their two prizes were still in the house. Three of them entered through the front door while Mr. Blanton waited outside. To their joy, they found Reggie and Anastasia in their makeshift bed sound asleep.

The colonel bellowed, "My oh my, what do we have hyeh'. Why look at 'dem, jus' like 'two peas in a pod' all nestled up together! Well, I hate to 'upset dah' apple cart', but I'm gonna' have to protect my interests. I knew I'd catch up to yu' two rapscallions! I orte' tan both of yur' hides right now, but thar' will be plenty of time fo' dat'. Mr. Eggers, chain both of 'dem! If either one of yah' move a peg, yu'll be reduced to cannon fodder."

Reggie thought he had thoroughly covered his tracks, and he couldn't figure out how they could have found them. Then Blanton entered the house, and Reggie knew he had followed him back to their hideaway. Reggie looked up in disgust and without regard to the consequences said, "I shoulda' known better. Yu' follered' me an' din' tipped dah' colonel off 'bout our whar'bouts. I'm a big fool to have ever trusted yu'.'" Reggie was staring directly at Mr. Blanton when he spoke.

The colonel stepped in. "Reggie don't ever address a white man like dat' in my presence. Yu' shoulda' known dat' white people 'round hyeh' stick together—'specially when dealin' wit' runaway niggahs'."

"Master, have yu' ever wondered how some of yur' field hands git' thar' whiskey?" Reggie defiantly asked. "It's Mr. Blanton! He gives 'dem whiskey in return fo' stolen merchandise from yur' plantation!"

Red-faced Mr. Blanton defensively blurted out, "Reggie, yu' really are a rascal. Yu' commit a serious crime an' din' yu' have dah' nerve to 'cuse me of wrongdoin'. Do yu' really 'lieve dat' Colonel Marshall would 'lieve a scoundrel like yu'? 'Sides, I don't have to take 'dis sass from any niggah'!" It was obvious to everybody that Reggie had struck a chord with Mr. Blanton, forcing him to protect his reputation.

"Look who's 'callin' dah' kettle black'!" Reggie glared back at him. "Yu' are a Judas! I saved yur' life, an' dis' is how yu' reward me!"

Colonel Marshall stepped in at this point. "'Nough of dis' talk. Suffice to say, I would never take dah' word of a niggah' over a white man. Let's git' goin'. Mr. Blanton, yu' come 'long as well, 'cuz' I want to give yu' yur' $500 reward—yu' earned it. Somethin' else, I guess we didn't need dah' services of Buzz Weaver atter' all."

Donald who had remained silent decided it was his time for his involvement. Positioning himself directly in front of Reggie, he slapped him in the face full force. "My father is far too kind to yu'—yu' 'yeller' niggah"! Yu' jus' can't git' it dat' yu' are a niggah' an' not a white man. Reggie, yu' should know dat' yu' can't make 'a silk purse out of a sow's ears'. Yu' kin' never be a white man—once a niggah', always a niggah'! Yu' cannot change dat', no matter how hard yu' try. An' 'bove all, yu' kin' never show disrespect toward any white man, even Mr. Blanton. Yu', a niggah', callin' Mr. Blanton a Judas, dat' is shameful. Dis' kind of behavior cannot be tolerated—such insolence! Jus' as soon as we git' back to Oak Manor, more 'schoolin' will be in order fo' our learned niggah'. Oh', I almost fo'got to tell yu' dat' yu' won't need a school book fo' dis' lesson," as he chuckled with an evil smile.

Anastasia had moved to a corner in the room shaking with fear as she watched and heard everything unfold. Their impending separation would be more torture for both of them than any punishment these men could concoct. If only, she would have listened to Reggie and left sooner when he arrived from Mr. Blanton's. A roar of laughter erupted at Donald's joke while tears ran down Anastasia's face as she sobbed over what she knew Donald had in store for Reggie.

Reggie and Anastasia in obvious despair were tethered together, and the six of them departed. They knew from this point on, the stakes had changed dramatically and that punishment would be swift, harsh and absolute. The chattel system required that runaway slaves had to face the wrath of the master, and extreme punishment would be handed down as an example to the other slaves of the consequences of fleeing and getting caught. In order to minimize an insurrection the slave master always had to be swift and decisive in the administration of punishment and Colonel Marshall would certainly follow that example.

The return trip to Oak Manor was painful, both physically and mentally for Reggie and Anastasia. The leg irons made it extremely difficult to travel at the pace that was required, but this was only minor to what would happen when they returned to the plantation. Reggie felt a terrible amount of guilt knowing that he was naïve enough to believe he could trust a "lowlife" like Mr. Blanton. They had tasted freedom for several days, and now they had to return to bondage. Pondering their fate made the difficult trek even worse as they tried to anticipate what punishment would be administered to them by their captor's. In addition, and more importantly, they were thinking about how their lives would be altered forever at Oak Manor, and how things could have been different if Reggie had never trusted Mr. Blanton.

Finally, arriving back at the plantation after a trek that seemed to last an eternity, Colonel Marshall was anxious to administer swift justice. Reggie was secured in the barn to a rope that was thrown over a wooden beam in the barn with his toes barely touching the floor. Colonel Marshall, Mr. Eggers, and Donald all gathered around Reggie while Anastasia was forced to watch the spectacle as part of her punishment. Meanwhile the colonel had taken a brief respite and went to the main house to get the reward money for Mr. Blanton so he could dispatch him on his way and then return with "vim and vigor".

Having returned, he was standing near Anastasia who was trying to contain her sobbing. The colonel said, "Anastasia, I wanted yu' hyeh' to see Reggie git' dah' opportunity to 'kiss dah' rod' of dah' master. We must impress upon our runaways dah' consequences of lettin' thar' master down. Dah' punishment has to be swift an' decisive. Yu' do understand dat', don't yu' Anastasia? If yu' don't, we'll jus' put yu' 'longside of Reggie."

Anastasia rebutted, "Master, if yu're goin' to flog Reggie, din yu' orte' flog me as well." She said it without hesitation, and it was obvious that she meant it.

"Not dis' time, Anastasia," the colonel angrily replied. "However, I do have some good an' bad news fo' yu'. Dis' blackguard who yu' are so fond of is only goin' to git' a light beatin'. Why? Now dah' bad news! 'Cuz' I have decided to 'put him in my pocket'. Mr. Eggers is goin' to transport him 'mediately to dah' auction house in Richmond."

Anastasia's knees gave way and she fell weeping at the colonel's feet. "Master, please don't sell Reggie, he'll be obedient—I promise!" It was evident that Anastasia's love for Reggie was deep, and in his own twisted way, Colonel Marshall was angered and jealous that Anastasia had spurned his affection so she could be with Reggie, and now he chose to get back at her in the most devious manner. He had decided that it would be wise to split them up forever by selling Reggie at auction.

"Too late fo' dat', Anastasia, an' if yu' don't stop cryin', dah' beatin' will be more severe."

"No master, please. I'll stop." Anastasia remained haunted at knowing she had encouraged Reggie that they should take a nice sleep before leaving and of course they were then subsequentially apprehended.

"I kinda' thought yu' would." He said with a sly smile.

Donald couldn't wait to whip Reggie yet again, and said, "Father, why jus' a light whippin' atter' dat' stunt he pulled? He should be beaten to within an 'inch of his life', an' I would like to be dah' one dat' would 'minister dah' punishment dat' he deserves."

"Donald, if he shows a heavy whippin' at auction, he'll go fo' less money." That type of beating would indicate that he was a defiant slave and that would definitely bring his value down. "'Sides I had to pay dat' white trash, Blanton, $500, an' I know damn well dat' Reggie tole' dah' truth when he said dat' bastard swapped my field hands whiskey fo' what dey' stole from me. I've known all 'long dat' thar' was some totens' goin' on 'round hyeh. Let's jus' say dah' apple doesn't fall too far from dah' tree. I jus' couldn't put my finger on it. 'Nough of dat', I'll worry 'bout dat' later. Right now, I need to make up fo' dat' money by gittin' as much as I kin' by sellin' Reggie at auction. Plus, I have to give Buzz Weaver some money fo' his trouble, even though his dogs never delivered—he doesn't work his dogs fo' nutten'! Dis' damn mess is costin' me a lot of money."

Donald was not happy with his father's decision. He looked Reggie squarely in the face and savagely told him, "If I had my way, Reggie, yu' would be beaten to wit'in an inch of yur' life."

Colonel Marshall turned to Donald saying, "Well, Donald, it won't be done yur' way. Now let's git' dis' ovah' wit'. Mr. Eggers, go 'head an' give him his stripes. As fo' yu', Anastasia, atter' dah' beatin,' I want yu' to go back to yur' cottage. An' 'member, don't plan on escapin' 'gain, or yu'll face a fate worse din' yur' worst nightmare. Liza is outside, an' she' will soon escort yu' back, an' she's gonna' watch yu' closer din' dah' nose on her face since she paid dearly fo' allowin' yu' to escape."

As Mr. Eggers was preparing to use his whip, he had a thought. "Colonel, I have an ider'. Donald wants him to suffer, an' yu' only want to 'minister a light whippin', why don't we 'put him in a buck'? Dat' way Anastasia kin' see jus' how miserable of a wretch dis' yeller' niggah' is wit'out 'fectin' his price at auction."

"Mr. Eggers, I have to hand it to yu'," the colonel responded with admiration in his tone. "Every once in a while yu' come up wit' a good one. Go 'head an' bring him down, an' 'put him in a buck'. Donald, go grab a pole."

The practice of putting somebody "in a buck" was used in the military as well. To put Reggie "in a buck" required him to roll up in a ball while a pole was placed between his arms and legs. Then he was tied at the wrists to the pole and knees thus rendering him completely immobile. The whipping would then proceed with Reggie on the ground positioned in a round ball and unable to move.

After the whipping began, Colonel Marshall with bravado intently stared at Anastasia and stated, "Anastasia, look at dis' pathetic creature yu' love all curled up in dah' dirt. How anybody could love such a specimen of a man—a miserable wretch all rolled up lookin' like a mealworm? It's a mystery to me!" It had to make the colonel feel good seeing Reggie in this condition, the man that Anastasia loved made to look foolish.

Anastasia's heart was broken for Reggie. Regardless of the situation that Reggie was put in, she had never seen a more beautiful or stronger man in her entire life. In her judgment the three of them with hate in their eyes looking down on a helpless Reggie, were spineless cowards while Reggie, even in this condition, remained the only man among them.

After the beating ended, Reggie was freed from the buck and left to remain on the ground until Mr. Eggers yanked him up and tied him to a post. Colonel Marshall faced him and said, "Take one long last look at Anastasia—it will be yur' last. We're goin' to leave yu' tied to dis' post overnight, an' in dah' mornin', Mr. Eggers will be takin' yu' to dah' main auction house in Richmond." Reggie was crestfallen as he looked at Anastasia's tear-stained face. He wanted to desperately hold her in his arms so he could lovingly soothe her. He knew their love for each other was so great that he would have to make one last plea to Colonel Marshall.

"Please, Master, I'm 'bery happy bein' yur' field hand."

"Shut up, Reggie, I can't have somebody like yu' whinin' an' settin' a bad precedent fo' dah' others. The damage is done, an' dah' decision has been made. My fondest wish is dat' yu' git' sold to someone who would take yu' down south to make yu' one of dose' Mississippi cotton niggahs'!" This represented a vindictive comment, since many would consider being sold to a Mississippi plantation owner a possible death sentence.

Donald broke in. "Yu' are goin' to have hell to pay, an' I jus' hope dat' dah' time comes sooner din' later," he said with a sneer.

Turning to leave the barn, Anastasia leaned in Reggie's direction wanting to touch him but was jerked around and forced to follow the others. Reggie's sense of helplessness at not being able to protect her was all consuming. His whole life seemed shattered. The forced separation from his wife, being auctioned off, and the prospect of possibly being placed in a much harsher environment than Oak Manor provided a dismal future. He sagged on the post in abject misery. Then without any warning, he suddenly began experiencing another vision similar to the one he had after his first beating. Unlike the earlier event, in this one Reggie could see much further into the future.

In the earlier vision Reggie was able to discern that in the near future a war between the North and the South would ensue bringing about the end of slavery. In this latest vision Reggie saw another struggle, only this time the main focus was on the inequality between the races. The theme of this vision made Reggie wonder—he had assumed the end of slavery would bring a reasonable amount of equality for the black people. However in this vision, he learned that black people were free but equality would continue to be evasive and much further into the future. Prejudice would remain a fixture that would not end.

What he envisioned appeared to be taking place in Washington, D.C. He could see a handsome middle-aged black man at the podium. It was a pleasant summer day, and this man was capturing the attention of a large mass of people of mixed races. It was very perplexing to Reggie to see a large statue of the man from his earlier vision behind the inspirational speaker who had captured everybody's attention. Suddenly, Halley's Comet could be observed churning overhead, appearing to protect the man—very similar to his earlier vision.

The speaker's address focused on the fight to end racial inequality nonviolently. The speaker, Dr. Martin Luther King, Jr. was giving his famous, *I Have a Dream Speech*, on August 28, 1963.

He stood proud and confident as he addressed the throng who were held spellbound by his booming voice, which resonated throughout the massive crowd. His words were directed at hoping to heal the injustices in our society. Similar to the great white man who addressed a large audience in his first dream, this powerful man gave a resounding and timeless speech. The theme reverberated—in Gods' eyes we are all equal. The power of non-violence, compassion, love, and understanding rose to a high level throughout the speech. The message resonated throughout the man's speech that the dream of equality, freedom, justice, and brotherhood would become the cornerstone for mankind to achieve.

The message for Reggie was evident. The struggle for complete equality would be a much longer struggle as prejudice would continue to haunt mankind long after slavery ended.

As Reggie's vision began to fade, the intensity of the beating and the heart-wrenching loss of Anastasia began to weigh heavy on him. This was clearly the most difficult time in his life. He knew that he had to generate the strength and determination to survive. The future represented an insurmountable hurdle in his life. He knew he had to prepare for it, both mentally and physically in order to make his way back to Anastasia. He wondered what it would take to bring the North and the South nonviolently together and end slavery. He knew it would first be necessary to end slavery followed by the long road to end racial inequality. The two life-like dreams he had experienced provided him with purpose for his future. Hopefully, he could convince others of a unifying direction for our country based on the spirit of compromise. He firmly accepted that we must never stop in our pursuit of equality as a sacred requirement of God. Furthermore, we must realize that in His eyes we shall always remain equal and that we are all His children.

CHAPTER NINE

Later that evening Colonel Marshall and Evelyn were taking their evening walk along the James River. There was an orange haze above the horizon that lit up the sky, and the colors seemed to dance on the ripples of the water. Even with the tranquility of the river, it was obvious that Evelyn's mood represented a contrast. She was very displeased with her husband and she could not conceal her anger. "I understand dat' Reggie is bein' sent to Richmond to be auctioned off. How cruel, couldn't yu' at least wait fo' a speculator to come 'long an' sell him hyeh' at dah' plantation?"

The colonel stood proud. "I jus' wanted dat' scoundrel out of hyeh' as quickly as possible."

"Are yu' sure dat' yu' aren't punishing him 'cuz' Anastasia loves him an' not yu'?" Evelyn's statement was calculated to evoke an instant negative reaction from Andrew.

"Dat' is insolence fo' yu' to imply dat' I could be jealous of a niggah'", he said angrily, while trying to control his temper as he leaned toward Evelyn demanding respect. The statement that Evelyn made and the colonel's reaction might be typical of a Southern white slave owner faced with the reality that a female slave could possibly love a slave over him. Of course Evelyn was well aware that Colonel Marshall's pride was shattered because of his tremendous ego.

"Andrew, I know how yu' think, an' I know yu' know I do.

I jus' have some regard fo' Reggie, an' I always thought yu' did as well. We all know dat' he had represented someone 'bery special to yu' and most certainly to Albert as well." Evelyn was venturing down a path that Colonel Marshall did not want her to travel— Reggie was his biological son, making him Albert's half brother as well.

"Evelyn, be careful what yu' say, 'cuz' yu're' goin' to create problems," the colonel shot back. "'Sides, I have what yu' will consider to be 'bery good news. I've decided to clean dah' house of dis' whole matter an' hire-out Anastasia."

Evelyn's voice turned shrill. "Andrew, dis' news is shockin'!" It was apparent that she was surprised, but it was evident by her response that she gladly welcomed the news that Anastasia would be off the plantation.

"It's true, an' furthermore, we know dat' 'hirin' out' is usually done on the first of January, but dis' will be an' 'ception. Yu' know dat' Mrs. Winter's husband recently died, an' she was forced to move from her plantation to a small home in Richmond. Her son tole' me dat' she is terribly lonely an' really needs company. I'm goin' to contact him right away an' make 'rangements. Anastasia will be helpful an' be a good companion in many ways fo' her. Also, Mrs. Winters will provide a welcome environment for Anastasia." The practice in the South of a recently widowed woman moving to a smaller home in town and leaving the plantation to her children to deal with was not at all uncommon. In those days special facilities for the elderly were not available.

"Why did yu' make dis' decision?" Evelyn was inquisitive, and she hoped the decision was made for the good of their marriage.

"I understand how yu've been feelin', an' I have 'cided dat' fo' dah' sake of harmony 'tween us, dis' would be a wise decision. Yu' know I'm putting Reggie in my pocket', an' I could have done dah' same thin' to Anastasia. Wit' her looks she would fetch a high price at one of dose' sportin' houses in New Orlens'. Of course, if things don't work out 'tween her an' Mrs. Winter's, I still have dat' option." Andrew wanted to remind Evelyn that he was keeping his options open.

Evelyn felt much better. "Sometimes I wonder 'bout yur' motives, but I do thank yu' fo' treatin' Anastasia fairly. I could not stand thinkin' 'bout her bein' sold fo' dah' delight of lecherous men. I still feel bad 'bout what yu' are doin' to Reggie, but I kin' live wit' myself knowin' dat' he will probably be a house servant fo' someone else an' if he stayed hyeh', it's likely he would remain a field hand." While Evelyn at first felt remorse for Reggie, when she found out that Anastasia was being hired-out, she felt a tremendous relief, which more then balanced out her sadness over Reggie.

"Evelyn, I'm glad yu' understand."

***

Early the next morning Mr. Eggers brought Reggie out of the barn wearing old rusted chains and fully prepared for the trek to Richmond. For Reggie, walking would be difficult since he was still in agony from the beating. Fortunately, it was milder than his previous beating. Far worse, he was grieving over the separation from his bride, especially since he did not know her fate. Reggie was cognizant the colonel could make a lot of money off of her sale or just lust over her for his own pleasure. He knew that most likely her fate would be one or the other and that weighed heavy on his heart.

Mr. Eggers knew it would not serve him well to push Reggie, causing him more bodily harm. Therefore, the trek went much slower than normal, allowing Reggie to rest at different intervals. It was nightfall when the two arrived in Richmond. Reggie, although in a haggard state made the trek none the worse for wear. Mr. Eggers went directly to the Richmond Hotel where other slave owners and traders often stayed. After an uneventful evening, where Reggie was allowed to sleep on the floor in the hotel room, he took Reggie to a dimly lit clothing store in the basement of the hotel where they stayed for the night. This clothing store was used by the slave owners to outfit the slaves they planned to sell. Mr. Eggers had dealt with this operation in the past so he knew the procedure. He approached the shop owner with Reggie right by his side.

"I'm Mr. Eggers, overseer fo' Colonel Marshall from Oak Manor plantation. I need to git' dis' fancy buck fitted fo' sale an' dey' tell me dat' yu' are dah' man who kin' git' dah' job done."

The clothier, who displayed the look of a city dweller, looking totally aghast, said, "Mr. Eggers you threw me for a loop. I thought this gent was your friend. Just joking, of course—I see the chains!" He realized by the look on Eggers face that he did not share his humor. "Originally, I'm from New York City so I guess I still have a lot to learn about the customs of the old South. Having said that, judging by his looks, I would say he should be sold definitely as a house servant."

"Dat' makes sense but 'tween yu' an' me, dah' rascal is no better din' a field hand." Mr. Eggers expressed his feelings of contempt with earnest.

"Well, my recommendation is that you sell him as a house servant. I have no choice but to make that recommendation since I personally have never seen anybody looking like him, going off at auction as a field hand," the clothier replied firmly.

"All right let's go 'head an' outfit him as a house servant, which is still 'gainst my better judgement," acquiesced Mr. Eggers.

"Mr. Eggers, this young man is quite the dandy, and I intend to make him shine in something quite colorful. He even strikes me as possibly having chutzpah, an' they don't often go through here as a complete package—don't you agree?"

"Hmmm. . . oh yeah—of course," Mr. Eggers mumbled.

"Hello Dandy. My name is Mr. Arnold Gilbert and what would be yours?"

"Sir, my name is Reggie."

"Well ain't that a cute name for a black man, but then you do look like a white man," Mr. Gilbert said sarcastically. "You know I almost expected you to come forward with a last name. You disappoint me, as I'm still waiting for a house servant or for that matter, a field hand to come up with a last name. I guess I'll just have to wait a little longer. Mr. Eggers, I still can't figure out why, just once they can't at least take their owner's last name and use that for an introduction." Coming from New York City, Mr. Gilbert had already learned to avoid using the word slave in the South. In addition he was injecting cynicism referencing a last name knowing full well that slaves carried only their first name, however, he did it with a smile and a little humor just to further aggravate Mr. Eggers.

"Well Mr. Gilbert, I'm not hyeh' to explain Southern customs," Mr. Eggers responded coldly.

The clothier knew he had come close to crossing the line. "Mr. Eggers, I didn't mean to walk on thin ice, so let's get on with our business. I think Reggie, being so dignified, should be sporting a blue velvet vest so he can stand apart from the others. They are in style but not many men can actually wear one. I believe he could be the fashion plate of the auction house, sporting a blue velvet vest when he steps up for sale.

Mr. Eggers finally found something humorous and began to laugh at the idea of a blue velvet vest. "Now dat's a great ider'. Now jus' pick out dah' clothes to go wit' dah' blue velvet vest an' we'll be on our way."

Mr. Gilbert quickly went about the business of picking out the clothing best-suited for Reggie with the approval of Mr. Eggers. When he was finished, Mr. Eggers sized up the new outfit on Reggie. "My, oh my, yu' do look dah' dandy wit' dose' fancy clothes topped off wit' a blue velvet vest," he said sarcastically. Finally, turning to Mr. Gilbert, he asked, "How much do I owe yu'?"

"Well, we didn't outfit your dandy with Negro cloth, so of course that would be an extra charge," Mr. Gilbert replied. At auction, most slaves wore Negro cloth, a low grade fabric. It's noteworthy that the complete division between the whites and slaves in the South would have to include the quality of the clothing.

"I see, din' how much do I owe," Mr. Eggers impatiently repeated.

"I would say four dollars and thirty cents."

"Cash down, it's a deal," Mr. Eggers said as he paid the man.

He then led Reggie down the street tethered in the rusty chains, "dressed to kill in his fancy togs" until they stopped in front of a very large, old rustic building. "Now dat' yu' look like a fancy niggah', it's time to git rid of yu'. Hyeh' we are at dah' main auction house—dah' Center buildin'," Mr. Eggers announced.

As they entered the building, a distinct and heavy foul odor was in the air. The two were approached by one of the personnel who slowly looked Reggie up and down. "I 'sume yu' want to auction off dis' fancy niggah'?" he asked Mr. Eggers.

"Yup, an' could yu' put him up fo' sale as soon as possible. He's dah' only merchandise I have to move at dis' time."

"Well we can put him on dah' block today," the man said. "Wait hyeh' while I take him to dah' holdin' pen. When I return yu' kin' tell me a little bit 'bout him. We should give our auctioneer, Shoutin' Frank Hanley, a little background on dis' dandy."

The auction area was a large, cold, bland room deep in the basement of the building. On one end of the room stood a large, rickety, old wooden stage where the auctioneer sized up the fully-packed room of men eagerly waiting to purchase slaves. Shouting Frank personified the look of an auctioneer. He was a large, robust man, nattily clad in a brown, large plaid, tweed suit accented with a white fringe shirt, and topped off with a wide brimmed matching brown hat. Somehow, his long, sandy-colored hair managed to stay in place. The outstanding quality that he possessed was his ability to draw people to him with his dominating voice and personality. Suddenly, he bellowed, "How do yu' folks do today! Kin' I have y'alls' attention for a moment? We've got a fine bunch of niggahs' to auction off today. So lets' not delay any longer an' bring dem' on up."

The first group, including Reggie, was brought in for inspection. In a booming voice, Shouting Frank yelled, "Y'all jump up an' down now to show y'all are in good health." Hanley then pulled forward a young male Negro who appeared to be strong and healthy—a perfect field hand. "Y'all he's ready to go, so come up fo' a close 'spection," Frank boomed.

The men who were serious about bidding came up to the poorly lit stage to take a closer look. They gazed inside his mouth and examined the general condition of his body. "Take off yur' blouse boy!" Frank ordered. "Show 'em yur' unmarked back. Open dat' mouth, nice an' wide. See his mouth is good an' clean. Jump boy, jump! Jump high, 'gain, jump, jump, jump, jump high. 'Bery good. Yu' see, fellers', he's good, clean, an' healthy. He'd be a good addition to yur' stock."

Frank turned to face the crowd of men waiting for the bidding to begin, which required going through his usual spin. "Now gentlemen an' fellow citizens," he called out. "Hyeh' is a perfect buck Negro, an' fo' all I know, he could be a Mandingo straight from dah' upper Niger River valley. He's stout as a mule, good fo' any kind a work an' he never gives no trouble. He's fully guaranteed. How much am I offered? Now, do I hyeh' six? Thank yu', six hundred is bid fo' dis' prime buck, but he's worth a lot more. Seven, make it seven. I hyeh' seven? Seven I have. Eight, do I hyeh' eight? Eight! Nine! 'Member he could be a great find. Nine! We have nine. Do we have ten, ten, I'm jus' gittin' warmed up? We have ten. Eleven, do I have eleven? I hyeh' ten-fifty. I got ten-fifty. Ten-sixty. Gentlemen, dah matter is slinkin' to an' end. Last chance. Goin' once, goin' twice, sold fo' $1,050. Move him out, an' bring up dat' fine wench wit' dah' two little niggahs'."

Handlers quickly grabbed the slave and escorted him off the stage as the woman and her two children were brought up. As she approached the front of the stage, she was visibly trembling. The poor woman's face reflected her fear and anguish over the possibility of being separated from her two young children.

As the three stood at the tip of the stage in terror, Frank began to shout. "Gentlemen 'spect dah' prime merchandise. Take off yur' blouse an' show us dose' nice firm breasts. Back is clean—dah' mouth is perfect. Jump, jump, jump high. Perfect! Now, she is a package deal wit' dah' two little wenches." She was forced to suffer the denigration of standing bare breasted in front of an almost all male crowd as they gawked at her.

The crowd demonstrated agitation when Frank said that the three had to be sold together. "I'm not interested in yur' package deal," somebody in the crowd yelled.

The woman dropped to her knees. "Please, I'd do anythin' but separatin' me from my little pickanannies. I'd go down south, anywhar', but please don't separate me from my pickanannies," she begged the crowd. It was obvious the thought of losing her two children would be more then she could endure.

Shouting Frank slapped her face. "Such insolence! Wench, yu're not goin' to be split from yur' little niggahs'. I never heard of a niggah' carin' 'bout thar' little niggahs' anyhow. Now gentlemen dah' reason I can't separate 'dem is 'cuz' dey' are dower niggahs'. I'm sorry gentlemen, but our women kin' be soft on thar' niggahs', an' in dis' case, dis' woman does not want des' little niggahs' separated from thar' mammy." Shouting Frank was alluding to the fact of Southern women having more compassion than the men.

Another bidder called out to Shouting Frank, "Well, if I purchased dose' niggahs', I would want to separate em', an' dat' would be my business," he said firmly.

"Mister, yu' are correct," Frank explained. All of yu' 'member dat' once yu' buy 'em, dey' are yurs' to do damn well what yu' please."

A loud interruption suddenly emerged from the back of the room. A young, well-dressed, very well-groomed man stood up in the rear and began shouting, "All of you are agents of Beelzebub. Hell will boil and overflow with joy at such works of this nature!" Beelzebub is a Hebrew word, which literally means lord of the flies as a reference to the devil.

Several men immediately grabbed the stranger, threw him to the floor and began throwing fists and kicking him. Shouting Frank jumped off the edge of the stage to intervene. "Stop dis' at once. Let me have a few words wit' dis' meddlin' 'bobolitionist 'fore yu' all kill him."

The men respected Shouting Frank and backed away from the beaten down stranger. "Mister yu' ain't drawin' cards in dis' poker game," Frank bellowed. "Yu' are in a heap of trouble. Don't yu' say 'nother word—yu' comin' down hyeh' to stir things up. What were yu' thinkin' comin' down hyeh' an' buttin' in on our business. Mister yu' must be crazier din' a loon comin' in hyeh' an' talkin' like dis' knowin' dat' yu' would git' a lickin', or worse yet—strung up an' danglin' at dah' end of a rope. 'Sides, I hear yu' got niggahs' runnin' wild up thar' in dah' North wit'out any supervision. Don't yu' think yu' would be better served takin' care of yur' own damn problems dat' are worse din' ours. I know who yu' are—one of dose' niggah' lovin' 'bobolitionists! Now yu' jus' shame dah' debil' an' tell us dah' truth?"

"Sir, I'm a man of God, not an abolitionist. I tend to stay far away from politics."

He could very well be telling the truth. In the North, Quakers like the famous author, Harriet Beecher Stowe, well known for *Uncle Tom's Cabin,* preferred being labeled antislavery—not abolitionist. Generally, Quakers were deeply religious and avoided being classified as abolitionists, a secular term, which would be reserved for people like Theodore Weld, Frederick Douglass and William Lloyd Garrison, editor of *The Liberator,* a publication that represented a total denunciation of slavery. The distinction between being antislavery and abolitionist was one of degrees. People who considered themselves antislavery usually took their position based on religion, not politics. They were moderate in their thinking and generally did not attach themselves to extremism.

Meanwhile, Southerners were generally not as much aware of the distinction between antislavery and abolitionists. Anyone who spoke out against slavery in the South would be automatically labeled an abolitionist and subject to harm. Religious motivation or social zeal would not be a factor as everyone was lumped together—abolitonists. Unfortunately, this communication gap along with others, continued to divide relations between the North and the South even further.

A large unkempt man in the crowd stepped forward and began poking the stranger repeatedly in the forehead. "Why don't we settle dis' wit' a nice, tight rope 'round dis niggah' lover's neck, an' we'll see if God kin' git' him out of dis' fix." The bully stared directly into the eyes of the outsider. "I kin' speak fo' all of us. We hate a white niggah' lover more din' if yu' was jus' 'nother niggah' bargin' in on us. 'Sides mister, what do yu' think dah' niggahs' would do to yu' if dah' boot was on dah' other foot? Dey' would probably have yur' white niggah' lovin' ass hangin' from a rope out of 'preciation fo' all dat' yu' have done fo' 'dem. I jus' can't understand a white man' cow-talin' to a bunch of niggahs'!"

Shouting Frank, knowing how out-of-hand the situation had become, responded. "We've got other business 'round hyeh' 'sides a hangin'. I have jus' one more thin' to say to dis' miserable creatur'—if yu' show up hyeh' 'gain we're goin' to hang yur' 'bobolitionist ass. Now skedaddle an' consider yurself' lucky, 'cuz' yu' came mighty close to meetin' yur' maker."

The stranger quickly fled the premises, knowing that he had come very close to being killed or at least seriously injured for a cause in which he so strongly believed in. One of the patrons commented, "My oh' my, jus' look at dat' fool, why he done shot out of hyeh' as quick as a bobcat jumpin' out of a gunny sack." The crowd laughed at the joke knowing that the stranger was long gone and probably not looking back.

Shouting Frank marched back up to the stage, the boards creaking beneath his heavy feet. "See hyeh', now let's git' back to business. Now she's a rattlin' good breeder wit' two little niggahs'. I say hyeh' is a wench dat' came from a good stock, maybe even another Mandingo. Dah' wench is young, well-proportioned, strong, an' a fine breeder wit' two niggah' babies. Let's start at $1,000. I have $1,000. Come on, gentlemen, I have 11, I have 11, now I have 12, I have 12. Thirteen, a bargain, I have 13. Now 14, come on gentlemen, loosen up, I have 14, now 15, now 16, 16 is cheap, 16 is cheap. Oh, I have 16, come on now $1,700. We have $1,700, now we need $1,800. Yu' could double yur' money. We have $1,750, come on folks, dig deep, let's make $1,800. Dah' matter is inchin' to an' end. Seventeen-fifty we have. Do I hyeh' seventeen-sixty, time is runnin' out? Now seventeen-fifty fo' three niggahs' is damn cheap. Seventeen-fifty once, twice, sold for $1,750."

Shouting Frank motioned to the mother and children to get off the stage and for the next slave to be brought up. "Now, let's bring dah' oddball specimen up," Frank yelled out, "dah' 'yeller' niggah'", all dressed up in his Sunday best, all togged up like a fancy white man, topped off wit' his fancy blue velvet vest—my oh my. Well gentlemen, we do have wit' us a gay Lothario. One of dose' fancy bucks dat' we seldom ever see! In fact, to my recollection I've never seen a niggah' wit' his carriage an' looks. He does look more white din' niggah'! He would be an ideal display niggah'— maybe even a butler. I mean he could do yur' plantation, right proud—struttin' 'round like he's somethin' special."

An interested bidder shouted, "Whar' did he come from, Shoutin' Frank—like yu' said he sur' don't look like a typical niggah'?"

Shouting Frank smiled. "I would guess dat' he's one of dose' camp meetin' babies—yu' know, a little hanky panky." Everyone responded with boisterous laughter at Shouting Frank's joke. They knew that at a typical camp meeting, a lot of social interaction took place when not engaged in religious services. Shouting Frank asked, "Jus' whar' did yu' come from boy?"

Reggie responded in a quiet stammer, "Sir, as far as I know..."

"Speak up, niggah'!" interrupted Shouting Frank.

Reggie cleared his throat and began again, a bit louder. "Sir, as far as I know, a turkey buzzard laid me an' dah' sun hatched me." This was a rather safe answer commonly stated by a slave with mixed blood that would hopefully diffuse any repercussions from being mixed blooded.

Annoyed by the answer, Shouting Frank replied, "Is dis' niggah' jawin' at me, handin' me some 'cock an' bull story'? We all know dat' niggah' talk. Whar' did yu' come from? Answer me, niggah', or I'll slap dah' spit right out of yur' mouth."

"Sir, I came from a plantation 'long dah' James River outside of Richmond," Reggie forcefully communicated, hoping he would not have to go any further where he would be asked about his father or mother.

"Ohhh', one of dose' dignified plantations?" Shouting Frank retorted sarcastically. The crowd knew that a James River plantation was of the elite.

Reggie nodded. "Yes sir, dat' would be correct." Reggie felt a bit of relief that the auctioneer ceased with the questions.

A member of the crowd loudly stated, "Come on let's git' down to nitty-gritty, dis' boy has got to be dah' product of a 'left-handed marriage'." This created an immediate and excited response from the crowd. A "left-handed marriage" is in reference to a socially unacceptable marriage or relationship. Interestingly, before eating untensils were common, people were taught to eat with their right hand and to discard the left overs with their left hand. As a result, the right-hand was treated as the "clean hand" while the left-hand became the "dirty hand". The term a "left-handed marriage" was then meant to imply a marriage that perhaps lacked fidelity. Notably, the aversion to the left-hand even extended to encouraging children to learn to write with their right hand.

"Gentlemen, I haven't had dis' much fun in a long time," Shouting Frank laughed. "We all kinda' git' a little bored at dah' usual run of niggahs' dat' comes through hyeh'. We jus' don't normally see some boy like dis'—sportin' a fancy blue vest, an' sur' in dah' hell not Negro cloth, an' he's struttin' his stuff like a real dandy wit' dah' women. Yu' must think yu' are better din' dah' other niggahs, comportin' yur'self like yu' are a blue blood when all yu' are is jus' 'nother damn niggah'. I would jus' love to give dis' niggah' a smack jus' to sorta' remind him of his place. I suppose yu' know yur' letters an' numbers? Answer me!"

"Yes sir, A, B, C, D, E, F, G, H," Reggie recited.

"Okay dat's 'nough. How 'bout yur' numbers?"

"Yes sir, two plus two equals four," Reggie went on. "Twelve minus two equals ten."

"Damn! Well we've got us a two-headed niggah who knows his letters an' numbers—a real smart one," Shouting Frank exclaimed.

Somebody in the back interrupted the proceedings,

"Shoutin' Frank, dis' really burns me up. Dah' niggah' knows his letters an' numbers, but hell, I don't, an' I bet dat' a good chunk of us in dis' crowd would have to say dah' same damn thin'! My oh my, jus' what in dah' hell is dis' world comin' to—a niggah' knowin' more din' a white man? Dat' sur' makes no sense to me, an' I don't like it. A niggah' always has to 'know his place'. White people must always rule dah' roost an' niggahs' jus' have to foller' 'hind. Dat's dah' way God intended it!" The message the stranger made regarding schooling was the truth. Since public schooling was not available, generally education was only in the reach of the minority of people—middle and upper class. The majority of the white people who were classified as lower class were usually illiterate while even a fair percentage of the middle class fell into that category as well.

Shouting Frank took control, "Okay, okay, dat's 'nough. Let's git' back to business. Gentlemen, dah' niggah' is smart. He'd be a real keeper, yu' know—a big fish on dah' hook, a prize catch."

Another member of the crowd commented. "He's pretty much white. It would be easy fo' him to run." Most were probably thinking the same thing.

Shouting Frank rebutted, "Jus' send him way down South whar' he'd have a hell of a distance to run." Everyone laughed, appreciating Shouting Frank's joke.

The crowd seemed to enjoy the novelty of this sale. They hadn't had this much fun at an auction in a long time. Finally, Shouting Frank got serious and turned toward Reggie. "Well, let's git' dah' show on dah' road. Mr. Dandy, take off dat' fancy blouse an' vest. Looks like dah' niggah came from dah' lap of luxury, but yu' never know. Yu' can't always judge a book by its cover. Des' men have dah' right to see what dey' are payin' fo'."

As Reggie removed his vest and shirt as ordered, the buyers were surprised to see the deep marks on his back. There were gasps and mumbling being generated throughout the crowd. They were completely shocked to find this light skinned Negro had been whipped.

Aghast, Shouting Frank said, "Whoa', whoa', what is dis'? I thought yu'd be clean. Why yu' got some pretty fresh stripes on yur' back. I can't guarantee yu' like dis'. Open dat' mouth—mouth is clean. Jump, jump, jump, like a monkey—very good. Are yu' sur' yu' aren't one of dose' refractory niggahs' out causin' yur' master trouble?"

"No, sir, I tried to avoid trouble. It more or less came my way."

"Men, did yu' hyeh' dat'! Say, dat's a nice, sweet answer. Maybe he even had a white woman or two give him dah' eye. Now gentlemen, I'm only jestin' wit' y'all on dat'. I know dat' if he had been caught sleepin' wit' a white woman, he wouldn't be hyeh'. He'd be dead an' buried." The auctioneer was addressing a very delicate subject.

"Let's git' serious, It sounds like one of yu' could git' a real deal since he may not be a troublemaker at all. Let's begin dah' biddin' fo' dis' fancy niggah'. Gentlemen, he's one of a kind. He would make yur' plantation look real prim an' proper. Do I have $600? I have $600—good. Seven hundred, come on, dis' is a one of a kind niggah'. He would dignify yur' plantation. Good! Eight, eight is cheap, do I have eight? Good, now nine, come on, he could give yur' plantation a touch of class. Good, I have nine. Ten, I don't want to close dis' off too soon—good, I have ten. Now 11, eleven, I have. Twelve, do I have 12? Come on gentlemen, y'all are gittin' awfully quiet. Do I have $1,150? How 'bou $1,130? I have $1,130. Is dat' all gentlemen? Matters are slitherin' to an' end. Well, $1,130 going once, twice, sold fo' $1,130!"

Reggie was quickly removed from the stage and taken to a dirty holding pen. Just like a horse led down a cobblestone path, Reggie did what he was told. The handlers put manacles on him, looped a chain through an iron ring on the pen wall, and then looped and relocked it into the manacles. They pulled hard on the chains making sure Reggie was securely held, then hit Reggie on the back of the neck and shoved him to the floor. Laughing at the sight of Reggie all curled up in pain, it was obvious the handlers were giving Reggie harsher treatment because of the color of his skin and handsome looks.

Reggie jammed himself into the far corner of the wooden pen, hoping someone would bring him a much needed meal. When dinner finally arrived, the handlers' resentment toward him was obvious. They spit on his plate and placed it on the floor, and for sheer meanness, they placed it slightly out of his reach. Once they left, Reggie's inventiveness took command, as he was able to maneuver his chains so that he could reach his plate and slide it over to him. Reggie assumed they were mistreating the other slaves as well, albeit not as harshly. Obviously, all he could be for now was the target of their cruelty, hoping that one day soon, things would change. He hoped it would be coming soon as his dream foresaw when the North would come and liberate the slaves.

Early the next morning, Reggie was awakened by the sound of boots clattering on the cobblestone. He was cold and shivering and not anxious to see who was appearing in the dimly lit room.

It was the agent for the company that had purchased him. He stopped when he spotted Reggie. In his mid-forties with a thick head of blond hair that was graying on the sides, he had pink skin stretched over his bloated face, and his eyes were tiny and almost colorless, appearing like slits between his cheeks and white eyebrows. Wet, red lips pursed above a chin strong enough to hold its shape in the blubber. He spoke to Reggie. "I'm Beau Collins, the agent for Miller and Hibbard. Shortly we will be boarding the brig, Three Carols, and we'll be heading toward New Orleans." His voice was high, almost feminine, and with no southern accent. These characteristics were comical to Reggie, since Mr. Collins exuded such a manly, authoritative look.

The slaves near Reggie overheard they were going to be shipped to New Orleans and immediately their despair became evident since they knew it was the worst place to be sent. This meant in all probability the slaves would end up in Mississippi, Louisiana, or Alabama where much harsher conditions existed than in Virginia or the Carolinas. These new states were a major part of the cotton boom of the South. Fueled by the destruction of the soil along the southeast coast along with the increase in the worldwide demand for cotton meant that slaves were being dispatched to these new states in large numbers. Unfortunately for the slaves, conditions in the new states were more haphazard, which made the exploitation of the slaves even greater.

New money in the hands of the nouveau riche had created a high level of greed, again, fed by worldwide demand for cotton, which meant that conditions were far more uncoordinated than they would be with the more established coastal states along the Atlantic Ocean. In addition to their usual soul-crushing situation, the slaves also knew the probability of escape to the North was far more difficult owing to the increased distance. Few ever made it to freedom from the "deep South". Unquestionably living in the "deep South" would place them in an extremely difficult situation, which would demand much harder working conditions and subsequently, higher suicide rates, a substantial drop in the quality of life, and ultimately a shorter life span.

One of the slaves shouted out, "Does dat' mean we are goin' to become cotton niggahs', master?"

"My experience with the New Orleans market does tell me that most likely you will be purchased for the cotton plantations to help in the expanding market," the agent answered. "When we arrive, all of you will be dispatched to the auction house, where you will be purchased by your new master." He failed to mention the sugar and rice plantations that required an intensive amount of labor as well.

Another slave muttered, "Does that mean I will never see my wife 'gain?" When the question was asked, Reggie could only think of the possibility of never seeing his Anastasia as well. A single tear ran down one cheek, exhibiting his growing despair as he looked to his new life knowing he had to find hope for a future that could be without the love of his life.

"I happen to be a Northerner," replied the agent. "However, I have heard that you people don't have the same feelings like white people. You can just pick up with somebody else and life goes on. So I guess with that in mind, it really won't matter that much—now will it?"

Reggie softly muttered just loud enough to be heard. "Why do yu' think we don't have feelings jus' like white folks? Aren't we human jus' as well? I have been split up from my bride an' every day I suffer ovah' not seein' her an' not knowin' how she is, or what has happened to her." In spite of his sadness and loneliness, he felt strength and pride knowing that he had defended his fellow slaves.

The agent was irritated with a slave talking back to him. "Well aren't you the spirited one. I did see the auction and saw those marks on your back. Now I understand why yu' were beaten. I take your comment to be insolent, and I'll be watching you. In the future if you value your life, you will learn to keep your mouth shut and do as you are told. By the way, sporting those fancy clothes makes you look like an organ grinder's monkey—all you need is a hurdy-gurdy." The agent laughed at his own joke, obviously enjoying the belittlement of Reggie.

CHAPTER TEN

The agent announced they would be leaving early in the morning to board the brigantine, Three Carols, causing Reggie's despair to only deepen upon hearing the inevitable news. Suffering the loss of his bride and now faced with the horrible imprisonment in the hold of a slave ship for some time was almost more than he could handle. His hopes of being purchased by a local plantation owner were dashed. From time to time he had grappled with the fear that he was claustrophobic, and now his survival instincts would be severely tested under conditions he may find intolerable.

During the night before the journey, Reggie and most of the other slaves lay shackled in the dark, pondering the horrible uncertainties in front to them. He knew white people falsely believed blacks could endure more physical suffering since God supposedly made them physically stronger. He wished they could be cognizant of the truth and develop compassion for slaves and their plight, instead of being so utterly brutal in their assessment of their needs.

A few could not sleep and talked about their families and their seemingly grim prospects. Reggie was silent, knowing that some of the slaves eyed him suspiciously thinking he might be an informant sent to report on any potential troublemakers.

As his next meal would not be until breakfast, Reggie decided that the easiest thing to do was to drown his hunger in sleep and face the impending morning with as much of a positive attitude as he could muster. After all he'd been through—his mind, body, and soul needed it desperately, and fortunately, he was able to sleep solidly through the night.

Daybreak came, and true to the words of the agent, one of his men arrived to provide breakfast and prepare the slaves for the long walk to the boarding docks and the brig.

The meal consisted of water and cornmeal boiled into a mushy liquid. Far from a complete breakfast, it still provided enough sustenance to give Reggie a little strength to start the day—like the others with him, the art of survival had been ingrained in him, which provided him with the skills to deal with the adversity he was now facing.

After a short time, the agent for Three Carols returned to announce that it was time to get moving. Connected together by chains, the slaves were told to line up into a normal slave coffle. It would be a long walk to the brig, which was harbored along the James River. From there, they would eventually sail into the open waters of the Atlantic Ocean.

The handlers were all business and not really interested in harassing the slaves. The march was quiet with the absence of singing. This appeared to be eerie since, traditionally, slaves in a coffle almost always sang. Perhaps, the sheer thought of heading for the New Orleans market was more than they could endure.

Arriving at the brig, they were unchained and individually placed in handcuffs. On board, the captain, Phillip Mason, opened the hatch, and they were instructed to go down into the hold.

As Reggie feared, his claustrophobia would make the voyage more difficult for him. However, he knew in his heart that he could endure, hoping for a chance to be reunited one day with Anastasia. In addition, his nautical background also reminded him that the Atlantic Ocean in the fall can be very tempermental.

Entering the hold, they were divided into two separate lines. Each line placed their backs against the hull of the ship, which meant through the entire journey they would have to look at each other across the center aisle. This particular configuration was different from many of the slave vessels that sailed from Africa. Far crueler, slaves on many of those ships were placed on shelves in chains at different levels. Nevertheless, the conditions in the hold of the Three Carols were still going to be extremely difficult.

Filling the air was a horrible stench of waste and body fluids from the previous voyages. That was only some of the problems. Lice, fleas and bugs infested the hold. Also, the planking was stained with filth, urine, and other stains. All combined, it created doubt as to how well Reggie was going to adjust to this situation since he had never been subjected to anything like this before. He hoped that after a short time he would grow accustomed to the conditions. Now he had to wonder if that would even be possible.

The hatch was secured tightly as the brig set sail headed for the Atlantic Ocean. The only lighting in the hold was provided by dangling whale oil lamps strategically placed from the bow to the aft. Instead of cushions, everyone sat on the rough, damp, filthy wooden planking.

As the brig sailed out, the individual personalities of the slaves began to emerge. Artemis provided the singing, and a few joined him as he sang, while Arthur, a self-styled preacher, conducted prayer periodically. Next to Reggie sat Agnes with her two children. Agnes was the slave who had been sold right before Reggie. She feared that she would lose her children, and as the brig sailed, she quietly talked with Reggie, only discussing her beloved "pickannies". The thought of losing them in New Orleans had completely overwhelmed her. Reggie spent time comforting her as much as he could. Agnes had to be a realist and knew the probability of holding her small family together was almost futile since they could now be sold without any restrictions. Others in the hold were also negatively preoccupied, discussing their fate as they would soon be sold at the New Orleans market. Reggie reflected that the atmosphere represented despair with little or no hope.

The odor of vomiting enhanced the prevailing stench and would continue to get worse as the journey progressed. Reggie took a small amount of comfort knowing his claustrophobia had not yet surfaced, but he knew this could change with his continuing confinement and the probable turbulence at sea.

Quite some time into the journey, Captain Mason, who appeared to maintain a unbiquitous presence opened the hatch to make an announcement. "How are you niggers doing down there? I'm Captain Mason, and my crew and I are from Boston. Looking the role of a captain, he was a large man with weather beaten features and a full white beard. I want all of you to know that my crew will not bother you as long as you do not cause any trouble. We are being paid to sail to New Orleans and that's where we are headed. Our goal is to protect our cargo and not harm it. I'll repeat, it's all business with us, just cooperate, and you will absolutely not have any problems with the crew." After this short message, the captain secured the hatch.

A little later, one of the crew members reopened it and ordered everybody out on deck for a few moments of fresh air. He yelled as the slaves, weary but eager, climbed out of the hold and onto the deck. Welcome sunlight greeted them, which immediately helped to rejuvenate their spirits. Mercifully, the captain ordered the manacles to come off since he felt they no longer represented a rebellious threat, and also in part because of their weakened state. Many had great difficulty emerging from the hold as they were sick and exhausted. They were in an unfortunate position to be able to appreciate what had been offered to them by being allowed on the deck.

While standing around on the deck, Reggie asked one of the crew members if he could get something to clean the vomit and other fluids as the odors were almost unbearable.

"I'm not the captain so I don't have the authority to order the cleaning of the hold. Besides, after a while everybody will only have the dry heaves, which should make it easier going." After a pause, the crewmember continued. "Damn, are you sure you belong with those niggers? I would swear you look whiter than me. I thought slaves were black. But then, I've heard that in the South, if you have any Negro blood, then you are considered black even if you look white. I guess that would be your situation.

You do represent the first true example I have ever seen of this."

Reggie assured the young man that his assessment was correct. He quickly added that it was necessary to make everything in the South black and white with no gray areas in order to effectively make the system work. He added, "In dah' South, if yu' have an ounce of Negro blood in yu' din' yu' are considered Negro. Dat' makes me Negro wit' no debate."

The crewmember had some thoughts on the subject. "I think the same rule would apply in the North. In fact, outside of not having legal slavery, it may not be that different up North regarding the treatment of Negroes." A friendly crewmember, he thanked Reggie for enlightening him on an aspect of the bondage system. The conversation ended as the slaves were placed back in the hold.

After two more days at sea, conditions were unbearable for Reggie and in desperation he thumped on the hatch in hopes of getting help.

A mate heard the thumping and yelled, "What's going on down there?"

"Sir I'm taken wit' claustrophobia an' I need to git' out of hyeh' fo' a short time," Reggie responded.

"Claustrophobia! How would a nigger know that word? Damn, it must be that white nigger—hold on, I'll open the hatch," he muttered to himself. The ships' watch came forward and opened the hatch. "Go ahead and crawl out of there. I'll give you a break only because you look out of place down there with those niggers. I do believe that being almost all white makes it more difficult for you. Only niggers could take those conditions down in that hold and you're not really a nigger."

The statement that the ships' watchman made is significant. Again it addresses a widely held belief amongst the white people that blacks could endure far more physical suffering. This belief helped to justify the white peoples' opinion that black people were better suited to pick cotton since they were able to undergo far more physical stress than white people. This would further be extended to accepting a degrading conclusion—blacks were gifted with physical prowess, while whites were gifted with the smarts and the ability to manage and take care of the blacks, who without the help of the white people would struggle through life unable to take care of themselves. A truly vicious and twisted circle that rationalized that the bondage system was good for both the blacks and the whites. It succeeded in providing an appearance of order and righteousness while hiding the true underlying depravity that allowed for whites to truly believe they were superior, and of course, the misinterpretation of the Bible provided the bedrock for their twisted logic.

Reggie pulled himself completely out of the hold. "Sir, I want to thank yu' fo' givin' me a break."

"I couldn't take being down there with those niggers even for a minute. I don't know how you can do it," the watchman said.

"Sir, no disrespect, but dey' feel dah' same amount of pain an' sufferin' as white people. It's a false belief held by white people, dat' black people kin' endure a lot more pain an' sufferin'. I believe wit' all my heart, God's laws would never condone dis' treatment of His children."

"I cannot continue this conversation with you—I could get in trouble. Here's some water, but be quick about it!" The watchman stated abruptly.

As the ship's watchman was making his warning statement, the captain suddenly appeared and saw Reggie sitting on the deck. In a fit of rage, he kicked Reggie and yelled at the shipmate, "Are you daft? Taking the hatch off after sundown is against my orders!"

"Captain, he was taken sick with claustrophobia, and I feared for his well-being. He's different, he's the white man."

"No, he's still a nigger, besides are you a doctor? This is gross insubordination. I'll deal with you later."

"Now, nigger, and notice I said nigger because that is what you are, get back in that hold," the captain ordered. The captain peered at the open hatch and, using his foot, pushed Reggie headlong down into the hold. It's notable that the captain, a Northerner would accept that Reggie was just another "nigger" even though he knew he could pass for white. This provides substance to what the crew member had told Reggie earlier.

As Reggie stood and struggled to regain his balance, a few of the slaves asked if he needed help. "I was jus' tryin' to git' ovah' claustrophobia, an' dah' captain threw me down dah' hatch like I'm an' animal." They gazed at him puzzled at the word he used.

"Mister, they treat hawses' better din' dis'," one man replied. "I say dat' cuz' dat' was my job, workin' wit' hawses'. I know it's true."

"Mister, I know yu're right," Reggie answered, "dah' treatment dat' we are given represents a blight on our so called democratic America." Reggie chortled to himself, democratic America. Isn't it more like democratic slavery?

"I don't know dat', but I reckon yu' are right."

Reggie then knelt to the floor and rolled onto his side trying to get over his claustrophobia. Weather conditions were getting a lot worse, and he could feel the endless motion of the ship riding the waves, growing stronger, which he knew meant turbulence at sea. Reggie warned, "I think dah' wind is kickin' up out thar'. I kin' feel it, an' I don't like what I think we could be in fo'. If all of yu' think dat' yu' have been through somethin', yu' ain't seen nuttin' yet."

On deck the captain was sizing up the situation. It was a cold, late spring afternoon; heavy dark ominous clouds had appeared overhead, and he could see his breath as he exhaled suggesting the temperature had precipitously dropped. The vessel tossed and turned as gale winds increased and heavy torrential rains battered the brig. Suddenly, he realized it was taking on water and help was needed. "Get those niggers out of the hold! We need them to work the pumps!"

One by one the exhausted slaves emerged from the hold and were put to work helping to man the pumps. After a few hours as a result of the unrelenting storm, water from the turbulence caused the vessel to take on even more water, and the situation was becoming critical. Without any prior notice, the captain, an experienced and weathered seaman, in desperation ordered, "Men, abandon ship! Bring your pistols and swords and abandon ship! But don't let any of those niggers on board, and if necessary—shoot!

A shivering frightened slave stuttered, "Cap, Cap, Captain, yu' can't leave us like dis'." He expressed the desperation the slaves felt when the announcement was made.

The captain demonstrated absolutely no compassion, pushing the slave backwards. "You're wrong—I can and if you take one step toward me, you'll be one dead nigger. Crew, lower the longboat. We'll leave this sinking ship to the niggers."

Panic spread like wildfire on the brig. After great effort, the longboat was successfully launched as conditions continued to worsen. Screaming resounded in the ears of each and every slave as an increased panic set in. They were witnessing the abandonment of the ship by the white crew and in their minds that meant almost certain death since they lacked leadership. Through it all Reggie remained calm, assessing the situation, knowing his nautical experience would be significant for the survival of himself and the slaves.

Safely aboard the longboat, the captain realized he had left his black satchel aboard the brig with his important papers inside. He yelled, "If any of you niggers sees my black satchel and can swim to me with it, you'll get roundly rewarded."

A desperate slave screamed back. "Captain, I found yur' satchel! I'll swim it ovah' to yu'."

Without any hesitation the slave jumped overboard and struggled to reach the longboat. Gasping for breath with one hand clutched to the longboat he handed the satchel to the captain. "Hyeh' it is—now kin' I board?"

The captain reached out his hand. "I did promise you a reward, and that reward is that you won't have to endure any more suffering." As the captain spoke, he quickly pulled out his gun and fired one round point blank into the forehead of the poor slave without hesitation.

It was obvious, the crew members did not appear to find this humorous as they were repulsed at the grisly scene.

It was an ugly and sad spectacle seeing the captain proudly puffing out his chest over shooting the slave while the crew was forced to witness the splattered brain matter that was everywhere. "We have too many on this boat now, let alone take on another a nigger. The added weight of the nigger could have made the difference between death or our survival. Right now men, we can survive by evaculating as much water out as possible," the captain stated all this with assurance. "Be happy that your captain had the strength to do what was necessary for our survival. After all, this exemplifies what leadership is all about." It was apparent, however, that not all the hands agreed with the captain, but they were not in a position to oppose him. Many believed the additional weight of one slave probably would not have affected the sea worthiness of the long boat. They sensed that his extolling words about leadership reflected an underlying sense of guilt for his actions.

The longboat slowly disappeared from the slaves' view, and Reggie stood motionless, assessing what he had witnessed. Most slaves aboard the vessel had believed that Northerners were more humane then Southerners. However, this horrible act demonstrated the barbaric treatment accorded to blacks in the South could be just as horrific in the North. Prejudice appeared to have no boundaries. This knowledge would serve Reggie quite well in the future as he would continue to experience the trials and tribulations of racism in the South, while recognizing the North harbored the same feelings against the blacks as well. He had always been falsely led to believe that the North was far less prejudice than the South and now he had cause to question that hypothesis.

Panic and confusion abounded on the faltering ship and Reggie knew it would have to be his knowledge and leadership that would represent the difference between the slaves making it or perishing at sea. This would present a major test in his belief that God had a plan for him. Quickly, he made an assessment of the situation. A jolly boat remained but he determined it would be inadequate to support everybody at sea. The best chance for survival remained by staying on the vessel and manning the pumps. Taking the wheel, he ordered the slaves to work the pumps even harder. It was absolutely critical they use their strength and energy to evacuate as much water as possible. He knew everyone's lives were now in his hands, and he accepted the burden and responsibility of saving the ship and his fellow slaves. He yelled to the crew, "Our lives are dependent on mannin' dah' pumps an' workin' together, now git to work an' we'll be jus' fine. Now pump knowin' yur' lives depend on it! So git' yur' backs into it!"

Responding to Reggies' orders, they manned the pumps, and everybody in unison, began singing. Reggie chanted, "Draw out my brothers, draw out fo' yur' lives. Draw out my brothers, draw out fo' yur' lives. Draw out my brothers, draw out fo' yur' lives!" The men followed in unison maintaining this constant chant.

A panic stricken man screaming over the singing bellowed, "We don't have a chance. Dah' faster we draw out water, dah' more water we take in. Why not man dah' jollyboat?"

Reggie confidently reassured the slave. "Don't git discouraged mate, jus' 'member to keep singin' loud an' clear. Cool heads prevail, dah' storm will abate! Fear not—we are goin' to make it. I kin' feel it. 'Sides dah' jollyboat would be inadequate fo' dah' number of people we have on board."

The slaves pulled together under Reggie's leadership as the waves tried to conquer the ship and it's crew. After what felt to be a lifetime, miraculously, the turbulent waters eventually began to recede as the rains and accompanying winds eased with eventual calm setting in. Reggie joyfully called out, "Dah' storm is subsidin', but, keep drawin' out an' singin', an' we will be home free 'fore yu' know it."

The storm eased, but left the brig badly damaged and listing helplessly. Reggie had kept their spirits high, sensing they were adrift in a shipping lane, which would be a major advantage. He knew that a ship would come along and eventually rescue them. Reggie explained the situation and the probable outcomes; however, a few slaves had the idea they could commandeer the brig and sail it to freedom. Reggie explained to them that in the vessel's condition that would not be possible. And even if they could, where would they sail to find a friendly port? Who would accept a ship full of slaves, absent of any white people? He was finally able to convince them their efforts would prove to be futile, but to not despair since on a positive note, the chances of ending up in New Orleans should be lessened.

Two days passed and just as the slaves began to give up hope, fortunately, a ship on the horizon was spotted. Reggie seized the moment and had all the slaves yell out in unison as loud as they could, "Hyeh' ye', hyeh' ye', ship in distress. Hyeh' ye', hyeh' ye', ship in distress. Hyeh' ye', hyeh' ye', ship in distress." They continued to chant this appeal over and over while waving fabric and canvas in the air.

Finally, their appeal was answered as the large sailing ship turned and approached the "Three Carols". Jubilation reigned as the crew celebrated their rescue. The ship pulled along side and the captain along with the carpenters in his crew quickly began to survey the damages to the brig. "Who's in charge of this brig?" the captain asked as he boarded the ship.

Reggie stepped forward. "Sir, I've taken charge an' I am responsible fo' dah' ship an' des' people. We got caught in a terrible storm, an' dah' crew 'bandoned dah' brig an' left all of us slaves to fend fo' ourselves. I'm dah' only person wit' any nautical experience so I had to take charge. I must admit learnin' how to git' everybody in sync' to run dah' pumps served as an on dah' job learnin' experience, an' fortunately, it worked."

"I'm a little confused—you are not a nigger, you are a white man. What did you do wrong to get abandoned by your mates?" the captain asked.

"Captain, I git' mistaken fo' bein' a white person all dah' time. I was born a slave, an' nobody ever bought my freedom an' so I have remained a slave. Fortunately, I was dah' personal servant to my close friend who found it difficult to acquire dah' nautical skills dat' were expected of him. My master saw fit fo' me to learn alongside of him since I was able to pick up dah' skills rather quickly."

"Well, it's a miracle that you are still afloat," the captain replied. "I'm sure you kept them at the pumps. It really addresses your skills that you were able to take this motley crew and bring them together. Combined with your leadership along with our timely rescue, your people can thank their lucky stars to be alive. It almost seems like a 'cock and bull story', and if I hadn't been a part of this operation, I never would have believed it myself."

Reggie appreciatively said, "Captain, we owe our lives to yu'. I don't think dis' brig would have lasted much longer. Incidentally, dah' original crew abandoned dah' ship when dah' sailin' got rough. Dey' decided to take thar' chances wit' dah' longboat. A man named Captain Mason commanded dah' ship, which I believe was out of Boston. I jus' hope dey' made it as well. I do pray dat' dey' made it."

"Personally, I would have attempted everything possible to have the crew maintain the ship before abandoning it for a long boat. Anyhow, why would you care as to the disposition of the main crew? They abandoned the ship thinking they had better odds while leaving all of you to die on a supposed sinking ship."

"Captain, I guess it's my Christian spirit hopin' dey' made it."

"Well I wouldn't worry about their welfare any longer. My carpenters will stop the leaks and repair the pumps. By the way, where was this brig headed?"

"Captain, we were headed fo' New Orlens'."

The captain, with a smile on his face stated, "Obviously, you cannot make New Orleans, but we can assist you in reaching Charleston." The captain knew the slaves would be happy to know their destination was no longer New Orleans.

His appearance was markedly different from Captain Mason. He was of medium build and was possibly in his early 40's. Clean shaven, absent of any weather beaten features, he lacked the stereotypical appearance of a sea captain.

"Captain, what is goin' to happen to us?"

"Well because of the situation, we can claim ownership of

the cargo. We will dispose of you and your crew in Charleston. The profits from the sale should be shared with the original owners. All that will be up to the authorities to decide."

Reggie breathed a sigh of relief. "I know dat' dah' crew will be 'bery happy to hyeh' dat'. I think I kin' speak fo' all of us when I say dat' nobody wanted to sail to New Orlens'. Charleston is a much better place. 'Gain we thank yu' fo' savin' our lives."

"Incidentally, I know all about the New Orleans trade. All of us Northerners involved in human trade are well aware of the harshness down there; however, we just move the cargo, and it doesn't matter to most of us how inhumane the conditions might be after we drop the cargo off. In this business, you learn to become emotionally callouse to everything. It's all about money and greed—pure and simple. By the way, what's your name boy?"

"Captain, my name is Reggie."

"Interesting name, well Reggie, I'm Captain Lawrence Nelson and our ship sails out of New York. I'm actually headed to Charleston to pick up a load of human cargo and take it to New Orleans. I shouldn't tell yu' this, but out of guilt, I will. Circumstances permit me to share this with you. I want you to know that I am not proud of what I do. I find the system of slavery to be inhumane. This is a dirty, messy business that just keeps going on and on. Let me give you a little history lesson."

Reggie was totally unprepared to listen to a history lesson, but nevertheless, he welcomed the opportunity to hear what the captain had to say regarding the importation of slaves.

The captain took a deep breath and went on. "You and your crew are a product of interstate trading between the states, which is legal. However, after 1807, Congress did make the further importation of slaves from Africa illegal. It had to do with the original Constitution of 1787 and represented a compromise between the North and the South. After twenty years, the further importation of slaves into the United States would legally end. In addition, they passed the Piracy Act of 1820 which allowed for even greater enforcement against the importation of slaves into the United States. However, because these laws are loosely enforced, they are almost entirely ignored and ships regularly travel to Africa for cargo where they are eventually dropped off at ports of call, off the coast of the United States. The ships originate almost entirely from the North, which points to just how much the North is involved in this filthy business. Hence, the North is culpable regarding slavery—they are directly tied into the whole evil system. As I said earlier, greed and money are the driving force for this messy business, which unfortunately appears to make the world go around. Just ask the Northern bankers who have their hands muddied in this filthy commerce as well." Captain Nelson's face displayed his guilt as he continued, "I sincerely wish someday when history objectively examines this inhumane trafficking of innocent people, we realize you cannot just blame the South—it rests heavily and equally on the shoulders of the entire country. Slavery is an institution of the United States and not just the South! Unfortunately, I am really concerned the South will have to bear the full brunt of it all. This can only continue to fracture the relations between the North and the South, not knowing where or when it will end."

Interestingly, history bears out Captain Nelson's assessment that the slave trade laws were loosely enforced. In fact in 1862 Nathaniel Gordon became the only person ever executed for violation of the slave trade laws and that was probably for political reasons since the Civil War was being waged.

Reggie recognized just how insightful Captain Nelson was with his diatribe. He found it ironic that he felt a certain amount of respect for a captain of a ship who was involved in the slave trade. "Captain, I can't say much regardin' dis' matter since I'm a slave; however, I'm goin' to take some latitude an' jus' say dat' I agree, especially when you state that slavery is an institution of the United States. Also, may I ask a small favor of yu, Captain?"

"Just what is it, Reggie?" the captain queried.

"On board is a slave named Agnes who has two small children. Since yu' have some influence over dah' disposition of dis' cargo, would it be possible fo' yu' to ensure dat' Agnes an' her two children could remain together an' not be separated at auction?

Dah' poor lady is frantic."

"As a reward for your bravery, I will take steps to make sure that your request is granted. I do applaud you for thinking of somebody else and ignoring yourself. You know that under these circumstances, people would almost always think of themselves first."

"Thank yu' so much, sir. It makes me feel good dat' Agnes will be able to stay with her children. As a Christian, I have dah' responsibility to think of others an' not jus' myself."

"Let me just make this clear, I want you to know that the only reason I'm involved in this business is because I need the money to cover my debts. When I get my debts paid off, I'm going to get out of this God-forsaken business. Why I'm telling my problems to a stranger, let alone a slave is a mystery to me. I will say that you have an easy way about you and that certainly helps. One other thing—I still can't figure out how you were able to organize this undisciplined crew. It's uncanny."

"Captain, our lives were on dah' line," Reggie modestly stated thinking that it appeared that the Captain Nelson was seeking absolution through him a slave—how ironic.

"Reggie it's more than that. I wouldn't think that under those conditions, they would accept taking orders from another slave at sea. Without the presence of a white man, they probably thought they would be lost at sea. However, you look white yourself, and maybe that was the difference, I just can't figure it out. Anyhow, your Negro crew can remain on deck without handcuffs. Besides, my carpenters need to work in the hold without being bothered."

After a relaxed time at sea under Captain Nelson's command, the ship arrived in Charleston. Unfortunately, all the slaves including Reggie were sent to a slave pen once again where they would be reintroduced to leg irons and sold. They were not accorded any special treatment that they could have been given under the unusual circumstances that brought them to port. For Reggie, the dreaded system, lacking any compassion would have no end.

CHAPTER ELEVEN

Anastasia and Reggie's forced separation had been painful for both. However, Anastasia's anguish and unhappiness was softened by her new assignment.

The colonel had recognized that he could have punished Anastasia by hiring her out to someone unscrupulous or by selling her. But out of respect for his wife, he honored his commitment for once to do the right thing and placed her with an elderly widow, Mrs. Agnes Winters, an old friend of the family. As the wife of a very successful plantation owner, she had maintained a socially elegant life. However, in her personal life she had also proven to be a very kind and modest lady who would be an ideal mistress for Anastasia.

Mrs. Winters had recently moved to an upscale part of Richmond. As stated earlier with the passing of her husband, her plantation was left to her son, and she knew it would be in her best interests to take up residence in town. Having made the decision to live alone she had clearly lost any interest in maintaining a regal life. Instead she looked forward to a more simple life, but needed someone who could take care of the home and act as her personal servant.

Most of the homes in her neighborhood were upscale. Again, she purposely sought out a simpler, more comfortable dwelling for her new life. The old style, brick-by-brick home featured a parlor, kitchen, and dining room with three bedrooms upstairs. The front porch provided an outstanding view of the neighborhood. In addition, the front and back yard provided evidence that the previous owners enjoyed gardening, which was very appealing feature.

From the beginning of their relationship, Mrs. Winters proved to be an ideal fit for Anastasia. Interestingly, it was almost as if Mrs. Winters preferred treating Anastasia more as a friend and not as a personal servant. As the months passed while living with Mrs. Winters, Anastasia's life changed immeasurably for the better.

One afternoon Mrs. Winters was talking to her good friend, Miss Jane Burwell in her parlor. The Burwell family was one of the most prominent families in the Williamsburg social set. It was a Burwell that had attracted the fondness of President Jefferson in his younger days.

Mrs. Winters had invited Anastasia to come in and sit down to join in their conversation. Awkwardly, Anastasia came and sat with the ladies. "Mrs. Winters, I'm dah' servant— dis' shouldn't be my position," she stated humbly.

Mrs. Winters reached over and placed her hand on Anastasias'. "Don't worry 'bout it, child. Once in a while we kin' make an exception."

"Anastasia, Mrs. Winters has spoken so highly of yu'."

"Anastasia, I told Miss Burwell dat' I find our situation so unusual."

"Why is dat', Mrs. Winters?" Anastasia asked.

"Well, Anastasia when Colonel Marshall 'hired yu' out' I was not expectin' somebody quite like yu'. I anticipated a much older Negro lady, not somebody who was so young, beautiful an' light skinned. As yu' know I even treat yu' more as a friend than a personal servant."

Miss. Burwell added, "Yu' are 'bery fortunate dat' dah' Colonel hired yu' out to Mrs. Winters. Servants like yu', who are quite fancy, often fall into dah' wrong hands an' suffer immeasurable harm."

Mrs. Winters became very serious as she turned to Anastasia. "I have news dat' I think yu' will like. 'Fore yu' came into dah' room I was tellin' Miss Burwell dat' I'm goin' to try to purchase yu' from Colonel Marshall. He would then no longer own yu'. Miss Burwell 'greed dat' it would be a good ider' to foller' through wit'—how would yu' like dat'?"

As soon as the words left Mrs. Winter's lips, a smile emerged that went from ear to ear on Anastasia's face. "I would much prefer bein' owned by yu' instead of Colonel Marshall, but won't it be difficult gittin' him to consent to dat' 'greement?"

Mrs. Winters peered into Anastasia's eyes with an assured expression. "Not at all, Anastasia, 'cuz' from time to time Colonel Marshall has needed favors from me. Even if he did not want to sell yu', I truly believe he will. Dat' is all I have to say Anastasia. Yu' kin' leave now, but please remain in dah' kitchen fo' clean up duties."

"Mrs. Winters, thank yu' so much fo' what yu' have done fo' me. I'm almost speechless wit' joy, an', Miss Burwell, it was such a pleasure meetin' yu'. I'll return to dah' kitchen now an' God bless yu' fo' thinkin' of me," as she nodded her head in gratitude—turned and went back her duties.

***

While Anastasia was receiving the best news possible from Mrs. Winters, Reggie's life was in complete turmoil. He was herded once again into a rusty old pen packed with slaves. The ever-present stench of body odor and general filth permeated the air, which Reggie had grown accustomed to. However, after accepting these conditions, Reggie was still very thankful to still be alive after his experiences at sea.

After a few days the disposition of Reggie and the other slaves had been settled and very soon he would be sold.

In a dejected mood, Reggie was left sitting alone in a corner wondering his fate. Suddenly, a slave driver beckoned him to come forward. "Yu', dah' yeller' niggah'! I have somethin' to say

167

to yu'."

"Yes sir!" Reggie respectfully replied as he made his way through the mass of slaves.

"See dat' man standin' over thar'? He's yur' new master—yu' were purchased privately. Fo' yur' actions at sea, dah' captain of dah' ship dat' brought yu' in rewarded yu' wit' a private purchase. Yu're a damn lucky niggah' 'cuz' dat' doesn't happen 'bery often. Now git' over thar' an' meet yur' new master. Oh, yeah, also I was tole' to tell yu' dat' dah' Negro lady wit' dah' two children will be auctioned off wit' her children an' will not be separated."

After receiving the good news includin' his friend's future fate, Reggie in leg irons, clumsily approached his new owner, a middle-aged gentleman with a slight build and a certain look that made him stand out in the crowd. He was nattily attired in all black with a round wide-brimmed black hat. He looked like a preacher with his most impressive feature being his long, flowing white hair hanging down over his back. He also had the pale skin of an albino—he was really quite a striking figure. He was opposite of Colonel Marshall in every way including his manners, which were more feminine. He spoke in an easily recognizable, high-pitched voice. He kindly, said, "Driver, please unshackle dis' man. I kin' handle him. He doesn't have dah' look of a menacin' character."

The slave driver unshackled Reggie, exposing bruises left from the heavy metal chains. "He is now legally in yur' hands."

Reggie and his new owner left the area immediately and went directly to a waiting buggy. They quickly boarded and headed out. On the road the man opened the conversation by asking, "Boy, what name do yu' go by?"

"Master, my name is Reggie."

"Reggie, what a good strong name—yu' even look like a Reggie. I like it—it's different. Not one of dose' Roman names like Caesar. I really hate it when a servant is 'signed a Roman or Greek name. I jus' can't explain why I feel dat' way but I prefer Biblical names, but Reggie is still perfectly 'ceptable. It's strange, but we all have our quirks. It jus' dawned on me dat' Greeks an'

Romans were pagans—dat' must be dah' reason. I'm definitely partial to Christians." His new master was obviously feeling him out through idle conversation.

"Master, I'm glad yu' like my name."

Soon his new masters' conversation took a more serious tone. "I wanted a niggah' who made a good appearance, a 'display niggah'', an' dey' did not disappoint me. However, I do think dat' yu' could cause quite a stir in des' parts. Yu' look white an' not at all like a niggah'. In fact, yu're handsome, an' dat' makes yu' even more controversial. Reggie, my name is Master Hibbard, an' I won't mince words wit' yu'. If yu' cooperate wit' me yu'll not have any problems. Fo' a niggah' yu'll be livin' in dah' lap of luxury."

"I kin' promise yu' master dat' I will be 'bery cooperative." Reggie stated with assurance.

"Dat's what I want to hyeh'! Yu' know, Reggie, yu' look an' act like one of dose' learned, 'two-headed niggahs''. Are yu'?" Slave owners frowned on slaves who could read and write knowing educated slaves would more likely question servitude and stir up trouble. Laws forbid the education of slaves, yet the slave owners were willing to violate the law if it would serve their own self interests. This represented yet another example of a more serious contradiction. Unfortunately, evidence exists of educated slaves who came under harsh punishment including death since they represented a threat to the system.

"Master, I do know my letters an' numbers."

"Have yu' ever studied dah' Bible?"

"Yes, I have studied dah' Bible extensively."

"Extensively, dat's a great word! Well dat's wonderful dat' yu' have studied dah' Bible extensively. Reggie yur' new master is not jus' a plantation owner. I'm proud to tell yu' I'm a Baptist preacher—a man of God."

"Master, I have great admiration fo' a man of dah' cloth, an' now I better understand why yu' are partial to Christian names."

"Well, I need an assistant, an' dat' will be whar' yu' will fall in. I'm a circuit rider, an' I hold services in a fairly wide area.

I do 'lieve dat' I have dah' duty to bring dah' word of God to not jus' dah' whites but also dah' niggahs'. My willin'ness to preach to our niggahs' requires help an' dat' is whar' yu' will come in. Yu' know not all my colleagues go 'long wit' me on dat'."

"Master, I'm sure dat' I kin' help yu', an' I do 'gree dat' God would want yu' to bring his word to dah' niggahs' as well."

"Reggie, I run a pretty small plantation, but yu' will like it. Yu' will be my personal servant, nothin' else other din' maybe assistin' a little on household chores. Well, we are approachin' yur' new home—it's in sight, right up yonder. We call it Hibbard Hall, an' we ain't ever been able to figure out why. Jus' jokin'! I know yu' must be a little tired atter' all you've been through so I want yu' to take it easy when we git' home 'til I call fo' yu'."

"Master, dis' is one buggy ride dat' I have truly enjoyed."

"I kin' imagine dat' it is a lot better din' bein' locked up in dah' hold of a brig at sea."

"Master, are yu' sure dat' yu' are not a carpenter as well?"

"I'm positive."

"Well, master, yu' sur' 'hit the nail on dah' head' wit' dat' comment. Suffice to say, I'm tickled to death to be hyeh' as yur' servant."

Both laughed at the joke and then Reverend Hibbard commented, "Dat' was a good one, especially since Jesus was a carpenter. Hey, yu' kin' be funny as well—I like dat' a lot. We all need humor in our lives."

As soon as they reached Hibbard Hall, Reggie could see that his new master's level of wealth was considerably less than Colonel Marshall's. He also noted the all-encompassing presence of cotton fields surrounding the modest plantation, which represented the typical look for the area. The home was very plain and simple, a two-story, white-framed dwelling in a bit of disrepair. The front yard had no foliage, highlighting the dry, dusty-looking red soil.

As they entered the front door, the main servant was there to greet them. "Master everythin' has been prepared as yu' asked."

"Good," Reverend Hibbard replied. "Oh, Egypt dis' is my new personal servant, Reggie. Reggie, dis' is my head servant,

Egypt."

"Pleasure to meet yu', Egypt."

"Pleasure to meet yu' as well, Reggie," he responded without any feeling, possibly thinking that his status might be diminished with the arrival of Reggie.

"Egypt, I want yu' to make sure dat' Reggie has something to eat an' din' take him to his quarters. He has been through a lot an' needs to git' washed up, an' git' a good nights sleep. 'Morrow is Saturday, an' I'm takin' my new personal servant wit' me to town. Kinda' like a hawss', we might as well break him in early— so to town we'll go." Reverend Hibbard laughed at his intended joke.

***

In the morning, Reggie was called into the dining room to see Reverend Hibbard as he finished his breakfast. The room appeared to be the main room of the house with a small dining table and a sideboard as its main furnishings, certainly what might be the furnishings for a bachelor.

Reverend Hibbard seemed very happy to be with his new personal servant. "Reggie, I hope yu' had plenty to eat. It's goin' to be a good day. I always look fo'ward to Saturday in town. Plus, I git' to top it all off by showin' off my new personal servant. Seriously, we need to purchase supplies an' pick up dah' mail an' dis' is good 'cuz' yu' kin' git' yur' feet wet right 'way. Incidently, I deferred on mornin' devotions, but dat' will be an exception." It was apparent that Reverend Hibbard was treating Reggie almost as if he was an out-of-town guest, which would not be acceptable by the locals. He was still a slave and that stigma could not be removed even as a bright, handsome man who looked white.

As the two departed in the buggy, Reverend Hibbard was anxious to delve into Reggie's background. "Heard yu' were born an' raised in Virginny'. Fo' a servant yu' must have quite a pedigree—maybe yu' were a fancy pants servant." Reverend Hibbard thought he was being very amusing and chuckled.

Reggie enjoyed the humor and laughed as well, then commented, "Yah' master, I was raised 'round dah' Williamsburg area, an' it's true dat' dey' are proud of thar' wealth, which in thar' own high-brow judgment makes 'dem feel dat' dey' are dah' crème de la crème of dah' entire country."

Reverend Hibbard smiled at Reggie as he spoke loudly and commented in an exaggerated, Southern drawl. "Reggie, I'm jus' an ole' down-home country preacher. I never heard of des' words 'fore. I guess it means dey' thought dey' were dah' top drawer."

"Master, dat' is exactly what I meant."

"Reggie, I heard something very commendable 'bout yu'—I guess yu' are sort of a hero. Seems yu' took charge of a sinkin' brig an' kept it 'float long 'nough fo' everyone to be rescued. Dat's really somethin' to be proud of."

"Master, it really wasn't dat' heroic. Dah' crew had 'bandoned dah' ship an' left it to sink wit' dah' niggahs' onboard, an' it became immediately obvious dat' nobody had any nautical 'perience 'cept me. I'm fortunate to have gone sailin' wit' my young master and learned my nautical skills from his instructor. So along with Albert, I learned the skillful art of sailin'. 'When push came to shove' my nautical skills served us all 'bery well fo' our survival."

"Well, Reggie jus' be glad yu' learned to sail," the pastor said with feeling. "I truly 'lieve dat' God works in strange ways, an' it looks to me like yu've been blessed. Yu' kin' do so many things dat' others cannot do. I don't know what it's like in Virginny', but down hyeh', an' I hate to say dis, but white folks are 'bery wary of a smart white niggah'."

"Master, I know dat' quite well. All my life, I have had to overcome some difficult obstacles wit' my skin color as well as wit' some of my 'bilities in Virginny'. But 'bove all, 'I know my place', an' I will keep it dat' way. I may be blessed, but I'm still only a niggah' an' 'cordin' to white folks I will always remain a niggah'," Reggie said with candor. He knew that when confronted with the issue of his skin color, he always had to state that he was just a common, household servant and above all—'he knew his

172

place' if he was engaged in conversation with a white person.

"Well put Reggie, but yu' don't have to act 'blue 'bout dah' gills'. Yu' are wit' me, dah' preacher man, an' I'll take good care to protect yu'. Speakin' of protectin' yu,' see dat' cart path right thar'? Well, deep in dah' neck of dah' woods back thar' is a settlement of people called dah' 'Backwoods Jimmies'—dey' settled back thar' 'fore dah' War of Rebellion." During the ante-bellum period the Revolutionary War was often referred to as the War of Rebellion.

Reggie quizzically asked, "Master, I've never heard of 'dem 'fore—who are dey', an' what's it like back thar'?"

"I don't know. Dey' don't mix wit' nobody, an' I mean nobody—dey' jus' keep to 'demselves. Folks tell me dey' don't even have any niggahs' wit' 'em. Crackers, I mean pure crackers, dat's what dey' are." The word crackers, was a condescending term used to describe poor whites. It probably originated in Georgia and the word was freely used by both whites and blacks.

"Master, have yu' ever thought of bringin' dah' word of God to 'dem?"

"Reggie, people don't go back thar'. I'd be 'fraid to do dat'. Dose' people kin' git' crazy wit yu', an' yu' may never git' out 'live. People call 'dem a bunch of heathens. I don't think even dah' constable go's back thar'. He jus' leaves 'dem 'lone. Dey' have thar' own justice. Maybe, I'll git' dah' courage someday, but we'll save dat' fo' 'nother time. We still have a long ride 'fore we git' to town."

Conversation was brisk as both continued to exhibit a positive mood while enjoying the ride to town. Reggie, not lacking for asking questions, decided to engage the preacher with a moot point. "Master, it has been brought up as to why our beloved South has not kept up wit' dah' march of progress dat' we see in dah' North. Dis' has led some to say dat' dah' standard of livin' in dah' North is higher. I hope I'm not bein' too forward askin' yu' to help me to understand what dis' is all 'bout?" Reggie was engaging the preacher in conversation hoping to learn a little more about his feelings on different topics.

"Of course not Reggie! I clearly know dah' answer to yur' question, an' it should be obvious to yu' wit'out me even tellin' yu'. Dah' people in our beloved South have been busy workin' fo' dah' Negroes, unlike dah' North, who have been workin' only fo' 'demselves. All of our money is spent housin', clothin' an' feedin' our Negroes. Take a look—we have nothin' fo' ourselves." Of course his explanation omitted the fact that slaves were paid in kind and not wages for their labor, and if they had been paid in wages, they would have been far better off.

Reggie, who was listening intently, knew it would not be wise to further question him. "Master, yu' raise a good point." Reggie had to bite his lip as he said these words.

Reverend Hibbard couldn't refrain from making an additional comment. "Somethin' else, Reggie. Years ago, des' Northerners were shrewd 'nough to unload all thar' Negroes on us leaving us wit' dah' expense of takin' care of 'dem. I think dat' is dah' sum total of dis' discussion." His answer was historically far from the truth. Southerners were willingly bringing in large numbers of blacks from Africa to provide the necessary labor for their agricultural needs. They were obviously not coming from the North. Meanwhile, the few free Negroes living in the North who would have prefered to live in the South were obviously not welcome in a society that abounded with slavery.

The anathema the Southerners held toward abolitionists was very similar to what they felt toward free Negroes who might venture South. The "peculiar institution" of the South rested on a "guardian institution". How do you fit "free Negroes" into a system that opposes citizenship for blacks? Obviously, you really can't find an easy solution and that continued to represent a difficult conundrum to a system that prefers only in dealing with absolutes. In addition to the abolitionists, the free Negroes represented a clear and present danger as well to the bondage system because of the dangerous possibility of fomenting an insurrection among the slaves. Many of the free Negroes were educated, and the white Southerners were well aware that being free and educated would put them in the position to lead an insurrection.

Reggie recognized that Reverend Hibbard wished to close this topic, and thought it would be wise to say nothing further. However, he mused to himself that Reverend Hibbard's assessment was totally absurd. He knew Reverend Hibbard's thinking was common in the South. Significantly, his beliefs highlighted just how deeply divided the North and the South was over economic differences while still recognizing slavery as the center of the problem. In the future Reggie recognized such extremism would only make it more difficult for both sides to compromise over their differences to avert a civil war.

Around noon, Reverend Hibbard and Reggie arrived in Summerville, a town that was rather typical for rural South Carolina. Most of the buildings were wooden, while an occasional brick structure stood out among them. The main street was a dry, dusty road with wooden sidewalks and hitching posts in front of the buildings.

As they approached the town square, there was a large throng of people with an unusual confrontation taking place. Ike Horn, one of the self-appointed leaders of the town, had just collared a white stranger. As quickly as possible, Reverend Hibbard and Reggie took the horse and buggy to the stables and returned to the square. Excitement of this magnitude seldom occurred in this small community.

Over the turmoil, Ike Horn spotted the preacher and yelled to him. "Well, preacher, yu' jus' 'rived in dah' nick of time fo' a little fun."

Reverend Hibbard quizzically asked, "Ike Horn what's goin' on hyeh'? We jus' 'rived in town an' noticed all dah' 'citement. Who do yu' have thar'?"

"Preacher, thar' stands 'fore yu' one of dose' meddlin' 'bobolitionists," Ike Horn answered with disgust in his voice, his red face flushed with anger and gritty sweat running down his brow. "Isn't dat' right mister, yu' impudent scounder'? Now, we don't git' many like yu' down hyeh', so we jus' wanta' offer yu' dah' best of hospitalities dat' dah' South has to offer—maybe in dah' shade under dat' tall tree over thar' whar' yu' kin' sorta' cool off.

And while yu' are relaxin', we might even bring yu' a nice cool glass of lemonade so yu' kin' quench yur' thirst. Oh yah, maybe dat' tree limb could support yur' weight, while hangin' from a nice tight rope to give yu' a once in a lifetime view of dah' place while yu' are coolin' off an' sippin' on yur' lemonade. Dis' will be all part of dah' reception, we want to give yu' a real treat as yu' jus' sorta' hang 'round wit' us Southern boys havin' a good ole' time, an' din' yu' kin' take a real long nap an' I mean a real long nap. Now doesn't dat' sound right cozy—us Southerners providin' yu, a Yankee boy, all dis' Southern hospitality!"

The crowd laughed and shouted approval of Horn's idea. Trembling with fear, the stranger turned to Reverend Hibbard and pleaded, "Like you, preacher, I'm a man of God who only came South as a missionary for God and certainly not as an abolitionist. In fact, I don't think I know any abolitionist." A Northerner apprehended in the South and accused of fomenting rebellion among the slaves was automatically considered an abolitionist even if his interests were purely religious absent of any political agenda.

Reggie had witnessed the same spectacle at the slave auction house in Richmond—another trespassing Northerner with good intentions who naively stirred up trouble without knowing the repercussions.

Ike Horn spoke so everyone could hear him. "Is dat' right, mister? Well explain what yu' were doin' in yur' room last night wit' dat' niggah' rascal, Charles. One of dah' boys jus' happened to be walkin' 'hind dah' tavern an' saw yur' face all lit' up. Yu' an' yur' new pal Charles, were jawin' near yur' window jus' as thick as thieves, jus' sorta' buddyin'-up together."

"Sir, I just met Charles, and I hardly know him," the stranger defended himself.

Ike Horn was in a near rage when he shouted, "Mister, we all know yu're a niggah'- lovin' Yankee!"

"It's true, I'm from Vermont, but I happen to have relatives who live in the South too," he answered.

"Mister, we don't care 'bout yu' an' yur' Southern roots. To us yu're jus' a damn Yankee—plain an' simple," Horn continued, "now let's git' down to brass tacks! I wanta' know jus' one thin'— what were yu' talkin' to Charles 'bout last night?"

"I was talking to Charles about Jesus," the stranger nervously replied.

Ike Horn was not about to believe the stranger. "Is dat' right, Jesus—nuttin' else? Now, yu wouldn't be tryin' to hornswoggle me an' my friends. Maybe yu' jus' sorta' take us fo' fools."

"Sir, we just talked about the Lord—that's all," pleaded the stranger.

Ike Horn yelled to the slave in the back of the crowd. "Charles, git' over hyeh'. I wanta' talk to yu'. What did dis' stranger talk to yu' 'bout last night?"

"Marse', he talked 'bout Jesus."

"Is dat' right?" Horn asked. "Charles, look yonder—see dat' buildin' over thar'."

"Yeah, Marse'," he replied, looking in the direction that was pointed out to him.

"Charles, jus' what is dat' buildin'?" Horn continued.

"Marse', dat's dah' calaboose. Dat's whar' dey' put niggahs' dat' aren't right."

"Now, Charles, it's time fo' yu' to shame the debil' an' tell dah' truth. If yu' don't fezz' up, dat's whar' yu're headed!"

Suddenly, Charles took on a terrified look. "Marse', he did talk 'bout Jesus, but he also talked 'bout why we niggahs' are treated so badly. He wondered why we jus' don't sorta' fight back," he said while sweating profusely.

As soon as the words "fight back" came out of his mouth the crowd immediately got stirred up. One of the main fears of the white Southerners was being showcased right in front of them—a perceived abolitionist showing up in their town, stirring up the slaves, and trying to foment an insurrection.

Ike Horn decided it was time to take further action. "Well boys, looks like Charles done 'spilt dah' beans' an' now we're goin' to have to 'throw some cold water on dis' damn Yankee's scheme'. Mister, when yu' tell dah' niggahs' to 'fight back', do yu' know

177

what dat' means? Oh, all of us white folks sur' do. We know what happened up in Virginny' wit' dat' Nat Turner. How many white folks did dose' niggahs' kill when dey' jus' sorta' 'fought back'."

Somebody shouted, "Ike, I heard 55 innocent white people, men, women an' children were killed by dose' blood-thirsty niggahs'!"

"Dat' would be 'bout half our town slaughtered by a bunch of niggahs' dat' were all fired up, an' inspired by dis' meddlin' 'bobolitionist," Horn yelled back while looking directly at the stranger.

The unwanted visitor was a good-looking, medium-built young man who appeared to be well-educated but perhaps lacking common sense. He was understandably terrified by what was unfolding as the situation continued to escalate, knowing his life was on the line. "Sir, I'm a man of God. I meant for them to raise their voices in a non-violent manner. What happened with the Nat Turner insurrection was horrible—I agree with you. I don't advocate any form of violence. The map that I follow in life is the Bible, which preaches nonviolence." Again, after the Nat Turner insurrection of 1831, increased paranoia gripped the South. They felt that this was only the beginning of more serious problems, which had to be countered by tightening things up with the slaves facing additional rules and regulations. The net effect was to further divide the whites and the slaves.

Horn listened intently to what the stranger was saying and sarcastically asked, "Oh, is dat' what yu' meant. Jus' protest? Is dat' what Nat Turner meant—jus' protest an' nuttin' more? Slaughter 55 people while yu' are protestin'—does dat' sound 'bout right, mister?"

"Sir, I promise you I meant no harm to anyone. Besides, Nat Turner was not a Northerner. That was an internal insurrection."

"Shut up mister—an insurrection is an insurrection, period! Mister, often times things kin' begin wit' a simple protest, an' din' things git' out of hand an' people git' killed," Ike informed him. "Now do yu' git' it?" Horn had raised an excellent point, supporting the Southerners' fear of any type of protest.

"Sir, I do understand what you're saying." The Northerner clearly understood Horn's position, but he also believed in the First Amendment's sacred right to protest. Nevertheless, he also knew that "discretion can be the better part of valor" and this situation required discretion. "I'm so sorry for all of this and I want to apologize for using such bad judgment in coming down here. Hopefully, I can be forgiven."

"Mister, yu' fell into a lot of hot water comin' down hyeh' an' tryin' to agitate our niggahs'." Ike Horn ignored the stranger's words, only concentrating on what he felt should be done to this abolitionist. He shouted as he turned to the crowd, "Mister, yu' are flat-out cashiered!"

One of Horn's supporters yelled, "Let's have a neck-tie party right now, an' we'll make dis' miserable bastard dah' guest of honor."

Another excitedly added, "I've got a nice strong rope in my wagon. We kin' git' dis' ovah' wit' right now."

One of the few women in the crowd called out to Horn, "Let's hang him ovah' thar', right whar' we hung dat' niggah' 'while back."

Ike Horn expanded on this. Glaring at the stranger, he stated, "Mister, Tilda's talkin' 'bout dah' free issue niggah' we jus' hung. Now a free issue niggah' is a niggah' dat' yu' would call a free niggah' up North. Well, now yu' kin' call him a dead niggah'. Are yu' ready to join dat' niggah' in Providence?"

The stranger panicked—sobbing and pleading for his life. "Sir, this is a terrible misunderstanding. I don't want to die. I'm still a young man with my life ahead of me. Please give me another chance and I'll ride out of here and go right back to Vermont— you'll never see me again, I swear!"

"Mister, yu' weren't thinkin' when yu' came down hyeh', were yu'?" Ike Horn then asked, "Yu' jus' sorta' thought yu' could come down hyeh' an' ride roughshod wit' all dah' niggahs', jus' stirrin' everythin' up like a kettle of soup an' din' tootin' yur' horn 'bout how good yu' are at managin' to git'dah' niggahs' to go on a rampage. Din' yu' would jus' sorta' soak it all up in fun—all dah'

179

damage yu' jus' caused—gittin' dah' niggahs' to kill innocent white people. An' like a typical cowardly Yankee, jus' ride out headin' due north knowin' dat' yu' done did yur' dirty work. Hey, yu' might even git' back to Vermont an' become a hero. Meanwhile, we all should jus' sorta' gleefully sit back an' let yu' perform yur' destructive deeds causin' a lot of sufferin' down hyeh'! Isn't dat' right, mister?"

Sobbing out of control, the stranger again pleaded, "Sir, I never meant any harm to anyone. This is just a terrible misunderstanding."

Ike Horn continued. "Mister, now yu' have to know dat'yu' gotta' 'nother thin' a comin'. Did yu know dat' yu' were comin' down hyeh' to die? In otherwords mister—yu' ain't goin' back home to become a hero! Instead yu'll be comin' home in a pine box! Now, how does dat' sit wit' yu'? What's dah' matter wit' yu'? Are yu' a little baby? Why, yu' strike me as bein' more scared din' a 'longtail cat in a room full of rockin' chairs'!" The crowd, while very serious, continued to be amused as Ike Horn stood center stage.

The stranger's pleading had now reached a fevered pitch. "Sir I'm begging you! I just want to go home and pretend this never happened. Please, please, let me go home. I apologize a thousand-fold—I was wrong, and I have learned my lesson."

"I do think you're learnin' yur' lesson, mister. Look at yu', a typical Yankee milksop jus' cryin' 'way." Ike let out a short, spasmodic laugh. "What a poor 'cuse fo' a man yu' are. Jus' a cowardly Yankee—a typical Yankee, I might add—no backbone 'bout yu'. Mister, we don't want yu' people down hyeh'! What does it take to git' yu' people to understand dat' yu' have yur' own problems wit' dose' free issue niggahs' up thar' committin' crimes?" Horn wasn't finished, " We don't go up thar' an' bother yur' niggahs'. All we want is fo' yu' to leave us 'lone. Damn, what does it take to git' dat' message 'cross. What do yu' have to say 'bout dat'?"

Ike Horn's words reflected the deep division between the North and the South, which was not being addressed—the idea that the North was bothering the South, while the South was leaving the North alone. In fact this perception would only get worse. Ironically, many Southerners' even believed that social decay in the North was a lot worse than in the South and that further left them wondering why the North didn't tend to their own problems and stay out of the South. Arguably, it represented a good case for the South to make.

"Sir, you are right! I agree. I don't see any Southerners' up there causing any problems." The stranger knew what he had to say if he had any hope of getting out of this situation with his life.

Ike Horn continued. "Yu' damn right yu' don't see us up thar'. Anyhow Mister, today is yur' lucky day, 'cuz' I've decided to spare yur' life. Dah' only reason I'm doin' dis' is 'cuz' I want yu' to tell dose' damn Yankees throughout dah' North what happens when dey' come down hyeh' causin' trouble. Yu' know, if dah' townspeople had thar' way, yu' woulda' been strung up already. "

One of the townspeople added, "Yu' know, mister, if yu' had been a free issue niggah', yu' would have been a dead niggah' by now. Dah' only reason yu' are gittin' out of hyeh' wit' yur' life is 'cuz' yu' are white. If yu' was a niggah', Ike Horn couldn't have saved yu'. In fact Jesus Christ couldn't have saved yu'—do yu' understand? Simply put—yu' had a mighty close call, comin' within an inch of yur' life."

"Sir, I understand," the Northerner quickly responded. "I want to thank all of you for sparing my life. I promise I will go home and tell the Northerners not to come down here and cause trouble." It was apparent that the stranger had just received the best news in his lifetime.

Another townsman stepped forward and commented, "I kinda' see it like dis'. Yur' cowardness shows jus' how spineless yu' people up North really are compared to us Southerners'. All of us proud Southerners feel dah' same way—yu' an' all yur' Yankee weaklin's make us sick."

Horn who was taking everything in and with a wide grin, exclaimed, "Mister, I bet yu' will tell everybody up North to stay outta' hyeh'. But we still have a little bit of unfinished business to tend to. I kinda' thought dat' we could show yu' some real fine Southern hospitality on yur' way outta' town. Yu' know mister, it jus' dawned on all of us dat' you've got dah' makins' of dah' best lookin' chicken in des' parts. All yu' need is some chicken feathers, an' we've got scads of 'em' right hyeh'. Charles, bring out dat' tar. We're goin' to let yu' annoint yur' new buddy wit' some fresh tar so dat' dose' feathers stick right tight."

Another woman in the crowd added, "Mister, what Ike is tellin 'yu' is dat' we are gonna' let yu' ride out of hyeh' as a free spirited Northern chicken!" Everyone laughed as the poor stranger endured a terrible anguish over what was about to happen.

Then Horn ordered Charles to stir the kettle of tar and told the stranger, "Mister, yu' are gonna' have to peel off dose' clothes now."

Obediently, the stranger took all of his clothes off and stood naked before the crowd. They were laughing and echoing what the woman had said. It was an uproarious event—almost a celebration targeting the stranger's humiliation and suffering.

The ridicule extended to even casting dispersions on the strangers sexual orientation. "Mister, jus' lookin' yu' over I'm havin' a hard time figurin' out if yu' are really a man or jus' a woman comin' down hyeh' all dressed up as a man." The crowd roared at the comment coming from an old man leaning against a hitching post.

Horn prophetically stated, "'Fore yur' friend Charles adorns yu', we want yu' to know two things. If yu' had been a niggah', yu' would be dead. Also, if yu' think dat' we're jus' tryin' to put dah' fear of God into yu'—'gain see dat' oak tree ovah' thar'? Well, like we said earlier, if yu' show up in des' parts 'gain, dat's gonna' be yur' final resting spot. We'll raise yu' up an' yu'll be center of 'tention jus' like dat' 'free issue niggah''. Wouldn't dat' be somethin' mister? It's obvious to all of us dat' yu' love 'tention or yu' wouldn't be down heyh' stirrin' up our niggahs' in dah' first place. Yu' an' dat' dead free issue niggah' could sorta' git' together up in heaven comparin' notes an' jus' talkin' 'bout how dah' two of yah' got to hang 'round town an' soak up some good ole' Southern hospitality. Now, mister, do yu' git' dah' drift? Do yah'?"

The crowd went into an uproar of laughter. The stranger, naked, embarrassed and frightened cried out, "Sir, when I get up North, I'll even take to the stump telling people to stay out of the South and to mind their own business."

With a wily look Horn replied, "I bet yu' will. Charles, go 'head an' make yur' friend a right smart chicken. Never let it be said dat' we Southerners don't know how to dress out a chicken." With that the crowd roared as Ike continued. "We all need a little fun in dis' town from time to time, an' dis' damn Yankee is gonna' be a real sport 'bout entertainin' us."

As directed, Charles went ahead and tarred and feathered the stranger, completely covering him from the top of his head to the tip of his toes. He screamed in pain as the tar was applied over his body. One could only wonder how he was able to breathe and see. He was fortunate the tar was only lukewarm and not hot, since it could have caused severe burns and possibly death. It's notable that tar and feathering was used up North as well. In addition, there are documented cases of death from the barbarous act.

Ike Horn then bellowed, "Now, mister, on dah' way out of town, we want yu' to sorta' act dah' fool. We all wanta' hyeh' an' see yu' jus' flappin' an' cluckin' as yu' leave. Somethin' else—see Slade over thar' in dat' wagon? Well, he's gonna' be right 'hind yu' wit' a shotgun loaded wit' bird shot jus' to make sur' yu' make a right smart chicken an' not git' to actin' up. I don't reckon dat' yu've ever been shot up wit' bird shot, have yu'? Well, we all know what it does to birds, so I kinda' think yu' may not like it pepperin' yur' Yankee ass."

"Sir, I would not, but I'm suffering right now even without the bird shot. I don't know if I'll be able to make it."

"Oh yu'll make it. Now mister, yu' better stop dat' Yankee whinin', an' jus' be happy yu're still alive. Yu' are dah' poorest specimen of a man dat' I've ever laid my eyes on. Damn, jus' cryin' like a little baby—yu' better not say 'nother word, or we may have to hang yu'! Damn, yu' make me sick jus' lookin' at yu', a damn trouble makin' Yankee. Now git' goin'!"

Under the circumstances the stranger quickly scurried away, flapping and clucking loud and clear as best as he could. On down the road, he tripped over his own feet and crashed with a loud thud to the ground. Slade began firing shots into the air. The stranger dazed and confused thought he was going to be shot. He immediately picked himself off the ground and resumed his clucking. This spectacle sent the crowd into a total uproar, lasting for some time.

Through the entire spectacle, Reverend Hibbard and Reggie stood silently watching, and once the humiliating scene had ended, Hibbard looked at Reggie and said, "It's downright sad what dey' did to dat' man, but he certainly deserved what he got. Yu' jus' can't come down hyeh' to cause trouble. What do yu' think?"

"Master, he's jus' lucky dat' 'Providence was on duty today'." Reggie was wondering if Reverend Hibbard, as a preacher, could ever understand what he had just witnessed was totally against the teachings of Jesus Christ.

"Yu' are right Reggie, he's indeed lucky. I thought fo' sur' dat' Ike Horn was goin' to have him hanged."

"Master, why didn't dah' constable stand up to dah' mob an' prevent anythin' from happenin' to dat' man?"

The reverend answered, "I jus' know if he had said a word, he would not be our constable. Dat's dah' way dat' justice is served 'round hyeh'—mob action takes ovah'. He's jus' sort of a figurehead 'round hyeh'. Dah' mob runs dah' show, not him."

"Master, it appears to be a lawless society when dah' constable cannot take control of a mob action."

"Reggie, I do believe dat' justice gits' served an' dat' is all dat' really counts. I jus' know dat' we still have to git' our supplies an' mail," and with that, they both continued on their errands.

CHAPTER TWELVE

While Reggie was upset with the unfortunate incident he had witnessed, he also knew the stranger was very fortunate to still be alive. Through it all, Reverend Hibbard remained in a positive mood knowing in his mind, the administration of justice toward the stranger was fair. Reggie wanted to be put into a more positive spirit and move into a another subject. "Master, whar' does dah' post coach 'rive at?"

"He makes his drop at our general store. Yu' kin' hear him comin' an' blowin' his bugle, soundin' dah' 'larm fo' fresh hawses' at dah' livery stable," Reverend Hibbard replied.

"What do yu' want me to do, master?"

"Nuttin', yu' jus' stay by my side. I wanta' show yu' dah' town even though I think it's dah' debil's workshop. Let's start wit' dah' tavern, an' please don't' say a word or look at anybody. Des' men, as yu' have seen today, have a short fuse, but I still have dah' responsibility of doin' dah' work of dah' Lawd'."

Reverend Hibbard was clearly lacking common sense and exercising poor judgment taking Reggie into the tavern. He just couldn't contain himself and wanted to show off his new personal servant, who conspicuously looked white, and was strikingly handsome. With some of the ruthless people who frequented the the tavern, a slave with Reggie's looks would certainly cause a stir, and Reverend Hibbard should have realized that. Reggie's common sense told him he should not go into the tavern but he was helpless to oppose the wishes of Reverend Hibbard. Normally, slaves would always wait outside in the back.

Reverend Hibbard and Reggie entered the rather typical wooden structure. The interior was in disrepair from the hard-living customers. The bar was on the left side. On the right side, several tables with chairs were scattered haphazardly in front of them, which provided for a sloppy but typical appearance.

Standing to one side, Boyd Rose, who had witnessed the tar and feathering, spotted the two of them. Boyd was a rough, middle-aged man who had developed a sordid reputation as a bully. Very similar to Ike Horn, he was the other self-imposed town leader. Typically, like so many others in the tavern, he was unkempt and wore dull, soiled, cotton clothing. Eyeing the preacher, Boyd grunted and cleared his throat and approached them to make conversation. "Well, if it ain't dah' preacher. Did yu' come in hyeh' to 'wet yur' whistle'? Hyeh', 'take a pull on dis".' Boyd then pushed a drink in Hibbard's face. It was obvious that he wished to make fun of the preacher.

"Boyd, yu' know I wouldn't touch dah' debil's brew. I jus' came to town to git' some provisions, dry goods an' my mail. The Negro wit' me is my new personal servant, an' I wanted to show him 'round town."

A patron standing at the bar shouted out so all could hear, "He looks more white din' me—not like a niggah'!" Based on his past experiences, Reggie knew that very quickly somebody would have a comment about the color of his skin.

Boyd Rose added, "Personal servant! Look boys, dah' preacher is all dressed in black wit' his long white hair an' his bootlickin' Sambo trailin' 'long all smartly dressed up. Now doesn't dat' 'beat dah' Dutch'? Don't dey' jus' sorta' look like a cute little couple—'two peas in a pod', jus' a lollagagin' 'round'? How sweet. What's yur' name, boy?" If Reverend Hibbard wanted to create a "buzz", he had certainly succeeded.

"Master, my name is Reggie."

"Reggie huh?" the inebriated Rose went on. "For a second I thought dis' niggah' might be givin' me a last name, yu' know, some 'ristocratic English last name like Kent—din' I woulda' cracked yu' upside of dah' head—a good one, boy!" Boyd paused a moment for effect. "Well, I may be a little 'in my cup', but I'm still sober 'nough to think dat' yu' don't look like a niggah'." It was quite apparent that the reverend had used very poor judgment bringing Reggie inside the tavern. Everyone was still riled up over what had just taken place with the stranger from Vermont, which only made matters worse.

Reverend Hibbard defended Reggie saying, "No, Boyd, he may not look like a niggah', but he is my bondsman."

"Preacher, yu' mean yur' niggah'. What dah' hell is dis' bondsman talk? 'Sides, it sorta' looks to me like yur' niggah' is a product of a left-handed marriage. He sure in dah' hell didn't come from two Afriky' niggahs'. But one thing fo' sur', yu' kin' take a pig an' dress him all up, but in the end, he's still a pig. Sorta' like yur' niggah'—boy yu're still a niggah', an' yu'll die a niggah', an' don't yu' ever forgit' it. Yu' sur' in dah' hell ain't no Englishman, a Kent or somebody like dat'! Hyeh' yu' already got dah' preacher man coverin' fo' yu', callin' yu' a bondsman. If yu' were as black as an ace of spades din' he would call yu' jus' what yu' are—jus' 'nother niggah'! Well 'round hyeh' jus' 'cuz' yu' kin' pass fo' white, yu' are jus' as much a niggah' as dose' darkies comin' hyeh' from Afriky. Fo'git' dis' bondsman talk." Boyd's wrinkled brow and facial expression reflected his mean-spirited attempts to be funny at Reggie's expense. Everyone gathered around their self imposed leader Rose, adding their own nasty comments and gestures, one suggesting, "Maybe we orte' take dis' clabber-colored niggah' outside an' work him ovah' a bit. Mark my words, thar's' nothin' worse din' a high-brow niggah' an' I'm lookin' at one, an' it jus' makes me sick!"

Another patron added, "What dah' hell is he doin' in hyeh' in dah' first place? I never felt quite right wit' any niggah' hangin' wit' me in a tavern while I'm enjoyin' my drink an' chewin' dah' fat wit' my friends. His place is outside in dah' back wit' all dah' other niggahs'—I'm really all riled up 'bout dis', Boyd! Jus' what dah' hell is he doin' in hyeh'?" The pleading tone in the man's voice prompted Boyd to take action.

Rose walked up to Reggie, pushing him backwards, and then led him around by his collar. Reggie was alarmed and visibly shaken as Rose continued to taunt him. "Niggah', what's dah' matter! Yu' look more nervous din' a pregnant nun." The laughter stirred up emotions and encouraged the bullying to escalate as Hibbard tried unsuccessfully to calm everyone.

Just when it looked like things couldn't get any worse, Boyd announced he was not quite through. He had something to offer to Reggie that he would always remember for the rest of his life. Without hesitation he turned and put his back toward Reggie, he pulled his pants down and bent over, exposing his rear end. "Guess what I'm fixin' to do—'break wind'? Now, who do yu' think has been selected to receive dah' full thrust of what I have to offer? I'll give y'all a clue. He is standin' right next to me, isn't dat' right boy?"

"Yes master, I know yu' have selected me." Reggie was disgusted at what was about to transpire, but as a slave, he had to stand there and let this evil person make him the butt of his ugly humor.

Just then another patron interjected to announce that he wanted to join Boyd. It was apparent that Jake Stone was inebriated as he quickly ran over and pulled his pants down as well. Of course, the patrons laughed even louder.

Boyd thanked Jake for joining him and resumed talking to Reggie. "Yu' damn right yu've been selected. Now, yu' better jus' stand thar', not move an' inhale dis'moment of joy when yur' Master Boyd an' Jake share what they have to offer!" At this point everybody in the bar was roaring with laughter as Reggie stood helpless with Reverend Hibbard standing by his side. Boyd and Jake then expressed a large amount of gas that proved to be loud and rancid. Everybody in the bar, except for Reggie, who was not allowed to move, quickly moved away from the area holding their noses.

One patron commented, "Boyd, dat' was really foul. I don't think I could take anymore of those. Yu' two really stunk up dah' place."

After the odor finally dissipated the crowd returned to face Reggie and continued their assault while Reverend Hibbard stood near him.

Another patron yelled over the taunting and laughter. "Well, preacher, yur' boy sorta' 'minds me of dah' spider dat' invited dah' fly into his parlor—welcome to our parlor, niggah', an' dat's no barroom josh! In fact we are all kinda' glad yu' brought yur' cute little Sambo in hyeh' preacher. All of us boys are always lookin' fo' a little fun as yu' jus' found out. I guess we didn' t git ' 'nough fun wit' dat' Yankee—an' yur' boy, preacher man is sorta' like 'Johnny on dah' spot'."

Reggie could see that these mean spirited men enjoyed inflicting pain and suffering—a replay of what he had jus' witnessed outside with the stranger. It was terribly disturbing as he had always applied Christian values in his life even while being subjected to the nightmares of bondage. Now at the hands of others who purported to be Christians, he was very near to having a physical beating administered on him, or possibly even worse, death as the patrons appeared to be intoxicated and looking for serious trouble. If the preacher had applied common sense, he would have known that he was inviting trouble bringing Reggie into the bar—a no-no in itself, let alone a house servant with Reggie's looks.

Reverend Hibbard saw the situation quickly deteriorating and knew it would only get worse. He fumbled beneath his shirt collar for his cross, which he located and clutched. "We're goin' to git' out of hyeh', Boyd, if yu'll please 'cuse us."

Boyd snarled back, "Dat' might be a good ider', 'specially since yur' niggah' doesn't even look like a half-breed—more like a white man. Yu' know we don't 'cotton 'round' hyeh' to a niggah' like him. He's liable to git wit' a white woman, an' dat' wouldn't be good—now would it, preacher? Let' jus' say it wouldn' bode well fo' yur' proud Sambo standin' ovah' thar' all full of himself—damn, I jus' can't 'lieve I'm lookin' at such a fancy niggah' who takes himself to be some English gent." Boyd shifted from Reggie and gave Hibbard a menacing look as he spoke. "Yu' kin leave. Let 'dem go, boys. 'Sides, dah' preacher knows he's comin' out to my plantation in a couple of weeks to preach dah' word of God to all my niggahs', an' I want his bootlickin' Sambo to 'rive all healthy an' wise wit' him. Now git!"

One of the patrons then made a very controversial comment. "Yu' know, preacher, what wit' dat' high-pitched voice an' girlish look 'bout yu' an' now carryin' dat' clabber-colored display niggah' wit' yu,' people are liable to start talkin' 'bout dah' two of yu' jus' sorta' cozyin' up together back at dah' ole' plantation at night. Yu' know, maybe a little hanky-panky." The man's comment drew a prolonged laugh from the crowd as the two hurriedly exited.

They stood outside the tavern visibly shaken from the event that had just occurred. Sweat was rolling down Reverend Hibbard's face. The suggestion of a homosexual relationship greatly troubled both men—Hibbard's reputation was being severely tarnished while Reggie, a happily married man, was upset at being drawn into a controversy that was not of his choice.

Reverend Hibbard assured Reggie everything would be fine. "Reggie, I tole' yu' dis' place was dah' debil's workshop,' but don't worry—barkin' dogs seldom bite. 'Sides, I'm dah' preacher, so dat' gives yu' a pass in most cases. But I want yu' to know dat' people don't fool wit' Boyd Rose. He's so flat-out mean dat' he could be dah' demon's watch-dog. In fact, I've heard it said dat' he is 'meaner din' a gut shot grizzly. People 'round hyeh' jus' know to give him a 'bery wide berth."

"Master, I clearly see why," Reggie affirmed.

"Come on Reggie, I wanta' git' goin'." He paused and then said, "Every Saturday, evil is really in full force in dis' town. It's all 'bout gamblin', chasin' women, gittin' liquored up, an' jus' general roughhousin'. Dey' have thar' cockfights, quarterhorse racin', card playin', an' dah' most barbaric of all—gander pullin'—a contest 'tween two men whar' people bet on who kin' pull dah' head off a goose first while everybody cheers on dah' victor. Dat's not all, frequently, dey' stage fights wit' two niggahs' battlin' it out 'til one of 'dem is knocked silly or dead, an' mind yu', while any one of des' events are goin' on, dey' are partakin' in dah' debil's brew, gamblin', an' usin' language dat' is pure sinful. Jus' dreadful—an' hyeh' I'm, a preacher man, tryin' to do dah' work of our Lawd', which He has blessed me to do, while I'm askin' myself—jus' whar' do I begin!"

"Master, may I have yur' permission to offer my opinion on all of dis'?"

"Go 'head, Reggie, I wanta' hyeh' it."

"Master, yu're so right, dey' are like a bunch of barbarians. Yu' know dah' Bible speaks of dah' ruthless Philistines. Well, dat's what dey' are. When I was in Virginny', I came in contact wit' all of dis' 'cept dah' gander-pullin'. Dah' whole thing jus' makes me feel 'bery unsettlin'."

"Reggie, I believe dat' yu' have dah' makin' of a man of God," Reverend Hibbard said. "I'm very impressed wit' yu'. I might be goin' out on a limb sayin' dis', but Matthew 22:14 says, 'many are called but few are chosen'. Maybe soon yu' will be called upon to preach to dah' niggahs'."

"Thank yu' master," Reggie humbly responded.

"Let's walk over hyeh'," Reverend Hibbard directed. "We kin' see dah' cock fightin' matches goin' on. We don't want any trouble, so let's stay at a distance."

They walked a few yards to a livery stable and stepped just inside a sliding door that was left partially open. They witnessed two cocks with two inch spikes attached to their feet pitted against each other in a battle to the death, while men were cheering for the bird they had bet on to win. Other cocks in wooden cages nearby were unknowingly awaiting their turn to go into the arena to fight.

"Master, I too find dis' blood sport to be vile. Those spikes on thar' feet—I can't understand why men find dat' excitin'. Notice one thin'—yu' don't see women participatin' in des' shenanigans!"

"I have observed dat'," Reverend Hibbard replied. "I think women are flat out more compassionate. To make dat' point strike home, last year we had two men settle a dispute by duelin', it's legal an' it's barbaric. One was killed ovah' somethin' dat' probably didn't amount to a 'hill of beans'. Dey' quit duelin' in dah' North but in our beloved South, we still have to fight a duel ovah' our individual honor. I talk 'bout all dis' on Sunday, an' dey' listen, din' on Monday dey' go back to thar' usual ways. It never seems to end."

"Master," Reggie asked. "May I say something 'bout dah' chattel system in dah' South dat' pertains to what we are talkin' 'bout?"

"Normally, I would say no, Reggie—be mindful of what yu' say."

"Master, do yu' think dat' all dis' violence an' general roughhousin' could be a spill ovah' effect from dah' bondage system in dah' South? Maybe a man has a difficult time knowin' when an' whar' to put dah' whip down."

"I have often thought dah' same thin'," Hibbard nodded. "But I warn yu', dis' kin' never be discussed 'round others. Even in dah' pulpit I have to measure my words to never say anythin' 'gainst our 'peculiar institution' of dah' South. Let's move on to somethin' else. Have yu' ever been to a quarter hawss' race? Let's walk ovah' to dah' track an' check it out."

As they walked, Reggie mused to himself that the preacher had acknowledged that he was limited in being able to speak the truth. That spoke volumes—society in so many ways avoids the truth and accepts the "road most traveled". A world where people could speak the truth—wouldn't that ideally make for a much better mankind?

"Master, I have been to both quarter hawss' an' thoroughbred races as well in Virginny'. In fact, I also had equestrian trainin' 'long wit' my young master. We frequently rode together— somethin' I truly enjoyed an' miss greatly. Wit' dah' exposure I've had, I have been 'bery fortunate to have learned a lot 'bout hawses'."

"Reggie, I certainly enjoy ridin', an' maybe both of us could do dat'. For now I wanta' show yu' our quarter hawss' race track. Dey' are racin' right now. Din' we kin' go to dah' general store whar' we kin' pick up our provisions, dry goods an' my mail."

The pair made their way across town to watch the quarter

horse races. The small grandstands were filled with a boisterous, seemingly happy crowd cheering for their favorite horse on the dusty quarter mile track.

"Reggie, since yu' have seen both types of racin', which is yur' favorite?"

"I went to a quarter hawss' race track near our plantation in Virginny', an' it was 'bery similar to dis' one an' to be honest wit' yu' master, I prefer thoroughbred racin'. I think wit' dah' quarter horse racin' dat' dey' kinda' push dose' hawses' a little too hard instead of pacin' 'dem. All out speed, even in a quarter of a mile fo' some hawses' kin' be too much."

"I 'preciate yur' opinion, 'though I don't fully 'gree. Let's git' to dah' general store as I wanta' leave as soon as we kin' so we don't git' caught ridin' home in dah' dark."

As the two neared the general store, the bugle sounded from the post coach, announcing its arrival. The large coach was adorned with red, white and blue colors and pulled by six handsome work horses. The largest and most colorful spectacle to arrive in town, it always attracted a crowd. The driver apologized for being late explaining that repairs at sunrise had disrupted normal mail delivery. He threw the mail gunny sack at the store owner, tipped his hat and rode off to the livery stable where he would get fresh horses.

Reverend Hibbard picked up his dry goods and provisions while the man who ran the general store was sorting through the mail, placing it in the mail slots. Meanwhile, Reggie had gone to bring up the horse and buggy. Reverend Hibbard was finally able to gather his mail and met Reggie in a timely fashion as he pulled up in front of the general store.

Loading everything quickly, they headed back to Reverend Hibbard's plantation feeling the effects of a full and exhausting day. As they rode home, Hibbard asked Reggie if the Carolinas were similar to Virginia.

"Master, I kin' observe several differences," Reggie began. "No offense to des' parts, but dah' people generally 'round hyeh' are a little coarser din' in dah' Williamsburg area. Also, we don't have cotton up thar'—it's all tabacca', cawn' an' wheat. Hyeh' it's pretty much cotton."

"Don't fret Reggie, yu'll adjust to dah' people 'round hyeh' as well as dah' cotton."

Reggie was getting bolder about sharing his opinions, and asked, "Master, kin' I confide in yu' 'bout somethin' else?"

Reverend Hibbard appreciated conversing with Reggie—it was as if he now had a confidante and not a slave as a companion. "Sur', what is it Reggie?"

Reggie started out slowly, carefully choosing his words. "Master, des' times have been difficult fo' me. I got married an' was forced to be separated from my bride." He paused briefly, took a deep breath and continued. "I do love her a lot, an' I miss her."

"Reggie I didn't know yu' were married! In fact, if I was yu', I would try to forgit' dah' past an' look fo'ward to dah' future wit' yur' new master. 'Sides in dah' eyes of dah' law yur' marriage is not legal. Personally, I never married, and I honestly prefer it dat' way. Gittin' back to yu,' aren't niggahs' different din' white people? Dey' don't have dah' same feelins' as white people. White people stay in love wit' each other, but niggahs' don't. Dey' jus' sorta' bounce 'round wit'out a care in dah' world. Yu' are mainly white, so yu' might be a little different din' most niggahs'."

"Master, black people do have feelins' jus' like white people. I dearly love my wife, an' it wouldn't matter if I was white, tan, brown or black. Yu' can't imagine dah' agony dat' black people have to suffer through when thar' loved ones are auctioned off an' separated from 'dem. In fact, if yu' talked to black people dey' will tell yu' dat' losin' loved ones at auction is dah' most dreaded thin' 'bout servitude. Black people love each other every bit as much as white people do." Reggie knew that stating his feelings could create problems for him, but he couldn't refrain from expressing his feelings when dealing with this sensitive subject.

While not surprised about Reverend Hibbard expressing his view that black people, unlike white people, were not troubled at losing a loved one, he was more concerned over his apparent annoyance at Reggie for being happily married. This troubled

Reggie as he recalled the patrons at the tavern had made jokes about Reverend Hibbard's sexual preference.

Hibbard changed the subject. "'Nough of dis' talk. What's dis' 'bout yu' savin' everyone at sea? I wanta' hyeh' dis' wit' a few details."

Reggie was glad to see a change of subject. "Master, not only was I equestrian trained, but I also received nautical trainin'. A mighty storm came up, an' when dah' ship started listin' in dah' water, dah' captain an' his crew jumped ship. I was forced to take command of dah' abandoned brig, an' I knew if all of us niggahs' did not panic, we could make it through dah' storm. I knew if dah' men could work dah' pumps at a feverish pace, we would survive. Incidentally, I wondered why dah' captain couldn't figure dat' out? We had to have been travelin' in a main sea lane, an' logic would suggest dat' eventually a ship would come 'long an' aid us as long as we stayed calm, cool, an' collected. Atter' driftin' at sea aimlessly fo' two days, a ship arrived an' rescued us. By remainin' calm we were able to avert a disaster, which surly' woulda' been dah' end of us had we panicked!"

"Reggie, yu' 'maze me wit' all yur' skills." Reverend Hibbard was indeed impressed that a servant would know so much about so many things. "I honestly believe dat' most white men don't have half yur' 'bilities."

"Master," Reggie explained. "I grew up amongst dah' Williamsburg crowd whar' all dah' finer things in life were available fo' dah' white people. My young master had difficulties wit' learnin' an' pickin' up things, so my master realized it would be easier fo' me to learn all des' skills wit' his son din' I could help him. Yu' could say dat' I sorta' tagged 'long. Normally, I would have never been allowed to be educated in so many ways, but it was 'sential dat' his son would learn to carry on dah' Marshall tradition by acquirin' a broad education, so dey' made an exception of me. Unfortunately, his son Albert died, an' I was extremely broken up ovah' his death as he was my best friend." Reggie knew that some things were left better unsaid, so he never told Reverend Hibbard that Albert was his half brother.

"Dat's some story. So, it was fo' practical reasons dat' yu' were educated along wit' yur' master's son."

"Master, dat' may be right, an' it has served me quite well," Reggie agreed. "But thar' is another part of my life dat' is really troublin'—kin' I tell yu' 'bout it?"

Reverend Hibbard was pleased that Reggie was sharing his background. "Sure, 'cuz' yu're makin' our return home more interestin'."

"Master, when I tell yu' dis' story, I want yu' to know dat' it is from God an' not from dah' dark side."

"Yu' have my 'tention, I'm all ears, Reggie."

"Master, I've had unusual visions," Reggie began. "Ever since Halley's Comet passed ovah' us, my life has changed. When it first 'peared, I watched it like everyone else, but somehow it jus' took ovah' me, an' I felt dat' God had entered my body an' soul. I'm confidin' in yu' master 'bout dis' matter since yu' are a man of God an' kin' understand."

"Well, dat' is really somethin'," Reverend Hibbard exclaimed. "Are yu' sur' yu' weren't excited an' merely hallucinatin'?"

"No, master, 'cuz' since din', I have had two lifelike dreams wit' Halley's Comet in each of 'dem."

"Maybe yu're' dah' immortal dreamer."

"Master, in dah' first dream I saw a tall white man deliverin' a speech as Halley's Comet churned overhead. He was dedicatin' a cemetery on a site whar' thousands of soldiers had perished fightin' a war 'tween dah' North an' dah' South. In dat' battle, dah' North was victorious an' went on to eventually end dah' war an' bring an' end to servitude." Reggie spoke his words with strength and conviction.

"Reggie, dah South has a lot of money tied up wit' servants an' field hands. Fo' dah' plantation owner, outside of his home an' land investment, his second greatest investment is his servants an' field hands. Now dat' would inflict a severe economic hardship on dah' South. I can't imagine a South wit'out our beloved bondage system. Reggie, it works—it's dat' simple an' it ain't goin' 'way." Hibbard's tone became even more serious as he continued. "'Sides, I personally don't believe dat' dah' North would ever have it in 'dem to be able to defeat my beloved South in a head-to-head war. We all know dat' we could outfight 'dem. In fact, I think dey' know dat' as well. Yu' yur'self witnessed dat' bobolitionist' who we jus' ran out of town. Could yu' honestly call dat' coward a man? In my book, he's jus' a typical Northerner. But go 'head— I'm listenin'."

Reggie knew he upset Reverend Hibbard, but he felt he had to finish explaining his visions. "Master, dah' second dream was different. It went much further into dah' future, I had another vision. I saw a black man deliverin' dis' 'portant speech 'bout equality an' he had throngs of people both black an' white 'round him. Everyone was spellbound as he explained dat' racial inequality is wrong an' must end in dah' eyes of God. He related dat' although dah' bondage system had ended long ago, dah' struggle fo' equality has had to continue. Somethin' else, Master—dah' black man was speakin' on a platform wit' a large memorial bearin' dah' image of dah' man I had seen in my first vision 'hind him. Again, Halley's Comet was watchin' over dah' man in dis' dream."

"Reggie, I must admit dat' yu' have a rich imagination. I do think dat' yu' might have a difficult time findin' anyone who would believe yur' fanciful stories. More important, it looks like we aren't goin' to git' back 'fore dark. Don't worry as I know my way 'round hyeh'. I kin' even find my way out of dah' bottoms' at night an' dats' a lot worse. Anyhow, 'nough of dis' talk of visions, I've got to worry 'bout gittin' us back to dah' plantation."

Reverend Hibbard maneuvered the horse and buggy, making several turns and driving on an inhospitable road until they finally arrived at Hibbard Hall. Reggie removed the provisions and took the horse and buggy to the stable while Hibbard prepared for evening devotions.

When Reggie entered the house after tending to the horse and buggy, Hibbard was anxious to discuss the importance of devotions. "Lawd' knows dat' atter' dah' day we had, we are gonna' have our devotions. As I tole' yu' 'fore, hyeh' we have devotions first thin' in dah' mornin' an' din' 'gain in dah' evenin'. It's dah' Christian way of life we're livin'. It's good fo' dah' heart an' soul!"

"Thank yu', Master, fo' givin' me dah' opportunity to share both evenin' an' mornin' devotions wit' yu'." Reggie recognized the relationship the two were developing could be positive. Again, it was obvious that Reverend Hibbard had no intention of treating Reggie as a personal servant, instead, more as a confidante. Under these circumstances, his life would be immeasurably better. It appeared he may have found himself in a rare situation where he might feel a small measure of freedom. He also realized, however that nothing could replace being truly free with Anastasia by his side.

CHAPTER THIRTEEN

Two weeks later on a Sunday morning, Reverend Hibbard surprised Reggie by informing him that today his committent to preach at the Boyd Rose plantation had arrived. With haste as Reverend Hibbard was always in a hurry, Reggie brought up the horse and buggy, and the two were on their way. Reverend Hibbard commented, "Today represents a test of your spiritual growth, an' I think yu' will do jus' fine. Boyd Rose is a true black hearted villain, but his niggahs' need dah' spirit of God jus' as much as anyone else. Most preachers steer clear of his plantation, but I'm prepared to test our faith, knowin' dat' we kin' put our safety in God's hands." Keeping his thoughts to himself, Reggie silently questioned if the reverend was once again exercising good judgment going to the Boyd Rose plantation to conduct services.

As they rode to Rose's plantation, Reggie said, "Master, it speaks highly of yur' faith in God dat' yur' callin' has brought yu'whar' others dare not tread."

Reverend Hibbard thought for a moment, then replied, "Reggie, we must not pick an' choose who we kin' bring dah' word of God to. Boyd's field hands need Jesus jus' as much as anybody."

"Master, I agree wit' yu'." Reggie would dare not say what he really believed.

"Thank yu', Reggie. At dis' pace it shouldn't take us long to git' thar'. In fact it's less din' a mile to dah' entrance of his plantation. Be prepared fo' dah' unexpected, an' be mindful of what yu' say an' do."

This warning came none too soon, as they witnessed the most appalling sight they had ever witnessed as they approached the property. Mounted on separate wooden pikes were the heads of three slaves, their decaying, grotesque leather-like remains suggesting they had been there for some time. Both Reverend Hibbard and Reggie had known this practice was used to create terror and fear, but they personally had never witnessed it. The message for the slaves on the Rose plantation was absolutely terrifying. It horrified slaves to see their friends and loved ones heads displayed on pikes for all to see, and they knew Boyd Rose would not hesitate to repeat the process to others as he deemed necessary to keep "them in line". While this level of cruelty was rarely used; nevertheless, it certainly ranked as one of the most barbaric and evil methods attached to the bondage system. A practice that was quietly kept secret in the South, the North would have very little knowledge of the use of this grotesque form of cruelty.

While the background and experiences of Reverend Hibbard and Reggie were completely different, their feelings and emotions remained the same as they moved forward. Neither knew where to look—their stomachs churned and their hearts were racing. Reggie wished Hibbard would turn the buggy around and go home, but he knew that Hibbard was steadfast in following his plans at the sacrifice of common sense. In the back of his mind Reggie knew he could be the next person to have his head mounted on a pike. As a slave that Boyd Rose loathed, he knew that Hibbard was putting him in harms way and he was helpless in stopping him. Instead, Hibbard took a deep breath, gathered his faculties and moved forward while Reggie prayed that Hibbard would suddenly come to his senses.

Pulling up front, Reggie was well aware that he was about to "face the music". It was also evident the plantation had been neglected and was in a dilapidated state. With anguish on his face Reverend Hibbard stated, "Well, Reggie, we have jus' 'rived at dah' gates of hell, but we're plowin' fo'ward—God's on our side. As a man of God, I must say, dis' is dah' most disgustin' an' evil plantation I have ever visited. I know Boyd Rose is a hardened pagan, but dis'!" Reggie rightfully remained terrified knowing what the consequences could be for him. He also knew that Reverend Hibbard had a lot of confidence in God.

They paused to collect themselves silently in front of the main house for a few minutes. Full of anxiety, they carefully got out of the buggy and knocked at the front door. A servant answered and invited them in, assuring Reverend Hibbard that his horse and buggy would be taken to the stable for proper care. They entered the parlor where Mrs. Rose sat waiting for them. Reverend Hibbard was shocked by her appearance since he hadn't seen her for some time. Once vital and attractive, she looked extremely thin, sickly, and had aged well beyond her years. Her condition suggested that problems on the plantation extended far beyond the cruel treatment of the slaves. Her looks were further compromised by a snuff stick in her mouth that protruded out about an inch and moved about as she talked. This habit could have affected her teeth, as many of them were gone, and those remaining were either decayed or discolored. A well-used spittoon was on the floor next to her chair.

"Preacher, it's so nice to see yu'. I'm sorry, I don't believe I ever met yur' friend. Both of yah' have a seat." She smiled directly at Reggie and then sat down.

Reverend Hibbard also sat down while Reggie remained standing.

"Sir, pull up a chair. Yu' do not have to remain standin'," assured Mrs. Boyd.

Reverend Hibbard intervened. "Dis' is my new personal servant, Reggie," Hibbard proudly informed her, leaving her flabbergasted. It would not be appropriate for Reggie to have pulled up a chair unless Hibbard had approved of it.

She quizzically responded, "Personal servant? He sur' doesn't look like a niggah'. Damn, he looks more like a white dandy, an' I mean a white dandy, not a niggah'!"

Hibbard, ignoring her remarks, quickly changed the subject. "Mrs. Rose, whar' is Boyd?"

Mrs. Rose stood up. "Who cares whar' dat' blackguard could be? Anyhow, one of dah' servants is goin' out to dah' quarters to bring him in now."

In a very soft, serious tone Reverend Hibbard asked, "Mrs. Rose, it's none of my business, but it looks like somethin' terrible happened 'round hyeh'."

"Preacher," Mrs. Rose proceeded cautiously, "I have to be very careful 'bout what I say 'cuz' my husband kin' be a real polecat. Are yu' talkin' 'bout dose' niggahs' mounted on pikes? Boyd tells me dat' dey' tried to git' all dah' other niggahs' to mutiny, an' yu' know Boyd! Dat's whar' dey' ended up. He done tole' me he didn't care how much cash it cost him, he had to show all dah' niggahs' what happens when yu' cross Boyd Rose. I reckon he got his message 'cross!"

"It sur' looks like he took matters into hand in a 'bery evil manner," Reverend Hibbard replied.

Suddenly, Mrs. Rose looked very serious, and in a pleading manner she followed, "Yu're a preacher, so I'm goin' to tell yu' dah' truth. Sometimes, I'm scared fo' my life as well as dah' children. He's always gittin' drunk—says dat' blood is his favorite natural brew. He gits' real mean, an' I mean real mean if he thinks I'm lookin' sorta' funny at him. He'll jus' 'whale on me' fo' no reason. He's jus' plumb crazy!"

"Mrs. Rose, it sounds like he is paranoid."

"What's dat' mean preacher?"

"It means dat' he thinks everyone is 'gainst him," Reverend Hibbard explained.

"Well, dat' would sound 'bout right, but still look at me an' my own home," she responded. "I'm livin' in hell 'round hyeh'. Jus' look how bad I look. Yu' know what I think? He can't tell us from his niggahs'. I heard it once said dat' if yu' give a man a whip, he'll have no boundaries. Please talk to him, but don't say dat' I had talked to yu'."

"Yu' have my word," Reverend Hibbard promised. "I have

a question fo' yu', Mrs. Rose. When did yu' take to dippin'?' I'm sorry to ask, Mrs. Rose, but yu' do look so sad an' withdrawn." It was a rather common practice for women in the South to dip a small stick in snuff, and then rub the snuff on their gums and then keep the stick in their mouths like a sucker.

Boyd Rose's wife had been through hell under his stern hand, and she shakily replied, "Preacher, I need some bad habits to take me out of my misery. 'Tween dippin', Laudenum an' liquor I kin' drown out all my miseries."

"Of course," Reverend Hibbard sympathized, but doin' all of dat' 'on dah' quiet' is 'bery serious. Mrs. Rose, yu' got to git' yur'self' out of dah' briar patch an' git' on wit' yur' life."

"Maybe I might seek salvation from God someday, but. . ." Her voice faded as she turned toward Reggie. She wanted to get off the subject of her obvious vices and discuss her curiosity about the light skinned servant. "I wanta' know more 'bout yur' niggah'. Damn, he sure could pass fo' white. I mean he looks more white din' most white people I know. To be honest wit' yu' preacher, he's so handsome dat' in these parts he could cut out all dah' men fo' dah' women. What do yu' have to say 'bout dat', Reggie?"

"Thank yu' missus'." Reggie answered meekly.

"Reggie, are yu' a brass ankle?" Mrs. Rose said it in an assuming manner.

"What's a brass ankle missus'? I haven't heard dat' term 'fore."

"Reggie, are yu' a mix of white, Indian, an' niggah'? Dah' three together makes fo' a person wit' a brassy colored ankle," she explained. "Is dat' dah' way yur' ankles look?"

"Well missus', dah' last time I looked, my ankles didn't have dat' appearance. Now I'm goin' to have to take a little closer look. I know my father was white, but my mother had Negro and mostly white blood in her an' possibly some Indian. I guess dat' would make me a brass ankle." Both Reverend Hibbard and Mrs. Rose thought that Reggie was being humorous and smiled.

White Southerners were always curious about people with mixed blood. It was important to know these details in order to maintain their official system of classification. A mulatto was one-half black and one half-white, which was not uncommon. The word mulatto was derived from breeding a horse with a donkey and delivering a mule—hence, mulatto. A quadroon had one-fourth Negro ancestry and three-quarter Caucasian ancestry while an octoroon was one-eighth Negro and seven-eights Caucasian. A "brass ankle" with Native American ancestry complicated the system by adding a third race to the mix. Nevertheless as stated earlier, the South's solution to the mixing of the races was simple—if a person had even a trace of Negro blood in them, they were officially classified as Negro—the bondage system always required that everything had to remain absolute.

As the three talked, Mrs. Rose looked at Reggie in a slightly flirtatious manner. "Well, I guess one thing is fo' certain, yur' daddy an' mammy must have been right smart-lookin'! Preacher, jus' look at dah' blush in his face!"

Hibbard began to shift the conversation to a less dangerous topic. "Mrs. Rose, shouldn't we talk 'bout somethin' else?"

Just when Reverend Hibbard and Reggie thought it couldn't get any worse, a house servant awkwardly shuffled into the parlor. She had a thread laced through her lower lip and sewn into her dress near her stomach, with the two ends tied together, forcing her to stoop over in order to not break the thread. This in itself had to be torturous. Finally, she continually slobbered from having her mouth forced open and not being able to close it in a normal fashion. Mrs. Rose explained, "Dis' is my splendid little Georgiana—jus' look at dah' poor creetur'. Boyd thought she might be givin' me some sass, so he did dis' to her. If she breaks dah' thread, din' she will receive addditional punishment."

Reggie wondered how she could avoid not breaking the thread in her sleep, but he knew not to ask any questions.

"Dis' is one of dah' cruelest punishments I have ever seen," Reverend Hibbard remarked. "Did she really sass yu' badly 'nough to warrant dis'?"

"Not really," Mrs. Rose quietly replied. "Boyd 'lieves dat' an ounce of prevention is worth a pound of cure. He always says dat'."

"How long has she been like dis', an' when will her discipline cease?" Reverend Hibbard asked, knowing cruelty this severe could not be endured indefinitely.

"I reckon 'round three days, an' I feel sorry fo' her—dah' poor thin' wanders 'round slobberin' everywhere. I can't say a word 'bout it to Boyd, or he's liable to haul off an' rawhide me! I can't even tell yu' fo' sur' when her punishment will end."

As she spoke, Boyd Rose charged into the room with a menacing look on his face, interrupting the conversation, slurring his words and bellowing, "Well, if it isn't dah' preacher an' his personal servant. My, yu' two do make fo' a fine pair—dah' preacher man an' his cute little gad-a-way flirt jus' cavortin' 'round wit' thar' special little ways 'bout 'dem." Mr. Boyd paused, briefly displaying a disgusted look. "Preacher, it jus' makes me sick havin' to look at yur' boy an' sometimes I wonder 'bout yu'. Anyway, did yu' enjoy dat' spectacle in town? If I had been callin' dah' shots, I would have hung dat' damn niggah' lovin' Yankee right whar' we hung dat' free-issue niggah'. It jus' sickens me dat' dey' didn't hang dat' niggah' lover."

"Boyd, he never caused yu' any harm," Reverend Hibbard carefully responded, hoping not to create additional problems with him.

"Preacher, yu' really need to be educated. I look at it like dis'. I have more sympathy fo' dah' free issue niggah' 'cuz' he was helpin' out his own. Now, dat' damn Yankee, dat's a hawss' of a different color. He's a white man an' was gonna' help' out dose' darkies. Dey' ain't his people. Dat' really bothers me. Preacher, kin' yu' imagine white folks cavortin' 'round wit' a bunch of niggahs'. Dat' jus' burns me up!" Boyd was not alone in his thinking. Many white Southerners were more sympathetic to blacks aiding their own people. Whites who aided slaves were branded as "turncoats" and were even more despised. Regarding this matter, a consensus may not be found. It still varied as to who was most hated of the two.

Reverend Hibbard tried to reason, "Now, Boyd, yu' know

dat' you're lettin' yur' booze do yur' talkin'.'"

"Preacher, yu're 'ginnin' to git' under my skin," Boyd looked at the preacher with disdain. "I'm still in a bad mood ovah' dat' damn niggah' lovin' Yankee gittin' out of hyeh' alive. Yu' know preacher man, I would have more sympathy wit' skinnin' yur' cat din' hangin' dat' niggah' lover dat' Ike Horn let run loose. Sometimes I wonder jus' whar' my beloved South is headed."

"Boyd yu' need to think 'bout bringin' more compassion an' love into yur' life through dah' Lawd, Jesus Christ."

"Don't be comin' 'round hyeh' tellin' me what I need to do when yu' got plenty of problems in yur' own house." Boyd was on the verge of losing control. "Preacher, I'm lookin' ovah' at yur' pretty little boy, an' if I see him laughin' or actin' up a little, I might jus' carve up his cute little face. Yu' know I jus' don't trust a clabber colored niggah, so I really don't want to look at him. He makes me sick. God only knows what could go on in yur' home wit' dah' two of yu' lookin' an' actin' dah' way both of yu' do."

Reverend Hibbard felt threatened and concerned about the welfare of Reggie but chose to not say anything for fear of further escalating the situation. "Boyd, yu' invited both of us to come over an' preach in dah' quarters, an' dat's what we are hyeh' to do. Yu' need not threaten my boy—he's not doin' anythin' wrong. 'Sides, my boy who is filled wit' dah' Holy Spirit assists me. Are we gonna' be able to bring dah' Lawd' into dah' lives of yur' niggahs' today?"

"Preacher, are yu' impressed wit' dah' plantation?" Boyd was baiting the preacher, knowing that he would bring up the heads mounted on pikes.

Reverend Hibbard quickly reacted. "Boyd Rose, lookin' at heads mounted on pikes at yur' entrance an' din' seein' dis' poor creetur' in dis' condition, how kin' I as a man of God be impressed wit' dat'?"

"Well, preacher man, what if I told yu' dat' dose' three niggahs' were tryin' to wipe out my family. What would yu' do? Yu' would probably slap 'em on dah' hand! Well, if it wasn't fo' people like me, dah' niggahs' would all be runnin' roughshod throughout dah' South. We've got to nip any problems in dah' bud an' do it right quick. Do yu' think my niggahs' will do anythin' atter' seein' dose' three heads on pikes? Yu' know damn well dey' won't do a thin'—nuttin' but shake like hell thinkin'dey' could wind up on one of dose' pikes. Preacher, yu' gotta' 'keep yur' niggahs' in thar' place'—not like dat' one ovah' thar'. Yu' know preacher man, it jus' dawned me dat' I could mount a white niggah' head on 'nother pike to sorta' offset dah' other three. Oh, I'm jus' jokin', don't worry 'bout it pretty boy." Boyd was sneering at Reggie as he spoke.

Notably, "the tables can always turn". There were examples of slave owners as cruel as Boyd Rose who would mysteriously disappear and never be heard of again. Boyd had to know that his actions put him at risk of being a target for his own slaves and of course, this only intensified his existing paranoia and shocking cruelty.

South Carolina had slave codes that were designed to protect the slaves against cruelty. However, local law enforcement, being sympathetic to slave owners, often looked the other way rather than enforce them. Additionally, the remoteness of the plantations made it difficult for law enforcement to visibly see what was going on even if they did want to enforce the laws. This inaction by law enforcement even extended to overlooking mob action at a public gathering. In the case of Rose, it would be very possible that the constable could know about the display of heads mounted in the front of the Rose plantation, but would choose to ignore it knowing that Rose would have a lot of support in the community. Simply, if he had taken action against Rose, it could cost him his job.

"Boyd, Reggie is obedient an' knows his place."

"Does he now?" Boyd mocked. "It jus' doesn't look like it to me. In fact, preacher, I kinda' think dat' yu' gotta' little of dat' niggah' lover in yu' like dat' Yankee dat' dey' shoulda' hung. Yu' got yur' display niggah' ovah' thar' trailin' 'long wit' yu'. Yu' two almost act like two lovers—jus' gallivantin' 'round lookin' sorta' like two court jesters jus' dancin' merrily away. I'm jus' waitin' to see dah' two of yah' holdin' hands—how sweet a couple dah' two of yu' would make. Din' I would kill both of yah' on dah' spot. Now, how does dat' set wit' yu', preacher man?"

"Boyd, I know yu' are 'in yur' cup', so I'm goin' to ignore what yu' are sayin'. Look, I didn't come out hyeh' to argue wit' yu'," Reverend Hibbard snapped, "I came out hyeh' to preach to yur' niggahs'—pure an' simple!"

"All right, preacher." In Boyd's evil mind he knew there would be another time to challenge Hibbard. "Let's git' out to dah' quarters—dey're all out thar' waitin' fo' yu'."

As Reverend Hibbard and Reggie had prepared to exit, Mrs. Rose made a farewell statement. "It was a pleasure seein' yu' 'gain, preacher. Be sur' to take good care of dat' 'bery special personal servant."

As soon as Mrs. Rose finished speaking, she knew that she had made a major faux pas that would bring the wrath of her husband down upon her. Her words had barely left her mouth when Boyd snapped and slapped her in the face, knocking the dipstick across the room. "Yu' little jade, I spotted yu' earlier lookin' at dat' clabber colored niggah', lookin' at him wit' a twinklin' in yur' eyes, an' now referrin' to him as a 'bery special personal servant. I'm gonna' deal wit' yu' later, an' it ain't gonna' be sweet. A married white woman flirtin' wit' a niggah'! Oh, I've jus' seen it all! I'm gonna' put some serious stripes on yu' lickety-split!" Rose's face was flush with color as sweat profusely ran down his face as he continued to rant and rave.

"Please, Boyd," she pleaded. "I know he's a niggah', an' yu' know I wouldn't flirt wit' a niggah'. I'm sorry if yu' thought dat'. I was jus' tryin' to be nice," Mrs. Rose pleaded.

"Yu' shut up, yu' niggah' lovin' wench—not 'nother word from yu'."

Mrs. Rose ran out of the room as Boyd turned to Reverend Hibbard and said, "Well preacher, let's git' out to dah' quarters, an' if yur' fancy niggah' causes any more trouble on my plantation, he will be dealin' wit' me, not yu'!" Boyd Rose quickly shifted his glaring eyes over to Reggie and stated, "Is dat' clear, half-breed?"

"Yes sir!" Reggie responded.

"Yu're damn right," Boyd blurted out while looking at Reggie and Reverend Hibbard. "Now say it wit' conviction! Yu' know it makes me sick to see my own wife flirtin' wit' dis' damn niggah' dat' I'm forced to look at. I jus' so badly wanta' kill yu' right now. Damn, I can't stomach yu'!"

"Yes sir!" Reggie respectfully and firmly responded a second time.

Boyd gained back some of his composure. "Good, yu'd better say, yes sir an' say it wit' conviction. An' 'member, I'll be keepin' my eye on yu'. Now let's git' out to dah' quarters," he gruffly commanded.

Reverend Hibbard stepped in front of Boyd at this point. "Boyd, we're leavin'. Yu're 'four sheets to dah' wind', an' I'm not goin' to preach under des' conditions. I know yu' are goin' to beat yur' wife when we leave, but 'member, if yu' harm her, yu'll have to answer to God."

"Preacher, yu' don't come on to my property an' threaten Boyd Rose or give him orders." Furious, he poked a finger into Reverend Hibbard's chest as he went on. "I only answer to dah' debil'. Besides, I kin' tell yu' an' yur' little Sambo are chompin' at dah' bit to git' out of hyeh'." Boyd knew he had successfully intimidated both of them, and he enjoyed every minute of it. "Preacher, yu' an' my wife are both niggah' lovers. Dah' two of yu' jus' make me sick! Now git' dah' hell out of hyeh' as quick as yu' kin' say 'jack splat an' don't look back'. Yu' know I've still got a good mind to dust dah' jacket of yur' half-breed. I wouldn't kill him, but it would be one beatin' he'd 'member. I guarantee he wouldn't look pretty fo' all dah' ladies anymore."

As Boyd spoke, he knew his nefarious reputation would not be called into question. Reverend Hibbard and Reggie didn't doubt that he was deadly serious. Rushing to the barn Reggie quickly hitched up the horses and they were on their way.

Once on the road, Reverend Hibbard turned to Reggie and spoke. "I had a sinkin' feelin' dat' we might not git' out of thar' alive. Dat' man is a bulldog from Hades! I think God will understand if we don't go back thar'. I knew we were 'skatin' on thin ice' when we were greeted by dat' display of heads mounted on dose' pikes—we shoulda' turned an' 'kicked dah' dust' to git' out of thar' at dat' time. I feel real pity toward his wife, poor thin'. Kin'yu' imagine livin' wit' dat' man. Yu' saw how his wife looks. She looks like a fugitive from dah' grave, an' I'm' 'fraid, it's only gonna' git' worse fo' her."

"Master, I'm jus' glad dat' yu' chose to 'ride hell fo' leather' an' git' us out of thar'." The relief in Reggie's voice came through loud and clear. "I began to wonder if Mr. Rose wasn't dah' debil' himself'. Master, yu' said earlier dat' barkin' dogs seldom bite, but dat's one dog dat' barks an' bites. Worse yet, master, I feel 'sponsible fo' what he might do to his wife."

Reggie had seen the horror on her face. The mere hint of fondness between a married white woman and a black man would be expected to bring about a reprisal that could very well be marked with violence and even death, while it would be acceptable for a white man to have a sexual liaison with a black woman. This double standard blatantly existed throughout the South. Reggie was keenly aware of this and took strident efforts to avoid any contact with white women.

Earlier, Reggie had to experience the wrath of this double standard in his own life with Colonel Marshall's actions toward Anastasia. Now Reggie could only pray that Anastasia had been able to fend off his advances. He agonized over this every day— wondering about the fate of his beloved wife.

Reverend Hibbard recognized it was time to lighten the conversation. "Yu' shouldn't be held 'sponsible for how yu' look, Reggie. I could see dat' Boyd disliked yu' a lot 'cuz' a little of dah' 'green-eyed monster' dey' call jealously, came up. Let me ask yu' 'bout somethin' more pleasant. Our day has been tryin' thus far. Did yu' know dat' eventually dah' Glorious Fourth will be comin' up? Do yu' know what dat' means?"

"It's dah' celebration of our nation's independence from England," answered Reggie. He really wanted to say a celebration of the white people's independence, but he knew that he could not. It illuminated how little white people thought of blacks. They could not possibly understand that the black people were always left out of any celebration.

"Reggie, have yu' ever been to a camp meetin'?"

"Master, I went to a camp meetin' wit' my young master, Albert, an' I really enjoyed it." If he expressed his true feelings on this subject he knew that Reverend Hibbard would not be happy.

"Well, dah' best camp meetin' in des' parts is dah' 'Ole' Timber Ridge Camp Meetin' Arbor' to celebrate dah' Glorious Fourth. I go every year, an' dis' year will be no 'ception—an' guess what? Yu're goin' wit' me."

"Master, I would be honored to 'tend wit' yu.'" Reggie knew he did not have a choice.

Toward evening, the buggy arrived back at Hibbard Manor. Reverend Hibbard chose to forego evening devotions. However, he assured Reggie that morning devotions would still be in order.

When Reggie retired for the evening, he gave some thought to Boyd Rose's conduct toward him. He pondered, could Boyd Rose in his own paranoia and cruel thinking be obsessed with black people in general? He had observed a pattern with evil people similar to Boyd Rose, who exhibited such deep racial hatred against black people that they became obsessed, almost to the point where in some fashion they were almost possessed by the very people they commanded. It was very ironic and it particularly disturbed him to recognize this paradox. Unfortunately, Reggie believed that only a few lucid thinking people could ever recognize this contradiction that was so apparent to him.

***

After a few months, Reggie had settled into his role as Reverend Hibbard's personal servant. Both felt comfortable with their relationship. Reggie's assistance on the plantation continued to be treasured by Hibbard. In late June as the two were chatting over breakfast, Reverend Hibbard decided he needed to solicit some advice. "I need yur' opinion—I'm jus' curious, Reggie, what do yu' think 'bout dah' way dat' I operate my plantation?"

"Master, I think yu've done a good job pastorin' throughout dah' area. Regardin' dah' operation of yur' plantation, I'd rather speak in general terms. Dah' overseer role in dah' South is based on how much dah' he kin' produce. Dah' more cotton the overseer produces, dah' more he makes. However, he doesn't own dah' field hands or dah' land, so he doesn't necessarily have an interest in dah' long term affects of the soil.' In addition, to the exhaustion of the soil, dah' field hands are often overworked resultin' in dah'eventual demise of dah' plantation. His interests, unlike the plantation owner are often not in dah' best interests of dah' field hands nor dah' long term conditions of dah' land. So who's left holdin' dah' bag—the plantation owner!"

"Reggie," Reverend Hibbard asked, "are yu' suggestin' dat' Mr. Wilkins, my overseer, is not doin' a good job?" The reverend sat expressionless as he digested Reggie's thinking and opinions and how they related to his property and his overseer.

"Master, I'm dah' servant an' I can't answer dat' question," Reggie replied. "I hyeh' yu' complain 'bout dah' fact dat' yur' plantation is failin'. Master, yu' need to ride over yur' crops an' see what's goin' on fo' yur'self. 'Member dat' Nero fiddled while Rome burned."

"Reggie, I have to admit dat' I'm fightin' to keep my place goin', an' it may be by dah' grace of God dat' I'm still hyeh'! I'm jus' gittin' by on borrowed funds, an' dat' could be runnin' out shortly. I'm prayin' to dah' good Lawd' fo' his help."

"Now, let's talk 'bout a better subject, dah' Glorious Fourth. Next week we will be leavin', an' I can't wait to git' out of hyeh' fo' 'while. Also, I'm gonna' take yur' 'vice 'bout my plantation an' 'mediately be more active on dah' business end of dis' operation. I'm gonna' ride from corner to corner on dah' property an' talk wit' all my people an' git' a handle on dah' situation directly from dah' field hands."

It was obvious that Reggie's well-chosen words regarding successful plantation management had a positive impact on Reverend Hibbard. Meanwhile, Reggie appreciated his master embracing his ideas. Applying the observations and experiences at the successfully run, and lucrative Oak Manor could help to reverse the adverse course at Hibbard's plantation. The relationship of the two men had become truly unusual—a slave dispensing business advice and the master not only accepting it, but also taking action on it.

Reverend Hibbard and Reggie worked from sunrise to sunset and into the evening, straightening out the plantation. Finally in a moment of relaxation, the preacher was able to once again talk about the Glorious Fourth and the impending camp meeting. The opportunity gave them a much needed break from their plantation activities. "Reggie, I'm so 'cited fo' us to be leavin'fo' dah' camp meetin'." He spoke in such a positive manner while always providing details of what they could expect to see.

Soon Reverend Hibbard announced, "I kin' hardly git' ovah' how fast dah' last few days have gone. Dis' is my absolute favorite time of dah' year."

"Master, I know I tole' yu' earlier dat' dah' camp meetin' I attended in Virginny' was enjoyable. I kin' 'magine dat' dis' will be every bit as good an' probably even better." Reggie refrained from expressing his view that the camp meeting in Virginny' was for the pleasure of the white people.

"Reggie, since our conversation, I have put more thought into how I run my plantation, an' I've considered somethin' else. I never used dah' whip, but sometimes I wonder. Seems like I might have some 'seein' eye niggahs' who need to be watched more closely—turn yur' head, an' dey' quit workin'."

"Master, I would never recommend dah' whip." Reggie spoke in a soft but very serious tone. He knew whatever he said to his master would be considered. He deeply felt it was his God-given duty to protect the slaves from the whip, and hopefully his honored position would help him convince his master that the use of the whip was not part of the teachings of Jesus Christ. "I personally think indolence kin' best be combated wit' kindness an' compassion an' not a whip."

"Reggie, yu' do have some 'bery meaningful ideas," Hibbard stated while totally engrossed in what Reggie had to say.

"Master, I don't want to be labeled a brown nosed sycophant who tells on others an' flatters dah' master, as I've been 'round dose' types, an' I don't like 'dem." At times Reggie felt uneasy and awkward advising and confiding in him, again, something very rarely done by slaves.

"Reggie, I know yu' are not like dat'," Reverend Hibbard assured. "Yu' are different din' any servant I've had, an' it really is a credit to yu'. Why would yu' even worry 'bout what dah' others think of yu'? Fo' now I'm goin' to heed yur' advice."

Reggie was pleased his master once again would listen to his suggestions since it meant that slaves on the Hibbard plantation would be spared the whip. With an obvious sigh of relief, Reggie asked, "Master, how did last year's camp meetin' go fo' yu'?" Reggie remained baffled that as a slave his recommendation to not use the whip was accepted—how ironic.

With a chuckle, Reverend Hibbard responded, "I hate to mention dis' since it could jinx me, but last year durin' dah' camp meetin' my 'piles' flared up, an' it was really uncomfortable on my bottom. I feel much better now, but when we git' to dah' camp meetin', dah' first thing I'm goin' to git' is some of Dr. Townsend's Sasparilla. Dey' say it kin' cure anythin'!" Reggie personally found the word piles to describe hemorrhoids distasteful.

Reggie hesitated to further discuss Reverend Hibbard's physical maladies and instead focused on the impending camp meeting that would be the highlight of the year for the preacher. "Master, observin' the Glorious Fourth wit' dah' revivals an' dah' camaraderie of mixin' wit' everybody at dah' various booths will certainly be an eventful experience. I share yur' 'citement in attendin' dah' camp meetin'."

The two men chatted late into the evening, shared devotions, and Reggie went to bed while Reverend Hibbard sat up and studied his Bible.

CHAPTER FOURTEEN

Finally the day arrived and the two arose early in the morning for breakfast, packed up and departed for the camp meeting. It was one of those typical summer days in South Carolina—sunny and hot, which didn't dampen the positive attitude the preacher displayed. Reverend Hibbard certainly appeared happier, which could only make Reggie feel better. Reggie asked, "Master, what makes dis' camp meetin' so 'bery special?"

"Reggie, how could it git' any better din' dis'—combinin' dah' celebration of dah' War of Rebellion wit' worshippin' God? It can't git' better din' dis'—wouldn't yu' 'gree?" Now dat's what makes dis' so 'bery special. I'm happier din' a lark. Right now I could jus' 'turn cartwheels'."

"Master, I do 'gree, but I jus' hope dat' God will still reign superior ovah' dah' Fourth of July in the hearts of the people," Reggie said this politely, knowing that most people would be there just to socialize treating the religious services secondary.

"Yu' are funny Reggie, anyhow, dis' day is beautiful an' in so many ways. Jus' look 'round—Virginny' can't top dis'. Take a look at all dah' cotton fields wit' dah' niggahs' happily singin' an' workin' 'way. Yu' know dah' niggahs' love it 'round hyeh'." He paused a moment. "Well, maybe we all love it, not jus' dah' niggahs'. Think 'bout how lucky dey' are to be hyeh' 'stead of stuck livin' in a hole somewhar' in Africky'. I say dat' 'cuz' I heard somebody say dat' dey' actually lived in holes. Maybe dat's' 'nother reason dey' are so happy, wouldn't yu' 'gree? We got 'dem out of thar' holes in dat' dark continent—Afriky', an' now dey' kin' be hyeh' wit' us livin' dah' good life. Isn't dat' true—we are doin' 'dem a big favor? Sometimes, I wish I could be jus' as carefree an' happy as all dah' niggahs' out in dah' field!"

"Yes, Master, dey' are fortunate to be hyeh' as we are doin' 'dem a big favor." As Reggie spoke, he had to bite his lip. He knew he was lying through his teeth as he parsed his words. Slaves sang as they worked trying to make the best of a terrible situation. Singing was a tradition handed down from Africa and was maintained here in the United States. It was used very effectively in maintaining a positive attitude. People were able to pass the time much easier while often working under unbearable conditions in the fields.

When Reverend Hibbard explained that Africans lived in holes, Reggie wanted him to expand on that and tell him the whole truth. Armed white slave raiders along with their black helpers would raid villages seizing people for enslavement. To escape being enslaved people fled, and if a hole was available that provided safety, it could make for an ideal hiding place. It was never intended as permanent living quarters—only a temporary refuge. This explanation would help to dispel the widely accepted falsehood that native Africans lived in extremely primitive living quarters. This particular misrepresentation of the truth by white folks was used to justify that Africans were so much better off living here. These false beliefs enabled the white Southerners to feel peace and comfort with the bondage system and help them to feel comfortable from any guilt for their actions against black people.

Reverend Hibbard failed to elaborate on another falsehood that white southerners harbored. As previously stated, white slave raiders commanded their black helpers to seize innocent Africans and forcibly drive them to the port cities off the coast of West Africa. They would then be transported by ship out of Africa and then to America. In telling this story, white Southerners always omit the white slave raider's involvement in seizing the black people in their native villages for enslavement. This belies the truth by falsely asserting that fellow blacks were "solely" responsible for seizing and driving blacks in chains to the West African port cities where the white slave traders waited for the black drivers to bring their captives. This unfortunate myth—entirely blaming fellow blacks for their initial enslavement continued to serve white people quite well. They were able to falsely believe that slavery was something that blacks were responsible for as the white people were mainly innocent bystanders who only agreed to "transport" them out of Africa where in their twisted thinking, they would have a better life out of Africa.

Correctly, Reverend Hibbard had assured Reggie they could reach camp by day's end. It proved to be a pleasant ride without any problems along the way. When stopping on occasion to rest and water the horses, they were also able to provide for their own needs.

Having established a positive relationship with Reverend Hibbard, Reggie felt he could ask a sensitive question. "Master, may I ask you somethin' dat' I have always wondered 'bout?"

"Reggie, what is it?" The weather was beautiful, and Reverend Hibbard was in a very good mood, more than ready to respond to Reggie's questions.

"Master, as a Christian, I wonder how yu' kin' justify dah' bondage system, which we know has come under criticism, especially up North an' in many parts of dah' world. President Jefferson, a Virginian, regardin' dah' bondage system once stated, 'but as it is we have dah' wolf by dah' ear, an' we kin' neither hold him, nor safely let him go. Justice is in one side an' self-preservation in dah' other'." Reggie hoped he had chosen the right quote so he wouldn't upset Reverend Hibbard.

"Regardin' President Jefferson, I respect his opinion but dat' is all it is—an opinion. Yu're askin' a delicate question but one dat' I'm more din' prepared to answer. For me personally, my father owned dis' plantation, an' yes, I inherited it from him, which also included my field hands an' personal servants. Now hyeh' we are today, an' I've become dah' guardian of my father's institution, a tradition dat's been handed down from his father to him an' now me. Dat' is dah' answer—short an' sweet. Now Reggie, yu' tell me, what would yu' do?" It was apparent that Reverend Hibbard felt very confident with the old "pass the buck" defense.

Reggie answered hesitatingly, "Master I really don't know." He wanted to say he would free them, but that answer could cause trouble for him. "Master gittin' back to yur' answer without steppin' on any toes, yu're sayin' dat' it has nothin' to do wit' bein' right or wrong. It's based on tradition. Is dat' correct?" The answer Reverend Hibbard had provided struck a painful chord with Reggie. He recalled "tradition" being played out seeing Albert having to give up his friendship with the black children on the Marshall plantation when they turned eleven. Tradition also included being pummeled by Donald for merely talking to one of the guests at Oak Manor in a so-called inappropriate manner. There were many other examples where "tradition" came to bear. Reggie pondered the significance of Reverend Hibbard's answer— not acknowledging any fault, instead, providing an answer to the question by merely shifting the blame on to his inheritance. Based on Reggie's experiences, he had to ponder the merits of basing decisions on "tradition" knowing that just because it is a "tradition" may not make it right.

"Reggie, I really want to git' off dis' subject. It's makin' me feel a little uneasy. Again, it's not a matter fo' debate. It's all 'bout tradition, an' let's jus' leave it at dat'." It was clear that Reverend Hibbard felt absolved, and he didn't want to have to explore the issue any further.

Reggie knew Reverend Hibbard meant what he just said and switched to another topic. "I'm really lookin' forward to dah' festivities comin' up today," Reggie stated. He realized he could have gone too far with Reverend Hibbard and he felt relieved when the subject was changed.

Later in the day, their excitement grew as they approached the camp grounds. Finally, Reverend Hibbard announced, "Reggie, we are hyeh', an' I jus' can't wait to pitch our tent!" Reverend Hibbard's excitement could rival that of a child left alone in a candy store.

Reverend Hibbard had purposely arrived early enough to stake out his yearly campsite, where for the most part, the same people camped near him. Camaraderie abounded amongst them since they knew each other fairly well.

The campsite was a desirable location outside of town in a large clearing surrounded by picturesque pines that provided ample coolness against the hot July weather. Situated along the banks of a river, the spacious grounds were sectioned off into four areas. The front section alongside the road was the vendor area where crude booths were set up. Everything imaginable could be found for sale with each merchant hawking his or her specialty. There was fodder for the horses, fresh fruits and vegetables, preserves and other foods. In addition, confections, dry goods, herbs, roots, salves, ointments, mementos, clothing, hats, and an assortment of medicines for whatever ails you. Finally, whisky, wine, lemonade, and water provided for those who needed to slake their thirst. In general, a wide variety of items were available. In addition, competition was keen as there would be several dealers "hawking" the same merchandise. Of course vendors were always prepared to negotiate.

Another section was provided for the camp grounds, which were located behind the booths. In addition there were the stables, which encompassed a large area. The entertainment and ministry section was at the far right—a crude amphitheater of pine boards and rows of elevated logs, which provided the seating. The stage area was strategically placed and was made out of crude materials with a railing around three sides. At one end of the center of the stage was a large pulpit and table, a roughly-made desk, a trunk for storage purposes and several chairs. Nothing of real value was represented on the stage.

The eclectic crowd was a true cross-section of the community. Christians were in abundance as well as non-believers and sinners who somehow all managed to mingle and tolerate each other. Then there were the wealthy plantation owners who came with their personal servants, which contrasted with the much greater number of poor whites who did not own a personal servant, nor for that matter any slaves at all. Finally, there was the presence of a very small middle class who were likely merchants from the nearby towns. They might own a slave or two, but more often their contact with slaves was usually confined to using "hired out" slaves at their place of business as needed.

An interesting conflict, which Reverend Hibbard was quick to address, was the endless battle of the church to save souls pitted against the large numbers who came to socialize and drink. The primary purpose of the camp meeting was always religious edification. Unfortunatly as a sordid contrast, alcohol represented the primary interest for many—their spiritual values were in the bottle and not at the pulpit. It was a never-ending battle for the church, which oftentimes they appeared to be losing.

"Reggie, look 'round—hyeh' we are in dah' land of milk an' honey. I've been comin' hyeh' ever since I was knee-high to a grasshopper, an' dis' event seems to grow in size every year. Yu' kin' count hundreds of people at any time. 'Nough of dat', let's pitch our tent an' git' set up. Reverend Hibbard paused and smiled as he looked around, almost inhaling his surroundings. "Reggie, I'm so excited to be hyeh' an' share all dis' wit' yu'. I want yu' to take dah' horse an' buggy to dah' livery an' din' git' right back hyeh'. When we git' set up, I'll take yu' 'round dah' grounds to sorta' help yu' git' yur' feet wet. We'll go to dah' vendor's section first—dat's whar' everyone kin' be found. 'Bery few stay 'round thar' tent, thars' too much to do. I can't blame dem', 'cuz' dey' are hyeh' to have fun but above all, git' spiritually cleansed. Of course I'm very troubled at how some people have fun. As a man of God, seein' people staggerin' 'round' all liquored-up, actin' the fool on wobbly legs, like a new born calf—well it's difficult to handle! Fortunately in dah' morning dey' aren't as bad. But wait 'til evenin'—then 'Katie, bar dah' door'!" Reverend Hibbard just shook his head as he continued to talk. "Oh Lawdy'! Dat's when dey' have had time to let dah' alcohol take ovah' an' din' dey' really let thar' hair down. Reggie, it's dah' liquor consumption dat' I hate 'bout dis' place! Quite often dey' don't know when to stop an' din' dey' git' sick out of thar' minds an' bodies! I've seen more din' one man, pukin' up his insides actin' like he was 'bout to turn inside out an' die. I git' so despondent when I see dah' likes of all dis' carryin' on—dah' debil's sanctuary, when I so badly want dis' place to be dah' land of milk an' honey."

Hibbard's emphatic position against alcohol was expected and fully understood. Reggie in a smaller scale had lived and witnessed the horrendous alcohol-related problems associated with the Southern ante-bellum period. In his heart, he fully agreed with Reverend Hibbard's assessment of the problem.

Reverend Hibbard and Reggie set up their campsite and still had ample time to visit the various booths as the sun began to set behind the pines. Reverend Hibbard was in a mood that Reggie enjoyed. "Reggie, do yu' have a sweet tooth?" Reverend Hibbard had a slightly mischievous look as he spoke with a twinkle in his eye.

"Master, I do enjoy confections, 'specially toffee." Reggie was very excited since candy was rarely ever given to slaves.

"Fo' bein' such a dutiful servant, I'm goin' to reward yu' an' buy yu' some toffee. Personally, I happen to have a fondness fo' lickorice' even though it tends to give me dah' runs. Do yu' git' my meanin', Reggie?" He displayed an embarrassing look as he snickered.

Reggie pondered why he couldn't just say diarrhea, but didn't want to appear disrespectful. "I think yu' are sayin' dat' lickorice' tends to act on yu' like a laxative, master."

"Reggie, yur' master is goin' to have a tough time puttin' one ovah' on yu'. Speakin' of my rear end, my piles have not flared up. I do believe God is rewardin' me fo' bein' such a good Christian."

After evening had descended, the two sat down on some tree stumps and continued their conversation. "Master, what really amazes me 'bout dis' camp meetin' is dah' number of pine tar torches givin' off so much light in dah' dead of dah' night. I kin' almost picture a Roman army encampment prior to a major battle." Reggie had always been impressed by the books he had read on the Roman Empire.

"What a rich imagination yu' have, Reggie. I do 'gree dat' it is somethin' to see." Reverend Hibbard recognized that Reggie's intelligence stood apart from anybody he had ever met.

"Master, I'm curious 'bout dah' activities an' events we are goin' to see."

"Reggie, dah most 'portant activity in my judgment is dah' ministry programs. Ministers from dah' Baptists, 'Piscopalians, Methodists an' Presbyterians will be heard. Of course, I'm mainly interested in dah' Baptist program. As a matter of fact, when Reverend Higgins, dah' Presbyterian minister, 'pears, we're leavin'—I don't 'gree wit' his teachins'."

"Master, kin' yu' elaborate on dis'?" Reggie's face reflected an interest in his comments.

"Reggie as a youngster, I was given an ample dose of James McGready an' Barton Stone, who preached throughout dah' Carolinnys'. Dey' called it dah' Second Great Awakening, which encouraged less formality an' a closer an' more intimate relationship wit' Jesus Christ. Reverend Higgins tends to be 'bery stiff an' formal, an' I firmly 'lieve dat' he does not have a close relationship wit' Jesus Christ. He's sort of opposite as to how I was brought up, an' I don't respect him." McGready and Stone had a profound influence on the Protestant church in the South, they believed that God can be reached with love and compassion and not just through fear of punishment as the old "hell fire and brimstone" teachings.

Reggie, nodding his head in agreement, stated, "My early master was an Episcopalian, an' his beliefs tended to be more dogmatic din' yurs', master. I 'gree wit' yur' relationship wit' Jesus, which is more intimate." Reggie early in life had learned to separate himself from those who he felt were more religious, often more authoritative and arrogant from those he felt were more spiritually led. He believed the slaves had to be more spiritual since their church would be no more than a shack hidden in the woods with only the bare essentials for comfort and all they could do was light the place up with joyful singing. He felt they could have a better opportunity to be more spiritual under these conditions.

"Thank yu'. I must admit dat' I never heard of dah' word dogmatic, but I think I know what yu' mean. Anyhow, Reggie, have yu' ever heard of Charles Finney?"

"Master, I have not."

"Well, Reggie, I have been mistaken fo' him an' I always take it as a compliment. He's a 'bery strikin' figure wit' long blond hair an' rivetin' blue eyes. He's also a major part of a movement called dah' Second Great Awakenin', but unfortunately he comes out of New York. My Christian values have directed me not to hold his Northern ties 'gainst him; atter' all, he is generally considered to be dah' leader of dah' Second Great Awakenin'. I would definitely put my stock in Charles Finney, even though he is a Northerner. He preaches dat' every person is free to choose if dey' want to live a Christian life or be sinner. If a sinner chooses dah' Lawd, dey' kin' seek salvation an' embrace spirtitual freedom. Now dat' is exactly what I preach."

"Master, I kin' understand why yu' feel dis' way. It really makes good sense havin' a free-spirited relationship wit' Jesus Christ." Interestingly, Reggie had known this was the method slaves had always used to communicate with God while often being mocked by whites for their outward passion. He found it ironic that many of the same people who would make fun of black people would end up worshiping God virtually in the same manner—especially the poor whites.

"Reggie, when I hear yu' talk like dis', it's music to my ears. An' speakin' 'bout music, dis' place is goin' to attract a big crowd since Harry Jones, dah' popular banjo player from North Carolinny' is goin' be hyeh'. Dey say he kin' even outstrum dah' great Joe Sweeney. Also, dey' are goin' to have a group of Negroes dressed up in patriotic clothin' who do a great song an' dance routine. Dah' black-face Campbell Minstrels are performin' as well. I'm tole' dey' are really a sight to see—a bunch of white men wit' thar' faces painted all black."

It had been a long day for Reverend Hibbard and Reggie, so they returned to their campsite for a good night of sleep. In bed, although exhausted, Reverend Hibbard was talkative. "Reggie are yu' lonely wit'out yur' wife?"

"Master, I love her so much, an' yes, it gits' lonely wit'out her. As we talk I'm thinkin' of her. We were separated from each other shortly atter' we were married. I'm extremely saddened thinkin' 'bout her welfare everyday."

"Reggie, I know yu' tole' me earlier dat' niggahs' have feelin' jus' like white people. I'm jus' not use to seein' or believin' dat'—niggahs' seem to be able to bounce from one to another, absent of any permanent commitments."

"Master, I've heard white people compare Negroes to animals. Even if Negroes were animals, which they are not, don't yu' believe dat' animals have feelin's fo' thar' young?" Reggie was stunned that Reverend Hibbard, a preacher, could be so ignorant of the truth.

"Reggie, yu' have a way of throwin' me fo' a loop."

Reggie added, "'Sides master, don't yu' think dat' I could be or would be more sensitive an' lovin' to my wife din' somebody like Master Rose is to his? We even witnessed him knock his wife 'cross dah' room."

"I must admit dat' some of dah' white people I have 'countered were a pretty poor representation of Christians. Take people like Boyd Rose or Ike Horn, dey' are as bad as it gits'. I guess times have sur' changed from dah' good old days when people weren't quite so mean." Reverend Hibbard knew that Reggie had presented his position very well and he could only come up with an answer that made little sense.

"Master, do yu' find in dah' South dat' dah' men are meaner din' dah' women?"

"As a preacher I kin' safely say dat' dah' women are dah' ones wit' compassion. We've probably talked 'bout dis' 'fore. Dat's what dah' white Southern males need—more compassion!" This touches on a widely-held belief that women do have more compassion than men.

"I would certainly 'gree wit' yu', master. Somethin' else, which may be a little personal. Have yu' ever been in love or come close to gittin' married?"

"Reggie, I'm glad yu' asked dat' question. I honestly never met a woman dat' I really ever wanted to git' hitched wit'. It's a funny thin'. God made me different an' all my life I have been attracted to men. I jus' can't help dah' way I am. I have always been able to control my emotions until yu' came along." As the minister spoke, he suddenly began to look a little differently at Reggie as he moved a little closer like a spider on its prey. Reggie felt very uncomfortable and knew the preacher was looking for something he was not willing to participate in. His tone of voice seemed lower—softer, almost like he was trying to charm him. Reggie regretted asking him the question concerning his feelings toward women, knowing that he had opened "Pandora's box".

He had recognized earlier that the preacher may have an affinity toward men, realizing that on occasion, he had found him staring at him in a most unusual manner. This represented a difficult situation since he was enslaved to this man. He tried to find the right words to politely avoid the reverend's advances. "Master, I kin' honestly say dat' I only git' 'cited ovah' my wife, Anastasia."

"Reggie, yu' know yu' are dah' handsomest specimen of a man dat' I've ever laid my eyes on!" The words were said in a very soft, sensuous way, the intentions quite obvious.

"Thank yu' fo' dah' compliment, master." Reggie knew that Reverend Hibbard's overtures were going to get more explicit and that he would have to find a way to defuse his advances.

"Reggie, I'm jus' curious, when yu' use to go swimmin' wit' dah' darkies an' all of yu' went jaybird naked, did yu' ever notice dat' dah' darkies were well-endowed?"

"Master, I never really took notice." Reggie had heard that white men liked to talk about black men having larger penises. Knowing this, he was not at all surprised that Reverend Hibbard would want to enter into this subject.

"Reggie, we all know dat' God made dah' Negro different from white folks, an' I'm curious 'bout yu'. I know dat' your blood is soiled wit' Negro blood, so dat' bein' dah' case, are yu' long at dah' penis like a big black buck?" Reggie ignored the negative connotation about his blood being soiled, knowing that he was enslaved to this man, making it difficult to challenge him.

"Master, yu' know dat' I love my wife!" Reggie responded nervously trying to restrain his anger and his discomfort with Hibbard's advances.

Reverend Hibbard's composure continued to change as he looked at Reggie, slowly moving closer, trying to gently touch his legs. "Reggie, I think fondly of yu' in so many ways. I have never been wit' 'nother man in my life, but way down deep as I tole' yu' earlier, I've always wanted to be wit' one—dah' right one, an' dat' man is yu'! Reggie would yu' slowly an' gently peel off yur' clothes fo' yur' master's joy an' stand close to me? I git' so 'cited jus' thinkin' 'bout it, an' I beseech yu' to fulfill my needs." Hibbard's hands trembled, his brow was moist, and he spoke just above a whisper as his excitement grew.

"I know dat' I cannot defy my master, but in dis' case I must. It's written in dah' Bible!"

"Reggie, I know dah' Bible, an' I know dat' God recognizes dat' we are all sinners an' fallible, an' He gives us all a little ground to error in our ways. Good Lawd', I'm only human an' I can't help how I feel." Then the reverend started to take off his clothing and ordered Reggie to do the same.

Reggie simply stated. "Master, I cannot!"

"Reggie, I've wanted yu' dah' day I set my eyes on yu'. Normally, I would have dah' strength to ignore dis' side of me, but yu' overwhelm me—yu' fill me wit' such 'citement. Touch me an' yu'll see! Don't deny me, please!"

"Master again, doesn't dah' Bible denounce dis' kind of behavior?"

"Yes, but as I jus' tole' yu' dah' Bible understands dat' we are only human! Let me make dis' clear—I'm dah' master, an' yu' are dah' servant—yu' have to obey me."

"Master, I'm not helpless to physically oppose."

"Reggie, do not disappoint yur' master, 'jus' cooperate dis' one time!"

"Master, I'm married, an' I love my wife."

"All right, din'!" The reverend feeling rejected and angry answered in a menacing tone, "If I ever hyeh' dat' yu' said anythin' to anybody 'bout what happened tonight, I'll put yu' in my pocket an' sell yu' cheap to Boyd Rose— now how does dat' sound to yu'?" It was obvious that Reverend Hibbard was acting defensively out of being rejected, and that he was going to take a very tough position against Reggie to ensure that his reputation would not be soiled.

"Master, I would never say a word to anybody, an' dat's a promise! Sellin' me to Boyd Rose would be a death sentence. Yu' know I want to stay wit' yu'!"

"Reggie, I don't bluff. If yu' tell anybody 'bout tonight din' yu' are goin' to have a new master, Boyd Rose. Meanwhile, I'm still goin' to have to decide what I'm goin' to do wit' yu' since yu' know 'bout a side of my life dat' must be kept secret."

Reggie knew how fortunate he had been to avert the sexual advances of Reverend Hibbard. He was also aware their relationship would be drastically altered after he had rebuffed his advances. This could lead to Reverend Hibbard selling him off far away from the community so that his homosexual tendencies would remain a secret. But he also realized on the other hand, if he did sell Reggie to Boyd Rose that he could inform Rose about Hibbard's sexual proclivity. Of course that would probably prove disasterous for Hibbard, so it serves his best interest to sell Reggie to a slave trader and Reggie could disappear.

With deep thought concerning the disturbing situation that had arose between him and Reverend Hibbard, he felt in his heart that the preacher should not be condemned for his fondness toward men. Reverend Hibbard had informed him in the tent that he was never attracted to women. He explained that God made him different and for that reason, Reggie as a Christian believed he had no right being judgmental toward Reverend Hibbard. With that rational, Reggie felt somewhat comfortable with the situation and hoped it could be forgotten and would not surface again.

CHAPTER FIFTEEN

A fter a sleepless night resulting from having to reject the advances of Reverend Hibbard, Reggie began the new day, well aware that his relationship with his master had significantly changed, and not for the better.

Putting the incident that had just occurred behind them, Reverend Hibbard and Reggie made the rounds of the various booths, neither saying a word about the previous evening.

Reverend Hibbard knew many of the people in attendance, and he enjoyed mingling with everybody. His gregarious nature, demeanor, and unusual looks tended to attract people. Even after being rebuffed by Reggie, Reverend Hibbard's resiliency was in evidence as he was still able to maintain a positive attitude as he made his rounds.

Toward Reggie, the preacher suddenly turned hardened and aloof, which Reggie hoped would eventually soften with time. Above all, Reggie knew it was important for him to be nice to the reverend while hoping that their relationship would improve.

Reggie observed that the crowd in general was a bit coarser than what he had seen in Virginia. Some were wealthy and well-dressed while many maintained an average look, and still a large number had an impoverished look about them, wearing old and worn out clothing. Obvious class differences were excluded for this event as everybody mixed as one. Additionally, the appeal of the camp meeting ran the gamut from the young to the old—it truly represented an interesting cross section of the ante-bellum South.

As Reverend Hibbard had pointed out when they first arrived, the most popular booths were the ones that sold whisky and wine. Reggie's own observation concurred that Reverend Hibbard was correct in just how serious the problem was—some patrons frequented the booths dispensing alcohol in the morning and were intoxicated before noon. On the brighter side, the booths that sold confections were also very popular—the lure of candy attracted many, especially the children while putting smiles on their faces. Those that sold necessities, such as farm implements, fodder, and clothing also had a drawing power; it was reassuring to know that a practical side existed with the crowd.

Interestingly, religious items were also popular. Hymnals, Bibles, crosses, and other related items were in abundance. In addition, prayer groups were also a part of the agenda.

It was quite a contrast—alcohol being sold adjacent to a booth offering religious items. What stupefied Reggie was witnessing a man who was intoxicated wander into one of the religious booths to get spiritually cleansed. He recalled Reverend Hibbard commenting on what the world was coming to.

Buskers in colorful garb could be seen roaming throughout the crowds playing their musical instruments, hawking for money, while beggars providing nothing but desperation pleaded for some small change while providing nothing but a thank-you in exchange.

Hucksters worked the people as well selling a wide variety of items, the most popular being drugs, and homemade remedies that were supposed to cure anything and everything. Reverend Hibbard was happy to get his ample supply of Dr. Townsend's Sasparilla. Reggie, unlike Reverend Hibbard, was skeptical of the claims being made by the barkers, knowing so many people were desperate to believe anything they heard since they were suffering from ailments that could not or were not being properly treated. He recalled Albert receiving only painkillers and not getting the proper medications that could quite possibly have helped save his life. Unfortunatly, Albert was never properly diagnosed almost precluding any chance for his recovery. From time to time, Reggie reminded himself of Sarah informing him that in Boston, he would have been given much better treatment.

Reggie and Reverend Hibbard continued to spend much of the late morning navigating through the crowd. With their adventuresome spirit, they roamed around the camp and eventually found their way to a large group huddled near a booth. They found themselves listening to what sounded like an apocalyptic message that the world was coming to an end. The discourse was being delivered by a tall, middle aged, black-haired man with dark, raven like eyes. The leader certainly played his role perfectly. Dressed in a black robe, he had a mesmerizing influence over the crowd. His followers, all dressed in the same black clothes, maybe not quite as fancy, looked perfectly content sitting in a circle on the ground, while surrounding him and softly chanting in unusual tones, which combined with his oratorical skills. All this provided for a riveting atmosphere. Conspicuously situated front and center to the circle of his followers was a kettle accepting donations from passers-by. Reverend Hibbard quickly dismissed the entire group as a bunch of wicked charlatans who were sponsored by Satan. It further disturbed him to see the amount of money that had been collected, knowing that a sermon delivered by him would not bring in nearly the same amount of donations.

On a much darker side, a slave trader could be seen lurking about, his slaves chained and well-guarded. They remained on the perimeter nearly out of sight. As Reggie walked, he kicked stones while quietly shaking his head in disapproval—the camp meeting that celebrated the Fourth of July—democracy based on freedom and equality with a slave coffle lurking in the shadows of the event—what a contradiction that speaks volumes for how you cannot justify this evil system. Reggie concluded that fortunately the sponsors of the camp meeting shared his observation of the slave coffle. The slave trader knew to keep his coffle off to the side where they were to remain inconspicuous. Reggie pondered what the crowd reaction would be if the leader of the slave coffle brought the group of slaves "adorned in chains" into the vending area for a little "fresh air". Would the camp meeting officials welcome the slave coffle as a display of our own "democratic slavery" to help celebrate our glorious Fourth of July?" Reggie knew the answer to his own question. He knew the slave coffle represented a necessary evil that many Southerners would accept but only at a distance. It was obvious that the camp meeting officials kept the slave coffle out of sight for an obvious reason.

On this subject, since communications between the North and the South were almost nonexistent, Reggie wondered if the Northerners understood just how the general population of the South really felt about certain aspects of slavery. Many uninformed Northerners believed slavery was welcomed throughout the South without any reservations, not realizing that it was only tacitly accepted as a necessary but "dirty" institution. Furthermore, it was such a small number of people that owned slaves. He knew it would immensely improve relations between the North and the South if the Northeners were made aware of the true situation in the South. Certainly, the people who controlled the media and politics in the South were slave owners as well, and they were able to paint a colorful picture of slavery in the old South. He had heard that the slave owners did in fact have political control of the South, which would provide at least a partial explanation for this false picture. It was truly an unfortunate misrepresentation of the truth, which had the egregious effect of further dividing the North and the South since the full truth would never be allowed to be disclosed.

Finally after enjoying the day, Reverend Hibbard and Reggie slowly made their way to the stage area, which was colorfully draped with red, white, and blue bunting. Proudly displayed in front of the stage area was a large twenty-five star flag waving on a flag pole. In addition to the main flag, many in the crowd wore brightly dressed patriotic colors, while waving small flags in support of the Fourth of July.

Reverend Hibbard and Reggie were impressed and excited by the pomp and display. "Master, dey' really go all out down hyeh' to celebrate dah' War of Rebellion.'"

"Reggie, why should yu' be shocked? Dis' is South Carolinny', an' we honor dah' foundin' of dis' great nation more din' anybody in dah' country.'"

"Master, I certainly 'lieve dat' based on what I kin' see." Reggie could not express what he was really thinking. He did recall Colonel Marshall eloquently enlightening everybody that Virginia was the greatest state in the union, and now, he is hearing the same thing said about South Carolina. Truly, "states rights" was in evidence.

"Reggie, jus' sit back an' git' ready to enjoy dah' show."

The master of ceremonies emerged and moved quickly to the center of the stage. He was an obese, middle-aged man with a booming voice, dressed appropriately for the holiday in red, white and blue colors with an American flag pinned into his hat. As the band played, he marched around the podium and shouted enthusiastically over the music of the small band. "My brothers and sisters, welcome to dah' Ole' Timber Ridge Camp Meetin' Arbor. Dis' is dah' biggest an' best extravaganza anywhere honorin' our nation's birth. Jus' take a look 'round hyeh'—yu' kin' feel dah' patriotism. If yu' can't maybe yu' belong up North!"

The crowd boisterously reacted to the humor and continued to laugh at the slur directed at Northerners. Reggie recognized this brand of sarcasm. He smiled, while pondering if the North at public gatherings, made similar quips targeted against the South? He believed perhaps the South was more vociferous concerning this matter since states rights were far more important.

"Brothers and sisters," the master of ceremonies continued. "I wish dat' Northerners could git' dah' spirit like we have hyeh' in Ole' Carolinny'. I'm goin' to bet dat' dey' have a long ways to go. It begins hyeh' at dah' Ole' Timber Ridge Camp Meetin' Arbor, an' it's gonna' spread all over dis' country. Hallelujah, glory be, we've only jus' begun!"

"Well, folks, I see our first entertainers comin' out, so I better cut dis' short. I want to remind yu' dat' dah' Presbyterian minister, Reverend Higgins, will be providin' a spiritual message 'bery soon.

Now, I know y'all need to be spiritually cleansed—dat' should be dah' main reason we are all gathered hyeh'. Y'all know dat', so let's make every effort not to leave atter' dah' musical show! Now, ladies an' gentlemen, nuttin' kin' be finer fo' dah' Glorious Fourth din' some upliftin' music sung by our Negro singers—hyeh' dey' are straight from Charleston. They're goin' to sing a short song, *Gal from dah' South*, an' din' return later. I guarantee y'all are goin' to find 'dem funny an' entertainin'. Well, 'nough, of dis' talk—let's bring 'em out." The excited crowd roared and clapped enthusiastically looking forward to the exciting entertainment that was soon to begin. The music started, and the Negro singers took the stage.

The singers were dressed in red, white, and blue, their clothing made from higher quality, well-tailored fabric and not Negro cloth. The right pant legs and right sleeves were red, the midsections of the shirts were white, and the left pant legs and left sleeves were a bright blue. The entertainers also wore matching red, white and blue cone-shaped hats and pranced about as the music played. An older white man dressed in a tan suit led the eight singers and dancers. The crowd cheered and applauded the colorful performance.

Everyone seemed highly amused and thoroughly entertained by the patriotic display except Reggie. In his eyes, the singers looked and acted like a bunch of organ grinder monkeys, representing the "sambo image" in all their glory as white people so much enjoyed. He knew that someday, based on his premonitions, things were going to change and this form of entertainment would become frowned upon, and eventually disappear.

The band, the music, and the singing seemed to grow louder.

Ole' massa' bought a colored girl,
He brought her at dah' South;
Her hair it curled so 'bery tight
She could not shut her mouth.
Her eyes were so 'bery small
Dey' both ran into one,

An' when a fly light in her eye,
Like a June bug in dah' sun.

Her nose it was so 'bery long,
It turned up like a squash,
An' when she got her dander up
She made me laugh, by gosh;
Ole' massa' had no hooks or nails,
Or nothin' else like dat'
So on dis' darkie's nose he used
To hang his coat an' hat.

One mornin' massa' goin' away,
He went to git' his coat,
But neighbor nor coat was thar',
Fo' she had swallowed both;
He took her to a tailor shop,
To have her mouth made small,
Dah' lady took in one long breath,
An' swallowed tailor an' all.

Immediately after they concluded their song the master of ceremonies ran out to the center of the stage. "How 'bout dose' little darkies. Let's give 'dem a round of applause, dat's right, an' we'll bring 'em back a little later."

The crowd booed and yelled, calling out for more.

"Now, brothers an' sisters, jus' 'hold on to yur' hawses'! Dah' Negro singers are comin' back fo' a longer show a little later on. Now let's bring out one of our featured entertainers, dah' Campbell Minstrels, straight from Charleston, wit' one of yur' favorite tunes. I have to 'pologize dat' dey' too kin' only sing one tune right now, but like dah' Negro singers, dey' will be returnin' atter' Reverend Higgins delivers his sermon. I do 'pologize fo' dah' inconvenience. 'Gain Reverend Higgins has 'nother engagement an' has to leave early."

The crowd was less than pleased with this explanation—

235

yelling out, "We don't care 'bout some spiritual message. Dis' comes only once a year. Yu' know most of us came hyeh' to have fun an' not have to listen to a sermon. We kin' git' dat' on any given Sunday."

The master of ceremonies assured the audience that both groups would be returning and quickly called to the Campbell Minstrels to come out, hoping to silence the crowd.

The black-faced Campbell Minstrels took center stage as they were introduced. The crowd applauded and cheered as this form of entertainment was very popular throughout the United States, and not just in the South. The men's faces were painted jet black, a sharp contrast with their clothing, which was primarily white. Unlike the Negro singers, their attire did not demonstrate a patriotic theme. Reggie thought it was ironic that the black singers wore patriotic clothing while the black-faced singers did not. He always found black-faced minstrels to be somewhat contradictory. White people believed they were superior to black people. Yet, the whites purposely painted their faces black as a form of humor. Interestingly, Reggie couldn't recall ever seeing blacks painting their faces white, but then, should he really be surprised as he laughed to himself?

When Reverend Hibbard informed Reggie about the universality of black-faced humor in the United States, he could no longer contain his feelings. "Master, it's so refreshin' to see dat' dah' North an' dah' South kin' finally 'gree on something, even if it is fo' dah' wrong reason."

Fortunately for Reggie, Reverend Hibbard did not recognize that Reggie was making a sarcastic comment, and he simply ignored it.

Four black-faced, white men appeared and unlike the Negro singers, they provided their own musical instruments—a ukulele, along with a fiddle, and sang to a song about a man named Jim Crow titled *Jump Jim Crow,* written in 1828 by Thomas Dartmouth "Daddy" Rice. He was a "black faced" white minstrel show performer from New York. He is supposed to have seen a young child or a black slave who walked poorly and somehow became inspired to create the Jim Crow character and with an accompanying dance. This required a certain amount of strutting along with some other innovative moves. He performed starting in the 1830's along the east coast along with others who soon copied him. Unfortunately, they further popularized the image of black people as being shiftless, stupid, and less human, which had the egregious affect of keeping the stereotypical concept alive and well.

Come listen all yu' gals an' boys
I'se jist' from Tuckyhoe,
I'm goin' to sing a little song,
My name's Jim Crow.
Weel' 'bout an' turn 'bout
An' o jis' so,
Eb'ry time I weel 'bout
An' jump Jim Crow.
Oh I'm a roarer on de fiddle,
An' down in old Virginny',
They say I play de' skyentific'
Like Massa' Pagannini
I'm a full-blooded niggah',
Ob' de real ole' stock,
An' wid' my head an' shoulder
I kin' split a hawss' block.

The crowd cheered for more as the Campbell Minstrels bowed and left the stage after singing the same stanza twice, and the master of ceremonies returned to announce the program for the rest of the day and evening. "How 'bout those Campbell Minstrels! Aren't dey' somethin'? It's jus' 'mazing what dey' kin' do. We will have a short break to prepare fo' Reverend Higgins, our Presbyterian minister, who will provide a spiritual message dat' yu' will not want to miss. 'Member, Harry Jones will 'pear wit' his banjo 'long wit' dah' Campbell Minstrels an' dah' darkies. They will all return fo' a much longer show atter' dah' spiritual message from Reverend Higgins. Finally at dusk, we will conclude dah' festivities fo' dah' day by celebrating our Glorious Fourth wit' a pyrotechnic display dat' will top all of our previous shows. Folks, it promises to be a spectacular show!"

Reverend Hibbard gave a quick tug on Reggie's arm as Reverend Higgins appeared on stage, "Reggie, dat's 'nough fo' me. I'm not goin' to sit hyeh' an' listen to dat' Presbyterian minister. We'll come back fo' dah' pyrotechnics display."

"Master, aren't yu' interested in dah' music an' dah' entertainers atter' dah' spiritual message?"

"Sometimes dah' debil' kin' git' in dat' music, an' me bein' a minister of God, I should know better din' to sit an' listen to it. I look 'round, an' it takes on dah' appearance of a crowd in a tavern. Now, yu' know how I feel 'bout dat' atter' dat' episode we had wit' Boyd Rose in dat' sinful tavern. Let's go have some good food, an' we'll git' back fo' dah' pyrotechnic display, which is one of dah' highlights of dah' camp meeting. Believe me, dat' should more than rival any entertainers."

"Master, dat' sounds good to me." As Reggie spoke he noticed they weren't the only ones who didn't want to hear the sermon. It looked like more than half the crowd had exited as soon as the emcee announced that Reverend Higgins was next.

"Reggie let's go," Reverend Hibbard demanded, and the two departed, heading directly for the booths. The two spent their afternoon people watching and sampling the food. Reggie also observed that Reverend Hibbard was beginning to loosen up, acting like he had forgotten what happened the other evening. This certainly represented an encouraging sign.

As dusk arrived, the announcement came for the fireworks display. The people knew that the fireworks show would soon begin as darkness arrived and returned in much larger numbers to the seating area. Reverend Hibbard and Reggie were part of the returning crowd as they were excited as school children. "Reggie, looks like dah' master of ceremonies is comin' out to introduce dah' pyrotechnics show. It's really somethin' to behold." Reverend Hibbard sounded more like a young boy than a preacher.

The master of ceremonies bellowed over his excited audience, "Now, I know dat' all of yu' came to be spiritually uplifted. Wit' dat' in mind, it's time to git' on wit' dah' pyrotechnic display." With the announcement, the fireworks began, and everyone was completely transfixed as they went off one right after another; each time appearing more spectacular than the previous one as they illuminated the sky and mesmerized the crowd. A clear area had been set aside to the right of the stage where the fireworks were launched. In the seating area, one had a good look at the fireworks as they were fired off.

"Reggie, looks like dah' heavens are openin' up an' Jesus is jus' sittin' up thar' callin' us home!" The reverend exclaimed. "What do yu' think?"

"Master, yu' have a rich imagination," Reggie called back over the noise. "I could sure hyeh' Him callin', but I don't know if I'm quite ready to join Him."

"Yu' know something Reggie? Yu' are nuttin' but a stick in dah' mud! Oh Lawd', I kin' feel yu' Lawd'. Yu' kin' take me right now! My own house servant doesn't want me—do Yu' want me Lawd'?"

Reggie ignored the backhanded comment knowing that to respond would only create trouble. Reverend Hibbard was pouting, and Reggie knew better then to go anywhere near this subject. Reggie instead raved about the fireworks. "Master, I sure am enjoyin' dah' show—it's truly breathtakin'!"

Reverend Hibbard joined in his enthusiasm. "Yu' know I'm enjoyin' it. I knew yu'd enjoy it too!"

After the grand finale, they walked back toward their tent. Reverend Hibbard in an unusually good mood, stated, "Reggie, I guess I'm not as tired as I thought. I don't wanta' go back to dah' tent jus' yet. Let's take a walk ovah' yonder an' git' some lemonade an' confections. We've got plenty of time, let's jus' have some more fun."

"Master, dat' sounds good to me."

As they walked toward the lemonade booth, a slovenly looking man who had obviously been drinking confronted

Reverend Hibbard. "Mister are yu' a minister of God? Yu' sur' look like one—all togged up in dose' black clothes, yur' wide brimmed black hat an' dat' long white hair!"

"Brother, I'm a Baptist preacher who recognizes dat' yu' are in yur' cup."

"Now preacher man, don't be so hard on me, I'm celebratin'." The man stumbled forward while smiling and said, "Dis' only happens once a year."

Reverend Hibbard looked into his face and sternly warned, "I hope yu' are speakin' dah' truth when yu' tell me yu' are not celebratin' everyday."

"I'm not—jus' once in awhile," the man slurred. It was obvious that he was telling a lie.

"Brother, what yu' need is salvation. Do yu' want to end up bein' wit' Old Scratch? He'll be happy to take yu' in, or would yu' rather be wit' dah' Lawd'?"

The stranger made a futile attempt to stand up straight. "Preacher, yu' make sense, an' I know yur' right. When I git' home I'll think 'bout what yu' tole' me."

It was a typical answer that the reverend had heard many times before this evening. "Well brother, I hope yu' are bein' honest wit' yur'self', 'cuz' yur' soul is dah' most precious thin' yu' have. Now, we have to move on."

"Thank yu', hope to see yu' 'gain." With that, the stranger stumbled off in the direction of the closest liquor booth.

As Reverend Hibbard and Reggie continued their walk, the reverend commented, "Yu' know, Reggie dat' man was all talk. He's not goin' to change. I've seen it too many times. He say's dat' he is goin' to change, an' says he's jus' celebratin' tonight. Dat's all poppycock. He'll wake up in dah' mornin' an' git all liquored up celebratin' a nice sunny day or a rainy day. People like him will find any ole' reason to drink—he's not kiddin' me, or dah' Lawd'!"

"Master, it looked to me like he was suffering from a serious ailment—dropsy. Dat' poor man's belly is badly swollen like a pregnate woman 'bout to deliver a child." Dropsy, properly called edema is an excessive accumulation of serous fluid in the tissues.

Reverend Hibbard was not lacking for words. "Reggie it's obvious dat' dah' poor man is not long fo' dis' earth. I even noticed his face looked almost like somebody had painted it yeller'. It was so painful to look at him knowing that he was in such bad shape." Today in all probability, he would be diagnosed with cirrhosis of the liver caused most likely from ecessive alcohol abuse.

"Master, back in Virginny, I knew of a man who came to visit my master an' he suffered from dah' same ailment. He was never sober, always in his cup, it was really sad 'cuz' he really suffered in dah' end. Death had to be a blessin' fo' what he went through."

"Reggie, I've seen others sufferin' wit' dis' disease as well. Dah' mischief of it is dat' dey' was all heavy drinkers. Dey' usually couldn't even stop drinkin' when it got whar' dey' were really sufferin'. Alcohol, kin' be so destructive."

"Master, I 'gree. It seems like once alcohol git's a grip on a man's life as dey' travel down dah' road to destruction and often times death. It really is a tragedy havin' to witness people runnin' 'round hog drunk destroyin' thar' lives an' affectin' others in such a destructive manner. I know dat' dah' alcohol becomes more important to 'dem din' thar' own family, thar' lies a tragedy."

"Take a look over thar' at dah' booth dispensin' whisky an' wine." The reverend pointed to one with about 20 people in line. "It's gittin' late an' dose' people want to be sur' dey' have time to consume all dey' kin' an' probably take a little back to thar' tent fo' a little 'pick me up' to git 'dem through dah' night. We're not goin' near dat' crowd, 'cuz' dey' scare me."

Interestingly, Reggie noticed very few women in line at the booth. He thought of Mrs. Rose drinking privately since it was not socially acceptable for a woman to be intoxicated in public.

Reggie, unable to contain himself had something to add. "Master, now yu' kin' see dah' problem wit' givin' a man a whip who gits' drunk all dah' time. Like Master Rose, dey' beat everybody, which includes thar' own wives an' children. On top of dat', dah' free use of a whip kin' be a steppin' stone to dah' grisly spectacle dat' welcomed us to dah' Rose plantation. It still makes me sick when I think 'bout it. It seems to me master, when we look at dah' 'bondage system' historically, we have a continual pattern of violence associated wit' people exercisin' unlimited power an' alcohol certainly has its place in dah' picture. Somehow, thar' power has to be reined in. Worse yet, I don't think thar'll be any improvement anytime soon."

Reverend Hibbard wanted to concentrate on enjoying the festival and ignored Reggie's comments even though he knew what Reggie stated had merit. "Reggie hyehs' dah' lemonade vendor. Let's git' our drinks an' din' we kin' go git' some confections." Mr. Hibbard thanked the man who served him, and then commented, "Brother, wouldn't it be nice if yu' could have dah' same crowd as dah' whisky vendor?"

The elderly retailer shook his head and said, "Mister, I've been doin' dis' fo' years an' I kin' guarantee yu' dat' it will never happen. I kin' see drunks staggerin' by my booth who I kin' 'member servin' a cup of lemonade to when dey' were jus' youngsters. Now look at 'dem—a disgrace. What's worse, I 'member when dey' were little children sippin' lemonade at my booth an' watchin' all dah' drunks pass by, an' more din' one of 'dem said they'd never allow 'dem selves to git' like dat'. Well, now dey' are grown men an' dey' too are staggerin' 'round—it jus' slays me to have to watch des' goin's on year atter' year knowin' it seems to never change."

"Thank yu' fo' sharin' yur' thinkin', bein' dat' I'm a man of dah' cloth. I 'preciate yu' bein' so candid. By dah' way, yur' lemonade is refreshin'—a touch of sweetness an' fresh squeezed lemons—a true nectar from heaven."

As Reggie and his master continued walking, Reverend Hibbard commented, "Yu' know Reggie I jus' wish dey' would sell buttermilk out hyeh'. Why dat' would even top lemonade on my list."

"I hyeh' yu' master. Dat' would surely hit dah' spot," Reggie agreed knowing he had only drunk buttermilk once in his lifetime. Buttermilk was a real Southern treat, but required being kept cool to prevent it from turning bad, which made it impractical at the camp meeting.

Soon Reverend Hibbard found a candy booth, "I'm goin' to git' some likorice'. Reggie, do yu' want some, or do yu' prefer toffee?"

"Master, I sur' would enjoy some toffee, an' I 'preciate yur' kind offer." Having toffee anytime was quite a treat for Reggie, and two days in a row was nearly overwhelming. It appeared that Reverend Hibbard was no longer angry with him. He hoped what transpired in the tent the night before would soon be overlooked and eventually forgotten.

As they walked back to their campsite, the reverend chatted about God. "Reggie, I know dat' yu' have said dat' heaven should be open to dah' niggah' jus' as much as dah' white man. Well, atter' careful thought I have come 'round to 'gree wit' yu'. It jus' doesn't make sense dat' a good Christian Negro man should be denied heaven 'cuz' of his skin color while yu' have all des' sinful white people who claim to be good Christians fallin' to dah' debil's ways an' 'pectin' to go to heaven as well."

Reggie warmly accepted this. "Master, it is true. I wish dat' more people could understand what yu' have come to realize."

"I respect yu' fo' yur' ability to see an' express things like dis'. However, I'm tired from all dah' runnin' 'round, an' now I'm lookin' forward to hearin' Reverend Smith tomorrow—time to turn in," Reverend Hibbard stated.

The two went about preparing for bed in silence, and they slept soundly through the night as Reverend Hibbard left Reggie alone making no further advances.

***

In the morning after breakfast, they continued to walk around and talk with vendors and people in the crowd.

After talking and doing some people watching for awhile, Reverend Hibbard and Reggie sat on a small bench and split a sandwich for lunch, while talking about what they had experienced so far for the day. Of course, religion, as always, became the center of discussion.

After lunch, they returned to the stage area, where the early afternoon spiritual message would be delivered by the Baptist minister, Reverend Smith. It was this message that Reverend Hibbard was looking forward to. Unfortunately, it appeared the crowd did not share Hibbard's attraction for Reverend Smith. The crowd was considerably smaller than the day before. There wasn't any entertainment scheduled and that always had the effect of drastically reducing the size of the crowd. A nicely dressed young man introduced the minister. The people in attendance gave a warm reception to Reverend Smith as he walked to his pulpit to begin the sermon.

As Reverend Hibbard and Reggie were intently preparing to listen to Reverend Smith, a pale man dressed in black that Reggie had never seen before approached Reverend Hibbard and asked if he could speak with him privately for a few minutes, and the reverend excused himself.

Reverend Smith began his sermon, while Reggie remained seated as instructed by Reverend Hibbard. "Thank yu', thank yu'—an' let it be known dat' dah' power of dah' Holy Spirit is upon us. Oh glory, glory hallelujah, fo' dah' power of God is upon yu'. Let's all sing a few words of our favorite camp meetin' song, *Rock of Ages*. Let's raise our voices to the heavens wit' dah' first stanza's—everybody sing!"

Rock of Ages, cleft fo' me, Let me hide myself in thee;
Let dah' water an' dah' blood, From thy river side which flowed,
Be of sin dah' double cure, Cleanse me from its guilt an' power.
Not dah' labors of my hands, Can fulfill thy law's demands;
Could my zeal no respite know, Could my tears fo' ever flow,
All fo' sin could not atone; Thou must save, an thou alone,
Amen.

The reverend began softly but raised his voice high every few words. "Dat' was beautiful. I first wanta' take a little time to talk 'bout what dah' Glorious Fourth represents. This is when we declared our independence from dah' British, touchin' off dah' War of Rebellion. Some say it was actually July 2nd, but I'm not goin' to 'split hairs'. Anyhow, dah' Glorious Fourth is dah' day dat' we should revere an' honor our Declaration of Independence, which states, 'We hold des' truths to be self evident dat' all men are created equal; dat' dey' are endowed by thar' Creator' wit' certain inalienable rights; dat' among dem' is dah' greatest of our democratic values. A land whar' all men are created equal like no other country.' Doesn't dat' jus' resonate—to all of us? Oh, glory be, glory be!"

Reggie was overwhelmed with an urge to convey his thinking regarding the minister's comments and bellowed out, "Reverend, I don't think dat' dose' words resonate to all in America."

The minister paused from his sermon and scanned the crowd, trying to locate his challenger.

Reggie continued, "Reverend, I'm talkin' 'bout America, land of dah' free an' home of democratic slavery!" When Reggie said democratic slavery, he realized he had expressed an oxymoron that would stir up a lot of trouble for him.

An elderly lady stood and yelled in Reggie's direction, we want to hyeh' dah' reverend—let him speak!" There was a buzz of support for the woman.

The reverend, not content to let matters rest, responded. "Let me speak to dis' young whippersnapper. I've never come 'cross anybody like him 'fore. Yu' referred to slavery. Well, young man, first dah' word slavery is a Yankee term used to stir up trouble. In dah' South we are God-fearin' followers of dah' Bible. The Bible mentions servants, not slaves. Hyeh' in our beloved South we abstain from usin' dat' word as it is not Biblical. Second, dah' South does have our own 'peculiar institution' which makes our Negro servants guardians an' not citizens, an', as such, dah' Declaration of Independence does not quite apply to 'dem."

Reggie knew he should now remain silent, but he couldn't help himself. He also felt the spirit of God urging him on, as before. "Reverend, are yu' sayin' a man born in dah' United States through parents who are guardians but not citizens must remain an alien to dah' country whar' he is born?"

As Reggie spoke, the audience became even more restless. One member shouted, "Reverend, we don't want to hyeh' dis' Yankee lover talk at our camp meetin'!"

The reverend was obviously angered and upset, but stubborn enough to continue. "No, let me settle dis' wit' dis' bag of wind 'cuz' he needs to be set straight. Young man, dat' is not true what yu' are sayin'. Someday, our guardians will be given dah' opportunity to establish citizenship in Afriky'. Dat' would include dose' born in dah' United States. Right now, in dah' North, largely through dah' efforts of dah' American Colonization Society, free Negroes are being sent back to Afriky' whar' dey' kin' civilize thar' people on dah' dark continent. Eventually, hyeh' in dah' South our servants will be foreclosed on an' sent back to Afriky' as well. Dey' will din' be given new opportunities in thar' native homeland. Now, do yu' understand, young man?"

Subjected to the same argument he had heard many times before, Reggie bellowed back, "Is dat' so reverend? Will these opportunities to be dispatched to Afriky', in order to whiten America, be similar to dose' jus' recently given to our Cherokee an' Creek brothers under dah' Removal Act of 1830 spearheaded by President Jackson? Reverend, one-fourth of dah' people perished under what dah' Cherokee called 'Dah' Trail Whar' We Cried'." The connection that Reggie made between the potential problems of the "back to Africa" movement and the "Removal Act of 1830" was novel, and it undoubtedly caught the minister completely off guard.

Reverend Smith realized this was the wrong arena for this debate. Besides, it was one he may not win. "Who are yu'—talkin' to me like dis' as if yu' have all dah' answers? I think, yu' are one of dose' cutthroat 'bobolitionists comin' down hyeh' to stir up trouble."

"Reverend, why don't yu' let me an' my friends take good care of him, an' yu'll never ever have to worry 'bout seein' dis' Yankee lover 'gain," a large surly looking man called out above the growing noise of the crowd.

Reverend Smith, a non-violent man replied, "No, I'm a man of God an' cannot advocate violence as a solution. Young man, I repeat, who are yu'?"

Reggie, without thinking of the consequences, exclaimed, "Reverend, I happen to be one of dose' guardian residents yu're talkin' 'bout."

The crowd angrily reacted as the reverend roared, "Shackle dis' servant 'mediately. Who is yur' master? Whar' is he? Yu' must be dealt wit' in dah' most severe fashion. Whar' is dah' constable?"

Fortunately, Reverend Hibbard had just returned, and immediately realized that not only was Reggie the center of all the turmoil—he had created it. Grabbing and dragging him through the angry whites, he let everyone know he was his master, and he would be severely punished. Forcing their way to the exit, the reverend shouted out, "Reggie, have yu' gone mad? If dey' find dah' constable, yur' in real trouble. Run, I mean run! Let's git' out of hyeh'."

They ran to their encampment, knowing they only had a short time to break camp and vanish. After they hurriedly broke camp, Hibbard told Reggie to hide while he retrieved the horse and buggy.

They hastily secured their belongings and left without detection. As soon as they were a safe distance away, Reverend Hibbard assailed him, "Reggie, my Christian thinkin' has always prevented me from usin' dah' whip, but yur' actions clearly make me think dat' I orte' change dat'. Do yu' realize dat' serious injury or even death jus' stalked yur' door? You're lucky we got out of thar' 'live. What's important is dat' yu' understand yur' actions today were wrong. Do yu'? Yu' more din' overstepped yur' bounds! Yu' endangered both of us wit' yur' boastful intervenin' ways!"

"Master, how kin' I admit to bein' wrong when I know dat' God is on my side?" Reggie stood up to Reverend Hibbard—his defiance was something he had previously avoided.

In a rage, Hibbard reached over and slapped Reggie across the face and responded. "I will not take yur' impudence. Yu're' 'bout as useless as a toothless ole' non-barkin' dog in a coon hunt! What value are yu' other din' to stir up trouble? Yur' actions have ruined my enjoyment of dah' one event of dah' year dat' I look forward to. I kin' never fo'give yu' fo' what yu' have jus' done."

"Master, what would Jesus say 'bout slavery? Yu're a minister of God. Haven't yu' ever given dat' some thought? Yu' even said dah' gates of heaven should be open to dah' black man jus' like dah' white man."

Reverend Hibbard was livid with rage. "Hold yur' tongue boy! Now I know what yu' are! Yu're a 'wolf in sheep's clothin'!'" As good as I've been to yu' an' now yu' do dis' to show yur' gratitude! First chance I git', I'm dumpin' yu'. Yu' are jus' too dangerous to keep 'round. From dis' point on I will have nothin' to say 'til I git' rid of yu'."

Reggie knew the recent events at the camp meeting had altered his life—most likely not for the better. A defiant slave would have to pay a grievous price, and he would have to be prepared accept the consequences.

CHAPTER SIXTEEN

Neither man spoke a word during the ride back to Hibbard Hall. Reggie surmised that as quickly as possible, Reverend Hibbard had plans that would not bode well for him.

Reggie's thoughts were swirling about. As stated earlier, he knew Reverend Hibbard feared his reputation would be destroyed if word ever got out about the incident in the tent. Fortunately, this should preclude him from selling Reggie to Boyd Rose even though Hibbard had threatened him with that option. Instead, his interests would best be served by selling him to a slave trader who would send him much further south where he would be rid of him forever along with the dark secret that Reggie kept.

For Reggie, his defiant actions, made it clear he could no longer stand-by silently and tolerate the evils of slavery. It meant he was now willing to accept the consequences of being insubordinate since he knew in his heart that in the eyes of the Lord, he was right. Realizing the results for being a defiant slave, Reggie knew his life would be forever changed. He would now be walking on very thin ice.

Within hours of their return, Reggie was informed of his new duties. His attendance for morning, and evening devotions would no longer be necessary. The status of personal servant had been changed to house servant, and he would now take orders from Egypt, the butler and head housekeeper. It was being made obvious that his days at Hibbard Hall were numbered and he was being made expendable.

Reggie's premonitions of trouble were soon confirmed a few weeks later when he was invited into the parlor by Reverend Hibbard. As he entered the room, he witnessed a sinister-looking stranger inspecting him. It was an ominous atmosphere that Reggie was beset with as the man continued to stare him down. He had the look of an evil slave trader—absent of any soul. Sloppily clad, he was short, thin, and unkempt, with a ruddy complexion and piercing eyes that penetrated straight through him. He looked pure evil. It was obvious that this was not going to be a social call. Reggie sensed that his life was about to change once again and not for the better.

Reverend Hibbard addressed him. "Reggie, it's been a full month since we returned from dah' camp meeting, an' since din' I have decided dat' yu' have become expendable. I had explained earlier to our guest, Mr. Cobb, dat' I need more field hands an' less house servants to turn dis' place 'round. Mr. Cobb is a speculator an' would like a good house servant to augment all of dah' field hands dat' he presently has in his stock. Take a look out dah' window, an' yu' kin' see his stock." Reggie complied and witnessed the full brutality of slavery—a slave coffle, one of the greatest forms of cruelty associated with the bondage system. He was aghast, knowing that very soon he would very likely be a part of this barbaric form of suffering. Furthermore, when the slaves were refered to as "stock" by Reverend Hibbard, a sickening feeling overwhelmed Reggie. The degradation of humans being lowered to the same level as cattle, brought home to Reggie another page in the full horrors of slavery.

Reverend Hibbard asked Mr. Cobb to remain in the parlor while he spoke briefly to Reggie in the hallway. The reverend, now looking piercingly at Reggie, said, "Yu' know I have to git' rid of yu.' I'm not in dah' habit of eatin' my Negroes but I have no choice. I could have sold yu' to Boyd Rose atter' what yu' put me through, but I actually have a Christian conscience. Instead, I'm goin' to let Mr. Cobb find a new master fo' yu' an' hopefully as far 'way from hyeh' as possible."

"Master, I do thank yu' fo' sparin' me a fate worse din' death." Reggie knew Reverend Hibbard's best interests were being served having him sold and sent far away from the area to help dispel any unwanted rumors. If sold to Boyd Rose, it could have proven to be a disaster for Reverend Hibbard. He had to keep his attempted affair with Reggie a deep secret.

Fidgeting, he said, "One last thing Reggie, I warned yu' dat' I was goin' to 'put yu' in my pocket', an' it wasn't jus' idle words. It was yur' own doins' dat' brought yu' down. I really tried hard to keep us together an' even wit' my reputation at stake. Yu' could have had a good life, 'specially fo' a personal servant but yu' chose to sew trouble an' dis' is what yu' have reaped. Dis' will be no picnic, bein' placed in a slave coffle an' marched to God knows whar'. I'm gonna' miss yu', but yu' made yur' own bed to lie in, not me. It's all yur' own doins'. Yet, even under des' circumstances, I'll still say it 'gain—yu' are dah' handsomest specimen of a man I have ever set my eyes on, but 'nough of dat'. It was yur' rejection of me an' yur' big mouth dat' messed things up. Now please hold yur' tongue an' foller' me back to dah' parlor."

Reggie knew from this point forward that his love for Anastasia and his deep religious convictions would have to provide him with the strength to persevere in the days that lay ahead.

In the parlor, Mr. Cobb made himself comfortable while looking forward to conducting business. Hibbard feeling tense, wished to lighten things up and asked him as he reentered the room, "Mr. Cobb, yu' seem to be an observin' an' knowledgeable man. Do yu' expect an average yield of cotton dis' year?" Perhaps, Reverend Hibbard felt a little guilt for what was about to transpire, and was attempting to make small talk.

"Oh, I reckon dat' dah' cotton will do quite well. But, I'm not hyeh' to discuss cotton, I'm hyeh' to discuss yur' niggahs'. Let's talk 'bout dah' sale of yur' prime merchandise." It was obvious Mr. Cobb was not an affable man—strictly business. He stood up and looked directly at Reggie. "Reverend Hibbard is dis' dah' niggah' dat' yu' want to sell?"

"Yes, I'm ready to sell my prime niggah'."

"Is dat' right?" Cobb asked, eyeing the merchandise almost menacingly, "Well, how much do yu' want fo' yur' prime niggah'?" He expressed "prime niggah" in a very sarcastic manner.

"I want to git' eight hundred dollars fo' him an' not a dollar less."

"Is dat' right now—yu' won't take a dollar less?" Cobb mocked, "Well, thar' are plenty of eight or nine hundred dollar niggahs' in dah' market, but dah' mischief is thar' are few buyers. Actually, dah' market is high fo' high grade niggahs' dat' kin' make yu' money. What kin' dat' dandy do ovah' thar'? He's jus' a display niggah' fo' somebody who wants to impress everybody. Who would give eight hundred dollars fo' dat' show piece niggah' dat' yu' want to unload on me?"

"Mr. Cobb, his looks are deceptive, why, he could be a good field hand. He's strong!"

"Now, Reverend Hibbard, yu' wouldn't be tryin' to hornswaggle me would yu'? Yu' know, Reverend Hibbard, dat' all dah' field hands would look at him like an informant sent to spy on 'dem. He' not even part niggah', he's 'bout all white. He jus' wouldn't fit in down in dah' quarters." Cobb wasn't going to make this easy.

"Well Mr. Cobb, he's certainly worth more than eight hundred dollars, but jus' to git rid of him, I'll take seven-hundred fifty dollars."

"Is dat' right now? Cobb responded. "Well, Reverend Hibbard, I kinda' got dah' feelin' dat' thars' more hyeh' din' meets dah' eye. Are yu' sure dat' dis' isn't all 'bout 'pourin' oil on troubled waters'?"

"I would normally never consider 'ceptin' seven hundred-fifty dollars, but I jus' don't have any time to take him to auction," Hibbard explained.

"Is dat' right Reverend Hibbard? Well, yu' drive a hard bargain, but fo' seven hundred-fifty dollars I could bail yu' out, providin' he's clean. Have him take off his blouse."

As Reggie revealed his back, Cobb circled him shaking his

head. "Goodness gracious Reverend Hibbard, dis' boy has felt dah' sweetness of cowhide. Yu' expect me to give yu' full value fo' damaged merchandise! I never expected dis'. He jus' doesn't look like one of dose' niggahs' who could be filled wit' rascality, but thar' it is—plain as day!"

"In my mind I had already discounted dat' he has stripes on his back. He tole' me dat' his master used dah' whip liberally on everybody, and he was no 'ception," Hibbard explained.

"Reverend Hibbard, I don't take to yur' bunk. Do yu' think dat' I'm a fool? I've come hyeh' in good faith, an' not to be insulted. I always check my merchandise 'fore I buy it. Yu' know Reverend Hibbard dat' dah' debil' is always in dah' details. Tellin' me dat' story 'bout a master jus' usin' dah' whip fo' no reason jus' doesn't hold water, but dah' details do."

"All right, I'll take seven hundred an' twenty-five dollars an' not a penny less. Mr. Cobb, I tole yu' dah' truth. I never used a whip on him and he never tried to run on me. Plus, he's a Christian. As I tole yu', I'm only partin' wit' him 'cuz' I have a surplus of house servants."

"Well, Reverend Hibbard, today is yur' lucky day. I might have a buyer fo' him jus' over dah' line in Georgia, so I'll take yur' offer fo' seven hundred dollars. I happen to have 'full cash on dah' barrel head'." Cobb pulled out a wad of money and paid Hibbard, who looked as if he was upset at the transaction but down deep, he was elated. Cobb cheated him out of twenty-five dollars but he wasn't about to argue. He needed the money, but more importantly, his reputation would be spared. In spite of his feelings for Reggie, he knew that circumstances dictated the move had to be made.

Cobb nodded to Hibbard and after the papers were signed, he then turned to his new purchase. "Well boy, now yu're my property. 'Let's git' our cows ovah' a bucket an' move on'." Reggie obediently followed his new master outside to the slave coffle.

The outlook for Reggie had sunk to a new low, knowing the coffle would be extremely difficult and inhumane, but he was still able to hold his head high as he approached Cobb's caravan.

This would be an experience he had hoped he would never have to encounter. At least forty slaves were in the coffle—the men shackled in the front and the women and children unshackled in the rear. The shackles were thick, nearly an inch in width, and secured together with thick chains. The slaves were generally barefoot or wore crude wrappings on their feet. Conspicuously, two white slave drivers with pistols and whips were present, one in the front and one in the rear, while a Negro fiddler knelt behind the white driver in the front. Leading the coffle was Mr. Cobb's horse and buggy. Finally, behind the rear driver were two covered wagons.

As they approached the rear driver, Cobb ordered that Reggie be placed with the other men and shackled. "Driver, it'll be gittin' dark soon, so we've gotta' git' dis' caravan a movin'."

As the procession started moving, the lead driver ordered, "Fiddler, start yur' fiddlin' an' I wanta' hyeh' all yu' suckers singin' loud an' clear all dah' way down dah' road. Now let's strike up lively, *Swing Low, Sweet Chariot.*"

I looked over Jordan, an' what did I see,
Coming fo' to carry me home?
A band of angels comin' atter me,
Comin' fo' to carry me home.
Swing low, sweet chariot,
Comin' fo' to carry me home;
Swing low, sweet chariot,
Comin' fo' to carry me home.
If yu' git' thar' befo' I do,
Comin' fo' to carry me home,
Tell all my friends I'm comin', too,
Comin' fo' to carry me home.
Swing low, sweet chariot,
Comin' fo' to carry me home;
Swing low, sweet chariot,
Comin' fo' to carry me home.
The brightest day that I ever saw,

254

Comin' fo' to carry me home,
When Jesus washed my sins away,
Comin' fo' to carry me home.
Swing low, sweet chariot,
Comin' fo' to carry me home;
Swing low, sweet chariot,
Comin' fo' to carry me home.

Many of the songs and expressions that slaves used such as *Swing Low Sweet Chariot* were coded. In the underground system, the Jordan River was the Ohio River, which separated Kentucky, a slave state from Ohio and Indiana where slavery was illegal. Ironically, the driver ordering that song probably would not have known the hidden meaning.

The procession of slaves continued to sing as they traveled south. Unfortunately along the route an old man was having great difficulty keeping his balance wearing his heavy manacles and collapsed. He was a sad figure who obviously had been ill for some time, and his body simply gave out. He weakly called out to the driver, "Marse', my legs—my legs, I can't move 'dem anymore."

The large, muscular driver briskly walked back to the old slave with his whip in his hand. "Damn yu', niggah, git' up an' git' movin', or I'll have yur' hide," the driver commanded.

"Marse', yu' kin' beat me 'til hell freezes ovah', I wanta' move, but I jus' can't."

"Niggah', yu' are holdin' up dah' whole damn train." The end of the driver's whip whistled through the air and sliced through the old man's back as the driver relentlessly whipped him. "Now git' up an' git' goin'."

The old man begged while in agony. "Marse', I can't move. My legs won't work no more. Yu' kin' keep beatin' me, but it won't do no good. I'm done fo'. Shoot me—please don't leave me to suffer." All the slaves had to witness this poor man suffering at the hands of these cruel men who had absolutely no compassion toward him.

Finally, the driver went to the front and brought back, Mr. Cobb. Cobb approached and bent over the slave, speaking to the driver and the old man, he said, "Beatin' dis' niggah' won't do no good, although he could be jus' 'shammin'' it. I've seen dat'—nothin' wrong, jus' wants to lay up in dah' wagon. Could be simple rascality—yu' jus' can't trust des' niggahs'. But in dis' case, I 'lieve him. Driver throw him into dah' wagon , 'cuz' we gotta' keep movin'. If he doesn't come 'round, we'll drop him off on down dah' road. He's worthless like dis', nobody would want him."

The slave was put into the wagon, and Cobb returned to the front of the train, and the march continued south.

Reggie was near the fallen, helplessly shackled slave, knowing he was unable to help in anyway, although he wanted to do so desperately. What he just witnessed further galvanized his determination to fight for the rights of the slaves.

Again, the lead driver yelled out, "Fiddler, start fiddlin'. I want to hear all of yu' loud an' clear. Sing *Poor Rosy,* an' strike it up lively." Obediently, they started singing.

Poor Rosy, poor gal, Poor Rosy, poor gal;
Rosy broke my poor heart, Heaven shall-a be my home.
Before I stay in hell one day,
Heaven shall-a be my home;
I'll sing an' pray my soul away,
Heaven shall-a be my home.
I got troubles on my way,
I got troubles on my way,
I got troubles on my way,
Heaven shall-a be my home."
Befo' I stay in hell one day,
Heaven shall-a be my home.
I'll sing an' pray my soul away,
Heaven shall-a be my home.

Toward evening, Mr. Cobb issued orders to halt the

procession, which came as a big relief to the exhausted slaves. Trudging ten miles in one day, with only an occasional drink of water and few bathroom breaks was even more difficult than Reggie imagined. To make matters even more demeaning for the women, they were not afforded any privacy when they relieved themselves. Meanwhile, the constant singing only masked the pain and sorrow of being herded together like cattle to the slaughter house. Ankles were cut, swollen, and bruised from the shackles as they marched and if anyone complained or delayed the progress, the driver was quick to appear with his whip and did not hesitate to use it. It amazed Reggie that somehow the slaves were able to muster the energy to keep moving—they endured sheer hell and for the most part did not break down.

They were close to total exhaustion when the procession stopped toward dusk. By the time their evening meal was finally prepared, they were further ravaged with hunger—even a cheap form of corn meal made without milk and eggs was still a welcome sight to the slaves. Served by two female slaves, this meager amount of food, along with potable drinking water, was the extent of their dinner. On a brighter note, the slave who sat next to Reggie informed him that on Sunday, Cobb would most likely purchase hogs from a local farmer and provide pork as a treat. Slave owners and traders always reminded themselves that it was important to provide some pleasure in order to maintain morale, strength and above all, prevent an insurrection.

The slaves tried to find a comfortable position on the ground to sleep, a few conversed quietly while others moaned and groaned throughout the night.

Reggie had spoken very little; however, one man lying near him asked, "Why are yu' hyeh', jus' to spy on us an' report back to Marse' Cobb? Yu' orte' feel shame fo' what yu' are doin'. If des' folks had thar' way, yu' would be dead. Dey' don't want yur' kind hyeh'. Take a look at dah' sufferin'. Dey' are so spent, dey' couldn't hurt a fly, an' yur' watchin' ovah' us thinkin' we could cause trouble. Yu' orte' to be ashamed of yur'self!"

"Hold yur' hawsses', I feel yur' pain an' sufferin.' I'm full of compassion. Take a look at my back." Reggie turned and pulled up his shirt. "Now, what do yu' see? Did dose' scars jus' happen magically on my back? In fact, if I had a gun on me, I woulda' shot dat' driver who was whippin' dat' poor ole' man."

The slave examined Reggie's back and was surprised at what he saw. "Mister, I didn't know—yu' jus' don't look like a colored man. I is sorry."

"My name is Reggie—what's yur' name?"

"My name is Steven." Steven's attitude had changed after seeing the scarring on Reggie's back.

"Well, Steven, I understand yur' questionin' me, an' I'm not angry wit' yu'," Reggie said. "I'm use to bein' called a turncoat by other slaves. It's like bein' in purgatory. I'm jus' 'nother niggah' to dah' whites an' a spy to dah' Negroes. In some ways I'm worse off din' yu' since I'm rejected by everybody. At least yu' are fully accepted by dah' slaves wit'out always havin' to prove yur'self like me."

"We're jus' not use to seein' somebody like yu' bein' one of us."

Another slave leaned close to Reggie and Steven. "Look, jus' 'cuz' yu' show us some scars on yur' back still doesn't convince me dat' yu' are one of us."

Reggie quickly responded, "I kin' understand yu' feelin' dat' way 'bout me but dis' is a slave coffle. Even if I was an informant, it wouldn't do anyone any good 'cuz' thar's' nuttin' back hyeh' dat' would ever amount to a hill of beans to report back on."

"I'm still goin' to keep a watch on yu'," replied the other slave with a dangerously suspicious look in his eyes.

"Look, my name is Reggie, what's yurs'?" Reggie was making an attempt to develop a warmer relationship with the man.

"My name is Abraham."

"I want both of yu' to know dat' I want to make dah' best of a terrible situation jus' as much as yu' do. Trust me dat' I have yur' best interests at heart. Let's work together an' not 'gainst each other."

Steven sensed that Reggie was an intelligent man. "Yu' talk like yu' are one of dose' two headed niggahs' who knows yur' letters an' numbers. I'm sur' thar' could be a time when dat' could prove helpful to us."

"Yes, Steven I'm educated," Reggie answered. "But what's important is dat' I'm gonna' help an' not hurt our cause in des' times of trials an' tribulations."

Steven had a genuine look of concern on his face. "Yu' know dat' dey' are gonna' dump dat' old man somewhar out' on dah' pike 'morrow. Dey' could care less 'bout dat' poor old man. He's of no value to 'dem since he'll never be able to work."

Reggie agreed. "Yu' are right, if he's become a liability, it's easier to jus' git' rid of him an' be done wit' it."

"Reggie, he won't improve, why don't dey' jus' shoot him an' do him a favor?" Steven asked.

Abraham agreed with Steven. "Why not jus' shoot him an' put him out of his sufferin'?"

"I can't say fo' sur' but thar' are dah' slave codes an' dey' prohibit shootin' slaves. However, jus' dumpin' him on dah' side of dah' pike would be no violation of dah' codes," Reggie stated.

"On my ole' plantation, marse' killed more din' one slave fo' causin' trouble, an' nothin' ever happened to him," Abraham interjected.

"Abraham," Reggie countered. "I'm listening to yu' but what goes on at dah' ole' plantation, stays at dah' plantation an' dah' plantation owner is none fo' worse to ever have to answer to justice. A lot of cruelty go's on out of dah' sight of dah' public, but shootin' dis' poor ole' man openly on dah' road could cause Cobb trouble. When Northerners visit dah' slaveowners, dey' always paint a picture' dat' everythin' is 'hunky-dory' 'tween dah' slave-owner an' his slaves. Dey' always hide dah' truth, an' when dah' Northern guests leave—all hell breaks loose. 'Lieve me, on most plantations dah' slaves would like to see dah' Northern guests stay year 'round!"

"My master never killed anybody dat' I kin' 'member," Steven added.

"Not all slave masters are mean an' cruel Steven, some are honorable men. It's like a lot of people, some are good an' some are bad. Yurs' was probably good—consider yur'self lucky," Reggie replied.

Abraham took a deep breath, paused for a few seconds and added, "My ole' slave master would git' drunk an' turn into dah' debil'. I was happy to git' out of thar' wit' my life. Whar'ever I end up, it can't be worse din' what I went through wit' Marse' Lacey."

"Well Abraham, Marse' Lacey is 'hind yu', an' yu' should look to dah' future wit' hope knowin' dat' dah' odds would favor dat' yur' next master will not be as ruthless." Reggie couldn't help but think of Boyd Rose, another drunk with an uncontrollable temper.

"It crossed my mind dat' I might be better off bein' dropped off wit' dat' ole' man who is 'bout to die. A Mississippi cotton niggah' workin' from sunup to sundown an' workin' till I drop dead—I think dat' hell would be better din' what I have to look fo'ward to," Steven sighed.

"Steven I hate to break dah' news to yu', but yu' could be workin' on one of dose' rice plantations, an' dat' could be worse din' pickin' cotton. Dose' niggahs' have to slough 'round in dirty water all day long, an' yu' know what dat' kin' do to yur' legs an' feet. 'Lieve me, I'll take dah' cotton fields ovah' havin' infected sores on my legs," Abraham injected.

Reggie realized the need to impart some positive thoughts into the conversation. He braced up and with strength and veracity in his words he spoke. "I want to share wit' both of yu' somethin' yu' might find hard to 'lieve or understand. I've been given a special gift—dah' power to see into dah' future. Not too long from now a war will be fought 'tween dah' North an' dah' South, an' dah' North will be victorious an' end slavery."

"Reggie, I hardly know yu', but I think dat' yu' are bein' honest wit' us. Normally, I might think yu' fell off yur' rocker, but yu' say it wit' such force." Steven went on, "Yu' seem to speak wit' wisdom—givin' us hope an' dat's what we need. Wit'out it a man has nothin'. Dat's what dah' conjurer talked to me 'bout, but, he didn't tell me dat' someday I'd be free! Freedom, sweet freedom—God, I do thank yu' an' I don't even know yu', an' I pray dat' yu' are right." Hearing the words of freedom in the future would invoke an immediate reaction from the slaves who so desperately held out for some hope.

"Steven, I'm jus' pleased dat' I'm able to spread dah' word to yu' an' as sur' as dah' sun rises in dah' mornin'—it's comin'!"

"Reggie, I'm jus' like every niggah' hyeh'—I need hope, dey' need hope, we all need hope. If yu' kin' bring it to us—hallelujah." As Abraham spoke he saw the tattered night blankets being passed out to the slaves. "Dey're' gittin' out dah' blankets now—it sur' beats sleepin' on dah' ground. Dah' other slave train I was in was worse. Dey' made us sleep on dah' hard ground wit' no blankets."

The night arrived and everyone, completely exhausted, quickly fell asleep. Reggie stood staring at the dark sky, his arms folded behind him, He had seen once again how important hope was to his fellow slaves as thoughts then turned to his wife, Anastasia. His heart ached, not knowing if Colonel Marshall might have sold her to a slave trader to be sent to the New Orleans market where she would be sold to serve in a brothel, unless, he just kept her for his own pleasure. Hopefully, her fate turned out better than those two options. One of his primary goals in life was clearly etched in stone—he would someday become free, find Anastasia and buy her freedom.

***

The following morning after the usual corn pone and water was served for breakfast, the slave coffle continued. After a short time on the road, Reggie had to witness a disgusting sight. He saw the old man being thrown from the wagon and onto the side of the road. He over heard the ensuing conversation. "Please don't leave me like dis', jus' go 'head an' shoot me," the old man begged. "I can't walk. I can't defend myself if animals come up on me."

The lead driver, the meaner of the two, yelled back with a malicious smile on his face. "Niggah', why should we waste a bullet on a worthless ole' field hand like yu'? We need to save our rounds fo' somethin' worth shootin' at—like a buzzard!" The two drivers heartily laughed as they turned away.

The slaves showed no reaction to what they had just seen and heard. Battered for so long, any cruel action perpetuated by the drivers would not surprise them. Reggie, always saddened by the atrocities of slavery, looked down at his manacles and the ground, wondering how much longer the slaves throughout the South could tolerate this level of cruelty without instigating more insurrections.

Reggie clearly understood the dynamics of what had just taken place. The slaves were not in a position to resist, or to protect one of their own. In addition, they were so beaten down that they were unable to display any feelings. Reggie knew, however that in their hearts, they felt compassion and love for their fellow slave but knew that resistance under these circumstances would be in vain.

As the slave coffle proceeded, the eerie cry of the old man could be heard in the distance, begging for somebody to shoot him and put him out of his suffering. It would not happen, and the crying only continued. For Reggie, it was extremely difficult to have witnessed something this cruel and inhumane and he felt even worse to be defenseless to do anything about it. Clearly, it would be an experience that he could never forget.

After endless days on the road, and intolerable suffering, the slave coffle crossed the Savannah River and into Georgia. A few miles down the road, Mr. Cobb stopped the procession at a large white stucco plantation with Greek revival columns across the front. The lawn was spacious and well manicured.

Mr. Cobb announced to the drivers, "I have to take care of some business. Make sure everyone is kept quiet. I'll return shortly." At the front door the butler greeted Cobb and asked him to wait in the entry hall while he summoned the plantation owner. A very dignified, tall, well-built man with a commanding appearance—someone Cobb had dealt with earlier, came down the circular stairway. He was immaculately dressed in gray, complemented by a white, ruffled shirt. In his mid-thirties, he was well manicured, while his medium length black hair enhanced his obvious good looks.

The man with a facetious look, stated, "Well if isn't dah' honorable Mr. Cobb. It's always a pleasure to see yu'."

Cobb knew the man did not respect him. "Captain Riley, how are yu' today? I know dat' yu' are always interested in my merchandise, an' I happened to be comin' through hyeh' an' kinda' thought yu' might wanta' see a 'bery special house servant 'long wit' my usual excellent merchandise. Yu' once tole' me yu' needed a good house servant, an' I have a young niggah' dat' might fill dah' bill."

"Yu' know, Cobb, yu' are Johnny on the spot. Last night I figured dat' I needed three more hands an' yu' pop in today jus' like a bad habit! I would prefer a house servant an' two field hands. Let's git' outside so we kin' git' down to business."

As the two men approached the coffle, Cobb confidently stated, "Take a look at dah' merchandise, as I've got quite a variety."

"Yu' do have some good merchandise dis' time, Cobb. Jus' 'member, yu' better not try to rook me, 'cuz' yu' know, I don't trust yu' Yankee soul drivers comin' down South to make money in a messy way, but unfortunately, yu' do serve a dirty need, an' I guess dat's why we tolerate yu' people." Captain Riley then took a closer look at the slaves a second and third time. Finally, he asked Cobb, "I wanta' see dis' one. Also, dah' one ovah' thar, an' let me see dat' light skinned one near dah' back. I kin' assume he is dah' special one yu' talked up."

After the three were unchained and separated, Cobb ordered. "I want all three of yu' to jump an' jump high fo' Captain Riley. Now do it 'gain an' touch dah' sky.

"Dat's good 'nough, Cobb. Now, let me check thar' teeth. By dah' way, I hope none of 'dem are 'blue-gum niggahs'". Once a niggah' bit me an' dat' was one 'blue-gum niggah'' I almost killed." The term "blue-gum" referred to the gums of very dark skinned blacks who had a blue tone to their gums. The expression was expanded to include any slave who might bite upon inspection.

"Major, none of 'dem is a 'blue-gum'. I know dat' 'cuz' I personally inspected thar' mouths wit'out any of 'em bitin' me."

"I 'lieve yu,' but if one of 'dem bites me, I will hold yu' personally 'sponsible. Once was 'nough." Captain Riley inspected their mouths without incident, and then demanded, "Take off yur' blouses, I got to make sur' yu' are all clean." All three took off their shirts, and after a quick inspection, Major Riley discovered a problem with Reggie. "Mr. Cobb, two of des' niggahs' are clean, but dah' yeller' niggah' is not."

Mr. Cobb addressed Reggie. "Boy, tell Captain Riley what happened to yu.' "

"Captain Riley," Reggie replied meekly. "I was beaten fo' a minor infraction."

Captain Riley was surprised by Reggie's response. "A minor infraction, damn, I knew yu' might be different din' dah' others. Yu' are one of dose' two-headed niggahs' who uses big words like infraction, aren't yu' boy? An' I'm jus' lettin' yu' know right now—I don't trust a two headed' niggah. Yu' know folks don't take too kindly to a niggah' like yu' who would have dah' knowledge to cause trouble. What do yu' have to say?"

"Yah' master," Reggie answered. "I know my letters an' my numbers. I also promise yu' dat' 'I know my place' an' I'm obedient an' will not cause any trouble."

Staring directly at Reggie, Captain Riley asked, "Well, knowin' yur' letters an' numbers didn't cause yu' to git' punished, which would make me doubt if yu' are really obedient. What happened?"

"Master," Reggie replied, "'One man may steal a horse while 'nother may not look ovah' dah' hedge'."

Captain Riley didn't like the answer. "Boy, dat' jus' brings tears to my eyes, yu' bein' unfairly treated. I don't give a tinker's damn 'bout yu' bein' treated unfairly, an' if I buy yu' I'm gonna' have fun, an' I may not be fair. In fact, I'm gonna' set yu' straight.

'Round hyeh' all dah' niggahs' are treated dah' same, so yu'll' be able to look ovah' dah' hedge."

"Master as yur' servant, I'll do whatever is asked of me." Whenever Reggie had to lower himself to this level it disturbed him, but he had no choice.

Then the captain called out, "Any of yu' niggahs' got flat feet?" Everyone remained silent.

Mr. Cobb stepped forward. "Major kin' we git' on wit' dah' business now?"

"Of course! Well, mister soul driver, jus' what do yu' want fo' dis' weak merchandise?"

"Well Captain Riley, I'll need four thousand dollars jus' to cover my expenses—an' dat' puts 'bery few dollars in my pocket," Cobb answered.

This amount infuriated Riley. "Mister soul driver, what do yu' take me fo', a pig in a poke, or some sorta' fool? Is dat' it?"

"Well, Captain Riley, I have 'penses," Cobb explained. "I had to dump a worthless niggah' off dah' wagon down dah' road, an' dat' cost me a lot of money. 'Lieve me dis' business is not all profit."

"Mister soul driver, dat's not my problem, dat's yurs'. Yu' know dat' I know dat' is part of yur' dirty business, so thar's no point in yu' givin' me a sob story. Let's git' down to brass tacks— I'm willin' to offer yu' thirty-two hundred dollars an' not a dime more."

Mr. Cobb was taken back at the low offer. "Captain, yu' know dat' thirty-two hundred dollars is not 'nough. Dat' would not even cover my expenses. I may jus' as well leave wit' my merchandise."

Captain Riley walked around the three slaves while he pondered the situation. "All right mister soul driver, I'll give yu' thirty-two hundred an' fifty dollars an' consider dah' matter closed."

"Captain Riley, I need thirty-five hundred dollars. Dat's my lowest figure an' dat' is a real bargain. I'm down five-hundred dollars from my original askin' price."

Captain Riley looked at the three slaves again and for one final time, than looked at Cobb. "Mister soul driver, yu' really take me to be wet 'hind dah' ears. Yu' know, I never met a Yankee who came South dat' I could trust, but I'm offerin' yu' thirty four-hundred dollars an' I'll take my merchandise so yu' kin' be on yur' way. Now, hyeh's your money—cash down! Captain Riley pulled out a large amount of money and counted out thirty-four hundred dollars as he spoke.

"Captain, it's a deal," Cobb said. "But one thing still disturbs me. How did yu' know dat' I'm from dah' North."

With a sneer Captain Riley replied, "I kin' always smell a damn Yankee! In fact, I dislike yu' more din' dose' niggahs' yu' got in yur' coffle. How does dat' set wit' yu', Mr. Soul Driver?"

Mr. Cobb with a stunned look, hesitatingly stated, "Well, on dat' note, I'll be on my way." Cobb was not entirely surprised at Riley's tirade directed at him as he knew that he represented one of the most despised class of people in the South, a Northern slave trader. Cobb reassembled his coffle and continued south as Captain Riley escorted his new slaves to their quarters.

CHAPTER SEVENTEEN

As they walked toward the slave quarters, a white man who looked the role of an overseer greeted them. Reggie had to assume he was the overseer, although he didn't quite fit the role in Reggie's judgment. Gangly, and much younger, broad at the hips and narrow shouldered, he wore his brown hair cropped short, while his clothing looked well worn. Reggie immediately felt cold vibrations as he looked at the man, but he had learned years before that you can't always "judge a book by its cover".

As they met a few yards from the quarters, the overseer, Jake Gibbons studied and evaluated the three field hands. "Captain Riley would dis' be yur' new merchandise?" It was obvious that Reggie's assumption was correct that he was indeed, the overseer.

"Jake, I picked up des' three fo' a fair amount. Dey' might need some seasonin', 'specially dah' clabber-colored niggah'. Now, we wouldn't want des' varmint's to think dat' dis' is goin' to be a picnic in dah' park, do we?" Riley stared at the three slaves as he spoke.

"No we don't, Captain Riley," Jake replied. "Yu' know dat' yur' merchandise will be in good hands wit' me. I'll git' des' boys shaped up in no time. Dey' will become a fine example fo' our field hands to look up to."

Captain Riley chuckled at Jake's humor. "I've always known dat' yu' have a special way of handlin' my merchandise, an' I know dat' des' boys will be no 'ception. Jake, why don't yu' introduce 'dem to yur' close friend, Judy." Captain Riley then looked at Gibbons whip.

"Captain, I'll do dat' right now." The overseer was eager to demonstrate his prowess with his whip. "Yu' niggahs', see dis' silk cracker, her name is Judy, an' Judy kin' git' real riled up at dah' drop of a hat. She has a hairline trigger 'bout her." He spun around and cracked the whip in the air, obviously done to intimidate the new slaves. "My name is Mr. Jake Gibbons, an' I kinda' think yu' boys know I'm yur' new overseer. Now what are yur' names? Yu', what's yur' name?"

"My name is Augustus, Mr. Gibbons," he quickly responded.

Captain Riley stepped back in feigned awe. "Whoa! Jake, doesn't dat' jus' take dah' cake? We got us one of dose' Roman niggahs' from times past. Sorta' comin' down hyeh' to bring us a little Roman dignity."

Jake laughed. "Yu' know Captain, we don't have any Romans in our special army hyeh' in dah' quarters. Augustus will be our first an' only one. Now, isn't dat' jus' peachy? Augustus I hope yu' are prepared to command yur' newly formed legion hyeh' on our plantation? Gibbons was starring at Augustus, "I'm talkin' to yu', Roman, answer me!"

It was obvious that Augustus did not know what Gibbons meant but he still knew that a reply was necessary. "Yes sir, I'm ready to command," he forcefully stated.

"Now, dat's better, an' 'member, when I speak to yu'—yu' answer. Got it?"

Augustus firmly replied, "Yes sir, Mr. Gibbons."

"Jake, dat's a pretty good one—yu' got dis' fool all riled up. I like dat'." The captain then looked at the next slave and asked, "Niggah', what's yur' name?"

"Marse', my name is Jimmy."

"Jimmy, well nothing special 'bout Jimmy—jus' 'nother niggah', but it sounds good to me. Yu' kin' keep dat' name." In the bondage system the master could change a name at his discretion.

Jake, while giving Jimmy a thorough examination, made an interesting comment. "Yu' know Captain Riley, jus' fo' a second I got to thinkin' dat' Jimmy was one of dose' sparrow eyed niggahs', an' dat' wouldn't be good. But on closer inspection, I realize dat' he is not." Jake was expressing a view held by the slaves that Negroes with close set eyes and sparrow like facial features were social misfits, bad luck, and often ostracized from the community.

"Jake yu' needn't worry 'bout me makin' dat' mistake." Then a wide grin spread across Riley's face as he turned to address Reggie. "Jake, I purposely saved dah' best fo' last. What's yur' name?"

Reggie answered with pride, "Master, my name is Reggie Marshall." As soon as he accidently uttered his last name, he knew he had just made a major faux pas.

Captain Riley glared at Reggie, "Is it now? Jake, am I hearin' things or do we have us a niggah' wit' a last name? What do yu' think of dat', Jake?" It was obvious the captain was going to have some fun at Reggie's expense.

"Captain, looks like we got us somethin' 'bery special hych'—one of dose' high-minded cavalier niggahs' who thinks dat' he was born in dah' purple, not in dah' gutter. He looks white an' has a last name to boot. Captain, kin' yu' 'magine dis' fool runnin' 'round in dah' quarters lookin' white an' tellin' all dah' niggahs' his last name? Dey' would probably kill him thinkin' he was fo' sur' a spy." Like the captain, it was very obvious by Jake's words and tone that he was planning something unfortunate for Reggie.

Reggie knew slaves weren't permitted to have a last name, as last names could establish family identification and even respect. This would definitely help to break the bondage system down. "Master, I spoke wit'out thinkin'. My name is Reggie, an' I well know my place. I only meant ..."

Captain Riley abruptly interrupted him. "Oh no niggah', we know what yu' meant. Yu' ain't gittin' by wit' a simple 'pology fo' gross insubordination. Like Jake said, yu' were born in dah' gutter, an' yu' have to know yur' place, an' in dah' gutter is whar' yu' shall remain. An' one other thin', 'round hyeh yu' never even look at dah' color purple let 'lone wear it, yu' high minded fool.

Come hell or high water, 'round hyeh' yu' will learn dah' rules 'bout life on my plantation. Jake, I think dis' niggah' needs to be taken down a peg or two. Let me add one thin' 'fore Jake 'ministers yur' lesson. Mr. Marshall, I purposely singled yu' out fo' eventual household duties, but 'round hyeh' yu' have to earn dat' workin' as a field hand. Now, Mr. Marshall yu' are off to a 'bery poor start. Yu' need to be taught a lesson, an' we know yu' are jus' dyin' to feel dah' sweetness of Judy gently stroked ovah' yur' back."

Jake had something to add. "Thar is nothin' worse din' a niggah' who thinks he is white. Jus' 'member dis' yu' miserable wretch—'yu' can't make a silk purse of a sow's ears's' an' don't yu' forgit' it." Jake was getting anxious to administer the beating and do less talking. "Jus' like yu' said Captain, I kin' feel Judy, an' she's jus' throbbin' to git' at dat' niggahs' back!"

Captain Riley glared at Reggie. "Boy, take dat' blouse off an' knuckle down fo' a good ole' whoopin'. Git' down in dah' dirt on yur' stomach. Jake, jus' 'minister a light whippin' on him dis' time, but next time it will be severe. Jus' 'member mister high brow, yu' are still a niggah' no matter how white yu' might look, an yu' will always be a niggah' till dah' day' yu' die. 'Bove all, yu' don't have a last name. In fact yu' couldn't have a last name any more din' a mule could own dah' plow 'hind him. Now, it's time fo' yu' to git' intimate wit' Judy."

Jake laughed loudly as he reached for his whip. "Captain, dat's a good one, but what disappoints me is dat' des' other two niggahs aren't laughin' wit' us."

"Yu' two niggahs, when yur' master tells a joke, yu' better laugh heartily. If yu' don't, din' Judy will come an' greet yu'! Now laugh!" Both slaves nervously began laughing.

Gibbons administered a few strokes on Reggie's back as Captain Riley supervised the punishment. The captain turned to the other two slaves, and asked, "Do yu' niggahs' understand what happens when yu' have a little sass in yu?'"

Augustus and Jimmy nodded that they understood. Captain Riley added, "It tickles me to death to know dat' yu' boys are so happy an' kin' comprehend dis' little lesson. Now Jake, git' 'em out of hyeh'—dey're beginnin' to stink dah' place up."

Reggie was relieved as he had been spared a harsh whipping. Fortunately, he was not nearly as sore as he had been from his previous beatings.

Quickly the three picked up their few possessions and followed Jake to their new quarters. Jake took Jimmy and Augustus to a small building and then led Reggie to his new home. "Reggie, you're 'signed to live wit' Willy an' Angie right hyeh'. Oh yes, Captain Riley has 'ssigned yu' to dah' plow gang, 'cuz' yu' are kinda' soft an' need toughenin' up. Dah' hoe gang would be too easy. Dah' captain wants dis' to be part of yur' seasonin' 'fore yu' kin' assume house duties in dah' future. Now let's go meet yur' new friends." Gibbons then departed with a sneer on his face.

Reggie looked around the quarters and then approached the small rustic cabin where Willy and Angie lived and knocked on the door. Reggie knew his skin color would be an immediate issue as soon as Willy and Angie answered the door.

A bewildered man looked at him and asked, "Marse' who are yu'?"

Reggie knew he had to respond firmly, "I'm not yur' master. I'm Reggie, a field hand jus' like yu'. Dey' 'signed me to live hyeh'."

"Dey' put ya' hyeh'? Yu' know niggahs' never trust a yeller' niggah' like yu'. We all know who yur' pa could be."

"Yu' will quickly find out dat' I'm not yur' enemy." Reggie knew he needed to bond quickly to avoid more trouble.

"Well, I've got no choice but to put up wit' yah', I'm Willy, an' dis' is my wife Angie. She's gonna' have her first little pickanannie. I guess dey' put yu' wit' us since we don't have any younguns' jus' yet."

"My name is Reggie, an' I'm glad to meet yu'," Reggie assured them, "an' please don't worry 'bout how I look, I can't help it if I'm light skinned."

"I've always given everyone a chance, even if dey' are white," Angie told him, which represented a form of guarded

271

approval. "Reggie, I have some hoe cake sittin' 'round hyeh'. Care fo' some victuals, or are yu' too good fo' niggah' slop," she said with a slight laughter and smile on her face "Oh, if dat' would be dah' case I think yu' are in trouble 'cuz' yu' ain't welcome at dah' big house."

"Angie, dat'll be great—thank yu'. I've been eatin' plain ole' corn pone fo' a long time an' sleepin' on dah' ground while in a slave coffle."

Angie was not surprised at what he just said. "Reggie, yu' are kinda' lucky, 'cuz' yu'll' git' dah' back room all to yur'self'. Lucky fo' yu' thar' is even a cot back thar' all ready to go," Angie assured him.

"Sur', dat'll be fine Angie." Reggie looked around the room where they were sitting. "Interestin' how des' houses are built."

"Des' are called shotgun houses 'cuz' yu' have three rooms all lined up like a shotgun. One day it'll be a comfortable place to raise a baby," Willy smiled as he spoke.

Reggie thanked Angie and Willy profusely as he dug into the food. After swallowing the first bite just to make conversation, he asked, "What's it like 'round hyeh'?"

"Not good! Dat' overseer is plum mean—dey' say dat' he is 'forty miles of bad road'. He carries dat' whip dat' he calls Judy, an' he'll put stripes on yu' fo' no reason—jus' fo' meanness." Willy's warm smile had been replaced by a very somber look as he spoke.

"I already met Judy. Hyeh', take a look." Reggie opened his shirt briefly and showed them his back so they would know he had already encountered the wrath of the overseer along with some bad scars from previous beatings."

"Well, I reckon yu' did find out who Judy is. Do yu' want some fat rubbed on yur' back?" Although Angie had seen and treated similar wounds before, she still winced at Reggie's injuries, as she went about to clean his wounds.

"Angie, I'll be fine, he jus' gave me a real light tannin', but I guess it wouldn't hurt fo' yu' to fix me up, although I've had it a lot worse."

Willy pulled his chair close to Reggie and asked, "What gang did dey' 'sign yu' to?"

"Dah' plow gang, he said somethin' 'bout it helpin' to season me. Incidentally, I'm prepared to take whatever dey' give me." Reggie continued to chow down as he talked.

"Reggie, dah' plow gang is harder, but yu' will be wit' Joseph, which is good. He's our preacher man an' our leader. Me an' Angie are both in dah' plow gang as well."

Reggie was somewhat comforted. "Willy, dat's good to know. When yu' said preacher, I sorta' figured dat' he was yur' leader. Dat's dah' way it is in dah' South. Dah' plantation preacher usually is dah' leader. Let's face it, what better leader is thar' din' dah' preacher man?"

"Reggie, I didn't know dat' dis' was dah' way it was everywhere." Willy was somewhat surprised at Reggie's comment. "I thought dat' Joseph was jus' special from dah' other preachers in dah' South."

"Willy, I don't doubt dat' he is a special man' an' may well be a great leader." Reggie continued, "However, it's common dat' dah' preacher does more din' preach in most slave quarters. It's important to have an' organizer in dah' quarters fo' dah' rights of dah' people." After listening to Reggie for awhile, both Willy and Angie were beginning to get tired.

"At day break, dey' sound dah' horn to git' up, which will come up all too soon Reggie, me an' Angie are goin' to git' some sleep now. She has set things up already fo' yu'." Willy took Angie by the hand and the two walked toward their bedroom. "I hope yu'll feel comfortable wit' me an' Angie in our home."

Reggie was very appreciative, "I want to thank both of yu' fo' welcomin' me into yur' home. I do feel so much better knowin' dat' I will be with yu'. Thank yu' 'gain."

Reggie got up and went into his back bedroom without disturbing Willy and Angie who were in the front bedroom. The long journey, compounded by his recent whipping left Reggie exhausted and weak. He fell onto the cot in sheer exhaustion from the day's events but he couldn't sleep—his mind was racing. First and foremost, he prayed that Anastasia was all right and safely watched over by God. Then he pondered about his first day of work. Unlike other slaves, he had to worry about being accepted because of his skin color. He tossed and turned most of the night, and at sunrise Willy knocked on his door, inviting him to have some hoe cake before the horn was blown.

Reggie was very tired and sore but happy as he returned to the kitchen. He was beginning to feel comfortable in his new setting. The aroma of hoe cake permeated the air as Reggie studied his new home. He complimented Angie for making the best hoe cake he had ever tasted.

The work horn went off to get to work, and Angie told him, "Reggie, yu' foller' Willy. I always help Aunt Wilma fo' a short time, as she takes care of all of dah' little pickanannies ."

Reggie noted a major contrast between Aunt Wilma and Mammy Bertha from Oak Manor. Aunt Wilma only took care of the black children while Mammy Bertha cared for only the white children. Even their titles were different—Aunt and Mammy. In addition, Aunt Wilma resided in the basic slave quarters, while Mammy Bertha lived in the main plantation home and eventually in her own cottage. Their paths would seldom cross even if they both had resided at the same plantation. It represented a clear structural difference, which Reggie recognized as yet another example of the codification within the American bondage system. This example further rendered credence to underground publications that he had read that stated the American bondage system was the most defining slave system in the world. This important social distinction, exemplified yet another example of the systemic foundation of servitude, which was far more defining than people realized. Reggie was further disturbed, knowing that those living in bondage were oblivious to just how much their lives were governed by this organized system, which was designed to keep them at a servile level. One of his missions would be to help educate the slaves to understand some of the evil nuances of the bondage system. Above all, it must be dispelled that the "good old boys" maintained a slave system based merely on "winging it", when in fact, they were far more calculating and above all— exacting in their methods. Matters were always taken into hand with a purpose in mind. Additionally, these extreme measures were implemented to help minimize the potential for any insurrection.

Reggie was staring down at his empty plate, deep in thought when Willy broke his trance. "Reggie, let's git' to work 'fore Walter dah' driver, comes in an' greets us." Reggie shook his head and snapped to attention. He followed Willy to the work site where Walter, the driver was awaiting their arrival.

"So yur' dah' new man. Yu' sur' don't look like a niggah'. I'm yur' driver, Walter, an' I will keep a steady watch, but I'm also 'bery fair. I must say it 'gain, yu' sur' don't look like a niggah'. 'Round hyeh' des' niggahs' may not trust yu'. I was tole' dat' yu' already met Judy but maybe dat' was jus' a setup to fool us niggahs'." Walter stood back, suspiciously looking over Reggie from head to toe. "Don't think dat' we won't be watchin' yu'."

Reggie defended himself. "I'm jus' as much a field hand as any man out hyeh'."

"Well, time will tell," Walter replied. "Isaiah is yur' lead row niggah', so yu' will listen to him as well as me." Cotton farming under the bondage system was fairly consistent. The driver, who was almost always a slave, was the assigned leader of the quarters and subordinate only to the master and the overseer. Below the driver were the lead row men who commanded the plow and the hoe gangs. The number of lead row men could vary with the size of the plantation. It clearly represented a type of rank system perhaps similar to the military. Incidentally, the preacher often represented the "true leader" of the quarters although not recognized by the plantation owner in that role.

Isaiah barked orders at the crew of workers, who were quickly dispatched to their duties. After a time, Jake Gibbons appeared riding a beautiful white horse, which clearly represented his pride and joy. Wearing a palmetto hat, a derringer in his belt, and a whip in his hands, Jake had some similarities to Mr. Eggers, his former overseer. The same garb and accessories—just a different colored horse and smaller in the waistline. He certainly looked the role of a overseer. He loudly ordered, "All hands, tumble up, tumble up, an' to work, all yu' niggahs'! Now make a noise, make a noise an' bare a hand. Sing—sing loud, an' don't stop. Let's hyeh' it, my favorite song, *Roll Jordan Roll.*"

Roll Jordan roll, roll, Jordan, roll, I want to go to
heaven when I die, To hear Jordan roll,
Oh, brothers, yu' ought t'have been thar', Yes my Lord!
A sittin' in dah' Kingdom, To hear Jordan roll.
Roll Jordan roll, roll, Jordan, roll, I want to go to
heaven when I die, To hear Jordan roll,
O, preachers, yu' ought t'have been thar', Yes my Lord!
A sittin' in dah' Kingdom, To hear Jordan roll.
Roll Jordan roll, roll, Jordan, roll, I want to go to
heaven when I die, To hear Jordan roll.
O, sinners, yu' ought t'have been thar', Yes my Lord!
A sittin' in dah' Kingdom, To hear Jordan roll.
Roll Jordan roll, roll, Jordan, roll, I want to go to
heaven when I die, To hear Jordan roll.
O, mourners, yu' ought t'have been thar', Yes my Lord!
A sittin' in dah' Kingdom, To hear Jordan roll.
Roll Jordan roll, roll, Jordan, roll, I want to go to
heaven when I die, To hear Jordan roll.
O, seekers, yu' ought t'have been thar', Yes my Lord!
A sittin' in dah' Kingdom, To hear Jordan roll.
Roll Jordan roll, roll, Jordan, roll, I want to go to
heaven when I die, To hear Jordan roll.
O, mothers, yu' ought t'have been thar', Yes my Lord!
A sittin' in dah' Kingdom, To hear Jordan roll.
Roll Jordan roll, roll, Jordan, roll, I want to go to
heaven when I die, To hear Jordan roll.
O, sisters, yu' ought t'have been thar', Yes my Lord!
A sittin' in dah' Kingdom, To hear Jordan roll.

Walter asked Reggie, "Have yu' ever stood 'hind a mule to plow a field?"

"Yeah, I have," Reggie answered.

"Good, now git' over hyeh' an' work dis' mule," the slave driver ordered. "Des' are cotton plants an' dah' soil has to be turned ovah' to keep dah' weeds out. But don't turn ovah' dah' cotton plants. Now, git' to workin'!"

Reggie took over the plow. The whipping from the previous day, only affected him slightly. He put his back into his work and had no difficulty moving the mule along—his previous experiences proved helpful. Walter looked pleased and left him to his work. Reggie concentrated on working hard to make a good impression on everybody knowing that his looks dictated that he had to do everything right.

Toward lunch, Walter called out, "All hands to eat, to eat, to eat." A mule emerged carrying a skid full of food. Jake Gibbons, who had been present, left to go take lunch in his cottage. Gibbons had a routine which required that he always left for lunch. It was rumored that he enjoyed a couple of drinks while at lunch. Needless to say, the field hands always looked forward to his absence.

Walter, hoping to learn more about his new worker, sat and ate with Reggie. As they were finishing their meal, a rather large, powerfully built man approached them. "Reggie, I want yu' to meet our preacher, Joseph. Joseph dis' is one of dah' new hands, but try not to let his color alarm yu'." Walter made the introduction with a smile on his face.

"Pleasure to meet yu' Joseph." Reggie had looked forward to meeting him so he could share with him the visions he had been having.

Joseph looked at Walter and then Reggie, and then he turned back to Walter. "I've jus' been thrown fo' a loop. We've never had a white man livin' in dah' quarters 'fore."

"Joseph." Reggie explained, "I happen to be of mixed blood. My mother was a slave, an' yu' know dah' system, I shall remain fo'ever a slave."

Joseph strongly responded. "Yu' better not be tied to Marse' Riley comin' down hyeh' to make mischief on us."

"Joseph, I have no ties to Captain Riley. In fact, on dah' first day of my 'rival I got to meet Judy. "

"Both marse' and his overseer are tyrants," Joseph stated. "Dat' overseer almost died last year, but he's too mean to die 'cuz' dah' Lawd' wouldn't accept him an' dah' debil' wouldn't take him!"

Both Reggie and Willy smiled at Joseph's comment, but then in a serious tone, Reggie said, "Joseph, isn't it unfortunate dat' in a country dat' expresses democratic values, we allow people to run roughshod ovah' others wit'out any 'tempt to check thar' cruel, evil ways."

"Sounds to me like yu' know yur' letters an' numbers," the preacher observed. "My speciality is dah' Lawd'. Are yu' right wit' dah' Lawd', Reggie?"

"Joseph, I'm 'bery fortunate to have studied dah' Bible, an' yes, I've found salvation."

"Reggie, yu' seem to be wise beyond yur' years. I've got a question fo' yu'. A lot of us niggahs' down hyeh' seem' to think President Van Buren will do 'way wit' slavery since he is from dah' North. What do yu' think?" Joseph was hoping Reggie would have an opinion that agreed with his.

Reggie thought for a moment before responding. He had gathered information from newspaper articles, editorials and social gatherings while with Albert at Oak Manor plantation. "Joseph, how I wish dat' could be true, but I think what yu' are hopin' fo' represents only a pipe dream. The truth is dat' fo' several complex reasons, most Northerners do not want slavery ended anymore din' Southerners. Dey' are 'fraid dat' if all dah' niggahs' were freed, dey' would swarm up North an' take 'way all dah' jobs from dah' white people 'cuz' dey' would work fo' less money. In fact dah' 'bolitionists who do want slavery ended are hated as much up North as dey' are down South. I hate to tell yu' dis,' but dah' North may not be as sympathetic to our cause as yu' might think, economics dictates keepin' things dah'way are."

"Dah' niggahs' down hyeh' only want hope," Joseph told Reggie. "Our faith in Jesus is all we have."

"I'll give yu' some hope. Mark my words, Joseph, slavery will end in a few years 'cuz' of a violent war 'tween dah' North an' dah' South. Dah' South will not want to end slavery, but dey' will have no choice. Unfortunately, while slavery may end, dah' struggle fo' equality will continue long atter' dah' war."

"Reggie, how do yu' know dis'? Yu' seem to be predictin' dah' future."

With conviction, Reggie stated, "I've got dah' gift to see into dah' future an' in a vision from dah' Holy Spirit, I saw a war fought dat' will end slavery."

The preacher was impressed with Reggie's revelations. "Reggie, I'm an old stump preacher who needs to bring hope to my people, an' it sounds like dat's what yu' are offerin'. God bless yu' fo' tellin' me dis'. On Sunday night we're gonna' have our 'hush harbor'. Will yu' tell all dah' brothers an' sisters what yu've seen? I'm kinda' taken back listenin' to a 'yeller' niggah" fo' dah' first time, an' fo' some funny reason, I kinda' trust yu'."

Reggie was very pleased with Joseph's acceptance of him. "I have tole' others of my visions, but Joseph, yu' are dah' first to really accept it. By dah' way, what's a 'hush harbor'?"

"Dat's a secret meetin' we have deep in dah' backwoods in an ole' shack," Joseph explained. "Us niggahs' git' wit' each other fo' our own Sunday service an' really git' down wit' dah' Lawd'. We foller' dat' wit' a good ole' meetin' jus' to talk 'bout what's goin' on 'round hyeh. Will yu' come an' be a part of our flock? Yu' could come an' add some of yur' 'bery own special touches."

Reggie accepted the invitation quickly, knowing this would be an opportunity to bond with the other slaves. "Of course I'll be thar'!"

The conversation ended as Walter returned from his lunch break. He smiled and clapped his hands as he walked toward Willy, Reggie and Joseph. "All yu' suckers, it's time to git' to work. Pick it up, pick it up, pick it up right now."

At Walter's command everyone went back to work.

Meanwhile, Reggie knew that developing a friendship with Joseph, Willy, and Angie would make a big difference in being accepted by the others in the quarters, and he looked forward to it.

CHAPTER EIGHTEEN

At dusk Reggie, Willy and Joseph met in front of Willy's home. Inhaling the fresh air of the early evening, Joseph commented, "Reggie, how do yu' like workin' 'hind dah' mule?"

"It's ole' stuff. It doesn't bother me," Reggie answered.

Willy seemed preoccupied as he looked throughout the quarters. "Thar' is something mighty fishy goin' on 'round hyeh'—dah' stocks are empty, an' nobody is in dah' box." Willy pointed in the direction of the stocks where slaves were forced to put their arms and head into a contraption that completely immobilized them. The box was a separate, wooden enclosure with only a few holes for air. Punishment in the box was considered more severe than the stocks since you were confined to a small dark enclosure and had to endure unbearable heat in the summer during the day. Both forms of punishment would be considered extremely cruel and unusual by any standards of correction today.

Joseph nodded his head in agreement. "I was wonderin' dah' same thin'. Dis' place is usually a hornet's nest 'round dah' punishment area. Reggie, we're tellin' yu' dis' is not normal."

"It sounds to me like dah' two of yu' are talkin' 'bout dah' calm 'fore dah' storm. I jus' hope dat' yu' are wrong," Reggie commented. "Let's talk on a positive note. 'Morrow is Saturday. Don't we git' off at noon, an' isn't dat' 'lowance time?" On most plantations in the South food allowance when the slaves received their food allotment for the week fell on Saturday when the slaves only worked a half a day.

"Yu' are right, Reggie, yu' kin' come wit' us to dah' big house an' git' yur' 'lowance. We'll teach yu' all dah' ropes," Joseph suggested.

"I don't know if yu' heard, but Saturday night we're gonna' have our 'frolic' in dah' barn," Willy announced. "Everybody always looks forward to dis', an' I hope yu' are gonna' be thar'. Reggie, I kin' proudly say dat' dey' tell me I kin' 'cut a mean pigeon wing'. Yu'll see me goin' at it wit'out stoppin'. Dat's not all Reggie, I also heard dat' in dah' atternoon', Cross'-Eyed' Sam, dah' conjurer is goin' to be hyeh' an' I wouldn't miss him fo' all dah' tea in China."

"I tole' yu' Willy dat' Cross'-Eyed' Sam an' his kind are no good. Dose' conjurers are in cahoots wit' dah' debil'." Joseph shook a finger at Willy as he spoke.

"Joseph, he only gives out roots an' herbs. He's not a hoodoo' man castin' evil spells on people," Willy responded.

"Hoodoo' man, conjurer, or trick doctor dey're' all dah' same." Then Joseph added, "He is doin' dah' debil's work." Voodoo, a French word, was a religious cult found primarily in Louisiana, which often practiced magic rites involving sorcery. Participants in voodoo communicated by trance with their ancestors while believing they could put a curse on others. Conjurers on the other hand, considered themselves to be a positive role model for society. Their primary concern was with medicine by primarily utilizing roots and herbs. This sharply contrasted with the practice of Voodoo, which was generally considered evil amongst most people.

Reggie ignored the argument, smiling as he told his two new friends, "I'm certainly excited 'bout Saturday night. Debil' or no debil', nothin' is gonna' spoil my fun."

The three talked a while longer before retiring for the night. The next morning they worked in the fields until Saturday at noon and then eagerly went to the plantation house to get their food allowances from Aunt Wilma. It rained in the morning, but fortunately by afternoon sunny skies returned.

Many of the slaves sang as they approached the big house. After they received their allowance they sang a song with an unknown title.

"I'm goin' to dah' great house farm, O yea, O yea, O yea
My old master is a good master, O yea, O yea, O yea
Today is 'lowance day, O yea, O yea, O yea
We niggahs' are happy, O yea, O yea, O yea."

After Willy and Reggie had picked up their provisions, Willy suddenly became excited as they approached the barn, "Reggie, I want yu' to meet Cross'-Eyed' Sam. I wanna' git' yur' opinion of him."

"I'll walk ovah' thar' wit' yu', 'cuz' I never met a conjurer, an' Lawd' knows I've been hyehin' 'bout conjurers fo' a long time. Willy, I want yu' to know dat' yu' are not dah' first one I've heard who swears by a conjurer. But Willy, somethin' more important troubles me. Why are dah' niggahs' singin' 'bout how wonderful thar' master is when in fact from what I have heard, he is nothin' more din' a no-good tyrant?" Reggie was somewhat curious about Cross'-Eyed' Sam but far more interested in discussing why his fellow slaves were so acquiescent to their master.

"Reggie, I never thought 'bout it. I do know dat' yu' won't hych' me 'singin' up a storm' 'bout him. I honestly think dat' dey' jus' don't know any better."

"Dat's dah' problem. Dey' have been hoodwinked fo' so long dat' dey' cannot 'see through dah' forest fo' dah' trees'. Dah' slaves lack organization dat' might help 'dem to do somethin' 'bout thar' plight. Get organized an' yu'll be singin' a different tune. Dey' need to git' outta' dis' bottomless pit." Interestingly, Reggie touched on the catalyst for organized labor in the United States.

"Reggie maybe yu' ought to talk to dah' niggahs' 'bout dis'."

"Dat's a good ider', but I'll have to defer fo' now Willy."

As they arrived at the barn, a crowd had gathered around the main attraction, Cross'-Eyed' Sam. Reggie soon realized that Willy was not the only person who looked up to Cross'-Eyed' Sam. His unkempt hair seemed to grow in every direction, and as expected, he was cross-eyed. He wore brown, tattered clothing, a large wide brimmed shapeless hat and shoes that looked like rags tied to his feet. Around his neck was a red scarf that seemed inappropriate for the weather along with his asafatatida necklace to ward off the evil spirits. He looked the role of the consummate ragamuffin.

As the slaves were welcoming Cross'-Eyed' Sam to the plantation, Cross-Eyed Sam noticed Willy from the crowd a few yards away and called out. "How are yu' doin' Willy? I see yu' have yur' asafatatida 'round your neck an' I kin' feel dah' evil spirits have been warded off in yur' life." Reggie found it interesting that Cross-Eyed Sam addressed Willy.

It was obvious that Willy was pleased that Cross'-Eyed' Sam spotted him and remembered his name, and was at a loss for words. He replied, "Yu' kin' do no wrong, Cross'-Eyed' Sam."

Cross'-Eyed' Sam accepted the compliment. "Thank yu', Willy, an' who is dis' white man?" It was apparent that he wanted to meet and speak with Reggie rather then to converse with Willy thinking that Reggie might be of importance.

"Cross' Eyed' Sam, dis' is my friend Reggie—he's one of us."

"What do yu' have to say fo' yur'self' mister."

"Cross'-Eyed' Sam, I'm jus' a common field hand, a hardworkin', spiritual man who's pleased to have dis' opportunity to speak wit' yu'."

"Well yu' sur' don't look like a niggah'." Cross'-Eyed' Sam, taken aback a little, continued. "It doesn't matter to me. I conjure white folks as much as I do niggahs'. White folks pretty much let me wander 'round wit'out a pass. However, I must admit dat' when I come hyeh' I have to be mighty careful. Captain Riley will run me off if he thinks I'm gittin' outta' line. He kin' be 'bout as mean as dey' kin' git'!" It was obvious to Reggie that Cross'-

Eyed' Sam socially put himself well above the other slaves, almost as a fellow peer to the white people.

Reggie's curiousity was piqued as he viewed Cross'-Eyed' Sam with suspicion. "Doesn't yur' master make yu' work?" Reggie was not aware that conjurers throughout the South were given special dispensation by the whites since their roots and herbs represented a hope of a cure rather than just a simple pain relief.

"I'm a conjurer. My work is in my roots an' herb's. Both blacks an' whites call me when dey're sick. Dat's my job. If yu' are askin' me if I pick cotton—no!"

Reggie's suspicion of Cross'-Eyed' Sam went unabated as he continued to wonder if he really knew how to medicate for people or if he was just another flimflam. Reggie queried, "What do yu' do fo' a snake bite?"

Cross'-Eyed' Sam quickly replied, "I use alum, saltpeter an' bluestar mix wit' brandy or whiskey."

"Dat' sounds reasonable. What do yu' do fo' smallpox?"

"Damn, I seldom ever have anybody question me like dis', but I'll tell yu' an' a lot more." The conjurer didn't much like being quizzed by anyone, but Reggie posed his questions politely with a slight smile on his face. "Roots fo' smallpox, bacon fo' mumps, an' sheep's wool wit' tea fo' whoopin' cough."

"Cross'-Eyed' Sam," Reggie chuckled. "I never would have guessed yu' were so scientific."

"Of course I am, but I kin' still cast spells if necessary. 'Member dat', mister smarty pants—'sides hasn't Captain Riley been nice lately?" The conjurer, feeling threatened by Reggie's intelligence and investigative mind, sought to end the questioning on a positive turn.

"Dey' tell me dat' he has been nice lately," Reggie answered.

The conjurer made sure the crowd could hear when he loudly proclaimed, "That's 'cuz' I cast a spell on him not to flog or hurt his niggahs' but instead, be kind!"

"Dat' was good of yu', Cross'-Eyed' Sam," Reggie mocked. "Now yu're sur' nobody tole' yu' earlier dat' Captain Riley has been nice lately?"

285

"Damn, yu' are a 'doubtin' Thomas'. I'm 'bout ready to cast a wicked hoodoo' spell ovah' yu' fo' questionin' me like dis'." Saint Thomas was one of the 12 Apostles. He at first doubted the miracles of Jesus Christ, hence the expression, "doubting Thomas".

Before the conversation heated up any further, Willy interceded, "Cross'-Eyed' Sam, we're leavin', 'cuz' I don't have any needs today. Reggie didn't mean to upset yu'—he's a good man." Willy was not happy with Reggie challenging Cross'-Eyed' Sam, and reminded him that he could still cast a spell over him. Reggie mentally dismissed the whole matter.

While the slaves socialized with each other, Captain Riley and Jake Gibbons walked around, watching the gathering closely. Jake appeared to be troubled since the slaves were having a good time. "Captain, I think letting' dah' niggahs' dance an' sing could eventually mean trouble fo' yu'."

Captain Riley quickly replied, "I've lived all my life in dah' South—my father was a plantation owner an' his father was a plantation owner. I learned what all dah' other plantation owners know—yu' have to give dah' niggahs' a little fun or yu' could break thar' spirits. Jus' a little an' not too much, or dey'll git' indolent. Let dah' niggahs' have thar' play time an' don't bother 'em." The slave owners throughout the South learned to give a little to deter a slave revolt. This calmed many fears and paranoia in the South, especially after the Nat Turner Insurrection. Allowing half-days on Saturday and Sundays off were typical on most plantations. Vacation time was given from Christmas to New Years day. In the thinking of the slave owners, this created a proper balance to maintain stability.

"Jake, what do yu' know 'bout Joseph?" the captain asked.

"Captain, I know dat' dah' preacher is thar' leader," Jake replied.

"I already know dat' dah' preacher man in dah' quarters is almost always dah' leader. What yu' don't know is dat' 'fore our preacher man got religion he was quite a fighter. In fact, I'm lookin' fo' a tough niggah' fighter to make me some money, an' I think Joseph is my boy. I want yu' to take him out of dah' field an' put him into a trainin' program usin' dah' barn startin' early Monday mornin'."

"Damn, Captain, dat's a good ider'," Jake agreed. "Use a niggah' to make yu' some good money. He lives by himself, which means no distractions. He would be perfect."

Gambling was a major preoccupation for male Southerners. Staging fights between two slaves was an extremely popular form of gambling. They fought—no holds barred, bare fisted, kicking, head butting and just about anything else being permissible. These fights were obviously not sanctioned through the state, which meant they did not have hard and fast rules. Throughout the area, they typically fought five-minute rounds and continued until one of the combatants could no longer continue, which precluded a fight ending in a decision. Wagering among spectators could be very large, the biggest fights taking place in New Orleans where people looked forward to seeing the best fighters the South had to offer.

"Yu' gotta' train him full time to git' him into top fightin' condition. I'm lookin' to git' back all dah' money I've lost gamblin'." Captain Riley was in good spirits and all excited as he spoke to Gibbons. He hoped he had a fighter who would make him money to recover his previous gambling losses. "I want everyone to enjoy a real shindig on dis' plantation as we plan fo' dis' new 'venture. In fact, Jake as we talk, dah' wheels have already been put in motion fo' our festivities." With Captain Riley's support the women were busy preparing pork and turkey with sides of corn bread and sweet potatoes.

While Riley and Gibbons were making the rounds, Reggie was making his own observation as the slaves were getting ready to enjoy the wide variety of food that would soon grace their presence. Interestingly, like Oak Manor, he observed raccoon and opossum stews found there way onto the menu. Reggie with "tongue and cheek" had to conclude that raccoon and opossum stews had to be a "gourmet dish" enjoyed by the slaves throughout the South.

The spirit of the slaves had been lifted in anticipation of this special event—they smiled and joked with each other as they went about this very special day working on their assigned tasks. Without any further fear of rain, everybody on the plantation was upbeat about the frolic. Soon everyone seemed to converge on the barn at the same time.

The oversized barn provided plenty of room for dancing. Musicians were set up in one corner with a fiddle, a banjo, a tambourine, and a set of bones. Interestingly with Jake Gibbons conspicuously missing, the music and the dancing carried a different theme—"freedom". Normally, Gibbons would be in attendance to watch over everybody and keep everything in line. The slaves remained puzzled at Captain Riley giving them this much autonomy knowing this was not at all normal. A rare festival, this truly represented a gala occasion on the plantation.

Everyone was in a joyous mood. Joseph and Reggie joined Willy in a circle of slaves who were dancing and singing *"Run Niggah' Run"*, a song enjoyed by the slaves throughout the South with its underground railroad theme.

Run niggah' run, Run niggah' run, de pat'roller ketch yo'
Run niggah' run, it almos' day. Dat' niggah' run, dat' niggah' flew,
Dat' niggah' tore his shirt in two, Dat' niggah', he said don't ketch
me, But, git' dat' niggah' he climb de tree, Dat' niggah' cried
Dat' niggah' lied, dat' niggah' shook his old fat side,
Run niggah', it's almos' day.
Run niggah' run, Run niggah' run, de pat'roller ketchy yo'
Run niggah' run, it's almos' day,
Dat' niggah' run, dat' niggah' flew,
Dat' niggah' tore his shirt in two,
Dat' niggah', he said don't ketch me,
But, git' dat' niggah' he climb de tree, Dat' niggah' cried,
Dat' niggah' lied, dat' niggah' shook his old fat side,
Run niggah', it's almos' day.

Dancing and singing continued at a frenetic pace until

Joseph interrupted the music to announce that it was time for the jigging contest.

Several slaves screamed with joy and danced about until Joseph quieted the crowd and stated the rules. "Y'all know how we do dis', but let me jus' refresh yur' memory. Two at a time will dance in dah' center at a fast pace. Each person has a full glass of water on thar' head as dey' dance. Dah' first one to spill thar' water is out of dah' contest. Din' 'nother takes it up 'til dey' spill thar' water. Yu' keep goin' 'til only one person is left an' dey' are dah' winner of dah' prize. Of course the prize shall remain a secret. Are yu' ready? Now start dah' music, an' let's git' two in dah' center an' git' started."

The contest went on for a long time with one after another eventually spilling their glass of water and having to drop out. Willy, who was an excellent jig dancer, loved to strut his stuff and made it close to the end before he fell out. Finally, a winner was announced by Joseph. "Folks we have a champion jig dancer—Wilbur! He never spilt his water. To dah' best high-steppin' niggah', step up an' git' yur' prize—a large chocolate cake." Wilbur proudly accepted his prize, grinning from ear to ear. Living under such deprivation as the slaves had to endure, it didn't take much to make them happy.

The slaves had a lot of respect for the winner, who was held in high esteem since singing and dancing were such a large part of their lives. Contests and festivities such as this provided a temporary escape from the bleak existence of servitude.

It was not unusual for a party like this to go on through the night and into daybreak. Like everybody else, Reggie, Joseph, Willy and Angie thoroughly enjoyed the event. Joseph, in conversation, turned to the other three and made an interesting observation. "Folks, it hardly seems possible dat' dah' master an' overseer didn't hyeh' all dah' freedom music in dah' barn, an' yet dey' let it go. I'm tellin' y'all—somethin' mighty fishy is goin' on 'round hyeh'! I kin' jus' smell a rat in dah' woodpile."

Willy shared what he thought had made the master so kind. "I was talkin' to Cross'-Eyed' Sam, an' he said dat' he had cast a good spell on dah' master. I kinda' reckon dat's what's goin' on. Jus' thank Cross'-Eyed' Sam."

Joseph disagreed vehemently. "Willy, yu' are plumb crazy believin' dat' conjurin' stuff! Dat's jus' dah' talk of dah' debil' an' would never bring sunshine to our lives. How many times do we have to tell yu'?"

"Willy, Joseph is right," Reggie interjected, "Yu' were standin' thar' when I tole' him dat' he had talked to 'nother slave who tole' him dat' dah' captain was bein' kind. Now he knows dah' captain is bein' kind, so din' he leads y'all to 'lieve dat' 'cock an' bull' story dat' he cast a spell on dah' captain to make him kind. Willy, he's nothin' but a charlatan."

"Reggie, what's dat' word mean—charlatan?" Willy asked.

"It means he is not what he claims to be. It means he's a quack, a fake—call it what yu' want!" Reggie tried to be polite but couldn't help but display his conviction as he responded.

"Reggie, I'll never 'lieve what yu' say 'bout Cross'-Eyed' Sam." Willy raised his voice as he responded.

Joseph added, "Yu don't have to 'lieve Reggie, but I know dat' Sam is no good."

**

Willy had nothing else to say and angrily walked away, exclaiming he was going home. It was late, and Joseph, Reggie, and Angie were tired, so they decided to walk back to their quarters while they followed Willy to be sure his anger didn't cause him to do something he would regret later. Just as they caught up with him, Joseph observed four men on the hill throwing dice.

As they came nearer to the gamblers, Joseph, who as a man of God knew that throwing dice was sinful, asked, "What are yu' men doin' up hyeh'?"

"Preacher, we jus' came up hyeh' to split a watermelon an' throw some craps," one replied.

"Yu' boys are gonna' let dose' craps take hold of yu' an' let dah' debil' git' yu'," the preacher exclaimed.

"Preacher, we're finishin' up. Don't yu' worry, we'll see y'all Sunday fo' dah' 'hush harbor'," another one of the gamblers assuredly stated.

"Well, I better see y'all atter' yu' had a night wit' dah' debil, yur' souls are goin' to need cleansin'," Joseph fiercely admonished.

"Ah, preacher, we ain't thrown craps fo' a long time," another said.

Joseph repeated his admonition. "I better see y'all on Sunday."

Joseph turned and rejoined his friends. "See dat', Reggie? I sometimes think dat' dah' niggahs' are jus' as bad as dah' white folks fo' gittin' involved in sin." He paused a moment and then looked at Willy. "Wouldn't it be a perfect night to go snipe huntin'? What do yu' think, Willy?"

"Joseph, I think yu' are right. It looks to be a perfect night. I'm sur' dah' snipe are runnin'."

Joseph turned toward Reggie. Reggie did yu' ever go snipe huntin' in old Virginny'?"

"I can't say dat' I have ever hunted snipe."

Joseph told Willy to go to the barn and retrieve a gunny sack, and then added, "Git dose' crap shooters over hyeh' fo' dah' snipe hunt as well."

Willy scrambled off after a gunny sack and then brought along the dice throwers who agreed to join them. "I know a good place whar' dah' snipe's are runnin'. It's right over dat' hill," Joseph told everyone. "In fact, I heard some niggahs' caught some jus' dah' other night over thar'. Let's git' goin' straight away an' stop dis' lollygaggin'."

Willy had forgotten all about the conjurer incident by now and was excited to get the hunt going, "I jus' talked to one of dose' niggahs', an' dey' 'greed dat' it was a good night to go snipe huntin'."

"Yu know, Reggie, we all kinda' like yu' 'round hyeh', so we are goin' to reward yu' by letting' yu' hold dah' bag." Joseph handed the gunny sack to Reggie. "Dat's dah' best job yu' kin' have on a snipe hunt. Yu' will be at dah' scene of dah' action wit' dah' most important job."

"What'll I do?" Reggie asked.

"Yu' jus' hold dah' bag an' yell, 'hyeh' snipe, hyeh' snipe'!" Joseph instructed. "Jus' keep yellin' 'hyeh' snipe' an' be sur' to keep dah' bag to dah' ground. Meanwhile, we'll do all dah' work, we're gonna' beat dah' bushes an' make a lot of noise. Jus' hold dah' bag facin' us. Usually, a snipe will run right into dah' bag if we make 'nough noise."

"Dis' all sounds a little crazy to me, but I'm ready fo' anythin', I'm a good sport." Reggie agreed, taking the gunny sack from Joseph. "I know y'all do things a little different down hyeh' in Georgia, but I didn't know it would be dis' different."

Everyone left Reggie holding the bag and ran up the hill. At the top everyone yelled and beat the ground with sticks while Reggie held the bag calling out, "hyeh' snipe, hyeh' snipe, hyeh' snipe."

Joseph came right up to Reggie furiously yelling and beating the ground. Then he paused and stated, "Reggie did yu' jus' see dat' snipe run by? I led him to yu' an' yu' missed him. 'Member to watch us, when we are near yu'. Yu' have to pay 'tention. Dat' was a good size snipe, an' yu' let him go right by."

"Joseph, I plumb missed him." Reggie was thoroughly disappointed in himself. "He must have really been movin' fo' me to miss him. Joseph, jus' what do dey' look like? Yu' never tole' me."

"Reggie, dey' look like a cross 'tween a rabbit an' a squirrel," Joseph answered in a serious tone. In truth, a snipe is really a longbilled wading bird.

"Joseph, I've never seen anything like dat' 'fore—least not in Virginny'," Reggie exclaimed. He had no idea what to expect.

"I'm headin' back up to dah' hill an' maybe even a little further. Yu' jus' keep yellin', 'hyeh' snipe, hyeh' snipe',"

"I'll give it another try, but I jus' can't git' a grip on dis' sport." Reggie wanted to impress Joseph, but he certainly had done poorly thus far.

"I'll see yah' shortly—so long," Joseph called out as he

took off up the hill to join the others.

Reggie continued yelling and listened for the others while beating the ground. Their voices were getting fainter and further away. He thought maybe the snipe were running in the wrong direction but soon would be driven back to him. Meanwhile, he continued to yell for the snipe as instructed. Eventually, he could no longer hear any voices at all and then he began to wonder if he had been tricked. Fifteen more minutes passed, and he knew it was time to abandon the game and get home since it became so quiet. He left at a quick pace and caught up with everybody. They were waiting fo' him and laughed boisterously as he approached. Reggie knew that his suspicions were correct—he had just been duped.

Reggie laughed at himself. "I've jus' had dah' 'wool pulled ovah' my eyes', an' I shoulda' known better. Joseph, yu', a preacher man workin' me ovah'—lyin' to me. Why yu' should be ashamed of yur'self."

"Now Reggie, dah' Lawd' says yu' kin' tell a little white lie every now an' din'! I jus' used up my little white lie. Jus' 'member dis', now yu' are one of us." Reggie now felt assured they trusted him, and he was now accepted as one of them.

"Well, white people would say I jus' had my initiation into dah' group an' I gladly accept. I knew somethin' wasn't right, but I still fell fo' it." Reggie continued to laugh even harder, his sides beginning to hurt.

Willy was laughing the loudest. "None of us knows our letters or numbers, but we know better than to fall fo' dat' old snipe trick. Doesn't dat' make yu' feel a little like a fool?" Willy was poking fun at Reggie to get back at Reggie for the Cross'-Eyed' Sam incident.

Reggie finally stopped laughing. "I want all of yu' to know dat' we deserve a little fun even at my expense. We have to know how to rise from oppression an' not let dis' evil system git' dah' best of us. Keep our spirits up an' soon freedom will arrive, dat' is dah' key to our success." This was a light occasion, but Reggie still found himself moralizing.

"Reggie, even though we've only known yu' a short time, yu' have a way of keepin' our spirits up even if we don't always understand yu'. We are fortunate to have yu' wit' us," Joseph gratefully added as he put his arm around him to accept him into their group.

Everyone laughed and nodded in agreement, ending a wonderful and enjoyable evening.

CHAPTER NINETEEN

Mrs. Winters asked Anastasia to sit with her in the parlor. Whenever Mrs. Winters invited her to sit down, Anastasia knew the conversation would be pertinent.

It was a comfortable, bright Sunday afternoon and Mrs. Winters looked excited. "Anastasia I enjoyed dah' church services so much—it's seems like I always come out feelin' filled wit' dah' spirit. I know dat' yu' have strong spiritual beliefs as well. Today, I want to share wit' yu' some good news dat' should have a profound affect on yur' life."

Anastasia nervously fidgeted in her chair wondering what was next as she asked, "Yes, Mrs. Winters?"

"I talked to Colonel Marshall 'bout buyin' yur' papers from him. Dat' way yu' will be protected from any possible harm."

"Mrs. Winters, will he 'gree?" If Colonel Marshall and Mrs. Winters could reach an agreement, the news would be exciting and wonderful for Anastasia. Having been hired out to Mrs. Winters, Colonel Marshall at his discretion could take her back at the end of the one year contract. The one year contract that Mrs. Winters agreed to was for $150 dollars, which was the usual amount charged throughout the area.

"Dat' won't be a problem as I have done some special favors for him through dah' years an' he owes me one or two in return. Besides, Evelyn would be all fo' it. An' dats' not all—I have decided dat' in my will I am includin' papers of manumission fo' yu' upon my death."

"Mrs. Winters, I think I know what dat' means," Anastasia responded. "I jus' want it explained to me a little further."

"Anastasia, dat' means one day yu' will be as free as me— no longer somebody else's property," Mrs. Winters imparted. Now, does all dis' news make yu' feel any better?"

When she heard the news, Anastasia suddenly became dumfounded with excitement. She was going to escape the dark and sinister side of slavery, which in her judgment was a blessing that had to be sent from the Lord. Exuding gratitude she imparted, "Mrs. Winters I can't thank yu' 'nough fo' all dat' yu' have done fo' me, an' now dis'!" Tears of joy flowed from her eyes as she continued to express her profound thanks.

Mrs. Winters acknowledged her sincere gratitude but took it all in stride. She was interested in discussing an issue that was dear to her heart. "Yu' know, Anastasia most Southern women deep in thar' hearts are 'bolitionists. It's dah' men who keep dis' evil institution 'live. I 'lieve dat' God never meant dat' one man should ever own 'nother man. I'm expressin' dis' to yu' in dah' strictest of confidence as it is somethin' dat' kin' never be discussed in public." Interestingly, Southern women were very careful in usually not expressing publicly their feelings dealing with any controversial issues such as slavery. This might suggest that the South was a very patriarchal society.

Anastasia, still in a state of shock from hearing the good news politely stated, "Mrs. Winters, I've sensed dah' same thin', but I could never mention it. I always felt dat' Mrs. Marshall only tolerated it. I too believe dat' Southern women have more compassion din' dah' men."

"Anastasia, dah' problem is twofold as I see it. First, we've got dah' plantation owner takin' advantage of his female servants—yu' are a product of dat' terrible stain. Second, we have dah' powerfully built Negro men—dah' breeders who move from one plantation to 'nother, 'signed to keep all dah' women pregnant. Incidently, usin' powerfully built men insures dat' dah' children should grow up to be powerfully built as well. More babies—more money fo' dah' slave master. An' tragically, most of dah' Negro children couldn't even tell yu' who thar' father is. It's simple economics over dah' good of humanity. It's evil, an' it all boils down to Virginny' raisin' Negroes like raisin' cattle— breedin' fo' sale. Yu' know as well as I do we don't need slave labor. Whars' dah' cotton grown in Virginny' to necessitate dah' gang system of labor? Maybe jus' a little in dah' southern part of Virginny', but dat' would be it—its got to be jus' to breed 'dem fo' sale down South since dey' have little agricultural value up hyeh'. Well, eventually dah' Negroes are sold an' do wind up further down South whar' dey' are used mainly in dah' cotton field's whar' dah' gang system is flourishin'. It's like one hand washes dah' other in our beloved South, an' it's all 'bout money."

Anastasia was a bit naïve regarding this subject. "I've always been a personal servant, an' I've never seen or heard much 'bout dis' subject. Fortunately, I've been in dah' 'big house' most of my life."

Mrs. Winters continued. "What disturbs me is dat' eventually all dah' Negroes will be free, but how will dah' Negro families be able to heal from all dis' turmoil? Dey' will be left wit' absolutely no foundation. I'm 'fraid a terrible injustice has been served. It will be a long, painful struggle fo' dah' Negro families to recover from dis,' an' even worse, I wouldn't ever expect white people to fully understand dah' harm dey' have caused. Also, as dah' Negroes struggle wit' freedom, whites will continue to 'lieve dey' have no responsibility fo' any of dah' social adjustments dat' Negroes will have to undergo dealin' wit' freedom. Dey' will continue to wanta' believe dey' are inferior to white people, an' whatever happens wit' dah' Negro race, dey' will say dat' dey' brought it on 'demselves. Well, 'nough of dat' talk fo' now—I think it would be 'bout time to prepare supper."

"Mrs. Winters may I say one thin' 'fore I return to dah' kitchen?" Anastasia meekly asked.

"Please do, Anastasia."

"I too have felt dah' terrible wrath of dis' system. I was separated from my husband right atter' we were married, an' I have no ider' whar' he might be now. He was sold at auction in

Richmond. I know dat' some white people think dat' I could jus' find somebody else to take up wit', but I deeply love my husband an' would do anythin' to have him back. I don't want anyone else. Dis' is dah' anguish I go through all dah' time. I apologize fo' havin' poured out my heart 'bout dis "witches brew",' but it's one more thin' dat' fits into what yu' were sayin'. I truly do love my Reggie, an' miss him greatly."

Mrs. Winters felt sorry for Anastasia. "I'm glad yu' shared dat' wit' me, Anastasia. I wish yu' would have tole' me dis' sooner. Anyhow, yu' would have one option available. Yu' could check wit' dah' auction house whar' he was sold, dey' keep a record of all sales. Dat' would be dah' best place to start."

"Thank yu', Mrs. Winters, for everythin' yu' have done fo' me. I don't know dah' right words to express how grateful I am. To know dat' I am now safe from bein' harmed is more din' a Godsend, 'cuz' I've spent a lot of agonizin' moments fearin' dat' I might be sold down South an' end up in New Orlens'. I also know what would happen to me once I was thar'—it's unspeakable. I'm so thankful to yu'. I jus' pray dat' one day soon I will find out if Reggie is 'live. I know he is—I kin' jus' feel it in my bones. I kin' start by checkin' wit' dah' auction house. Anastasia purposely avoided mentioning Colonel Marshall's sexual advances toward her knowing that certain things were left better unsaid. Even among white women in conversation, this was a topic that was almost always kept "underground".

***

Reggie's life in servitude had also improved as he had gained the confidence and friendship of Joseph and Willy. Their acceptance of him assured him that he would most likely be well received by others on the Riley plantation.

Lately on Sundays, Captain Riley did not require the slaves to attend services with the whites. The slaves were elated, since they deplored having to listen to a white minister. What they did look forward to were evening services conducted by Joseph in a small shack located in the woods away from the quarters.

Sunday evening quickly arrived along with the "hush harbor service", and Reggie, now in the inner circle, was invited to attend.

Joseph explained to Reggie the importance of the "hush harbor". "A white preacher will take dah' Bible an' try to tell us dat' in Gods eyes, we aren't as good as 'dem. Din' he will go on an' on 'bout us folk obeyin' our master an' how dah' white people are able to take good care of us helpless black people. But hyeh' in our hush harbor we kin' 'steal a meetin'' an' tell dah' real truth."

"Joseph in two separate sentences yu' have directly brought up dah' bedrock fo' slavery in dah' South dat' white people use to justify dis' evil system. First, yu' mentioned dah' white preacher tellin' us dat' in God's eyes we aren't as good as dey' are. Well, if we look at Genesis 9:21 through 27, dah' Bible says dat' Ham walked in on his drunken father, Noah who was lyin' naked inside his tent. Instead of immediately turnin' his back, Ham looked an' gazed at him while his two brothers entered an' covered thar' father wit' a garment. Unlike Ham, dey' turned away from him. When Noah awakened from his stupor an' found out dat' Ham had stared at him in dah' nude, he cursed Ham, an' condemned all of his descendents fo' all time. Usin' dat' condemnation, Southerners have misused dah' Bible by usin' dah' dictionary to conclude dat' Noah had blackened Ham's descendants since blacken quite literally means to defame or sully, which also means to disgrace an' disgrace similarly means to condemn. So condemn can mean blacken, an' din' blacken would apply only to black people an' not white people. Yu' see, dah' dictionary also provides a second meanin' fo' blacken, which is to make dark or black. So what dah' Southerners have done is to take dah' two meanings of blacken an' combine dem' into one, which would din' justify condemnin' black people fo' all time as dah' pariah on mankind. Now yu' kin' see how white people manipulate dah' Bible in conjunction wit' dah' dictionary to suit thar' own needs an' falsely condemn us."

Joseph listened intently and interrupted, "Reggie, dat' really places all of us in a bad light wit' little or no hope fo' equality. What kin' we do?"

"Joseph, dat' is a 'bery difficult question to answer. Now we know whar' dah' magician has performed his trickery. It really is clever but horribly evil to make dis' one of dah' 'bedrocks' fo' dis' shameful system dat' we have to live under. Misusin' dah' Bible an' dah' dictionary in itself is a sin. Yu' know dat' God would have never intended to wrongfully twist dah' interpretation of blacken. In order to directly answer yur' question an' git' me off my diatribe, I personally think dat' knowledge an' education are dah' key, but din' as a slave, we are fo'bidden to learn to read an' write. Joseph, I kin' summarize dis' horrible system as a vicious circle dat' jus' keeps goin' round an' round, an' we kin' only pray it will eventually stop wit' dah' truth."

"Reggie, dats' a mouthful to swallow. Somehow, I have to explain dis' to our people, an' it is a bit confusin'," Joseph stated almost in a bewildered state.

"Joseph, dah' ramifications of dis' are enormous. Dis' means yu', a Negro kin' never be equal to a white man. Yu' could even be a paragon fo' Jesus Christ while a white man could be a model fo' dah' debil', yet in dah' end, 'cuz' yu' are a Negro an' he is a white man, yu' shall remain fo'ever his inferior. Atter' all, yu' have been blackened. No matter how great yu' may be in makin' a contribution to society while dah' white man could be a total failure, yu' have to fall short! Dah' curse of Ham is on yu'! Hopefully when slavery does end, dis' dreadful miscarriage of dah' Bible will be put to rest, but I'm 'bery fearful 'dat' white people will want to continue 'lievin' dat' Negroes are inherently inferior to 'dem. I'm beleaguerin' dah' point Joseph, but a Negro could do great deeds an' yet he'll still be jus' a niggah', an' not even equal to a drunken, worthless white man. In fact, dah' worthless white man will say to dah' successful black man dat' he is a white man an' as such, better din' any niggah'! It really is soberin' since yu' know dat' yu' are gonna' have to be a much better man din' dah' white man to git' anywhar' in life. I do pray dat' I'm wrong in portendin' dis' shameful prediction, but in my heart, I truly 'lieve dat' white people will continue to feel superior to black people. Unfortunately Joseph, dis' awful miscarriage of the Bible has created a shameful division 'tween dah' two races, which will only continue.

Joseph was flabbergasted while listening to Reggie. He wanted to hear more. "Even though yu' use such big words, it still makes sense to me. Now as a preacher I would like to hyeh' dah' second part of yur' response to what I had said earlier."

"Joseph, I'll answer yur' question. When dah' white Southern preacher warns us dat' as servants we must obey our master, he correctly has used dah' Bible to justify dis'. Ephesians 6:5 states, 'servants be obedient to 'dem dat' are yur' master accordin' to dah' flesh wit' fear an' tremblin' in singleness of yur' heart as unto Christ'." Reggie remained fixated on Joseph as he stated this verse. While showing anguish on his face, he recalled reading this same verse earlier at Oak Manor when he was a personal servant to Albert.

Joseph, looking confused, responded. "Reggie dat's' 'nother tough pill to swallow."

"Again, not to despair, dat' is not all of it. Yu' see dis' is only half dah' story. If yu' read on in Ephesians 6:9, it says, 'an', masters, do dah' same things to dem', an' give up threatenin', knowin' dat' both thar' Master an' yurs' is in heaven, an' thar' is no partiality wit' Him'."

Joseph was taken back at this last verse that Reggie recited. "Why doesn't dah' white preacher read dis' verse as well?"

"Joseph, I think yu' kin' answer yur' question yur'self. Joseph, now yu' are gittin' to dah' crux of dah' problem. Dey' only want yu' to hyeh' what's important fo' 'dem to support thar' evil system. Why would dey' want to tell dah' whole story? Yu' will only hyeh' half —dah' part dat' dey' use to justify dat' God intended the servant to obey his master while omitting the part that says the master has an obligation to be impartial. Impartiality touches on equality an' yu' can't have dat'! Why dat' would be a breakdown of dah' whole evil system."

Joseph was mesmerized by what he had heard. "Reggie, I wish more people knew what yu' jus' tole' me."

"Joseph, I guess yu' are gonna' have to deliver dah' word at one of yur' 'hush harbors', an' my fondest wish is dey' all will want to hyeh' an' profit from dah' truth. 'Member Joseph, education is dah' key an' it is up to us to try to educate ourselves an' others 'cuz' dah' white folks sur' ain't gonna' do it fo' us."

"If dat' ain't dah' truth!" Joseph refreshingly stated, "I'm really anxious to spread dah' truth."

Reggie replied wit' conviction, "Yu' know dat' bad people kin' always find a way to justify thar' evil doins'—even a killer kin' justify killin' 'nother person. In fact, I kin' recall hyehin' 'bout a man who took dah' lifes of children an' justified his actions on dah' grounds dat' dah' world was evil, an' by takin' thar' lifes dey' could be wit' dah' Lawd' in heaven whar' in his wicked, an' twisted mind he could reason dat' dey' were in a better place. Dis' is dah' most horrible justification of usin' pure evil dat' I kin' come up wit', but it is true dat' it is done. Well, dah' South has concocted a way to justify thar' evil ways—misusin' our sacred Bible. I'm tellin' yu' Joseph, dah' bedrock fo' American slavery rests wit' a horrible misapplication of dah' Bible. Our bondage system is disgustin', an' horribly evil! It jus' ain't right an' I'll leave it at dat'."

"Yu' rightfully got' worked up ovah' dis'," said Willy, who had been listening but not saying a word.

Reggie said with some frustration, while exhibiting deep concern. "Willy, dis' is a subject dat' is dear to my heart, an' I dare say dah' truth should be known to all."

"Yu'll see, Reggie, what Joseph was sayin' earlier 'bout dah' white preacher," Willy interjected. "Yu' haven't been forced to attend Sunday services hyeh' wit' dah' white people, but yu' will. It's bad, Reggie, 'cuz' dey' make us niggahs' sit up in dah' galley while all dah' white folks sit down in dah' front. We know it ain't right, but dat's dah' way it is. One day yu' will be forced to go to thar' church an' din' yu' will see it fo' yur'self what shouldn't be allowed in a house of dah' Lawd', but fo' now let's jus' enjoy our hush harbor."

Reggie with a smile on his face had a meaningful joke to tell. "Look at sittin' in dah' galley from 'nother angle. It's dah' one time of dah' year when yu' will be ovah' dah' white folks." Reggie paused for a laugh and then went on. "I personally kin' recall a personal experience when I was a personal servant an' had to sleep on a small cot jus' barely off dah' floor while my master slept on a bed 'bove me. I always wanted to sleep equal to my master, but it could never happen. In fact, he wanted it too, but it was prohibited. 'Member, dah' clear separation 'tween a niggah' an' a white man cannot be breached."

It was apparent that Joseph and Willy appreciated the discourse that Reggie provided.

As they entered the shack, Joseph made sure everything was set up correctly. "Git' dose' pots turned up." The pots absorbed the sound, so singing wouldn't carry as far. Joseph continued, "Charley yu're our trusted raid-fox. Did yu' git' dah' grape vines stretched out whar' dose' pattyrollers like to ride?"

"Preacher, I sur' did, an' I'm goin' out thar' right now," Charley answered. "If I hyeh' 'dem comin', I'll yell loud an' clear as I run dose' fools into dah' vines."

In many parts of the South, slaves met secretly at night. Sunday evenings were the favorite time because they could combine the Sunday church services with their general meeting to discuss various affairs they needed to know. To avoid the whites being "tipped off", the slaves used code words when whites were present. Notably, they were more popular with house servants who were constantly in the presence of whites. One thing for sure, they all knew their code words as it was another must for their survival.

The "hush harbor" was the meeting house, and the "raid fox" was the man who watched out for the patrollers. The "pattyrollers" as the slaves called them, were men paid by the county to catch runaways while patrolling the quarters to make sure that nothing else unusual was taking place. Interestingly, they were also attached to the active militia. This helped to explain why the militia in the South was far more active than in the North. Further, a "hush harbor" meeting was illegal since a white man was not present to preside. That made the "hush harbor" a favorite target of the patrollers. It was a "cat and mouse game" between the owners who used the patrollers to police the slaves and the slaves who were involved in activities deemed illegal.

As soon as Charley secured himself in his position outside, Joseph began the evening services. "'Fore we start singin', I wanta' ask Reggie if dey' ever patted juba in ole' Virginny?"

"I can't say dat' I know." Reggie looked bewildered and asked, "What does it mean?"

"Us niggahs' don't need musical instruments," Joseph informed him. "We kin' make music jus' hittin' different parts of our body or objects as well. Jus' join in—yu' will' see." Pattin' juba" became a traditional way of making sound to produce music.

Joseph smiled at Reggie and raised his arms toward heaven asking everyone to sing one of their favorite songs, *Oh, Freedom.*

Oh freedom! Oh, freedom!
Oh, freedom over me;
An' 'fore I'll be a slave,
I'll lie buried in my grave,
An' go home to my Lawd' an' be free.
No more mournin', no more mournin',
No more mournin' over me;
An' 'fore I'll be a slave,
I'll be buried in my grave,
An' go home to my Lawd', an' be free.
No more mournin', no more mournin',
No more mournin' over me;
An' 'fore I'll be a slave,
I'll be buried in my grave,
An' go home to my Lawd', an' be free.
Oh, freedom! Oh, freedom!
Oh' freedom over me;
An' 'fore I'll be a slave,
I'll be buried in my grave.
An' go home to my Lawd', an' be free.

After singing everyone chanted "we shall overcome" for some time until Joseph lowered his arms to his side.

Joseph began his sermon: "Brothers an' sisters of dah' Lawd', we are gathered hyeh' to bring thanks knowin' dat' one day we will be free at last, free at last. Praise dah' Lawd, we will be free at last. Free at last, free at last. Oh, Lawd, free at last. Oh, Lawd, we kin' see it. Oh, Lawd', we kin' feel it comin'. Free at last. Oh, Lawdy', one day we'll be free at last."

Joseph had more to say. "Brothers an' sisters, y'all know we have a new man wit' us, Reggie, an' I wanta' have him tell us 'bout what he has seen in des' visions dat' he has. God has given him dah' gift of seein' into dah' future."

Reggie had not planned to speak but gathered his thoughts and stood up and said, "Brothers an' sisters, as I stand hyeh' 'fore yu', I want all of yu' to know as yu' sing out dah' words 'free at last' yu' better start thinkin' 'bout eventually bein' free, as it's not dat' far in dah' future when we will all be 'free at last'."

Everyone encouraged him to continue as they gasped in disbelief and anticipation. "Oh, Lawd' keep talkin' an' don't stop. We wanta' hyeh' some more of yur' sweet words to dah' ear. Keep goin'. Praise dah' Lawd', an' bless me, Jesus!"

"Brothers an' sisters, dah' Lawd' has given me dah' gift to look into dah' future an' I kin' see what's gonna' happen. In my first vision, I saw a gangly lookin' white man deliverin' a speech honorin' dah' dead at a gravesite fo' a battle dat' was waged 'tween dah' North an' dah' South. In dat' battle, thousands of soldiers had died, but dah' North 'ventually won. Other battles follered', but in dah' end, dah' war brought down slavery, an' all of our brothers an' sisters were made free. Fo' us, all of dis' is comin' soon, an' y'all will be 'free at last'. I know dah' vision is real, an' I know it's goin' to happen. I know we all want hope, an' I'm bringin' dah' message of hope. Don't give up—keep fightin' an' hang on, 'cuz' freedom is comin', an' dah' mean old master won't have any choice but to step back an' let freedom roll." Throughout the South, amongst the slaves the words—Jesus, hope, and "free at last" resonated constantly.

As Reggie finished, the crowd was overtaken with joy at what they had just heard. What Reggie had said raised their spirits. The emotions ran high throughout the fellowship, realizing this man was bringing the message they wanted to hear, "free at last" and "we shall overcome" could be heard resonating throughout the room.

Even Charley, the "raid fox", could hear them and entered the meeting. "I could hyeh' y'all way out in dah' woods. Lawdy', what's goin' on hyeh'? I was 'fraid y'all would brin' dah' pattyrollers fo' sur' wit' all dat' infernal shoutin'."

"Charley, don't worry 'bout dose' pattyrollers," Willy told him, "we are gonna' be 'free at last'. If dose' pattyrollers show up, we'll jus' fight back!"

"I wouldn't go quite dat' far jus' yet," Reggie interjected. Everyone smiled, knowing their celebration could be a bit premature.

Joseph stated, "Reggie, maybe dah' Lawd' sent yu' hyeh' to bring hope an' His light into our lives. Hope, Reggie, dat's what we all need—hope an' more hope. Brothers an' sisters, we all are gonna' make it 'cuz' we know dat' we will be 'free at last'."

After services Joseph, Angie, Willy and Reggie walked back to the quarters in a more spirited mood, even though Monday morning would bring another long work week. Joseph stopped and turned to Reggie, "Yu' are really special. When I heard yu' talk, it dawned on me dat' a man's words can be much stronger din' his fist. I couldn't git' over how the niggahs' were so drawn to yu'. Yu' look like a white man, yet yu' could tell dat' dey' trusted yu'. Dat' really is a gift, Reggie. Use it wisely, an' yu' will be able to do a lot of good fo' all of our brothers an' sisters."

It was highly unusual for native, full-blooded African slaves to have any trust in anybody who was of mixed blood. Reggie's talents transcended the normal and allowed him to gain implicit trust. He truly represented an anomaly among the slaves.

"Thank yu' Joseph," Reggie humbly said, "but really I jus' spoke dah' truth an' related to what I have seen, jus' be sur' y'all are ready fo' dis'!"

"Reggie, all of dah' sisters were spellbound by yu'. I could tell yu' put 'dem in a bigger trance din' any conjurer could have." Angie looked directly at Willy as she spoke.

"Now, Angie, yu' are bein' too kind," Reggie replied, "but I want yu' to know dat' we are all in dis' together, an' dah' Lawd' gives all of us somethin' special. It's jus' dat' dah' Lawd' gave me dis' visionary gift, an' I have to use it fo' dah' good of all. I jus' can't 'lieve dat' I could have put my people in a bigger trance din' Cross'-Eyed' Sam," Reggie said with a wink and a smile.

"Yu' know, Reggie, if yu' wanted to study roots an' herbs, yu' could become a conjurer an' be better at it din' Cross'-Eyed' Sam." Willy was trying to compliment Reggie, naively believing that Reggie might be interested in becoming a conjurer.

Everyone laughed at Willy's comment. "Now, Willy, don't be comparin' Reggie to Cross'-Eyed' Sam," Joseph added. "Do yu' really believe dat' Cross'-Eyed' Sam, who is filled wit' dah' debil', could ever hold a candle to Reggie? Come on now—stop joshin'!"

"Willy, I know I'm married to yu'," Angie joined in, "but sometimes I do wonder. I never say much 'bout yu' an' dat' conjure talk, but to compare Reggie to dat' creepy Cross'-Eyed' Sam—why all dah' women 'round hyeh' would think yur' nuts. Reggie is truly handsome an' bery' wise. I don't know what yu' would call Cross'-Eyed' Sam other din' a creepy ole' scarecrow!"

"I'm sorry dat' I ruffled everyone's feathers," Willy said defensively. "I jus' 'lieve dat' Cross'-Eyed' Sam has brought me good luck."

"All right, Willy, yu' 'lieve what yu' want to 'lieve, but don't compare him 'gain to Reggie." Angie and Joseph said almost the exact same thing at the same time, and then laughed it off.

Reggie excused himself and went to bed, sleeping restlessly, while pondering over Anastasia, and her fate.

***

Early Monday morning arrived with the horn blasting—

307

Reggie and Willy went directly to the field while Angie went to help Aunt Wilma with the children.

Reggie was breaking the ground with the mule when Captain Riley and Mr. Gibbons appeared riding up. Captain Riley yelled out, "I want all yu' niggahs' over hyeh' right now. Y'all know dat' nothin' dat' go's on 'round hyeh' gits' past me. Well, I know dat' all yu' niggahs' got together in dat' shed last night an' were out thar' raisin' a ruckus. I shoulda' sent dah' patrollers to break it up, but I didn't. Y'all know why? 'Cuz' I'm dah' good-hearted master, an' I'm jus' gonna' let it pass, but I got somethin' else to say. Saturday, when yu' pick up yur' 'lowance, I want all yu' suckers to take yur' annual spring cleanin' concoction of molasses, sulfur, an' sassafras tea to purify yur' blood. Also, git' yur'selves cleaned up. I could smell all yu' suckers comin' hyeh'—nothin' worse din' a bunch of stinky niggahs' all filled wit' body lice an' bed bugs."

Jake added, "Yu' niggahs' are lucky dat' Captain Riley kin' be so nice."

Then Captain Riley ordered Joseph to approach him.

"Yes, Marse', "Joseph asked.

"We know, Joseph dat' yu' are dah' leader who takes dah' niggahs' up to dat' shack in dah' back woods to pray every Sunday evenin'," he began. "Well, I kin' let some things slide 'round hyeh' an' dat's one of 'dem. Yu' see, Joseph, I got dah' word dat' yu' use to be quite a fighter 'fore yu' got religion. Well, I want to help revive yur' interest in fightin'."

"Marse', when I was saved, I gave myself to dah' Lawd an' quit fightin'." Joseph thought he knew what was coming next and hoped the captain would accept what he said.

Captain Riley glared at Joseph. "Is dat' right now? Well, I'm gonna' make yu' an' offer yu' can't resist. Now Joseph, I know dat' yu' kin' lead a horse to water, but yu' can't make him drink it. But I also know yu' kin' salt dah' oats, an' guess what? He'll drink dah' water an' lots of it. Now, how might I salt dah' oats to git' yu' to fight?"

"Marse', yu' couldn't put 'nough salt in dah' oats to git' me to fight 'gain," Joseph replied.

"Is dat' right now, Joseph?" Riley queried. "I guess I'm gonna' have to prove yu' wrong. I'm tellin' yu' dat' if yu' don't fight, din' all hell is gonna' break loose 'round hyeh', an' it will be yur' fault fo' not listenin' to yur' master. Joseph, haven't yu' noticed things have been so nice 'round hyeh' lately?"

"Marse', we all have noticed dat' dah' stocks an' box are empty," Joseph replied in agreement.

"Well, Joseph, dah' reason dah' stocks an' box are empty is not by accident, 'cuz' I kinda' knew dat' yu' were gonna' set an example fo' all dah' niggahs' 'round hyeh' an' show 'dem how yu' could make yur' master some extra money." Captain Riley looked directly into Joseph's eyes so there would be no doubt as to how serious he was.

"I understand dat', Marse'." Joseph's heart sank.

"Well, take yur' choice," Riley shouted at him. "Fight or let all hell break loose 'round hyeh', an' let me promise yu' dat' yu' ain't seen nuttin' 'round hyeh' like what I will do if yu' don't fight fo' me. Y'all will think dat' y'all died an' went to hell!"

Joseph knew a quick decision was required. "Marse', fo' my people I will do it. I jus' hope dah' Lawd' will be forgivin'."

"Good, I kinda' thought yu' would see dis' my way. I kinda' thought I might be able to salt dah' oats 'nough to git' dat' old hawss' to drink up a storm at dah' trough." Captain Riley's face reflected how pleased he was with the decision Joseph had made since it could bring him a lot of money. "Jake, take my fighter to dah' barn an' start his trainin' right away."

Jake took Joseph directly to the barn to begin his training as Jake had already set up the facility, and everything was ready to go.

"Captain wants me to treat yu' wit' kid gloves. First thin' he wants yu' to do is take a slug of dis'. It's 'Dr. Puffer's Elixir of dah' Water of Life', which is 'pose to cure anythin' an' everythin'. He swears by it."

Joseph drank the concoction, wincing in disgust at the taste. "Mr. Gibbons, I'm not in shape to fight—it's been a long time."

"Joseph, dat's why yu're hyeh'," Jake gruffly explained. "I'm gonna' help git' yu' in shape, an' yur' gonna' make yur' master money an' make all yur' people happy at dah' same time. Yur' master has lost a lot of money gamblin', an' he figures yu' kin' git' it back fo' him. Now let's git' started." Immediately, Mr. Gibbons put Joseph into a training regimen.

***

As promised, Joseph's rigorous training schedule brought very favorable times for the slaves. Captain Riley and Jake improved working conditions—a welcome respite for the slaves who had been subjected to prolonged cruelty. Meanwhile, through the entire period of favorable times on the plantation, Joseph remained in training. Largely sequestered from everybody, except for weekends, his schedule required him to exclusively train for his fight that would soon be coming up. Joseph could be seen jogging throughout the plantation and even out on the road. Captain Riley gave him special dispensation to leave the plantation without a pass.

After a month of training, the time had arrived for some action. Captain Riley knew that experience in the ring remained an absolute necessity. He approached Joseph. "Joseph, yu' are gittin' in good shape an' yu' are ready to git' some fightin' experience right hyeh' on dah' plantation. We've looked 'round fo' a worthy opponent an' 'cided on dah' Roman niggah', Augustus. It's time to git' yur' feet wet. Saturday evenin' yur' gonna fight him, an' yu' better impress yur' master. Yu' go out thar' lookin' like a fool an' trouble will lie 'head fo' everybody on dis' plantation, includin' yu'!"

The news was a surprise to Joseph as he had no hint he would be fighting so soon. However, he was pleased with his training program, which in a short time had helped him to hone his skills. It also improved him physically while providing the confidence he would need. Although the thought of fighting one of his own people on the plantation was disturbing, he knew the captain would give him no choice. He was anxious to give him some ring time before putting him up against an experienced fighter.

Joseph sought out Augustus in the quarters a couple of days before the fight. It was important for him to talk to Augustus ahead of time. "Augustus, I feel terrible 'bout dah' scheduled fight 'tween yu' an' me. I'm well 'ware dat' our paths have seldom crossed, but we are still friends."

Augustus looked puzzled. "What are yu' talkin' 'bout, Joseph?"

"Augustus, yu' are goin' to have to fight me in dah' ring Saturday night fo' dah' entertainment of dah' white people," Joseph explained, "but whatever happens, I will try not to hurt yu' 'cuz' yu' are my friend. Who knows, maybe yu' might even take me down—try not to hurt me too badly if yu' do!" Joseph smiled as he said this. Then he had more to say, "I hate to say dis' but if I don't fight, din' Marse' is gonna' make life real nasty 'round hyeh'. I have no choice."

"Joseph, I'm no fighter. I don't wanta' go in dat' ring 'gainst yu'. Why, I don't think I was ever in a fight in my life."

"Yu' have no choice. Put up dah' best fight yu' kin' come up wit'. Marse' means business. We are gonna' have to go out thar' an' fight," Joseph replied.

The two men looked at each other for several awkward and fear-filled moments before Joseph turned away and left. With a heavy feeling in his heart, he knew that Augustus would not be a match for him. He just hoped he could pull off the fight without hurting him too badly and that God would forgive him for whatever the outcome may be.

CHAPTER TWENTY

Saturday night arrived—the fight was scheduled for sundown. A circular ring had been set up near the quarters with ropes tied around poles that were driven into the ground, which formed the perimeter of the ring. Pine tar stacks strategically placed clearly illuminated the area. Aunt Wilma, the trusty cook, provided pork, chicken, and a few of her specialty side dishes. A generous amout of whiskey was also available, although many of the men brought their own as it was clearly the most popular item amongst the crowd. The configuration was set up for the white people to sit on improvised seating a few feet from the ropes while the slaves stood toward the rear. It had been quite awhile since a fight was staged in the area, so a large crowd was anticipated for the sporting event.

The weather provided ideal conditions for the fight, which would only enhance the number of people in attendance. The crowd was male-dominated since women had such little interest in prizefighting and were certainly never encouraged to get involved. After everyone had assembled, Captain Riley entered the ring to introduce some instructions to the audience regarding the fight. "Gentlemen, we all know dah' procedure. I'm providin' dah' facility 'long wit' dah' food. My interest in all of dis' will be served by 'pinchin' dah' pot' an' receivin' dah' standard ten-percent fee on dah' total amount bet on dah' fighters. In 'dition I 'gree dat' I will not make a wager since both of dah' fighters are mine.

No one in the crowd really listened to what the captain had to say—they just wanted the fight to begin. A fight always generated excitement and anticipation and this particular fight would be no exception even though the combatants were unknown.

The owner of a nearby plantation was standing at ringside and shouted out, "Captain Riley, we jus' hope des' two ain't little softies. We came hyeh' to see some real men fight."

Somebody else called out, "Captain, I don't know nuttin' 'bout des' fighters other din' one fighter has some 'perience—bring 'dem out 'fore I place my bet. Right now, I almost feel like I'm bettin' on two blind hawsses' in a county race." While laughing and enjoying the festivities, the crowd naturally demanded the opportunity to look over Joseph and Augustus to get a visual look before placing a bet.

Captain Riley ordered Jake to bring the combatants from the barn. They both jogged toward the ring, throwing punches and short jabs in the air. Wearing white Negro cloth trousers with no shirt or shoes, they approached the ropes as the audience quickly began to make their assessment of the fighters.

They stood in opposite corners awaiting instructions and the order to begin the fight. The crowd soon recognized that Joseph appeared to be more confident than Augustus, who unlike Joseph stood silently in his corner, looking for any crowd support he might muster up. It was quite evident that Augustus did not want to be there, and the crowd was able to pick up on that. Since Joseph had fought previously in the ring and Augustus had no experience, this tipped the odds decidedly toward Joseph. In addition, Joseph, who was larger and stronger looking had the appearance of being in good fighting condition. Unfortunately for the betting crowd, they did not know the background of these two men, but based on what they could see of the two men, they had to know that Joseph had a big edge. It was obvious that Joseph had all the attributes to win the fight while Augustus looked the role of a "patsy".

Captain Riley introduced the two combatants to the spectators while interjecting an obvious hyperbole hoping to encourage more betting. "Dah' man in dah' west corner is

Augustus, dah' Roman Niggah', who comes straight from dah' coliseum whar' he triumphed ovah' lions."

One man yelled to Captain Riley, "Captain, we may not have much education, but damn well, we sur' ain't fools. If dat' man fought a lion an' won, din' I fought dah' entire Roman army an' won." The humor drew laughter from those who heard the quip.

The captain restored order and introduced Joseph. "In dah' east corner is Joseph, dah' Preacher Man. Now gentlemen, rumor has it dat' it wasn't David who slew Goliath. It was Joseph, dah' Preacher Man, a true pugilist. Incidentally, dah' Preacher Man does bring some 'perience to dah' ring." As the captain introduced the combatants, it was almost as if he was reading from a script that he had memorized earlier.

Fred Stevens, who owned the tavern in town, stood and addressed Captain Riley, "Captain, yu' ain't funny. We know dat' yu' are only promotin' des' two stiffs so we kin' put our money out thar'—dah' more we wager dah' more yu' make. I swear dat' yu' take us fo' damn fools."

Luke Jones, a man with a big reputation in the fight game, reacted in a more serious manner to the captain's claims. "Captain, if des' two fighters are so good, din' let dah' winner take on my Congo Assassin." The crowd quieted, knowing the Congo Assassin was owned by Jones, and his fighter had a big reputation. Jones had campaigned him in New Orleans where he had fought only the top fighters in the ring. Meanwhile, the captain chose to ignore the intimidating challenge of Luke Jones and moved on with the program.

Captain Riley called the two combatants to the center of the ring. "Gentlemen, we all know dah' rules 'round hyeh'—nothin' is barred, five minute rounds, an' may dah' best man win." Only risk takers went with Augustus. Finally, the bets were in, and after the odds were set, the fight was ready to begin. The betting decidedly leaned toward Joseph at ten to one. After the usual agenda had concluded, the captain exited the ring in order to sound the gong to start the fight.

315

The audience was really excited about seeing a good long fight. Prizefighting was unquestionably one of the favorite sports of the men in the South. It would never take much to get them excited, especially when they hadn't seen a fight in such a long time. The boisterous crowd was as usual, obnoxious in their behavior, while cheering madly for their favorite. It was pretty evident that the whiskey had been flowing as soon as the crowd started mingling—persuading the men to enjoy their whiskey was never a problem.

The captain sounded the gong and two fighters came out, sizing each other up. As it appeared before the fight, it was obvious that Joseph was in good condition while Augustus was quite the opposite. After simply tapping each other's fists, quickly both men stepped back three or four feet. Augustus cautiously moved toward Joseph throwing short, ineffective punches that would do little more than keep Joseph a foot or two away from him. Even at this early stage in the fight, it was clear that Augustus had no business being in the ring.

Joseph sidestepped his opponent, hitting him below the ribs as he circled. It was evident that Joseph was just playing with his opponent as Augutus continued to throw wild punches that Joseph was able to sidestep with ease while he continued to size up when and where to throw a solid punch that could end the fight. Then, maybe four minutes into the fight, a solid well aimed punch to the jaw connected, and Augustus fell to the ground. Joseph quickly jumped on him and switched to throwing combination punches at his head. As Joseph continued to pummel Augustus, it became obvious the fight was over and should never have been staged. Joseph quickly whispered to Augustus to pass out, and the fight would end. Augustus complied ending the fight. The crowd responded by loudly booing, which by all standards would be understandable since it was such an obvious mismatch.

The spectators were rightfully upset over the outcome since Joseph was quite superior to his opponent, and even for a mismatch, the fight didn't last long enough to satisfy the appetite of the crowd who came for some blood. The smaller than normal amount of money waged indicated that the crowd had doubted it would be an exciting fight. Knowing this, they still felt rightfully cheated out of a good night's entertainment and they wanted the captain on no uncertain terms to realize why they were booing.

After the winner was announced, the crescendo of booing kept rising, becoming louder until Luke again taunted Captain Riley. "Captain, yu' think yu' gotta' good niggah' fighter in dat' 'Preacher Man'. Well, why don't yu' put him up 'gainst a real niggah' fighter—my own Congo Assassin, dah' cream of dah' crop? In fact, Captain, dis' could be a real treat fo' all dah' locals 'round hyeh' since dah' Assassin needs a tune-up fight 'fore he git's back to New Orlens'. Atter' dah' crowd got taken by dis' phony fight, dey' have a right to a real treat wit' a real fighter—not two play actin' hacks fightin' like little girls. Well Captain, are yu' gonna' stand tall or back down! Yu' need to make up fo' cheatin' des' men! Gitin' 'dem' ovah' heyh' fo' dis' joke—why yu' orte' be ashamed of yur' self! Now, I'm callin' yu' on yur' honor to stand up to dah' challenge an' put yur' Preacher Man into dah' ring wit' a real fighter, dah' Congo Assassin, or are yu' jus' goin' to slink 'way in a cowardly way."

The direct challenge extended by Luke silenced the crowd. An opportunity to see the Congo Assassin fight in a local arena would be a "dream come true" for many people. They forgot all about being taken in with a bad fight, and now they became excited about the challenge extended to Captain Riley. They assumed he would coyly back down. However, Riley accepted the challenge. "Luke, yu' think dat' my Preacher Man would cower or git' cold feet? Yu' keep tootin' yur' horn 'bout dah' Congo Assassin, well dah' Preacher Man will put yu' both in yur' place. 'Sides yu' are right dat' I owe dis' crowd somethin' more—dat' will be my Preacher Man sendin' yur' Congo Assassin back to dah' Congo whar' he belongs." Captain Riley's ego would always get the best of him. He could never let anyone insult him. Unfortunately, he sometimes let his emotions get the better of him when he might be better off just keeping quiet.

Luke was surprised the captain accepted his proposal so

quickly. "Well, Captain Riley, I'm a little 'fraid 'bout puttin' my man in dah' ring, knowin' dat' yur' fighter slew Goliath, but din', I'm willing to take dah' challenge. 'Sides I wanta' see yur' man send dah' Congo Assassin back to dah' Congo." The crowd knew that Luke was being cynical and was poking fun at Captain Riley knowing that in his mind, the Preacher Man did not have a "snowballs chance in hell" of winning the fight. Many were enjoying the dialogue between Captain Riley and Luke more than the fight. It was rewarding to the crowd, creating a tremendous amount of hype after just viewing such a disappointing fight.

The captain was so pleased with the ease in which Joseph manhandled Augustus that perhaps he had not given much thought to the fact that Augustus was not the Congo Assassin. "Luke, we are more din' ready to fight in dah' face of all odds. We are not turnin' tail an' runnin'. In fact, I honestly 'lieve dah' 'Preacher Man' will whoop yur' boy as I tole' yu' earlier." The crowd went into a frenzy listening to the captain making such bold statements. It took a few minutes to finally settle the crowd down. Unquestionably, the talk would be raging throughout the county and beyond about the impending battle, which many assumed would end with the death of the Preacher Man.

Fred Stevens, who had been listening to all the hype, issued an offer. "Well, Captain, if yu' are so cocksur' yur' man kin' stand up to dah' Congo Assassin, din' let 'dem square off at my tavern— say Saturday, four weeks from now at noon. How does dat' sound to y'all? Captain is dat' 'nough time to high tail it out of dah' county 'cuz' I still can't 'lieve dat' yu' are goin' to put dat' runt up 'gainst dah' Congo Assassin who's twice his size! Incidentally, Captain, it will be yur' man bein' sent to purgatory an' maybe yu' orte' join him fo' puttin' him in dah' ring like a sacrificial lamb." Stevens thought about what he had just said, realizing he could make a lot of money staging this fight. He would be better served by encouraging the fight and not talking it down.

Although the crowd had been let down in the fight they had just witnessed, they were electrified at the opportunity to see the "Congo Assassin" in action against the "Preacher Man". It wouldn't matter who the "Congo Assassin" was pitted against, they just wanted to see their black hero fight. They now had something to really look forward to, which provided them with some much needed excitement that did not come along very often in the community. To see the legendary Congo Assassin fight, even the Preacher Man for many, would rank as the highlight of their year since their lives were so relatively mundane.

Luke Jones had some additional comments to make. "Captain, why would yu' even think dat' yur' man could hold a candle to somebody like dah' Congo Assassin? Yu' are a bigger fool din' I first thought."

"Don't yu' be concerned 'bout my man—yu' better worry 'bout yur' own man, 'cuz' dah' Preacher Man is gonna' knock dah' daylights outta' dah' Congo Assassin. Yur' man may have the size, but my man has the smarts. If dis' crowd had any sense, dey' would bet on brains over brawn." Riley's comments were directed at Luke Jones, but he looked at the men standing around him as he spoke.

One called out, "Captain, what's dis' talk 'bout brains over brawn? It would take a fool to bet 'gainst dah' Congo Assassin, an' everybody knows dat'! Luke's man has a reputation in New Orlens'—dis' Preacher Man is jus' a local boy an' a patsy at dat'."

The captain's braggadocio statements did not go entirely unnoticed. While it was assumed that the Congo Assassin would win the fight, many were somewhat surprised at the confidence Captain Riley exhibited in his fighter. Did the captain know something they didn't know, or was it merely build-up?

The crowd was reluctant to want to break up the gathering— they were now having a wonderful time. With all the "after the fight hype", the crowd was just settling in for a good time. Food was plentiful and of course there was no threat of running out of whiskey. The combination of the two along with discussing the upcoming prizefight made for a perfect evening. Soon the crowd forgot all about the poor fight they had just witnessed and now they were excited about the impending fight. It was obvious they were determined to get their moneys worth with whiskey and conversation before they left. Discussion was flowing with the crowd, trying to determine if the Preacher Man had a chance against the Congo Assassin. Could he hold his own against the Congo Assassin? It was obvious this fight had the makings of an event, which would bring in a huge crowd. Word by mouth along with posters placed throughout the county and beyond, would almost guarantee a large crowd for the event. Without a doubt, knowing that the Congo Assassin would be in the ring would almost create a mania since he had already been assigned a heroic status by the people.

After the crowd had finally quit reveling and dispersed late into the night Augustus was left standing alone, bewildered at what had transpired. Joseph, who was nearby, approached with a smile on his face to lend comfort. Walking back to the barn, they chatted about the evening—Joseph apologizing and expressing his relieve for the brevity of the fight since Augustus had not been given the opportunity to train for the fight. After a comfortable walk, they shook hands, and Joseph excused himself to join Reggie, Willy and Angie.

Joseph entered Willy's home anxious to talk to them about the fight. Angie first spoke up. "Joseph, yu' don't have a mark on yur' body."

"Angie, yu' are right," Joseph admitted. "I never got hit even once. I felt bad 'bout Augustus, 'cuz' he didn't know how to fight. I had to tell him in his ear to jus' lay up an' pretend dat' he passed out so I wouldn't have to hit him anymore. He'll be fine—I jus' roughed him up a little to make it look good."

"Joseph, aren't yu' scared 'bout dis' fight comin' up wit' dis' man dat' dey' are callin' a monster?" Willy asked.

"I fear no one wit' dah' Lawd' on my side, dah' bigger dey' are, dah' harder dey' fall. Willy, I'm gonna' outsmart dis' big niggah', 'sides, I heard he is not dat' young. I 'lieve I kin' wear him down, an' when his arms feel like lead, din' I'll move in an' put him 'way."

Reggie, who was standing nearby, entered the conversation. "Sounds like yu've already figured out a strategy," as Reggie placed a hand on Joseph's shoulder.

"I'm a thinkin' fighter, Reggie—maybe a little of yu' is rubbin' off on me," Joseph said, "dis' man is jus' a brawler, an' when he sees me, he's gonna' think he has dah' fight in dah' bag, an' dat' is what I want him to think. I jus' hope he gits' cocky, 'cuz' din' he'll let his guard down. I'm gonna' watch fo' dat' one openin'."

Reggie was amazed at Joseph's brave plan. "Joseph aren't yu' at all worried? We are all worried fo' yur' safety, but yu' seem to be fearless."

"I told y'all dah' truth. I'm not scared, an' I'm probably dah' only one dat' feels dat' way, but I mean it. Truth be told, I have to win or dah' captain will severely punish us all. It's dat' simple—I have to win! 'Sides, Reggie, I've got a 'bery special person watchin' ovah' me—dah' Lawd' Jesus Christ, an' I sense he wants me to win dis' fight. So yu' see, I have nothin' to fret 'bout. He knows what's at stake."

"Joseph, I'm jus' glad yu' are so confident. But, if yu' win dis' fight, thar' will be others, an' 'ventually yu' will lose. Din' what?" Reggie asked.

"Reggie, I guess I'll have to cross dat' bridge when I git' thar'. I can't think 'bout anythin' else. Right now, I intend to keep things as smooth as possible fo' my feller' people."

"Well put, Joseph," replied Reggie. "I guess we'll jus' have to take all dis' in as it all comes 'long—one day at a time."

"Marse' tole me dat' he wants yu' to come 'long wit' us fo' dah' big fight, Reggie. Yu' are gonna' be my handler, 'cuz' he thinks dat' yu' are smart an' could help me out."

"Joseph, I'd be honored to be yur' handler. An' yes, I hope to have a few ider's' fo' yu' on how to outsmart dis' guy. We are not goin' to git' into a brawl—jus' fight smart an' wear him down till he's all tuckered out! Like yu' said, he's a big guy, an' has to carry a lot of weight. 'Sides I understand yu' are younger. See dat', Joseph, I already know what to do to win dis' fight. How is dat' fo' a handler? Of course I heard yu' say dah' same thin' earlier," Reggie said with a sly smile.

"Reggie, wit' yu' on my side I can't lose. Yu' are a special man who dah' Lawd' has anointed to see into dah' future." Joseph went on, "Yur' powers are God given, an' are special, dah' Lawd' doesn't jus' give 'dem out to everyone. Speakin' of powers, I once heard a man speakin' in tongues an' another man stood by interpretin' what he was sayin'. Kin' dat' be true?"

"Joseph, whar' in dah' world do yu' come up wit' askin' me 'bout speakin' in tongues? But, yes in Acts II, dah' Bible states dat' dah' Lawd' gave dah' Apostles dah' power to speak in tongues since dey' did not have a common language amongst 'dem. I have heard it said dat' dis' gift is not exclusive to dah' Apostles and it is has been handed down to others," Reggie explained.

"Reggie, I'm only tellin' yu' what I saw. I couldn't understand him, but dah' other man was able to state exactly what he was sayin'."

"I learned while some have dah' gift of speakin' in tongues, others have dah' gift to interpret what dey' are sayin'. Honestly, Joseph, I've never been witness to dis', but I do look forward to dah' day when I kin' see dis' gift first hand. Well, it's late, an' I know yu' are tired an' need yur' sleep." Reggie found himself confused, trying to understand why Joseph would bring up speaking in tongues at this time, but he sensed there must have been a purpose that he would find out later on.

Joseph left for his home, while Willy, Angie, and Reggie retired for the evening. Reggie through it all fell fast asleep thinking of Anastasia, his beloved wife, and their short lived honeymoon. It seemed so long ago, but at times, he could almost feel her presence, just thinking about her, especially at night, when all was quiet, and he lay in bed.

***

The next four weeks were quite civil and comfortable for the field hands on the Riley plantation. The usual harshness of servitude had been somewhat replaced by Captain Riley and Jake Gibbon's continued attempts to be kind. However, the slaves knew this manufactured atmosphere reflected Captain Riley's desire for Joseph's fight to succeed and to make him money. Everything seemed secondary to the impending fight, while the plantation maintained a tranquil environment. Both Captain Riley and Mr. Gibbons payed little attention to what was going on in the quarters. Captain Riley was especially excited over the impending fight. He could continually be seen in the barn assisting in Joseph's training program. As stated earlier, Joseph had been given special status and freedom to do whatever he might wish. Walter was given complete autonomy to run the slave quarters with little or no input from Captain Riley or Mr. Gibbons as they concentrated on Joseph.

Soon the day of the fight arrived, representing a festive occasion in itself on the plantation as everyone gathered to send a warm sendoff for Captain Riley, Jake, Joseph and Reggie. They confidently departed early in the morning in a surrey for Clarkesville, a nearby town where Fred's tavern was located. A positive feeling, helped along by the warm sendoff helped to ignite the four men who maintained confident that Joseph would be victorious. On the negative side, Captain Riley reminded Joseph that a loss would bring severe harm to him and his fellow slaves. Furthermore, Captain Riley informed Joseph that if he lost the fight to the Congo Assassin, Riley stood to lose a lot of money, along with his reputation. All of this news was intended to put more pressure on Joseph to win the fight at all costs.

It was a cool, sunny day, which made for a perfect day for the fight, which would only help to spur even more interest. A sight seldom seen, hundreds of people were clustered throughout Clarkesville. The mere mention of the Congo Assassin created frenzy amongst the crowd. They were all eagerly awaiting the presence of their black hero.

Vendors lined the streets selling confections, food and of course, the main staple, whiskey. There were local musicians who added to the holiday atmosphere as a fight of this magnitude could arguably be the number one sporting event of the year in the county.

While a strong turnout had been assured by the drawing

power of the Congo Assassin, the savvy of Fred Stevens an excellent promoter, only enhanced the numbers. The site for the fight was ideal since the Crossroads Inn clearly represented the most successful and popular place to congregate in the area.

For miles around, posters were conspicuously posted promoting the event. Between the Congo Assassin's wide following and the fight lover's thirst for blood, Fred, the promoter was assured that he would not have a problem getting the word out. Gamblers were especially excited, believing they could not lose betting on the Congo Assassin—a sure thing. The hype was well received as an event of this magnitude was thrilling in a community where people lived with such a humdrum existence.

Captain Riley's surrey slowly moved through the crowded main street as they pulled up to the front of the inn. As the four tried to innocuously step out from the surrey, one member of the crowd yelled, "Captain, so dis' is yur' sacrificial lamb fo' dah' Congo Assassin? Now yu' know dat' dis' niggah' may as well roll ovah' an' die now than face dah' Congo Assassin!" The crowd chortled at the comment. Unquestionably, the arrival of Joseph represented only an after thought, compared to the entrance of the Congo Assassin, who would be accorded celebrity status.

Captain Riley defended Joseph. "Mister, have yu' been to hell to find out how cold it kin' git' down thar'. I don't think so— all yu' kin' do is jus' shoot yur' mouth off! None of yu' saw dah' Preacher Man destroy a capable fighter—dah' Roman Gladiator. If yu' had seen dat' fight, yu' wouldn't be so cocksure dat' dah' Congo Assassin will win dis' fight, so stop yur' jawin' an' put yur' money whar' yur' mouth is!" Perhaps the captain was stretching the truth a little in order to "save face".

Another man interrupted the captain. "Now wait a minute. I jus' happened to have seen dat' fight, if dat' is what yu' wanta' call it, an' I think it should have been called a minstrel show. What I saw was not what yu' saw—I saw a throw-in. Yur' so-called Roman Gladiator was a patsy. Any one of us out hyeh' could have taken him on an' won dat' fight. Tryin' to hornswoggle us ain't gonna' git' it. Yu' know dat' niggah' was a stiff—jus' tell dah' damn truth, Captain, an' it will set yu' free!," he said in a sarcastic tone.

"I'm tellin' yu' all dat' Preacher Man will win dah' fight," Riley roared. "If yu' bet 'gainst him, yu' are gonna' lose yur' money. I'll put it to yu' men like dis'—I'll be standin' tall wit' my man 'til dah' last dog comes home. An' yes, I'll put my money whar' my mouth is." Captain Riley was a bit evasive since he avoided answering the question.

Another stranger asked, "Captain, are yu' really goin' to put up a lot of money on yur' man to win?"

Someone else added, "Yur' jus' tryin' to git' more money into dah' pot. Now, shame dah' debil' an' tell dah' truth. We all know yu' git' money from promotin' yur' fighter, an' dat's fine wit' us, but don't try to tell us dat' he is goin' to be 'nother David who slew Goliath. Dis' is all jus' hogwash, an' Captain, yu' know it!"

The captain was obviously miffed at this comment and his emotions took over. "Look, y'all kin stand ovah' me an' watch me place my bet. Dat' will shut y'all up. I'm tired of all dis' poppycock—I don't lie." The captain's pride always got the best of him as he placed a large amount of money down on the Preacher Man to win the fight. He had not planned on making such a large bet, but his emotions once again got the best of him.

"Captain, good luck, I'm sure dat' dah' odds will be great 'gainst yur' niggah'." Who knows, wit' a lot of luck, yu'll be in line to win handsomely," one sympathetic stranger stated.

The crowd was getting restless until an official looking cavalcade of three buggies arrived. A hush descended over the crowd knowing that their black hero would soon be in their presence. In the lead buggy were Luke, the Congo Assassin and his two handlers. The rest of the entourage included friends and relatives. It was quite a spectacle as they all got out of their buggies—everyone dressed in black and looking quite professional, almost as if the fight were being staged in New Orleans amongst the crème de la crème of society. Certainly, based on the appearance of the Congo Assassin and his entourage, the Preacher Man did not look to belong in the same ring. The Congo Assassin, who was an enormous looking man projected fear thoughout the crowd and they were not the ones who would be facing him in the ring. The very sight of him convinced the crowd that the Preacher Man would be best to back down, and give up on his ambitions of ever being a prize fighter. Many thought he should be praying for his survival in the ring, and wondered if his prayers could be answered.

Interestingly, Reggie, always the thinker, pondered why white people would revere black people for their physical attributes. Will the day arrive when they would accept black people for their mental prowess as well?

The sheer size of the crowd made it obvious that Fred's Tavern would not be able to accommodate all these people. This was not a problem since outdoor activities were common throughout the South so the people came prepared. Throngs of people were circulating, which created a carnival like atmosphere.

Fred's tavern had a lot to offer. It was a large wooden structure with a spacious bar and dining area. Upstairs several overnight rooms were available as well.

Inside the tavern, Captain Riley called Fred to the side. "I want to make sur' dat' dah' ring size is adequate." The captain knew the Preacher Man would need a lot of room to move to evade the power of his opponent. A small ring could only spell trouble for him.

Fred confidently assured Captain Riley that his needs were served. "Come on out to dah' back an' check out dah' size. Yu' will not be disappointed."

One of the patrons overheard the conversation and said, "What's dah' matter Captain, are yu' 'fraid dat' yur' boy won't have 'nough room to run? I reckon if I was him, I would jus' run to dah' next county an' not stop to look back!"

Captain Riley failed to see the humor in the joke. "Mister, since yu' are so cocksur', go 'head an' bet a bundle on dah' Congo Assassin, an' din' yu' kin' watch yur' money run 'way!"

Luke was in a gleeful mood, taking everything in while talking to one of the members of his entourage. "Fred asked me 'bout dah' size of dah ring—said dat' Captain Riley would want a larger ring fo' his man. I tole' him I'll 'gree to dat'. It doesn't matter how big dah' ring is, dah' Congo will catch dah' Preacher Man an' put him 'way in short order. Let us jus' say dat' he'll have a lot to pray fo'." The crowd laughed as Luke continued to confidently deliver barbs directed at the captain. He was really enjoying the limelight since his man was a sure thing to win the fight, a bet for the Assassin was money in the bank.

Meanwhile as promised, Fred escorted Captain Riley outside to show him the size of the ring. After inspecting the ring, the captain was satisfied and everything moved along as planned.

Fred announced it was time to start accepting bets. One of the members of the crowd announced, "I'm placin' my money down on dah' Congo Assassin. I do feel like I'm takin' confections 'way from a baby." The tenor of the crowd echoed exactly what the gambler had just said. However, there were a few who were taking the long shot, knowing strange things could happen in the ring that could tip the advantage to the Preacher Man such as the Congo Assassin getting accidently hurt, and they would cash in on a tidy profit. As the betting progressed, as expected, the odds were clearly favoring the Congo Assassin. Because of the large number of people betting, Fred had two additional aides helping him to collect the money.

Luke sought out Captain Riley and couldn't resist taunting him further, "I'm really surprised dat' yu' would show up wit' dat' weaklin' of yurs'. We kinda' thought yu' might be headed fo' parts unknown. Take a good look at dah' Congo Assassin. Do yu' really think yur' man has a chance? Judgin' by dah' bettin'—it 'pears dat' nobody else does either! Let me call a spade a spade. Dah' Congo Assassin will polish off yur' boy in no time flat, an' yu' kin' bet on dat'. I even hyeh' dat' yu' did put yur' money whar' yur' mouth is an' bet a good 'mount of money on yur' boy. I respect yu' fo' dat', an' I guess it's even possible to show respect fo' a fool," he said as he laughed and walked away in the opposite direction.

Not given to taking criticism, Captain Riley quickly retorted, "I don't give a tinker's damn what yu' say, or think—callin' me a fool! Last I heard, yu' can't aways judge a book by its cover. Yu' jus' better git' set to eat crow." The captain as well then turned and swiftly walked away.

While the crowd was busy placing their bets, Joseph and Reggie were left alone mapping out the strategy that Joseph would employ to win the fight. Joseph exclaimed, "Reggie, I'm tellin' yu' dat' I'm gonna' win dis' fight. I kin' feel it 'cuz' I know dah' Lawd' is in my camp."

Reggie got serious, "Joseph, let's git' down to brass tacks. It's my job to make sur' yu' win dis' fight. He is huge an' mean lookin', but he might be easier fo' yu' to handle din' if he was smaller, younger, an' quicker on his feet. He may prove jus' to be a big, lumberin' oaf."

"I think yu're right, Reggie," Joseph agreed. "I sorta' thought dah' same thin' when I saw him. He really does not scare me, an' I mean dat'. Reggie, I'm sorta' like a dog, I'm not 'fraid of size."

"Hyeh's' how yu' do it. First, stay away from him as much as yu' kin'. Let him chase yu' 'round. Atter' lookin' him ovah' I kin' safely say dat' he's carryin' a lotta' weight an' he'll wear down. Second, yu' have to slide 'way from his punches. If he throws a lot of empty punches, it won't take long fo' his arms to feel like lead. When dat' happens, yu' got him dead to rights. Dat's when yu' start uncorkin' punches an' I guarantee yu', it'll be all ovah'. The key fo' yu' is to not allow him to git' any hard shots on yu'. If yu' kin' git' him to throw roundhouse punches, an' not straight jabs, dat' will also help. They'll be easier to block. But watch out, 'member, one hard punch, an' he will knock yu' out. Third, stay 'way from him as much as yu' kin' until he begins to tire, an' din' yu' got dah' fight goin' yur' way. If he is able to engage yu' in a wrestin' match dat' could be a disaster. Yu' cannot out wrestle him—stay 'way. He'll break yur' bones. 'Member, avoid takin' any hard shots an' no wrestlin' an' yu' kin' win. Got it Joseph? No brawlin'. It all comes down to what we first said—outsmart dis' oaf an' yu' win dah' fight. Last thin' to 'member is dat' yu' must stay calm an' collected at all times, an' conserve yur' energy, gittin' excited will actually expend yur' energy. Yu' have to be dah' fighter an' let him be dah' brawler, fight yur' fight, not his."

"Reggie, I know I have to outsmart him an' dat' is whar' yu' come in wit' yur' smarts. I trust yur' thinkin'." Joseph felt even more confident than before since his own strategy closely paralleled Reggie's.

As Captain Riley and Jake Gibbons approached Joseph and Reggie, the captain announced, "They have finished takin' bets an' everyone is outside waitin' fo' us to git' out thar' an' git' dah' show on dah' road. One thin', Joseph, I put a lot of money on yu'—yu' have no choice, yu' have to win 'gainst all odds. If yu' don't, yu' are gonna' make a lot of niggahs' back on dah' plantation 'bery unhappy. I jus' know yu' don't want dat' to happen, so git' out thar' an' show all dah' nay sayers how to win a fight."

With that final message, the principals involved in the fight went outside to the ring. Meanwhile the crowd was pouring out, all clamoring for a good view. The crowd was enormous. Luke and his aides were busy counting the wagers so they could announce the odds. Because of the heavy betting, it took some time. Eventually the odds were set at fifteen to one, which was exceedingly high.

With some additional fanfare, the combatants finally entered the ring along with their handlers. Fred, holding his megaphone, had already assumed his role as the ring announcer. He called the fighters to the center of the ring and ordered the handlers to take their positions outside the ropes. The Preacher Man and the Congo Assassin were clad in standard white Negro cloth trousers with no shirt or shoes, which was typical for these fights. The Assassin towered over his opponent, which assured many of those who had bet on the Congo Assassin that they were sure to make money. Some were already pondering how they were going to spend their winnings. Those who had taken the long shot had to be wondering if they had just thrown their money away. A victory for the Preacher Man appeared to be more remote then ever. For a moment, the crowd was silent as they assessed the situation. It was obvious that the crowd was mesmerized by their hero—the

Congo Assassin.

Reggie recognized that even in a fight of this magnitude the fighters were not provided with better clothing. Instead, they had to wear standard Negro cloth, which might address that no exceptions could be made to upgrade their clothing since they were still slaves—absolutism always had to prevail.

Fred bellowed, "Gentlemen we've got dah' Congo Assassin goin' 'gainst dah' underdog, dah' Preacher Man. Are dah' black gladiators of Georgia all ready to do battle? We have five-minute rounds an' no holds barred—punchin', kickin', bitin' an head buttin' are all permissible. All bets are in, are we're ready to git' dis' fight on? Last man standin' will win and yes yu' kin' be saved by dah' bell. Now let's git' dah' show on dah' road."

Reggie mused over the attention accorded the Congo Assassin. In a sporting event such as a prize fight that requires great physical prowess, a black man can be well respected and well received. Again, Reggie was left wondering when white people would be able to judge black people for more than picking cotton, their physical prowess, and musical talents.

As Fred sounded the gong, the Congo Assassin quickly came out of his corner and confidently began his attack with a flurry of jabs. It was apparent that he wanted to end the fight as quickly as possible as he threw roundhouse punches along with some straight jabs. Joseph skillfully ducked, slid and backpeddled as his opponent continued to throw errant punches. While he avoided his punches, Joseph sized up the Assassin, trying to determine where his weaknesses might be. Meanwhile, he was able to see that the Assassin was beginning to tire ever so slightly and it was still only the first round. Joseph, the smarter fighter of the two, was content throwing body punches as the Congo Assassin continued to concentrate on throwing head shots to end the fight. Joseph soon realized the Congo Assassin was not waging a smart fight. He was expending a lot of energy in his frustration as he was unable to immediately take Joseph out of the fight like he assumed he would do. Meanwhile, all he had to do was duck and feint, and avoid head shots, and so far that proved to be not too difficult. It was a little perplexing to Joseph that somebody with his experience would not conserve his energy and above all, fight a smarter contest.

At the beginning of the bout, the crowd seemed confident the Congo Assassin would take Joseph out in short order, but as the first round went on, they became quieter, knowing that the Preacher Man was holding his own. It was also apparent that the Preacher Man demonstrated absolutely no fear which had to further frustrate the Congo Assassin. The bell rang, ending the first round, and the two combatants went back to their corners. Their handlers shoved water at them and wiped the sweat from their foreheads, all the while pumping them with verbal strategy for the second round.

The second round began pretty much as the first round ended—the Congo Assassin continued his relentless pressure on Joseph. It was apparent, he was disappointed at not being able to land a knockout punch or even just a solid jab, and finally frustration began to show up in the Assassin's actions. Joseph continued to land body punches at will as the Assassin provided little defense to his midsection. Joseph had arrived at his final plan of attack as the fight dragged on. His tactics would be to punch his opponent's body until he eventually dropped his guard to defend his midsection. Then he could start throwing some solid shots to the head.

Joseph had to keep light on his feet, always moving as he punched, knowing that he could very well win the fight as long as he continued to "fight his fight". As the second round neared an end, the Congo Assassin was noticeably starting to slow, and began to put less pressure on Joseph. Predictably, he threw more roundhouse punches out of sheer desperation. He attempted to wrestle with Joseph, but his energy level had dropped, making it more difficult to get a hold on him. Joseph knew if he continued to fight his fight, eventually, he could go on the attack when the Congo Assassin dropped his guard from exhaustion. The round ended, and although Joseph had been hit with a few glancing punches, nothing really solid had landed, leaving him in excellent shape.

The time between rounds enabled the Congo Assassin to catch his much needed breath as Luke anxiously called out to him, "Kick, punch, an' swarm Assassin." It was beginning to appear that Luke was beginning to lose his patience since things were not going as planned. He also knew the Congo Assassin had done little training, confidently thinking the fight would be over in the first round, and this is where the big mistake was made—underestimating the opponent.

In Joseph's corner the instructions were simple. Continue as he was doing while avoiding any possible roundhouse punch directly to the head.

As the third round began, the Congo Assassin followed Luke's instructions and attempted to kick, swarm, and punch at Joseph, but everything he did was going awry, allowing Joseph to continue hitting the midsection while stepping and moving away from his roundhouse punches. Meanwhile, Joseph realized he no longer had to worry about the Congo Assassin manhandling him with wrestling maneuvers as he was tiring and quickly running out of energy. Joseph continued to measure his punches while conserving his energy. The audience looked stunned as they watched the Congo Assassin weaken. He tried to respond as the crowd cheered him on, hoping he'd land a lucky punch that would put Joseph down. The round ended, and the Congo Assassin failed once again to land any solid punches while exhibiting even more signs of desperation, and exhaustion.

Between rounds, total frustration was evident in the Congo Assassin's corner while in Joseph's corner—calm and confidence prevailed.

The fourth round was uneventful, with little action as Joseph continued to avoid his opponent, yet never underestimating his power. Some in the crowd were so shocked that they began to yell out that the fight was fixed. In their minds, it was simply not possible for the Preacher Man to stand up to the Congo Assassin. They began to realize that an upset could very well be in the making, which could only shock the crowd since they had assumed they had bet on a sure winner.

The fifth round proved to be pivotal for Joseph. The Congo Assassin came out throwing wild punches. It was evident he was really desperate, allowing himself to be more vulnerable—completely frustrated at not being able to intimidate his opponent. It wouldn't be long until the Preacher Man could change his tactics by going on the offensive, moving closer and delivering stronger blows to the head. His punches were a lot harder than anyone realized, and coming out of nowhere, Joseph sent a hard right to the temple, which put the Congo Assassin down. He struggled up from the ground and fortuitously, the round ended giving him a chance to gather his senses. The crowd was in total dismay at what they were witnessing. Many knew that quite possibly they had "counted their chickens before their eggs were hatched".

Joseph confidently told Reggie that the fight would be over in the next round, and he knew how he planned to end it. It would remain a surprise. In the other corner, Luke was desperately attempting to revive his fighter and instill some confidence, knowing the situation was turning dire since there was a lot riding on this fight and no one knew it more than he. If the Congo Assassin lost this fight, his reputation would be ruined and he would be relegated to the status of a "has been".

The crowd continued to cheer for the Congo Assassin as the sixth round began. Most could see he was clearly exhausted but were still hoping for a miracle, hoping their support would possibly help to provide him with his second wind. Joseph let the pace of the round slow as he continued to measure the Assassin for a second or two and then spun around and delivered a tremendous head butt so devastating that the big man simply crumbled to the ground without moving. The head butt came out of nowhere and suddenly, the fight was over. Many sat in silence and disbelief—most seeing their money go down "the drain" with the Congo Assassin.

Luke and his handlers ran into the ring to administer help to the Congo Assassin, who was still lying on is back, motionless. Something shocking had just occurred in the ring. It soon became obvious that no amount of reviving would work. The Congo

Assassin was not breathing—he was dead. The head butt to his nose drove the membrane bone directly into his brain, which proved to be fatal. Joseph had carefully and intelligently conducted his fight and then, unintentionally, he had administered the lethal blow.

Luke knelt along side of the Congo Assassin. "My niggah' is dead—he's dead! Captain, yur' niggah' killed my boy." He apparently forgot how he had bragged that his man was unstoppable.

The captain jumped up and stood next to Luke and the fallen fighter and said. "Luke, sauce fo' dah' goose is sauce fo' dah' gander. You kinda' let it out of dah' bag dat' dah' Congo Assassin was goin' to kill my boy, didn't yu' now!" The display of bravado exhibited by the captain at the outcome of the fight spoke volumes for his feelings. He showed absolutely no remorse for the death of the Congo Assassin. In fact, he knew that Joseph was now a name fighter who would be billed as the man who killed the Congo Assassin in the ring and that would speak volumes for him.

Luke was remorseful. "Well, I didn't mean dat' he would actually kill him, an' yu' know dat'. Dis' is a 'hawss' of a different color'. My boy was worth a lot of money to me, an' now he is worthless. I jus' lost a good chunk of my income." Interestingly, the monetary loss associated with the death of the Congo Assassin was the only thing that mattered to Luke—the absence of any compassion was apparent.

"Look, Luke, yu' know dat' my boy wasn't fixin' to kill dah' Congo Assassin. It was purely an accident. Don't worry yu'll' git' ovah' it."

Fred, who was standing by, attempted to console Luke. "He's only a niggah'. Yu'll git 'nother one an' he'll take care of the Preacher Man in right fashion."

The crowd was still left totally aghast at the entire spectacle, attempting to understand how this could have happened. It was such a silent crowd, now the opposite of the carnival-like atmosphere that had been on display earlier. You could almost hear a pin drop, it was so quiet. They were so shocked that they hadn't even started to disperse. It was a fight that would not be forgotten anytime soon.

Reggie walked around the inside perimeter of the ring with his arm around Joseph's shoulders. Joseph was visibly shaken. "Reggie, I killed dat' man. I didn't mean to kill him, but I did. Me, a preacher, killin' a man—I have to beg fo' fo'giveness. I know dah' Lawd' intended dat' I win but not to kill dah' Congo Assassin doin' it. Somethin' else, I don't even know dah' poor mans real name—I'm sur' his mammy didn't name him Congo Assassin. Reggie, all of dis' jus' ain't right."

"Joseph, yu' can't punish yur'self, God understands an' will fo'give yu'. Yu' were forced into it, an' yu' accidently killed him. Notice I said accidently. God does not cast sin on accidents. 'Sides he could have done dah' same thin' to yu'."

Joseph walked over to the body of the Assassin and wept aloud. "Reggie, I can't do dis' 'gain. Dis' is truly my last fight. The Lawd' would not want me to fight 'gain."

"Joseph, yu' are a money maker, an' dah' captain will not let yu' off dah' hook wit'out a terrible price." Reggie was aware of what the captain could do.

Meanwhile, Reggie stood quietly along side of his friend Joseph, as Fred directed his attention to Captain Riley. "Well Captain, yu' were right an' probably dah' only person who was right. Yu' have quite a man. He cost me a lot of money 'long wit' jus' 'bout everyone else. I also know he made a few people 'bery rich who had dah' guts to bet on him dah' Preacher Man. I suppose you're gonna' take yur' niggah' to New Orlens'. He'll come wit' a big reputation—dah' Preacher Man who slew dah' Congo Assassin. Yu' kin' bet dat' yu' got yur'self' a real money maker. Incidentally, if yu' want to continue fighting hyeh', dah' welcome mat is always out at my tavern."

"Fred, speakin' of money," Riley asked, "how 'bout my winnins'? How much is it?"

"Well, Captain yu' really hit dah' jackpot," Fred replied. "Dah' niggah' made yu' ovah' three thousand dollars at fifteen to one on yur' bet an' one thousand dollars fo' yur' entrance fee. Incidentally, yu' wagered dah' most money on dah' Preacher Man of anybody. Now, dat's a hefty haul of over four thousand dollars.

I hope yu' got a gun wit' yu' when yu' leave? I'm serious, 'cuz' we have a lot of men dat' would kill fo' far less money din' dat', an' dey' know yu' will have all dat' money wit' yu'."

"Don't worry 'bout it, Fred. We came well-armed." The captain tried to hide his excitement as Fred counted out over four thousand dollars. The captain raised his right arm above his head to signal for Jake, Joseph and Reggie that it was time to return home.

Once they were on the road, Captain Riley congratulated Joseph. "Joseph, I owe yu' my gratitude, as yu' made yur' master a lot of money. As long as things go on like dis', I'll be happy, an' everyone on dah' plantation will git' 'warded as well. I'll jus' continue to be lax on everybody, an' yu' won't have to do anythin' but train. Also, dat' was a stroke of good luck dat' yu' killed dah' Congo Assassin. Now yu' will have a big reputation dat' will bode well fo' us in New Orlens'."

Looking downward at his feet Joseph sadly and softly replied, "Marse', I killed dat' man, an' me a preacher, a God-fearin' man."

"Joseph, yu' only killed a niggah'—nobody cares! What counts is dah' kind of money yu' kin' generate fo' yur' master while providin' a cornucopia fo' all dah' niggahs' on dah' plantation. I gotta' hand it to yu'—dat' head butt did dah' job. Yu' know Joseph, white folks talk 'bout niggahs' usin' head butts. Dey' say dat' it's a tactic dat' comes from Afriky'. I've even heard it said dat' niggahs' have a tougher head din' white folks. I jus' know it worked right fo' us dis' time."

"Marse', my fightin' days are ovah'." It was apparent that Joseph had definitely made up his mind, an unwelcome decision that shocked the Captain and Jake.

The captain was stunned at what he'd just heard. "Joseph, I'm yur' master, an' as yur' master, I command dat' yu' fight 'gain, or yu'll taste dah' sweetness of yur' masters whip ovah' yur' back, not to mention what's gonna' happen to everybody else on dah' plantation." It was obvious that the captain meant exactly what he said.

"Marse', I have to answer to a higher master, God, an' he wants me to stop." Joseph knew the full ramifications of his words.

In a rage the captain turned and slapped Joseph across the face. "No niggah' kin' defy me. If I say yu' will fight—damn it, din' yu' will fight!"

"Marse', dah' Lord has directed me not to fight."

"Joseph, dah' laxness will end in dah' quarters. Things will go from heaven on earth to dah' unleashin' of hell on dah' plantation if yu' don't fight." The captain believed Joseph would eventually agree. He quickly enlisted Reggie's help. "Reggie, since yu' are so thick wit' Joseph, talk to him, an' let him know dat' dah' welfare of all dah' niggahs' on dah' plantation is in his hands. An' Joseph, yu' have till' Monday mornin' to make yur' decision."

Jake like the captain, was visibly upset. "Joseph, I want to remind yu' dat' Judy's jus' itchin' to git' busy, an' all dose' niggahs' in dah' quarters will suffer a fate worse din' death. I guess we'll find out Monday mornin' in dah' ole' barn, won't we, Joseph?" Joseph lapsed into a sullen silence as Jake spoke. Reggie agonized about what could happen because of Joseph's announcement.

"Mr. Gibbons, I'll think 'bout it." Joseph answered only to pacify him since he had already made up his mind.

Captain Riley continued to display his rage as Joseph could do little more than hang his head and remain silent. He was "damned if he did, and he was damned if he didn't". Joseph was caught squarely in the middle of a predicament that would result in serious repercussions if he didn't relent to fight.

Reggie blocked out everything but the hoofbeats and the sounds of the wheels of the buggy on the road. He thought about how the tragedy of a man accidentally killed in the ring could be so devastating to witness, especially since it was his dear friend who had administered the lethal blow. In a reflective mood, Reggie was shocked not only at the death but the reaction of the crowd who remained speechless as the Congo Assassin lay motionless. Mumbling audibly at the fallen giant, "Jus' 'nother dead niggah'," could be widely heard. Reggie found all this to be chilling. The chants, "Kill him, kill him, kill him," had been answered. In the end that's what they got—a dead man, albeit, the wrong man in their eyes. The majority had unfortunately bet on the Assassin. Betting on a prizefight, like any form of gambling, always has risks even when it is assumed that you cannot lose. Most folks walked away, visibly upset, while only a very few managed to leave in good spirits—those who bet on the Preacher Man.

For Reggie it represented a time for more deep thought. Once again, he had witnessed the sadistic side of mankind that consistently needs feeding as it malingers and resurfaces. The continual call for blood and even death rose throughout the contest. Reggie's acumen went well beyond the crowd with his visionary scope, coupled with his understanding of the past. Prophetically, it played itself out when he saw a correlation between the fight scene he had just witnessed and the gladiators waged in mortal combat at the Roman coliseum. He knew the barbaric pleasures of the paganistic Romans were still ever present in mankind. Further, the South prided itself on its Christian environment, which denounces paganism, but ironically, he witnessed the crowd at the prizefight engaged in a practice that was almost as barbaric as the gladiator fights.

Reggie concluded that the teachings of Jesus Christ— nonviolence, kindness, compassion, forgiveness and love are often compromised for the pleasures of the dark side of humanity.

He honestly wondered if he and Joseph were walking on a higher plane where they could see and understand the frailties of society. With that understanding, their purpose in life would become even more apparent. They had to remain a positive role model, while promoting and teaching Christian values.

All these thoughts swirled through Reggie's mind until he was totally exhausted from it all. He sat in silence for the rest of the journey home, staring at the side of the road, wondering if mankind would ever understand the expectations of God, and better yet, if mankind would ever be able to fulfill them.

CHAPTER TWENTY-ONE

The following afternoon, Joseph, extremely upset and needing advice, visited Reggie, Willy and Angie at their home to discuss his decision to quit fighting.

Disconsolate, he sought Angie's opinion first. "I need a woman's opinion—Angie, I'm caught 'tween a rock an' a hard place. I can't fight 'gain. I jus' killed a man an' me a Christian, yet if I don't fight dah' master is goin' to severely punish all of us. Angie, yu' know I'm a preacher man, an' 'bove all, a Christian. What should I do?"

"I have always 'lieved dat' I have to foller' what my heart tells me to do. If yur' heart says don't fight 'gain, din' don't," she advised

"Angie, what 'bout my people? Dah' master will hurt a lot of us if I don't fight."

"Yu' know, Joseph, dat' even if yu' kept fightin', 'ventually yu're goin' to lose," she calmly answered. "Din' what? Yu' don't think dat' Captain Riley won't unleash his bitterness an' anger on all of us? I think yu' have to consider dat' too."

Clearly troubled by his dilemma, Joseph looked at each of his three friends. "What if I flee to dah' swamp an' join one of dose' maroon colonies? Dose' niggahs' have been out thar' fo' years an' no white man kin' find 'dem."

"Fo' now, Joseph dat' wouldn't make sense—dey' would still punish us. 'Sides, yu're our spiritual guide an' leader, dah' man we need most in times of trouble, an' yu'd be gone. Joseph, one way or 'nother, yu' have to stand tall, an' I know yu' will not run. I'll stand wit' yu' through thick an' thin," Reggie assured him.

"Reggie, yu' are right—I won't run. But believe me, Monday mornin' is right 'round dah' corner, an' I'm gonna' have to face marse' an' Mr. Gibbons. I'm gonna' tell 'dem dat' I'm not fightin' 'gain. Like Angie said, I should foller' my heart an' dat' is what I'm goin' to do." Willy had suggested that he consult Cross'-Eyed' Sam before he makes a decision. He quickly dismissed the suggestion.

They all respected Joseph's decision, despite knowing the far-reaching consequences. There was little else to say regarding this matter. So the rest of the afternoon was spent chatting about church and Angie's small garden while Joseph sat quietly pondering over his decision. The weekend proved to be quiet without any further incidents. However, in the quarters, there was a lot of rumbling going on knowing that a lot was at stake based on Joseph's decision.

***

Monday soon arrived and Joseph went directly to the barn to face Captain Riley and Jake Gibbons. On the way over, he started vacillating over his decision not to fight again. Would his actions bring immediate harm to the lives of his fellow slaves? But, as Angie said, he would eventually lose a fight. Then what would happen? Maybe it would be better to face the consequences now. Anxiety overtook Joseph, knowing the stakes were so very high.

Captain Riley and Jake greeted Joseph when he entered the barn. Captain Riley stepped toward Joseph and confidently said, " Yu've had some time to rethink yur' decision, an' we all know dat' yu' are anxious to resume trainin' fo' yur' next fight."

Captain Riley and Jake were eagerly awaiting what they thought would be good news that Joseph had decided to fight.

"Well, what is it, Joseph?" The captain had a warm smile on his face as he posed his question.

Joseph defiantly stated, "Marse', I'm follerin' dah' Lawd's will. I will not fight 'gain."

"Damn yu', niggah'!" Captain Riley spat at him as his face turned from warmth to rage. "Jake, git' Judy out an' show dis' niggah' dat' we mean business. But jus' a mild whippin' in case he changes his mind—right, Joseph?"

"Marse' I won't be changin' my mind. I'm truly sorry, but I see no other choice."

Jake's warm grin turned sinister. He ordered Joseph to remove his shirt. Then Joseph was bound and chained to a large post even though it was to be only a light whipping—probably more for intimidation than anything else. The whipping was soon administered, while Joseph stood tall, without demonstrating any reaction to the beating even though it was painful.

Jake was gloating as he said, "Oh, I'm jus' lovin' dis'. Yu' might be a big name fighter, but to me yu're jus' 'nother flat nosed niggah'. I know yu' are enjoyin' dah warmth of yur' master's whip over yur' back. It's kinda' good fo' yu' to not git' big headed ovah' dat' victory yu' had at Fred's. Yu' know dat' yu' need to be reminded from time to time dat' when yu' are 'round hyeh', yu' are jus' 'nother niggah'." Psychologically being able to punish Joseph made Jake feel powerful. It represented the white mans dominance over the black man, even though he knew in a one-on-one fight he would be no match against Joseph.

Captain Riley angrily put his face a few inches from Joseph's. "Niggah', 'member dis', yu' will cause yur' master to suffer huge losses by yur' actions. Dah' wheel will come to a full circle an' all hell will soon break loose 'round hyeh' if yu' don't fight 'gain. 'Sides all yu' niggahs' are gittin' soft 'cuz' of my recent kindness. It's time to put a change to dat'. Boy, tell all dah' niggahs' what's goin' to happen 'round hyeh', an' let 'dem know dat' it was 'cuz' of yur' decision!" Joseph was unbound and he sank to his knees.

"Git' up an' git' outta' hyeh' yu' damn worthless niggah'!

Oh yah' niggah', yur' stock 'round hyeh' dropped to nothin' since yu' made dah' decision not to fight fo' yur' master." As Joseph departed as a parting shot, Jake kicked him in the buttocks, causing Joseph to stumble and then fall face down in the dirt, adding further insult to injury.

***

Everyone in the quarters knew trouble was coming from Captain Riley and Jake, and it didn't take long to begin. That afternoon, while the slaves were out in the field working, Gibbons approached on horseback—prepared for action wearing his palmetto hat, white duster jacket, derringer pistol and of course, Judy. He stopped a few feet from Reggie. "Reggie Marshall, I wanta' talk to yu'! Foller' me to dat' grove ovah' thar'!"

Quickly Reggie followed Gibbons to the grove. "Yes sir, Mr. Gibbons, what do yu' want?" He knew there was going to be trouble when he was addressed by his first and last name since a slave could not have a last name.

"Niggah', what is dah' matter wit' yu'. Yu' never learned yur' lesson from 'fore. Yu' high-brow niggahs' think yu' should have a last name wit' yur' noble presence, don't y'all? Yu' jus' responded to a last name an' dat' is a serious breach of rules."

"Mr. Gibbons, if I had ignored yu', din' what would yu' have done?" Reggie tried to be polite and non-threatening with his answer.

Jake pretended he was enraged at Reggie's answer, when in fact there was no response that would have avoided the beating he was about to receive. He called Walter over. "Walter, git' over hyeh', I need yur' help. We're goin' to put dis' smart niggah' down right now. Shuck dat' blouse. Dis' niggah' is a serious troublemaker an' dat' calls fo' a severe beatin'. 'Member Reggie Marshall when Captain Riley warned yu' dah' next beatin' would be severe? Well maybe yu' done fo'got 'bout it, but I didn't, I don't forgit' things. Walter run ovah' to dah' barn an' bring back one of dose' barn cat's 'long wit' some rope. We got somethin' in store fo' dis' rascal—a real treat! I'll put Judy on him first while yu' run to dah' barn. In dah' meantime, I'm gonna' finish dah' job I had started on dis' damn niggah'. Dis' is one beatin' he'll never forgit'." Walter was shaken as he carried out Jake's instructions as he knew what he had planned with the cat.

Reggie respectfully pleaded with Gibbons. "Yu' know Mr. Gibbons, I don't think I did anythin' to deserve dis'." His words fell on deaf ears. He knew he would be beaten no matter what he said.

"Now is dat' right, boy? Well git' on yur' stomach so dat' Judy kin' have a conversation wit' yu'." Jake paused and smiled at his whip. Dat' was a joke! Why aren't yu' laughin' at my humor? Laugh, yu' miserable blackguard! We all know 'bout yur' type. We kinda' think dat' yu' encouraged Joseph not to fight. Dat' is a 'bery serious offense an' yur' master has to suffer dah' consequences 'cuz' yu've got a loose lip an' a workin' jaw. As I said, matters like dis' have to be dealt wit' severely an' not jus' casually. Now, it's time fo' yu' to take yur' medicine from Judy."

The end of Jake's whip whistled as it swirled high above his head, and moments later found its mark as Reggie lay on the ground. It was a prolonged beating, intended to cause great pain and suffering. With each strike of the whip the pain intensified. The agony surged unabating throughout Reggie's body.

Gibbons was grinning from ear to ear as Reggie agonized on the ground. It was obvious that he was taking great pleasure in seeing Reggie suffer. After the beating had been administered, he turned his attention to Walter, who had returned with a cat and a rope. He then directed Walter to help set up the cat and the rope for the next round of torture. Gibbons stated to Reggie, "Yu' think dat' was bad Reggie Marshall, have yu' ever seen anybody go 'cat-haulin'"?"

"I never have, Mr. Gibbons," Reggie feebly replied.

"Well, 'round hyeh' we like to make our troublemakers really pay the price, an' yu' happen to be our number one troublemaker. It's time fo' yu' to 'perience some real pain. Now Walter, yu' pick him up or jus' drag him ovah' to dat' tree an' put him directly under dat' low lyin' big limb."

Walter complied and slowly dragged Reggie, who had been lying helpless on his stomach over to the tree. He then swung the rope over the limb so that both ends hung just above Reggie's back. Then he tied one end of the rope to the cat's rear legs and then pulled the cat up by the rope so the front paws dangled directly over Reggie's back. As the cat would feverishly try to get free, his front claws would inflict deep wounds on Reggie's back. This extremely painful experience was considered to be one of the cruelest forms of punishment administered to the slaves in the South. Not only would the claws inflict serious pain but they also were known to cause serious infections, one that was called appropriately "cat scratch fever". It was a type of blood poisoning that could be fatal.

Walter adjusted the height of the cat over Reggie's back as Gibbons yelled out instructions. "Don't try to give dis' scamp any slack wit' dose' cat's claws. I wanta' see 'dem diggin' deep to make sur' dat' he'll carry dis' beatin' wit' him fo' dah' rest of his life. He'll be able to show his beautiful scars to all dah' wenches dat' jus' might fall in love him." Gibbons knew this type of punishment would cause deep permanent scarring on Reggie's back, but in his own sadistic way, he was overjoyed to inflict the damage.

Reggie was on the ground agonizing over the painful whipping he had just received while sensing that the worse was yet to come. In this horrible situation, his only solace was in thinking about being reunited with Anastasia and putting his life into the hands of the Lord. That was his only comforting thought as he awaited the "cat-hauling". Walter soon adjusted the rope at the right height to inflict maximum harm as Gibbons rendered instructions. The torture began and went unabated as Reggie screamed while suffering unimaginable pain that continued until he fortunately passed out. Finally, Gibbons ordered Walter to release the cat.

When the "cat-hauling" ended, Mr. Gibbons shoved Reggie with the heel of one of his boots forcing him to awaken. "Reggie,

I hope yu' kin' hyeh' me. Fo' dah' rest of yur' life yu' will be able to show people dah' scars dat' come from defyin' yur' master. Dey' will call yu' dah' handsome man wit' dah' ugly back. Now is dat not a' contrast? Also, I heard yu' received a 'Negro plaster' sometime ago. Well, dat's nuttin' to what yu' jus' got rewarded wit' right hyeh' from yur' master fo' causin' us trouble. Dis' is one of dah' best 'minders dat' we kin' come up wit' to keep niggahs' like yu' in line—a lot better din' 'Negro plaster'. Yu' best be ready fo' work 'morrow," he said triumphantly, "an' one other thin'—next time I might jus' fix up yur' handsome face to match yur' back. Now, yu' wouldn't like dat' since all dah' women wouldn't find yu' quite so fancy. In fact, dey' would think yu' were downright ugly. 'Member, I do have dah' power to transform yu' into a candidate for a freak show—now, wouldn't dat' be a cryin' shame? Dat' would sur' knock dah' cockiness out of yu'. Yu' would have to run 'round in shame hidin' from people, knowin' dat' people couldn't stand to look at yur' ugly puss."

As ordered, Walter freed the cat from the rope. Their mission had been completed regarding Reggie, and it was time to tend to other business.

Reggie, now alone at the base of the tree continued to lapse in and out of consciousness as the agony continued unabated. The pain was so agonizing that Reggie felt that he may not make it. His whole back felt as if it were on fire. Regardless, he still understood what Jake had just said. As he squinted and tried to focus and clear his head, bright rays of light and sunshine appeared in front and above him. Miraculously, through all the suffering that he had just endured, Reggie was peering through a bright light and witnessing Jesus Christ crucified on the cross at Golgotha with two common criminals along side of Him. Similar to his two other visions Halley's Comet was circling overhead.

Reggie could hear Jesus say, "Father, forgive them, for they know not what they do."

He heard a soldier call out, "He saved others, let Him save Himself if this is the Christ of God, His Chosen One."

Another soldier mocked Christ while offering him wine.

"If You are the king of the Jews, save Yourself!"

One of the criminals added, "Are You not the Christ? Save Yourself and us!"

Reggie could hear the other criminal say, "Do You not even fear God since You are under the same sentence of condemnation? And we, indeed, for we are receiving what we deserve for our deeds, but this man had done nothing wrong. Jesus, remember me when You enter into Your Kingdom!"

Then Jesus said, "Truly I say to you, today you shall be with Me in Paradise."

The fire and light enveloping the ground before Reggie and the sky seemed to fade as Jesus cried out, "Father, into Thy hands I commit My spirit." Jesus Christ took His last earthly breath. Through it all, Reggie witnessed Halley's Comet continuing to streak overhead, watching over Him through it all.

Reggie tried to collect his thoughts and interpret what he had just witnessed. His previous two visions related to seeing into the future; however, this revelation took place far into the past. He wondered how his vision of Jesus Christ on the cross related to the other dreams. For now it would just have to remain a mystery. However, as powerful as the two previous apparitions had been, this one was far more intense and thought provoking. Perhaps, this vision would eventually bring the entire enigma to a full circle. Yet all three visions were directly related and could not be separated with each involving Halley's Comet. It weighed on his heart, even as he lay there in unbelievable pain and suffering as he attempted to unravel the mystery. Above all, he now knew that it would remain for him to continue to bring the message of his revelations and hope to others.

Word eventually reached Joseph, Willy and Angie late in the day about Reggie's beating. Without any hesitation, they rushed to his side after work. They witnessed him, lying in dire straits on the ground with severe back wounds exposed to the grit, dirt, and flies. It was critically important that they get Reggie home, and tend to his painful wounds as soon as possible.

Joseph quickly examined Reggie's back before helping him

stand. "Willy, I don't see how he's gonna' work 'morrow atter' goin' through both a whippin' an' a cat-haulin'.'."

"Joseph yu' know dat' if he 'lays up' Mr. Gibbons will only bring him more trouble. We'll have to cover fo' him. When Gibbons is 'round, we'll jus' sorta' make it look like he is really workin'." Willy stated.

Joseph, who was feeling guilty said, "Maybe I should go back to fightin'. What happened to Reggie wouldn't have happened if I had 'greed to fight. Kin' yu' imagine how guilty I feel?"

Willy spoke up. "Joseph, yu' did dah' right thing. We all said yu' should foller' yur' heart. What happened to Reggie will pass." Willy wished his words were more comforting.

"I know dat' it will pass, an' he'll be fine, but his back will be badly scarred," Joseph replied.

As the men assisted Reggie, Walter returned. "I'm dah' beast dat' had to do dis' to him. I feel terrible—sorta' sick to my stomach. At least nobody has to see his back, but what if it had been his face? I don't even want to think 'bout dat'."

"Walter, yu' had no choice. If it hadn't been yu', it would have been somebody else picked to do dah' dirty work. Yu' were only follerin' orders. If yu' had refused, din' we would have lost yu' as our driver, an' we need yu'," Joseph told him.

Angie was angered and saddened by Reggie's condition and chose to provide some positive direction. "None of us have to take dah' blame fo' what des' evil men kin' come up wit'. We will jus' have to continue to struggle to survive an' fight in our own little way, an' 'ventually we'll win our freedom."

***

At home, Angie cleaned Reggie's wounds and rubbed lard over his back, and then she wrapped a clean cloth around his torso. This helped soothe the pain and promote healing. Finally, Reggie was helped into his bed where he endured a night of excruciating pain with very little rest. Through it all, the thought of Anastasia,

347

and his recent vision of Christ on the cross, together, still brought about a feeling of hope and contentment to his heart. He realized he would get through this period of suffering and move on with his life. It behooved him to remain positive through all the adversity that he was facing.

When the horn sounded the next morning, everyone left for work, including Reggie. He was unable to walk on his own, but with Willy's help, he was able to make it to the work area. Reggie believed it was only through God's intervention that enabled him to make it. Certainly in no condition to work, fortunately Walter managed to successfully allow Reggie to rest.

Everything appeared quiet and normal through the morning hours without the presence of Captain Riley or Jake Gibbons, but it didn't remain like that for too long. Sometime after lunch, Captain Riley and Jake Gibbons rode up to the work area with a devilish look about them. Gibbons yelled from horseback so all could see and hear him. "Niggahs', I've got some good news fo' all of yah'. Yur' master has decided dat' all of yu' need some entertainment to sorta' take dah' edge off of work. He wants all of yu' suckers to gather ovah' at dat' hill near dah' quarters. Now hurry up an' git' over thar'. Yu' rascals better git' a move on! Git' goin'!"

Knowing that this would be bad, everybody apprehensively scrambled over to the hill. After they were assembled, Captain Riley called for Augustus. "I'm jus' lettin' y'all know dat' I'm generously providin' a little recreation. Our legion commander, Augustus, has so graciously volunteered his services to provide all of us wit' a little entertainment."

Shocked at the news, Augustus speechless, stood trembling in front of Captain Riley and Jake. Riley stated, "Well, well, well, we all know yu' are jus' so excited dat' yu' can't even say a word 'bout bein' selected to be dah' featured entertainer fo' all of us. Now Augustus, yu' haven't been hyeh' long 'nough to see dah' barrel ride have yah'?" Riley took delight in his sick devilish ways. "Well, yur' not jus' gonna' see dah' barrel ride, but yu're' gonna' git' to participate an' ride in it! Now, ain't yu' jus' tickled pink to be hand selected to be dah' center of attention fo' all yur' feller' niggahs'? Yu' know opportunities like dis' don't come 'long 'bery often whar' yu' kin' be center stage. Me an' Jake jus' heard dat' yu' like to be dah' funny man 'round hyeh', an' we wanta' give yu' a good chance to show us yur' comedic skills. I hope jus' one thin'—dat' yu' are a better barrel rider din' fighter!" He paused for effect and then stated, "Well, aren't yu' 'cited to be able to make up fo' yur' terrible outin' as a fighter." Octavious, quite the opposite of a "funny man" was retiring, preferring to keep to himself. Captain Riley knew the truth about Octavious, but he was just looking for a "fall guy".

"Master, I's 'bery 'cited to go barrel ridin'." Augustus replied, trembling. He knew what to say.

"Now ain't dat' jus' ducky dat' yu' are so 'cited to go barrel ridin' fo' everybody's enjoyment," Gibbons drawled. "I've got jus' one question to ask yu', Augustus. Do yu' git' real dizzy easily, 'cuz' yu' are gonna' be rollin' down dat' hill at a pretty good clip? Now, dat' really isn't too bad if yu' sorta' girder up an' take barrel ridin' wit' a grain of salt—nuttin' to it, even a dog kin' do it. Well, yu' might git' a little dizzy, but dat' would be it. Now dat' doesn't sound so bad. What do yu' have to say fo' yur'self?"

Augustus took a deep breath and nervously agreed, "I'm ready to do it." Way down deep, the poor man was absolutely terrified.

Gibbons sneered as he spoke. "Oh, Augustus we fo'got to tell yu' dat' dis' isn't jus' any ole' barrel. Dis' is a 'bery special barrel, which provides an even more excitin' challenge fo' a high minded niggah' like yu' wit' a Roman pedigree. It's sorta' of a custom made barrel, made jus' fo' yur' likins' 'cuz' yu' always runnin' 'round braggin' 'bout wantin' a challenge." In reality, Augustus was very quiet and kept to himself.

Walter brought the barrel up from the barn and positioned it at the top of the hill. To everybody's amazement nails had been pounded into the barrel at various points so that as the barrel rolled the down hill, the occupant would be repeatedly stabbed and pierced by them. The slaves stared in disbelief, as Augustus felt his knees buckle—he almost passed out in anticipation of his

349

fate.

It was horrifying for Augustus as he gazed at the barrel, knowing he was about to be subjected to such torture. Captain Riley gleefully added, "Don't look so crestfallen, Augustus, today is really yur' lucky day. I flipped a coin comin' ovah' hyeh'. Heads yu' was goin' down dis' hill an' gently comin' to a halt at dah' base of dis' hill. If it had been tails, dis' would have been yur' last barrel ride. We woulda' set yu' up ovah' on dat' hill wit' dah' pond at dah' bottom whar' yu' woulda' gently rolled down an' settled into dah' water all sealed up in dah' barrel. In fact, based on what I have seen in dah' past, yu' would have had plenty of time to pray an' git' wit' dah' Lawd' since yur' barrel would take in water ever so slowly." Captain Riley was pleased that he had Augustus absolutely terrified. Watching him shake with fear gave Captain Riley great pleasure as he sadistically kept reminding Augustus about how "lucky" he was.

"Augustus, we feel kinda' bad dat' we forgot to tell yu' dah' whole story dat' dis' wouldn't be any ole' barrel ride," Jake interjected. "Dis' is a barrel ride dat' should give yu', a legion commander, a special challenge. We know fightin' is not yur' game, but we jus' thought maybe barrel ridin' wit' nails puncturin' yur' body might be somethin' right up yur' alley, maybe an even better challenge din' fightin'. Yu' know, Augustus, 'one man's cup of tea is 'nother mans cup of poison'. Who knows, maybe dis' could be yur' tea, an' possibly, yu' might be so good at it an' want to give lessons later on. 'Sides Augustus yu' caught a break, dah' nails are not as long as dey' could be, jus' keep dat' in mind!" Gibbons and Captain Riley laughed at his sadistic joke.

The impending torture that was soon to be administered put absolute terror into all the slaves. They knew the stakes had significantly risen. Many were begging Joseph to fight again for the captain. Only a few remained supportive of his decision to not fight. The debate created a division among the slaves.

Augustus was shaking uncontrollably as Captain Riley explained why he was being punished. "Augustus yu've been preselected fo' two reasons. First, yu' disappointed me wit' yur' performance as a fighter, but yur' master kin' fo'give yu' fo' dat'. Secondly, I can't allow yu' to hang 'round wit' dah' wrong people. Yu've been observed hangin' wit' dah' troublemakers 'round hyeh'—Joseph, Willy, an' Reggie. Well dat's jus' not good. Maybe yu' should choose yur' friends more wisely. Dat' I cannot fo'give yu' fo'. What do yu' have to say fo' yur'self'?"

"Master, yu' know what dey' say, dey' say us niggahs' all look alike. I'm not in dah' plow gang. I never see 'dem," Augustus pleaded. "Yu' got me mixed up wit' somebody else."

Joseph stepped forward and respectfully spoke. "Why don't yu' punish me? He never hangs wit' us. I hardly ever . . ." Captain Riley cut Joseph off in mid-sentence. "Now aren't yu' chivalrous, goin' to bat fo' yur' close sidekick? But, it ain't gonna' work, 'cuz' he's been hand-picked to do us dah' honor, an' jus' look at how 'cited he is to roll down dah' hill—aren't yu' boy? In fact he's so 'cited dat' he's gonna laugh all dah' way down dah' hill."

"Yes'um marse', I's excited." Augustus hung his head, his voice quivering.

"'Member, boy, yu' better be laughin' all dah' way down dah' hill or yu'll be goin' 'gain," the captain warned. "Git' it? Now it's time fo' yu' to hop into yur' own custom made barrel."

Augustus was paralyzed with fear, shaking and unable to speak. To make matters much worse, he wet his pants as he stood trembling. When Captain Riley and Gibbons spotted the puddle, they laughed even louder. Captain Riley turned to Gibbons, speaking so everybody could hear him, "Look at dat' niggah'—he's wettin' his pants, now dat' takes all. I can't 'lieve what I'm seein'. Damn, I thought he was so happy. I guess he jus' wants to impress his master wit' his abilty to do so many things—like pissin' in his pants."

"Well, Captain Riley, I can't say as if I've ever seen anybody pissin' in thar' pants, although I've heard of it. I must say dat' thar' is a first time fo' everythin'."

"Yu' know, Jake, Augustus could become our clown—Augustus, dah' Roman clown. It's sorta' sad Jake, 'cuz he's bein' demoted from legion commander to a complete fool, but dat' sorta' fits yu' boy—a loser. A fool like him kin' really make my day. What do yu' think of dat', Augustus?"

"Marse', I don't know much 'bout bein' a Roman clown," he responded in an apologetic tone, his voice hardly audible.

Captain Riley elaborated, "Well, a Roman clown is like yu', Augustus—a complete fool shakin' an' pissin' in his pants. I'll say one other thin' to all of ya'. Do yu' think a white man would ever piss his pants like dis' niggah'? Of course not, he would take his punishment like a man. I jus' wish yu' niggahs' had half dah' manliness in yu' as white folks. 'Nough of dis' talk. Let's git' dis' ovah' wit'."

Gibbons added, "Like yur' master, I find it sad to have to be 'round such a coward as yu', Augustus. Yu' niggahs' have no fight in yu' at all—a bunch of cowards 'fraid of yur' own shadow lest it might be a ghost. Why don't y'all git' a little manliness 'bout yu'? Why don't yu' jus' watch me or yur' master an' y'all will learn how to git' a little gumption 'bout yah'?" Smiling as he spoke, Gibbons obviously believed his own words.

Joseph wondered how manly Gibbons would be if he were the one taking the barrel ride or if he were the one who had been chosen to step into the ring with him—one on one.

Finally, Captain Riley ordered Augustus to get into the barrel. Once he was inside, the nails appeared to be bigger and sharper. Augustus rightfully believed he was about to die. The terrified slaves were absolutely silent. Captain Riley and Jake looked at each other and laughed as Walter sealed the top and placed it on its side. The slaves stood at the top of the hill and cried out for Augustus, knowing the suffering he was going to be going through.

Captain Riley yelled at Augustus, "I tole' yu' to laugh! 'Member, I don't want to hyeh' yu' scream. If yu' rile me up, I'm liable to give yu' a second run down dah' hill, an' yu' would make yur' run jaybird naked. I hope dat' my words sink in. Yu' jus' be a man fo' once in yur' life time. Hey I have an ider', jus' pretend yu' are a white man an' yu' might muster up dah' strength to take it like a man."

A fabricated laugh emerged from the barrel as Augustus tried to respond to the orders.

Gibbons couldn't help but make an additional comment. "Captain Riley, I kin' hyeh' Augustus change his tune from screamin' to laughin'. I guess we kin' say dat' it sounds like Augustus is jus' goin' to have a barrel of fun!" Gibbons smirked as he directed his humor toward the black faces around him.

Captain Riley, added, "All yu' niggahs' aren't laughin'. Yur' overseer jus' tole' one hell of a joke an' yu' suckers jus' stand thar'! Dat' really disappoints me. I wanta' hyeh' all of yu' niggahs' laugh."

Walter was ordered to put the barrel in motion as manufactured laughs emerged, which could not hide the terror the slaves were feeling, knowing what Augustus was going through. As the barrel rolled and bounced down the hill, Augustus could be heard making noises similar to forced laughter. Mercifully after the barrel rolled to a halt, Walter was sent to retrieve Augustus and bring him back up the hill. A silence pervaded the slaves as Walter pried open the barrel. Augustus fell out, blood covering his clothes and dripping onto the ground. It was a horrible scene for everybody to witness as Augustus lapsed between two worlds.

Able to muster the strength to say something to Walter, he cried, "Dose' nails stabbed me all ovah' my body. I'd be blessed to die, Walter," Augustus moaned in sheer agony. For the slaves, it represented an absolute terror to see this spectacle unfold knowing that each one of them could receive the same fate.

Walter, feeling deep sympathy for Augustus, was forced to inform him they had to immediately walk back up the hill or face more punishment.

Walter aided Augustus as the two slowly stumbled up the hill to Captain Riley and Gibbons who were waiting for them. A few yards from the top, the captain yelled, "Augustus, tell all dah' niggahs' 'bout dah' barrel of fun yu' jus' had. Come on now tell 'dem!"

Augustus manufactured just enough energy to respond.

"Marse', I had a barrel of fun." He knew what he had to say.

Riley sneered and said, "Damn right, boy, yu' had a lot of fun givin' yur' master an' Mr. Gibbons a little entertainment. Jus' thank yur' preacher man an' his fellow rascals, especially Reggie fo' yur' ride. An' 'member, things are gonna' continue like dis' since dah' preacher quit fightin' fo' me. One other thin', Augustus fo' bein' a sportin' man an'providin' all of us wit' a little fun, I've decided to provide yu' wit' a Roman sidekick. Jimmy git' ovah' hyeh'! When yu' first 'rived hyeh', I kinda' thought din' dat' yu' lacked a backbone so I've decided to give yu' dat' backbone dat' yu' lack. Scipio, dat's yur' new name, an' now I'm jus' servin' notice to y'all dat' Jimmy's new name is Scipio, named atter' a Roman general, an' if I hyeh' dat' anyone calls him anythin' else, dey' will have to answer to me. Now, git outta' my sight, General Scipio, 'fore I git' upset at havin' to look at yur' ugly puss any longer. I'll jus' say dis' 'bout yu', Scipio, damn when dah' Lawd' passed out dah' looks yu' sur' weren't 'round."

Gibbons had a final word. "Now, all yu' niggahs git' back to work. Oh yes, yur' master an' me will be visitin' yu' in dah' quarters at dusk. We promise to bring yu' some more fun. One other thin'—if yu' niggahs' were smart, y'all would talk to Joseph 'bout fightin' fo' his master. At dusk it will be too late to take it back." Gibbons had an ominous look on his face as he spoke along with the evil glint that was always present in his eyes.

***

As Reggie, Joseph, Angie and Willy walked back to the fields, Joseph, obviously distraught, said, "Reggie, all hell has broke loose. What should I do? I can't stand to see everyone hurt 'cus' of me, an' dey' promise more sufferin' at dusk."

"Joseph," Reggie told him, "Dah' Captain is an evil man who is usin' terror to control yu' an' everybody else. Unfortunately, it kin' work. Take a look at me. Do yu' think I want to mess wit' dat' man? I don't know how I'm able to git' 'round wit' my painful back, but 'gardless, stick to yur' guns Joseph. Everythin' will pass an' we'll find our way back to normal."

"He's right, Joseph." Willy agreed with what Reggie had said, and Angie nodded her head in support.

"It's better to face dah' music now since, eventually, yu're gonna' lose a fight anyhow. Jus' stick to yur' guns! We'll all git' through dis'," Reggie said.

"Reggie, yu' know thar' are a lot of niggahs' dat' want me to fight. Yu' folks are pretty much 'lone in yur' view. All I have to do is step back into dah' ring an' everythin' will be peaceful 'gain, an' I still have time. I jus' don't know what to do."

Willy supported what Reggie had said, "Look, Joseph, we are all 'hind yah'." He then looked at Reggie with compassion, and added, "Reggie, we kin' all feel yur' pain. It's a wonder to me dat' yu' kin' still walk. Yur' wounds look mighty bad!"

"I'm in terrible pain, Willy, an' I kin' thank Walter fo' lettin' me rest up, an' Angie fo' tendin' to my sorry back dat' has taken on an infection. Jus' give it time as dey' say, 'time heals all wounds'." Reggie tried to make light of his suffering as he was more concerned for the others.

Joseph took a deep breath. "Pray dat' Augustus is all right. Yu' know we jus' saw dah' debil' in action. We hardly know Augustus an' yet dey' blamed dat' poor man fo' hangin' 'round wit' us as dah' reason fo' punishin' him, jus' to git' at us. May God grant him strength."

When quitting time arrived, everyone returned to the quarters, knowing and fearing Captain Riley and Jake intended to visit. Not to disappoint, before long they appeared on horseback. It was evident, judging by their demeanor that it was not going to be a pleasant social call.

Gibbons called out, "All yu' niggahs' git' over hyeh'! Yur' master wants to talk to yu', an' he's not happy. Thar' is some toten's goin' on 'round hyeh'." "Toten's" was a slang word for thieving.

Captain Riley bellowed, "All yu' niggahs' hyeh' dis'. Dah' other night one of my swine was taken. Din' I heard dat' Willy's wench was out in dah' back roastin' pork. Now, how far does dah' apple fall from dah' tree? Whar' would she git' dat' pork unless it was fleeced from her master? Kin' yu' 'magine—a niggah' woman stealin' her master's swine! Why, she's a little snake in dah' grass an' needs to be taken down a peg or two fo' her actions. Walter, bring Angie ovah' hyeh', she's gonna' have to be reckoned wit'."

Quickly, Walter took Angie by the arm and walked her to the captain, still seated on his horse to have her answer to the charges.

"A niggah' stealin' wench, dat's what yu' are. Des' are 'bery serious charges. What do yu' have to say fo' yur'self?"

"Marse', I'm wit' my baby an' soon to deliver. I wouldn't be out in dah' back roastin' a pig." Angie was visibly shaking as she spoke.

"Come right hyeh' along side of my hawss'. Do yu' take me fo' a damn fool, girl?" He reached down and slapped Angie full force in the face. "Take dat' yu' little black thief! I mighta' given yu' a little bit of a break if yu' hadn't tried to hocus me. Nuttin' worse din' a niggah' lyin' to her master. One of my trusty hands spotted yu' out in dah' back, Angie—yu've done been caught red-handed. I jus' said thar' was some toten' goin' on 'round hyeh', I jus' had to catch dah' culprit. Who woulda' 'lieved dat' yu' would do somethin' like dis'? Walter, go git' a shovel fo' Angie to start diggin'."

Walter hurried to get a shovel and returned as Gibbons dismounted his horse and took over, giving her the shovel. "Niggah', dig yur' own hole over thar'. Jus' make it belly size."

"Marse', Angie's gonna' have her first pickaninny. She is petrified of yu', an' she would never steal one of yur' hogs. 'Sides she couldn't 'cuz' she's pregnant an' couldn't do it. Please let her go!" Willy begged while crying uncontrollably, his friends tried to hold him back so there wouldn't be an excuse for the captain to make it even worse.

Captain Riley was not sympathetic. "Shut him up, Walter. If he gits' out of line one more time, we're gonna deal wit' him, too, an' it will be severe. Now, yu' little wench, git dat' hole dug! I'm in a hurry."

Willy could not help himself from trying to protect his wife. The captain had some of the slaves seize him and drag him out of the immediate area. When Angie completed digging the hole the captain said, "I want all yu' niggahs' to see what happens to anyone who steals from yur' master. Wench, git' 'jaybird naked', an' din' lie down an' put yur' belly in dah' hole. Walter, tie her arms an' legs together atter' she is in dah' hole."

After Angie was positioned in the hole with her arms and legs tied together, the captain ordered, "Jake, I know yu' have been unhappy dat' Judy has not been kept busy. Well let's give ole' Judy some work."

As Walter and the others restrained Willy, Joseph broke in pleading, "Marse' I'll do what yu' want!"

"It's too late, Joseph, yu' done missed dah' deadline, she has to take her medicine. Yu' had your chance an' yu' chose to see yur' feller' niggahs' suffer while yu' jus' gleefully watched. Anyhow, yu' niggahs' from time to time y'all have to be taught a lesson."

On the captain's order Gibbons proceeded to whip Angie. The screaming was pronounced at first, and then it got quieter and quieter until there was little more than a soft whimper—and then silence as the beating ceased. "Next time yu' suckers will think twice 'fore yu' fleece from yur' master. Jake, let's go." The two rode away, leaving Angie on the ground, not giving a thought to her condition.

Willy, Joseph, and Reggie rushed to assist Angie while quickly untieing her and covering her up, but she was not moving. Joseph, clearly distraught, cried, "Willy, she's not movin' or breathin'! I don't think she is wit' us hyeh' on earth—she's joined dah' Lawd' in heaven wit' her pickaninny!" Joseph sobbed as he looked over Angie's lifeless body.

Willy was hysterical as he picked her up in his arms and held her close. "Joseph, I blame yu' fo' dis'. Why did yu' quit fightin'? Now my beloved Angie an' dah' little one are both dead, leaving me wit' nothin' to live fo'! Dis' is all on yu'!"

"Willy, Joseph is already grievin' an' blamin' himself fo'

dis'. It's not his fault. Blame dose' murderin' tyrants who jus' left, don't blame yur' friend Joseph." Tears started to streak down Reggie's face as he walked with his friends.

"Reggie, I know yu're right, it's not his fault, but yu' kin understand why I feel dis' way. Dey' made dat' story up 'bout Angie killin' thar' swine, an' I can't blame Joseph fo' dat'. He couldn't have known dat' dey' were goin' to kill my Angie an' her pickaninny. 'Sides, he said he would start fightin' 'gain an' dey' ignored him. It's mighty tough not to blame Joseph, but I know dat' dey' are on a rampage, an' my Angie got caught in dah' crossfire."

Reggie provided a message, "Yu' cannot allow des' tyrants to divide our people—we have to stick together. Yu' know dat' Angie would not want yu' to blame Joseph. If dey' don't pay fo' thar' actions now, din' someday dey' will have to answer to dah' Lawd'. Thar' day of reckonin' will come sooner, or later, one way or dah' other."

"Reggie, if I ever git' a chance, I will kill either one or both of 'dem an' not even blink an eye. All I kin' think of is my darlin' Angie an' our little pickaninny murdered. Dis' is not of dah' Lawd'—dis' is nothin' but pure evil—dah' debil'!" Willy cried, cradling his beloved.

"Hyeh Willy, I've said dis' 'fore—how kin' dey' call 'demselves Christians an' commit acts dis' horrible. I understand why yu' want revenge fo' what dey' did, I honestly believe dat' dah' Lawd' would 'ventually come to fo'give yu', if yu' took action 'gainst 'dem, but dat's not gonna' bring Angie back." Reggie stood close to his grief-stricken friend, hoping his words would give both strength and support.

"Willy, dah' burial must be 'morrow evenin'." Joseph interjected. "We can't wait any longer din' dat.' We'll take Angie back home, an' yu' kin' tend to her as long as necessary. Luckily, we have a pine box all lined up with black cloth, an' dat' would be nice fo' Angie an' her little pickaninny."

Willy trying to pull himself together added, "I wanta' clean her up right nice an' put her best dress on her. I couldn't bear it if my last vision of Angie was of her naked an' in dis' tortured, bloodied condition. I want her to be meetin' her Maker in her Sunday best!"

"Dat'll be fine," Joseph assured Willy. "I'll go back wit' Reggie, jus' let us know when yu' are ready." Joseph continued to carry guilt, "Reggie, I had no ider' dey' would kill Angie an' her pickaninny. I even stepped in but dey' said it was too late. I'll be sorry fo' dah' rest of my life—I'll be mighty sorry. I'll have to shoulder dis' horrible burden fo' dah' rest of my days."

"Joseph, yu' told 'dem dat' yu' would be willin' to fight 'gain but dat' wasn't good 'nough, an' now we can't bring her back. I blame dose' two wicked men, not yu'!"

Willy took his Angie into their small house where he cleaned and dressed her. He wept throughout the night as he lovingly remained her guardian by her side.

Jake Gibbons arrived early the next morning blowing his horn to announce the new work day. He had absolutely no interest regarding what might have become of Angie after her beating the previous evening.

Joseph immediately approached Gibbons, "Angie didn't make it an' we need to bury her an' her baby tonight atter' work. May we borrow a couple of shovels to dig dah' hole, Mr. Gibbons?"

"Joseph, dat's too bad 'bout Angie, 'cuz' dat' costs yur' master a lot of money. Yu' kin' have dah' shovels—now git' to work." He had absolutely no feelings of guilt for taking the life of two human beings, expressing sorrow only for the monetary loss. Captain Riley's thinking was that the monetary loss was great, but the lesson taught to the field hands, over-rode any obvious financial loss. This belief was really not that uncommon. As much as a slave owner might pay for a slave, sometimes it was more important to set an example even if it was costly. This refutes a commonly held belief that a slave owner would not damage costly "property".

Reggie who was standing by, overhearing the conversation could recall Mrs. Rose stating that "if you give a man a whip he will have no bounds".

Gibbons spotted Reggie and asked, "How's dah' trouble

maker feelin'?"

"Mr. Gibbons," Reggie answered. "I think an infection has set in on my back. I can't pick up anythin' wit'out severe pain, an' dah' only reason I'm able to git' 'round now is 'cuz' I'm able to force myself wit' dah' help of dah' Lawd'."

"Well, dat's too bad. I could smell dah' sour stench of yur' hide as I came upon yur' pathetic self," Jake mocked. "What do yu' want me to do 'bout it? I could rub a little salt on it or even send yu' cat-haulin 'gain." With that comment he started laughing.

"Mr. Gibbons, I'm goin' to work right now!" Reggie distanced himself from Gibbons as quickly as possible so he didn't have the opportunity to make good on his earlier threat. He knew another "cat-hauling" would cripple him more, or worse, give him "cat scratch fever" which could end his life.

Walter assured Reggie he could rest but added, "If dat' cruel overseer returns, git' 'hind dat' mule an' git' to work."

"Walter, I 'preciate yur' kindness, but I'm havin' problems. Dah' infection has taken all my energy, an' I'm 'bery weak. I kin' barely walk." It was obvious that Reggie was sweating profusely and suffering; but he had to continue, knowing that any sign of weakness would likely bring more harm than good.

Mid-morning, Joseph located Reggie and Willy. He then consulted with them about their future on the plantation.

Joseph pleaded, "Fo' some reason dey' didn't mention me fightin' 'gain. Dat' has me worried, an' I think I know what we have to do. Tonight, atter' dah' burial, let's flee to dat' maroon colony out in dah' bottoms. Dey' seldom nab anybody out thar'— some of dose' niggahs' have been out thar' fo' years. If we stay hyeh', it will only git' worse fo' everyone, includin' ourselves."

Reggie's face suddenly showed relief. "Truthfully, I was thinkin' dah' same thin'. Fo' dah' sake of everyone, we have to git' out of hyeh' now. 'Sides, I know dat' dah' next time dey' go atter' me, it's gonna' be real bad. In spite of all dah' pain an' sufferin' I'm goin' through, I'll make it through dat' marsh, knowin' my life depends on it. What do yu' say, Willy?" Reggie hoped Willy as well would participate in the escape as he had developed such a close relationship with him.

"I'll go, what do I have to lose? I have jus' one wish. I'd like to kill both of dose' tyrants wit' my bare hands!" Willy knew his anger at the overseer and the captain would cause him to act in a manner that could jeopardize his life and bring harm to others if he stayed. It would be less risky and much wiser for him to leave.

"One last thing—yu' cannot trust anyone. It would take jus' one informant an' dey' would kill all three of us. 'Member, not a word to anyone." Joseph made sure his words made an impression on each of his two friends.

Reggie turned to Willy. "Joseph is right. We have to high tail it outta' hyeh' now while dah' gittin' is good. Yu' know we are grievin' yur' loss, but Willy, dah' three of us have to stick together. I truly believe dat' Angie would want yu' to do dis'."

"I'll be ready, but dis' is really tough, I have to bury Angie an' my pickaninny an' in dah' same evenin', I have to flee! But don't yu' fret none, I'll be ready!"

Joseph had the final word. "'Member, do not talk 'bout dis' wit' anyone. Yu' know dat' Captain Riley will send Mr. Gibbons to be wit' us fo' dah' funeral. It's dah' same old ritual, a white person has be wit' us fo' a social gatherin', even a funeral. As soon as he is gone, din' we will skidaddle outta' hyeh'. We need all dah' time we kin' git' to put some distance 'tween him an' us."

That evening everyone gathered at the quarters for the funeral. Joseph slowly drove the ox cart to the cemetery carrying the coffin that was adorned with beautiful purple and yellow wild flowers that had been Angie's favorite. Mr. Gibbons was present with his trusty whip and derringer. As the cart moved along, the slaves softly began singing their beloved hymn, *Swing Low Sweet Chariot*.

Swing low, sweet chariot, Comin' fo' to carry me home,
Swing low, sweet chariot, Comin' fo' to carry me home.
I looked over Jordan, an' what did I see,
Comin' fo' to carry me home? A band of angels
comin' atter me, Comin' fo' to carry me home.

Swing low, sweet chariot, Comin' fo' to carry me home.
Swing low, sweet chariot, Comin' fo' to carry me home.
If yu' git' thar' befo' I do,
Comin' fo' to carry me home, Tell all my friends I'm
comin' too, comin' fo' to carry me home.
Swing low, sweet chariot, Comin' fo' to carry me home.
Swing low, sweet chariot, Comin' fo' to carry me home.

Jake mouthed the words to *Swing Low, Sweet Chariot* and then directed them to get the ceremony moving. "Come on, all yu' niggahs'. Let's git' goin'. I've got to git' my sleep. Damn all of yah', we have to bring a white man to a niggah' burial 'cuz' yu' can't be trusted. Let's git' dah' 'cession goin'. Jus' sing, *Lay Dis' Body Down*. Dat's what yu' always sing anyway."

Gibbons ordered the cortege to keep in motion—pine tar torches illuminating the area. First came Joseph who was driving the ox cart, followed by Reggie, Willy and the slaves who paid their last respects. Mr. Gibbons brought up the rear on his horse, as the slaves sang:

"O graveyard, O graveyard, I'm walkin'
troo de' graveyard; Lay dis' body down.
I know moonlight, I know starlight, I'm walkin'
troo de' starlight; Lay dis' body down.
I know de' graveyard, I know de' graveyard;
When I lay dis' body down.
I walk in de' graveyard, I walk
troo de' graveyard; To lay dis' body down.
I lay in de' grave an' stretch out my arms;
I lay dis' body down.
I go to de' judgment in de' evenin' of de'
day; When I lay dis' body down.
An' my soul an' your soul will meet
in de' day; When we lay dis' body down."

The cortege solemnly walked along the cart path continuing

to sing, *"Lay This Body Down"* with Angie's killer directly behind them. It was very difficult to keep their anger contained since Angie was so loved and well respected by everyone.

It was a long walk to the graveyard since it was located deep in the woods, quite a distance from the quarters. In preparation, some slaves had gone ahead of everyone to light pine tar torches along the route and in the cemetery. Without proper lighting it would have been extremely difficult to conduct the service. Fortunately, the slaves kept the cemetery in good condition, never overgrown in spite of the surrounding area being heavily wooded with pine trees and wild vegetation.

Gathered around Angie's final resting place, Joseph began the services. "Brothers an' sisters in Christ, we're gathered hyeh' to mourn dah' loss of our sister Angie an' her unborn pickaninny. We all know she's up in heaven now wit 'her little pickaninny watchin' ovah' us as we all pray. Like all of us, times have always been hard hyeh' on earth fo' our sister, but we all know dat' she an' her pickaninny are in a better place wit' dah' Lawd' in heaven whar' she kin' be 'free at last'. Amen."

The pallbearers shut the lid of the casket, drawing an emotional outburst from Willy, who begged to keep the lid open a little longer. Willy's wishes were granted, and he wept with the others, knowing this would be the last time he would ever lay his eyes on her in this life. Finally, Joseph asked for the closing of the lid and the lowering of the body. He then recited the "Lords Prayer":

Our Father, who art in heaven, hallered be thy Name,
thy kingdom come, dey'will be done, on earth as it is in heaven
Give us dis' day our daily bread. An' forgive us our trespasses,
As we forgive those who trespass 'gainst us.
An' lead us not into temptation, but deliver us from evil.
Fo' thine is dah' kingdom, dah' power, an' dah' glory,
fo' ever an' ever. Amen.

Pallbearers shoveled dirt into the grave as Joseph continued to read the prayer, followed by Willy, who added a few words. "Everyone hyeh' knows how deeply I loved Angie an' was so proud to be dah' father to her pickaninny. Oh' Lawd', I wish I could understand why yu' would take 'dem from me, but I know yu' have yur' reason. Lawd', dis' seems like it's jus' a bad dream— dis' can't be happenin'. Angie, I love yu' an' our tiny pickaninny an' I know someday I will be united wit' dah' two of yu' 'gain in heaven. Amen."

The crowd resumed singing, *Lay This Body Down.*

O graveyard, O graveyard, I walkin'
troo de graveyard; Lay dis' body down.
I know moonlight, I know starlight, I'm walkin'
troo de starlight; Lay dis' body down.
I know de' graveyard, I know de' graveyard;
When I lay dis' body down.
I walk in de' graveyard, I walk
troo de' graveyard; To lay dis' body down.
I lay in de' graveyard an' stretch out my arms;
I lay dis' body down.
I go to de' judgment in de' evenin' of de'
day; When I lay dis' body down.
And my soul an' your soul will meet
in de' day; When we lay dis' body down."

Their singing continued as the grave was filled with dirt. Willy offered one last message. "In dah' spirit of our Afriky' ancestors I'm placin' on her grave dis' little bowl, which was dah' last thin' Angie used. All yu' know Angie will 'preciate what yu' put on her grave as well." He set the bowl at the head of the grave signaling others to place broken glass, fragments of pottery, shells, and rocks around the grave in her honor, part of a traditional African burial ceremony.

No one made any attempt to leave and reverently kept singing until Jake Gibbons on horseback pushed his way to the center of the mourners. "Come on, all yah' niggahs'. I have to sound dah' horn in a few hours. Y'all are in America, not in Afriky', so forgit' all des' ole' hoodoo' customs." Apparently, Gibbons did not know that voodoo is a cult practiced in Haiti.

As Reggie walked back to Willy's home, he kept thinking about three things—Angie's sweet face, and how callous Jake Gibbons was, even in times of grief and sorrow. Also, that black people have every bit as much compassion, caring and love as whites. How could the white people not see this? An indelible impression had been made back at Oak Manor when he observed the slaves showing more emotion toward the passing of Albert than the white people, which suggested to him that overtly they certainly demonstated as much compassion as the white people. Deep down, he believed they also had every bit as much compassion as the white people.

Suddenly, the time to leave was imminent. In his heart he knew this was the right choice, considerin' the alternative—stay and suffer, and quite possibly lose his life next time, or flee with Joseph and Willy and take his chances on the road to freedom. Prepared to depart, immediately Reggie, Willy and Joseph grabbed their gunny-sacks and vanished into the night. For Reggie, he felt a relief he hadn't experienced since he fled with Anastasia from Oak Manor. In spite of the pain he was suffering, Reggie knew he could make it. He had to keep up with Joseph and Willy, while gaining strength as his adrenaline kicked in, providing him with the necessary strength to make it. His heart soared as he forced himself to move along, knowing that he had made the right decision.

For the three of them, they knew there would be no turning back—almost certain death awaited them if they were apprehended. Somehow, a positive zeal overtook them as they moved out knowing the "road to freedom" was ahead.

CHAPTER TWENTY-TWO

Time was of the essence. Fortunately, Joseph and Willy knew the route through the marsh, like the back of their hand. They had six to seven hours of travel before Gibbons would learn they had fled. They hoped this would provide the necessary time to get comfortably ahead.

With confidence, they were successful in being able to travel almost nonstop through the marsh. It proved to be extremely difficult terrain with vegetation pushing through tall grass and low-growing shrubs that lacerated their arms, legs and faces. Insects, especially mosquitoes, and flies were attracted to their exposed flesh, forcing them to rub mud over their bodies. For Reggie, the escape was made even more difficult since he was dealing with festering open sores on his infected back. Reggie had to believe that it was only through the grace of God that he was able to continue in the condition he was in. However, he was painfully aware of the alternative to not keeping up with Joseph and Willy. Unfortunately, they all knew that Gibbons on horseback would be in hot pursuit, which gave him a huge advantage.

By late in the afternoon, the three men, feeling they had put sufficient distance between themselves and a pursuing Gibbons, decided to take a much needed break thinking it would be safe. They were resting at length when they heard a dog barking in the distance. They then realized they had underestimated Gibbons determinism and horsemanship in thinking that perhaps a six hour time lag would be sufficient to put them safely out of danger.

"We're not gonna' outrun dose' dogs, but din' I hyeh' only one, so we may as well stay put an' let me take care of it. It's dat' niggah' hunter bloodhound marse' is so proud of. I know dat' dogs bark, yu' can't miss it. I also bet yu' dat' Mr. Gibbons is drivin' him on his white horse. Hopefully, he was so cocksure of himself dat' he came 'lone." Joseph expressed optimism and confidence as he spoke.

"What should we do? We don't have any firearms!" Reggie stood and said nervously as he looked in the direction of their pursuer.

Joseph boldly stated, "I brought my prize Case knife. I'll catch dat' hound's 'tention an' provoke him to attack me, an' don't worry, I'll win dah' fight. 'Member Reggie yu' have dah' brains, but I have dah' brawn. 'Sides, I'm dah' one wit' dah' knife, givin' me an edge. I'm not one bit 'fraid of dat' bloodhound."

Reggie and Willy quickly located some good sized sticks to offer an additional defense while Joseph stood tall awaiting the dogs' arrival.

The dog emerged, snarling, lunging at the most obvious target, Joseph, who had positioned himself in front of Reggie and Willy. Without hestitation the dog attacked Joseph. Showing no fear, Joseph quickly plunged the knife into the animal's heart in midair. The dog let out a yelp as he crumpled to the ground. What appeared to be an extremely precarious situation for Joseph was made easy by his ability to stand tall and remain calm and collected in the face of adversity. He knew the exact spot to plunge the knife into the dog and the fight was over as soon as it began.

At that precise moment Jake Gibbons appeared with his derringer, ready to fire. Confidently he addressed the slaves as he pulled up near them. "I knew I would catch up to yu' three scamps!" He looked around at each of the men and then witnessed his dog lying motionless on the ground. "Who killed my dog?"

Joseph stepped forward.

"Well, yu're one dead niggah'!" Enraged, he pointed his derringer at Joseph, and without thinking of the consequences pulled the trigger. However, miraculously the weapon misfired. Willy knew it was time to go on the offense. He attacked from the rear, pulling Jake off his horse and onto the ground as Reggie grabbed the derringer from him. Within a few brief moments they had successfully disarmed and subdued him—the chase and fight had successfully ended in their favor. It was certainly not expected to be so easy as they all looked at each other in disbelief.

Reggie stepped on Gibbons chest and with bravado, commented, "My, oh my, Mr. Gibbons, yu' do look like a fish out of water. Wasn't it rather foolish of yu' to attack us single-handed wit' jus' one dog? Yu' must really take us fo' fools an' weaklins' to boot comin' out hyeh' all by yur'self' thinkin' yu' could handle dah' three of us. I believe dah' derringer dat' yu' tote chambers only one round. Mr. Gibbons, even if yu' had successfully brought Joseph down, it would still be yu' wit' a useless pistol, 'gainst dah' two of us. I would call dat' short-sighted plannin'. I really don't know what yu' were thinkin'. I do think yu' actually believed dat' foolish talk yu' use to come up wit' 'bout how much stronger dah' white man was. Dat' said, I think we would all 'gree dat' dah' shoe is now on dah' other foot—yu' bein' so foolhardy to think yu' could overcome dah' three of us! Isn't it somethin', how dah' tide can turn so quickly, Mr. Gibbons?" Reggie exaggerated the pronunciation of his last name, mocking and belittling him as he spoke.

Gibbons was well aware of his perilous situation, which he had foolishly put himself into. "My intent was not to cause harm to anyone, jus' give y'all dah' good news dat' Captain Riley is willin' to fo'give all of yah' as he wants everythin' to fall back to normal on dah' plantation." Jake desperately tried to talk his way out of the situation.

"Normal!" Willy spat in Jake's face, "Fall back to normal! How do yu' do dat' atter' my wife an' pickaninny were killed by yu'. Haven't yu' ever heard of an eye fo' an eye?"

"Now, Willy, please be reasonable. I was follerin' orders an' it was an accident. I didn't mean to kill Angie an' yur' baby. Yu' know me better din' dat'."

Joseph, who had remained silent, was enraged and he looked directly into Gibbons eyes while still recovering from the effect of having a gun misfire that was pointed directly in his face. "Of course, an' yu' didn't intend to harm me when yu' pulled dah' trigger wit' yur' derringer pointed at my head, did yah'? An' now yu're askin' us to go quietly back wit' yu'—what do yu' take us fo'—blame fools?"

"Joseph, I wasn't aimin' to hit yu'. I was pointin' dah' gun ovah' yur' head. I only wanted to scare yu' fo' killin' dah' dog, dat's all it was. Now let's all jus' quietly go back an' let 'bygones be bygones'. Better yet, I could let y'all return at yur' own pace."

"Mr. Gibbons, if I believed dat', I would believe dat' hell is filled wit' nothin' but fruit an' honey." Joseph replied as he circled Gibbons.

"I 'member when I trusted a white man with my safety, an' he double crossed me, causin' my life to fall into an upheaval," Reggie interjected. "Are yu' askin' me to 'lieve dat' yu' would not double cross us?"

Willy spoke up, "Now, I like yur' answer dat' yu' only want to be nice, so I've decided to make yu' happy too. Mr. Gibbons, I know how yu' hate yur' job 'cuz' marse' makes yu' kill people so I'm gonna' give yu' a better deal."

Jake displayed a slight smile on his face. "Willy, I thank yu' so much fo' yur' understandin'. What kind of a deal are yu' talkin' 'bout?" Mr. Gibbons was very nervous as he addressed Willy knowing that a lot was at stake.

Willy in a mocking manner stated, "I'm gonna' make yur' life comfortable, 'cuz' I'm gonna' have dah' debil' set' yu' up wit' a mansion in hell so yu' kin' live in grand style fo' 'ternity while I 'ventually join my family livin' up in a shack in heaven. Now isn't dat' sportin' of me—yu' wit' a mansion an' me wit' a shack? It's only right—yu' know, a white man in a mansion an' a niggah' in a shack."

The hint of a smile on Jake's face was replaced by fear. "Please, Willy, I don't wanta' die. Do dah' Christian thin' an' let me go." Jake was in terror now realizing that he may not come out of this situation alive.

Reggie wanted to get in a few more remarks. "Looks to me like yu' are frightened out of yur' wits, Mr. Gibbons, or kin' I call yu' Jake? Oh yes! And yu' kin' call me Reggie Marshall. Is dat' a problem?"

Mr. Gibbons, unhesitatingly, said, "Reggie Marshall, it's no problem an' Reggie, yu' kin' call me Jake, I'm always lookin' fo' a friend. No reason we can't develop a friendship. Now, my friend, convince Willy to quit talkin' foolishness."

"Now Jake how would dat' sit back at dah' quarters? Jus' yu' an' me—lollygaggin' 'round as best of friends—wouldn't dat' jus' take dah' cake, yu' dah' overseer an' me dah' slave chummin' up together. Also, Jake yu' forgit' dat' yu' sent me 'cat-haulin'' fo' acknowledgin' my last name. I'm in constant agony wit' my back, which will be permanently scarred. Also, I 'member dat' atter' dah' beatin' yu' said dat' dah' next time yu' would disfigure my face to match my back. I was semiconscious, but I still heard yu' say dat'. An' yu' are now askin' me to be yur' friend, knowin' dat' yu' would want to transform me into a side show freak? I normally 'lieve in bein' fair an' considerate, but in dis' case, I stand wit' Willy."

"Yu' men should target dah' captain, not me. I only follered' orders." Jake pleaded.

This blame-shifting infuriated Joseph. "Dat' is dah' second time yu' have brought up dat' yu' were only follerin' orders. In other words, if dah' captain jumped off of a cliff, yu' would foller' right 'hind him. Yu' must take all of us fo' fools!"

Reggie wanted Jake to know exactly how he felt. "Yu' say yu' follered' orders, but didn't yu' put yourself in dah' position to carry out all dah' captain's instructions? Yu', Mr. Gibbons—are an evil tyrant, comin' from dah' North to extract blood money out of dah' South. Everybody throughout dah' South despises dah' likes of yu', even dah' plantation owner yu' work fo'. All yu' represent is a tool fo' Captain Riley, dat's all! Now yu' are goin' to die fo' a man who probably despises yu'. Dat' should really make yu' feel good, Jake. When yu' git' to hell, yu' kin' wait 'round to see yur' good friend, Captain Riley, who sent yu' off by yur'self' to apprehend us single-handed. Dah' two of yu' should be reunited friends in hell. Yu' know, yu' are even a bigger fool din' I thought," Reggie stated, and he wasn't finished. "I guarantee in no time dah' captain will have a replacement fo' yu' an' din' make a disparagin' comments 'bout how worthless yu' were to jus' disappear an' not bring us back, an' worse yet, allow his favorite dog to vanish! I guarantee yu' Jake, dat' he will be more upset 'bout dah' dog din' yu'. Dat' ought to make yu' feel better. Jake, Captain Riley is dah' consummate of evil, an' when yu' hang wit' dah' debil', yu' will likely die wit' dah' debil'!"

Jake's begging intensified as he felt his throat tighten with fear. "Please, Reggie, I beg yu' please—yu' are a compassionate an' intelligent man."

"Jake, history has recorded dat' when tyrants have to pay for thar' evil deeds, dey' always pass dah' buck, an as I jus' said, yu' are no 'ception, 'cuz' yu' knew what yu' were doin'." Reggie retorted.

As Willy held the gun on Jake with intent, he said, "Yur' time is runnin' out. I'm gonna' give yu' five minutes to try to right yur'self' wit' dah' Lawd', an' din' I'm gonna' put one round right into yur' head. How does dat' sound to yah', Mr. Gibbons? Oh, by dah' way, Angie will be watchin' in heaven, an' dah' gun won't misfire dis' time." Willy spoke slowly, punctuating his comments with clenched teeth and a sneer.

Reggie added with passion, "When a man dies at dah' hand of his own pistol, it means dat' he had to have done somethin' wrong."

Gibbons was terrified. "Please Willy don't scare me like dis'. I know yu' wouldn't kill me. We kin' patch everythin' up—it's not too late."

"Mr. Gibbons I'm not jestin' wit' yu'. I tole' Reggie dat' I prayed to be dah' one to kill yu' an' Captain Riley. Well I guess I'm gonna' fulfill half dat' prayer right now. Mr. Gibbons, if yu' have some unfinished matters wit' dah' Lawd' dat' yu' have to take care of—git' it done—time is runnin' out. Yu' are a dead duck!"

Willy did not mince words.

"Mr. Gibbons do yu' want me to pray over yu'? Dah' Lawd' kin' be fo'givin' to dose' who ask fo' salvation. Would yu' like dat'?" Joseph asked with sincerity in his voice.

Jake, realizing he was about to die, humbly stated, "Joseph I never got religion, so yu' better pray ovah' me now."

Joseph placed his hands over Jake's head to give him his last rites. "As a sinner, are yu' prepared to ask dah' Lawd' fo' his fo'giveness?"

"Joseph, please stop, I don't want any last rites administered ovah' me. I meant fo' yu' to pray ovah' me dat' I kin' git' out of hyeh' 'live. I never meant to kill anybody. Lawd' I don't wanta' die. Please intervene an' help me—save me from dyin', skip dah' last rites." Gibbons begged.

Joseph directly eyed Gibbons and said, "Yu' kin' only be saved from goin' to hell, Mr. Gibbons, but yu' have to ask fo' salvation. Yu' won't be spared from death hyeh' on earth—it's too late fo' dat', Willy is 'chompin' at dah' bit' to git' dis' ovah' wit'. Mr. Gibbons, I 'member when yu' an' marse' had Augustus pissin' in his pants, an' it came up dat' Augustus was jus' 'nother weak spined niggah' an' dat' a white man would be able to take his medicine much better din' a black man—somethin' 'bout a black man havin' no spine. I think dat' was dah' gist of what was said." Joseph thoughtfully, paused and went on, "Now, Mr. Gibbons, it's yur' chance to stand tall fo' all dah' brave white men out thar' an' show us how gallant yu' are as thar' representative. How does dat' set wit' yu', Mr. Gibbons?"

"Joseph, we were jus' kiddin'. I know dat' black men are every bit as manly as white men. I sur' didn't mean it. I felt pressured to act dat' way wit' Captain Riley next to me. If yu' took it dah' wrong way, let me 'pologize right now!"

"Talk comes easy, Mr. Gibbons, when yu' got all dah' power, but now yu' ain't got nuttin', an' thar' yu' are, a coward, pure an' simple," Joseph exclaimed. "Stand tall as a white man an' show us some gumption." Joseph smiled at the humor that he just interjected into the conversation.

Gibbons was desperate as he looked to Reggie. "Please, Reggie don't let Willy commit dis' horrible deed. I promise I won't say a word 'bout yur' location to anyone. Jus' let me go an' I'll make somethin' up 'bout losin' dah' dog in dah' marsh— everythin' will work out fo' all of us."

"Do yu' take us to be fools?" Reggie snapped. "I tole yu' earlier dat' I trusted a white man, an' it almost got me killed an' caused dah' separation from my wife. We all know dat' we cannot trust yu'. Dah' second yu' got back, yu' would tell our exact location. Din' dah' captain would reward yu' fo' yur' duty to him. Dey' would high tail it outta' thar' an' come at us in full force. We all know dat' come hell or high water, Captain Riley would be in hot pursuit of us an' yu' taggin' right 'long."

"I swear on a stack of Bibles dat' I won't say a word. Please, jus' give me a chance. I'll even leave my hawss' wit' y'all an' I kin' walk back."

Reggie glared at him. "Look what yu' have done to each of us, an' din' yu' tell us dat' yu' deserve fo'giveness? Start prayin' Jake an' stand up an' take it like a strong white man. Oh dat' reminds me, try to avoid pissin' in yur' pants."

"Reggie, wit' death stalkin' at my door I'm too weak an' scared to stand. I always thought dat' I could take death like a man, but I can't. I'm scared like a young lad, maybe I'm a poor representative fo' a full grown white man," Jake moaned. "I'm prayin' dat' Willy realizes dat' I won't tell on yu' men. I know now dat' I was wrong an' I ask fo' dah' fo'giveness' of dah' three of yu'. I'm truly sorry, fo' I have sinned. If yu' men jus' give me one more chance, I'll come back hyeh' an' supply yu' wit' food an' provisions as yur' friend. Nobody will ever have to know."

"Mr. Gibbons, yu' are goin' to die in a very short time. All dis' talk will do yu' no good, 'cuz' it's too late. Do yu' wish to be blindfolded while administered dah' last rites?" Joseph spoke in a quiet but serious tone.

Jake cried uncontrollably. "Yes, yes, blindfold me, an' give me last rites. Please. I jus' wish I had stayed in Pennsylvania an' never came down hyeh'. Why am I hyeh'? I jus' wanna' go home whar' I came from." Willy was able to retrieve a rag from the saddle on the horse, which could serve as a blindfold.

Joseph administered the rites. "Mr. Gibbons, I truly believe dat' yu' will be able to go home in spirit," Joseph said in a forgiving tone. "Father, dis' sinner in his final moments hyeh' on earth has asked fo' yur' fo'giveness. We know yu' are a fo'givin' Lawd', an' he says he never 'tended to kill anyone. Yu' are dah' final judge of dat', but I think dis' sinner 'cepts penance fo' his evil ways hyeh' on earth. Amen!"

Reggie observed something of importance while the men prepared for the execution. Neither Willy nor Joseph could bring themselves to call Mr. Gibbons by his first name. This demonstrated psychologically to Reggie just how beaten down the black man was in the South. Even when the white man is totally subjugated to the black man, the black man still demonstrates respect toward him.

Jake wept loudly. "I don't wanna' die. Please, please, I don't wanna' die. Everythin' I did dat' was wrong, I had to do it—I was follerin' orders. Please, please, I don't wanna' die!"

Talk was over and the time for the execution had arrived. Without any hesitation, Willy coldly placed the the barrel of the pistol on Jake's forehead and pulled the trigger. Blood splattered as Willy stood motionless, watching Gibbons who was on his knees, further drop to the ground dead. Willy looked up with relief and stated, "Dat' was one of dah' easiest tasks I've ever completed. I jus' wish I could have Captain Riley in my cross hairs as well."

Reggie stoically commented, "It's eerie. I once witnessed a poor slave shot in dah' head while at sea. I saw blood an' brain matter splatter all ovah' dah' place. Now I see dah' same sight 'gain. I find it amazin' how violence can shift from a black man goin' down an' din' witnessin' a white man goin' down. An' guess what? A white man dies jus' as easily as a black man. I guess dis' would be jus' one example of equality amongst dah' races. Now, let's do somethin' wit' dis' corpse an' dead dog an' move on." Reggie just couldn't help invoking his own brand of humor at a very somber event.

"Without a shovel, it won't be easy. Let's put 'em both in dah' marsh an' place rocks on top of 'em so dat' thar' bodies don't float back up. Mother nature will take care of dah' rest." Joseph suggested.

"Wait! How 'bout takin' des' fancy clothes from Mr. Gibbons an' give dem' to Reggie? Make a swap." Willy grabbed Gibbons by the heels as he spoke.

"Willy, I was a little surprised by yur' ider', but it would make good sense. As we travel dah' freedom road I could be dah' slave master an' dah' two of yu' would be my slaves." Reggie quickly made the switch, knowing that his Negro cloth would have revealed his true identity. Fortunately, the clothes fit.

"Even though Reggie kin' pass fo' white an' even if we take yur' advice Willy, we still gotta' travel a long way from Georgia to make it to freedom. Dat's a mighty long haul!" Joseph looked Reggie squarely in the face and continued. "Reggie, I 'lieve wit' dis' steed yu' could ride to freedom—yu' could make it on horseback as a white man. Me an' Willy will slow yu' down and we would probably git caught anyhow. From Georgia, it would be a mighty long haul to freedom, but I honestly believe dat' yu' kin' make it."

"I can't leave my two best friends out in dis' marsh," Reggie pleaded.

"Don't worry 'bout us. We're gonna' stay out hyeh' in dah' 'bottoms' an' hook up wit' dose' maroon runaways. Our business of servin' dah' Lawd' is down hyeh', an' yur's should be in dah' North whar' yu' kin' work toward our freedom while findin' yur' loved one. Please git' goin', an' don't worry 'bout us. We'll be fine," Joseph stressed.

"Jus 'member to foller' dah' North Star by night an' dah' moss side of dah' trees by day—both will lead yu' north. Try to sleep in graveyards as much as yu' kin' since white folks are 'fraid to go into 'dem, 'specially at night." Willy walked Reggie toward the horse as he spoke.

Reggie found humor in Willy's advice. He had always

heard that black people were afraid to sleep in graveyards at night since they were more fearful of the supernatural than white people. Now he's learned from Willy, it's the other way around. Reggie accepted that would just have to remain a mystery.

"Yu' know, Reggie, dat' Willy an' I are gonna' miss yu' a lot, but I'm sur' our paths will cross 'gain. Now please git' goin,' an' 'member not to stop ridin' until yu' are completely out of dis' area. One more bit of advice; foller' a northwest route through dah' brush an' yu' will shortly come to a by-path headed straight west, which will soon lead to the main pike headed straight north. Do not stray from what I tole yu', it'll git' yu' out of hyeh."

"Reggie, we have gotten mighty close, I'm really gonna' miss yu', but someday we will be together 'gain," added Willy.

Reggie's eyes watered as he stood next to his two best friends. "I promise both of yu' I'll be back to help yu'. John 15:13 tells us: 'Greater love hath no man din' dis', dat' a man lay down his life fo' his friends'. Yu' two men are riskin' yur' lives while I ride to freedom. I can't thank both of yu' 'nough."

He mounted his horse and waved goodbye to his beloved friends, knowing this could be the last time he would ever see them. Tearfully, and gratefully, he rode off, hoping he was beginning an entirely new chapter in his life—one of freedom for himself and eventually for his wife and those he left behind, Joseph and Willy.

CHAPTER TWENTY-THREE

Reggie took charge of Gibbons white stallion and calmly navigated through the marsh. Following Joseph's instructions, Reggie traveled a northwest route where he should find a by-path that went straight west, and would intersect the main road that would lead him straight north. He knew Joseph's directions provided him with the best opportunity for his escape to freedom and the rest would be left up to him. With no money, Reggie was at a major disadvantage at this juncture as he lacked the funds that would provide for the basic needs of the horse and him.

He defied advice and decided his chances were better served traveling during daylight hours. He appreciated the advice he was given, but he knew having a horse dictated a different strategy then traveling on foot. He could make much better and safer time by day since this would reduce the chances of an encounter with robbers and also eliminate the perils of unseen hazards in the road.

Reggie estimated that if he traveled twenty miles a day, it would take him approximately fifty days to reach Boston. He knew the odds were great, but he had no other choice. As an above average rider, he realized he would still have a better chance of defying the odds than if he had lacked horsemanship skills. He also knew that taking his time and allowing his horse to dictate the pace would reduce the risks of an injury. To his advantage the risk of Captain Riley catching up to him was far removed since he was on horseback as well, which helped to negate any advantage Captain Riley could have. This served him well as his main concern would be the immediate welfare of his horse.

Retrieving the money he had hidden at the abandoned plantation, remained a priority. With the proximity of Oak Manor so close to his hidden funds, the risk of riding at night would have to be made for that one occasion. Fortunately, he would only have to veer eastward a few miles from his northward route. The hidden money would be essential for the necessary care needed to complete the long journey.

For Reggie, things were fortunately working out for him. Successfully finding the by-path westward made travel much easier than through the marsh, but it was imperative that he get to the main road. Fortunately, the directions given by Joseph proved accurate, and not far up the by-path, he fortuitously came upon the main road that went north. He knew the road existed since he had traveled this very road with Reverend Hibbard and then later on when he was in the slave coffle. A memory he would like to forget, and wished he'd never experienced, but he could now take solace in knowing that under these circumstances, he felt free and everything was looking up for him. Traveling the road under these circumstances provided a completely different feeling.

Conditions would prove to be immeasurably better along the main route. Traveling at a good pace, he crossed the Savannah River into South Carolina, which in itself proved to be a minor accomplishment as the first leg of the journey to conquer. Leaving Georgia represented the first sense of relief but not the last. However, he felt that he could now put Captain Riley behind him and that represented a warm feeling. Finally after three additional days of riding at a comfortable pace, he neared Reverend Hibbard's plantation. At this point, he picked up the pace lest he should be recognized. This leg of the journey brought back some painful memories that he didn't want to dwell on, especially when he rode by the camp meeting site that he and Reverend Hibbard had stayed. Pushing further north, Reggie finally felt situation was safe and he was able to slow the pace down for the good of the horse.

As he rode along enjoying his freedom, he realized that he had never given his horse a name. "Hawss', yu' deserve a name, an' since I'm ridin' to freedom, din' Freedom should be yur' name. Now dat' we are talkin', I must tell yu' dat' I find yu' to be an 'ceptional hawss'." He paused for a moment knowing he was talking out loud to Freedom, but he smiled because it was such a refreshing conversation even though it was rather one-sided. "Mr. Gibbons took very good care of yu' an' fo' dat' I have a lot to thank him fo'. I'm sur' Freedom, a large white stallion like yu' was his pride an' joy, an' now yu' have become mine, an' I promise I will take good care of yu'." Reggie couldn't believe that he was having such a warm conversation with Freedom, which helped to make the trip more enjoyable. Humorously, Reggie even believed that Freedom even kept one ear back to listen to him.

Reggie found the frequency of talking to Freedom increased, especially when he was in high spirits. "Freedom, we've been ridin' at a good pace since we made dah' initial push out of Georgia. As we ride to freedom, I jus' can't believe dat' we have made it all dah' way to Richmond an' have not encountered any problems 'long dah' way. I jus' know dat' dah' Lawd' is watchin' ovah' us."

Thus far, the twenty mile a day goal had been maintained; however, he dared not push Freedom any harder knowing his horse would need to be well rested in order to successfully complete the journey. Meanwhile, Anastasia remained at the forefront of his mind, and he prayed that she was still safe. He could only dream that circumstances would allow him to be with her. For now, his first priority had to be his horse Freedom and a new life. Eventually with good fortune, he could concentrate on finding the means to locate Anastasia and secure her freedom.

Just when Reggie began to think that "things were too good to be true" one late afternoon two horsemen emerged and rode up. They did not demonstrate any menacing manners, but instead, appeared quite friendly. One pulled up along side of Freedom to make conversation. "Mister, we spotted yu' on yur' beautiful white mount an' sorta' thought yu' kinda' looked a little familiar. We jus' wondered whar' yu' might be headed."

"I'm from Emporia an' was notified dat' my grandfather had taken sick in Fredericksburg, an' I thought dat' it was prudent dat' I check on his condition." Again, Reggie's mind and intelligence served him quite well, and he was able to think quickly.

"Yu' do look 'bery familiar. Are yu' sure yu' didn't live 'round hyeh' at one time? I have a flair fo' 'memberin' faces." The second stranger positioned his horse on the other side of Freedom as he questioned Reggie.

"Yu' have me confused wit' somebody else."

"Damn, I swear dat' I have seen yu' somewhar'," the first man stated with a puzzled look.

"Must be déjà vu," Reggie stated with confidence.

"What's dat' mean? Is dat' French or somethin' like dat'? The first man wiped his brow and brushed the dust from the brim of his hat as he talked.

"Yes, it's French. It means dat' yu' think yu' met me when in fact it's only a distortion of yur' memory."

The other stranger was impressed. "Mister, it sounds like yu' are a man of dah' world an' all 'bout books. Actually, we don't know dat' many edgecated' people 'round hyeh', which leads me to believe dat' yu' are probably not somebody we would likely know."

The other stranger laughed at his partner's humor. "Hate to admit it, but damn, he's right! Maybe we should go git' edgecated' so dat' we know what is dah' meanin' of déjà vu or any other Frenchy' words dat' someone might spring on us. Mister, jus' what is yur' name?"

"My name is James Hibbard, an' gentlemen, what would be yur' names?"

"My name is Alex Adams," one of the men stated. "An' my friend is Harold Jackson. Look mister, we don't want to take up any more of yur' time. Up dah' pike 'round ten miles thar' is a nice inn dat' serves good food, an' yu' kin' git' a room. Jus' watch out fo' dah' bed bugs!" They all smiled at the remark, knowing that bed bugs were a major problem in many of the inns. Reggie smirked to himself that since he was sleeping outside, he didn't have to worry about the bed bugs getting to him, maybe snakes but not bed bugs.

"Gentlemen, thanks so much fo' dah' advice—I'll certainly take yur' suggestion." Reggie tipped his head. "Good day gentlemen, an' thank yu' 'gain."

As he rode away Reggie whispered to his horse, "Freedom, who would ever think dat' knowin' a simple French term could bail us out of a potentially serious problem? I would say it was by dah' skin of our teeth dat' we got out of thar'." In his thoughts, Reggie vaguely recognized the two men, but he couldn't remember the circumstances.

At dusk, Reggie grew excited as he realized he had arrived at the intersection that would put him on the road that would eventually take him to the abandoned plantation where he could retrieve his much-needed money. He believed this should not be a risky adventure—taking the required eastward road, which put him very near to Oak Manor. But under the cover of darkness, he was confident he would be successful.

As he had hoped, the night ride proved to be easy as he was able to locate the abandoned plantation where he had hid his money. The old plantation looked pretty much the same, overgrown with weeds and saplings, which would prove to be a good sign that he would probably not have to worry about any human occupancy. Quickly, he went to the back of the plantation and dug up the money and put it in his gunny sack. Mounting Freedom, he rode back to the main road and headed north without looking back. Experiencing no problems, he breathed a sigh of relief as he resumed his journey. The funds would now make it much easier to complete his mission.

Continuing north, he finally crossed the part of the Potomac River that separated Virginia from Maryland at Bethesda, west of Washington D.C. He found himself in a rejoiceful mood leaving Virginia knowing that Pennsyvania was not that far ahead. However, Maryland was still a slave state so he was in no position to "throw caution to the wind". By his calculations he figured he could now make Pennsylvania and freedom in three days. Without encountering any further problems, he skirted Baltimore, and traveled through Towson, putting him even closer to Pennsylvania. Psychologically, even at this seemingly short distance from freedom, Reggie became more apprehensive about the related obstacles he might encounter. It had been ingrained in him from listening to fellow slaves that escape from bondage was next to impossible, and yet, he was nearing freedom. Fortunately, the ride from Towson to the state line proved even easier than he had imagined. As he traveled, he still envisioned armed guards along the way who would apprehend him. Of course, they proved to be nonexistent. It confounded him that he still subconsciously harbored all the beliefs and feelings that a slave on a plantation in Georgia might have even when he knew the truth was right in front of him.

He wished he were able to relay to all of his brothers and sisters in the South that while it was a difficult journey, it was still attainable. However, he was also well aware that while as a fugitive slave he was also blessed with several advantages. Five factors enabled him to be successful and minimize problems: he could easily pass for a white man; possessed ample funds; traveled on horseback; was literate; and he was not wearing Negro cloth. Having all these advantages enabled him to "buck the odds". Unfortunately, these advantages were simply not available for the vast majority of slaves, which might explain why slaves who were living in the "deep South" rightfully so had such a negative perception of ever being free.

Reggie had a lot of time to think and he thought back to what he had seen and learned thus far during his trip. What really stood out was the topographic differences between Maryland, which was hilly and totally absent of any cotton fields, opposite of the coastal regions of South Carolina and Georgia, which were often swampy, fairly flat and agriculturally engaged almost entirely in cotton production. It was also evident that in Maryland, the gang system of agriculture associated with cotton farming was nonexistent—there were very few people in the fields. In the rural areas of the North, corn and wheat were the main crops, which did not require intensive labor. In addition, he had read that the North had invested much of its interests in manufacturing, opposite of the South, where the main economic interests were tied to agriculture, which precluded any diversification. These differences became even more visible as he traveled through the North. In his judgment, it further explained why the North and the South, with separate economies maintained such a dichotomy between each other.

The South had staked its future on cotton for their economic stability. As such, Reggie realized the millions of slaves used in the South were an economic necessity because of the cotton production. This was further compounded as the world demand for cotton dramatically increased after the economic recession of 1837 ended, which then helped to further create a "cotton boom" in the South. Southerners now found cotton to be very profitable and likely would not be amenable to diversifying their economic interests. The old adage, "if it works why fix it" certainly applied to the South. Of course, the increased demand for cotton encouraged the increase in slaves coming into the United States from Africa. Reggie had just read a publication that stated the number of slaves in 1820 was around 1,500,000; grew to 2,000,000 in 1830; and reached 2,500,000 in 1840. This dramatic rise in the number of slaves would continue in the future, which would only further dampen any hope of reconciliation.

Meanwhile, the employment demands up North were being met by a large influx of European immigrants, especially from Ireland. In fact, token measures, political in nature were being extended to send blacks back to Africa through the efforts of the American Colonization Society. These two positions—as stated earlier, "whiten" the North and make the South "darker" were driven by economic interests, which left such little room for compromise.

Reggie's journey to the North provided him with a better perspective on the differences between wage labor in the North and slave labor in the South. He had read that wages in the South were typically one-third less than in the North since slave labor had the effect of bringing wage labor down. This became evident to him as he studied the situation. This also would explain why workers in the North supported the bondage system since it would confine black labor to the South where they would not pose a threat to bringing wages down in the North. Incidentally, to blame black people for this economic problem would be wrong as they were not the ones that had any control over this matter. This would dispute the belief that black people willingly worked for less, they had no choice.

***

While enjoying his ride on Freedom, he was beginning to find a new outlook on life, when a sudden revelation overtook him. He found himself crossing the state line into Pennsylvania and into immediate freedom. Where was the opposition that he had expected to encounter? It was an exhilarating moment as great as his marriage to Anastasia. Still, a true and deep feeling of freedom flooded through him—no longer would he have to look over his shoulder, fearing further harm from a tyrant. Unfortunately the full joy of the moment would have to be tempered by not having Anastasia with him.

Not wanting to make things look too obvious, he rode onward and began to digest what had just occurred in his life. He dismounted and kissed the ground and then looked over the countryside. Was this all just a dream? It was now time to move on to Boston and to seriously focus on his hopes of one day being united with his wife. Hopefully, he would be able to take the necessary steps to attain freedom for the both of them. Always thinking of Anastasia, he wondered how long it would take before he could celebrate with his wife beside him. Before he continued, Reggie had to take just one more deep breath of the Pennsylvania air, just to seize the moment. Fittingly, he said to himself "carpe diem".

Now in free territory and feeling a complete sense of freedom, he finally felt comfortable with being able to start up a conversation with a stranger. He soon came upon an old black man walking along the road and rode up alongside of him. Feeling joy in his heart, he could not contain himself, "Excuse me sir, my name is Reggie, an' I wanted to say dat' I jus' rode to freedom, an' yu' happen to be dah' first stranger dat' I've talked to since I made my 'freedom ride' from Georgia." When Reggie opened the conversation with the gentleman it was readily apparent just how naïve he could be. The stranger reacted to Reggie with complete surprise. His surprised appearance indicated that he doubted the veracity of Reggie's statement since Reggie looked like a carbon copy of a white man, hardly on the "road to freedom".

"If yu' are tellin' me dah' truth din' Mister let me straighten yu' out. Yu' really won't be free 'til yu' git' to Canada." The old man shook his finger at Reggie as he spoke.

Reggie was completely bewildered and taken aback by what the old man said. "I'm in Pennsylvania, not Maryland. Dis' is free soil." Reggie was still confused and asked, "What in dah' world are yu' talkin' 'bout, and why are yu' talkin' 'bout Canada to me?"

"Listen to me, Mister. Yu' have a few things to learn. First, don't tell anybody dat' yu' jus' rode to freedom. 'Round hyeh', people are hard up, an' dey' wouldn't hesitate to report yu' hopin' fo' reward money an' I'm talkin' 'bout niggahs' informin' on yu' too! I will say dat', if yu' are what yu' say yu' are, din' wit' yur' skin color yu' kin' pass as a white man. Yu' are lucky to be able to pass fo' white. Jus' forgit' 'bout bein' a slave an' 'cross ovah' an' become a white man right now, an' yu'll be jus' fine. 'Lieve me, if I could, I would. I escaped from Merryland', an' oh Lawd', my master was wicked, but I can't say dat' I'm any better off now, other din' bein' free. I kin' say dat' if I looked white like yu', din' it would be a whole lot easier, an' I really do mean a whole lot easier. Jus' one thin', yu' won't have any of dis' in Canada—it's really free up thar'!"

Reggie couldn't believe his ears—he had ridden 600 miles to freedom and now he was being told he'd have to continue on to Canada to be totally free or run the risk of being turned in as a runaway.

"Hyeh' me out, " the old man went on, "a lot of niggahs' up hyeh' will tell yu' dat' at least down South as a slave dey' had a roof over thar' head, clothes, food an' care when dey' were sick. Hyeh' a lot of us are homeless. How free kin' yu' feel when yu' are homeless?"

Reggie confided, "I once heard 'bout dis' from some white girls from Boston. I kinda' thought dey' were exaggeratin' a little."

"Dey' were tellin' yu' dah' truth Mister! Don't git' me wrong, I don't wanta' go back to bein' owned by anybody. As bad as dis' is, I'll take it ovah' bein' owned an' beaten. I jus' wish dat' I could have a chance to earn my keep. I need a job, nuttin' else, jus' a steady job wit' wages."

Reggie responded with genuine compassion. "I don't blame yu' one bit fo' wantin' a job wit' wages. Dat's what it's all 'bout, wage labor an' not slave labor."

"I've worked fo' wages but dey' never keep yu' 'round 'bery long—dat's dah' long an' short of it." The old man rubbed his forehead as he spoke. "Mister, somethin' else, yu' say yu' came all dah' way from Georgia?"

"Dat's what I said Sir."

"Mister, don't call me sir," the old man told Reggie firmly. "Now let me tell yu' somethin'. I guarantee yu' dat' if I tried to make Pennsylvania from Georgia, bein' a darkie, I woulda' never made it. I don't think I've met anybody who made it to freedom from Georgia. Yu' are dah' first I've met but din' yu' look white—I swear y'all are white. 'Lieve me, if yu' was a darkie like me, yu' wouldn't have made it. See Mister, 'bout all of us darkies 'round hyeh' came outa' Merryland', whar' we only had to cover a few miles—Georgia, Oh Lawdy', no way. Yu' won't see any cotton niggahs' 'round hyeh' Mister. Dat' orte' to tell yu' somethin'.'"

"Well, I'll be on my way to Boston. I still have a long ride 'head, but I've got a great mount," Reggie said with a reassuring smile.

The old man felt compelled to repeat his warning. "Look

mister, I can't figure out yur' game, but I still wish yu' good luck. 'Member what I tole' yu' earlier. Unless yu' know dah' person, don't be talkin' 'bout escapin' from dah' South. Present yur'self' as a white man an' not a niggah', an' yu'll be jus' fine. Mister, I love my people, but I'm tellin' y'all dis' fo' yur' own good. Put yur' trust in yur'self an' nobody else. Dah' stakes are always high on dah' 'road to freedom'."

"I 'preciate dah' advice, now it's time to move on." Reggie was grateful the old gentleman had shared his thoughts with him. He unfortunately felt that what the stranger had to say helped him validate what he had suspected earlier—serious discrimination existed throughout the United States and not just the South. It was now time to resume his journey having a better perspective on the level of discrimination up North.

He looked down at Freedom as they rode northward. "Freedom, yu' would know dis' better din' anyone else. 'Does' dah' grass always look greener on dah' other side of dah' fence'?" In an amusing way, he thought he had just heard a whinny coming out of Freedom. Needless to say, he concluded that he was just hearing things—or was he?

Sarah and Emily had told him that life quite often is very difficult for blacks up North. Now he was informed he should proceed into Canada if he wanted total freedom—that came as a complete surprise. Could the grass metaphor be accurate, he wondered? This much was certain—his life in the North was going to offer a new and dramatically different adventure and perhaps not all for the good.

***

Since money was not a problem for Reggie, he had ample funds to provide for Freedom, and himself. His number one concern would have to remain being apprehended as a fugitive, and the welfare of his horse. It was still another 350 miles to Boston and he had put around 650 miles behind him. Reggie decided at this point that it would be wise to reduce the number of miles Freedom covered to 15 miles each day. This would further reduce the potential of an injury to Freedom. Besides, he found himself enjoying the scenery and the feeling of freedom, which only encouraged a slower pace.

Confidently, Reggie continued on his journey, now talking more frequently to people, both black and white as he traveled through Rhode Island, New York, and Connecticut. Finally, he crossed into Massachusetts, which meant that he was nearing his objective. Boston was only approximately one hundred miles away, which seemed like a relatively short distance, considering he had already ridden over nine hundred miles.

His thoughts now began to turn to his Northern connection, Sarah Clark. Would she still be willing to help him out as she had indicated when they first met a few years ago? He needed her support and continued to believe that she was a lady of her word.

Finally, after another week of riding, he reached his destination, Boston without any further incident. He was stunned that he actually made it against all odds. Reggie took a deep breath and exhaled—he couldn't believe the size of the city. Until now, he had purposely avoided any large communities. He now found himself completely in awe at what was before him. Riding through Boston, he naturally made comparisons to Richmond, the only other major city he had ever visited. The contrasts were enormous as he looked at a city which he felt expressed more wealth, vibrance, and freedom than he had ever witnessed in Richmond.

Suddenly without any warning an epiphany swept over Reggie, more intense than anything he had ever experienced in his life. With the old South still firmly wedged in his mind, the full weight of the "bondage system" came down upon him as he envisioned seeing a slave coffle trudging through the streets of Boston. How would the Bostonians react to seeing slaves mired in filth, locked in leg irons, and guarded by drivers on horseback anxious to bring the full wrath of their bull whip down upon any one of them if they perceived they were doing anything wrong? Obviously, this scenario would not be welcomed by Bostonians who were used to being part of a free society. The thought of a slave coffle in Boston, which realistically would have been well beyond absurd, yet what was illogical in Boston, was common throughout the South. Perhaps this startling revelation, which captured a major difference between the North and South might explain just how far the division between the two regions had grown, which was headed on a course that would be irreparable.

Reggie sat pondering atop Freedom knowing that his imaginative power had just supplanted what was reality. By creating a false scenario with the inclusion of a slave coffle, what had been a free society now took on a whole new malevolent atmosphere that sent a chill down his spine. Sadly, his fondest wish would be that everybody could be given the opportunity to see this scenario so they could better understand just how critical the situation had become, but unfortunately he knew this was not going to happen. It was truly the hardships that he had regrettably endured that enabled him to see what others could never visualize.

Reggie was reminded of Matthew 12:25 which states, "Any kingdom divided against itself is laid waste, and any city, or house divided against itself will not stand." Reggie recognized that this verse is very significant since it is apropos to the situation that existed in the United States during the ante-bellum period. Sadly, the North and the South were being barely "civil" to each other making it very difficult to administer the compromising measures, which would be necessary to prevent a civil war. Instead, a popular political canard became widely accepted, which subscribed to the belief that slavery would somehow just gradually end peacefully and with time everything would work out for the good of our country as everybody went about their "merry way". Unfortunately, he never heard or read of any specifics that would be applied to make for a "peaceful end". Instead, Reggie foresaw the tragedy of our country being led down the road to a "sorrowful struggle", far short of a "peaceful end"— ending in a civil war that could have been prevented. Could he help to change the course of American history, and prevent a horrible conflict? He asked himself, "Why does the North and the South persist to wear "blinders", which can only preclude society from seeing just how egregious the situation had become? This was the awesome assignment that awaited him.

Finally, Reggie speculated on the number of wars fought between adversaries throughout the world as they were unprepared to understand the gravity of the situation they were in until it was too late. And now this same secenario was about to overtake our country. He even contemplated the possibility of grabbing and shaking people in hopes of "pounding some sense in their heads"! That is how frustrating and desperate his thinking had become.

CHAPTER TWENTY-FOUR

R eggie located Sarah's residence and not to his surprise, found himself in an area of affluence. The home was large and very tasteful, yet not nearly as pretentious as some of the plantations in the South. The style was Federal—practical, but not massive looking. The red brick façade had a light appearance— elegantly simple with a flat rectangular shape along with a small covered porch with a light over the door. The front yard was fairly large with a well-maintained, picturesque flower garden, which represented the landscaping motif of the period.

Looking around and taking stock of the situation, Reggie knocked on the door, realizing that his life could quickly change. Nervously, he continued to have doubts about being well received. Had he bitten off more then he could chew? Would all of this end in futility? These were questions racing through his mind as he reminded himself that even if he was rejected, he could still make something of himself without the help of Sarah. When at Oak Manor, Sarah had appeared sincere when she offered to help him if he reached freedom and made it to Boston. He was hoping her earlier sentiments would still be genuine. It would certainly make it easier to transition into his new life. She could have possibly married and may not reside with her parent's any longer. Perhaps her friendship toward Reggie lacked sincerity. Negative thoughts entered his mind as anxiety continued to build up awaiting an answer to his knock on the door. He would have preferred notifying her in advance of his arrival, but obviously, circumstances dictated otherwise.

After a brief time, which seemed like an eternity, the butler opened the door and asked, "May I help you?"

Knowing a critical time in his life was ahead of him, he confidently stood tall as he proudly announced, "Yes sir, I happen to be a friend of Miss Sarah Clark's."

"You know Miss Sarah?"

"Not only do I know Miss Sarah, but she 'vited me to come an' see her if I was in Boston."

"May I have your name Sir and I'll let her know you are here?"

"My name is Reggie Marshall," he proudly stated. It was obvious that he was doing a good job of hiding his nervousness.

"Please wait here in the vestibule while I notify Miss Sarah."

Moments later, Sarah appeared in the vestibule, staring at Reggie. She was in total disbelief, flabbergasted and delighted all at the same time! "Reggie, I never thought I would ever see you again. You've escaped that horrible life! I'm so happy and very proud of you. I know it took a lot of strength and courage for you to leave! I'm almost speechless. Here, give me a big hug." As he hugged her, she said, "Oh, it's so good to see you again." Reggie enjoyed the feeling of affection, something he had not felt since being separated from Anastasia. After a long hug, Sarah said, "I've thought about you so many times. I prayed over and over for your safe escape from bondage, and here you are. What a blessing!"

Reggie was stunned by Sarah's greeting. He knew she would be surprised, but this was definitely more than he had expected. "Thank yu' so much Miss Sarah. It's so comfortin' fo' me to be received by yu' in such a joyous manner."

Sarah led Reggie into the parlor. "Reggie, first you must stop addressing me as Miss Sarah. Reggie, you are a free man, no longer living in bondage. Now, please just call me Sarah. That said, I have so much I want to ask you! I just can't believe that you actually made it out of the South." Sarah took Reggie's hand and motioned for him to sit down. She shut the parlor door while excitedly asking, "Tell me every detail of your journey—and don't leave out a stitch!"

"Sarah yu' have no ider' how difficult it is fo' me not to address yu' as Miss Sarah. Trust me when I say dat' I was ingrained to always foller' proper' respect, an' sayin' anythin' other din' Miss Sarah would have gotten me in trouble. Okay, now I got dat' out of my system, Sarah, thar' is so much to say," Reggie began, "I rode my horse, whom I dubbed Freedom ovah' one thousand miles from Georgia to git' hyeh'. I know yu' expected me to say from Virginny' but I was sold at auction an' ended up in Georgia, which of course made the journey 'a horse of a different color'." Reggie could not resist injecting a little humor. "Anyhow, naturally, my biggest fear was gittin' caught along dah' way, but fortunately everythin' broke my way. I said ovah' an' ovah' 'gain, 'come hell or high water', I was goin' to make it to freedom. I took real good care of my hawss', Freedom, 'cuz' wit'out him it would've been next to impossible to make the 1,000 mile trip! I know God was smilin' on me an' Freedom all dah' way." Reggie paused with a look of relief. "I was meant to be hyeh', an' God willin' hyeh' I'll stand! I was challenged only once by two men outside of Richmond, but I convinced 'dem I was jus' travelin' through dah' area, an' dey' never really questioned me."

"Reggie—glory be! You are so fortunate to have had such a great steed. By foot, I would think it would be next to impossible." Sarah clasped her hands together. "To this day, I'm still haunted by the memory of seeing you getting beaten by that tyrant, Donald."

Reggie exclaimed, "Sarah it was through dah' grace of God dat' I was able to make it hyeh'."

"Reggie, I'm standing here utterly amazed. You mean to tell me that you rode Freedom over one thousand miles without changing horses? I've ridden all my life and I've never heard of anything like this—absolutely incredible!"

"Yu' kin' understand why Freedom has become such a big part of my life." Reggie was relieved and very appreciative.

"I just thought of something else, Reggie. I'm going to contact the newspaper. They'll run your story and the entire city will greet you almost like a hero for traveling 1,000 miles on the 'road to freedom' on a horse.

"Sarah, please, no, yu' can't do dat'. I'm classified as a fugitive slave an' dah' last thin' I want is to have my present situation an' location carried throughout dah' press."

"Reggie, I'm sorry! I didn't know that the system worked that way. I guarantee that your secret will remain with my family. But I do wish you could get the recognition you deserve, but I guess it will have to come later."

"Thank yu' Sarah, I would 'preciate dat' very much. I want yu' to know somethin'." Reggie took a deep breath, smiled and then explained, "Our original Constitution of 1787 contains a fugitive slave clause dat' legally allows a master to reclaim his or her property an' return 'dem back to servitude, even though dey' are recaptured in free territory."

"Reggie, I'm glad you enlightened me as to the legal implications. After such a long journey, you must be exhausted." Sarah thought a moment. "I'm so excited for you to meet my mother. I talked about you in so many positive ways. I know she will want to extend a warm welcome. It's just so good to see you!" Excited, she gave him another big hug. "I'm just so glad you remembered me, and came here!"

Reggie feeling a little awkward continued, "I do feel a little funny as I allowed my hygiene on the road to slip. Sarah, I would reach an inn an' put Freedom up in dah' livery stable while I would bed down outside even though I had ample funds to git' cleaned up an' git' a good nights sleep in dah' inn. I was so bamboozled an' beaten down by dah' system dat' I couldn't bring myself to sleep in an inn even in a free state. The indoctrination was so complete an' successful—me, a slave sleepin' as an equal to a white man at an' inn was more din' I could fathom! It would be unheard of." Applying the bondage system to his own actions after careful thought, Reggie could better understand why Willy and Joseph gave special consideration to Mr. Gibbons, the white overseer, even when he was captured and in their hands.

" Reggie, it's time for you to meet my mother and don't worry, you will find her very kind. Besides, you certainly look fine to me." Sarah excused herself, and called a servant to fetch her mother and then resumed her conversation with Reggie.

"Thank yu' Sarah, I really do 'preciate yur' confidence in me." Reggie realized that she was excited for him to meet her mother. However, he was just getting comfortable in his new surroundings and would have preferred meeting her after he had a chance to clean up so he could present himself clean and refreshed.

Just then Sarah's mother, Alice Clark, entered the room, looking startled at the stranger clad in worn-out clothing. "Sarah, may I ask whom do I have the pleasure to meet?"

"Mother, this happens to be somebody I have often and fondly spoken of, Reggie Marshall, my friend from Virginia. He rode his horse from Georgia to get here."

Mrs. Clark regained her composure and displayed an accepting smile. "Hello, Reggie, my name is Mrs. Alice Clark. It's such a pleasure to meet a friend of my daughter. Sarah has talked so admiringly about you.

"Mrs. Clark, it's such a pleasure to meet yu'. I must admit dat' I didn't expect such warm hospitality—it makes me feel good dat' I'm wit' friends. I have to add dat' I'm still in disbelief, an it may take me sometime to adjust to all des' new found surroundins', so please fo'give me."

"Reggie, you are so special to my daughter. You became an immediate and dear friend to her right after she met you, and that alone is enough for me to want you to be our special guest. I'm really anxious to hear more about your life since it's so different from what we have experienced up North. Reggie will you please excuse me since I have to oversee the preparation of dinner. I'm sure a nice home cooked meal would be enjoyable. Reggie you will be our very special guest. Excuse me while I call Daniel to make sure your horse is taken care of." After summoning Daniel, she requested that he see to it that Reggie's horse was bedded down, fed, and watered for the night.

397

Reggie, grateful that his horse, who was responsible for him making it to Boston would be properly stabled in appreciation stated, "If it wasn't fo' Freedom, I wouldn't be hyeh'. Thank yu' fo' takin' such good care of my hawss'."

Mrs. Clark smiled and said, "Incidentally, you're welcome to stay with us in our home as long you need. Daniel prepare the guest room, including a nice warm bath and see to it that Reggie has all of the necessities including something suitable for him to wear in place of his traveling clothes." Mrs. Clark didn't want him to feel out of place and hoped this would help him feel more at ease and truly welcome in their home.

"Thank yu' so much Mrs. Clark," Reggie responded, completely taken aback by the warm hospitality and offer extended to him.

Sarah's mother then excused herself to the kitchen so she could supervise the preparation for dinner.

Reggie, realized it was necessary to be candid with Sarah concerning his personal life and felt it was important to explain, "Sarah, I want to tell yu' dat' I married Anastasia. Yu' 'member her—she was Abigail's personal servant."

While trying to hide her disappointment about Reggie being married, she managed to congratulate him with a fabricated smile, "Reggie, I'm so happy for you. I do remember her very well. In fact I mentioned to Abigail just how kind and beautiful she was."

Reggie could tell Sarah was both surprised and saddened to hear he was married, but he felt it was imperative to tell her now rather than to lead her on if she did have any designs on him. "Thank yu' so much fo' yur' kind words as yu' kin' imagine how difficult it has been bein' taken from my bride, but I truly hope someday we will be united. Now I'm free, but only half free since Anastasia has been forced from my life. I don't even know fo' sur' her present fate. When I left, Colonel Marshall had reassigned her."

"I do understand your plight. Reggie, now we'll have plenty of time to talk about these matters later. For now, I'm sure you will appreciate your nice warm bath. I have so much to learn.

Right now, I am just so excited that my mother has extended an invitation for you to stay with us. Also, tomorrow we're going to the haberdashery shop and buy you some new clothes! Yours are tattered after such a long and grueling trip, and I want to assure you that the condition of your clothing is not your fault. It would just be my pleasure as a friend to take care of the expenses of new clothes as a gift to you and your new beginning here in Boston. Now please don't say another word. It's also time for you to think about your nice warm bath. Your belongings have been taken to your room, your bathwater will soon be ready shortly, and towels have been put out for you." Sarah purposely ignored responding to Reggie's comment that Colonel Marshall had Anastasia reassigned. She had heard the rumor at the Marshall plantation that Anastasia had been moved to separate quarters, which could mean something, which was intended to be not discussed.

Reggie chose not to further discuss Anastasia. "Wait a minute Sarah, 'jus' hold dah' fort', I don't expect yu' to pay fo' my clothes, I have funds wit' me."

Sarah was emphatic. "I insist on doing this as an appreciation for what you have had to endure to get here. It's such a very small thing to do. Remember, I consider you a close friend."

"Sarah I do understand an' I really do appreciate yur' kindness but let me jus' share one thing 'fore I go upstairs. I do have to tell yu' dat' dah' last time I came in contact wit' a haberdasher was when I was bein' prepared fo' auction in Richmond. My overseer bought a silly blue velvet vest fo' me to wear to top off my new outfit, and I might add, it was not Negro cloth. However, I was really disappointed dat' dah' vest wasn't purple to show everyone jus' how important I could be as a slave." As soon as he finished talking about the vest he started laughing. He also knew that he was to get upstairs for his bath, but he just felt compelled to tell this story.

"Reggie what are you talking about? I don't understand." Sarah missed the point of the humor. She knew the difference between regular cloth and Negro cloth. Northerners were generally aware that servitude was defining, measured even by the quality of their clothes. Still the comment about wearing a purple vest instead of a blue vest was confusing. Now she found herself intrigued by the story he was telling.

"Sarah I'm havin' fun wit' yu'. I despised dat' vest—I'm only makin' a joke. Kin' yu' imagine dose' good old Southern boys havin' me, a slave strut 'round sportin' a purple vest at auction—dah' color of royalty! Sarah, dat' is so far fetched dat' it's really funny. See, Sarah, dah' Virginians kin' be 'bery upholdin' to dah' monarchy of Britain by maintainin' dah' tradition of royalty. Purple, dah' color of nobility, is reserved fo' only dah' 'bery privileged in thar' minds. A slave wearin' purple would represent a complete mockery of ole' Virginny' an' its social stratum. It jus' would not happen."

"I'm getting a history lesson. Your bath can wait a little while longer. Please tell me more, as I find all this so fascinating."

"Sarah, did yu' know dah' Virginia House of Burgesses in 1677 allowed dat' dah' meanin' of indentured servitude could be extended from a defined period to lifetime. Hence, we had dah' beginnin' of slavery in dah' United States. Lifetime indentured servitude is 'nother name fo' slavery, pure an' simple."

Sarah queried, "Reggie, why do you think they did this?"

"Dat's a good question, I've heard it said dat' dah' upper class Virginian's fascination toward dah' monarchy extended to creatin' a limited monarchy in Virginny' wit' slaves bein' utilized as serfs. Indentured servitude is socially gray while bondage is definin'—black an' white, hence, an absolute division, wit' no possible upward social movement. Historically, authoritative systems always attempt to remove the gray area an' indentured servitude would certainly represent a gray area."

"How sad, it sort of reminds me of the caste system of India." Sarah thought of this, knowing Reggie had been a part of the bondage system, which replicates the caste system—black and white with no gray.

"Sarah, I know all dis' sounds far fetched, but history does tell us dah' South was more sympathetic to England in dah' War of Rebellion. Ironically, whar' we sit right now, hyeh' in Boston as yu' well know was dah' 'bery hot-bed of dah' revolution. Of course dah' primary aim of dah' revolution was to be free from English dominance wit' a complete rejection of dah' monarchy. Now, contrast dat' wit' livin' in Richmond situated near dah' Williamsburg area—whar' dah' monarchy is almost revered!"

Sarah was completely taken aback by Reggie's scope of knowledge. In addition, she was especially curious about the slave auctions and couldn't wait to ask him about it. "People up North are well aware of the slave auctions, and quite frankly, find them to be repugnant but a necessary part of the evil system. They actually talk a lot about the slave auctions, but know very little about it. Like most of us up North, I have a limited amount of knowledge. If it wouldn't be too difficult to share, I'd like to learn more?"

"Sarah, it doesn't bother me to talk 'bout it. Have yu' ever been to a livestock auction? If yu' have, well din' yu' pretty much know dah' basics of a slave auction. Dey' bring yu' out an' put yu' on display jus' like a hawss. Dey' make yu' jump, check yur' mouth, an' din' examine yur' back, checkin' fo' scars from a whippin'."

"Reggie, do they present the women in the same way as the men?"

"Of course, dey' are presented in dah' same manner," Reggie said without hesitation, "All slaves have to be inspected by potential buyers an' dat' means removin' thar' clothin'! Fo' women, it is particularly demeaning. It represents yet another example of our women being violated!"

Sarah tried not to show how shocked she really was. "I find all this to be so upsetting. However, even with all the difficulties you've suffered in your life, I have a feeling you are prepared to move forward with a new beginning in the North. Let's move on an' try to put all these sordid experiences behind you while you start to build a new life for yourself here in Boston. For now, I'm sure you will appreciate a nice warm bath, which is awaiting you, come back down when you're cleaned up. Now go!" She playfully led him toward the stairs where Daniel was patiently waiting for him with a warm smile.

Sarah then went to the kitchen to be with her mother. Clearly upset, Sarah needed to confide in her mother. Standing close to her she whispered, "Mother, I just found out that Reggie is married. It really upsets me to hear this."

Although Sarah's mother was busy, she recognized that her daughter needed her attention. "Sarah, why should you care, you have David in your life?" She was referring to David Waters, Sarah's long-time boyfriend. Sarah had purposely not mentioned him to Reggie because he might think she had a serious relationship. In spite of only knowing Reggie briefly at Oak Manor, her feelings for Reggie had always been much greater than they had ever been for David. "He really adores you," Sarah's mother went on, "why would you want to muddy the waters by bringing another love into your life? Reggie can still remain your dear friend, besides, I don't want to upset you, but Reggie is still a slave. True, he can pass for white, but he has to be tainted with Negro blood and because of this, you never would be allowed to have a serious relationship with him. Your father would put his foot down."

"Mother, I can't believe that you would talk to me like this," Sarah stammered in disbelief. "You sound just like a Southerner! His blood is tainted! Is that what you said? Then you bring up father putting his foot down. How dare you dictate whom I can fall in love with! You sound like Colonel Marshall or worse yet, his son Donald, whom I really despise."

"I will admit that Reggie is as handsome of a specimen of a man as I have ever seen, but you should know the difficulty of getting involved with someone with his background," Sarah's mother warned.

"Just for the sake of argument" Sarah replied indignantly, "his father is Colonel Marshall, who comes from a very prominent Virginia family. In fact, Colonel Marshall is related to former Chief Justice John Marshall. But, that doesn't matter, does it mother, because he is still tainted with Negro blood? Furthermore, Reggie is married, and you can be assured that he loves his wife, Anastasia, so you won't have to worry about anything happening between us. I know you want me to marry David, but I think I would rather be an old maid than to risk an unhappy marriage. In fact, the next time I have to see him, I'm going to tell him that I only wish to be his friend."

"Sarah don't talk to your mother like this," she scolded.

Sarah was getting her second wind. "I can't help but talk like this—I'm beginning to think I'm still in the South. I heard Southerners say the Northerners harbored their own form of a bondage system even though slavery was not legal up North. They call it a *de facto* form of slavery. Not legal slavery, but by fact it exists as we witness how Negroes are forced to live as second class citizens up North as opposed to a *de jure* or legal form of slavery that they have in the South. Now, I understand it. If I fell in love with Reggie and married him, it would be difficult to explain at one of your socials that Reggie was a former slave. Wait, you couldn't even say it like that. Technically, he's still a slave and could be brought back to Georgia as a fugitive slave, so the love of my life would be removed from me only because he was owned by someone a thousand miles away. I just know you would have a solution! You would want him to assume a whole new identity, a white man absent of any Negro blood who would just willingly forget his past. Doesn't that make you wonder? Wouldn't you agree on how artificial that would make him? Personally, I could never "crossover" knowing I would have to live with my conscious, but then, that is just how I feel. What I'm saying mother, is that I just hope that you understand there are many sides to this issue."

"Sarah, please don't talk like this. You are only talking in the abstract. He's married! We really don't have to worry about a picture like the one you painted. Now get a hold of yourself and stop letting your imagination run away with you!"

"You are right mother," Sarah sighed, "but I want you to know I abhor the bondage system, and I will fight 'tooth and nail' against it. I could see what it was like when I visited the Marshall plantation. What frightened me most was just how narrow the Southerner's perspective was. They tried with every trick in the book to justify their system to me, and I still think they failed miserably! The word compassion is not even in their vocabulary!

How can you practice kindness while holding a whip? How do you think I would have fared if father had liberally beat me with a whip?"

"Why are you being so harsh on the Marshalls, a family that was so hospitable to you and your friends? It's not really all their fault."

"I'm sorry, mother." Sarah apologized but needed to make her point. "A system that violates the very foundation of our Christian values and morals absolutely infuriates me. Another thing that really disturbs me arose when you made the point that Reggie was very handsome but still tainted with Negro blood. I know I am being redundant, but on this topic, I can't help it. As a Northerner you talk just like a Southerner. It doesn't matter to you how handsome and intelligent Reggie could be since he is not pure white. In otherwards, either you are black or white—no gray. If you are 99% white and 1% black then you are black. Mother, that is exactly what you are saying and spoken like a true Southerner! You are my mother, but regrettably. We'll have to agree to disagree. That is all I am going to say on this subject. Sometimes, I think Northerners in general are every bit as bad as Southerners in their thinking that Negroes are inferior to whites."

"Sarah, enough is enough! I understand your feelings, but you cannot change anything! Accept that eventually, changes will be made to abolish slavery. For now it is ensconced in our society, and we just have to learn to live with it. Incidentally, your father might have a different perspective on this matter." She paused and then added, "I do have something more to say. I fear Reggie might quickly become sympathetic to the abolitionist movement. We certainly do not want you to associate with those radicals—those people are dangerous! They advocate violence as a means to end slavery. Your father and I agree that people like that represent a significant disruption to our whole democratic process. We both accept slavery will eventually die a slow death—yet a painful one in many ways."

Again, Mrs. Clark's position on slavery, "the slow death theory", was a moderate position in the North and certainly the most popular position. The abolitionist, on the other hand, wanted an immediate end to slavery. The two positions were clearly opposite of each other, which created a lot of friction

"Mother, I never said anything about getting involved with the abolitionists." Sarah was not at all happy with her mother's thinking. "I just can't believe that you feel so strongly against it. Besides, you don't know how Reggie feels about the movement. However, I have a feeling that he would be against any form of violence."

"Let's quit mincing words," Mrs. Clark firmly stated. "Your father owns a large company, and we travel in very important social circles. This abolitionist movement harbors radicals whom we would not want you associating with—now, that ends this little discussion. Could you imagine them, coming around here to visit? Remember your station in life!"

"My station in life—what is this, the Middle Ages? Mother, I do understand why you feel the way you do. You have to protect the family position, but don't you understand, someone like Reggie who was born a slave might have a different perspective? The rich have their way of seeing things, based on their experiences as rich people, while the poor have another perspective, based on their experiences as poor people. Isn't that the truth, Mother?" She paused to see if her reasoning had made any impact on her mother and then went on. "Wouldn't it be a better world if we used compassion to understand another person's point of view? In fact, I even remember Colonel Marshall talking about how the North and the South have to learn to be more compromising."

"Sarah, I can't believe that we are still having this conversation while your friend is under our roof. Perhaps, if I could put myself in Reggie's shoes I would be more sympathetic to any cause he might pursue. However, with his looks and talents, he has a lot going for himself, regardless of his current position in life. Why would he want to throw all that away by getting involved with a bunch of radicals?" As the conversation ensued, it seemed ironic, indeed to Mrs. Clark that a recently arrived slave from the South was bathing in her home and enjoying all the amenities while she prepared dinner. Mrs. Clark thought of the expression that the "truth can be stranger than fiction", and it certainly applied to this situation.

"Thank you for understanding how I feel," Sarah replied. "I will respectfully honor your advice, although I may not agree with it."

"Reggie will be downstairs soon, so it would be best to end this conversation and not mention it to your father. We best forget about this conversation altogether, as neither of us should test or challenge his views. Anyhow, Sarah, his take on everything is very fair and honorable."

"I won't bring it up," Sarah agreed. "I certainly don't want to cause Reggie more problems than he already has by 'upsetting the apple cart' with father."

After enjoying his bath, Reggie dressed, and came downstairs to meet Sarah. Sarah warmly greeted him and then they went into the parlor where the appetizers Mrs. Clark had prepared, were placed. Decorated in both Federal and American Empire style furniture, the room was accented with imported furniture of very high quality. Quite common among the wealthy, European furniture tended to be looked upon as being more prestigious than American made home furnishings. Located on one side of the room were a beautiful harp and a Viennese-style piano. Many of the accessories had been imported from the Orient as the Asian trade market was in vogue at that time. A striking red Persian rug with matching red and tan plumed wallpaper helped set the tone, and the crowning piece was a large Waterford crystal chandelier imported from Ireland. The harp, piano, and chandelier defined the atmosphere of the room, which helped to create an overall ambience that could only be described as stunning.

Reggie gazed with wonder at the opulence. "I have never been in a room more beautiful. It is truly breathtakin'." He could only try to compare it with the parlor of Oak Manor, which could not approach the beauty and luxury of this.

"Thank you, Reggie. Mother hired a decorator, and it took a long time to come up with just the right design and touches to create this wonderful room." Reggie stood there in a daze confused about hiring somebody to decorate your home, but accepting it as Boston and a new life.

"An', Sarah, if I might take liberties to pay yu' a compliment," Reggie said shyly, "I jus' want to say how nice yu' look since I last saw yu' at dah' plantation."

"Why, thank you, Reggie," Sarah responded. "It's the Graham diet—no meat, alcohol, tea or coffee. The diet includes only healthful foods and of course Graham bread. Quite a few Bostonian women who watch their weight are following this regimen." Sylvester Graham was an early nutritionist who is famous for the graham cracker.

"Sarah, yu' jus' left me at sea wit' dis' diet talk. I kin' further assure yu' dat' I don't have a weight problem. I jus' came off a plantation in Georgia, an' outside of an occasional house servant who has access to a lot of food, yu' won't find black people overweight down South. I kin' guarantee yu' dat' livin' dah' life of a field hand will keep dah' weight off." Reggie and Sarah laughed as he spoke. Dieting to regulate your weight and hiring a decorator to beautify your house—he realized he had a lot to learn about his new life.

Sarah explained, "We might be a little overweight in the North because of the plentiful supply of food along with perhaps living a more sedentary life. Reggie, I do find this most interesting— one that most of us in the North would never be aware of."

"In dah' South livin' in dah' quarters our staple was cawn'meal. Din' once in a while dey' would throw in some meats, fruits an' vegetables," Reggie added. "Trust me, Sarah, it's really hard to gain weight on dat' diet." Even the most casual conversation seemed to bring out the plight of the black people in the South.

Sarah shifted to another topic. "I failed to mention my brother Lucas to you. He works for my father's company as a supervisor directly under the plant superintendent. I want you to know that he is quite conventional and may not be as accepting of your overall situation as my parents are. Some of his opinions may upset you, but I know you can handle whatever comes your way."

"Thank yu' fo' dah' warnin'—yu' are a true friend. However, I kin' assure yu' I'm more din' equipped to take care of myself. My survival has depended upon it." Reggie demonstrated an air of confidence that impressed Sarah.

"Wonderful! Incidentally, my father's company manufactures machines used in the garment industry in the northeast. Who knows, maybe he will make you an offer to work for him? It wouldn't surprise me, as you have a look about you that would well represent the Clark Manufacturing image, and also, your intelligence and Southern accent won't hurt. It brings a bit of uniqueness to you. Besides, my father will do anything for his daughter and soon he'll learn that I would like to have you work for the company," she said with a gentle smile. Sarah wanted him to know that since her father owns the company, he would be in a position to give him a good job.

Reggie's face was beaming hearing the excellent news. "Well, thank yu' fo' dah' support, I'm really overwhelmed." Reggie had been in Boston just a few hours and already there was a possibility brought up of employment. Things like this could only happen in the dreams of a slave. He also remembered the old black gentleman he met on the road who could not find a job and described how difficult it was for even free black people to find employment.

Reggie had learned the importance of common sense through his struggles, which dictated that at times he knew he had to be positive when opportunity "knocked". "Sarah, if dah' opportunity presents itself, it would be an honor to work fo' yur' father."

Sarah then asked in a more serious tone, "I have one more question for you, and I know you'll understand I'm asking it because of my interest in you and our friendship. My mother already extended an invitation for you to stay until you can get your feet on the ground. I truly hope you will accept her offer? I say that only because I desperately want you to be able to transition into your new life without experiencing too much difficulty."

"Sarah, I'm ovah'whelmed at yur' kind offer. Of course, I would be honored to be a guest of yur' family while I adjust to my new life. I jus' want to be able to repay yu' an' yur' folks fo' bein' so thoughtful an' kind."

"Reggie, don't worry about it. While we have the time, if you can, tell me more about what you had to go through and how it affected you."

Reggie was humbled at Sarah's genuine concern. "Mentally, I have refused to allow myself to be defeated by dah' deprivation I've had to endure. Dat' would represent a victory fo' dah' tyrants. Instead, I want to pride myself in bein' able to rise 'bove everythin' an' look fo' dah' positive an' a better life 'head. Let me add, I do carry dah' horrible physical scars of slavery on my back as a 'membrance of whar' I came from."

Puzzled, Sarah asked, "Your back is permanently scarred?"

"While, I'd never want to show dah' scars to anyone, I want yu' to know, Sarah, in spite of it all, I'm still proud of my disfigured back. It's a symbol of what all my black brothers an' sisters have to endure." Reggie's strong feelings toward slavery suddenly emerged, which indicated that Reggie was a highly principled man who would probably never think of "crossing over".

"Reggie, I had no idea. I want you to know, I have a tremendous amount of respect and affection for you, and I will always stand with you." Sarah was overwhelmed to hear about the horrible suffering Reggie went through, and upon reflection, she recalled when she visited Oak Manor that some of the experiences she witnessed appeared to be staged, which further led her to believe that Reggie was being very truthful.

"Thank yu', Sarah, I appreciate dat'. Worse yet, when I was lyin' in a semi-coma, I heard dah' tyrant who brutally tortured me say dat' dah' next beatin' would include disfigurin' my face. He told me while I was in sheer agony that it would give him great pleasure to transform me into a freak show candidate. I knew din' dat' I had to git' out of thar'. Incidentally, I do want yu' to know dat' dis' incident did not occur at Oak Manor.

"That man's more than a tyrant—he's a monster," Sarah exclaimed. "Thank God you escaped, Reggie!"

"Now yu' kin better understand my present mental an' physical state. So desperately I want to fight 'gainst dah' oppression dat' would be capable of causin' such unbelievable harm—even death to people who cannot fight back. I've seen heads impaled on pikes, an' one of my best friends, Angie, who was wit' child was brutally beaten to death in my presence. In God's name, how could anybody do dat'?"

Sarah was shocked to hear about heads being impaled on pikes and the death of Angie. She could only feel for the pain that Reggie had to endure, knowing her life has been one of comfort. She knew that stories of slave torture had surfaced in the North but, like most Northerners, she had accepted the saying "out of sight, out mind" and went about her life without giving it much thought. Hearing Reggie's story brought the horrors of slavery "to a full circle" for her. "Reggie, what you just described had to be the work of the devil!"

Sarah recognized that Reggie was becoming upset and appeared to be a little drowsy describing what he had endured and knew it was a good time for him to rest up. "Reggie, I know you have to be physically and mentally drained. Please allow Daniel to see you to your room where you can take a nap before dinner."

Reggie was stunned at the suggestion that he needed to take a nap. A slave being invited to go take a nap would be unheard of. It was definitely a first in his life, and more important to him, it was significant since it was the first time where he truly felt that he was being treated as a free man.

Daniel was summoned, and he accompanied Reggie upstairs. Once again, he was very pleasantly surprised when he entered the room. Decorated in white and blue, the room was very stylish and, ironically, even more refined than the master bedroom of Oak Manor. Reggie was stunned, while he laughed to himself—a slave sleeping in a bedroom fancier than his former master's. Interestingly, this was the first time that Reggie began to feel that he was beginning to move into a higher station in life. He then disrobed and slowly crawled into bed, pulled the covers up to his chin even though he was not cold. Reggie studied the room thoroughly and smiled—this was truly the beginning of a new life. Sleeping on such a high bed with a feather mattress and silk sheets in the past could have only taken place in a dream. Since slaves were always required to sleep on a cot or on the floor in recognition of their lower status, he was taken back by this new experience. If only Anastasia was here, his dream would be complete.

After a much-needed nap, Reggie prepared for dinner, knowing he would soon meet Sarah's father and brother. He feared they would not accept him, but he knew he had nothing to lose and everything to gain.

His clothes that had been provided for him by Daniel were once again pressed and placed next to his bed for him to wear for the evening.

Symbolically as Reggie was getting dressed, he examined his worn and tattered clothing and realized he should keep them as another symbol of his freedom. He also pondered why he didn't buy some new clothes along the route since he had more than adequate funds. Again, it was the realization that he was unable to bring himself to understand that he was a free man—the indoctrination was complete.

Just as he had finished getting ready, Sarah knocked at the door, summoning him for dinner. As Sarah led him down the stairs to the dining room he was extremely nervous, not knowing if his standards of etiquette would be adequate. He knew that as the personal servant to Albert, he had been fortunate enough to acquire good manners that would never have been available to most slaves who lived in the slave quarters or even in the main house. Sarah assured him there was no reason to worry since her family would be very understanding, and besides, she would be there alongside of him to help guide him along if necessary.

CHAPTER TWENTY-FIVE

Reggie knew his presence would generate curiousity and conversation as he entered the dining room. Nervously, he stood near the table anticipating the introductions, which would be followed by questions about the South and his background.

Sarah's mother, father, and brother arrived within minutes, exchanging cordialities as Sarah introduced Reggie to her father, Mel Clark, and brother, Lucas Clark and once seated an immediate discussion ensued.

As Reggie had expected, Mr. Clark did not mince words. Immediately, he brought up the color of his skin as he settled into his chair, which did not surprise Reggie. "Reggie I must admit I am surprised at your features. When I think of a slave, I don't think of someone who is as light skinned as you. In addition you conduct yourself as a well mannered gentleman, which I frankly find quite extraordinary. You certainly do not have the appearance of a worn down slave. I have to assume that your overall looks posed quite a problem for you when you were living in the South. Is that true?" Since Reggie had been victimized by stereotyping throughout his life, it was a question that he was prepared to answer.

"Yes, Mr. Clark, dat' is true, an' I think it's important dat' yu' know dat' in dah' South, I had to be reminded of my skin color almost every day. Dah' South is paranoid 'bout color identification—people are either black or white. Mix-blooded people like me remain an' enigma who dey' have a 'bery difficult time catalogin'." Dey' know 'bery well mix-blooded people like me kin' could cause a break down of dah' bondage system as it exists today, which makes us a potential danger. The bondage system operates smoothly as long as absolutes remain in force. Dah' problem can only grow as dah' mix-blooded people grow in greater numbers. Let me elaborate. Currently dah' back-to-Afriky movement, popular up North is sendin' free blacks back to Afriky who voluntarily want to relocate in thar' native homeland. Dah' mischief lies in mixed blooded people who can't claim Afriky' as thar' native land. What do yu' do wit' 'dem—or wit' me—we are not wanted by dah' whites or dah' blacks—we jus' remain in limbo, an' our numbers are growin', makin' it an expandin' problem dah' South will eventually have to address as well an' in some ways, dah' North as well."

Mr. Clark was duly impressed with Reggie's understanding of some of the problems associated with the bondage system and the "back to Africa movement". "I was particularly impresssed by your insightful summary of the differences between the Negro in the North and in the South. Reggie, it is so nice to see how intelligent you are, in fact, I can certainly see why my daughter is so fascinated by you. You are a very handsome young man with a sturdy carriage, and a sharp acumen. All of this bodes quite well for you to achieve success here in Boston."

Lucas, who had been observing Reggie, was quite frank when he expressed his initial impression of him in a sarcastic tone. "It's interesting that outside of your Southern drawl, which I personally find to be rather simple-sounding, your command of the English language would suggest to me that somewhere along the way you were able to acquire an education. Can you explain this?"

With an upbeat in his response Reggie replied, "My master, who I was 'signed to as his personal servant had learnin' difficulties. When dah' tutor came to dah' plantation, I always 'companied my master so I could later help reinforce what dah' tutor taught him. Not only did I aide him wit' academics, I also aided him wit' boatin', hawss'manship, an' nature studies. In dah' end, I was fortunate to be provided wit' a broad education dat' I'm so thankful to have."

Lucas, in an attempt to further intimidate Reggie, asked a rather derogatory question. "Reggie, as a slave, isn't it true that you wouldn't accurately know your background or your father's history?"

Silence dominated the room, as this bordered on being an insult. Reggie, however, was well-equipped to respond. "Lucas, on dah' contrary, to answer yur' highly-salted question, I know 'bery well who my father is. He is Colonel Marshall, who comes from one of dah' most elite families in Virginia, which would include dah' likes of former Chief Justice John Marshall. Hyehs' dah' caveat, it's agonizin' fo' me to know dat' I'm dah' son of such a prominent man, an' yet, I kin' never be acknowledged by my own father."

"Well put, Reggie," Lucas answered curtly, realizing that Reggie would not back down from any question he might pose.

Mrs. Clark, aware her son was purposely making an effort to make Reggie feel uncomfortable, shifted the conversation. "Enough of this conversation about family history, I would like to know the one aspect of slavery in the old South you found interesting and might be relatively unknown about up North?"

Her question excited Reggie. "I'm so glad yu' asked dat'. As horrible as slavery really is thar' is an occasional bright spot. From Christmas to New Year's Day, dah' slaves are given vacation time in dah' South. Now yu' might have an occasional tyrant who will not honor dis' tradition, but dey' are dah' 'ception. I've heard it said dat' slaveholders recognize dey' have to give dah' slaves some time off or risk insurrection. Dey' like to say dat' dah' slaves need some balance in thar' lives. Dis' is no more din' 'nother example of Southerners carefully thinkin' out everythin' jus' to keep dah' system runnin' as smooth as possible. It is not based on kindness or a reward fo' hard work but more out of necessity. Jus' give dah' slaves 'nough freedom to prevent an insurrection. Yu' might say it represents a form of give an' take wit' dah' slave

THE EYES OF THE COMET

owners doin' most of dah' takin'.'"

"Reggie, that's interesting, but I'm still curious to hear about something else you might find that might be relatively unknown up North."

"Well Mrs. Clark, as I jus' said, it's dah' only vacation time fo' dah' slaves fo' dah' entire year an' dey' have to make dah' best of it. I must tell yu' dat' it is dah' most colorful time of dah' year in dah' South. It's a beautiful sight to see dah' women in thar' native dress of Afriky' walkin' down dah' road. Incidentally, yu' will see many of 'dem not wearin' Negro cloth. Somehow dey' are able to git' thar' hands on a better quality of cloth at dah' general store. Dah' women wear colorful, bold-patterned, wrap-'round skirts easily seen from a distance. Bandannas, kerchiefs or head wraps are proudly worn, while dah' men wear cotton trousers an' straw hats. Not nearly as colorful as dah' women, dah' men nevertheless display a bright festive appearance while providing a sense of dignity."

Reggie realized he had something else to say. "In addition, slaves are always required, throughout dah' year to have a pass to leave dah' plantation. Dah' 'ception to dis' rule is durin' des' few days of vacation when slaves kin' visit other plantations wit'out a pass. Saunterin' down dah' road dey' sing an' dance wit' a feelin' of freedom. My regret is dat' dah' feelin' of freedom has to end so soon but 'bove all, it still brings some form of hope, an' hope is extremely important to thar' lives."

"Reggie, I didn't visit the Marshall plantation during Christmas, so I wasn't aware of what you just told us. However, I was there for the corn-shucking party, and I was really impressed." Sarah was pleased that she could add a comment to the conversation.

"Well," Reggie turned to her and went on, "dey' make a special occasion out of dah' corn-shuckin' party. It's a wonderful gala, but Christmas is far different since it is very religious, an' dah' slaves have their time off to really enjoy it. I wonder if dah' people up North realize jus' how fervent dah' slaves are in thar' belief an' passion fo' Jesus Christ an' how strongly dey' believe in prayer an' fo'giveness. Fo' 'dem, Christmas is a 'bery solemn day—it's a celebration of dah' birth of Jesus Christ. It's a bit ironic dat' so many of dah' customs of Afriky are still retained amongst 'dem, but when it comes to religion, dah' slaves are firmly rooted in dah' spirit of Christianity. Why can't dah' white people accept 'dem as true Christians an' not a bunch of heathens? To add further insult, I have heard it said God never intended fo' Negroes to be allowed in heaven. I find dis' extremely upsettin'. Whether I'm hyeh' or in dah' South; perceived as white, light skinned or black; free or in bondage, my heart is dat' of a slave, an' I know in God's eyes we are all equal, an'. . . .

Lucas interrupted Reggie before he could complete his thought. "How magnanimous, but you're getting into a diatribe now. You were talking about the days between Christmas and New Year's, not white people's failure to respect slaves. I think you strayed a little from the subject."

Changing the subject, Mr. Clark pushed his chair back a few inches and looked at his guest. "Reggie, I've been giving it some thought and I'd like to help you. I know this is a bit premature but let's talk about you having a future with our company. I'm offering you a job right now. Four things really bode well for you—your intelligence, looks, and friendship with Sarah. The fourth has to do with your ability to succeed against all odds. Anyone who can ride a horse over 1,000 miles on the 'road to freedom' represents an individual who has achieved quite an accomplishment. Reggie, you have a lot of fortitude. That said, what do you think?"

Reggie was stunned at the offer from Mr. Clark but was still able to muster up an answer. "Dey' talk 'bout Southern hospitality, well dis' jus' leaves me speechless. Maybe dey' orte' to talk 'bout Northern hospitality. Kin' yu' folks imagine dat' a short time ago I was livin' an absolute nightmare dat' nobody 'round heyh' would ever 'lieve? Now I'm bein' given a chance dat' few even up North are ever given. Mr. Clark of course, I accept yur' offer."

Sarah was overjoyed. "Father, I'm so happy that you are going to consider Reggie for a job with the company."

Mrs. Clark interjected, "Of course Sarah and I want to again affirm that I support Reggie staying right here with us until he gets settled."

Mr. Clark smiled. "Well, Reggie, you deserve the chance to succeed, and we want to give you that opportunity. There are no strings attached other than we expect you to work hard. I've heard enough and I want to see you succeed, and I have all the confidence in you."

Mrs. Clark saved the best for last. "Oh, there's more Reggie. We know you are married to a woman who is being held in bondage. Well, if things work out with your employment, we'll take legal steps to secure her freedom and bring your wife up here. Separate papers will be legally drawn up to buy both you and your wife's manumission. It would not be difficult for our attorney to make all this happen, and I know I am also speaking for my husband when I make this statement." It was apparent that Mrs. Clark was a warm and giving lady.

Reggie could not speak for several minutes. He simply shook his head in disbelief but finally said in a choked voice, "Mrs. Clark dis' can't be happenin' to me. Yur' wonderful hospitality—bein' wit' my wife an' both of us livin' free in Boston—I jus' can't contain myself any longer. I jus' 'rived hyeh' an' all of dis' is happenin' to me so suddenly." Reggie was totally overwhelmed, caught off guard as tears of gratitude and joy rolled down his face. An offer of this magnitude being extended to a fugitive slave was beyond his belief.

"Sarah is very dear to our hearts, and we know this will make her happy." Then Mr. Clark looked at Lucas and continued. "My immediate thoughts tell me that Reggie might have the makings of a terrific salesman. Even his Southern drawl could work to his advantage."

Meanwhile, Reggie was so excited by all that had taken place that he paid little attention to the delicious dinner being served. Instead, he sat spellbound attempting to digest the recent turn of events. Immediately after dinner, Reggie asked if he might be able to retire a bit early. He was blissfully worn out from all the events of the day. After thanking everyone, he bid a good night, and then Sarah cordially walked him to the stairwell. "I'm thrilled for you, Reggie!" she exclaimed. "And remember that tomorrow we'll go to the haberdashery for your new clothes, and then you are going to get a haircut and a shave! Then you will be set to paint the town. Just joking of course." Out of sheer joy for him, she pecked his cheek with a kiss goodnight.

Reggie smiled from ear to ear. "Sarah, I can't thank yu' 'nough fo' keepin' yur' word to help me atter' I made it up to freedom. I'm speechless, so much is happenin' so quick, I jus' can't 'lieve all dis' is true."

Sarah nodded and said, "It is true, and so—welcome to the North and a new life where you'll have the opportunity to fulfill all your hopes and dreams! And remember, you deserve this for all you've been through. Goodnight, Reggie."

She returned to her family as Reggie climbed the stairs to his guest bedroom—not his slave quarters. Once there he took his clothes off and crawled onto the feather mattress, pulling the soft blanket up to his chin as he reviewed the events of the day, feeling both relief and secure. He couldn't believe that Sarah's family would help reunite Anastasia with him. This was more than he could fathom. Furthermore, he had been offered a position in Mr. Clark's company. However, Mr. and Mrs. Clark did imply that everything rested on him performing well for Clark Manufacturing. This caveat came as no surprise, but it would put a lot of pressure on him even though Reggie was still confident that he could handle anything put before him.

One thing still troubled him, which he had no control over—the unfairness of society. He recognized all the wonderful things happening to him could only be possible because of his looks and intelligence. He still had to take advantage of this unbelievable opportunity and keep moving forward. However, it would have to remain for him to fight for equal justice for all those who could not have this opportunity. He finally began to drift off to sleep, smiling with thoughts of Anastasia on his mind.

***

As promised, the next day Sarah took him shopping for new clothes. As they walked into a haberdashery shop, she reminded Reggie that as a salesman for her father's company, his appearance would be very important. For someone who had only worn Negro cloth, high quality clothing would represent quite a change. Seeing the high priced clothing on display throughout the store was rather shocking and overwhelming. Also, he still had to overcome the tendency to feel out of place in the shop since technically, he was still a fugitive slave. At first he even caught himself shifting toward the back of the store, feeling a predilection to being outside in the back where slaves waited for their master. Sarah recognized he was nervous and assured him that in time, he would get used to enjoying his freedom. She then helped him to relax as they selected his wardrobe. After being properly fitted, Reggie was left in total awe of the whole procedure and the results. He profusely thanked Sarah both for all her help and for paying for the clothes. The entire experience was very positive in helping Reggie to begin to think like a free man living in Boston. It made him feel proud—life was suddenly good and about to get better.

***

In the days before beginning work at Clark Manufacturing, Reggie spent a lot of time riding his loyal friend, Freedom through the streets of Boston and into the surrounding countryside. It served a practical purpose since he could learn so much about Boston just from touring the streets and seeing the sights of the city and the surrounding area. He felt free and happy knowing how his life had changed and all for the good. He was especially pleased at being able to ride Freedom at a very comfortable pace and not having to worry about covering 15 or 20 miles a day!

As Reggie and Freedom rode throughout the town, he discovered many historical sights. On Beacon Street was the Old State House built in 1713. It was here, in 1770, that the Boston Massacre took place, which was a prelude to the Revolutionary War. Near the corner of School Street and Washington Street was the Old South Meeting House with its steepled bell tower. Here in the front, the Boston Tea Party was organized. This area, so rich in history was the nerve center of Boston. Situated along North Street in the hub of Boston was Faneuil Hall and Quincy Market. This area had been the hotbed of the Revolutionary War. This represented such a dramatic contrast from Richmond where the revolutionary zeal was never present. These sights and sounds continued to amaze Reggie as he rode on his trusted steed, Freedom. Now, if only Anastasia could be by his side, his life would be complete.

CHAPTER TWENTY-SIX

On Monday morning, the beginning of the much anticipated work-week, Reggie eagerly reported to Mr. Clark to begin his new job.

As he nervously walked into Mr. Clarks's office, he was taken aback by the spacious interior that greeted him. A large, custom-made black walnut desk located at the back of the room served as a focal point, and the bookcase along the right side featured a notable collection of books. A deep, red beige colored Persian rug accentuated the dark, imported European furniture. Nautical accessories accented the room, apropos since the corporation was located on Atlantic Avenue alongside Boston harbor. The office certainly left no doubt about who was in charge of the corporation.

Mr. Clark, with a warm smile, shook Reggie's hand and formally welcomed him to the Clark Manufacturing facility. Graciously, he asked Reggie to be seated in a comfortable-looking black leather chair that was directly in front of his desk. Reggie tried to appear confident, but inwardly he remained nervous not knowing what would be expected of him. His immediate fear was of Mr. Clark sending him out on the job with little or no training. He had dealt with dilemmas all of his life but nothing like what he could possibly be facing now. Coming from plantation life in Georgia, and now working for a large manufacturing corporation in Boston represented such a departure that naturally he felt apprehensive.

Mr. Clark was extremely friendly and professional while reassuring Reggie that he was in good hands. Reggie's nervousness began to subside as he conversed with Mr. Clark. The first thing brought up was good news for Reggie. "Reggie, let me be honest with you. You have no knowledge of the textile business, but I can assure you, this will not be a problem. In fact that could be an asset since some men with previous experience have had difficulty making adjustments to the Clark system. History has demonstrated this could work to your advantage and ours as well. Now that should make you feel better about being a greenhorn in our company," he said with a smile on his face.

"Mr. Clark, it certainly is gratifyin' to know dat' my inexperience kin' be rewardin'. I kin' further guarantee dat' I will foller' yur' system an' not deviate." It was obvious Reggie was comforted by Mr. Clark's words and was eager to learn and to succeed.

"Now Reggie, don't get me wrong, I appreciate your desire to follow our system. However, you have to learn how to capitalize on your own particular assets. In our system, you will always maintain your autonomy to operate within your own personality and have the disgression to make some adjustments as you will see fit on the job. You have some strong assets about you that I mentioned a few days ago. Your Southern drawl and calm demeanor should be a tremendous asset in your performance, contributing in your ability to gain the confidence of your customers. For some reason Northerners are fascinated with Southern drawls. Perhaps with your Southern drawl you will be able to lull them into feeling confident that they are dealing with somebody who is honest, trustworthy, and more 'down home'."

Reggie thought to himself that it was interesting that a Northerner liked the way a Southerner talked, but felt it was a bit of a puzzle that a Southerner might not like to hear a Northerner talk. That thought would have to remain a mystery.

"Mr. Clark, I honestly never gave it a thought, but it is a 'bery good point. I hesitate to make too much of it other din' dah' fact dat' dah' Southern drawl is uniquely different from dah' way dey' speak up North. But din', dah' British have thar' unique way of speakin', which is different from either one of us." Reggie wanted to agree with Mr. Clark, but he felt he should take the middle of the road where it might be safer.

"That sounds about right," Clark stated. "I like the way you think and reason. Reggie a building must have a solid foundation, or it will topple, and that metaphor applies to you. If you don't have a strong base, you will probably fail working for Clark Manufacturing. I'm going to ask you a fundamental question before we get specific about the job. What do you think makes for a good salesman?"

Reggie had not rehearsed for the questions Mr. Clark might ask, but his ingenuity came to the forefront. "Mr. Clark in my opinion, thar' are four important qualities dat' are necessary to be successful. First, yu' have to have common sense."

Clark interrupted, "Please elaborate on that."

"If I enter a customer's office and he displays accessories on dah' wall indicating he enjoys fishin', I would somehow let him know dat' I enjoy fishin' as well—which I honestly do. Dat' type of openin' discussion should create a relaxed, friendly atmosphere to eventually move into to discussin' Clark Manufacturin'."

Mr. Clark beamed as he listened. "I like that answer a lot. What's the second quality?"

Reggie was prepared to answer the question. "A balanced personality is a must. A good salesman has to be a good listener 'fore bein' a good talker. In fact, too much talkin' can be dangerous, 'cuz' it opens up dah' possibility of sayin' dah' wrong thin'. It would be better to let dah' customer feel comfortable doin' dah' talkin'. Dah' more a customer talks, dah' better he will feel 'bout me an' our company. Bein' a humorist is a good asset, but first a balanced personality allows yu' to know when to listen an' when to talk wit' dah' emphasis on always listenin' to what yur' customer has to say."

"Again Reggie, I like that, and I think you are the first person to express that at times good listening skills can be more important than good talking skills. As with your first point, I heartily agree with you. Now let's get to number three."

"Mr. Clark, it's really important to concentrate on finding solutions an' less on jus' worryin' 'bout problems."

"Reggie, I really do find your first three points to be outstanding! It says to me that you possess the uncanny thinking of someone who has the abilty to drive the company forward. Now that is exactly what I am looking for. That said, in the context of the other two points you made, it gives you the complete package, but I still haven't heard your fourth prerequisite for a good salesman. In fact I don't want this to go to your head, but your answers are as good as I have ever heard. You have an amazing ability to answer a question right off the top of your head. I have to take my hat off to my daughter. I think she knows how to choose good friends. Now let me hear your fourth point."

Reggie's confidence level peaked at this point as he calmly stated, "Mr. Clark, I think dat' it's especially important dat' yu' believe in dah' product dat' yu' are sellin'."

Mr. Clark reacted quickly to the answer. "Reggie, you just said a mouthful. That is so true, and fortunately for you, Clark Manufacturing will provide the products you will believe in wholeheartedly."

"Mr. Clark, thank yu' so much for havin' trust in me," Reggie humbly stated. "I look forward to havin' a chance to live up to yur' expectations."

Clark briefly outlined what was expected of him. "Reggie, you are officially in our training program, and have been classified as an apprentice and officially assigned to work under one of my top salesman. His name is Kenneth Miller. Now this program will take several weeks to complete. Learning about the products we manufacture will require a tremendous amount of knowledge and hard work. Later you will have to familiarize yourself with your assigned territory, which could be Lowell, Lawrence, New Bedford or Fall River to name a few of the main textile centers in the area. While I can't say how long the training program will take, Mr. Miller will know when you are ready and advise me accordingly. Oh yes, you will be compensated while in training—

wage labor and not slave labor! Congratulations, Reggie." Mr. Clark was injecting a bit of humor with Reggie when he referenced wage labor and not slave labor and insightfully pointed out one of the fundamental differences between the North and South since slave labor is confined to the South.

"Thank yu' Mr. Clark. Dis' will be dah' first time I have ever been paid fo' my labor, which really is a bit bizarre when I think 'bout it as a former slave. Reggie paused and then addressed the training program. "I must admit, Mr. Clark, dat' I feel a lot better knowin' dat' I'm goin' to be properly trained. I was afraid dat' I could be thrown to dah' wolves, but I swore dat' whatever happened I would work hard fo' yu' an' Clark Manufacturin' while acceptin' all challenges."

"Trust me Reggie we would not throw you to the wolves. I've enjoyed our conversation. You've got a lot of spunk, and we can always use that around here. Reggie, I'll see you here at eight sharp tomorrow morning. You will meet Mr. Miller, and we'll get you started. I can only say that I look forward to both our friendship and a working relationship.

"Thank you, Mr. Clark. Yu' have already instilled confidence in me in such a short time, I'll be hyeh' at eight sharp." As Reggie left the office he found himself already having a different perspective toward work. Being paid for his labor and abilities would be unique. He genuinely looked forward to everything about his new job.

The rest of the day was filled with a carefree ride on Freedom while touring the areas of Boston he had previously not seen. All he could think about was Anastasia and his new job. He sometimes felt that all of this was only a dream, and if it was a dream, he was certain that it was one he didn't want to wake up from.

The next day Reggie arrived promptly at Mr. Clark's office, eager to make a good impression. Mr. Miller was already there, and Clark introduced them. "Reggie, I want you to meet Kenneth Miller. He will be responsible for your training program. As I said earlier, Kenneth just happens to be one of our top salesmen. When you get done with your training program, then and only then, will you be ready to go out on your own. I can assure you that under Kenneth's tutorage, you will be properly prepared." He paused a moment, and turning toward Miller said, "Kenneth this is Reggie Marshall, your new trainee."

Both men smiled as they shook hands. Reggie had a very good first impression of him. He quickly surmised that this pleasant, clean cut man, who personified the stereotypic salesman—thin, middle aged and slightly balding with an affable personality would be somebody he would enjoy working with.

"I think it's time for you to get to work. This should be the beginning of a successful business relationship between you and Mr. Miller." Clark stood and shook the hand of each man as they prepared to leave his office, and wished them luck.

Reggie wished Mr. Clark a good day and then walked down the hallway with Ken Miller to his office. As they entered, Miller wanted to make sure Reggie felt comfortable. "Mr. Clark has given me some insight on your background. I understand you had to endure a lot of suffering in your lifetime. I would think all of this will probably make you more appreciative of your new job. Obviously, you don't have any experience in this business since you've lived on plantations all your life, but that doesn't matter. Word has it that you are a quick learner, and besides, I sense you are mighty hungry to want to learn, and I'll be your buffet of knowledge," he said in a light hearted manner with a grin.

"I kin' assure yu', Mr. Miller, dat' I will work as hard as possible to grasp everythin'. I'm used to hard work, so whatever I'm required to do fo' Clark Manufacturin', it can't be more difficult din' what was expected of me in dah' past."

"That's great but please, do me a favor and call me Kenneth, not Mr. Miller."

"I will, if dats' what yu' want, but I must be honest. As a former slave, it's rather difficult fo' me to call yu' by yur' first name—I'm goin' to have to git' used to it. I have one favor to ask of yu'. Technically, I'm still classified as a fugitive slave 'til my papers of manumission are official, so please don't mention to anyone 'bout my background 'til I've been notified dat' I'm legally free."

"Believe me, I won't say a word," Miller promised. I know Mr. Clark thinks highly of you, and he would not be happy to find out that I meddled in your personal life. That said, may I ask you a gut-level question that has been on my mind?"

Reggie nodded that he could.

"You don't have any Negro features. Why not just "crossover" and disavow your past? It would make your life immeasurably easier."

"Yu' are right 'bout dat'," Reggie stated. "It would make my life easier on dah' outside, but I'd have to deal wit' my conscience. All my brothers an' sisters who are in servitude need hope an' help, an' someday I would like to be in a position to improve thar' lives an' help give 'dem dah' hope dey' need. I cannot abandon dose' who were so good to me in dah' days when I had to suffer so much. I hope yu' understand why I feel so strongly 'bout my people."

This reasoning made sense to Miller. "I do understand, and I truly respect you for feeling the way you do. Believe me your attitude speaks volumes about your character. Unfortunately, I would think you might find yourself in the minority with your thinking."

"Thank yu', Kenneth fo' understandin' jus' how important dis' matter is to me." Reggie felt better, knowing that Mr. Miller respected him for his commitment to his roots.

Miller showed Reggie his office. "Temporarily, my office will also serve as yours until your training has been completed and you are on your own. It's rather compact and simple but has an empty pedestal desk for you to use."

Miller then explained the main elements of the Clark training program. "First, we'll spend a lot of time in the plant simply learning about all of the products we manufacture and sell. It won't be easy, and it may prove difficult at times, but I know you're a fast learner. You will be meeting others in the plant, such as the engineers, supervisors, production people, and repairmen. Believe me you will be in contact with everybody. They will enlighten you more about their specific products and responsibilities."

Reggie listened intently as Miller continued explaining the training program regarding information relative to his new position as a sales representative. "After learning about our products, and sales techniques, you'll be ready to go on the road since you won't make the company money just sitting here at your desk. I think you would agree," he jokingly said with a smile. "This will require being on the road a lot of the time. Don't worry as you'll get used to it. My personal route covers Lowell, which happens to be one of the busiest routes. You will serve as an apprentice salesman for me until I feel you are ready to be on your own. I have no idea where you will eventually be assigned; however, I can assure you that you'll be staying overnight in various inns on the road. Lowell, my area is about forty miles northwest of Boston, which has fairly good lodging throughout my route. You will become familiar with the inns and the hotels on your route. Although sleeping away from home is not like sleeping at home in your own bed, you'll at least find most accommodations adequate. Naturally, you'll develop both business and personal relationships as you travel, which makes the job even more interesting."

Reggie laughed to himself as Miller described the inns and hotels on the road as only adequate as he remembered sleeping on a little cot in a tiny room in the slave quarters—anything would be almost "heavenly" compared to that.

Kenneth continued to tell Reggie what his job entailed. Reggie, your work in the field has three aspects. First, you will be responsible for selling our equipment to new textile plants within your route. Second, you will have to make calls on all of our existing accounts that we presently service. They may need new equipment or parts for existing machines. Lastly, if you have any surplus time, which I might add, you should have, you will be expected to call on the mills that are serviced by other companies. Sometimes you can convince them into doing business with us, especially if they're not satisfied with the company that has been servicing them. Do you think you can handle all of that?"

Reggie stood up and nearly shouted. "Of course, an' I'm anxious to start dah' trainin' program immediately."

"That's great. Your positive attitude is an asset. Now that you've heard what is expected of you, let's go meet your supervisior who is in charge of sales."

Reggie moved to the office door and held it open for Miller. "Atter' yu'," he stated.

Reggie and Ken Miller entered an adjacent office where Reggie was introduced to his immediate superior, James Wicklund who was in charge of the sales department.

Wicklund introduced himself to Reggie and commented that under normal circumstances, he would have interviewed him, but this procedure had been by-passed in this case. A tall, thin, middle-aged man, almost a clone to Mr. Miller, he had a warm smile that made Reggie immediately feel comfortable. Reggie thought to himself that everything was working out better than he could have expected.

"Working with Ken will serve you very well. He's one of our top salesmen. Under his tutorage you will learn how to represent yourself, our product and our company at the highest level. For now that is all I have to say, but I will very soon be in contact with you to give you more information and see how you're getting along."

"Thank yu', Mr. Wicklund. I kin' assure yu' dat' I will put forth every ounce of my energy into helpin' dah' company to become more successful."

***

True to his words, Reggie pursued his training program, vigorously demonstrating a tremendous amount of drive and energy. Each day he arrived early—alert and ready to absorb as much knowledge as possible. His ability to prove he was a quick study became evident very early.

After two months into his apprenticeship, which passed

very quickly, Mr. Clark summoned Reggie into his office. "Please sit down, Reggie. I have some very good news for you! Mr. Wicklund and Mr. Miller have both given you very high marks and think you are getting close to being able to be on your own as a sales representative for Clark Manufacturing." Mr. Clark smiled proudly at Reggie. "Normally we would want you to have more preparation before going out on your own; however, you seem to have an exceptional ability to quickly grasp everything. Along with your acumen, Mr. Miller informed me that you have the makings of a natural salesman. He was very impressed with the way you conducted yourself when the two of you visited his accounts. It was evident that his customers felt very comfortable and trustworthy with you. Do you feel comfortable with that assessment?"

"Mr. Clark, I'm more din' ready to prove dat' I kin be a valuable salesman fo' Clark Manufacturin'."

"Excellent! Now, I have some additional good news. I have decided to take action on the letters of manumission for both you and Anastasia. Would that meet with your approval? I just want to get this process moving along. I'm doing this even though you haven't been tested in the field on your own, but I anticipate you will do quite well."

Reggie was overcome with emotion as tears of joy rolled down his face. He tried to compose himself and then said, "Mr. Clark, I jus' can't 'lieve what I'm hyehin'. Yu' can't imagine how happy I am. Day in an' day out I think 'bout my wife an' our freedom. I'm stunned to learn dis' news. I apologize dat' I'm gettin' a little choked up, but I can't contain my feelins'. Of course dis' would meet my 'proval!"

Clark pulled his chair round to the front of his desk and sat down next to Reggie. "Don't worry about it, Reggie, I fully understand. Now, I'm going to need some information from you. I want to know the address of the man who formerly held your papers and Colonel Marshall's address as well. Hopefully we can track your wife's location. I might add, my attorney has an uncanny way of successfully getting things done."

Reggie's crying abruptly halted—replaced by a look of panic. "Mr. Clark, dah' current fugitive slave act still gives my former master, Captain Riley, dah' power to have me 'rested an' deported back to dah' plantation. If he knew my location, he might dispatch somebody up hyeh' to git' me."

"Don't worry about that." Clark was determined to assure Reggie he had nothing to worry about. "You are protected by me. I gather that Captain Riley owns your papers. Again, just give me his address along with Colonel Marshall's, and our attorney, Mr. Joseph, will contact them and take the necessary actions to buy the papers of freedom for the both of you. It's that simple."

"I jus' can't believe dat' it kin' be dat' easy," Reggie stuttered in pure disbelief.

"With influence and money, a lot can happen," Clark said flatly, and then he added, "Reggie, I will expect to be paid back— is that fair enough for you?"

"Of course to have my wife wit' me an' both of us free." Reggie's voice rose with excitement. "I jus' can't believe dis' is happenin' to me. To pay yu' back, Mr. Clark, fo' what yu' are doing fo' me an' Anastasia is such a small request. I'll always be indebted to yu'.

"Reggie, it's almost always true that power and money are very effective and this is no exception. My family and I feel that you are a fine young man, and we want to help you in any way we can."

Again, Reggie was well aware that he was being treated differently than other fugitive slaves since the special attention given to his situation would rarely ever be accorded to others. Being literate and able to pass for white provided a major advantage.

Reggie truly enjoyed working for Mr. Clark. The contrast between picking cotton as a slave in Georgia and working for a large, well respected corporation as a salesman in Boston was a huge contrast. In addition, with Mr. Clark's support and effort to secure his freedom along with Anastasia's, Reggie's life was about to become immeasurably better.

Reggie continued to hone his skills with Ken Miller. After

traveling back and forth with him from Boston to Lowell for another six weeks, Mr. Miller felt he was ready to go out on his own.

Reggie was surprised to find out that he was assigned to the surrounding suburbs of Boston. Remaining in the Boston area pleased Reggie with the relatively close proximity to his home. However, he would still have to stay overnight at inns on a regular basis, which Reggie looked forward to.

Soon Reggie was thoroughly enjoying his job and all the responsibilities that went with it. Very soon into being on his own, it was also becoming apparent that Reggie's job performance was outstanding. Further, while he truly enjoyed calling on his customers, he particularly enjoyed staying at the various inns available to him along his route. Very quickly, the Munro Tavern in Lexington became Reggie's favorite inn. Boston was so rich with history, and the inn represented a big part of it. It's most famous customer was George Washington, who visited in 1775.

The Munro Tavern was located on an old stagecoach road at the historic Green where the Colonials mustered to pursue the British fleeing from Concord.

The quaint brick inn featured a bar room with a large fireplace and brick oven. Behind the fireplace was the kitchen that provided food for the spacious dining area. In addition, both men and women were always present, quite often in large numbers who enjoyed the company of the crowd who frequented the tavern. Upstairs, was a grand dance hall used to entertain the drovers in the evening who were passing through the area. On occasion, Reggie could even see herds of cattle and sheep grazing in the surrounding fields. It represented quite a contrast from the cotton fields of the South. The bucolic character, combined with the fine dining and comfortable sleeping rooms put Reggie at ease when he visited the inn.

On one occasion he had the pleasure to meet three gregarious, well-dressed gentlemen at the tavern, all of whom had the look of being well-educated. They had finished their dinner and were indulging in a fine white wine when they invited Reggie to join them. Reggie congenially accepted their offer and sat down at the table with them. As he introduced himself the men expressed their fascination with his drawl. They quickly became curious about his life in the South. The gentleman who sat in a chair that faced Reggie smiled and asked, "Could you tell us a little about yourself, as we rarely ever get any Southerners up here to converse with.

"Gentlemen, my name is Reggie Marshall, I presently reside in Boston, but originally I came from Virginny'."

A second man seated at the table turned his chair toward Reggie and made the introductions. "Reggie, my name is Ralph Sanders; this is Joseph Martin and this is James Johnson. The three of us are from New York City, and we're here on business. Truthfully, we come to Boston more often than we want to, and we've been doing this for quite some time. Thankfully it's a lot easier to get here now. We would have to take a stagecoach to Springfield and then another one to Watertown where we could rent a buggy. Thankfully, we can now travel by railroad. Years ago we would arrive here exhausted, skip dinner and go to bed—times have changed for the better."

Joseph Martin, who was nattily attired and appeared to be the oldest of the three, asked Reggie where he now lived and what he did for a living.

Reggie proudly answered the question, "I have taken up residence hyeh' in Boston an' I work as a salesman fo' Clark Manufacturin', a textile equipment maker." Even in a friendly conversation with the strangers it would not be wise to inform them that he was also a fugitive slave.

James Johnson, a very distinguished looking man, posed an interesting question. "I'm a curious person. Mr. Marshall, coming from the South, other than agricultural and topographic differences, what is the most startling distinction you find between the North and the South?"

Reggie enjoyed answering the question. "I think dat' is a good question. I have two points to make. First, I find dat' dah' material wealth dat' separates dah' North an' dah' South to be quite pronounced. Dah' South has committed its economic well-bein' wit' cotton, while dah' North has diversified wit' a concentration in manufacturin'. It's so obvious—yu' kin' visually see dah' differences in dah' infrastructure in industry an' in housin' 'tween dah' two. Unfortunately, dah' commitment to cotton in dah' South has put thar' wealth into dah' hands of a 'bery few. Further, I believe dat' dah' South's continuin' dependence on cotton will further weaken thar' economy in dah' long run. Dis' economic gulf 'tween dah' North an' dah' South will only git' greater an' make relations 'tween dah' two more strained an' difficult. Point two, I'll summarize wit' one word—slavery."

"Mr. Marshall, you fired that answer out like a speech," Johnson said. "It's a real interesting synopsis that you have just given. I for one, would like to hear more since I rarely ever get to talk to a Southerner, and I might add, somebody who appears to know what he's talking about."

"Gentlemen, I personally 'lieve dah' South overestimates thar' resources an' economic strength. However, what dey' might lack in resources an' economic strength dey' kin' more din' make up fo' in thar' bravado."

"Mr. Marshall, I have heard they are committed to having a strong militia. Is that where their bravado emanates from?" asked Mr. Sanders.

"Dat' is true. I think dat' thar' swagger is reinforced by thar' more din' ready militia. Other factors of a lesser degree relate to manhood, which is extremely important to 'dem. Duelin' is still an accepted practice to settle thar' differences, an' in addition dey' are 'bery proud of thar' outdoor lore while dey' feel dat' manliness is lackin' in dah' North."

Sanders bristled at Reggie's response. "Are you being foolish? Granted, we no longer allow dueling in the North, but do the Southerners really believe the men living throughout Indiana, Illinois or Michigan spend all their time in the kitchen behind their wife's skirts?" The humor drew an immediate laugh from everybody. He continued, "That's pretty raw country that requires a lot of outdoor work. Or for that matter, what about the men of

Pennsylvania, New York or elsewhere in the North? Incidentally, hunting and fishing abound throughout the North. For a lot of people that is their entire life. It is ridiculous for Southerners to think that Northerners lack manliness, an' this thinking could get them in trouble later on. I'm sure that in case of an improbable war the North could put up an equal fight against the South."

"Mr. Sanders, I think dat's what dey' are sayin'. Dis' goes 'long wit' state pride, which is 'bery important as well. In fact, most feel thar' state pride is more important din' thar' respect fo' our country. Yu' could say dey' are highly principled. What I'm sayin' to yu' an' yur' friends are only my observations. Simply put, state rights are more important to dah' South din' dah' rights of dah' federal government, an' I really don't think dat' would even be a moot point."

Johnson agreed with Reggie. "I have heard that the South puts a lot of pride in their beloved Southern heritage. I do find your comments and interpretations quite interesting since they do parallel what I have read and heard. You mentioned earlier their emphasis on having a strong militia. What is the purpose in having a strong militia?"

"Mr. Johnson, I would bet dat' yu' could answer yur' own question. In 1831 in Virginny' thar' was dah' Nat Turner insurrection. It was quickly put down, but not wit'out fear of future rebellions. In fact Virginny' tightened up dah' slave code laws right atter' dat'. Dis' insurrection reinforced dah' paranoia throughout dah' South dat' a strong military presence was a must in order to keep dah' slaves from revoltin'. Think 'bout dis! In God's world, what is natural 'bout subjugatin' people an' turnin' 'dem into slaves? So yu' have to create a system of repression to keep 'dem down. Gentlemen, allow me to answer my own question— nothin'! As a Christian, I deplore man twistin' dah' Bible 'long wit' other things in order to justify an unnatural existence, which creates all dah' sufferin' dat' we now have to witness in dah' South fo' dah' profit of a few. I think yu' gentlemen know dat' only a few Southerners even own slaves. It amazes me why so many white people in dah' South would defend a system that provides no positive good fo' 'dem. In fact, dah' system is 'bery harmful to thar' economic well-bein'. Dah' most obvious example is dah' wages of white Southerners, which are far less din' Northerners 'cuz' slavery clearly holds wages down. Yet all des' poor white Southern boys will fight 'tooth an' nail' fo' dah' dignity an' honor of dah' ole' South. Also, jus' 'member dat' dah' slave system holds wages down, not black people—don't blame 'dem. Dat's a real sore spot wit' me, 'cuz' dey' are dah' victims, bein' used fo' dah' benefit of a few."

"Gentlemen, this man is very perceptive and can be quite vociferous in his answers. I can't speak for my friends, but what you are saying makes sense." Mr. Johnson turned to the other two men who nodded their heads in agreement.

Reggie, never afraid of a political discussion, looked at each of the three men as he continued. "How do yu' gentlemen see dah' issue of slavery?"

Sanders stood up and walked toward the bar to order another glass of wine as he responded to Reggie's question. "I have some understanding of it, and it's a ticklish but practical situation. We need cotton for our mills, and the cotton comes from the South. Without it our economy up North would suffer greatly, which means we have to support slavery in order to provide for the raw cotton that we need for our mills," said Mr. Sanders.

"Gentlemen, let me be dah' debil's advocate in dis' matter. Wouldn't free Negro labor in dah' cotton fields produce dah' same results—black men an' women who could work as tenants or sharecroppers, or better yet, own thar' own farms an' plantations."

Sanders challenged Reggie's answer. "Mister, now 'that is a horse of a different color'! I would personally be against that. Look, we don't need to rock the boat, as the system seems to be working quite well for them in spite of your personal observations."

Joseph Martin, who had only asked Reggie where he lived and what he did added some information he felt was relevant. "Here in the North we have the American Colonization Society which is presently shipping free Negroes back to Africa. They could even begin to expand the program to include slaves in the

South."

"Well, dat' sounds like a magnanimous plan, but what 'bout dah' costs? Who's goin' to pay fo' dis' ambitious project? Who pays fo' thar' settlement in Africa? What 'bout dah' white Southern slave owners who have a tremendous investment in thar' slaves, which is second only to thar' investment in thar' land an' property? What 'bout all dah' slaves born in dah' United States who have no physical ties to Africa—do they have to be shipped out? Lastly, dah' number of slaves in dah' South is increasin' dramatically an' at a far greater rate din' dose' who are bein' shipped back through dah' efforts of dah' American Colonization Society. Finally, I think dat' dah' 'back to Africa' movement dat' I hyeh' people talk 'bout all dah' time reflects a political policy but not reality. My observation of it, tells me dat' it doesn't 'amount to a hill of beans'!" Mr. Martin's comment obviously stirred up Reggie.

Mr. Sanders, who had been enjoying every minute of the conversation added, "You do raise a lot of questions that give credence to how complicated the issue of slavery really is and further explaining why there is no easy resolution. Perhaps these questions will have to be solved in the future. To your credit, it certainly sounds like you have given this some study."

Reggie had more to say. "What do yu' think of dah' conditions dat' dah' slaves are forced to live under? Wouldn't yu' agree dat' it is cruel an' inhumane? An' 'bove all, should dat' problem have to wait fo' dah' future to be addressed, a country based on democracy, which means equality fo' all dah' people. Isn't dis' what our Declaration of Independence stands fo' as we celebrate our independence from Great Britain on July 4th.

"Look, young man none of us have been to the South, and I've heard thar' may be an occasional slave owner who is cruel, but as a whole they are very humane. Think of it this way, it's like owning a horse. The horse costs money—why would you abuse it?" Sanders thoroughly enjoyed the debate and lit a cigar as he awaited a reply to a comment you would often hear a Southern gentleman make.

"Mr. Sanders, a horse is completely different from a human

an' has needs dat' do not offer serious resistance like a human, which could manifest in an insurrection. Yu' also mentioned how humane dah' plantation owners can be; however, people really don't know what goes on since dah' plantations are largely isolated. Even in dah' South, dah' people livin' in dah' city know 'bery little 'bout plantation life. Thar' contact wit' slavery is confined to hired-out slaves who are workin' in dah' city fo' non-slave owners. Dey' never git' to dah' plantations, so how would dey' know? Also, I believe from my own obversation, dah' rate of alcoholism is higher in dah' South. Dat' problem becomes magnified when yu' consider dat' a drunk kin' legally use a whip at his own discretion." Reggie paused to take a deep breath and enjoy a sip of wine. "In fact I have observed dat' dah' level of disorder, drunkenness an' violence is less up North din' in dah' South. Could dat' be attributed to dah' residual affects of dah' bondage system creatin' a negative affect on dah' South? Now, I'm only posin' dat' question based on my own study an' observations."

Martin thought for a few moments and then added, "I've read that each Southern state has its own slave codes to protect the slaves. Is that not true?"

It was becoming obvious that these intelligent men in the North had flawed information and needed to hear more. "Do yu' know what des' slave codes are all 'bout, Mr. Martin?"

Martin responded, "Aren't the codes designed to protect the slaves similar to the laws protecting animals from cruelty? I think it is legally based on a 'peculiar institution' that recognizes the rights of animals and slaves."

"I find it interestin' dat' yu' compare a human bein' to an animal. Dah' slave codes may very well vary from state to state in dah' South wit' dah' deep South havin' dah' harshest codes. Let's take a closer look at a few. Yu' are correct dat' dah' slave codes do have a provision dat' is suppose to protect dah' slaves from extreme cruelty from thar' master or others. Of course dat' provision is often ignored. But what 'bout dah' majority of slave codes designed fo' dah' master's benefit? Des' may not arise in conversation up North. Marriage 'mong dah' slaves cannot be legally sanctioned by dah' state. It's simply 'tween dah' couple gittin' married in the eyes of God an' thar' master who grants it. To leave dah' plantation a slave is required to have a pass. How 'bout not bein' able to legally carry a gun even for huntin' unless yu' are wit' a white person. Also, yu' are not suppose to have any money. In addition, slaves are restricted from congregatin' in groups at night unless a white person is present. Dose' are dah' more minor restrictions, an' dah' list gits' worse from hyeh'. Of course, yu' have to know all des' provisions are intended to make it more difficult to incite an insurrection. Also on a more minor scale to prevent runaways."

The three men sat quietly, their expressions clearly frozen with surprise but insisted that Reggie continue.

"Mr. Johnson, would you like to be legally restricted from learnin' to read an' write? Yes, yu' are not 'lowed to learn to read an' write. That's right, yu' must remain illiterate throughout yur' life. Mr. Martin, as a slave yu' have absolutely no right to file a law suit—yu' have dah' same rights as a hawss'—none, dat's what yu' have! That means, if somebody physically harms yu', as a slave yu' cannot take dah' party who harmed yu' to court. An' Mr. Sanders, how would yu' like to not have any family identification since yu' are not 'lowed to have a last name? Yur' first name is all yu' kin' use, an' dey' kin' change dat' on a whim! I personally knew a field hand whose name was instantly changed from Jimmy to Scipio, simply 'cuz' dey' wanted another Roman soldier in dah' quarters. Fo' 'dem it's jus' a big joke. How denigratin' is dat'? Dis' significantly demoralizes a slave, an' helps to destroy dah' quality of family life an' any family history dat' a person would have. Add to dis' dat' family life an' history has already been compromised accordin' to whites since Afrikans' identify only to thar' native tribe an' not thar' country of origin like Europeans. Simply put, yu' kin' say I'm German an' I'm from Germany, an Afrikan' might respond by sayin' I'm Mandingo from dah' Mandingo tribe 'long dah' upper Niger. He very likely would not be able to acknowledge dah' name of his country. He may not even know dah' country or tribe he originally was from, especially if he was taken from his mother, which happens frequently in dah' South. Families bein' broken up an' sold wit' little or no regard of their feelins'. Gentlemen, would it not break all of yur' hearts to see a mother an' child torn from one another an' each sold separately at a slave auction? In fact if yu' asked slaves what dah' most feared thin' was dat' could happen to 'dem, it would have to be bein' sold an' separated from thar' family. Dis' is dah' answer dat' I personally have always heard."

Mr. Martin interrupted, "I admit that here up North we fail to give much thought to what could be the dark side of slavery. I do find what you are saying more than troubling."

Reggie was not quite through. "That is true Mr. Martin—a big dark side does exist. Now let me just finish what I was saying. For a black man, his primary pride is his tribe an' not his country. I don't want to be repetitious, but in general, white people have a difficult time understandin' an' acceptin' dis' cultural difference an' I fear it will continue to create problems fo' dah' colored people in dah' future. It will make it more difficult to assimililate into dah' white culture. A little black child may ask, why can't I be like dah' white people an' say I'm German, or English? I have to say I'm Afrikan', which identifies to a large continent, not a single country like Germany or England. Again, even his tribal identification has been lost in time. Let's put it another way, would yu' hyeh' a German child say he is European? Of course not—he's German! Now, can't yu' see dah' confusion?"

Mr. Martin commented. "Mr. Marshall your perspective on this matter is very deep and inciteful. I do like the way that you have successfully explained the plight of the slaves."

Mr. Martin's comments made Reggie feel good, but he still had more to say. "Getting' back to dah' slave codes, break dah' law an' legally be prepared to be punished wit' a whip or some other form of corporal punishment dat' could be 'bery severe an' even death. Gentlemen, thar' is so much more I've seen an' heard 'bout—dah' word 'cruel' isn't good 'nough to cover all of dah' inhumanities bestowed on dah' slaves. It's absolutely appallin' an' cold blooded at dah' very least."

Reggie paused and then added, "Personally, I pride myself in bein' objective an' avoidin' takin' a side on issues while understandin' dat' 'thar are always two sides to a coin'. However, in dis' case I clearly take a position—our system of bondage in our country is inherently cruel an' violates God's laws dealing wit' compassion, love, an' moral rights fo' mankind."

Mr. Johnson, who had intently been listening, agreed. "All this talk about slavery does sound pretty harsh to me—in fact, downright cruel. I must admit that I never knew too much about these slave codes. They appear to be legal methods to empower an evil system to continue.

Reggie couldn't resist adding another point to what Mr. Johnson stated. "Mr. Johnson, I admire yur' insightfulness. However, I have to add jus' one more thin', which incidently is not spelled out in dah' slave codes. Could referin' to a human bein' as a fine pet or creature be cruel? Simply put, jus' whar' does cruelty begin an' whar' does it end! I believe the dictionary defines cruel as inflictin' sufferin'. Could dis' not be handin' out mental sufferin'? Think 'bout dah' little ole' white woman in dah' South who truly believes she is so kind an' gentle to her fine creatures or pets as she calls 'dem, an' of course she would never lay a hand on 'dem. Is somethin' wrong wit' dat' thought? Let's put it dis' way. How would any of yu' gentlemen like to be somebody's creature or pet? I bet not! Finally, would Jesus Christ refer to feller' humans as fine creatures or pets? Now if yu' foller' dah' teachin' of our Father, thar' is no way yu' kin' justify dat' line of reasonin', an' I'll leave it at dat'."

Mr. Martin realizing that he was losing the argument, switched to another topic. "If slaves were freed as you would suggest, then wouldn't we have a devil of a time in the North? We would have an onslaught of darkies pouring in and taking away jobs that would drive wages down. It could create a high unemployment rate along with economy spiraling out of control, and consequently create another depression. Incidentally, I already knew as you yourself stated that wages presently in the South are on average one-third less than in the North due to slave labor holding down wages. So I am not simply stating this based on opinion but facts. Remember, we just got over the crash of 1837!"

"I understand yur' point 'bout dah' onslaught of darkies dat' would pour into dah' North takin' jobs 'way while drivin' wages down, however thar's' some mischief to dat' premise, Mr. Martin," Reggie had more he wanted to add. "In 1787 eighteen men sat in a little room on Wall Street an' drafted dah' Northwest Ordinance. Much credit has been given to 'dem since dey' prohibited slavery in dah' Northwest Territory. Dat' said, dey' deserve to be congratulated fo' thar' decision; however, thar' is a caveat to dis' decision. We would like to think dah' determination fo' dis' conclusion represents a humane offer 'gainst dah' institution of slavery an' a clear effort to keep it banished from dah' Northwest Territory fo' humanitarian reasons. Unfortunately, dah' debil' lies in dah' details."

Reggie paused to see if the three men were still interested in what he was saying, and then went on, "Abundant evidence exists dat' indicates dah' primary motivation was more economic an' less humanitarian. An', Mr. Martin, din', yur' assessment of dah' problem is correct—dah' fear of takin' away jobs an' drivin' down wages was dah' primary motivation to keep slavery out of dah' Northwest Territory, which in addition reflected public sentiment. Had anybody thought of jus' makin' all dah' Negroes free so dey' kin' compete at a 'wage labor' in dah' absence of 'slave labor'? Dah' truth be known, today black people in dah' North work fo' far less din' white people, an' mostly doin' odd jobs dat' dah' white people don't want."

Before anyone else spoke, Reggie added, "Gentlemen, allow me to make one last point dat' needs mentionin'. Do you all 'member dah' Missoura' Compromise of 1820, which solved a dilemma? Maine wanted to be admitted into statehood an' dah' South said wait a minute, dat' would tip dah' advantage to dah' North by havin' more free states din' slave states, puttin' dah' South in dah' minority in Congress. Well, fortunately fo' dah' South, 'long came Missoura', which already had slaves mainly in dah' southern part of dah' state, so dey' petitioned fo' statehood as a slave state to keep dah' balance. It has worked temporarily, an' hyeh' we are in 1841, puttin' off a potential problem dat' could blow up in our faces by not dealin' wit' dah' full ramifications of extendin' slavery or not extendin' slavery further west, knowin' a resolution will not come easy.

"I feel like I'm getting a history lesson. That said, you might have a good point—actually, you have made quite a few good points on this matter." Sanders raised his glass as he spoke, indicating that the information Reggie presented was quite good and thought provoking and then continued. "So Reggie, what do you see for our future?"

"Gentlemen, it's goin' to git' dirty, real dirty! Dah' North will stay disillusioned into believin' in 'out of sight is out of mind'—keepin' dah' messy business of slavery confined to dah' South. In addition, ovah' dah' long haul dey' will continue to 'lieve slavery will jus' miraculously go 'way like it always has in dah' past throughout dah' history of mankind. I should preface dat' by mentionin' dat' Haiti was an exception. In a fight fo' independence dey' successfully drove out dah' French an' ended slavery. Meanwhile, in dah' South dey' will be goin' full speed ahead wit' an increase in dah' slave population due to dah' demand fo' an increase in dah' production of cotton. Now hyeh' lies dah' mischief!" Reggie's face suddenly demonstrated an even more concerned look as he continued, "Dah' South, wit' its bravado an' need to stay equal wit' dah' North will want to maintain a balance of power in Congress in order to remain equal in strength. Dah' problem fo' dah' South will be findin' more potential slave states—presently dey' are runnin' out—now what? We already know, based on dah' prohibition of slavery in dah' Northwest Territory, future states not involved in growin' cotton in all likelihood will also not accept slavery. Simply put, westward expansion will eventually dictate dah' South's representation in Congress will become dat' of a minority, an' dat' will not set well wit' dah' South."

Mr. Johnson demonstrated interest toward Reggie's statement and said, "I feel I am pretty well read and yet I have to admit that probably not enough has been written on this subject.

That being the case, I am curious Mr. Marshall, how do you see this problem being resolved?"

"Mr. Johnson, while I hesitate to give yu' my opinion or assessment, I think yu' will all wanta' hyeh' it. The question of dah' extension of slavery will unfortunately be solved in dah' most horrific way. Westward expansion represents 'dah' fuse, which will ignite dis' powder keg' ovah' slavery, leadin' our country, I 'lieve into a horrible civil war." Reggie showed displeasure with his own words.

Mr. Johnson threw his hands up in the air as he responded. "Mr. Marshall, I think the comment you just made represents an outrageous assessment. Our country is too smart for a civil war. Two things have to be considered. First, we are not a small, weak country—you are talking about the United States! Secondly, slavery will die a slow, peaceful death like it always has previously throughout the world with perhaps Haiti being the exception as you stated. All you've done is 'go out on a limb' with your crazy observations. Now, what do you have to say?

Reggie quickly reacted, "Mr. Johnson, I have to make two observations. First, yu' mentioned Haiti. Led by Toussaint l' Overture in 1804, dah' largest an' most successful slave rebellion in dah' world took place wit' dah' Haitians proclaimin' thar' independence from France. Dis' is 'bery relevant since dah' Southerners like to bring up dah' Nat Turner rebellion an' often times, Haiti as examples of why day' have to be vigilant 'gainst a slave insurrection in thar' dear ole' South. It jus' fits into thar' paranoia."

"More important, I want to share a powerful, lifelike visionary dream dat' came to me while watchin' Halley's Comet. What I saw was a tall man dressed in all black, who appeared to be dah' President of dah' United States, deliverin' a speech consecratin' dah' grounds of a cemetery created from a terrible battle dat' had been fought 'tween dah' North an' South. Dis' civil war was won by dah' North, an' as a result of dah' defeat of dah' South, slavery ended in dah' United States. I'm speculatin', but probably dah' South did not git' any compensation fo' losin' thar'

446

slaves. As awful as dis' may sound, it's goin' to happen in dah' near future unless we take steps to prevent it."

Mr. Sanders couldn't believe what he was hearing. "Wait a minute, Mr. Marshall, now you are talking loony! I thought you were a level-headed young man, but now you have me thinking you were dealt a few cards too short. You are talking like one of those crazy abolitionists, and they are dangerous people who advocate a violent end to slavery. They want to destroy the very fabric of democracy with their violence for their own perceived benefit. It simply makes me shudder. Is this what you want?"

Reggie stated his position on violence. "I do not advocate violence of any kind. I would first say dat' a clear distrust exists 'tween dah' North an' dah' South an' dis' distrust has continued to exacerbate relations 'tween dah' two. Somehow dey' are goin' to have to establish a positive dialogue based on compromise.

Mr. Sanders in the spirit of discussion, stated, "Compromise, I think the North has already met the South halfway. What else can we do?" It was apparent that Mr. Sanders was interested in hearing Reggie's rebuttal.

"Good question Mr. Sanders. Let's first examine what dah' South calls dah' 'tariff of abominations'. We all know dat' dah' purpose of dah' tariff is to protect Northern manufacturin' from imports undercuttin' 'dem. In order to compete wit' dah' added competition, dey' have to lower thar' prices, which means less profit! True, dah' tariff has been modified to placate dah' South, but obviously not eliminated. Meanwhile, dah' South, even wit' dah' modification will continue to have to face a stiff tariff on thar' exported cotton as retribution to git' back at us fo' our tariff imposed on countries importin' goods to dah' United States. To summarize, dah' South rightfully so, looks at dah' 'tariff of abominations' as a 'monkey on thar' back' dat' needs to be completely eliminated."

Mr. Sanders had a retort, "Mr. Marshall, you raise an excellent case, but it may not be easy to find a compromise on this problem. Besides, the North did lower the tariff, now wouldn't that be a fair compromise?"

"Mr. Sanders, anyway yu' cut it, dah' South is payin' a

higher import tax on thar' exported cotton an' gittin' absolutely nothin' back," Reggie quickly responded.

Reggie had more to add. "Gentlemen, I need to tell yu' 'bout one other big problem dat' troubles dah' South. Jus' to fully understand the Southern position, dey' look at dah' abolitionists comin' down South as major troublemakers. The question dey' ask is why dah' North doesn't tackle thar' own problems wit' thar' own black people? Besides, yu' don't see Southerners comin' up North tryin' to stir up trouble. Gentlemen, I'm not sayin' dat' I agree wit' dah' South on dis' particular issue, but I certainly see whar' dey' are comin from."

It was becoming apparent that an easy solution was not at hand on these issues. Mr. Sanders, made a conciliatory statement, "Perhaps, only time will solve these problems, and I guess we will just have to leave it at that."

Reggie couldn't restrain himself. "Lets put dah' tariff issue off fo' dah' future 'long wit' all dah' problems associated wit' slavery. I jus' wonder what dah' future kin' provide solvin' des' serious problems dat' we can't solve now?"

Mr. Johnson, who was intently listening to Reggie added, "I must admit that I never looked at how the South might see these issues. It is rather interesting. So what is your summary?"

Reggie quickly retorted, "Simply put, dah' problem of slavery has to be solved wit'out' fightin' a war. All signs should point to manumission. Dah' freein' of dah' slaves would have to include both sides makin' concessions resultin' in givin' some serious type of compensation to dah' slave owners. I also believe future states not involved in cotton production would be more acceptin' to havin' free blacks din' slaves in thar' state. All dis' would remove dah' problem of dah' extension of slavery since slavery would be eliminated. Dis' in turn would take 'way dah' most direct cause of dah' impendin' civil war in dah' United States. We all know how difficult it could be since nobody likes to give ground, but it sure sounds better to me din' dah' alternative—civil war. Gentlemen, dat' would be my plan of action."

Mr. Johnson quickly responded, "That was well said and

certainly would deserve to be examined. I like your idea that both sides have to give in and make concessions, but giving compensation to slave owners for releasing their slaves would mean that almost all the money would have to come from the North for the compensation. I just don't think many Northerners would support ponying up the funds. Besides, I personally believe the South is as stubborn as a mule and wouldn't go along with any compromise, even with jus' compensation for their slaves."

"Mr. Johnson, trust me when I say dis'. We better start 'dah' ball rollin' now' in dah' spirit of compromise or face a future wit' a horrific war—'brother against brother'," Reggie emphatically stated.

Mr. Johnson smiled, realizing Reggie made a very good point. "I see what you mean. We do take a position based on our own side without allowing for what the other side might see."

Reggie succinctly stated, "Gentlemen what I really see is a Southern mule tied to a rope dat' is tied to a Northern mule an' both mules are pullin' 'gainst each other an' gittin' nowhar' wit' one mule pullin' South an' one mule pullin' North. I'm jus' gonna pray dat' somebody kin' come 'long an' redirect dose' two mules to walk together right down dah' middle whar' dey' kin come to an 'greement. If we don't have a compromise din' a terrible war is on dah' horizon, which will occur to solve dis' dilemma an' dah' South will have thar' honor shoved right down thar' throats by dah' North who will have all dah' military an' economic advantages to win dah' war. An' I dare say, dis' will only make future relations 'tween dah' South an' dah' North 'bery difficult. Dah' South will continue to more din' jus' resent dah' North fo' forcin' thar' will upon 'dem. 'Member, dis' is dah' South wit' all thar' states rights, honor, an' manliness."

"Mister, we respect your opinion, but we don't agree," Mr. Johnson interjected.

Reggie added, "I'm not goin' to beleaguer dah' point. Jus' 'member someday yu' kin' tell people dat' yu' met a man who warned all three of y'all 'bout a comin' war an' how it could have been prevented. Incidentally, earlier I took an absolute positon dat' slavery was inherently cruel, now I'm takin' a second absolute position an' warnin' yu' dat' a war 'tween dah' North an' dah' South is in dah' cards. These are two definite positions I take 'cuz' I adamantly believe dey' are true. We are destined fo' a civil war if we don't compromise on our differences." After Reggie said this, he mused to himself that he had more than vented his anger, repeating himself, and perhaps with a little too much bravado, but he hoped at least they would recognize his sincerity. After all the word compromise was never spared in his position.

Mr. Johnson responded, "Now Mr. Marshall you are sounding rather blustery, but only time will tell, but I am sure you will be proven to be wrong."

"Gentlemen, I have truly enjoyed yur' company an' our thought provokin' conversation, but I think it's time fo' me to retire." Reggie shook hands with each of the men and departed to his room. As he climbed the stairs of the inn he thought about the conversation, feeling he had fallen short to convince them of the impending danger the country faced. He sensed that of the three, Mr. Sanders who at first appeared to be the most argumentative, turned out to be the most open minded, especially regarding the slave codes. He seemed to understand them more objectively than the other two gentlemen. Also, Mr. Johnson did appear to understand how difficult a compromise would be between the North and the South.

As he entered his room his thoughts ran the gamut. He was deeply concerned that he had to do a better job of convincing people of an impending civil war that weighed so heavy on his conscience.

CHAPTER TWENTY-SEVEN

Reggie's sales numbers continued to climb, motivated mainly by his passion to succeed. In addition, the challenge was exciting, and of course he wanted to ensure Mr. Clark that he had made a good decision in hiring him. He was always aware that Mr. Clark had high expectations, and he knew he would not want to disappoint him.

Only annoying problems arose for Reggie in his life. Sarah's brother, Lucas, persisted to have reservations about him and in conversation continued to make sarcastic comments. He liked to open discussions at dinner trying to "bait" Reggie into saying something he would later regret. Reggie had become use to this ploy, which forced him to carefully measure his words when talking to Lucas. In Reggie's mind, and rightfully so, the stakes were very high, which meant he could not afford to fall into a trap that Lucas might set that could imperil his relations with the Clark's.

At dinner one evening, Lucas purposely drew Reggie into an uncomfortable position when he asked, "Reggie, now that you are devoting your time and energies to your success as a salesman, have you completely disengaged yourself from the black community? In fact, do you support any Negro causes?"

This was a subject Reggie had purposely avoided, knowing that outside of Sarah, the Clark family embraced the widely held belief that slavery would eventually and quietly die a slow death. He feared that his true convictions could potentially cause problems with his relationship with the Clark family. Tactfully, he replied, "Lucas, under dah' circumstances of my background, I should, an' I do have a lot of sympathy fo' black people."

Lucas continued his questioning. "Just how far or how deep does your sympathy for black people go? I am curious. Let me put it this way—have you ever considered 'crossing over' and embracing the white community and disavowing your background?"

"Dat's a good question, but I honestly 'lieve dat' yu' cannot disavow yur' past even if yu' wanted to. I wouldn't 'cuz' dah' past is an important part of me." Reggie answered with conviction.

"Reggie, I have to give you credit for coming up with a good answer," Lucas responded.

Mr. and Mrs. Clark along with Sarah listened intently to Reggie's answer. If he "crossed over" and disavowed his roots they might think he was transparent and lacking loyalty. On the other hand, if he demonstrated sympathy toward the abolitionist movement, they might think he was a radical. It appeared as another "Hobson's choice"—a choice without a choice, exactly the position he did not want to be in but seemed to arise more frequently then he wished when talking to Lucas.

Sarah often wondered if Lucas was jealous of Reggie in some way as he continued to try and trip up Reggie in conversation. "Can you explain to me your position on the abolitionist movement? Wouldn't all slaves be in support of the movement since they are trying to secure their freedom?"

Reggie knew that Lucas had been leading up to this question. It was a clear attempt to put him in a corner. "Lucas, yu' ask a good question dat' requires an answer dat' hovers in dah' middle. I understand dah' movement, but I could only 'cept an 'bolitionist movement dat' decries any form of violence. When Nat Turner an' his followers killed 55 innocent white people in an attempt to foment a slave insurrection, dah' paranoia dah' South harbored toward a slave insurrection was dramatically intensified. In addition, in retaliation ovah' 100 slaves were killed as well, follerin' dah' attack. Furthermore, I strongly 'lieved at dat' time dat' it would significantly fracture relations 'tween dah' North an' dah' South as many Southerners believed dah' revolt was inspired by the North, which only created much more tension."

Lucas, confident of his position, pushed Reggie further. "If you support a nonviolent abolitionist movement, than you are saying that slavery should be peacefully abolished. You can't have it both ways—either you want slavery abolished peacefully or you don't. Which is it?"

Reggie was displeased with this line of questioning, but he knew that he had to provide an answer that would not upset the Clark's while maintaining his own honor at the same time. "Lucas, yu' ask a 'bery insightful question dat' I feel I'm qualified to answer." Reggie answered with a sly smile to let Lucas know he wasn't going to be "pulling the wool over his eyes". "Slavery itself is inhumane; however, we cannot simply extirpate slavery wit' one swift axe. It would have to be done sequentially so as to not catapult us into a terrible recession. It would have to involve dose' Negroes who want to optionally go back to Africa. Regardin' dah' slave owners, dey' would have to be remunerated fo' thar' losses. Dat' would represent a very fair conciliation."

Lucas was suddenly taken aback and at a loss for words. He could comment no further because he failed to quite understand the answer. Rather than admit this, he preferred to maintain his pride. "I really can't criticize your answer. Let's just say it makes sense to you and impresses me to some degree. Let's talk about something else. I know that you are quite a salesman. Reggie, how do you like being in sales?" It was clear to Lucas that he was engaged in a discussion with a highly intelligent man who could more than hold his own, and it might be wise to change the subject.

Reggie was relieved that Lucas had decided to give up his attempts to make him look bad and was more than anxious to discuss his work record. "I feel privileged to have yu' as a supervisior an' to work fo' yur' father an' an' be a loyal worker fo' Clark Manufacturing, an' I will continue to show my gratitude wit' my excellent sales production an' service to our clients." As a slave, Reggie had learned a long time ago the art of being tactful and above all—humble. In addition in this particular discussion he might have said some things he truly did not believe, but the purpose of what he said was to move the conversation into a "lighter side", and he had succeeded in that effort. Once again, his wit served him quite well. He would be quick to note that the "pen is mightier than the sword",

Mr. Clark recognized that Reggie had successfully held up to his son's barrage of questions and was satisfied that the discussion ended amicably. He smiled warmly at both of them.

After Reggie successfully outmaneuvered Lucas, he mused to himself about his potential capture when confronted outside of Richmond by the two men who swore they knew him. Using the words *déjà vu* worked, as it threw the two men into confusion. The ploy was successful and Reggie was able to continue his journey. His limited command of the French language served him well in being able to finesse himself out of a difficult situation. Now, employing his broad vocabulary he was successful in getting out of another potential problem.

Mr. Clark had another reason to smile, as he had some excellent news to share with Reggie. "Mr. Joseph, my attorney, contacted me yesterday. The paperwork to secure your freedom, as well as Anastasia's is ready, and I can assure you that we are close to announcing freedom for both of you." He could see that Reggie was exhilarated to learn of this as he turned to his wife and daughter and winked.

Reggie's heart leapt. These were the words that he had so desperately wanted to hear through all of the suffering he had been through.

"You are very fortunate," Mr. Clark went on to explain. "Colonel Marshall hired Anastasia out to a Mrs. Winters who resides in Richmond. She is very fond of her and has her best interests at heart, which will make the negotiations for her freedom much easier. As a gift to the two of you, I will pay for Anastasia's passage from Norfolk, Virginia, to Boston. You will only have to pay for the papers of manumission. It couldn't get much better than that. You are so fortunate that Anastasia had not been sold further down south where she most likely would have disappeared into thin air. Sometimes I think Reggie that you were born in a field of four leaf clovers."

A tremendous weight had been lifted from Reggie's shoulders. His precious Anastasia was safe, and she would be with him soon! "Mr. Clark, I'm nearly speechless ovah' dah' good news, I was so 'fraid dat' yu' wouldn't be able to find her or worse yet, yu' found out she was dead." While always thinking positive about locating Anastasia, he also knew the odds had always been much greater that he would never find her. Yet, he always held out that she was in God's hands, and he maintained hope that He would protect her until somehow they could be reunited. Reggie considered that maybe Mr. Clark was correct in his assessment that he is lucky.

"Understandably so," Clark replied. "Reggie, remember, you deserve the great news you are getting—you've earned it. I'm pleased to be the one to deliver it. Incidentally, Reggie as I just told you regarding your situation, I haven't heard anything, but I remain confident that some good news is forthcoming."

Eyes watering and voice trembling, Reggie stood up. "What yu' have done fo' me an' Anastasia is far more din' I could even comprehend. I know, Mr. Clark yu' an' yur' family will receive a high reward from dah' Lawd' someday fo' yur' kindness."

Mr. Clark stood up, and as he did, Reggie walked over to him and gave him a hug. He thanked him profusely for all he had done. "Stop, that's' enough, Reggie. The only thanks I need right now would be you playing the piano for us. You've been practicing since you've been here, and we'd love to hear you."

"I'd be happy to entertain all of yu', as I am in such a great mood."

The family followed Reggie into the parlor where he quickly positioned himself at the keyboard. Having first learned to play the harpsichord at Oak Manor with Albert when they were young, the Viennese piano proved to be quite comfortable for him. He began with a soft, gentle tune, and could see from the corner of his eye the Clarks smiling while Mrs. Clark was nodding to her husband.

As he played, his thoughts drifted to his beloved about their broomstick wedding and their attempt to flee Oak Manor. In addition, he mused about being cheated out of so much after they were apprehended. Soon new plans could be made, hopefully for an exciting and bright future—in Boston with Anastasia, where they would be free.

Throughout the performance Reggie avoided playing the classics, instead, staying with light music fearing they might think he was showing off. It was a legacy of the bondage system to always remain humble and subservient to white people and it always persisted to "dog him" even when now safe. Reggie had been taught as a slave to never appear to know more than white people when dealing with matters such as formally playing the piano, which only rarely slaves would ever be given access to.

One by one everybody related how much they enjoyed the evening—thanked Reggie for playing the piano and retired for the evening. Sarah remained and he turned to her. "Sarah thank yu' fo' stayin' so long, an' thank yu' fo' bein' such a dear friend. I do have one other favor to ask of yu' before Anastasia arrives."

"Anything, Reggie," Sarah responded.

"I know it will be proper fo' me an' Anastasia to have our own home. Do yu' think yu' would have time to help me locate a home suitable fo' dah' two of us? Yu' have a good knowledge of Boston, an' I know so little 'bout dah' city an' gittin' settled in a home."

Sarah smiled. "Of course, Reggie, I'd be happy to help you find a home."

"Thank yu' so much Sarah. I'll be eternally grateful."

The two of them talked a while longer and made plans to begin their search the very next day.

***

Upon Sarah's recommendation, Sarah and Reggie spent

several days canvassing an area called the South End one she felt had nice quality rentals at reasonable prices.

Reggie was looking for two levels in his new residence along with an accompanying front and back yard. In addition, Freedom necessitated having a fair sized barn and a small paddock. Reggie believed he should provide nothing but the best for his beloved Freedom. They continued to look at homes and finally located a two-story brick structure on Pearl Street, which they both found appealing. The minute they walked through the front door, Reggie knew Anastasia would love it. The foyer had a stairwell to the upper floor bedroom with a spacious sitting room. The kitchen downstairs looked out over the small yard. Regarding the welfare of Freedom, a good sized barn and a small paddock were nestled in the rear under some large shade trees. It represented a dream home for Reggie, and he knew that Anastasia would share his passion.

Sarah encouraged him to put a deposit down immediately knowing that he wanted it. She knew this town home wouldn't be on the market very long.

He quickly acted, and put down a deposit to hold the home. He knew it was a stroke of good luck to find a town home of this quality at such a reasonable price. It was more than he and Anastasia could ever hope for to start their new life together. Meanwhile, their landlord was very cooperative, allowing them to take possession of the property in two weeks.

After such a wonderful turn of events, Sarah and Reggie rode back to the Clark's, eager to share their exciting news with everyone.

***

Mr. Clark learned from his attorney that Reggie's "broomstick bride" should arrive in Boston in the next two to three weeks. He gave Reggie a rather light work schedule, which afforded him the time to spend shopping with Sarah for some furniture and all the other accessories necessary to properly outfit the home before Anastasia arrived.

When not shopping or not on the road, Reggie spent time maintaining his paperwork related to his job while still allowing down time for playing the piano and reading the classic books in the Clark library. He was anxious to resume his regular work schedule, but he certainly enjoyed the time off to prepare for Anastasia.

As the days passed, he was able to maintain his positive spirit, although he was very concerned about Anastasia's impending voyage at sea. He didn't like the idea of her traveling by herself. He also felt guilty when he thought about his two friends—Joseph and Willy, who had been left behind and most likely, were still living in the maroon colony in the marsh. Hopefully, they wouldn't get restless and venture out of the swamp and into harms way. He knew that time was of the essence, if Captain Riley captured them, it would likely mean death. The sooner Reggie could secure his friend's freedom, the better off they would be. While reuniting with his bride was of paramount importance, his deep concerns regarding Joseph and Willy greatly troubled him.

As Reggie had already purchased much of the furniture and accessories he and Anastasia would need, he resumed his regular work schedule realizing he would need more funds to pay for the impending attorney fees. Reggie was excited to tackle the challenges that would lie ahead.

After careful thought Reggie made the decision to defer moving into the town home on Pearl Street until Anastasia arrived since the Clarks graciously allowed him to stay as their guest. He knew he would not feel comfortable living in the town house without Anastasia's presence.

***

One late afternoon, as Mr. Clark and Lucas returned home from work, Mr. Clark called to Reggie when he walked through the front door. As Reggie came down the stairway to see why he was paged, Mr. Clark announced with a broad smile on his face, "Your wife is on a steamship and will soon arrive in Boston. Papers were signed by Mrs. Winters, who, incidentally, required only $700.00. You well know this is a pittance to the amount Anastasia could have brought at auction. Most importantly, she will be with you very soon, my friend. Congratulations!"

Reggie was numb with joy, "Oh my Lawd', everythin' is happenin' so fast!" He grabbed Lucas, who was completely caught off guard and danced around the front entry hall with him as Lucas blushed red. Reggie was unable to contain the emotions that he had stored up inside for so long. It truly represented the most exuberant news he had ever received in his life.

"I'm so happy for you and Anastasia," Sarah exclaimed when she saw what was taking place. "You have become my best friend, and I'm so pleased to see you this elated! My father has given you a wonderful opportunity, but I want you to know you have been a fabulous employee for my father as well. Be proud and remember, whatever has come your way, you've earned it."

In tears, Reggie responded, "Sarah, I place yu' an' yur' family equal wit' Anastasia, Joseph, Willy, Albert an' Mammy Bertha as equals to my best friends on dis' earth."

"Reggie, do you know what you just said? You have successfully stripped us of all our material wealth and placed us as equals to your friends who are all enslaved excepting of course Albert. I must admit that most people would think you insulted us with your comment, but I know in God's eyes you brought us up." Sarah paused briefly to look at her family and then she turned back to Reggie. "I have never known anyone I would call a true egalitarian until you came along. Anastasia has been in bondage all her life; Joseph and Willy are dirt poor, downtrodden slaves; and Mammy Bertha, is a slave as well; yet, even today when your lot in life has socially risen, they still remain your best friends who you so humbly respect as your equals. Of course your half brother, Albert, who was your best friend growing up and sympathetic to the slaves, will always harbor a tremendous amount of love and respect from you. When someone seeks the meaning of Christianity, they'd better come to your door. Again, I have heard all about the trials and tribulations you went through and especially those with Joseph, Willy and Anastasia and now for you to feel that we are their equal. I consider that as something I will always cherish." The intensity level of Sarah's words continued to grow. "Reggie, you have positively impacted my way of seeing life. I can't speak for my family, but I personally never ever thought I would feel this way. Why can't more people understand that spiritual wealth is far more important than material wealth? I now realize that spiritual wealth makes me feel so warm and satisfying, and helping others in need would be a good example of sharing spiritual wealth. Certainly, gold represents a commodity that one might covet and feel secure with, but in the end, can I really feel all the warmth and satisfaction from coveting gold that I can get from helping others? Oh, I well know there are those who would laugh at that statement and I further presume that could be the problem—coveting money and power." Tears welled up in the corners of her eyes as she gazed at Reggie, still harboring deep, respectful affections for him.

Reggie deeply understood and appreciated what Sarah had said. "Indeed, yu' should feel pleased wit' yurself' to feel dis' way since dis' exemplifies dah' embodiment of dah teachins' of Jesus Christ—having compassion, love, an' grace. Sarah, I want yu' to know dat' I have so much love an' respect fo' yu'—I honestly feel yu' are walkin' in dah' kingdom of dah' Lawd'. Yes Sarah, spritiual values will always triumph ovah' material values. This deals wit' one of dah' greatest sins dat' mankind has to deal wit'— avarice, an' unfortunately, mankind is on course to continue to covet greed, money, an' power while spiritual values for so many will only remain in dah' background. How complicated kin' it be, askin' fo' fo'giveness while givin' yurself' to dah' Lawd'? 'Nough of dat' Sarah, but sometimes I jus' can't help myself."

"Reggie, thank you so much for helping me see the light of Christ in myself," Sarah humbly replied.

"Sarah, assignin' dah' word egalitarian to me is very gracious of yu' an' I thank yu'. I try so hard to look at people devoid of color, money or status. Instead, I look to see what is in thar' heart, an' Anastasia, Joseph, Willy, Albert, an' Mammy Bertha all embody dose' spiritual values dat' I respect. I do apologize for being so emotional in front of yur' family, but I jus' can't help it. Knowin' I have a friend like yu' who truly understands how I feel 'bout Christ is truly overwhelmin'." As he talked, Reggie felt truly overwhelmed.

Mrs. Clark stood up and walked toward Reggie. "Having you here in our home has been an inspiration. Not only have you been very successful as a salesman for the company, but more importantly, you have also gained a very special place in all our hearts as a salesman with another very special talent—helping us to see the importance of spiritual values over material things. Reggie, I share my daughter's sentiments that, as an individual, your life is exemplary of what all of us should strive for. Do you realize how much you have taught our family? I must admit I have enjoyed our material wealth, but you have provided us with something more important that we must realize—spiritual values do outweigh money. And I want you to know, I never thought I would ever say that!"

Lucas took a sip of water to clear his throat and spoke. "I must concur, and I do apologize for my reserved behavior earlier toward you. Hearing all these accolades accorded to you makes me want to join in with further congratulations. You helped me better understand that all men are created equal. I salute you because I know you did not purposely want to affect our family's attitude on life—it manifested itself through your own actions, which is a reflection on who you really are. I have often heard that actions speak louder than words, and you are a living example, and I thank you. In addition, I must admit that you could be a master of elocution." He said the last sentence with a smile.

"As your mother, I can hardly believe my ears. I am so happy to hear you talk like this, Lucas. I never knew if it was in you to fully understand the meaning of compassion. I am so proud of you." Mrs. Clark radiated such a warm smile as she spoke to her son.

Reggie was clearly embarrassed by all the attention and plaudits. He pondered that his life was dramatically changing in

461

such a short time. How could he, a simple slave have swayed this wealthy family to realize that spiritual values are more important in their lives? Now he knew that the Lord had granted him the power to minister to others, and that would remain his calling through life, and it was being played out, right here at the Clark household.

"It is genuinely nice to hear my family talk like this," Mr. Clark added. "They are correct. We need to be reminded of our Christian values—compassion, understanding, grace and love. For such a young man, you do have a way of touching the hearts of people. Now, not to change the subject but Reggie, Sarah reminded me that you also enjoy playing classical music on the piano, and we'd love to have you perform for us after dinner. Besides, I have heard from time to time, classical music played on our piano—I just never quite understood who could be playing classical music in our house and then it dawned on me that it was only my imagination." Mr. Clark then smiled and winked at Reggie.

Through the entire meal, it was obvious that everybody was looking forward to hearing Reggie play the piano. When everybody had finished, Mr. Clark led his family into the parlor.

Mrs. Clark requested that Reggie play Bach's Brandenburg concerto No. 3 G, which Reggie acknowledged as one of his personal favorites. She remained somewhat stunned that he knew her request.

The family marveled at Reggie's talents. Mr. Clark made a request for a Mozart piece as soon as Reggie completed the Bach concerto, which he performed effortlessly.

Mozart was Reggie's favorite composer, and he selected Mozart's Sonata in C Major first movement for the family. After a flawless performance, he continued with more of Bach and Mozart and concluded by playing Bach's Toccata and Fugue in D Minor.

He then asked to be excused, as he had an appointment in Waltham early the next day and had to get some much needed rest. Disappointed that Reggie was finished for the evening but thoroughly entertained, the Clarks bid Reggie a good night. Reggie assured them it would be a pleasure to play the piano again for them at any time in the future.

Mr. Clark found it amusing that Reggie put his work schedule ahead of playing the piano. He certainly could not question Reggie's drive to succeed on the job, as he was the boss. It did put Mr. Clark in a strange position. He found himself almost encouraging Reggie to place pleasure over work, certainly something that was out of the normal.

It took a long time for Reggie to fall asleep that evening as he tossed and turned. He found himself mulling over all the compliments given to him by the Clark family. Other than Anastasia, Joseph, Willy, Albert, and Mammy Bertha, no friendships had offered praise and encouragement like the Clark's. Raised in bondage, he was never provided with a family structure, which made it a little difficult to accept all the attention that had been accorded to him. Fortuitously, Colonel Marshall had put Reggie in a unique situation—helping with the education of his son Albert, both academically and socially. It was very rare for a slave to have had the broad experiences he had undergone and now he was able to reap the rewards of this unique combination of adventures, which provided him with being able to adjust to his new life.

CHAPTER TWENTY-EIGHT

When Reggie departed for his business trip the following morning, he left with the anticipation that Anastasia would be awaiting him when he returned home. Reggie's new life with his beloved Anastasia at his side was now imminent. He still would have to face the next three days of work knowing that he would be unable to keep Anastasia out of his mind. In his judgment, it would have to be the most difficult days he would ever have experienced on the job. His concerns for Anastasia were further compounded fearing that problems could arise at sea.

The first two days were very difficult while Anastasia dominated his mind. Naturally, the third day proved to be the most difficult of the three since he so desperately wanted to leave work early, but his work ethic required that above all else, he maintain his schedule. What felt like an eternity, the end of his third work day finally arrived, and he was able to quickly climb into his buggy to return home. Normally, he would have stayed at an inn overnight and left early the next morning, but he was too excited at the prospect of being reunited with his wife. Reggie reckoned, "'Come hell or high water', he was headed home".

He arrived at the Clark home around midnight and nervously took care of the horse and buggy. Reggie also took the time in the barn to pay his respects to Freedom, knowing that without Freedom this would never have been possible. This was a ritual he always observed. After saying farewell to Freedom, he went to the front door of the house where he eagerly anticipated seeing Anastasia. However, it was quiet throughout the house and no immediate sign of his beloved's presence. He went to his room to take a quick sponge bath knowing he would be tossing and turning all night thinking of Anastasia, and deeply disappointed that she was not there.

All Reggie could do was to lie in bed and look up at the ceiling and listen—hoping to hear anything or anyone stirring in the house. It was painfully quiet at the Clark house that night. She must not have arrived, but he still prayed that she would appear. He couldn't help but fear that something unexpected could have occurred, it was imperative that he keep the negative thoughts from overtaking him.

The silence was broken by what he thought was a slight tapping at the door. He thought it was just his mind playing tricks on him as it has from to time to time. But then, sitting upright in his bed, he heard the sound again and again and there it was again—a louder rapping at the door! Could it be? He wondered as he jumped out of bed and ran to the door. He anxiously started to open the door still believing that all of this was just his mind playing tricks on him, but then he flung the door wide open, and there, clad in a floor-length nightgown, stood his beautiful Anastasia—the love of his life. Reggie blinked his eyes a couple of times in utter disbelief, thinking it was only a miracle while gazing at her standing there and then swept her up into his arms while passionately kissing her, and pressing her as close to him as he could. He was so weak with joy, he almost passed out.

As they embraced, Reggie lifted her off her feet, and he swept her into the bedroom. He spun her around in his arms, pushing the door closed as he turned. He gently set her on the bed, and finally spoke, "Anastasia," he breathed, "I can't 'lieve yu' are hyeh'. I know dis' has to be jus' a dream. Oh Anastasia, I love yu' so much. My love, I've missed yu' every minute of every day."

"Reggie, my love, I love yu' wit' all my heart," she responded, gently stroking his hair. "I desperately prayed fo' dis' moment. I suffered fo' so long jus' thinkin' 'bout yu', wonderin' if yu' were still alive. I'm jus' tryin' to preserve dis' moment knowin' we are finally together."

Reggie held her at arm's length briefly so he could see the face of his angel. They then warmly embraced and intensely kissed, laughed and cried, and then finally gazed deeply into each other's eyes. "Is dis' really real or jus' a dream? I've had some pretty strong dreams in dah' past." Reggie wiped the tears from his eyes and pulled her close.

"No, my love," Anastasia whispered softly, "Dis' is not a dream. Dis' is real, an' it's only dah' beginnin' of our wonderful life together." Compassionately, she kissed him again and then said, "Love me tonight as yur' lovin' wife—I've missed yu' so much. Reggie, I love yu' wit' all my heart an' I want to feel yu' throughout me. I jus' do not want dis' night to ever end!"

As they continued to embrace each other, Anastasia went to remove his night shirt, and Reggie suddenly showed some resistance, displaying a grimace on his face. "Anastasia, I hate to show yu' my back. I was badly beaten by a tyrant who used a cat fo' his dirty work, havin' dah' cat claw up an' down my back, an' now it's horribly disfigured. My back will be like dis' way fo' dah' rest of my life. It's unfortunate but thar' is nothin' I kin' do 'bout it."

Anastasia with unconditional love unhesitatingly moved toward him and took his nightshirt off. She lovingly caressed and than gently kissed his back as he continued to fear her being repulsed looking at him. Anastasia looked at Reggie lovingly. "I will always be gentle to dah' man I most deeply love. I love yu' so much, an' of course it doesn't matter to me dat' yur' back is scarred. In fact yur' scars only make me respect an' love yu' even more. Yu'had to triumph over far more adversity din' I ever had to endure. But I know it could have been even worse. My love—yu' could have been killed, an' if dat' had happened, dey' may as well have killed me too."

"Anastasia, it means everythin' to know dat' yur' love is so real. Yu' are my first love an' yu' will be my last love. I have to be dah' luckiest man in dah' whole wide world to have somebody like yu'. Something else, yu' didn't exactly have a "bed or roses yur'self, but 'nough of dat'."

"Reggie," Anastasia breathed, "I want to feel yur' skin next to my body, come an' lay down beside me."

"Dis' is dah' most wonderful night of my life," Reggie sighed, gazing at Anastasia as she removed her nightgown. "An' jus' think, Anastasia, it doesn't ever have to stop. We will be together fo'ever now." As they lay in bed together in each other's arms, they passionately continued to fulfill each other's desires.

Their lovemaking continued until it reached a crescendo and then they fell back into peaceful exhaustion and total bliss, finally drifting off to sleep still holding one another.

The reunited couple awoke at dawn, making love and showering affection on one another. They had a lot of catching up to do, since they had last been with each other—spending the first days of their broomstick marriage on a honeymoon at the abandoned plantation while on the run. After being captured, they were then separated for the next several years.

Morning passions spent, they turned to each other to simply talk about everything but neither one knew where to begin as so much had happened during their time apart.

Before Anastasia and Reggie were able to make up for lost time together, it was time for breakfast. "We have been so busy wit' our lovemakin' dat' we lost sight of dah' time. Breakfast is bein' served in dah' parlor, an' I know dat' dah' family is jus' dyin' to talk to yu'. We should wash up an' join 'dem fo' a proper introduction, an' some breakfast." Reggie began to think that he was the practical one of the two since Anastasia showed no inclination of leaving their room. As much as he wanted to continue to make love, he was aware they had to come back down out of the clouds and deal with reality.

Anastasia quickly donned her nightgown and hustled out of his bedroom. Her clothes were in the room Sarah had made up for her the night before. It was notable that Mrs. Winters had provided her with nice clothing for the trip, and certainly not of Negro cloth.

Reggie called out, "When yu're ready, meet me at dah' top of dah' stairs," as he quickly washed up and put his clothes on and scurried after her. He was so excited at being with her and being able to formally present her to the family, he could hardly contain his composure.

They reunited at the top of the stairway, arm-in-arm, and nervously descended. Anastasia had arrived the night before and met everybody, but exclamations of surprise and glee still greeted the two as they found their seats at the dining table.

"Welcome, Anastasia, your husband has told us so much about you," Mrs. Clark bubbled with enthusiasm. "Massachusetts awaits you, and I know both of you will enjoy your new lives as 'Bostonians'."

Anastasia was overwhelmed with the warm welcome and thanked each of the Clark's repeatedly. "Mrs. Clark, Mr. Clark, Lucas an' Sarah, I know I said dis' last night when we met briefly but I can't say it 'nough—thank yu' fo' all yu' have done for me an' my Reggie. Wit'out all of yu' dis' would never have been possible. We owe so much to y'all. I know dat' we will never be able to pay yu' back fo' all yur' help an' generosity."

They all assured Anastasia that she and Reggie didn't owe them anything since Reggie was now a member of their family. Rising to become one of the top sales representatives for Clark Manufacturing was no small matter either. "Believe me," Mr. Clark beamed, "Reggie is showing his gratitude in so many ways, and even far beyond his excellent performance at Clark Manufacturing, all of us are simply so proud of him."

"Your husband has also managed to help reintroduce the meaning of compassion, understanding and Christian values in a way we have never experienced before," Mrs. Clark added. "We had all but forgotten our Christian values since we were far too wrapped up in our material possessions. Reggie has made an indelible mark on us. I have to say that I have a great deal of respect for the way he has gained strength and wisdom from his roots and has continued to build on this as he has found a new life in Boston. We thought that since he could pass for white, he would take on a new identity, but we were dead wrong. He's proud of his heritage, and you can be proud of him too, Anastasia."

"I'm not surprised to hear dis' 'bout my Reggie," Anastasia responded. "I've known all 'long dat' in dah' scheme of life, I married a man who has such respect fo' all dose' who have given him dah' love an' affection dat' he never had by not havin' a mother an' a father in his life."

"'Nough talkin' 'bout me," Reggie interrupted. "I want everyone to know how fortunate I am to have Anastasia as my wife. Through thick an' thin she did not fo'git' our love even though we hadn't heard from each other fo' several years. Dat' was quite an 'complishment on her part. An' 'lieve me, it was not easy fo' either one of us. Even though I was separated from her an' didn't know her location or situation, I always clung to hope. I knew dat' she held dah' same convictions as me. Reality kin' spring from hope, an' it was dah' hope dat' we both had dat' someday we would both be together dat' made it all happen. Of course Mr. Clark, yu' an' yur' family are directly responsible fo' makin' our hope a reality."

Sarah turned to Anastasia and said, "I remember, when I visited the Marshalls I saw you assisting Abigail, and I thought you looked out of place. Like Reggie, you had the features of a white person, and I also surmised that, like Reggie, you too were educated."

"Bein' dah' personal servant to Abigail proved a blessin' fo' me," Anastasia replied. "Abigail wanted me to be literate, an' she convinced her family dat' I be schooled 'long wit' her—similar to Reggie bein' educated 'long wit' Albert as to better serve him. Both of us were treated differently din' dah' other house servants 'cuz' of our color an' education, which put us in a rather unusual situation. To thar' friends dey' always refered to us as thar' display niggahs'."

Mrs. Clark chose not to further explore what Anatasia said and moved on to another question, which proved to be a little surprising—she was up-front and extremely candid. "Do you have any idea about your family background?"

Anastasia took a deep breath before she responded. It was just as well to get this awkward question over with right away. She thought to herself and then said, "Well, my background is somewhat similar to Reggie's." She looked over at Reggie, as it was obvious he was concerned about how she would answer.

"My father was a white slave owner an' my mother was his slave mistress." Anastasia paused before she continued, taking another breath. "My mother was a quadroon, which I'm sur' yu' already know, means she was one-fourth Negro. My father of course was all white, making me an octoroon, which simply means I'm one-eighth Negro." Those were the only details she provided.

Since her father was Colonel Marshall's brother and Colonel Marshall was Reggie's father, that meant she and Reggie were first cousins. In the South it was not uncommon for first cousins to marry, especially among the whites since plantation owners wished to keep property and wealth within the boundaries of family members. This liberal practice extended to the slaves as well. Of course she wisely with-held this information

Mrs. Clark seemed satisfied with her answer, and let it rest. "It's so nice that you and Reggie have similar backgrounds." As she spoke, both Anastasia and Reggie breathed a sigh of relief, as they knew their first-cousin bloodline might not be acceptable in the North. Reggie thought to himself that some things are left better unsaid.

"One last thing Anastasia, we were all fearful that you might have encountered some probems at sea being by yourself," Mrs. Clark added.

"I must admit dat' I first I was a bit nervous, but I could only think 'bout what I was leavin' 'hind an' whar' may future was headed so dah' voyage became a pleasure trip. In fact, I met a couple from Boston ''long dah' way, an' dey' provided me wit' some valuable company. Thar' names were Mr. an' Mrs. Robert Jamison. Dey' asked dat' I contact 'dem atter' I git' settled so we kin' all git' together. I have so much gratitude fo' thar' kindness. Also, dah' weather was fine an' we really didn't experience any problems."

Mr. Clark, who was beaming, stated, "We are so happy to hear that your trip proved to be problem free. We were all worried about you." Eventually, the pleasant conversation gave way to the demands of the day, and after extending another warm welcome to Anatasia, everyone went their separate ways.

With the free time to enjoy each other, Reggie was particularly excited about surprising her with their new home while showing her the sights of Boston. Reggie then said eagerly to Anastasia, "Well 'fore we let dah' rest of dah' day grow too long in dah' tooth, we'd better git' goin', thar's lots to see hyeh' in Boston, an' I'm jus' dah' one to show yu'!"

Anastasia had never been in a big city other than Richmond, and she reacted like a little girl as they rode the streets of Boston taking in all the sights, sounds, and movement of the city. She laughed, pointed and grabbed Reggie by the hand repeatedly in her excitement as they rounded the bend to Pearl Street. She gasped loudly. "Oh, Reggie, I love dah' quaintness of dis' neighborhood! Jus' look at all dah' lovely, well kept homes."

"I'm so pleased yu' like dis' street," Reggie said, pulling up to the front of their new town home, "'cuz' yu' are lookin' at our new home." He mused to himself that it was so rewarding that she would like the street that he had chosen earlier for their new residence and now, hopefully she would like the new home.

Anastasia was speechless, and she could barely wait for Reggie to help her out of the buggy. She ran through the gate and up the front steps onto the porch while he calmly and proudly walked behind her until he reached the front door, unlocked it and opened it for her.

"Wait! I want to carry my wife over dah' threshold of our new home." With that he picked her up and spun her around—a sweeping gesture that took Anastasia by surprise. In fact everything that day had taken her by surprise. Everything was so fresh and new, and she loved it!

When Reggie put her down, he barely had a chance to kiss her as she was off and running, beaming over all the furnishings and the rooms. They both laughed out loud as they scurried about, investigating each room and every corner in it.

"I absolutely love it!" she declared after her brief, joyous inspection. "Jus' think, Reggie, it's ours, all ours! Dis' jus' has to be a dream. We were enslaved, an' now we are free an' kin' live in dis' beautiful home whar' slavery doesn't exist! Nobody 'round hyeh' could ever understand what we are feelin', could dey'?"

"No, I don't think dey' could. In order to fully understand what we had to endure, yu' would almost have had to walk in our shoes."

"When kin' we move in?" Anastasia asked, eyes gleaming and sparkling with anticipation. At this time, she was not interested in dwelling on their past life since she was too excited about her future.

"Well," Reggie began with a little trepidation in his voice, "I'm still waitin' on my papers of manumission, but dey' are on dah' way. It keeps me on edge 'til I kin' actually see dah' formal papers an' hold 'dem in my hands."

"I'm not worried an' neither should yu'! You've got an excellent job an' wit' influential friends like dah' Clark's standin' behind yu', I don't foresee any problems," Anastasia replied confidently. "So when kin' we move in?"

"Very soon! I could have moved in earlier, but I wanted to wait fo' yu', so we could both welcome our new home together."

She ran to Reggie and jumped into his arms, and kissed him all over his face. "I hope dis' isn't jus' a dream. Everythin' is happenin' so fast since I've been hyeh'. I have a wonderful husband, whom I deeply love, an' now a new home dat' is our' own."

Reggie gently stroked Anastasia's hair and gazed into her eyes and kissed her. He then walked her to the kitchen and they set down at the table to talk about their immediate plans.

"Since I've been hyeh', I stayed wit' dah' Clarks an' maintained a traditional lifestyle but as soon as I git' my formal freedom, I jus' might look into dah' 'bolitionist movement—but not till I'm free. 'Member, unlike yu', I'm still a fugitive slave. However, I did go to dah' Afrikan' Meetin' House on Beacon

473

Street, which is one of dah' hotbeds of dah' 'bolitionist movement, jus' to sorta' git' my feet wet."

"While yu' wait fo' yur' final papers, yu' kin' be my personal servant? Don't worry, I'll be kind an' let yu' leave dah' property wit'out a pass. How does dat' sound, my love?" It was obvious that Anastasia was being facetious.

"Anastasia are yu' goin' to put me on a cot at dah' lower level from yu' 'til I git' my freedom papers? I guess it makes sense dat' I should have to sleep lower din' yu' since I'm not yur' equal yet. Hmmmm, maybe I oughta' think twice 'bout all dis'!" Reggie was willing to play along with her.

"My love, yu' kin' be so funny. In dah' dead of dah' night as long as yu' are good I might jus' have to crawl onto dat' cot wit' yu'. Now, if yu' are bad, I might have to order yu' to sleep on dah' porch."

"Oh, Missus', I promise to be a good boy."

Then Anastasia grew quiet and said, "Reggie, let's not joke 'round 'bout dis' any more. It saddens me to think 'bout yu' bein' technically a slave. It really makes me uneasy thinkin' dat" I am free an' yu' still do not have yur' papers of freedom."

"Fear not as I already tole' yu', dah' papers are on dah' way. All dah' legal work is being handled by an attorney named Mr. Joseph, an' he knows how to git' dah' job done. He's dah' same lawyer who handled yur' situation. Captain Riley, my former slave owner, is a 'bery wicked man, but Mr. Joseph will know how to deal wit' him—money an' influence kin' work miracles!" Reggie paused and then added, "I can't 'lieve I said dat', but unfortunately our modern society has gone increasingly in dat' direction."

"I still have purposely avoided askin' yu' 'bout dat' man, Captain Riley. I'm thankful yu' got 'way from him 'live," Anastasia said with a great sigh of relief.

Grimly Reggie related, "If I hadn't fled when I did, I would have probably been killed, an' I'm not exaggeratin'. Dat's how bad it was."

Anastasia took his hand in hers and said, "Don't think 'bout it anymore," as she comforted him. "Yu' will never have to answer to him 'gain."

"I have one bit of unfinished business I haven't tole' yu' 'bout an' it is important." Reggie released her hands and then gently pulled her into his arms. "When I fled from slavery, I had to leave behind my two closest friends, Willy an' Joseph who were holed up in a swamp. We had captured a hawss', which dey' gave to me since dey' felt I would have dah' best chance of makin' it North. Think 'bout it, dey' gave me dah' hawss' dat' brought me to freedom. Wit'out dat' hawss' I never would have made it."

"An' what haven't yu' finished, my love?" Anastasia had a feeling she knew the answer to her question.

"I made a solemn oath to myself an' to 'dem dat' I would go back someday an' find 'dem when I gain my freedom. In fact, I have purposely avoided discussin' our honeymoon since I felt it was imperative dat' I take care of my unfinished business first. Time is of dah' essence to git' 'dem out. Delayin' our honeymoon is such a small sacrifice to save our dear friends."

"Reggie, I perfectly understand yur' passion to rescue 'dem an' I support everythin' yu' want to do fo' thar' welfare, but jus' how are yu' goin' to do dat'?"

Reggie was very pleased that Anastasia was cooperating with him. "As I said, I'm first goin' to go down thar' an' try to round 'dem up, hopin' dey' are still 'live. Mr. Joseph knows of an attorney in Georgia who kin' help buy thar' freedom. 'Tween dah' money I have saved up an' Mr. Clark's assurance dat' he could help me wit' some additional funds, I feel confident dat' I kin' financially git' dah' job done."

"Reggie, through thick an' thin, we are together an' I want to be wit' yu' when yu' go down thar' to git' 'dem. Atter' all yu' done fo' me, I would travel dah' universe wit' yu' to help yu' fulfill yur' promises."

"My love, dis' is 'bery serious business, an' I'm ecstatic to hyeh' dat' yu' want to come 'long wit' me. Dat's like Mozart to my ears," as Reggie gave her a quick peck on the cheek.

"Yu' are so clever," Anastasia commented, "but I always thought Bach was yur' favorite." She knew it was Mozart, but she was just having fun with him.

The two laughed and then sat down at the kitchen table and continued talking for quite some time.

***

Anastasia had been lived at Oak Manor and than with Mrs. Winter in Richmond. Now, with a new life, her freedom and no restrictions, she was anxious to continue to explore Boston and the surrounding areas. Sitting at the kitchen table, Reggie told her he planned to take her on some of his business trips where they could spend time together in the evening after he had completed his work day. For Anastasia the opportunity to travel with Reggie even when he was working was wonderful. Meanwhile they discussed plans to move into their home chatting like two children planning the many wonderful and exciting adventures that lay ahead for them.

Reggie then got up and walked around the table, glanced out the kitchen window and sighed, "Well, my love, I think it's time to git' goin'. We'll be back as soon as I kin' git' time off to finally move in."

"Oh Reggie, I'm so elated an' kin' hardly wait. It's goin' to be quite a change fo' me, adaptin' to des' beautiful surroundins', knowin' it's actually ours."

Somewhat reluctantly, they left their home to go exploring. Outside, Reggie helped Anastasia into the buggy and hopped up next to her. With a faint smile on his face he said, "I have somewhere I'd like to take yu' 'fore we head back to dah' Clark's."

"Reggie, what are yu' up to now? Yu' are so full of surprises!"

Reggie laughed, assured Anastasia she'd like what was next and then lightly cracked the whip. The buggy bounded off through town to a small park where Reggie brought the buggy to a halt. Once out of the buggy, Reggie led her to a nearby bench. Anastasia sat down, having no idea what Reggie was up to as he positioned himself on one knee in front of her.

"Thar' is 'nother matter I'd like to 'dress so we kin' start our new life together properly." He looked deeply into Anastasia's eyes. "I know we were married in dah' eyes of God wit' dah' broomstick weddin', an' dat' was all we could do at dah' time, but when I git' my papers of freedom, I think it would be wonderful fo' us to git' married in a church through dah' Clark's minister. Mr. Clark told me dat' people up North tend to frown on couples jus' livin' together, an' 'sides we have to think of our future family." Suddenly while still on one knee, Reggie proposed, "I'd like to ask yu' formally Anastasia, if yu' will have me as yur' husband, all legal an' proper?" In addition to the proposal, Reggie slipped an engagement ring on her finger.

Anastasia was overwhelmed as she accepted the engagement ring from Reggie. "My love, dis' ring is absolutely beautiful, but I must say dat' I'm overwhelmed wit' dah' meanin' of dis' ring. Reggie, I 'gree wit' Mr. Clark dat' we need to git' formally married. Of course I want yu' fo' my husband fo'ever! Yu' well 'member when yu' tripped ovah' dah' broomstick Carl was holdin? Well, I never fo'got dat', an' dat' means I'm still dah' boss of our marriage since yu' fell an' I didn't. Now, if we git' married legally, am I goin' to have to relinquish my right to be dah' boss in our marriage?" Anastasia then laughed out loud and said, "Now give me a kiss, yu' big clumsy oaf to consummate dah' love surroundin' dis' ring." Reggie then rose kissed Anastasia, and sat alongside of her on the bench.

Reggie still had more to say about their broomstick marriage. "Anastasia quit bein' silly, yu' know dat' Carl lifted dat' broomstick up on my side deliberately so I would trip ovah' it. 'Sides, I can't 'lieve dat' hyeh' I'm proposin' to yu' an' yu' makin' jest—let's try to be serious." Reggie was able to fashion a wink as he spoke.

A smiling Anastasia stated, "Reggie I never knew yu' could be so serious. Since I love yu' so much, I'm willin' to give up my position as boss when we git' married legally—how does dat' sound?"

"Anastasia, I will agree to dat' bargain. Din' our broomstick marriage would be abrogated, an' both of us will be dah' boss."

Reggie again smiled and shook her hand as they both laughed at the joke.

"Whar' do yu' always come up wit' des' fancy words? Abrogate, I have never heard of dat' word, sometimes I think yu' carry a dictionary wit' yu'.

"I jus' said dat' word 'cuz' dat' is what popped up in my mind," Reggie responded.

"It amazes me dat' yu' kin' always come up wit' an' answer to everythin'," Anastasia said. "It would really be hard to put one ovah' on yu'."

"Anastasia, I may not be as smart as yu' think." Reggie humbly recounted the story about the snipe hunting mission he'd been sent out on while he was in Georgia. "I was made a fool of," he said in a subdued voice. "Dey' tole' me 'bout dis' wild animal dey' called a snipe. Dey' screamed an' yelled while I held dis' bag waitin' fo' dah' snipe to run ovah' so I could catch dah' varmint. Like a fool, I was out thar' yellin' 'hyeh' snipe, hyeh' snipe, hyeh' snipe' while dey' were all laughin' at me. An' me standin' thar' holdin' dat' gunny sack an' waitin' fo' some animal dat' doesn't even exist. Dat's how smart yur' husband kin' be."

"Dat' is funny!" Anastasia laughed. "I don't know what snipe huntin' is, but I guess dey' left yu' holdin' dah' bag, an' I think I've heard of dat' expression 'fore."

"It seems like every time I got dah' wool pulled ovah' my eyes it was my feller' slaves who did it. I kinda' think dat' des' Northerners would be hard pressed to out-smart my Southern friends."

"I wouldn't be too sure of dat', my love," Anastasia warned.

"Yu' are so right. Now dat' I think 'bout it, I'm reminded 'bout dah' Southern white men 'lievin' dat' dey' are manlier din' dah' Northern men. I know it's jus' a bunch of poppycock, an' hyeh' I'm sayin' somethin' jus' as silly," Reggie admitted, as they both laughed about it.

They spent a few more minutes sitting in the park talking and simply watching the sunset. Finally, they discussed how rewarding the day had been as they rode back to the Clark's to retire for the evening. Their hearts were full of anticipation of what the future was going to hold for them. Whatever it was, at least they knew they would be together, through good times and bad, they would now face them as one.

CHAPTER TWENTY-NINE

Making plans to move into their new town home was truly exciting for Anastasia and Reggie. They had lived their entire lives under the bondage system, and now they were setting up housekeeping in a comfortable town home in Boston—their own home, free and as man and wife. It was almost more than they could fathom.

Mr. Clark generously gave them more time to get situated in their new home, which they warmly appreciated. Household tasks abounded but through it all, Reggie was particularly proud to have with him his wife Anastasia along with the symbol of his freedom from bondage—his horse Freedom. Reggie was also proud of his "freedom clothes", which he chose to keep, lest he should forget where he came from and get a little "full of himself". All of these wonderful reminders were blending in with his new life. Meanwhile, the papers of manumission from Captain Riley would soon be arriving. Reggie was in a pensive mood when he said, "Yu' know Anastasia we should write a book 'bout dah' dramatic changes in our lives—from livin' as slaves in dah' South to a comfortable lifestyle in dah' North. Dis' is a fairy tale dat' people would want to read. Only a very few are livin' dis' dream dat' we are now livin' after coming through all the trials and tribulations we had to endure to get here. In my judgment, livin' wit' such extremes in yur' lifetime kin' make fo' an interestin' book. Seriously, Anastasia dat' would be a project dat' yu' could take charge of since I am so busy right now wit' so many other things. 'Sides I think yu' would be a 'bery good writer. More important, half dah' battle of writin' is havin' somethin' interestin' to write 'bout, an' I think yu' have dah' material yu' need. What do yu' think?"

Anastasia was fascinated at just how her husband's creativity seemed to have no bounds. "Reggie, I think yu're right, an' I'm goin' to give dis' some serious thought. It would be a project dat' I could thoroughly enjoy.

"I jus' threw dah' ider' out thar' since I honestly 'lieve a lot of people would enjoy dah' book. Anyhow, let's git' back to workin' in our new home, we've still got a long ways to go."

They poured all their energies into getting settled in on Pearl Street. Sarah proved to be indispensible. With her domestic abilities she helped to choose their window coverings and other household necessities that would compliment their home.

The week passed quickly, and still the manumission papers had not arrived, much to Reggie's vexation. Unfortunately, Monday morning came all too soon, and Reggie had to return to work," as he departed, he commented, "Dis will be a difficult trip since I can't git' dose' freedom papers out of my head."

"I understand, Reggie, I'm confident yur' papers will soon 'rive. Yu' have nothin' to fret 'bout. Meanwhile, Sarah is goin' to help me work on dah' house, an' hopefully dah' house will be ready when yu' git' back home." Anastasia always had a way of calming Reggie.

"Yu' will be in great company wit' Sarah. Incidentally, I'm happy dat' yu' two have become such good friends." Reggie's attitude suddenly improved after Anastasia talked to him.

"I'll be fine, my love. I have to git' use to bein' separated from yu' at times, an' yes, Sarah has quickly become a close friend," Anastasia confirmed. "Now git' goin' so yu' kin' git' yur' work done an' git' back home soon, an' hopefully yu'll be able to joyously examine yur' 'freedom papers'."

"An' yu' know," Reggie winked at her, "absence does make dah' heart grow fonder."

Anastasia, standing inside the stable to see Reggie off,

giggled as they kissed goodbye. She then said, "Yu' know yu' can't git' back home—if yu' never leave!" They both laughed and Reggie prepared the horse and buggy for the trip. He then rode off and silently she prayed for a successful trip and his safe return.

Anastasia walked back into the house and busied herself arranging the pantry and cabinets, and sweeping the floors before sitting down to a simple lunch. Afterwards she explored her back yard for a few minutes to think about different types of flowers and vegetables she could grow in the spring. When she returned to her kitchen she began listing all the items she would need to begin the project.

The afternoon passed, with dinner time quickly arriving. Anastasia, content to not have to worry about dinner, instead, found herself sitting and musing over all the developments that were occurring in her life.

Unexpectedly, a knocking came at the door and Sarah appeared with an excited look on her face. She had brought muffins and fresh fruit to share, but that was not all—she had important news for Anastasia and could hardly wait to tell her.

"The papers arrived for Reggie's freedom!" She could not contain her excitement as she put her packages down on the table, "Here they are!"

She pulled them out of an official looking envelope and presented them to an astonished Anastasia. "Oh my Lawd'," she exclaimed and then stated, "bless me Jesus!"

"I know Reggie is headed for Wakefield right now," Sarah went on, "but I couldn't wait to get the papers to you! I wish I could be here when you tell him."

"Dis' is dah' greatest news, Sarah. Yu' well know dat' Reggie has been anxiously awaitin' dis' moment, an' I know dat' he will be ecstatic when he sees des' papers. It's really been difficult fo' him thinkin' dat' somethin' unfo'seen could occur dat' would prove to be awful."

"On that note, I must tell you that it was not easy to get Captain Riley to agree to the sale. Mr. Joseph, our attorney, had to pay a pretty penny to get the deal done. At one point he even thought he would have to close the negotiations; however, Captain Riley relented and agreed to a premium price. A man like Riley wasn't the easiest man to deal with, but Mr. Joseph was prepared to do whatever was necessary to secure Reggie's freedom. One way or another, the deal was going to get done."

"Reggie will be so happy to know dat' he is finally free! Sarah—dis' is all so unbelievable! As Reggie likes to say, it's like livin' dah' dream an' now everthin' will glow wit' freedom!"

The two embraced joyfully and danced around the kitchen table celebrating the wonderful news, and when they calmed down a bit, Sarah had a suggestion. "Let's really celebrate! Let's get out of the house and have some fun riding around the city and later I'll take you somewhere nice and interesting for dinner. What do you think—will you accept my invitation? My treat!"

"Sarah, I would love to, but I wouldn't know what to wear."

"Anastasia, we can take care of that. Besides, you need to venture out of the house every once and awhile when Reggie is not here. I'm sure that Reggie would agree."

"Yu' are right, Sarah. I really know so little 'bout Boston. Now, would yu' help me choose what to wear, I still find myself feelin' rather backward?" The two ladies ran upstairs and in no time at all had chosen a simple outfit for Anastasia to wear from her modest selection of clothing.

Quickly, they were soon in Sarah's buggy navigating the streets of Boston while joyfully celebrating Reggie's freedom. Acting as a tour guide, Sarah pointed out Faneuil Hall. "You are looking at a three-story structure that was built in 1740. Can you imagine that? It's over 100 years old and was built by a man named Peter Faneuil, who later donated it to the city for use as a market and meeting house. The top story was later added to hold town meetings. If you are interested in hearing speeches on politics or just about anything else, then this is the place to go. During the War of Rebellion, John Hancock, and Samuel Adams frequently came here. In fact, President George Washington attended a banquet here, which was held in his honor in 1789. Things have not changed since then as the building still serves the city in the same way. You are looking at a big part of Boston history," Sarah proudly stated.

"Dat' is really somethin' to know an' see." Anastasia was in awe. "I'm lookin' fo'ward to spendin' a whole day jus' at Faneuil Hall wit' Reggie, an' hopefully yu' will want to come 'long. I know he would enjoy dat' as he has a true fondness fo' history 'long wit' hyehin' speakers discussin' current political issues. Understandably, Reggie has a penchant fo' politics."

"Oh, but there's more," Sarah went on. "Notice the cupola topped by a grasshopper weather vane. If you can figure out why a grasshopper adorns the cupola, please let our mayor know? Boston is all about the sea, not the grasslands of the west where you would find grasshoppers. This is still the biggest mystery in all of Boston."

"Dis' is all so fascinatin'," Anastasia exclaimed. "I must say dat' Boston has so much more to offer din' Richmond. I really do love it hyeh', an' not jus' 'cuz' of my circumstances."

"I'm glad you like your new home, Anastasia." Sarah felt a deep satisfaction in knowing she had played a strong part in helping Anastasia and Reggie establish their new life.

Eventually, they found their way to the Oyster House, a fine establishment Sarah had recommended for dinner. Riding up to the tavern, they secured the horse and buggy and ran up to the entrance like schoolgirls. Settling down as they walked through the front door, Anastasia told Sarah how impressed she was with the establishment. Whale oil lamps illuminated the walls and table providing a colorful ambience, which fittingly expressed a nautical theme. The two young women attracted a lot of attention by walking to their table unescorted. Sarah had instructed Anastasia to ignore any gawking male patrons and any potential comments they might hear since sailors had a reputation for being flirtatious, and they would possibly be dominant among the patrons. On this particular evening the men were mindful and once seated, Anastasia and Sarah enjoyed a spirited conversation without any interruptions. Anastasia, who was intimidated at first, soon relaxed and savored the evening—another new experience in her life. They each enjoyed their wine and an excellent seafood dinner and with the view, the evening was complete.

Anastasia had so much to learn and felt very fortunate to have Sarah as her friend. The transition from being a servant to the role of the wife of a successful young businessman in Boston was almost more than she could bear. However, with Sarah's guidance, it was made much easier.

Sarah passed along valuable information to Anastasia; she wanted her to know that Reggie's new life would require a certain amount of socializing and of course, this would be expected of her as well. Anastasia found it all very interesting but laughed to herself as her thoughts drifted to a simpler life. She mentioned to Sarah that at home she had plans to have a vegetable garden in the back and a flower garden in the front. In addition, because of Reggie's urging, she was going to write a book about their lives as he felt it would provide her with a worthwhile project to fill the day. Providing encouragement, Sarah agreed that their experiences were so unique that it would make for a very interesting book.

After a good conversation, they got up and departed, heading back toward Pearl Street. On the way home Sarah asked Anastasia if she would like to go shopping with her the next day. She accepted the invitation knowing that she needed to learn more about how the ladies of Boston filled their day when shopping. Arriving at her town home, Anastasia thanked her good friend Sarah for everything and walked quickly to the front porch. She turned and waved good night with tears of joy and gratitude filling her eyes. Sarah politely waved back and waited to be sure Anastasia entered her town home safely before leaving. Meanwhile, Anastasia mused to herself that she had enjoyed her brief tour of the city and enjoyed her exciting dinner, but was still glad to be back in her home to retire for the evening and then think of Reggie being a free man.

***

As promised, Sarah arrived the next morning for a day of

shopping. Knowing Anastasia would soon be formally married, she knew a trousseau would be in order, which would require Sarah's expertise. As they departed in their buggy, both were very excited and looked forward to Anastasia's very first shopping spree! With a long list in hand, Sarah and Anastasia shopped through many of the better stores in Boston looking for everything she would need for her wedding to accommodate her new Bostonian lifestyle.

Anastasia was mindful of her friend's advice not to tell Reggie. But she knew that she couldn't wait to show him all the lovely items Sarah had helped her purchase. In addition, she was anxious to tell him about the restaurant they dined at along with all the other new sights she saw. But by far the major thing of course was to present him with his papers of freedom.

They finished up late in the afternoon and opted to eat at Anastasia's home. After Sarah departed, Anastasia's mind was trying to absorb all she had seen, done, and learned. Exhausted, she went to bed early knowing she had a lot to do before Reggie's return the following evening.

Sarah came back the next day to help Anastasia get her home organized for the big event that night—Reggie's return and his reaction to knowing he was now a free man.

A special candlelight dinner was planned with some of Reggie's favorite foods. She couldn't believe that soon she would be handing Reggie his papers of freedom, which would be so exciting for him that she could hardly contain herself. Sarah, knowing Anastasia needed some down time, left in the middle of the afternoon. After Sarah departed, Anastasia continued to prepare herself for her husband's return. As the time neared, Anastasia's excitement continued to build up knowing how joyous this occasion would be for Reggie.

She had just finished putting on the new dress they had purchased, when she heard Reggie enter through the rear door. Her heart pounded with excitement as she checked her appearance in the mirror. Earlier she had wrapped her hair up into a simple chignon, a popular style, the way Sarah had shown her and now she was ready and scurried downstairs and greeted her husband in the foyer. After an affectionate kiss, Reggie gazed at Anastasia with joy, seeing his wife looking so beautiful.

He was thrilled with the natural beauty of his wife whose looks were enhanced with her beautiful new dress and a blush of rouge on her cheeks. He felt great joy and appreciation knowing his friend, Sarah, must have had something to do with the touches to his wife's new radiant appearance.

Anastasia stood in front of him awaiting his response. Reggie circled her, carefully sizing up the soft gown with her upswept hair, and came to a full stop in front of her. "My beautiful Anastasia," he breathed, "What in dah' world have yu' done to yur'self? Yu' look so beautiful. Somethin' funny is goin' on 'round hyeh'." Reggie sensed that Anastasia was going to inform him that his papers had arrived.

Anastasia was crushed, and her shoulders slumped. "Oh no!" she exclaimed. "Yu' don't like it!"

"On dah' contrary, my love, I find it excitin', I jus' said yu' look beautiful, but I'm questionin' dah' timin' fo' gittin' all dressed up like dis'. Somethin' is in dah' air." He smiled and took her in his arms, then kissed her softly. "I missed yu' so much des' last few days. I love comin' home to yu'." Reggie was filled with anticipation that Anastasia was going to surprise him with the all of the important news he had been anticipating for so long.

"And I missed yu' too," Anastasia answered breathlessly. "Oh my Lawd', Reggie, I have such wonderful news fo' yu'!"

"How could anythin' be better din' comin' home to yu'?" As he hugged Anastasia he was hoping she was going to spring the good news that he was now a free man.

She wiggled free from his embrace and rushed to the kitchen to retrieve the large envelope from a drawer. Quickly handing it to him, she beamed and said, "Reggie, yur' papers of manumission are right heyh'—yu' are a free man!"

Stunned and speechless for several moments, he recognized the required official seal and then read over them just to be sure they were bona fide. "We are truly both free now—'free, free at last'! I never knew it would feel dis' good! We are free to do whatever we want to do wit' nobody standin' ovah' us wit' a whip. Anastasia, I have now lost my status as an adult boy— no oxymoron intended, now I'm a man. I'm nobody's 'boy'—I'm a man—period!" Reggie just couldn't resist making some humor out of the situation. "Anastasia, it really feels good to be able to say dat'. And jus' think, together we've made it! I finally know how it really feels to be really 'free at last'. I never knew it would feel dis' overwhelmin'. It does make a big difference to know dat' like yu' I'm now legally free. I'm dumbstruck. Oh Lardy', I have to sit down an' digest all dis'. Isn't dis' really somethin'! I jus' can't 'lieve all dis' is happenin' to us—isn't dis' really somethin'?"

Reggie thought about all his brothers and sisters in servitude, who, when given the chance, chanted the words "free at last", hoping it might become a reality for all someday. His fondest wish would remain—the complete abolition of slavery, so they too could feel the exuberance of being forever—"free at last". His unselfish feelings dictated that even in this moment of finding freedom for himself, he had to be thinking of his fellow "brothers and sisters", deeply concerned that they too should know freedom.

He sat down on a kitchen chair and pulled Anastasia on to his lap. After an affectionate embrace coupled with passionate kisses, the two of them enjoyed the quality time together knowing that both of them were now free. She finally asked Reggie to freshen up while she set the table for dinner.

When he returned, dinner for two by candlelight was waiting for Reggie. "My beautiful wife, my freedom, my hawss' Freedom an' my favorite food, what more could I ask for? Oh, I fo'got somethin', maybe I should run upstairs an' slip into my 'freedom clothes'—jus' jokin' of course." Anastasia shared in his humor and then Reggie stared at the table and then Anastasia, and pulled the chair out for her. Reggie was taken aback with joy. First, he learned he was free and now being treated to a home-cooked meal. Soon after giving thanks to the Lord, they were enjoying their meal, and the two lovingly talked about the day. Reggie said, "Look at dis' candlelit dinner yu' prepared." Reggie was still overwhelmed. "It's all my favorite foods! When did you git' time to do all of dis'. I thought yu' were spendin' all yur' time shoppin' wit' Sarah?"

"Reggie, yu' kin be so special, I'm jus' wonderin' if yu' are more excited ovah' yur' special dinner or yur' papers of freedom." She winked at him as she said the words.

"Anastasia, I would have to say dat' dah' meal comes first an' dah' freedom papers come maybe a distant second," as he returned the wink along with a smile.

"Reggie I'm learnin' how to shop an' cook an' I love every minute of it. Some would say I'm learnin' to budget my time."

"Anastasia I think it's all so great. I must say dat' I never realized how different I would feel when I found out I was legally free. I'm tryin' to make sense of all dat' has jus' occurred. It's wonderful. My love, we went from bein' in bondage to all of dis'. Jus' 'member dat' it's still important fo' both of us to realize our broomstick marriage is still as valid in dah' eyes of God an' will always be. Anastasia, dah' reason I feel dis' way is 'cuz' dah' broomstick marriage represents our past, which we should remind ourselves of everyday, while our formal marriage will represent our new future."

"I think thar' are degrees to everythin'," Anastasia suggested. "Dah' degree of sufferin' yu' underwent was much greater din' what I went through. I think dis' has made yu' a lot more compassionate to dah' plight of others, whar'ever dey' may be. Certainly our broomstick marriage reflects dat' side of yu'. My fondest wish is dat' I learn to fully share yur' passion an' love fo' all of our 'brothers an' sisters'."

"Now, Anastasia, yu' suffered too. Colonel Marshall assigned yu' to his special little cottage. Dat' had to be terrifyin'— knowin' he had sexual designs on yu'."

Anastasia shuddered at the picture that came to her mind. "Yes, dat' was dah' worst of it dat' I had to undergo, an' honestly, dat' was more din' 'nough. I would lie in bed thinkin' 'bout dat' tyrant ravagin' himself ovah' me. Thank God nothin' happened, fortunately dat' whole situation only lasted 'til I reminded him I was his brother's child. As yu' already know, he slapped me in anger an' din', fortunately, he later hired me out to Mrs. Winters, maybe out of guilt. But Reggie, yu' were put through hell an' back!"

He reached for her, and she responded lovingly as he held her close. "No matter whar' life leads us, I will always love yu' wit' all my heart an' soul, but I feel a strong personal bond fo' Willy an' Joseph, an' I kin' take solace in knowin' steps are goin' to be taken to free 'dem as well. I have to do dis' to fulfill my wishes dat' dey' too may experience freedom. It's all part of bringin' our freedom to a full circle."

"Yes," Anastasia agreed, "I truly understand how yu' feel 'bout Joseph an' Willy. I never met 'dem but I think of 'dem a lot, an' din' I feel a little guilty 'bout our good fortune."

"Anastasia, do not feel any guilt. Dis' is dah' way dat' Joseph an' Willy wanted it to be. Dey' are unselfish an' would only want us to succeed—'member dey' are true friends! Dey' know we have not fo'gotten 'dem an' we'll be back to free 'dem as well. Everythin' is goin' as planned." Reggie understood why Anastasia might feel guilt. He knew it was important for her to understand that under the circumstances, things were going good as expected.

As the couple slowly made their way upstairs, Anastasia reassured Reggie, "All dah' sufferin' is now behind yu'. It's time fo' us to share our lives together knowin' dat' a bright future is 'head."

"Anastasia, I'm ready—dis' is what I have been livin' fo' since we became separated. Right now, I jus' want to love all of yu' in bed knowin' dat' both us of will remain together fo'ever," as Reggie slowly closed the bedroom door.

Once more, she knew they would share another night of bliss, together with uninterrupted love as they both lay back onto the bed knowing they were both truly "free at last".

CHAPTER-THIRTY

Each new day for Anastasia and Reggie was a new adventure. Both were now legally free and able to live their dreams without fear of repression. Much time was spent just filling one another in on the years they were apart while getting acclimated to their freedom and new lives in the North. They both realized that the formal papers of manumission did make a tremendous difference and much more than they could have ever imagined. They now felt truly free, confident, and absent of any paranoia, knowing "beyond a shadow of doubt" that nobody should ever have to live their life under the bondage of another person.

They openly discussed slavery, now willing to let others know they were once held in bondage. It would remain important for them to be candid about their past and above all to be supportive toward the abolition of slavery.

The practice of miscegenation in the South was a subject frequently discussed in the North. Of course, the persistent rumors involving miscegenation that always surrounded President Jefferson's lifestyle helped to "fan the fire". When it became known that Reggie and Anastasia were both former slaves and obvious products of miscegenation, people wanted to know more about them while many were still thinking in the back of their minds about President Jefferson. There was no question that miscegenation was an issue that generated a tremendous amount of gossip in the North as well as the South and would not go away.

Concerning Reggie and Anastasia, many still wondered when they would "cross over" and assume the identity of white people; however, they had absolutely no intention of ever disavowing their roots. Reggie's convictions ran especially deep. He would proudly state to whoever would listen that he was just as proud of the little amount of Negro blood in his veins as that of his white blood. However, he adamantly believed that the Negro blood in him was inconsequential to the tireless effort he was putting forth for the abolition of slavery. Physically, the scarring on his back would reflect that he also had paid a terrible price while living in bondage. Continuing to fight for the total abolishment of slavery, while working first to secure the freedom of Joseph and Willy, would remain as his immediate concerns. He further felt that in a modest way, his destiny was to act as an ambassador for his people.

***

Living in Boston proved magical as Reggie and Anastasia continued to transition into their new life together. Meanwhile, a lot of time was being spent with Sarah and her family as they were planning for their formal wedding. Of course, Sarah would be maid of honor. Emma, now married to a Mr. Paul Brown, resided in Lowell, Massachusetts and was fittingly chosen to be the bridesmaid. Invitations had been sent and Emma's, Aunt Opal would also be attending. This was particularly pleasing to Reggie and Anastasia since Sarah, Emma, and Aunt Opal would be the only people present at the wedding who knew Reggie and Anastasia while they were enslaved at the Oak Manor plantation. In addition, Anastasia made sure to invite Robert and Alice Jamison who she had befriended on her voyage.

The date of their union was set for a Saturday morning in late October. Reverend Hicks would be presiding and it was to be held at the First Unitarian Church, which was originally an Anglican Church named King's Chapel, located on Tremont Street at the south end of Boston. This prestigious and historic church was built of granite slabs with a portico supported by massive gray wooden columns. The interior was elegant with a Georgian influence. Notably, it included the first church organ in New England.

When Reggie learned that George Washington had attended services there, he humorously made the comment that President Washington maintained a ubiquitous presence in Boston since it appeared that he had been honored in so many different places throughout the city.

Sarah and Anastasia found her wedding dress at one of the finer shops in Boston. They selected an off white gown that reflected an understated elegance. It was fashioned of beautiful silk with a V-neck bodice and long fitted sleeves, which ended in points over her hands. The skirt was graceful and full, creating a billowing effect. The fine lace veil would be held in place by a coronet of trailing mayflowers, the fragrant, shell-pink blossoms streaming downward over an ample train. Anastasia's nosegay was of mayflowers infused with pink roses and baby's breath. Her shoes matched the color of her dress with a pink strap over each instep.

Sarah and Emma, Anastasia's Maid of Honor and bridesmaid respectively, had chosen the same pink, floor length dresses but with high Victorian style necklines. Their sleeves were long and their shoes were pink with off white ribbons at the instep. The flowers they would carry included a blend of white roses and wildflowers.

Reggie's ensemble included a frock coat of mulberry, an off-white ivory vest with a silk shirt and a white rose in the lapel. Finally, a light grey tie and grey trousers finished it off. Lucas Clark would serve as best man and Kenneth Miller would be the usher. They would wear light grey frock coats and trousers with mulberry vests and neckties, accompanied by an off- white silk shirt with a white tea rose in their lapels.

Emma had been in town for a week prior to the wedding. She was staying at the Clarks' so that she would be available for fittings on her bridesmaid gown. Her husband, Paul, would be joining her there a couple of days before the ceremony. She also wanted to be available to assist Anastasia and the Clark's in any way necessary as they had graciously offered to have a traditional wedding meal served at their residence.

Normally, a breakfast or brunch meal was served after a wedding at this time of day, and the Clark's would follow custom.

Sarah had ordered a traditional wedding cake and several miniature replicas. The day before the ceremony, Sarah supervised the arrival of the flowers and cakes. She and Emma decorated the church and put flowers on the front pews. She also asked Emma to help box the smaller cakes and place pennies inside of them, an old tradition for prosperity and good fortune. After the brunch, the miniature boxed cakes would be given to the guests as they left. The large cake was a dark, rich, fruitcake with ornate white frosting, decorated with models of the mayflowers that Anastasia would wear on her veil.

The night before the wedding, Anastasia stayed at the Clark's home and spent the evening with Sarah and Emma, showing them her engagement ring and doing all of the things that girls do to prepare for a wedding. Mostly, there was a lot of giggling and very little sleep as would be expected. Both Reggie and Anastasia had difficulty sleeping apart from each other but bowing to custom, they did so on the eve of their wedding.

The morning of the wedding day arrived, and everyone rose early to prepare for the ceremony. Sarah, Emma, and Anastasia helped each other get ready and into their gowns. Fresh flowers were arranged in Anatasia's hair and placed on her veil. Sarah put the finishing touches on Anastasia's gown and the veil was finally pulled down over her face for the ride to the church.

A white carriage with white horses took the bride and her attendants to the church. The two groomsmen rode in a separate coach while Reggie chose to ride Freedom. Reggie knew all of this would have never been possible without his horse, Freedom. His loyalty drove him to insist that Freedom should be ridden at the front of the groom's coach, which was highly unusual, but he felt so strongly that it was necessary to override tradition as he allowed his conscious to be his guide. Freedom did play a notable role, people watching the procession were in awe viewing Reggie, a handsome specimen of a man all dressed in his wedding attire, sporting a top hat and riding a beautiful white stallion. It was said by one of the spectators that Reggie rivaled Don Quixote. Yet it was such a significant paradox—a former slave and now to be looked on as the picture of royalty. Only this could occur in a fairy tale, and the time had come at last for the rest of this fairy tale wedding to unfold.

Reggie arrived early and took his place at the front of the church along with Reverend Hicks. The groomsmen were at the back of the church preparing to line up with the bridesmaids. The anticipation was great. Reggie couldn't wait to see Anastasia, his bride, coming toward him to become his wife before God and man.

As soon as the bride and bridesmaids arrived, they lined up at the back of the church along with the groomsmen to begin the procession. The organ began playing Jeremiah Clarke's *Trumpet in Voluntary in D Major,* and then with the groomsmen on the right and the bridesmaids on the left they slowly walked, arm in arm down the aisle. As they reached the altar, the bridesmaids went to the left and the groomsmen took their places at Reggie's right side.

The moment had arrived as Anastasia appeared, walking toward him on Mr. Clark's arm. Reggie was overcome with emotion; he heard no music, and saw nothing around him, only his lovely Anastasia. It appeared to him that she floated toward him, a vision beyond words. Mr. Clark placed her hand in Reggie's when they reached the altar, then kissed her cheek and took his seat.

The music stopped, and Reverend Hicks began the service using the revised *Anglican Book of Common Prayer.* "Dearly beloved we are gathered together here in the sight of God, and in the presence of those gathered here to unite this man and this woman in holy matrimony, . . ." The beautiful couple pledged their love and exchanged wedding rings, looking into one another's eyes, while tears of pure love appeared on their faces. Reverend Hicks concluded by saying, "Forasmuch as Anastasia and Reggie have consented together in holy wedlock, and have witnessed the same before God and this company and thereto have given and pledged their troth, each to the other and have declared the same by the giving and receiving of a ring and the joining of hands, 'I now pronounce that they are man and wife in the name of the Father, and the Son, and of the Holy Spirit. Amen. What God hath joined together let no man put asunder'."

He then turned to Reggie and said, "You may kiss the bride." Reggie raised the veil and then kissed his beloved Anastasia. The reverend then announced to the congregation. "I'd like to present to you Mr. and Mrs. Reggie Marshall." Those words were very special to Reggie and Anastasia since as slaves they could not have had a last name.

The organ played Johann Wagner's *Bridal Course,* and the wedding entourage marched back up the aisle and outside where they formed a reception line to greet the guests and receive their congratulations.

Passers-by stopped to look at the beautiful couple, and the attractive wedding party. Heads turned as they asked about the lovely couple and Mr. Clark proudly told them, "This is Reggie and Anastasia Marshall, a picture-perfect couple."

Maintaining the Victorian tradition, the couple made their way to the carriage to take the short trip back to the Clark home where servants had decorated the house and had everything prepared for the reception. Reggie had made prior arrangements to have somebody ride Freedom back home.

The short trip back to the Clark home proved to be an exhilarating experience for Reggie and Anastasia as people along the way waved and cheered them as they proceeded in their fancy white carriage. It was such a very special occasion that one could not have imagined it—again, former slaves being accorded the same respect given to the affluent. This could only happen in a dream; and here it was unfolding as a reality for Reggie and his bride.

***

Finally, everyone was back at the Clark home where the reception was about to begin. After they had been properly seated and with emotions running high, Mr. Clark cleared his throat to get everyones attention so he could make a toast as everybody had been given a glass of champagne to start the festivities. "I would like to congratulate the new bride and groom. Anastasia and Reggie, may you live a long, peaceful and happy life together." As he spoke it was obvious how heartfelt his words were. Everyone cheered and took a drink of their champagne. Reggie and Anastasia sipped theirs and kissed as Mr. Clark went on, "As your wedding gift, I am sending you on a honeymoon to Niagara Falls!" The guests cheered while Reggie and Anastasia were so overcome with joy that if they hadn't been sitting down, they might have fallen over. Reggie expressed their gratitude and Anastasia wiped tears from her eyes with a handkerchief Emma handed her.

Anastasia gathered her wits and stated, "It is indeed an honor to receive dis' gift from dah' Clark's. Niagara Falls, dah' honeymoon mecca in our country, an' fo' us to be goin' thar' is somethin' we never expected or dreamed possible. We sincerely thank dah' Clark family from dah' bottom of our hearts fo' everythin'." It was difficult for Anastasia to speak to a large audience, but the words of gratitude came right out, and were heartfelt.

Reggie added as Anastasia regained her composure and stood at his side. "I want to personally thank everybody hyeh' as well fo' yur' warm generosity an' yur' friendship. I join my wife when I say dis' goes beyond any dream we ever believed could be possible."

Mr. Clark stepped forward, beaming from ear to ear, and had more to say. "Thank you all for being a part of this glorious occasion, now let's eat, drink and be merry!"

Reggie and Anastasia held hands, looking around at the spectacle of the occasion, remembering where their journey began and where that venture now found them. It was an exhilarating and daunting experience to comprehend the path that brought them to this day. It was even more difficult to believe that all of this could have ever happened to them.

It was apparent that the guests enjoyed the celebration and the Clark's hospitality too. Proud of Reggie, Mr. Clark urged him to entertain the guests by playing classical music on the piano, which he gladly accepted. It was apparent from the reaction of the guests that they were impressed with how talented he was.

It was mid-afternoon when the guests began to leave after enjoying the wonderful reception that had unfolded without any problems. Finally, Mrs. Clark recognized the newlyweds were emotionally spent from the day's events and recommended they go home and rest, assuring them everything would be tended to without needing any of their assistance.

After thanking the Clark's and their guests, they departed for home. When they arrived home, passion outweighed their exhaustion and they made love before even making it to the bedroom. The sight of the carpet in the foyer would forever more bring a gentle smile to their faces when they thought of it. Before going to sleep, Reggie reminded Anastasia of their first wedding night, making love in the old, abandoned plantation house and then trying to compare that to this night in their own home. Anastasia said, "When it comes to us, whar' we make love doesn't matter, only dat' we're in each others arms." Reggie respected her insightful comment that demonstrated her love and wisdom.

They stayed in bed until sunset, their naked bodies woven among the sheets and blankets. After fully enjoying the night of their honeymoon, Anastasia put on her robe and Reggie donned a nightshirt to slowly walk down to the kitchen where Anastasia put together a light meal. They sat at the kitchen table reliving the activities of their wedding day and marveling at the way they felt now legally married and free. Serenity enveloped them as Anastasia sat in Reggie's lap, admiring her beautiful diamond wedding ring and how much it meant to her. She turned her face to him and said, tenderly, "I love yu' so much, Reggie Marshall!" She couldn't resist putting a little emphasis on Marshall.

He warmly answered, "Not half as much as I love yu' my dearest Anastasia." They embraced and Reggie kissed her, assuring her that he loved her with all his heart. So deeply in love, they returned to their bedroom, never even finishing their meal.

The following morning as they cleaned up the kitchen, Reggie talked about some of his experiences in Boston before

Anastasia's arrival. "As I tole' yu' earlier, 'fore yu' got hyeh', I had some free time, an' found myself goin' to dah' Afrikan' Meetin' House on Beacon Street. It's located in dah' First Afrikan' Baptist Church. Dah' black community's life revolves 'round thar' as it's one of dah' strongholds fo' dah' 'bolitionist movement. I really felt at home thar' since it was as close to being in dah' 'quarters' as I could git' wit'out actually bein' down South. It was funny Anastasia, when I first went to a gatherin' at dah' church, dey' looked at me like I didn't belong, but atter' I talked to 'dem an' dey' got to know me, 'din dah' red carpet was rolled out. I hope yu' will go thar' wit' me sometime soon."

"Reggie, trust me, I do share yur' passion to stay connected to our roots. Of course I'll go' wit' yu'!"

"Anastasia, I have to make a confession. Truthfully, I would have preferred gittin' married in dah' First Afrikan' Baptist Church, but out of respect to dah' Clarks an' what dey' have done fo' us, I realized it would be best to graciously 'cept thar' offer. Honestly, I must admit dat' dah' feelin' dat' I have from dah' weddin' is much better din' I had ever anticipated."

"I would have understood yur' wishes had yu' wanted to git' married in dah' First Afrikan' Meetin' House. I love yu', Reggie, an' I only want to make yu' happy. However, like yu', I was thrilled by our weddin'. Everythin' 'bout it was truly wonderful. It was jus' like a fairy tale weddin'." Anastasia's eyes just sparkled as she spoke.

"I love yu' so much, an' I'm pleased at how supportin' yu' kin' be. Anyhow, dah' Afrikan' Meetin' House amongst our people is also known as dah' Black Faneuil Hall. 'Gain, I do feel 'bery comfortable when I'm thar'." Reggie's enthusiasm was bubbling with joy.

"I never spent time in dah' quarters," Anastasia remarked, "but I do have a profound respect fo' my brothers an' sisters who had to endure so much sufferin'. Trust me Reggie, I could fit in ovah' thar' an' be 'bery comfortable as well."

"Anastasia, I'm so happy dat' yu' feel dis' way. It's so important dat' we remain committed to our roots. I have to tell yu' something else. I have had an opportunity to read what some consider inflammatory materials dat' are supported by dah' 'bolitionist movement, an' I want to share 'dem wit' yu.' Recently, Timothy Weld, a very intelligent an' passionate 'bolitionist, wrote American Slavery As It Is. Atter' readin' his' book, I could only think dat' it comes 'bery close to what I saw an' had to endure. It exposes dah' brutality of dah' bondage system. In my judgment, dah' book tells dah' truth. What's wrong wit' dah' truth? I say dat' Anastasia, 'cuz' I have observed dat' people really don't want to know dah' truth! 'Out of sight, out of mind', it truly disturbs me."

"I would like to read dis' book, as I know it would mean a lot to yu'." Anastasia responded knowing Reggie was extremely sensitive to this problem.

"Oh yes, Anastasia I do think yu' will find dis' book more din' enlightenin'." Anyhow, thank yu' fo' yu' support an' understandin'. I have one other book to talk 'bout. In 1829 David Walker, who was a free black man, wrote, Appeal to dah' Colored Citizens of dah' World. Although it is a short read, dis' book really caught my attention. As yu' know, I have tole' many people 'bout my dream dat' slavery will end 'cuz' of a bitter an' bloody war fought 'tween dah' North an' dah' South, but it seems as if no one, white or black, would believe me." Anastasia walked around the table and stood along side of her husband as he spoke, kissing the top of his head when he paused to gather his thoughts. Reggie went on, "His book sees a major insurrection 'tween dah' whites an' dah' blacks. He died in 1830, which gave him little time to defend his thinkin', an' outside of him, I have not read any other author who kin' see a war or major insurrection comin' ovah' slavery. I put David Walker in 'bery high esteem fo' havin' dah' knowledge an' insight to predict dah' horrible violence dat' lies 'head ovah' dis' terrible institution of slavery. While his prediction 'bout violence deals wit' a race war an' not a war 'tween dah' North an' dah' South in my judgment, it still represents a major effort in understandin' slavery."

"Reggie, from what yu' are tellin' me, it sounds like he is like yu'. He is a visionary who kin' see serious trouble 'head ovah' slavery. Unfortunately, both of yu' represent dah' minority in yur' thinkin'.'"

"'Gain, he is dah' only person I have read who shares my opinion 'bout a comin' civil war ovah' slavery right hyeh' in our beloved democratic United States. Personally, when I have been engaged in conversation about our Declaration of Independence, I sarcastically emphasize dah' word democratic, as dat' door to democracy is closed to dose' who are of color."

"Reggie, why are people so blind to dah' truth? I even thought of our weddin' an' everythin' 'fore it. Do yu' think dat' all of dis' would have happened to us if we looked Negro?"

"Dah' answer to dat' is obvious—of course not! Now, let me say somethin' 'bout people bein' blind to dah' truth. I'm not sur', but people today are really not any different din' others in dah' past, set in thar' ways, not willin' to realize dat' we have to be active an' open to change an' 'bove all, compromise!"

Anastasia continued to listen while admiring Reggie's perception and intelligence.

Reggie went on to explain, "Dey' don't really want to communicate or compromise. Dah' North an' dah' South have to realize jus' how much dey' have in common an' not jus' thar' differences. It's essential dat' we keep our nation together as one while we recognize dah' unique social, political, an' economic differences dat' are presently dividin' us in half. An' 'bove all, we cannot allow dah' forces of greed, power, pride, and stubborness to muddy dah' water an' destroy' dah' chance to heal our wounds. I've said all of dis' 'fore. It's jus' so important to git' dah' message 'cross while we still have time."

"Reggie, it's late afternoon, an' we still have to go visit dah' Clark's an' open our gifts. Doesn't dat' sound excitin'?" Anastasia beamed. "Still, I could listen to yu' all day an' night, I do have such a profound respect fo' yur' visionary skills. I jus' wish yu' had a bigger an' better stump to orate from. Our country desperately needs people like yu' to lead us—men an' women who kin' look at a problem an' objectively seek a solution an' make a decision while takin' into account dah' different interests dat' people might have—'bove all, bein' willin' to compromise when necessary." It began to sound like Anastasia wanted Reggie to seek a political office, which Reggie found humorous.

"Thank yu,' my love," Reggie replied. "Yu' are a 'bery eloquent, young lady an' I know like me, yu' carry such a heavy heart fo' our country. It's goin' to be such a struggle to end slavery, but dah' real tragedy is dat' even when it does end, dah' fight fo' equality will be far from ovah'. I tole' yu' 'bout dah' other dream I had, which ventured into dah' distant future. Dah' distinguished black man was preachin' equality to thousands of people. I felt dat' his greatest wish on earth was to git' people to understand dat' 'in God's eyes we are all one'."

"Reggie, yur' wisdom goes far beyond what others kin' see. No child of God, man, or woman in dah' eyes of God should ever be owned. We all have an inherent right to be free an' equal. Reggie, des' thoughts an' emotions ran deep inside of me when I was a slave, now I'm free to release 'dem an' I feel much better fo' it."

"Anastasia, dat' was powerful statement an' I might add, well put! As yu' jus' said, it is time to git' ready an' visit dah' Clark's. We better git' goin' while dah' goin' is good." Reggie said with a smile.

***

As days passed, Reggie continued his hard work, and spent many nights away from home. On occasion Anastasia was able to travel with him, but generally she stayed at home and took care of domestic duties or worked on her book. Of course, Reggie always looked forward to her accompanying him on the road. Reggie liked to say that "it was like having your cake an' eating it too" when she was on the road with him.

One evening at the Wellesley Red Lion Inn in the Berkshires, where they planned to be for business purposes for two to three days, they were having a glass of wine after dinner and noticed a gentleman who seemed to be peering at them while attempting to listen in on their conversation. He appeared to be in his late 30's, of medium build with long, dark hair, and a penetrating look. His eyes stood out as he rose and slowly toddled toward their table. "It is most unusual hearing a Southern drawl up North. I just couldn't resist approaching the two of you. I hope you two don't find me too forward?"

"Not at all sir," Reggie answered respectfully. "My wife an' I are originally from dah' South, an' have since relocated to Boston." It was obvious to Reggie that the gentleman had been drinking to an excess, but he still appeared to be able to properly conduct himself.

"My name is Isaac Knapp," the stranger offered. "At one time I was very close to William Lloyd Garrison. Yu' do know William Lloyd Garrison?"

"Yes, I do. Mr. Knapp, he is dah' editor of *The Liberator*, dah' number one 'bolitionist publication," Reggie stated, thinking that Knapp was a name-dropper.

"Well, that is good. For a second I feared you might excuse yourself when I mentioned William Lloyd Garrison. After all, you do come from the South, and he is not exactly a household favorite down there. Anyhow, we were boyhood friends, and eventually I became his business partner and co-publisher of *The Liberator*," Mr. Knapp proudly announced.

"Mr. Knapp, I'm Reggie Marshall, an' dis' is my wife, Anastasia, I have enjoyed yur' paper an' I find it 'bery intrigin'. Incidentally both of us have a profound respect fo' Mr. Garrision."

Mr. Knapp did not "mince words". "I had a falling out with the editors and was forced out," Knapp related to Anastasia and Reggie. "I have to be honest with you. I'm not doing very well as I'm having a difficult time with alcohol. That said, I must add that I'm surprised and very pleased to meet a Southerner who would find *The Liberator* intriguing. Believe me the two of you represent the exception."

"Mr. Knapp, it may surprise yu' to learn dat' both my wife an' I are former slaves, an' we are now free an' livin' in Boston." Reggie knew this admission would immediately get Mr. Knapp's attention.

Mr. Knapp's eyebrows rose as he pondered the veracity of Reggie's statement. "Well, if that's true, I hope the two of you get involved in the abolitionist movement. We can always use your support." Mr. Knapp avoided mentioning their skin color, which was unusual.

"We have been so occupied wit' work an' gittin' settled, dat' we haven't had time fo' anythin' else. Wit' our backgrounds, we happen to be 'bery sympathetic to dah' movement, but why do yu' think we should git' involved?"

Even though Mr. Knapp was intoxicated and slurring his words, he immediately reacted. "Let me give you the facts to illustrate why we need a call to action and must continue to rally support. The abolitionist movement has had to overcome a lot of serious obstacles. In 1836 Congress passed the gag rule that prohibited discussing or undertaking any business about slavery in Congress, which I might add, was done to placate the South. This rule is definitely anti-democratic, preventing Congress from doing its legal business. Now how do you react to a suppressed Congress? Doesn't that alone just frustrate the hell out of you, sir?"

"Yes, it does," Reggie replied. "An' I'm certain dat' Anastasia would also 'gree."

This positive response is what Knapp had wanted to hear, and he gestured in the air as he continued. "In Alton, Illinois in 1837, Elijah Lovejoy was dragged out of his office and beaten to death by a mob simply because he was the editor of the local anti-slavery newspaper, and they did not want the paper published in their town. Notice, I said this took place in Illinois! Last I heard Illinois was a free state! Don't get it in your head that slavery is just an institution of the South while the North remains squeaky clean. The evil institution permeates our entire country like a messy bird cage, to paraphrase William Lloyd Garrison."

Anastasia and Reggie finished their wine and ordered a cup of coffee. Reggie asked Mr. Knapp if he could get anything for him but he declined and continued talking. "Those of us who call ourselves abolitionists are looked on as pariahs. Southerners think the North sends abolitionists down South to stir up trouble. That's not true. Northerners can't stand us any more than Southerners. I think they would all prefer for us to disappear from the face of the earth. Remember, they think we are the troublemakers who want to start an insurrection that will lead to a bloodbath. That makes us radicals, pure and simple! We know that's not the truth, but that's our reputation, both in the North and the South."

"What's interestin' is dat' dah' Southerners honestly 'lieve dah' North supports dah' 'bolitionist movement," Reggie added. "I also know from experience thar' are groups or individuals dat' act on thar' own to stir up trouble an' don't represent dah' 'bolitionist movement at all. Regardless of who dey' might represent, dey' are automatically tagged as a 'bolitionist by dah' Southerners. Talk 'bout miscommunication, it really is blatant an' destructive."

"That's true," Knapp affirmed, "a lot of them are religious zealots who are against slavery, but have absolutely no connection to the abolitionists."

Reggie told about a scene from his past. "I once saw a religious zealot in a small town in South Carolina who was tarred an' feathered fo' talkin' to some slaves. I know dah' townspeople thought he was a spokesman fo' dah' North, a rabid 'bolitionist. I heard 'dem say it even though he maintained several times that he was not connected to the abolitionist movement. Most of dah' people wanted to hang him. He had to have had a four leaf clover in his possession, 'cuz' he was 'bery lucky to have gotten out of thar' 'live. Of course it did not go easy fo' him since dey' still tarred an' feathered him." Reggie found himself respectfully mimicking Mr. Clark using his four leaf clover expression, which made him ponder if he was beginning to think like a Northerner as well.

Knapp pulled a chair up to their table and nodded in a way that requested approval for his action. They smiled, and he sat down with them. "That's interesting. Are you suggesting that Northerners should stay out of the South?"

"Not at all, Mr. Knapp, however, I do think when dah' 'bolitionists or religious zealots who come down to dah' South should not encourage any type of insurrection. 'Member Nat Turner, who incidentally was not involved in dah' 'bolitionist movement up North? Now dat' was a real bloodbath. I 'lieve thar' is a place fo' 'dem down South, but dey' have to be 'bery judicious 'bout what dey' say or how dey' conduct 'demselves. Violence begets violence, an' dah' South is jus' waitin' fo' any rebel rousin' 'bolitionist. Dey' will hang a 'bolitionist in a heartbeat—dose' Southerners don't mess 'round. Dah' wrong approach will only further exacerbate dah' situation. Let's jus' say dey' are 'bery sensitive to any outsiders comin' 'round."

"What are you saying?" Knapp queried.

"I'm saying dah lines of communication 'tween dah' North an' dah' South are closed, yet nobody wants to take any action to alleviate the problems associated wit' slavery so dah' matter will remain closed. Wouldn't yu 'gree wit' me when I say dis'? The truth is dat' slavery is a United States' institution wit' dah' North goin' 'long wit' dah' South in dah' ugly system as long as dey' keep dah' ugly system down South an' not have to look at. Dat' said, dah' other countries find it difficult to understand why nothin' is bein' done to end slavery hyeh' in dah' United States. In 1833 Britain ended slavery. I hate to put it dis' way, but support 'gainst slavery is pretty strong amongst dah' Negroes, 'bolitionists, Quakers, Indians, an' white women. Unfortunately support is 'bery weak amongst white males fo' endin' slavery hyeh' in dah' United States. Of course all dah' power is held by dah' white males, which means dat' things are not goin' to change.

Knapp smiled politely, as he liked how Reggie presented his position. "Keep talking, Mr. Marshall, I'm listening. By the way, I do agree with you so far."

"I'm suggestin' dat' people in dah' North as well as dose' in dah' South are satisfied to keep dah' evil system goin' while maintain' a status quo. Dah' North an' certainly dah' South see dah' economic benefits an' dat's dah' mischief. It's all 'bout greed an' power. What dey' are doin' to des' poor people is secondary to dah' money. I do think dat' dah' power brokers have thar' long tentacles clutchin' at dah' 'bery fabric of our society, an' dey' are not 'bout to let it go."

Mr. Knapp, not at a loss for words even in his inebriated condition added, "I do like your take on this. I know the abolitionists are bemused at being considered troublemakers when they believe they are only following the teachings of Jesus Christ. They see this whole thing as a contradiction. On the other hand, what you are saying is that economic interests outweigh what is morally right for our country with greed and power outweighing our spiritual values."

"Exactly!" Pleased he had found someone who could understand his views, Reggie continued. "In fact, historically dis' is jus' a reflection of dah' way it has always been worldwide. Truthfully, I think slavery would have died a slow death even in dah' United States, but good ole' cotton became king. I 'lieve 'round 1800 Eli Whitney invented dah' cotton gin, which made growin' cotton far more profitable. Dis' called fo' a much greater increase in production. Of course dah' world cotton boom certainly reflected dah' other part of dah' equation. All dis' made it necessary fo' more slaves to be brought in to feed dah' gang system of labor required fo' growin' an' pickin' cotton. Mr. Knapp, it's all 'bout greed 'long wit' power, pure an' simple, an' I know I'm bein' redundant! In fact, puttin' dah' blame on greed should be obvious since greed is almost dah' driver fo' all dah' other problems in our country an' fo' dat' matter, the entire world. Mr. Knapp, I believe a fool kin' see what I'm sayin' an' knows it is true."

Reggie just couldn't resist relating a personal experience. "I jus' tole' yu' what I think is dah' backdrop fo' why we needed more slaves. Mr. Knapp, I kin' relate to yu' jus' how twisted dah' minds of Southerners kin' be when it comes to slaves. A minister who I was enslaved to, tole me dat' it was through dah' kindness of dah' Southerners dat' Negroes were privileged to come hyeh' an' leave dat' dark continent whar' dey' were livin' in holes. Now how far-fetched is dat'? I git' upset jus' thinkin' 'bout it. Dey' always come up wit' des' stories to make it sound like everythin' is jus' 'peaches an' cream' hyeh' in dah' United States, when we all know dah' truth. He really suffered from delusions. As we were riding in his buggy, he would always comment on how happy dah' field hands were in dah' cotton fields. He observed thar' singin' reflected how happy dey' were wit' pickin' cotton. Dah' fool never realized dey' only sang fo' thar' survival in order to make dah' best of a horrible existence. Sadly, Mr. Knapp, what he espoused is what most of dah' plantation owners throughout dah' South thought."

Mr. Knapp confessed, "I was going to teach you and your wife a lesson or two, but I think you're the one enlightening me. That doesn't happen very often. I must admit, you have a lot of fervor in yu'!"

Anastasia smiled as she addressed Reggie and Mr. Knapp. "I think yu' have both learned things dis' evenin' an' so have I."

Even though alcohol had taken its toll on Mr. Knapp, he still had one more important salvo left in him. "Well, there is one bright spot to relate about slavery. Last March, Justice Joseph Story freed the African prisoners who were on the *Amistad* slave ship; however, there was a caveat, and it was a big one—his brief clearly established they were not being freed because they were slaves. Instead, they were determined to be kidnapped citizens from Africa, and as such, under international law had to be freed from their kidnappers. I also wish to point out how former President John Quincy Adams acquitted himself quite well as their counsel."

"Dat' is an interestin' twist," Reggie said with a touch of anger and sarcasm in his voice. "In other words, if dey' had been considered slaves, din' dey' never would have been freed?"

"That is correct, Mr. Marshall. Court decisions have not been favorable toward ending slavery; however as I said, we have a bright spot here. They were still freed, regardless of why. That alone is significant. Maybe this could be the start of something." Knapp reached for his drink, nearly tumbling out of his chair. Reggie caught his arm, just in time to prevent his fall.

Reggie, unable to contain himself exclaimed, "Mr. Knapp, I think it was truly a magnanimous decision, which moved our country into dah' right direction. However, take a closer look at dah' decision, an' 'member, 'dah' devil kin' be found in dah' details'." Reggie drew a deep breath and went on. "We need to really examine dis' further since it only goes halfway."

Mr. Knapp broke in. "I don't quite know where you are headed but I hope you are not bringing in any mischief?"

"On dah' contrary Mr. Knapp, I merely want to enlighten yu' on somethin'. By yur' own admission dey' were released an' freed since dey' were determined to be kidnapped citizens from Africa, an' as such fell under international law and had to freed from thar' kidnappers. Now, Mr. Knapp, let's assume dat' under similar circumstances dey' were captured after dey' had been previously in Puerto Rico whar' dey' had been held fo' 'seasonin'' to be eventually sent to the South to serve as 'full blown slaves'. Technically, once dey' git' to Puerto Rico, din' wouldn't dey' become enslaved an' as such internationl law would no longer apply so dey' could not be freed an' din' would have to be sent back to Puerto Rico for enslavement?"

Mr. Knapp was engrossed in what Reggie was saying. "That is a very good point and I believe that the scenario that you have just laid out is correct and indeed scary. Yes, they would probably have to be sent back to Puerto Rico."

Reggie quickly stated, "I find all dis' rather interestin' or should I say revulsive."

"Mr. Marshall, I think you know the courts move rather slowly," Knapp's reply appeared to be defensive.

Reggie somberly replied in the most emblematic manner. "Mr. Knapp let us not sugar-coat dis' important issue. Anyway yu' slice it, slavery is immoral—a direct contradiction to what God commands from His people—period! Now, dah' reason we continue wit' dis' immoral system is obvious—it's economic consideration's overridin' spiritual an' social justice. We twist an' misrepresent dah' Bible—whatever is necessary to justify our selfish needs. I know I'm bein' mundane but, meanwhile, look at what we are doin' to des' poor people who have to immeasurably suffer under dis' horrible system. However, puttin' dah' truth 'side, dah' repercussions on dah' court would be far too great to make dah' right decision, which would be to simply 'bolish slavery. In fact, I would wager in a hypothetical ruling dat' any member of dah' court who would vote to abolish slavery would find ' himself ostracized wit' many people wantin' him impeached. I also 'lieve' dat' if yu' could git' dah' ear of some of des' Supreme Court members in privacy dey' would 'gree dat' it should be 'bolished, but dey' want to keep thar' jobs an' not make waves. Mr. Knapp, I usually 'lieve in compromise, but in dis' case I have to take a more radical approach. Rich people who benefit from dah' evil system have a lot of power an'dat't power extends to dah' court. I personally don't think dat' dis' pernicious system will be overturned in a soft an' gentle manner. It's goin' to take somethin' big to turn dis' 'round."

"Oh, Mr. Marshall you have the makings of a real firebrand don't you? Let me say, I agree with you a hundred percent on everything you have just said. Unfortunately, it's unrealistic to even think about a court decision outlawing slavery. It will have to end in some other manner."

"Mr. Knapp, yu' are right an'dat' other manner will be war. But let me pique yur' interest yet on 'nother matter. I'm sur' yu' know yur' history quite well, so I'm only reacquaintin' yu' wit' dis' information. In 1692 in Salem, Massachusetts, 20 innocent people were executed by hangin' fo' witchcraft. Incidentally one man, Giles Corey, was pressed to death. Now, I have a strong feelin' dat' dis' 'trocity will be studied in American history as well as it should be. However, what troubles me is dat' today we know of documented cases in dah' South whar' slaves have been put to death by burnin' at dah' stake. Now, we all know dat' death by burnin' is absolutely one of dah' worst forms of death, if not dah' worst. Mr. Knapp, how familiar are Americans wit' what I jus' tole' yu'? I dare say not too familiar, an' I find dat' extremely troublin' as one day I believe dat' children will be taught all 'bout dah' Salem witch trials an' nothin' 'bout dah' slaves who were burned to death at dah' stake! It will simply end up bein' fo'gotten in American history. How do yu' feel 'bout dat', Mr. Knapp? Doesn't dat' jus' turn yur' stomach? I guess it's jus' not as important since it only involves black people bein' put to death. Let's put it 'nother way, if dey' were puttin' white people to death in dah' South by burnin' at dah' stake, do yu' think more would be said? I think yu' kin' answer dat' yur'self. I'm sorry but dis' is really a sensitive subject fo' me.!"

"Mr. Marshall, hearing this makes me shudder. Why I'm the former co-editor of *The Liberator* and I never made this connection and I did read Weld's book, <u>American Slavery As It Is,</u> which discusses this very issue. The burning of Negroes on the stake has to represent one of the greatest blights on America, simply put—unconscionable! You are correct in saying that young people will be taught all about the Salem witch trials while the deaths of slaves being burned at the stake in the South will probably go relatively unnoticed. That truly upsets me. It addresses that certain parts of history can be emphasized while other parts are forgotten—especially black history! I really have to hand it to you. Mr. Marshall, your compassion and insightfulness goes far beyond the normal. Even though I've had too much to drink, I know when I've had an insightful conversation. Thank you, Mr. and Mrs. Marshall, for providing me with such a thought-provoking evening."

Reggie assured him, "Mr. Knapp, it's been a true pleasure an' a real privilege to have had dis' conversation wit' somebody of yur' stature. I know dat' both of us will always cherish dis' meetin'. We want to thank yu' as well. Oh yes, earlier I did say dat' dah' issue of slavery would be settled by war an' I meant it. I don't want to further indulge yu' on dis issue as it is late, but suffice to say, we will have a civil war wit' dah' North victorious ovah' dah' South an' dah' South will be forced to accept dah' end to slavery."

Knapp was intrigued by what Reggie just said, but surprisingly, he had little to say. It was apparent that he was so intoxicated that he was about to pass out. Instead, he appeared to be somewhat embarrassed by the accolades being handed to him as he slurred his final words. "Again, it was a real pleasure and I hope that we will run into each other again sometime in the near future. I wish you both nothing but good fortune in the future."

"We certainly enjoyed dah' conversation, an' likewise, hope to see yu' 'gain some time soon. Good evenin'." Anastasia's words brought a smile to Knapp's face, and the couple rose to wish him well and retire for the evening.

As they walked out of the dining room, Reggie turned to his wife and quietly said, "I would have liked to have picked his brain a little longer an' in more depth, but I could sense yu' were uncomfortable wit' his drunken state. It is unfortunate his drinkin' caused him to lose his job as dah' co-editor of, *The Liberator.* He really does have so many good qualities goin' fo' him."

"He's such an interestin' an' intelligent man. Yu' jus' wish dat' he could git' his feet back on dah' ground." Anastasia agreed.

"Let's git' some rest. We'll be headin' home early in dah' mornin'."

"That sounds perfect," Anastasia smiled warmly at her husband and added. "It's really somethin' dat' we kin' combine yur' work schedule wit' some pleasure."

Reggie added, "Bein' wit' yu' is always a pleasure my love, no matter whar' we are, or what we're doin'." With that, they had reached their room and retired for the evening.

CHAPTER THIRTY-ONE

The holidays quickly descended upon Anastasia and Reggie. Sarah's enthusiasm and knowledge helped immensely in preparation for the upcoming holidays. Her graciousness even went further as she was able to help them decorate their new home as well.

In addition to spending time together enjoying their new home, the Clark's insisted they spend time with them during the holidays. This included enjoying both Thanksgiving and Christmas Eve at the Clarks with traditional meals served for both holidays. In addition, gifts were exchanged for Christmas. Both of the holidays were warmly accepted and proved to be wonderful experiences for Reggie and Anastasia. Only a few privileged Bostonians would ever have the opportunity to celebrate Thanksgiving and Christmas at the level afforded to Reggie and Anastasia through the Clark's generosity. Coming from a life of servitude made all of this even more amazing. This was truly the beginning of a "rags to riches" story.

The holidays passed by very quickly, and before they knew it, the winter of 1842 had descended upon them. Even with their Southern roots, they had no problem maintaining a positive attitude through the dreary winter months knowing on the other hand, they now had so much to be thankful for. In spite of the extreme cold, which was new to both of them, they enjoyed taking short walks and watching the neighborhood children romping in the white fluffy snow. Meanwhile, Anastasia continued to faithfully work on her book. In addition, she was hoping in the back of her mind that sometime in the near future she would be having a family with Reggie and seeing her own children playing in the snow. Diligently, Reggie continued to maintain his constructive work ethic. In spite of weather conditions, which made it extremely difficult to travel, he was still able to cover his territory and do an excellent job. Also, at Reggie's urging, their support for social and political interests remained in the forefront.

Nationally, the political scene was interesting. President Van Buren's term of office had expired. Meanwhile, the country survived the economic crash of 1837, which was primarily caused from a plunge in world cotton prices.

Reggie thought it was unfortunate rememberng that some slaves falsely believed that Van Buren, himself a Northerner from New York, might take some measures to end slavery. However, nothing changed, which of course was of no surprise to Reggie. He well knew this represented yet another example of the slaves clinging onto some far fetched hope. He mulled to himself, what else do they have to live for? After Van Buren finished his term, William Henry Harrison, a Virginian, was sworn into office in March of 1841. After a lengthy inaugural address in the cold, he died a month later from pneumonia that was alleged to have been contracted from his carriage ride to Washington D.C. Harrison held office approximately one month, and John Tyler, another Virginian, succeeded him. Incidentally, Tyler was a neighbor to Reggie's father, Colonel Marshall. Like the colonel, his plantation was also along the James River outside of Richmond. Considered to be a weak President, Tyler's Presidency reflected the continuing tradition of the government avoiding any controversial issues including slavery. It would just have to remain a very hot issue nationally, but not to be addressed by the government. Meanwhile, slavery was woven into the entire fabric of our economic infrastructure, which only encouraged maintaining its status quo. It appeared that it wouldn't matter who was President, circumstances were not going to change. For most Americans, this issue would continue to cause some concern with the general public. But the country was clinging to the false belief that slavery would eventually die a slow death, which made the issue much easier to deal with.

Reggie pondered over the "money changers" in the Bible who rebuffed Jesus Christ over greed. Regarding slavery, certainly greed stood in the forefront just as much as in Biblical times when money was being made in the temples. Does mankind's drive for greed and power ever improve? This was a burning question that Reggie examined and concluded that things were pretty much the same as always—no change, business as usual!

***

After a particularly grueling week, while calling on accounts and battling snow-laden roads, Reggie returned home in time to attend a speech at Faneuil Hall given by the leading abolitionist speaker, Frederick Douglass, he had been looking forward to this event for some time.

Anastasia, who was beginning to develop a little interest in politics wanted to go as well. Of course, Reggie was excited to bring her along. They quickly readied themselves and they departed knowing this was the first political event the two would attend together. It was a cold buggy ride to Faneuil Hall, but the thrill of the impending event made their discomfort a small sacrifice. As they entered the building, they knew they hadn't arrived too early as a large crowd was already present. Both were taken aback by the size of the hall. The interior of the hall was interesting. Brick and wood was in dominance with large chandeliers providing the necessary light. A mixed crowd of people could be seen roaming throughout the building socializing as they awaited the festivities to begin and of course to hear the keynote speaker, Frederick Douglass.

As the couple inched their way through the crowd, Reggie couldn't help but notice two prominent abolitionists, William Lloyd Garrison and Wendell Phillips. He had seen pictures of them and recognized them. The two men both stood with the look of confidence. Garrison had very pointed features was bald, bespectacled, and slight of build. Phillips was balding slightly, and like Garrison, was also slight of build. The two men who looked to be in their thirties had somewhat similar appearances and were standing together just surveying the crowd as Reggie and Anastasia walked up and boldly, yet politely, spoke to them. "Mr. Garrison an' Mr. Phillips, I would like to introduce ourselves. I'm Reggie Marshall an' dis' is my wife Anastasia, I thought yu' might find it interestin' to know dat' dah' two of us are former slaves. We are now free an' wanted to meet dah' two of yu'—men who have tirelessly fought 'gainst a horrible system we had to endure fo' so long." After Reggie spoke, he wondered if they might take offense at his forwardness, or worse yet, if they thought he was acting as a sycophant. He might be guilty of assuming they would find it interesting to know they were former slaves.

Garrison spoke first. "I would normally find it very interesting indeed to meet two people who have actually been enslaved and are now free. However, I must admit that neither of you have any Negro features, which calls into question your credibility as I'm sure you'll understand." It was obvious that Garrison was not a man who would mince his words.

Phillips looked over Anastasia and Reggie from head to toe and sarcastically added. "This appears to be a hoax almost like the two of you are making mockery of us. I understand why Mr. Garrison would doubt your integrity. If you two were former slaves, then maybe I'd better take a closer look at my own roots." Mr. Phillips and Mr. Garrison smiled when the comment was made.

Anastasia, insulted by what she had heard, stepped in front of Reggie. "We have no intention of provin' our credibility, but Mr. Garrison, yur' former partner, Isaac Knapp, was very courteous to us, an' didn't find any humor associated wit' our backgrounds. In fact, we enjoyed a most fruitful conversation wit' him." Reggie was surprised at Anastasia's strong offensive posture.

"You met Isaac?" Garrison and Phillips spoke at the same time.

"Unfortunately he was in his cup," Reggie answered, "but

he was 'bery engagin' an' cordial to us."

"Regrettably, Isaac has a serious drinking problem," Garrison remarked. "He is my dear boyhood friend and I still think a lot of him, but we had to part ways because of his abuse with alcohol." Garrison and Phillips appeared to warm up to them after they found out both of them knew Isaac Knapp.

"Miscegenation is very common in the South. The two of you have to be a product of that practice, and quite frankly, you surprised us. At first I thought you might be a couple of quacks—my apologies. As abolitionists, William and I have been confronted with people, who let's just say, lack sincerity." Phillips' tone was almost apologetic as he smoothed things over.

"Wendell is right," Garrison added. "I owe you an apology. Sometimes I can be presumptuous, and it gets me into trouble. The two of you could prove to be valuable members of our organization, and we would certainly welcome you both."

Frederick Douglass suddenly approached and joined the conversation. Both Reggie and Anastasia were surprised but very pleased at the opportunity to speak directly and so easily with a black man of such stature.

Phillips made the introductions. "Frederick, I want you to meet Reggie and Anastasia Marshall. They both were former slaves and now live, I believe, right here in Boston."

A young man in his twenties, good looking, tall, and of medium build, Douglass had riveting eyes with a commanding appearance. He was effusive regarding Reggie and Anastasia's enslavement. "It is an honor to meet anyone who was formerly shackled. I know yu' would have a 'bery special feelin' in yur' heart dat' must be 'bery difficult to comprehend."

"Mr. Douglass," Reggie responded, "we went through hell an' back, an' I personally have deep scars dat' remind me every day of my experiences. If anyone ever doubts me, dey' kin' look at my back as it is horribly disfigured from what dey' call a cat-haulin' in Georgia." Reggie wanted to show the three men but he knew this was not the right time or place.

Douglass looked at Phillips and Garrison and said, "I have

heard of dis' practice. It's one of dose' thins' dat' is buried in dah' South an' would seldom, if ever, be discussed up North." Turning to Reggie, he asked, "Mr. Marshall, are yu' familiar wit' Negro plaster? I had dat' administered on me."

"Yessuh', I am. I also received dat' treatment. It's a concoction made up of vinegar, pepper, mustard, an' salt dat' dey' rub ovah' yur' back atter' a whippin' to sorta' 'sooth dah' pain', as dah' overseer would say! Jus' more torture, dat's all it is."

"Yu' really do know," Douglass was taken aback by Reggie's knowledge, "I 'lieve yu' went through even more din' I did, an' dat' would make yu' exceptional. What 'bout yu', Anastasia?" Douglass reached out to hold her hands as he addressed her.

"Mr. Douglass, I was always a personal servant, but at a certain point I had to repel dah' advances of my owner as he had transferred me to my own private cottage. Fortunately, he backed off from his attack. Out of anger he slapped me in dah' face an' din' threatened to sell me down South whar' I would probably end up in one of dose' sportin' houses in New Orlens'. I honestly must say dat' I was 'bery fortunate dat' he saw fit to hire me out to a kind lady in Richmond an' I was spared a horrible fate."

Mr. Douglass was empathetic. "Yu' are truly fortunate as dat' would have been such a destructive experience fo' a young woman to have to go through. Emotionally yu' would have been ruined, not to mention dah' physical consequences. In my judgment, dat' would have been far worse din' receivin' a severe whippin'." He thought for a moment about this pair of former slaves, now free, and wondered if his probing into their past would allow him to ask a relevant question. "Let me ask yu' a question, Reggie. What is yur' thinkin' 'bout slavery an' dah' relations 'tween dah' North an' dah' South?"

Garrison and Phillips were a bit surprised at the interest Douglass gave to Reggie and Anastasia; however, they both knew there had to be some bonding going on since the three were former slaves.

Reggie wasted no time, seizing at the opportunity to be heard. "Gentlemen, I know we would all 'gree dat' slavery must end. It's a horrible, inhumane institution dat' should not reflect what our country is all 'bout. In fact, dah' Lawd' has shown me in several visions dat' thar' will be a violent an' costly civil war 'tween dah' North an' dah' South. Dah' North will win an' 'bolish slavery unless we do somethin' different to alter dis' course. Dah' vision came to me through a tall man who presented himself as dah' President of dah' United States speakin' to a crowd at a cemetery to honor dah' fallen soldiers who gave thar' lives at dat' great battle."

"In all of history there has never been a war fought to end slavery," Phillips argued, a comment Reggie was not surprised to hear.

"Yu' are correct wit' perhaps Haiti bein' dah' exception but do not fall into dah' trap dat' says thar' cannot be a civil war fought in dah' United States ovah' slavery." Reggie looked at each of the men as he responded.

"I'm sorry, Mr. Marshall, but it is difficult to accept that slavery will end in a violent civil war. That really is a tough scenario to embrace." Phillips looked at Douglass as he spoke, hoping to see an indication of his agreement.

Mr. Garrison asked Reggie a pointed question, "Do you support the abolitionist society? I can only assume you do."

Reggie quickly reacted. "I do support dah' 'bolitionist society but not dah' use of violence as a means to an end. Dah' Nat Turner rebellion is a good example, an' unlike other Southerners, I don't blame dah' 'bolitionist movement fo' dat' incident in any way. Turner operated independently of any movement other din' his own. We know it ended in bloodshed an' further divided our nation. Unfortunately, dah' South attached Nat Turner to dah' 'bolitionists, which meant dey' thought he was gettin' support from dah' North. Violence always makes matters much worse—creates distrust, hate, division an' din' more violence. Again, dah' North had nothin' to do wit' Nat Turner, yet dah' North will shoulder dah' fault fo' what he did an' only further widen dah' gap 'tween dah' two. Incidentally, I realize he was actin' out of sheer frustration an' to dat' degree he kin' be fo'given."

"Mr. Marshall, dat' is level headed an' insightful. Wit' dat' in mind, what road do yu' suggest we travel?" It was obvious, Douglass was impressed with Reggie.

With the leading abolitionist in the country giving him an audience, Reggie continued. "Again, I suggest we travel down dah' road of nonviolence. Let me add somethin' else 'bout dah' use of violence. In dah' second vision, I saw a black man way off into dah' future deliverin' a speech 'gainst inequality in our nation's capital. Yes gentlemen, slavery had long ended but not inequality, an' he proposed usin' only nonviolence to reach equality. He knew violence would not solve dah' problem as dah' nation was in some ways still recoverin' from dah' violent civil war dat' had been fought much earlier dat' had legally ended slavery. Now dah' battle was bein' waged ovah' gainin' equality, which had proven to be elusive as so many barriers had been constructed followin' dah' Civil War to prevent equality. He preached dat' faith, love, fo'giveness an' 'bove all—nonviolence are dah' paths we must use to end inequality an' racial division."

Phillips, Garrison and Douglass stood quietly, awaiting more from Reggie.

Reggie took a deep breath. What he was about to say represented very radical thinking for its time. "I would support dah' government gittin' actively involved in buyin' out every slave in dah' United States at fair market price. I also realize it would cost millions of dollars, an' most of dat' money would have to come from dah' North since dah' South does not have nearly as much capital as dah' North. Also, dah' North would see dah' newly freed slaves pourin' up North fo' a job as a real problem since dey' would possibly drive down wages an' create unemployment. Yes, I kin' see dah' obvious problems."

Garrison quickly confirmed what Reggie said, "That would be true about the wage issue, and that represents one of the major obstacles in abolishing slavery. You also mentioned paying off the slave owners—that will not happen! Also, keep in mind the importation of more slaves continues to move at a rapid pace even as we are now speaking which leads me to believe that your plan will only get increasingly more difficult."

Reggie quickly responded, "But it would be a lot cheaper din' dah' alternative—a civil war. Dah' newly freed slaves could remain on dah' plantation as tenants or sharecroppers so dah' labor supply on dah' plantations would stablilize. Frankly, I'm only guessin', but 'gain I would think dat' most of 'dem would stay in dah' South an' continue workin' in dah' cotton fields since dat' is all dey' know. Mr. Garrison yu' mention dat' dah' government would never agree to compensate dah' slave owners an' dat' is whar' dah' problem lies. In addition, slave owners would never agree to give up a good portion of thar' wealth, which is tied to slaves wit'out jus' compensation. Unfortunately, dah' sheer amount of money we are talkin' 'bout is so great dat' it would almost preclude dah' possibility of any peaceful resolution. Nevertheless, gentlemen, compensation has to be 'on the table' an' wit'out it, dah' only alternative will be war." When Reggie talked, his actions represented a prophetic appeal for the men to listen and fully understand the consequences of "business as usual".

"That's plumb crazy! I've never met a man who was in the business of telling the future and yet, could be so wrong. Your argument assumes we are headed for a civil war. Again, most people believe slavery will just die a slow death. We in the abolitionist movement are in the business to hasten that process, but we must be realistic, a civil war will not happen in our country." Phillips stepped back a few feet as he talked while preparing to leave the conversation.

"Again, unless we choose a different path din' dah' one we're currently on," Reggie reiterated, "we will have a violent civil war in dah' near future wit' thousands an' thousands of Americans dyin' in dat' war. In addition, all dah' sufferin', death an' destruction, an'dah' monetary cost of dis' war will be far greater din' to jus' compensate dah' slave owners. Further, we cannot be taken in by dis' horrible canard dat' subscribes to slavery jus' dyin' a slow death wit'out any repercussions. Dis' is based on never havin' a major war, out side of Haiti, ever fought over slavery but 'gain, history does not always have to repeat itself. Folks, our own universe cannot always be predictable, why do we think dat' humans kin' go beyond dah' universe an' predict dah' future? Dat' is really narrow minded thinkin' an' frankly—absurd!"

"Anythin' else to add, Mr. Marshall? I must say yu' make a compelling case." Douglass was pleased with the manner in which he presented his position and held to his beliefs.

Reggie pleaded, "Gentlemen, let me briefly say one other thin' regardin' dis' matter. As I have stated more din' once, almost everybody supports dah' slow death theory regardin' dah' end of slavery. However, I'm havin' a difficult time findin' any evidence dat' supports dat' things are gettin' better. Looks to me as if yu' should be lookin' fo' some trend dat' would substantiate dat' slavery is headed to jus' die a slow death. Realistically, things are only lookin' worse as we see more slaves 'rivin' from Afriky' compoundin' dah' problem. Meanwhile, dah' North will remain content wit' 'out of sight an' out of mind' an' not deal wit' dah' reality of dah' situation. Just show me one trend demonstratin' dat' things are actually improvin' 'tween dah' North an' dah' South? Good luck findin' dat' positive trend dat' could bring all of us some hope. Personally, I'm still lookin' fo' it, I jus' havn't found it!"

It was obvious that Reggie had done his homework and was making everyone uncomfortable as he laid out a strong case that was certainly worth examining. Douglass knew it was time for him to say something. "David Walker has said we are goin' to have a war 'tween dah' blacks an' dah' whites, an' if yu' an' David Walker are right, maybe we better start doin' somethin' to prevent a major conflict now. I think dat's what yu' are sayin' as well."

Reggie's voice rose emphatically. "Gentlemen, dah' debil' is in dah' details! Regrettably, all dah' different self-interests, 'long wit' greed, power, pride, an' stubbornness will work to prevent a peaceful end to slavery unless we move immediately on overcomin' these difficult barriers. Yu' men have dah' power to git' things movin' in a positive direction. I would give dis' some serious thought an' 'take dah' bull by dah' horns' an' git' slavery 'bolished through compromise an' not war. 'Member gentlemen, dah' clock is tickin'!"

Phillips' manners demonstrated that he had no intention of accepting Reggie's conclusion. In the spirit of compromise he did state, "There could be some merit in what you've said, but right now, I just can't support your thinking."

"It's a possibility," Garrison added, "but right now, I'm going to have to see more evidence to support your theory."

Douglass took the role of the contrarian and commented, "I think yu' might 'bery well be onto somethin' Reggie, an' I would certainly not rule anythin' out. I want a little more time to see how events unfold, but if relations 'tween dah' North an' dah' South continue to git' worse wit' no end in sight, din' maybe what yu' predict will happen. Hopefully, thar' will still be time to initiate some of yur' remedies." Garrison and Phillips were taken aback at how supportive Douglass was regarding Reggie's position.

Reggie was a little displeased for having only convinced one of these three influential men to seriously consider what he had said. Still, it only takes one voice to help put things into motion and it did appear that Douglass, the most influential of the three was supportive of Reggie's position. Knowing he had support from Douglas, he said in closing, "Gentlemen, I do hope y'all give what I have said some consideration. We need to take bold measures in dah' spirit of compromise, which could eventually lead to unity an' a resolution. 'Gain, please give it some consideration fo' dah' good of our nation an' it's people are at stake."

"Thank yu, Reggie an' Anastasia. What yu' have said could be dah' most insightful words I have heard in a long time, but if yu'll please excuse me, I have a speech to give as Wendell and William will be joinin' me on stage. Thank yu', brother an' sister, an' by dah' way, I think dah' two of yu' in a 'bery special way might be able to relate to dah' short speech I'm givin'." Douglass then smiled, nodded and winked. For Reggie and Anastasia it was a special compliment for Mr. Douglass to have referred to them as "brother and sister".

Everyone shook hands and the three men departed for the stage area. Reggie and Anastasia were left awestruck at what had just ensued, a spirited conversation with three of the leading figures of the abolitionist movement. Now, they both recognized the need to relax and find something else to talk about. It struck Reggie just how cosmopolitan the crowd was compared to anything he had ever witnessed in the South where the people were generally more provincial. In fact this was even quite different then what he had observed in the North when on the road making sales calls. He had witnessed in the North that the blacks and whites seldom mixed. This eclectic gathering here at Faneuil Hall actually reminded him more of the South, where the blacks and whites mixed quite frequently. Reggie reminded Anastasia about his observation.

Anastasia astutely explained to Reggie that he left something out of his equation. "Reggie yur' assessment was true exceptin' yu' fo'got to mention dat' while dis' mixed gatherin' might be rare in dah' North at least dah' Negroes are treated equal hyeh' at Faneuil Hall wit' dah' whites. Yu' well know, Reggie dat' down South, when dah' Negroes mix wit' dah' whites dey' are thar' as slaves—a far cry from bein' fellow peers. My love, need I say more?"

"Anastasia, more frequently din' I sometime realize, yu' have a way of correctin' me when I make a faulty observation. Thank yu', 'cuz' yu' are so inciteful in yur' comments." He then nodded and smiled in agreement.

***

Music was provided by a string quartet accompanied by a piano. Absent of any vocalist, it was a little different from small Southern bands. In the South, Reggie and Anastasia had grown accustomed to music with lyrics at social functions that often would cast dispersions on people of color. They were led to wonder why the music of the South seemed to be preoccupied with black people if they felt blacks were so inferior to white people. It was just one of many inconsistences they had noted about the South. Meanwhile, Reggie and Anastasia wanted to just enjoy the classical music while awaiting the start of the program.

When the program was about to start, the couple moved through the crowd to find seating as close to the stage as possible. A pastor began the event with a prayer, followed with words about the headliner, Mr. Douglass. He made it clear the theme for the evening was abolition and assured everyone they would find themselves highly informed and quite moved. It was most unusual for Reggie and Anastasia to attend a gathering with this theme after having to listen to quite the opposite all of there life—words and messages that extolled servitude with an emphasis on obedience and respecting the superiority of white people.

After several inspiring speakers, the pastor walked to center stage and spoke only six words, "Ladies and Gentlemen, Mr. Frederick Douglass." A long spirited applause followed Mr. Douglass as he approached the podium. All eyes were riveted on him, everyone anxiously anticipating his message.

He stood at the podium not saying a word, drawing the audience in with his demeanor. Finally, he was ready to deliver his satirical message on "obedience" for the slaves to follow, which represented a complete mockery of most white Southern preachers.

"Yu' too, my friends, have souls of infinite value!
Souls dat' will live through endless happiness or misery
in eternity. Oh, labor diligently to make yur' callin' an'
election sure. Oh, receive into yur' souls des' words
of dah' holy apostle—Servants, be obedient unto yur'
master. Oh, consider dah' wonderful goodness of God!
Look at yur' hard, thorny hands, yur' strong, muscular
frames, an' see how mercifully He has adapted yu' to
the duties you are to fulfill, while to your masters, who
have slender frames and long, delicate fingers, He has
given brilliant intellects, dat' may do dah' thinkin'
while yu' do dah' workin'."

It was obviously meant to be a satire, and the audience cheered and applauded as Douglass delivered his final words. A satirical sermon, this was the prelude to a longer address, but this oration proved to be far more dramatic and, ironically not just a satire to Anastasia and Reggie as the message was one they were forced to hear and accept in the South when they were required to attend church services conducted by a white minister. They recalled, all too well, of being reminded by the preacher just how fortunate they were as Negro servants and field hands to have the white people over them so they could be properly taken care of since on their own they were utterly helpless. The key to these sermons always dealt with God's intent for the slaves to realize just how inferior and needy they were to the white people, who of course always had their best interests at heart. Hence, the bondage system was almost synonymous to the guardian institution of a horse owner who has a guardian responsibility to his animal. Again, the "peculiar institution" of the South was indeed shaped by the misinterpretation and the "cherry picking" of the Bible, which led to socially justifying that slaves fell into a "guardian institution", which God accepted since black people were treated ridiculously, not equal to white people.

Other activities and speakers followed, but this short satirical message delivered by Frederick Douglass was the highlight of the evening. The rousing speech by Douglass would one day be considered as one of the greatest satirical speeches ever given in American history. He had successfully crafted and delivered his words so they truly moved the audience humorously, but seriously.

When the program ended many found their way to nearby taverns to further discuss the events of the evening. However, Anastasia and Reggie rode home in near silence through the streets, declining to make conversation with others. The satire given by Douglass reminded them of their past, which brought back such unhappy feelings. Further, Reggie was displeased with himself for not making a better impression on Garrison and Phillips. "Anastasia, it really troubles me to have an audience wit' people of thar' caliber an' walk away feelin' like I failed. My love what does it take to git' people to listen an' act while we still have time? Dey' are dah' leadin' abolitionists. Of all people who should listen an' maybe sign on—dey'should be dah' ones. Other din' Frederick Douglass, dey' largely dismissed me as dah' eternal dreamer!"

"Reggie don't be so hard on yurself'. Yu' still have time to git' dah' word out."

Little more was said as they rode home. However, Reggie had something else on his mind that would remain unsaid until they got home.

Once home, he sat Anastasia down and shared his intentions with her. He wanted to return to Georgia as soon as possible to free Joseph and Willy. His tone was very serious. "It's been some time since I left dah' South. My love, yu' have always been on my mind from dah' moment I started my journey to Boston an' fortunately through dah' efforts of Mr. Clark, yu' have rejoined me. As yu' know, however, I still have some unfinished business. I dream of findin' Joseph an' Willy an' freein' 'dem from slavery as well. Listenin' to Mr. Douglass has fired me up even more. Recently, I have talked to Mr. Clark 'bout my intent to find 'dem, an' he understands why I feel dis' way an' respects me fo' honorin' my commitment to my friends. Wit' Mr. Clark's support, I'm goin' back in dah' spring to git' 'dem, an' I think its imperative dat' we start makin' preparations now. I do hope yu' understand why dis' means so much to me. I need to git' dah' wheels in motion now!"

"Yu' know I support yu'. In fact, as I tole' yu' 'fore, I will go wit' yu' to dah' farthest ends of dah' world. I dearly want to meet yur' two best friends."

"Dis' could prove to be a dangerous mission. Yu' have to realize dah' risks involved. I certainly want yu' to come wit' me, but it's yur' decision to make." Reggie could see in her eyes how excited she was to accompany him. "As a reward fo' both of us, I think we should go on our honeymoon to Niagra Falls, when we git' back," Reggie stated.

With that, they both turned in for the night with the hopes and dreams that weighed heavy on their minds. They both were able to fall into a much needed heavy slumber.

CHAPTER THIRTY-TWO

Reggie spent most of his free time engaged in planning their trip to Georgia to rescue his friends. Meanwhile, with Mr. Clark's influence, a merchant ship with an extra cabin had been located and passage from Boston to Savannah was secured.

Through his effort, Reggie's sales were rewarding and he was able to substantially reduce his debt to Mr. Clark while saving a fair amount of money to purchase Joseph and Willy's freedom. In addition, Mr. Clark, knowing that Reggie could be trusted, said he would back him with additional funds to insure that he could cover the costs for the manumission of his friends.

Careful planning dictated that he should carry a money belt strapped under his clothing while knowing the risks involved in carrying such a large sum of money. As he knew it was paramount for him not to fail, the mission would have to require special attention to details.

Arrangements had been made to ensure everything at home was taken care of. If necessary Mr. Clark made plans to have Kenneth Miller available to service Reggie's customers.

Reggie and Anastasia had rehearsed a plan in the event that they might be challenged. Their strategy if questioned required them to remain calm and collected without demonstrating any anxiety. If under question, they would further provide they were simply everyday people from Richmond who were interested in possibly purchasing some land for investment purposes. If their credibility came under question after all of this, he carried their papers of manumission in his money-belt. Tragically, there were documented cases where free blacks even with papers were unlawfully seized and forced into slavery. This represented just another dark side to slavery. They were aware that with their skin color, the probability of being challenged was very slight. Nevertheless, Reggie and Anastasia knew the stakes were still very great knowing the element of chance and uncertainty required that you can never be absolutely sure that everything is 100% foolproof. Reggie was reminded of Robert Burns as he stated to Anastasia, "'Dah' best plans of men and mice often go awry'. Anastasia, simply put, we have to always remain vigilant against any carelessness."

The time between the planning stage and the day of departure came quickly. Mr. and Mrs. Clark, and Sarah accompanied Reggie and Anastasia to the merchant ship, *The Hampshire*. After their farewells and good wishes, they boarded the ship where they were greeted by a Captain Smith. To their pleasure, he appeared to be quite friendly. To no ones surprise, he had the stereotypical look of a middle aged sea captain—a long flowing white beard, shoulder length white hair and a ruddy complexion weathered from years of life on the sea. Very affable, he assured them that while at sea he would enjoy a conversation with them when time permitted.

On board, very quickly Reggie felt anxiety as he found himself undergoing a minor flashback from his earlier sailing adventure at sea while enslaved. But with Anastasia by his side, it soon subsided.

Earlier they had considered traveling by carriage, but then they weighed their options and decided ocean travel would be better. Reggie's nature was fearless but he still harbored some concern about Anastasia. However, she had "tasted the salt in the air" of her earlier ocean voyage and pleasantly enjoyed it. She assured Reggie that she had absolutely no fear. They were now eager to begin the voyage and with it, a new adventure in life. Exploring Boston and the suburbs and now a journey at sea back to the South, provided them with so many new and intriguing adventures.

The departure proved to be very smooth. Soon they were both acclimating themselves to the ship. While at sea, much of the time was spent sleeping or just reading in their tiny cabin, where they felt very comfortable. In addition, Anastasia had time to work on her book.

Reggie felt that spending too much time in their cabin was not healthy, so they decided to spend a certain amount of time on the deck and take in some fresh air. Often after breakfast they sat out on the deck simply enjoying all the sights at sea. It provided some quality time together where they could give some more thought to their future.

One calm sunny morning as they were sitting on the deck enjoying the good weather, the captain approached them to chat as he had promised. Usually, Reggie liked heavy political conversations, but he had promised Anastasia that he would avoid any controversial discussions with the captain, which would include their prior servitude.

The captain greeted them with a warm smile as he leaned against the side rails and looked over the side of his ship. "Hello folks, I'm pleased to finally have a few minutes to speak with the two of you. My name is Captain Wilbert Smith and it is a pleasure to meet both of you.

"Captain Smith, my name is Reggie Marshall an' dis my bride, Anastasia, an' we take great pleasure in havin' dah' opportunity to talk wit' yu' as well."

"I do think good fortune is with us, as we are experiencing excellent conditions at sea for March and hopefully, it will continue. I will qualify that comment with a knock on wood since I don't want to jinx us. The Atlantic can be very temperamental—you just never know. I have seen it too often where you have a beautiful day and then a few hours later you have a horrible storm. The weather in the spring can be particularly unpredictable. Incidently, I do detect a Southern accent. May I ask where you two are from?"

Reggie responded, "We are originally from Virginny', but

we now reside in Boston. What is yur' background, Captain?"

Captain Smith was excited to share his past. "I'm from Nantucket Island where I'm proud to say, I was born with salt water in my veins. I came from a whaling family. My father was a whaler as was my grandfather—doesn't that tell you something? I will say I had a tough life growing up, because my father would be at sea for up to two years at a time, leaving my mother to take care of my two brothers, two sisters and me. Like most boys on Nantucket, I spent my time along the Atlantic honing my skills for boating, sailing and fishing. You really can't avoid it as there's nothing else to do on the island. Add to that the weather, which can be very harsh as you might surmise."

"Captain, didn't yu' want to foller' in yur' father's an' grandfather's footsteps an' 'come a whaler." Reggie was more than just curious as it was a subject that he knew so little about.

"No as I saw what it did to my poor mother. It's indescribable how difficult her life was away from my father most of the time. Whaling is much tougher than what I'm doing. In fact, I know of more then one whaler who was gone for years at sea and returned home to find his wife remarried. Trust me when I say this practice took place. Whalers are a strange breed. My father would return home from being at sea for an extended time and act like he never left home. In fact, he would take over as the head of the household and my mother would meekly follow along. He really gave her such little respect. He had absolutely no feelings. He could be so ornery while at home. It was like he had to be at sea all the time. It amazes me how my mother managed to raise her five children— she had to feel abandoned most of the time. It truly was a hard life for all of us."

"Do yu' enjoy yur' life at sea, or do yu' wish yu' had done somethin' else?"

"Mr. Marshall, I have lived a good life, and I can't complain about anything. To answer your question, I love the sea. Besides, it is really all that I have ever known."

Reggie had sworn he would not ask a political question, but he had to acquiesce to his curiosity regarding slave trade. "Captain

Smith, may I ask yu' a sensitive question?" Anastasia, sitting along side Reggie knew he could not resist asking a political question; so she quietly gave him a pinch to remind him to watch his tongue, which Reggie chose to ignore.

"Sure, I'll try to answer it if I can."

"As a captain of a Northern merchant ship, what is yur' thinkin' 'bout slave tradin'?"

"I find the people disgustin who are involved in that messy business! I personally avoid associating with them. I am so adamant about my feelings on this subject that I tend to avoid even discussing the matter. However, I will say that the overseas slave trading is illegal in the United States, as it should be! In fact, it wouldn't bother me if they banned interstate slave trading as well. Fortunately, most of us who make a living at sea are far removed from that unscrupulous activity and really don't think much about it. However, I do know of a few seamen on Nantucket who are involved with slave trade. Believe me they are looked upon by all of us as a pariah on mankind. Again, I have absolutely no respect for these people who are involved in that messy business and that's all I have to say on the subject." It appeared that the low level of respect that the captain accorded to slave traders might be compared to how one would address the drug dealers of the future.

"Captain, I whole-heartily 'gree wit' yu' dat' it is a 'bery messy business." Reggie was pleased with the captain's answer.

Soon Captain Smith excused himself to return to work. After he departed, Reggie tried to evaluate what he personally knew about slave trading at sea while taking into account his brief discussion with Captain Smith. The captain helped affirm what Reggie had already known. It was an evil, immoral, and messy business, deeply involving the North as well as the South. Slave trading did represent one of the most depraved elements of the bondage system. Some fellow peers in the slave trading business even looked upon the trafficing of slaves with disdain. Reggie recalled the slave trader who rescued him at sea exhibiting remorse and even embarrassment for his occupation. Captain Nelson who had rescued him at sea sounded apologetic as he explained how he wanted to get out of the dirty business of slave trading. It was the good money that drew him in. He had confided in Reggie that he needed to get out of debt, and as soon as his debts were paid off, he was going to quit. In some way, Reggie sensed the captain was seeking absolution for his transgressions by confiding in him since he was a common slave. What better source to seek forgiveness from, than the main sufferer of the evil oppression? Reggie saw quite a contrast between Captain Nelson and Captain Smith. Captain Nelson exhibited a defensive posture clearly remorseful, exhibiting guilt for being a slave trader. Captain Smith, on the other hand, demonstrated a very positive view on life even though he had been brought up under such difficult circumstances.

When Captain Smith was out of range of their voices, Anastasia said, "Reggie, yu' jus' can't help it. Yu' jus' had to say somethin'."

Reggie smiled, "Yu' are right my love. Yu' should 'member dat' my passion for dah' subject of slavery is almost as great as my love fo' yu'. Reggie smiled, winked and then continued, "Now, let's take advantage of dah' weather an' dah' calm sea, enjoy a short walk followed by a good nap." Anastasia took his hand as they strolled along the rail before returning to the quiet of their cabin where they discussed what might happen when they arrived in port.

The captain's prediction proved to be correct. The weather remained very mild for spring as they arrived in Savannah, Georgia on calm seas. They had packed their luggage and were now prepared to debark from the ship. They courteously thanked Captain Smith and the crew at his side for a most pleasant voyage at sea as they debarked. Reggie would forever remember his conversation with the captain, which helped to confirm what he had earlier believed concerning slave trade. The next task ahead was to secure a horse and buggy.

It took a bit of doing, but Reggie found a horse and buggy for the next leg of their journey. After they shopped for supplies, and enjoyed their first meal on land, they were able to leave Savannah by early afternoon. For obvious reasons, they avoided making any conversation with strangers unless it was absolutely necessary. Having been former slaves, they still harbored a certain amount of paranoia since they were on Southern soil even though they probably had very little to fear.

Once on the road, Reggie's excitement was obvious. "Anastasia, we're takin' dah' Broad Path Road, an' toward dusk we oughta' come 'cross dah' Quarter Horse Inn. It's a 'bery popular place 'round des' parts."

"Sounds good to me, Reggie. I will say dah' roads an' countryside are so much different din' outside of Boston or fo' dat' matter Richmond, but dey' do have thar' own charm an' beauty."

"I will say dis,' my love. Yu' will be seein' a drop off in dah' quality of inns down hyeh'." Reggie explained that the South simply lacked the resources of the North.

The uneventful buggy ride eventually brought them to the Quarter Horse Inn, a plain, two-story structure offering only the most modest accommodations. Reggie tied off the horse and buggy, and they entered the small bar area. The tavern appeared to look like it needed some work on the interior, but it was clean. A few patrons sat at the bar that also served as the reception desk for overnight guests while others were dining, playing cards or checkers at the rustic tables.

The proprietor, Gerald "Fuzzy" McCubbins, had a warm, affable look about him. He came from behind the bar to greet Anastasia and Reggie with a broad smile. "An' may I have dah' honor of knowin' wit' whom I'm addressin'?"

"Yes sir," Reggie proudly announced. "I'm Reggie Marshall, an' dis' is my wife, Anastasia. We need a place to stay fo' dah' evenin', an' we were wonderin' 'bout dah' 'vailability of a room." Reggie chose his words carefully as he was addressing a Southerner. He never felt inferior in the North when addressing people, but here in the South a small amount of his deep seated feelings of inferiority resurfaced. Interestingly, he realized he was feeling somewhat like Joseph and Willy who continued to call Jake Gibbons, "Mr. Gibbons", even when they had complete control over him.

"Well, I'm Fuzzy McCubbins, dah' proud Irish proprietor." The stumpy, round-faced man had an unusual look about him with rosy cheeks and squinty blue eyes. "Yu' folks are lucky, as I have one room left, an' dat' is it. My boy will put yur' hawss' in dah' livery stable while dah' two of yu' relax. An' 'fore yu' retire, he'll heat up a bowl of hot water so yu' kin' freshen up. We provide nothin' but first-class treatment." Reggie felt a bit uncomfortable in the role of a master while the servant waited on him. The slave to master indoctrination was so complete that similar to Joseph and Willy, he found himself victimized by it as well.

Reggie and Anastasia were amused that Mr. McCubbins thought his service was of such top quality, as they had experienced much better service up North. Reggie thanked the inn owner and then went to get their luggage. He was not fearful of leaving it briefly unattended since he had strapped the $2,500 and papers of manumission into his money belt leaving nothing of value in he buggy.

"As yu' talk, my boy is bringin' yur' grips in," McCubbins smiled. "I'm one step 'head of yu'."

"Thank yu' Mr. McCubbins, an' let me say dat' we are so happy to be stayin' at such a fine establishment."

McCubbins nodded and ushered them to a nearby table. "Please sit down—yu' an' yur' lovely wife must be famished. I kin' proudly say we have dah' finest food dat' is served 'round des' parts." Anastasia pondered to herself that it is probably the only food served around these parts.

Reggie thanked the owner again, as he and Anastasia sat down. They were given a menu and ordered their meals.

"As yu' know, Southerners are 'bery leery 'bout any outsider askin' questions," Reggie whispered to Anastasia. "If I ask anyone directly 'bout Joseph an' Willy, dey' might question why a white man would be wonderin' 'bout a couple of niggahs'. Somehow I have to bring 'dem up wit'out causin' any suspicion. In dah' North my questions would create little concern fo' me, but in dah' South, a paranoia exists wit' blacks an' whites, an' yu' have to measure yur' words 'bery carefully. Anastasia, yu' know dis' as well as I do, we gotta' watch ovah' our 'P's' an' 'Q's'."

McCubbins returned to the table with two different bottles of wine. "Which is yur' pleasure? I'm sur' two fancy folks such as yur'selves will want some wine wit' yur' dinner."

Anastasia thought how ironic that they were called fancy folks when only a very short time ago Mr. McCubbins would have accorded them absolutely no respect as slaves. Reggie laughed to himself about how their circumstances had changed—recent servitude and now a peer to this short, overweight typical white Southern innkeeper.

What they were uniquely experiencing was so rare and unusual that it would be difficult for others to comprehend, a transition of this magnitude, they almost felt as though they were characters in a play.

Reggie chose a red wine to go with his dinner, while Anastasia chose a white wine with her order. Soon McCubbins barked their orders into the kitchen. He then asked, "Mind if I sit an' chew dah' fat wit' dah' two of yu' fo' a minute? Maybe I kin' offer a little extra Georgian hospitality. I must admit, I'm curious to find out whar' yu' folks are from."

Reggie eagerly accepted. "Certainly—please join us. We are from Richmond, Virginny'. By dah' way, Mr. McCubbins, what do people 'round hyeh' do fo' excitement?" He was hopeful this conversation with the owner of the inn might offer an opportunity to obtain a little information on his friends.

"First off, call me Fuzzy. To answer yur' question, not much goes on 'round hyeh' mister. But, if yu' are lookin' fo' a little excitement, dey' are goin' to string up three niggahs' fo' tryin' to start an insurrection. Let's face it, we don't need 'nother Nat Turner situation on our hands, now, do we? I know yu' two understand, 'specially since dat' Nat' Turner thin' happened near yu'.

"Nuttin' worse din' niggahs' tryin' to cause an insurrection," Reggie replied. "What exactly did des' niggahs' do?"

"I understand dey' were maroon niggahs' who lived out in dah' swamp," Fuzzy said. "Dey' would drop in an' out of dah' swamp an' spread trouble 'mongst dah' other niggahs'. Dey' finally got nabbed—most of 'dem were shot. Dah' leader, a niggah' named Joseph was captured alive an' he will dangle from a rope 'long wit two of his followers as soon as 'morrow."

Reggie's heart sank when he heard the name Joseph as he knew it had to be his dear friend. He knew he could not exhibit his true feelings. "Jus' whar' are dey' goin' to hang des' niggahs'? I haven't seen a good lynchin' in a while." He realized the odds of him arriving just at the time of Joseph's impending execution were so great that it had to be God's intervention making all this happen.

"Ovah' in Hinesville, an' I'd git thar' early if I was yu' to enjoy all dah' festivities. Yu'd think dah' circus was in town. Hinesville is close by, which explains why I'm plumb filled up— no more vacancies. Yu' folks are jus' lucky, 'specially since I had held dah' room yu' are gittin' fo' somebody else who didn't show up. By dah' way, what is yur' business down hyeh'?"

Reggie had repeatedly rehearsed his answer. "We are down hyeh' lookin' fo' a plantation to buy, possibly jus' as an investment. So much of dah' land in Virginny' is worn out from overuse."

"Good luck wit' dat', "McCubbins said sarcastically. "I think yu' will find a lot of dah' land 'round hyeh' is jus' as bad. Talk to dah' land agent ovah' in Jesup. He'll help yu' fo' a small fee."

"Thank yu', Fuzzy, I think we'll take yur' advice." Their food arrived, and McCubbins left the couple to enjoy their meal.

In a very somber tone, Reggie stated, "Anastasia, we have to git' to Hinesville an' see Joseph 'fore dey' hang him, Willy may be thar' too. I'm at a loss fo' dah' right words dat' express how sad I am to hyeh' such horrible news. I'm simply crushed."

"My love, I share yur' deep sorrow fo' dah' bad news, but please eat yur' dinner, 'cuz' yu' are gonna' need all dah' energy yu' kin' muster up to git' through dis' ordeal."

They ate slowly, only picking at their food as their appetite had diminished with the horrible news. Reggie paid for their meals, and they went to their room immediately. He slumped into a small chair and placed his head in his hands and grievously stated, "I can't 'lieve we are too late to save my friends." He cried, "How could dis' have ever happened? Good God, I've failed 'dem."

"Reggie, we have to cling to hope 'til we git' to Hinesville, an' I know dah' Lawd' will guide us. Also, yu' did not fail 'dem. Yu' kept yur' commitment, arrivin' hyeh' as quickly as possible."

"I sense dat' Willy is already gone. Yu' know how I feel 'bout both of 'dem. An' of course, Joseph has such a 'bery special place in my heart. Thar' is almost somethin' Christ-like 'bout him, Anastasia."

"Dat' is quite a tribute, my love."

"What am I gonna' do?" Reggie sobbed as he poured out is feelings. Then he got up and walked over to the bed and pulled Anastasia close. She held him tight and stroked his hair in anticipation of the next day, which would represent a true test of their faith. They prayed together for God to give them the strength to make it through what awaited them. With that, they went to bed. Reggie had a restless night as he awakened several times, his head full of images of his two friends and their fate. He had to see Joseph. Hopefully, Willy was not one of the other two and was still on the run, even though his gut told him something else.

***

In the morning Reggie and Anastasia awakened at sunrise and ordered two homemade muffins to take with them. McCubbins had a response, "Normally people take breakfast 'fore dey' leave. Why dah' rush?"

Reggie paid the bill and told him they had to get going. "Thank yu', Mr. McCubbins—we 'bery much enjoyed our stay at yur' inn."

Mr. McCubbins walked with them to their rig and gave them directions to Hinesville. They then hurried to the stable. Quickly, they placed their luggage in their buggy and were back on the road. The directions proved to be correct and they had no problems getting there. Nevertheless, the uneventful ride proved very difficult for Reggie as he was extremely upset knowing what they soon would be facing.

They arrived in Hinesville without any problems, and rode to the center of town where they saw what they had feared—a recently constructed scaffold. Townspeople slowly walked about absorbing the venue, while vendors had set up their stands and wagons to sell whiskey, confections, and food. Not to be out-done, hucksters selling cure-alls were also evident.

A platform had been erected to accommodate musicians. All this was somewhat reminiscent of the camp meeting Reggie had attended in Georgia with Reverend Hibbard. Reggie stared in silence at the chilling sight around him—outdoor recreation at the expense of three innocent black men who were to be hanged as a spectacle for the white people to mock and enjoy.

They had secured their horse and buggy and Reggie then confronted a man who had set up his goods. "Excuse me, sir, could yu' please tell me when dey' are goin' to have dah' hangin'?"

"'Morrow' dey' are goin' to strin' up dose' three nasty niggahs', an' not a day too soon I might add," the stranger responded gruffly.

"Thank yu' sir. An' if yu' don't mind, could yu' tell me whar' dah' local jailhouse is?"

"Sur' yu' can't miss it. It's right 'cross dah' street an' to dah' right. I don't blame yu' for wantin' to take a peek at dose' niggahs' 'fore dey' take thar' last breath of air."

"We'll be on our way din', thank yu' 'gain." Reggie nodded politely and took Anastasia's arm, as they walked in the direction of the jail.

As the man turned away, Anastasia quietly asked, "Reggie, what are yu' plannin' to do?"

"I have a plan dat' may give us a chance to see Joseph. Fuzzy McCubbins said dat' he was scheduled to die today. Fortunately, we have one more day 'fore dat' happens. Dat' gives me time to put my plan into action."

"It doesn't matter when dis' takes place. Reggie, it still won't be easy to talk wit' Joseph." Anastasia smiled and squeezed his hand as she spoke, while she had conveyed her concern and support.

"Joseph an' Willy are the reason we came all dah' way down hyeh', an' I plan to do whatever I kin' to see dem'. Hyeh's dah' plan. Let me do all dah' talkin', 'cuz' we're goin' to ask dah' constable if we kin' speak wit' Joseph 'bout dah' disappearance of my uncle, Jake Gibbons."

***

After a brief hesitation, Reggie and Anastasia took a deep breath and confidently walked into the jailhouse. A robust-looking man sat at a large desk, and he looked up warily from his book as the two entered.

Reggie stepped forward to introduce them, "I'm Reggie Marshall, an' dis' is my wife, Anastasia. I assume yu' are dah' constable 'round hyeh'—is dat' right?" Reggie's manners demonstrated little respect toward the constable. In his judgment the constable in most of the Southern towns represented only a figurehead for the town and this man was the very personification. He recalled earlier in his life having witnessed the treatment accorded to the Northerner who was eventually tarred and feathered by the townspeople. Reverend Hibbard had admitted to him that the constable, lacked authority and was helpless to do anything to prevent the lawlessness from continuing. In Reggie's judgment the ineffectiveness of the constable revealed the strength of the bondage system in being able to override the law, which arguably, could represent a form of limited anarchy. The consequences were somewhat similar to other forms of anarchy—often people unjustly convicted and executed for crimes for the benefit and pleasure of others.

The constable stood up and stretched his hand out to shake Reggie's. "I'm Constable Harris, what kin' I do fo' yu'?"

Without hesitation Reggie launched into his fabricated story. "Well, sir, dah' two of us are from Richmond, Virginny'. We're down hyeh' lookin' fo' information concernin' dah' disappearance of my uncle, Jake Gibbons. We have reason to 'lieve dat' one of des' three niggahs' dat' yu' are goin' to hang had somethin' to do wit' dat', an' we'd like to have a few words wit' him.'"

"I 'member when Gibbons came up missin'," the constable replied as he rolled a toothpick from side to side in his mouth. "But I thought Gibbons was from up North. I suppose he could have a relative or two from Richmond. It's been some time since he jus' up an' vanished—lock, stock an' barrel. An' nobody ever found out why. Which one of dah' niggahs' do yu' want to talk to?"

"I believe his name is Joseph," Reggie answered.

The constable had sat up straight in his chair and then leaned forward when he heard Joseph's name. "Yu' jus' mentioned dah' worst of dah' three an' dah' one I figure most likely would have committed such a dastardly deed as to kill yur' uncle. He's dah' ringleader an' dah' one who deserves to die dah' most. Who knows—he jus' might talk? I'll take yu' to him, but first I got to check yu' an' yur' wife fo' weapons. It's a precaution. Dis' Joseph is one tough, mean debil', an' I'm not takin' any chances."

"Of course," Reggie agreed. "Go right 'head an' check us." Fortunately, a token inspection was made, and the money belt was overlooked.

Satisfied they had not concealed anything, the constable escorted them to Joseph's jail cell. As they approached, his contempt of Joseph was obvious as he glared at him. "Try anythin', an' I'll put a bullet in yur' head—do yu' understand yu' dirty rotten niggah'?"

"Yes sir," Joseph answered in a tone, which suggested that he was mocking him. "I'm a Christian—why would I want to harm 'dem? 'Sides, it really wouldn't matter much to me if yu' did put a hole in me, 'cuz' I've got a date wit' dah' hangman 'morrow. Do yu' want to deny dose' lovely folks gathered outside dah' thrill of watchin' me dangle from dah' rope? Go 'head, I welcome it."

"I'm givin' des' people five minutes to talk to yu', an' dat's it," the constable barked back at Joseph as he returned to his desk leaving Reggie and Anastasia in front of the locked cell.

"Reggie, my dear, dear friend," Joseph softly cried out, holding the bars of his cell, "I never thought I'd ever see yu' 'gain."

"Every day of dah' week I've wondered 'bout yu' an' Willy." Reggie wrapped his hands around Joseph's hands. "Joseph, yu' are my brother, an' I have missed yu' an' Willy so much dah' last few years." He continued to squeeze Joseph's hands firmly as he spoke.

Sadly, Joseph told Reggie what had happened to Willy. "Dey' caught up wit' us in dah' swamp, an' I saw Willy take three or four rounds as we were lookin' fo' a safe place to hide. Dey' searched 'round an' finally found me. Reggie, I jus' wish dey' would have shot me din'—I'm more din' ready to meet dah' Lawd'."

He looked at Anastasia and asked Reggie, "Is dis' yur' broomstick bride yu' always talked 'bout?"

"Yes, Joseph, dis' is my precious Anastasia." Reggie put an arm around her as he spoke. "We were also formally married in Boston recently."

"Reggie thinks yu' walk wit' dah' Lawd', Joseph. He tells me dat' he never met a man who rose to yur' level of faith in dah' Lawd'. We hope to git' yu' outta' hyeh'." Anastasia's soft, sweet voice was very comforting to Joseph.

Joseph reached for her through the bars as his large weathered hand gently squeezed hers as he spoke. "I understand how yu' two feel, but yu' must realize dat' God has a plan fo' me to meet up wit' Willy an' Angie in heaven. Someday, we'll all be reunited thar', but Reggie, yur' callin' is right hyeh' on earth fo' now. Me, I'm rejoicin' now. I'm already so close to my Lawd'. In fact I feel kinda' like dah' Lawd' did when dey' put him on dah' cross. I'm eager to be wit' Him. Dat's how I feel—it'll be a reward! Don't worry 'bout me—celebrate dat' I'm goin' to be wit' our Lawd' in heaven. Besides I think it'll be a celebration yu' won't soon forgit'."

"Yur' work hyeh' on earth is so important, Joseph. Do yu' realize how many people yu' have inspired an' have helped?" Reggie felt the frustration of Joseph's situation and a course that he feared he could not alter. He also had to ponder why Joseph appeared so happy and content to die.

"Reggie, thank yu' fo' dah' kind words, but dah' Lawd' wants me. It's my time. I knew dat' I'd be found sooner or later. I want yu' to continue to work fo' dah' Lawd' as I have hyeh' on earth. It's time dat' yu' realize dat' yu' have been chosen by dah' Lawd to work fo' Him an', yur' callin' will carry yu' to a new level dat' will give yu' dah' wisdom to see what only a 'bery few kin' understand."

Joseph continued, "Bein' mixed gives yu' a tremendous advantage—understandin' why people hate each other. An' of course one color has to feel dey' are superior to dah' other. Yu' kin' freely move 'tween both sides. I can't do dat' 'cuz' I'm all black. Have yu' ever wondered why yu' have been able to easily move about on both sides of dah' fence? Well, now you know— yur' skin color, but more important, dah' Lawd' has been wit' yu' to help yu' along dah' way. I know yu' are not gonna' let Him down. Again, Reggie, the Lawd' is wit' yu'—He's always wit' yu' an' yu' will feel His presence. He has given yu' both dah' power to work wit' both sides an' to be able to see into dah' future. Use yur' powers wisely, an' wit' dah' Lawd's support yu' will carry on His work in a 'bery productive manner."

Reggie and Anastasia began to weep, trying hard to not let the constable hear them. They wiped away their tears as they stood quietly for a few minutes looking into Joseph's eyes.

Reggie composed himself. "Joseph, I promise yu' dat' I will do as dah' Lawd' wills. Yu' have always been an inspiration to me, an' I have nothin' but love an' respect fo' yu'. Yu' are my brother, an' I will not disappoint dah' Lawd' or yu'. "

"Reggie, I have somethin' to say, I personally never felt dah' purpose of a burial ceremony. I do not want yu' an' Anastasia at my burial as my dead body is only a shell. Instead, I want both of yu' honorin' my ascension into heaven to be wit' my father. Simply—look up to see me, not down at my burial plot—I won't be thar', I will already be in heaven wit' our Lawd, Angie an' Willy lookin' down at y'all!"

In awe of every word Joseph had said, Reggie realized that Joseph's unique belief on death made a lot of sense. "Joseph of course we will honor yur' wishes. I must also admit dat' I have so much respect fo' how yu' think. It makes so much sense. It's funny, when I'm wit' others, I'm never at a loss fo' words, but 'round yu', right now I almost feel speechless."

As Reggie finished speaking, Joseph saw that the constable was returning. "Now don't forgit', yu' got to be stern wit' me, like yur' cross-examinin' me or sumpthin' like dat'." It had been such a highly emotional confrontation. Reggie had so regretted not being with Joseph earlier, and now he had to be present when he died. Now in his final words with Joseph, he felt so sad being forced to talk to the man he most respected in such a demeaning manner to satisfy the constable, and to keep himself and Anastasia "under cover".

Reggie complied with Joseph's request and stated, "'Fore I leave I'm gonna' ask yu' one last time, yu' rapscallion, do yu' know anythin' 'bout dah' disappearance of my uncle, Jake Gibbons an' don't give me any rigamarole?"

"Fo' dah' last time," Joseph pleaded, "I wish I could help yu', but I don't know nutten'."

The constable intervened, and led the couple away from the jail cell area and sat down at his desk once again. He had looked curiously at Anastasia and asked her, "Ever since dah' two of yu' came in hyeh', somethin' has piqued my interest. Miss what might be yur' background? Yu' have an interestin' skin tone." Very likely he had hinted that she might have Negro blood in her.

Anastasia and Reggie had looked at each other and showed no emotion. Anastasia's slightly darker skin seldom attracted any attention before, and the question caught her a little off guard. However, she never lost her composure. "My father is English. He met my mother in Lisbon, Spain, an' my mother is of course of Spanish descent."

The constable fumbled briefly for the right words. "Oh, I see! Of course! Pardon my curiosity. Anyhow, stick 'round fo' dah' 'citement 'morrow. It ortea' be quite a show."

Anastasia and Reggie thanked him for his time and quickly left the jail. Reggie was disgusted at the constable's reference to the three men being hung as "quite a show". He felt sickened as he wondered how people can find pleasure in witnessing the deaths of three men executed by hanging, and only guilty of being the wrong skin color. How can Christianity dwell in the hearts of people who madly cheer watching men lose their lives at the gallows? This question raced through his mind. What was further disturbing was the reality that historically things tend to stay the same. What is the difference between the Romans who cheered over watching the gladiators die, or the locals who would watch three men die on the scaffold? In his judgement—none! The only real difference might be that the Romans were pagans while the people who would be viewing the hanging were "proud" Christians, who on Sunday will be attending church services.

CHAPTER THIRTY-THREE

The approaching finality of Joseph's life on earth was near. All they could do was helplessly standby and pray. It was now a matter of accepting Joseph's fate as Reggie and Anastasia comprehended and digested the positive influence he made on others. The recent turn of events had precluded any hope of being able to free him from his impending execution. Instead, they were forced to have to witness people celebrating the death of an inspirational gentleman, which deepened their despair even more. Reggie was reminded of the taunting Jesus Christ had to endure on the cross. Reggie kept chastising himself, thinking he failed by not arriving sooner to locate his friends before the authorities found them.

It was his beloved Anastasia who gave him the courage and the support to work through his guilt. She reminded him of Joseph's words about carrying on the Lord's work after he was gone. They proved to be calming—almost healing, and exactly what he needed to maintain his strength and spirit. Besides, it was apparent from talking to Joseph that he had absolutely no trepedations. Instead, he rejoiced his impending death knowing he would soon be with the Lord and his loved ones.

As Reggie and Anastasia walked around the town, he thought about what Joseph had said to him. The Lord had carefully designed the events that had happened to them, and more of His will would be revealed each day. Joseph's "common sense sagacity" gave Reggie the peace of mind that he so desperately needed to get through these difficult times. Reggie remained mesmerized at Joseph's wisdom and just how much closer he had grown to the Lord since they had become separated.

He and Anastasia after walking around, thoroughly disgusted at what they were seeing, finally relented to their hunger and went to the main tavern in the community. With the large crowd in town they were forced to wait for some time for a table to become available. Finally after they were seated, they attempted to enjoy their meal, but instead it was futile as they were consoling each other, pondering Joseph's fate and what would lie ahead for the two of them after all of this was over. Eventually, Reggie changed the subject. "Anastasia, when dah' constable asked 'bout yur' skin color, it scared me half to death! But yu' recovered nicely, an' I was 'mazed by yur' answer. Yu' remained as 'cool as a cucumber'."

"I knew we had papers, but I didn't want to be bothered by him questionin' us any further. Dat' road could become risky. Dah' easiest thing to do was jus' tell a little fib an' dat's what I did, I'm sure dah' Lawd' will fo'give me," she said with a sly smile and a little wink.

"Anastasia, yu' know dah' Lawd would fo'give yu' under dose' circumstances. I'll say it 'gain—yu' were wonderful, my love. I would have never thought of dat' answer. It was brilliant— by dah' way dat' was not dah' first little fib yu' ever tole'. 'Member when yu' had to answer Mrs. Clark, an' yu' avoided disclosin' dat' we were first cousins?"

Anastasia smiled. "Well, thank yu', Reggie fo' remindin' me of all dah' little fibs I have tole'. Besides, I didn't know dat' not tellin' Mrs. Clark everthin' represents a fib. She spoke with confidence, "I might add dat' over dah' years, yu' well know wit' Abigail's tutorage I was given dah' opportunity to learn my letters an' numbers as well as certain social skills, which have come in 'bery handy." It was apparent when Anastasia spoke that she radiated an intelligence and confidence that reached Reggie's level.

As they finished their meal, Reggie reminded Anastasia about how crowded the town was. "We'll never be able to find lodgin' 'round hyeh' tonight. We are gonna' have to camp outside on dah' outskirts of town. What else kin' we do?"

"Yu' are right, my love. We'd best git' goin' 'fore it gits' dark an' becomes difficult to find a good location. Reggie, do yu' know dat' dis' will be our first experience truly campin' out? At least when we were on dah' run, we had a roof ovah' our heads."

"It's such a small sacrifice havin' to sleep outside when compared to Joseph, knowin' dat' dis' is his last night of sleep hyeh' on earth," Reggie remarked with a chill in his voice.

"Yu're so right, my love. Nevertheless, I'm so happy dat' I had dah' opportunity to meet yur' dear friend, Joseph. I kin' truly understand why yu' admire an' respect him so much. Reggie, it's also apparent dat' he would not want yu' to feel sorry fo' him. He's so fearless 'bout death. Meanwhile, he wants yu' to carry on dah' work of dah' Lawd' hyeh' on earth. He knows dat' we'll all be meetin' up in heaven someday. Unquestionably, he is dah' most fearless man I have ever met. It certainly is obvious to me why yu' feel he rises to 'nother level in life dat' only a 'bery few could ever 'chieve. In fact I have never met anybody quite like him, an' other din' yu', I doubt dat' I ever will. He simply stands apart as an icon from dah' world like a 'beacon of light on a stormy sea'."

Reggie sensitively replied, "One of dah' reasons I love yu' more an' more each day is how priceless yur' insight an' compassion are to me, Anastasia."

"I do know how important it will be fo' yu' to carry on yur' dear friend's work. Now let's find a place whar' we kin' camp tonight an' git' some sleep. It's goin' to be a 'bery difficult day tomorrow," Anastasia reminded Reggie. It appeared that a little bit of Reggie's "practicality" was beginning to rub off on Anastasia as he knew, she was right.

As they left the tavern, they were confronted with a cacophony of sounds—people milling about in the street drinking and acting disorderly while eagerly awaiting the hangings. It was clear they the crowd was treating the whole spectacle as a celebration. Disgusted, Reggie took Anastasia's hand and moved quickly through the crowd to their buggy. Knowing the worst was yet to come, he felt a deep sadness as he helped Anastasia into the buggy. They departed as the sun was setting. They hurriedly moved out of town, not wanting to continue to witness the scene that was being forced upon them prior to the hanging.

To no surprise, outside of town they observed a large number of people who were camping out as well. After a lengthy search they located a spot which provided the necessary privacy. Retiring for the evening, they were not in any mood to make any further conversation. Following an expected sleepless night, they tidied up in a nearby stream and prepared for the ride back to town. Without any fanfare they quickly got into their buggy and departed. Lacking any appetite, both were content to simply eat a few crackers as they slowly traveled down the road. They carried heavy hearts, saying very little, knowing this dreadful experience was not nearly over, but just beginning.

As they arrived in town, Reggie tied his horse and buggy at the first place he could find and then stared up the dusty main street. At quite a distance they could see the ominous platform and the ropes of the gallows—the structure seemed to rise out of the crowd above the activities. The overall scene cast a gloomy and foreboding atmosphere. Was this just a nightmare? Obviously not—the crowd was enormous as they descended on Hinesdale like locusts on wheat during Biblical days. It was apparent they were morbidly looking forward to being entertained by the deaths of three helpless black men who were being victimized by an evil system.

As Reggie gazed into the crowd, negative thoughts ran through his head. The carnival-like atmosphere mirrored the bloodthirsty mob when Joseph fought the Congo Assassin. Both events had one common, chilling thread—whites being entertained through the pain and suffering of black men.

Reggie pondered another question. Would the crowd celebrate at the same intensity if the three men to be executed were white? He suspected that perhaps more compassion would have been accorded to them.. He knew that he had never attended a hanging where the men to be executed were white, which determined he could not answer his own question with certainty.

Their only "crime" had been that they were born black and now they were being executed for fighting against a system of oppression that violated the very moral fiber of mankind. Regretfully, only a very small minority in the crowd could have the compassion and understanding that Reggie and Anastasia possessed. Worse yet, most lacked the insight to understand this spectacle violated their own Christian tenets, which made them hypocrites.

As no one was aware of Joseph's involvement in the disappearance of Jake Gibbons, Joseph was instead being executed presumably for "trumping up" an insurrection. The other two were labeled as his followers. Rustic gallows crafted from old barn siding beams now represented their "death trap".

As Reggie led Anastasia, they passed folks in their Sunday best; children playing tag and people enjoying the fiddler. There was also a main entertainer playing the piano with an accompanying ukulele all adding to the cacophony of sounds. It all provided for the appearance of a "joyous" event. Chillingly, it might even appear to be one that might be seen at a Christian inspired gathering—how ironic. Finally, the piano player boldly made a loud announcement. "Come closer, everyone, 'cuz' on dis' joyous occasion, we want to introduce a song y'all are gonna' like, *Ole' Dan Tucker*, written by Daniel Emmitt. We've purposely been savin' dis' tune fo' when dah' action heats up."

Reggie could no longer restrain himself from speaking out as he boldly announced for others to hear, "Sir, it's a hangin'— three men are goin' to die—dis' should not be considered a joyous 'casion accompanied by music an' singin'. I shudder to think dat' dah' debil' has taken ovah' in dis' place."

The piano player recanted quickly. "Well, I guess yu' are right. I didn't mean to say a joyous occasion, but anyhow, let's jus' enjoy dah' song." Perhaps the piano player could have even felt a little guilt.

I come to town de' udder' night.
I hear de' noise an saw de' fight
De' watchman was a runnin' roun'
Ole' Dan Tucker's come to town.
So git' out de' way!
Git' out de' way! Git' out de' way!
Ole' Dan Tucker you're too late
To come to supper.
Ole' Dan Tucker an' I git' drunk
He fell in de' fire an' kicked up a chunk.
De' charcoal got inside his shoe
Lawd' bless yu' honey how de' ashes flew.
So get out de' way!
Git' out de' way! Get out de' way!
Ole' Dan Tucker you're too late
To come to supper.
Tucker was a hardened sinner.
He nebber' said his grace at dinner.
De' ale sow squealed. De' pigs did squall
He 'hole hog wide de' tail an' all.
So git' out de' way!
Git' out de' way! Git' out de' way!
Ole' Dan Tucker you're too late
To come to supper.

Everyone seemed to enjoy the lively tune while keeping time to the music and trying to follow with the chorus. Reggie and Anastasia remained repulsed by the entire scene, thinking only of Joseph and the other two slaves who were condemned to hang shortly. Meanwhile, they barely noticed the two men who had come up alongside of them. They weren't laughing or clapping like the rest of the crowd—they appeared to be watching Reggie and Anastasia and in all probability were conversing about them. Finally, Reggie turned to find out why they were staring at him and Anastasia. As he stood there, he realized he was standing face-to-face with Captain Riley, once his cruel master—now a fellow peer.

Irony reigned as Reggie gazed at Captain Riley, realizing their paths were crossing at Joseph's hanging. To Reggie's amazement, he felt absolutely no fear—only power. He had his freedom, his bride and the strength of the Lord infused into his mind and body as he stood tall in the crowd with his cowardly nemesis eyeing him, realizing that Reggie, nattily attired, had the look of a man whose stature was every bit his equal. Captain Riley, maybe a little intimidated by Reggie's appearance, his voice dripping in sarcasm, asked, "'Cuse me, haven't we met 'fore?"

"Unfortunately, I do believe we have met in dah' most difficult circumstances," Reggie proudly replied, "Aren't yu' dah' man who can't accept dat' every man is entitled to a last name? Dat' said, my name is 'Reggie Marshall', jus' in case yu' fo'got it! I repeat, 'Marshall, a prominent name in Virginny' circles!" Reggie proudly rolled the words out without hesitation.

Somewhat surprised, embarrassed, and at a loss for words, Riley simply turned to the man accompanying him and said it was time to move on. It was obvious that he "had bit off more than he could chew" with Reggie.

The entire incident lasted a very short time but would be indelibly imprinted in Reggie's mind as the day he stood "toe to toe" with Captain Riley and more than perservered. He remembered Joseph informing him that God had provided him with unusual strength and that he should no longer have any fears. This was the first time he truly felt Him, and when he saw Captain Riley cower, he was mindful of what Joseph had told him was true. This entire scene represented a significant phenomenon in Reggie's life, one that would forever change the direction he and Anastasia would take from this point forward—they would never look back, only ahead with their Lord as their leader.

Anastasia in a low tone, asked, "Reggie, who was dat' man?"

"Dat' man is pure evil in human form! Anastasia, it's not even worth my time or energy to tell yu' who he is." Seeing Captain Riley, even briefly, reminded him of the devil's work. He did not wish to share with Anastasia who this man was since he was the horrible representation of the past that he had successfully put behind him. Besides in his judgement, he could not tell Anastasia who he was since he would have to acknowledge the control this man had over him. He truly realized that he had now vanquished all his previous fears and was preparing for a future serving God. "Anastasia, I'm joinin' Joseph by puttin' my trust in God's hands while castin' out all worldly fears."

"I've never heard yu' talk like dis' 'fore. It's almost as if at dis' 'bery moment a part of yu' is wit' Joseph." Anastasia wrapped an arm tightly around Reggie's as she softly spoke to him, realizing her husband was walking with the Lord at the same level as Joseph.

"Right now I'm standin' wit' Joseph in spirit, an' what I see is a man who is larger din' life, an' I kin' feel him helpin' bring me even closer to dah' Lawd, an' I know dah' Lawd is wit' us right now. He is right hyeh', my love!" Reggie was speaking with absolute confidence, but yet, wonderment. It appeared that he had an aura about him.

Suddenly, the music stopped, and the crowd went silent as the three slaves without fanfare appeared and were brought forward to the scaffold. Absolute silence reigned in, broken only by the horses tied along the street and the sound of the wind.

"Look, Anastasia," Reggie whispered, "dey' have Joseph in dah' middle jus' like Jesus at Golgotha when dey' placed him in 'tween dah' two thieves at dah' crucifixion! It was more din' a premonition when I said somethin' is happenin' hyeh' dat' cannot be explained. I always sensed dat' Joseph had special qualities 'bout him dat' could not be defined as dey' were at a level 'bove my comprehension, an' now I'm seein' an' feelin' 'dem fo' myself. Perhaps earlier, some of dose' special qualities had not yet emerged to thar'fullest, but I guarantee dey' have 'rived now, an' yu' an' I are witnesses to dat'."

"Look how strong an' proud Joseph looks, even wit' death stalkin' at his door. I'll try to say dis' respectfully—while dah' other two demonstrate fear, Joseph has a broad smile on his face exhibitin' confidence," Anastasia added.

Reggie knew Joseph's complete lack of fright demonstrated his inner strength and his feelings of joy knowing he would soon be with his Lord. He looked into Anastasia's eyes and then lifted his head upward to scan the cloudless, perfect sky. He envisioned the face of the Lord and Joseph's—he now understood his vision of Jesus Christ at Golgotha. What he had perceived to be in the past was really a representation of this day. His vision of Jesus Christ at Golgotha had transcended from the past to now. The entire representation went far beyond the descriptive word "powerful".

While the crowd was looking up at the gallows in a rather confused manner, Joseph with a smile on his face climbed the wooden steps to face the hangman's noose. An emanation far beyond the normal was ever present as Joseph stood tall.

Chub Andrews, a local activist, shouted, "Look at dat' damn niggah' up thar' wit' a smile on his face! He's too dumb to know dat' he's 'bout to die. It jus' ain't normal to be smilin' in dah' face of death." This brought a rumble of assents from many in the crowd as they heckled the condemned. Andrews yelled out again. "Why doesn't someone take dat' damn smile off his face? I wanta' see dat' damn niggah' scared to death knowin' dat' he is bound fo' hell—he can't go to heaven, he's a niggah'—dah' Bible tells us so!"

The ranting and raving directed toward Joseph continued unabated. An older woman sitting on a bench in front of the general store with three small children at her side yelled to the executioner, "I do believe dat' niggah' is mockin' us wit' dat' smile on his face. Dis' jus' ain't normal—it's creepy. I ain't ever let a niggah' mock me." It was beginning to appear that the heckling was partly defensive perhaps out of fear of what may come.

Anastasia tugged at Reggie's arm and nodded, while hoping he'd remain silent. However, he couldn't. Reggie freely yelled out. "Maybe he knows somethin' none of us have figured out."

"Shut up, mister, we don't need anybody supportin' dat' dirty niggah' up thar' who's laughin' an' tauntin' us wit' dat' stupid grin," an old man responded, shaking a finger and pointing at Joseph and then Reggie.

The condemned were lined up directly in front of their respective nooses while the crowd continued to stir about, unable to quite understand why these executions were developing into something they had never seen before. The constable, executioner and minister took their positions, near them. The constable spoke first knowing that under these trying circumstances, he wanted to get things moving. "Preacher, yu may as well deliver dah' last words to des' black scoundrels."

Somberly, the minister opened his Bible to give the three condemned their last rites. "Almighty God, look on these men, yur' servants, lyin' in great weakness, an' comfort 'dem wit' dah' promise of life everlastin', given in dah' resurrection of yur' Son, Jesus Christ, our Lawd'. Amen." When the preacher said "lying in great weakness", Joseph looked straight into the face of the minister, his smile broadening even wider.

Chub Andrews reminded the preacher about what he had said earlier. "Preacher, why are yu' talkin' 'bout heaven to des' damn niggahs'? Niggahs' can't go to heaven—dah' curse of Ham is on all des' damn niggahs'. Condemned to hell, dat's whar' thar' are headed—dah' Bible tells us so."

Many began to chant as if they were at a sporting event. "Preacher, condemn 'dem to hell! Condemn 'dem to hell! Condemn 'dem to hell! Hell! Hell! Hell! Dat's thar' lot in dah' hereafter."

The constable finally intervened. "Now, folks, we're not goin' to allow dis' to descend into a mob action. Let dah' preacher finish so we kin' git' dis' ovah' wit'! Dey' are goin' to be dead in a few minutes, so quit frettin'." Then he stepped forward, smiling, "Why do yu' folks care what dat' old preacher man says? Jus' sit back an' enjoy dah' show!"

Reggie loudly interjected, "Dah' constable is right. Jus' sit back an' enjoy dah' show. It might be even more din' yu' bargained fo'—jus' 'member dat'!" As Reggie was mockingly speaking, he didn't realize that Captain Riley was looking at him in disbelief, knowing this is not the same man he once knew.

The constable moved to one side of the gallows as the

preacher began reciting the Lord's prayer.

Our Father, who art in Heaven, hallowed be thy name,
Thy kingdom come, thy will be done, on earth as it is in heaven.
Give us dis' day our daily bread. An' forgive us our trespasses,
As we forgive dos' who trespass 'gainst us.
An' lead us not into temptation, but deliver us from evil.
Fo' thine is dah' kingdom, dah' power, an' dah' Glory fo' ever.
Amen.

The constable thanked the preacher and then walked in front of the slaves. "Now each of yu' have a right to say yur' final words. Preacher, take over 'gain an' let dah' rascal on dah' left go first."

The slave to the right of Joseph sputtered, "I know dat' I'm right wit' dah' Lawd'." He was shaking and could barely get his words out. "Lawd', I'm scared 'cuz' I don't wanta' die. I jus' wish I could git' back home Lawd' an' forgit' dis' ever happened." He broke down, sobbing uncontrollably.

"Yu', on dah' right—now it's yur' turn, an' make it quick," the constable ordered.

The slave to the left of Joseph was defiant as he spoke. "Yu're' hangin' an innocent man. I did nuttin' wrong. Dis' is jus' dah' way yu' treat us niggahs'."

The constable quickly stepped in and stopped him from saying anything further. "Dat's what dey' all say! Now let's git' to our prized catch—dah' niggah' wit' dat' insolent smile on his face. Go 'head, we are jus' dyin' to hyeh' from yu'—boy!"

One person near the gallows had witnessed Joseph as the Preacher Man who killed the Congo Assassin. He confidently screamed out to him, "Hey, niggah'! If yu' are dah' Preacher Man wit' so much power, why don't yu' power yur' way out of dis' mess?" Reggie then confirmed to Anastasia that the continued taunting of Joseph replicated the crowd at Jesus Christ's crucifixion at Golgotha when they jeered Him.

"I first want to correct dah' preacher's last rites, which

were directed at me as well." Joseph began, gesturing toward the preacher. "I'm not lyin' in great weakness—I'm lyin' in sacred strength—I'm already wit' dah' Lawd'! Jesus Christ had a choice—a throne or dah' cross. He chose dah' cross. Dat' represents dah' strength dat' I look up to." Joseph then bowed and prayed, "Jesus, I've already fo'given des' people fo' takin' our lives. Dey' are part of an uncontrolled evil system run by dah' debil', which dey' have unknowingly accepted an' do not understand but must come to grips wit' some day. Now, God, I'm more din' ready, an' I welcome bein' delivered to Yu' in heaven." Joseph's head turned upward as he continued. "Lawd', I'm prepared to commit my spirit to yu'!" A broad smile remained on his face as he then looked directly at the people gathered around him, his strength of spirit evident in his face.

The constable, visibly upset, made a final statement to Joseph. "Oh, how touchin' boy. Yu' jus' keep dat' smile on yur' face, an' we'll see how long it remains as soon as yu' are danglin' from a rope in midair." As he spoke this time, it didn't appear that he was as cocksure of himself as earlier.

The executioner stepped forward with three black hoods, the next to last procedure before the execution. Normally a mere formality, a problem soon developed since Joseph refused to be hooded for his execution.

The executioner, taken aback, stated. "Dis' is unheard of—no man has ever refused dah' hood when I have offered it. Niggah', what's wit' yu' keepin' dat' smile on yur' face an' refusin' yur' hood? Yu' are beginnin' to scare me, an' I'm dah' executioner!"

Joseph responded, "When I 'scend to heaven, I wanta' see dah' sights on dah' way up. It promises to be dah' greatest ride I'll ever take!" Joseph radiated a look of love and confidence that transcended any earthly look. The crowd appeared to be awestruck at Joseph, knowing that he was reacting to his impending execution in a manner that appeared to be programmed from heaven, absent of any fear with a comment that could only be made from a truly inspired man.

The last procedure had finally arrived. The condemned

were asked to move slightly backwards so the ropes could be placed around their necks and then tightened.

Under normal circumstances the executioner remained silent. However, in a departure from the normal, and perhaps even out of fear, he hesitatingly looked at Joseph and stated, "'Nough of dis' talk—yu' had yur' final words! When dat' rope breaks yur' neck, we kin' all see dat' grin come off yur' black face!" The executioner was not fooling the audience as his demeanor had changed significantly. It was obvious by his actions that he was becoming uneasy and having second thoughts about finishing the job and the crowd recognized it.

The tension continued to build as Joseph stood proud with his smile radiating for all to see. Then, just when nothing more could be expected from Joseph that could shock the crowd, he began praying loudly in a strange language that nobody could understand. Many in the crowd were familiar with the gift of "speaking in tongues" from their Christian background, but never was it expressed to them in this fashion. If some had doubted this execution would be unique, now they all knew this hanging was going to be very far from normal. Most in a fearful manner felt Godly power emanating from the words Joseph spoke. This strange language that he was loudly, and yet so proudly declaring, went far beyond any style of deliverance that anyone of them had ever heard in church. That reality had a very unsettling affect on the crowd. They were left spellbound, not able to quite comprehend what was unfolding in front them, perhaps mystified that Joseph might be speaking in a language sent directly from God. They had become mesmerized by him to the point where nobody intervened as he prayed in his own mystical language.

Reggie recalled Joseph asking him about "speaking in tongues", having observed a man in church talking in a strange language. Reggie had explained Acts II of the Bible to Joseph, which recognizes the gift of "speaking in tongues". In addition, it was understood that others have the power to interpret the words being spoken. It now became crystal clear why Joseph brought this subject up to him. Joseph was now "speaking in tongues", and shockingly, Reggie was given the gift to interpret what he was saying. In an excited manner, he uncontrollably shouted out a translation of Joseph's words. "Fools, dah' man is radiatin' a Messianic appeal fo' y'all to hyeh' an' 'member! Now listen to des'words emanatin' from God through Joseph. Dah' greatest record of slavery throughout all history of time is 'mankind's slavery to sin', whereby dah' only source an' hope fo' freedom is God. True slavery, which millions of us now have to endure would end, along with all other sins. Din', mankind through God will finally be able to triumph ovah' evil an' finally recognize dat' 'in God's eyes we are all truly one'! Amen!" Reggie was stunned that he was able to lucidly interpret what Joseph was saying and to his amazement, the crowd stood silent as he spoke, transfixed to every word. In fact, he imagined that under normal circumstances he would have been pummeled by the crowd for speaking out. It was surrealistic! You could almost 'hear a pin drop' as Reggie spoke knowing the very words that he had just uttered held the audience completely mesmerized.

Reggie turned to Anastasia. "Anastasia, Joseph is a martyr 'fore our eyes, but I still don't know what's goin' to happen. I feel dat' God will send an important sign as he welcomes Joseph home. Also, isn't it fittin' dat' his last words were in a prayer language given to him by God an' not in English. How powerful is dat'? I know we can't understand dah' total relevancy of dis'. I kin' only pray dat' dis' crowd assembled hyeh' understands dah' importance. I personally 'lieve dis' could be dah' same common prayer language given to dah' apostles by dah' Lawd'—Anastasia, dat' would really be somethin'!"

Anastasia glanced at Reggie and then looked back to the three men about to hang. As she looked at Joseph, he looked directly at her and managed to tip his head in her direction, all the while maintaining his confident smile.

The executioner announced that it was time to get down to business. He then nervously placed the assigned rope around each of their necks, which he quickly tightened. They were now ready for execution. The crowd became completely silent as the executioner approached the lever. Even at this point, Joseph never flinched, his smile was ever present. Meanwhile, the executioner hesitatingly fumbled about as he put on his black leather gloves and appeared to pause almost as if he had "second thoughts" before finally releasing the trap door.

When the executioner finally released the trap door, the three men dropped downward with a loud thump. The crowd had been cheering—now complete silence overtook everyone. It was almost as if the crowd had surmised that something highly unusual had occurred. Not a word could be heard as the other two men dangled in the air, their bodies twitching while Joseph, exhibited absolutely no fear or pain on his smiling face, casting an enduring radiance over the crowd while not exhibiting any sign of twitching. To the crowd his actions were definitely eerie and not of this earth. They were left numbed and unable to react.

With her eyes partially covered, Anastasia slowly looked at Joseph hanging from the rope. "Reggie, Joseph still has dat' smile on his face, even in death." Unable to look away from the three black men dangling on the gallows, she held Reggie tightly, and then nervously stated, "What's really sad is dat' Joseph, who was so close to God had to die wit'out a last name. Did anyone know who he really was?"

As Reggie looked to the sky he replied, "Anastasia he does have a last name an' a mighty big one at dat'—but only one person other than Joseph knows dat' name!" Anastasia understood what he meant.

Normally, the crowd would be cheering and celebrating the hangings; however, Joseph's continual smile and his prophetic words had the affect of "putting a damper" on what would normally be a festive occasion. Everyone knew this execution that was played out in front of their very own eyes was sinking deeper and deeper into an area they could not begin to comprehend as fear of the "unknown" began to mount throughout the crowd. They remained silent hoping the smile on Joseph's face would just go away and everything could return to normal just as if this aberration had never occurred in their lives. It was all so unearthly and continued with no signs of abating.

The silence was finally broken by vendors hawking their goods and street musicians providing music, attempting to distract the crowd away from the three corpses that dangled on the scaffold. It was obvious they were having a difficult time moving the crowd away from gazing at Joseph. His corpse remained frightening to the celebrants—his ubiquitous smile emanated a strange life form not of this earth and had the affect of mocking the crowd even in death. Out of complete fear, some began asking the executioner to cut the ropes so they wouldn't have to look at Joseph's face any longer. It was obvious to the crowd that something had gone amuck—something frightening beyond any earthly description.

The executioner complied, and Joseph's body, along with the others crumpled to the ground at the bottom of the scaffold. Just then from out of nowhere, a lightning bolt severed the sky with a loud crack of thunder even while the sun continued to shine. This apparition was far from meteorologically normal. Everyone fell silently in awe at what they were witnessing—it was not of this earth.

All eyes turned upward toward the sky—toward heaven, where a large, gray, ominous looking cloud was forming directly above them. A sunny late afternoon, an azure skyline, with a dark cloud and a bolt of lighting piercing its center was more than a simple anomaly. Many went to their knees in prayer, others crouched down, and still others stepped backward hoping their simple reflex actions would shield them from the unexplainable.

Just when the crowd thought this occurrence would possibily abate, a much louder thunderclap sent further terror through the crowd. The deafening thunder continued, absent of rain. Panic took over as it sounded as if several trains were passing through the sky. Some ran, some in prayer, some men fumbled to open their flasks for a quick "pick me up", and children clung to their mother's skirts. It was an aberration nobody could even begin to comprehend.

The scene appeared to get even more unearthly and frightening. Just when it seemed it could not get any worse, a comet appeared from the center of the cloud and moved in an arch overhead. Someone in the crowd shouted, "It must be dat' comet dat's been seen lately, an' it's comin' straight down to earth! We're doomed!" Obviously, this type of language buzzing throughout the crowd could only stir up more panic.

Was this the Great Comet of 1843 which had recently been observed in the skies or simply God welcoming Joseph home? Many accepted the Great Comet theory, especially since they were quick to point out that the Great Comet was said to have illuminated brighter than Halley's Comet that had visited the earth eight years earlier. Most questioned the scientific explanation; they believed this had to be God's intervention welcoming Joseph home with his own creation and had nothing to do with the Great Comet.

Reggie stood tall, scanning the sky and watching the people cower around him. Strangely enough, he felt even more strength as the event unfolded. He knew that the Lord had a carefully scripted a plan for the both of them now that Joseph had ascended to heaven. Meanwhile, Anastasia stood close to his side, calmed, and strengthened by his demeanor knowing this was all part of God's plan.

Many quit running in panic and became enthralled by the comet, knowing there was nothing more they could do but to submit to the will of the Lord—God's intercession was complete.

Interlaced within the cobalt-colored comet were whispy orange threads and a white streak behind it. As the comet passed slowly above the town, a yellow circle began forming within the core. The blazing tail descended into a small point from the main body of the comet. Everyone stood gazing at the comet as it passed above them with a yellow circle continuing to develop within the core of the main body.

One member of the crowd was overheard loudly saying, "I'll never see 'nother pyrotechnic display to match dis' one." It appeared that he was only attempting to inject a little humor to cover up the fear that he was going through.

People continued to drop to their knees in prayer, some, possibly the first time in their lives, but Reggie and Anastasia remained standing while observing the orb as they tried to digest all that was occurring. Reggie continued to feel God's presence sweeping through him—he knew He was watching over everyone. Finally, Reggie began to piece together his life with all of the human cruelty he had been subjected to, and he now realized it was God's way to prepare him for the difficult journey that awaited him as a "spiritual shepherd" in His ministry. He knew how difficult it would be to convince people that in God's world we are all equal on this earth. It was so lucid and so clear to Reggie that he could only pray that all could see and feel the divine spirit, which illuminated a world where human greed for power and money would one day succumb to spiritual wealth. He knew the ideal righteous path must be clearly understood and followed if we are to be together and not divided in God's eyes. The events of the day brought everything to a full circle. Reggie could now further understand why Joseph welcomed death, absolutely without any fear, but only joy. It was apparent that Joseph must have known what would unfold immediately following his death.

As quickly and drastically as events had built up, they subsided as the apparition began to mysteriously fade away. First, the comet vanished, then the lightening and thunder ceased. Finally, the large cloud rolled away as the sun brightened the skies once again. The total apparition lasted only for a relatively short time, but in that short occurrence for what seemed a lifetime, an indelible event was left for all those who witnessed it.

Slowly, those kneeling stood and joined those staring at the heavens, their lives forever changed by what they had just witnessed. The message was loud and clear—God is in charge. Reggie knew what it all meant as he prepared himself to be a "spiritual shepherd" for the Lord, following in the footsteps of his beloved friend Joseph, who would remain forever as his mentor.

After Reggie and Anastasia said a prayer, Reggie walked over to look at Joseph lying on the ground, his smile replaced by a serene peacefulness. He had now ascended to heaven. Most now recognized Joseph's smile as a sign of forgiveness and knew he was at peace with the Lord. Reggie knelt beside his dear friend and gently closed his eyes as others walked close to him to quietly pay their respects. This certainly represented a miraculous change in how they had first viewed him. But then, how else could they view this very special man who helped to forever reshape their lives in such a very positive manner. In Reggie's judgment, it was a miracle beyond description to see white people paying homage to a black man, certainly something he had never witnessed in the past.

The constable approached Reggie and assured him that Joseph would be quickly buried in a field, along with the other two men who were executed with him. They would be laid to rest in a Negro graveyard directly across the road from a church regularly attended by whites as a symbol of oneness with God. It particularly pleased Reggie that respect was being accorded to all three men, which is the way that Joseph would have wanted it. The constable further assured Reggie that proper steps for the deceased would be accorded at the funeral and burial site.

As Reggie and Anastasia had mourned over the departure of Joseph, Reggie, not lacking in confidence, looked directly into the eyes of the constable, and confidently stated with a smile on his face. "Constable, I love and respect Joseph in so many positive ways. But 'bove all I kin' honestly say dat' he didn't do bad fo' himself hyeh' on earth considerin' he was one of Ham's condemned descendents." Reggie couldn't resist making one last cynical comment believing the constable would probably not grasp what Reggie was really saying to him.

When these words rolled out of Reggie's mouth, Anastasia with loving gentleness looked upon Reggie and stated, "My love, yu' jus' said it all. Thar' kin' be nothin' to add to dat' other din'—kin' mankind ever understand what yu' jus' said an' begin to grow from it?"

The constable stood dumbfounded and clueless unable to grasp the significance of the ironic statement Reggie just made. Unfortunately, he would probably continue to aimlessly conduct his life without ever realizing just how close he came to greatness with Joseph while regrettably failing to understand the importance of his encounter with Reggie and Anastasia.

The time had now arrived for their departure. Reggie and Anastasia walked to their buggy to begin their long journey home while observing Joseph's wish for them to celebrate his ascension into heaven in spirit only, not wanting them to witness his corpse being interred since the corpse only represented a shell. Reggie and Anastasia viewed their departure from Hinesville as two "spiritual shepherds" that God anointed to help watch over his sheep. And above all, through their profound odyssey, Joseph would always remain in the forefront as their spiritual guide and mentor.

Finally, they rode beyond the edge of town and stopped on an old wooden bridge. Reggie stepped out of the buggy with Anastasia at his side and glanced up the road they had just traveled and then looked down into the stream and listened and gazed at the water trickling below them. He saw his reflection with a broad smile on his face and a rainbow in the sky shimmering in the flow of the creek, hoping to see Joseph with his wide smile as well. Then he realized that Joseph had departed and had indeed risen to heaven. With his passing Reggie could clearly see that Joseph's spirit emanated as a positive force to help mankind find God through "spiritual filled hearts".

Now it was left to Reggie and Anastasia to do the "shepherd's" work here on earth for the Lord, knowing they would be reunited with Joseph at a later date. Finally, they looked to the heavens to ponder about the events of the last two days. The message was quite clear! It was not by accident that the Lord would find in the most oppressed people here on earth—a strong black man who was truly "spiritually filled"! That man was Joseph, who was selected to be the messenger—God's power will always remain supreme over mankind's "slavery to sin" and that "in God's eyes we are all one"!

ABOUT THE AUTHOR

Dennis was born and raised in South Bend, Indiana, the youngest of three boys. The "seeds" for his passion for history were "planted" early in life. As a child residing in an older section of the community, Dennis was "held captive" visiting historical sites near his home. Riding his bicycle, he vividly recalls on numerous occasions visiting a Civil War training site. In addition, he particularly enjoyed admiring a huge oak tree called Council Oak where LaSalle conferred with the Miami Indians. While at these various historical sites, his imagination could run wild seeing Native American Indians, French explorers, and soldiers training for the Civil War.

In the evenings, history remained in the forefront as Dennis would read and travel the world fantasying about Sherwood Forest in The

s of Robin Hood, or the Himalaya Mountains in
just to name a few. Through his imagination, he
e to grasp the significance of reading to "open the
adventure, understanding, and knowledge.

is entered Ball State University in Muncie, Indiana and
eived a bachelor's degree in social science. He then completed
a tour of duty in the United States Marine Corps, serving in Viet
Nam. After leaving the Marines, he returned to Ball State as a
teaching assistant and completed his master's degree in world
history.

During the next thirty-two years Dennis taught United States
history and future studies at Wheeling High School in Wheeling,
Illinois near Chicago. His love for history and working with young
people never subsided. He would always say that his "work was
his passion".

Dennis currently lives outside of Lake Geneva, Wisconsin where
his fondness for teaching history has now been extended to writing
historical novels.